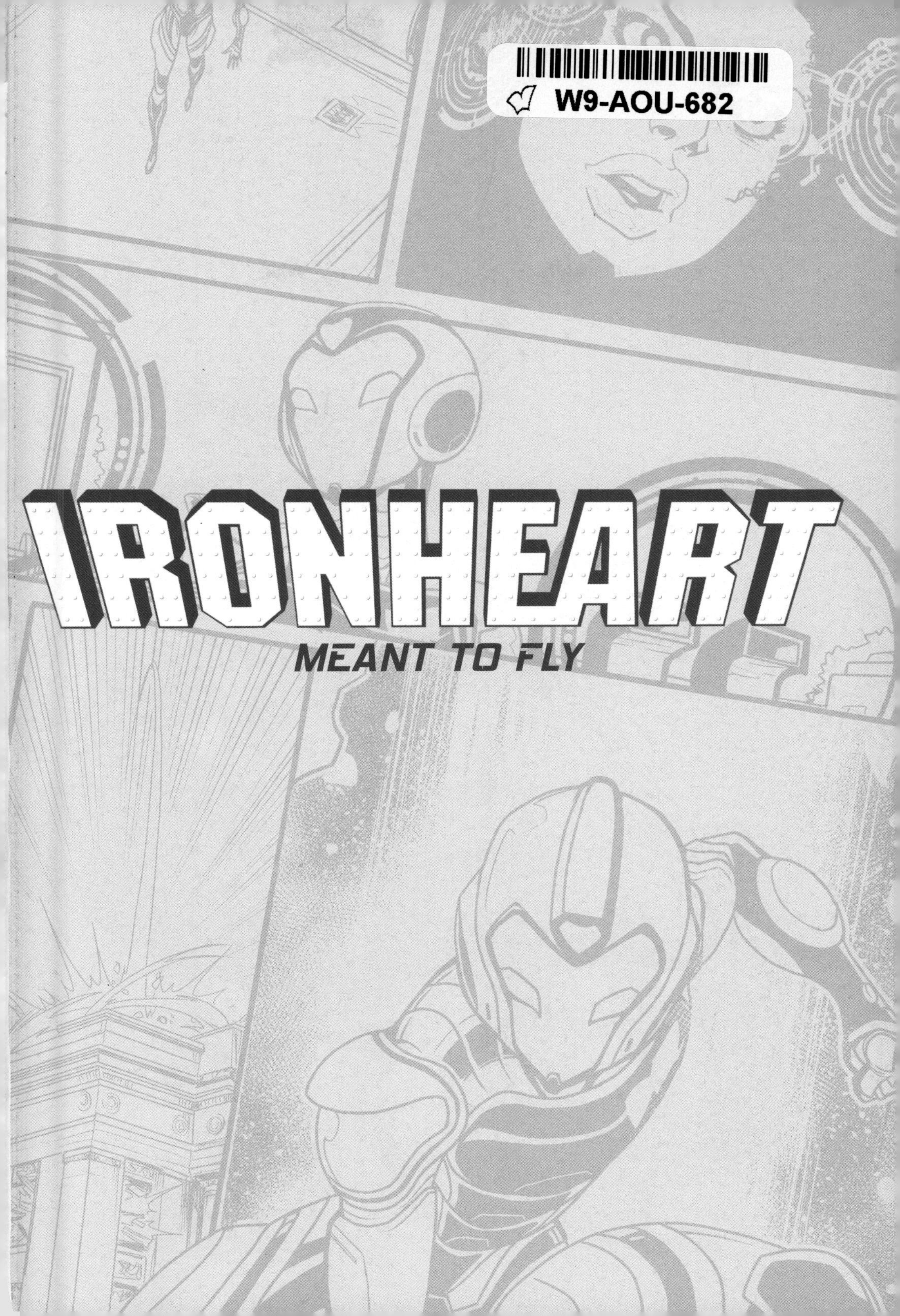
IRONHEART
MEANT TO FLY

CONTENTS

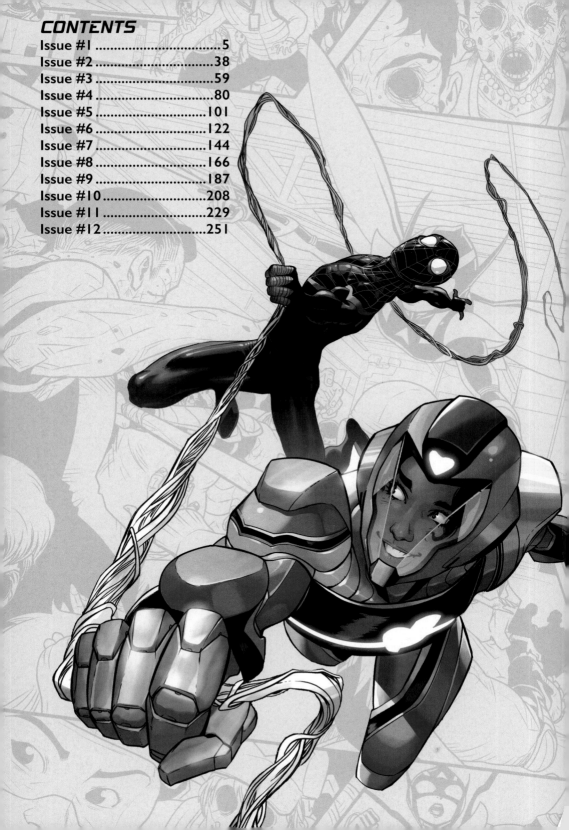

IRONHEART

MEANT TO FLY

WRITER
EVE L. EWING

ARTISTS
LUCIANO VECCHIO (#1-5 & #7-12)
& **KEVIN LIBRANDA** (#1, #6)

LAYOUTS
GEOFFO

COLOR ARTIST
MATT MILLA

LETTERER
VC's CLAYTON COWLES

COVER ART
AMY REEDER (#1-7),
STEFANO CASELLI & MARTE GRACIA (#8-9)
AND **LUCIANO VECCHIO** (#11-12)

ASSISTANT EDITOR
SHANNON ANDREWS BALLESTEROS

EDITOR
ALANNA SMITH

collection editor JENNIFER GRÜNWALD
assistant editor DANIEL KIRCHHOFFER • assistant managing editor MAIA LOY
associate manager, talent relations LISA MONTALBANO • vp production & special projects JEFF YOUNGQUIST
director, licensed publishing SVEN LARSEN • svp print, sales & marketing DAVID GABRIEL
editor in chief C.B. CEBULSKI

IRONHEART: MEANT TO FLY. Contains material originally published in magazine form as IRONHEART (2018) #1-12. Second printing 2022. ISBN 978-1-302-92352-5. Published by MARVEL WORLDWIDE, INC., a subsidiary of MARVEL ENTERTAINMENT, LLC. OFFICE OF PUBLICATION: 1290 Avenue of the Americas, New York, NY 10104. © 2020 MARVEL No similarity between any of the names, characters, persons, and/or institutions in this book with those of any living or dead person or institution is intended, and any such similarity which may exist is purely coincidental. **Printed in Canada.** KEVIN FEIGE, Chief Creative Officer; DAN BUCKLEY, President, Marvel Entertainment; DAVID BOGART, Associate Publisher & SVP of Talent Affairs; TOM BREVOORT, VP, Executive Editor; NICK LOWE, Executive Editor, VP of Content, Digital Publishing; DAVID GABRIEL, VP of Print & Digital Publishing; SVEN LARSEN, VP of Licensed Publishing; MARK ANNUNZIATO, VP of Planning & Forecasting; JEFF YOUNGQUIST, VP of Production & Special Projects; ALEX MORALES, Director of Publishing Operations; DAN EDINGTON, Director of Editorial Operations; RICKEY PURDIN, Director of Talent Relations; JENNIFER GRÜNWALD, Director of Production & Special Projects; SUSAN CRESPI, Production Manager; STAN LEE, Chairman Emeritus. For information regarding advertising in Marvel Comics or on Marvel.com, please contact Vit DeBellis, Custom Solutions & Integrated Advertising Manager, at vdebellis@marvel.com. For Marvel subscription inquiries, please call 888-511-5480. **Manufactured between 7/1/2022 and 8/2/2022 by SOLISCO PRINTERS, SCOTT, QC, CANADA.**

10 9 8 7 6 5 4 3 2

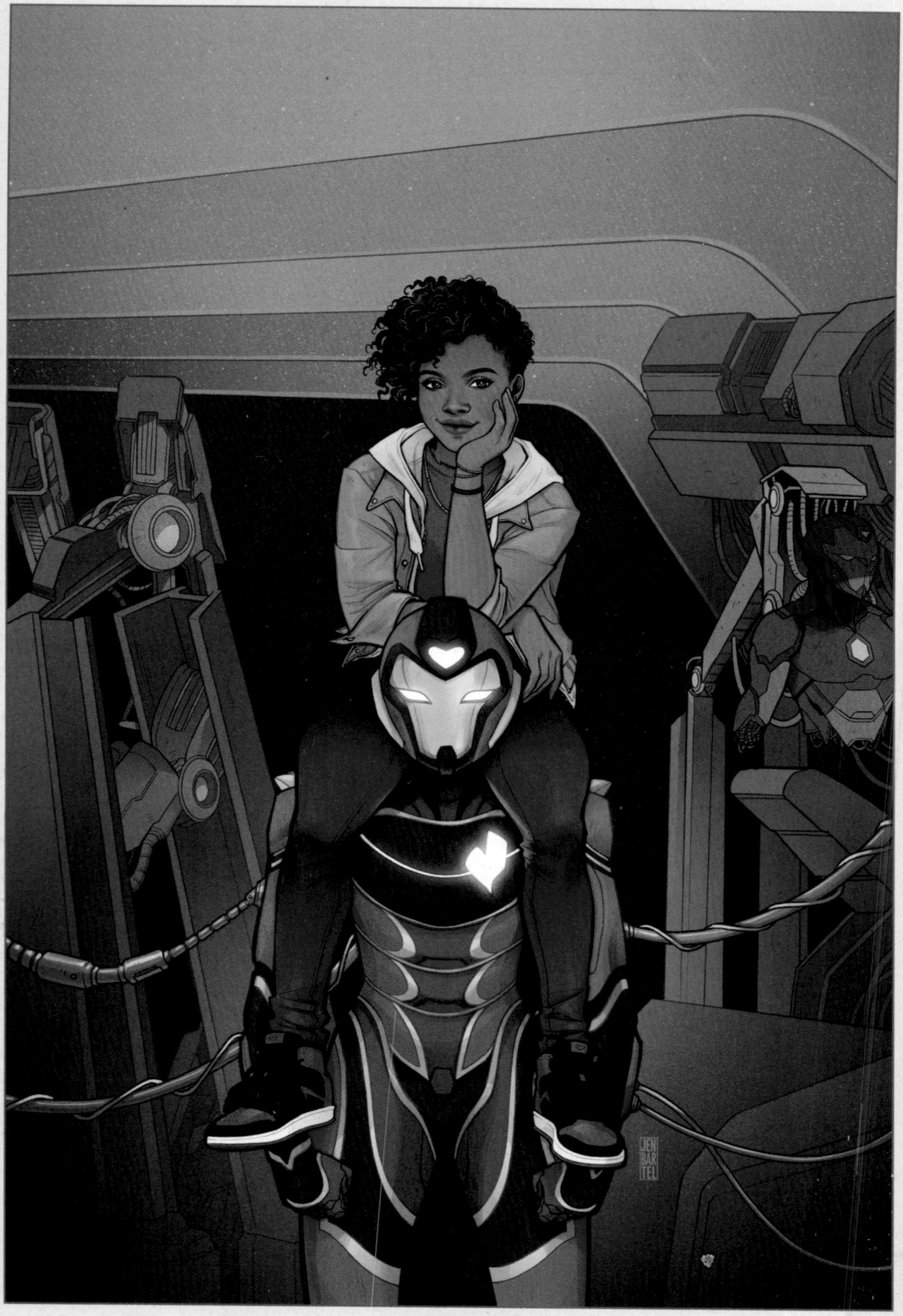
JEN BARTEL

#1 VARIANT
BY JEN BARTEL

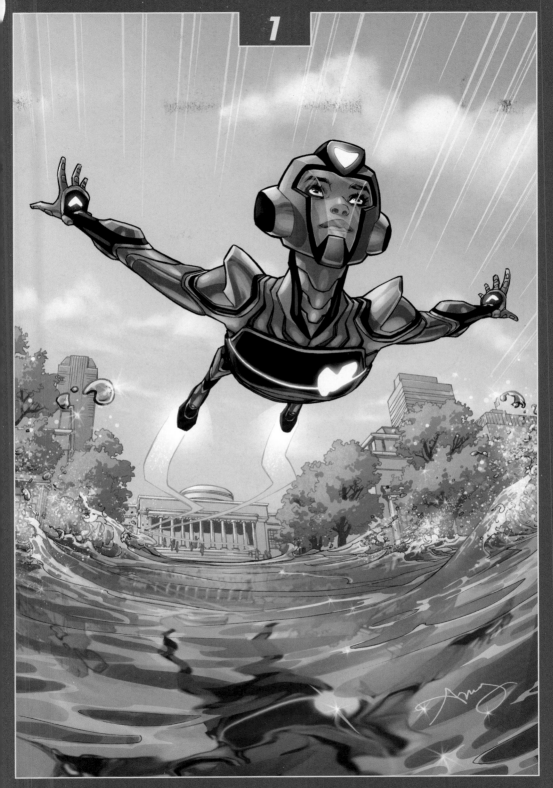

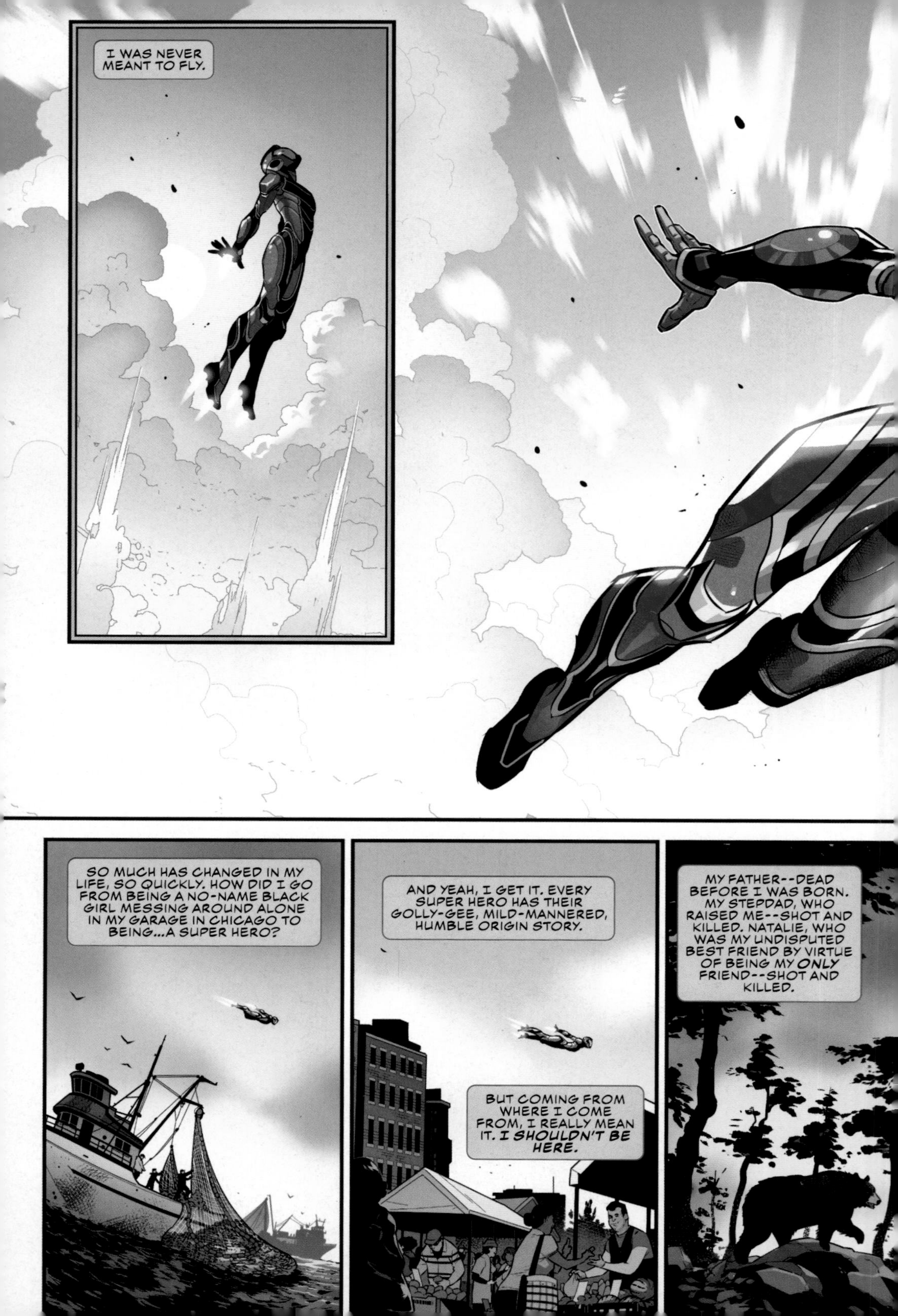
I WAS NEVER MEANT TO FLY.
SO MUCH HAS CHANGED IN MY LIFE, SO QUICKLY. HOW DID I GO FROM BEING A NO-NAME BLACK GIRL MESSING AROUND ALONE IN MY GARAGE IN CHICAGO TO BEING...A SUPER HERO?
AND YEAH, I GET IT. EVERY SUPER HERO HAS THEIR GOLLY-GEE, MILD-MANNERED, HUMBLE ORIGIN STORY.
BUT COMING FROM WHERE I COME FROM, I REALLY MEAN IT. *I SHOULDN'T BE HERE.*
MY FATHER--DEAD BEFORE I WAS BORN. MY STEPDAD, WHO RAISED ME--SHOT AND KILLED. NATALIE, WHO WAS MY UNDISPUTED BEST FRIEND BY VIRTUE OF BEING MY *ONLY* FRIEND--SHOT AND KILLED.

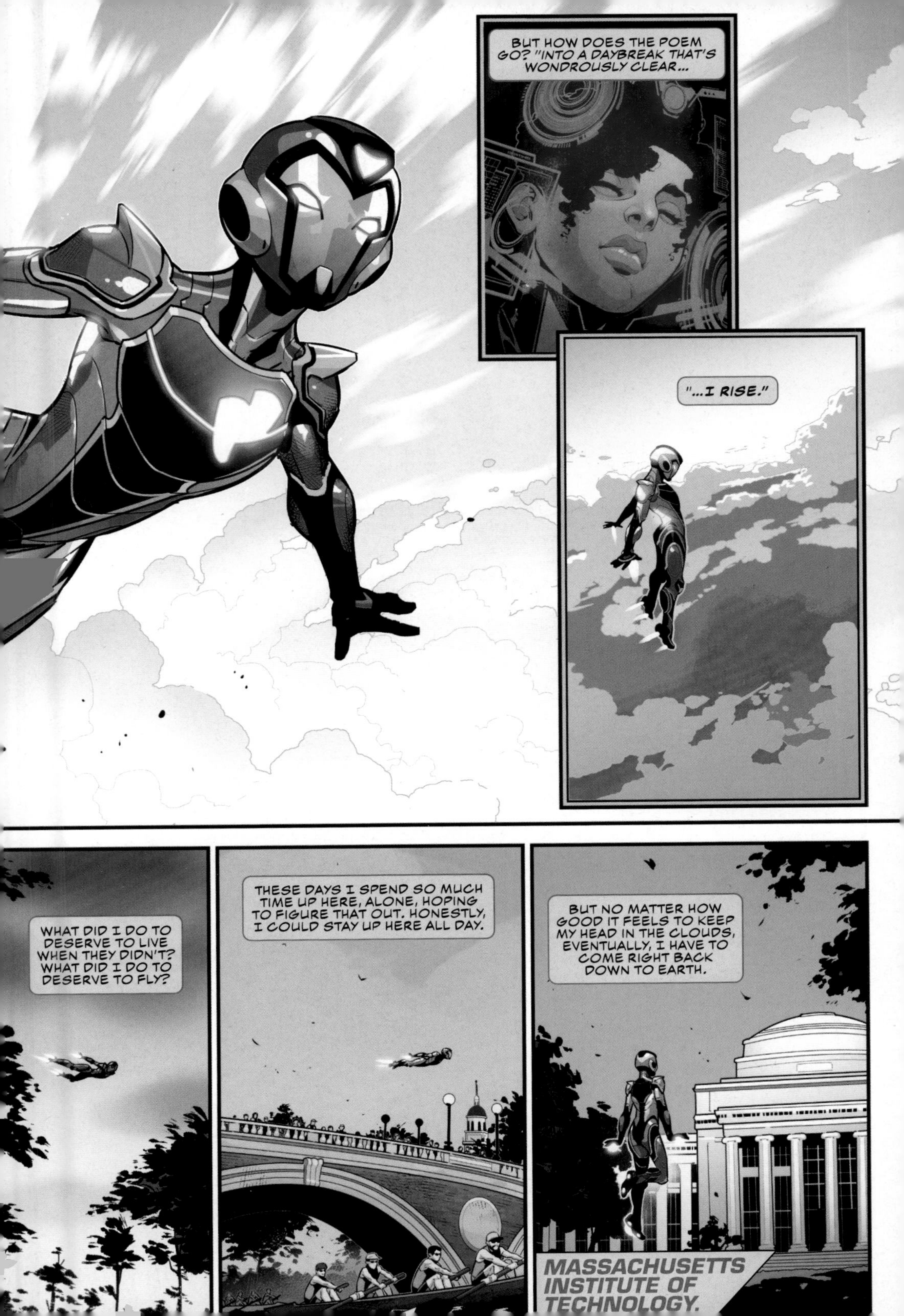

BUT HOW DOES THE POEM GO? "INTO A DAYBREAK THAT'S WONDROUSLY CLEAR...
"...I RISE."
WHAT DID I DO TO DESERVE TO LIVE WHEN THEY DIDN'T? WHAT DID I DO TO DESERVE TO FLY?
THESE DAYS I SPEND SO MUCH TIME UP HERE, ALONE, HOPING TO FIGURE THAT OUT. HONESTLY, I COULD STAY UP HERE ALL DAY.
BUT NO MATTER HOW GOOD IT FEELS TO KEEP MY HEAD IN THE CLOUDS, EVENTUALLY, I HAVE TO COME RIGHT BACK DOWN TO EARTH.
MASSACHUSETTS INSTITUTE OF TECHNOLOGY.

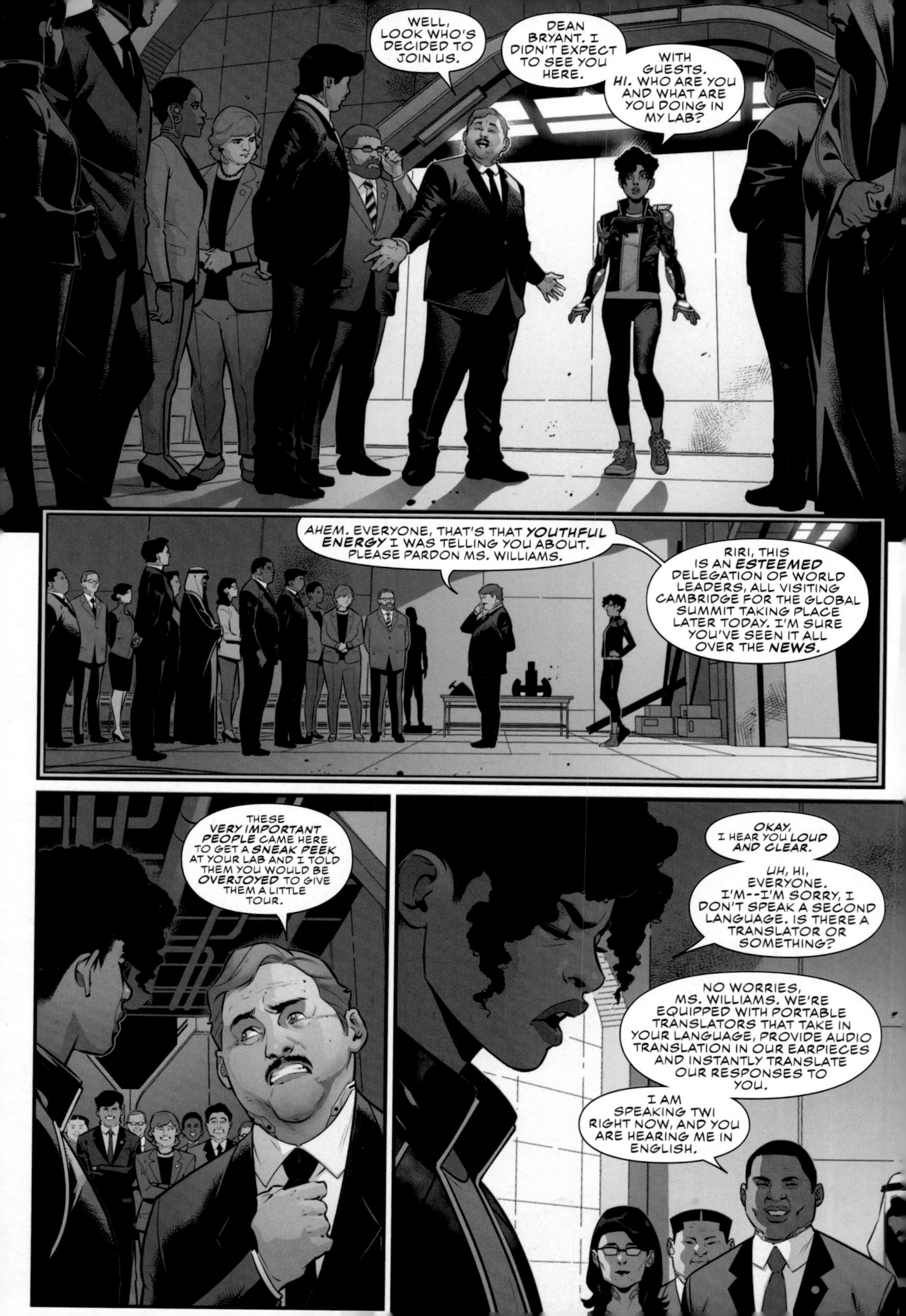
WELL, LOOK WHO'S DECIDED TO JOIN US.
DEAN BRYANT. I DIDN'T EXPECT TO SEE YOU HERE.
WITH GUESTS. HI. WHO ARE YOU AND WHAT ARE YOU DOING IN MY LAB?
AHEM. EVERYONE, THAT'S THAT YOUTHFUL ENERGY I WAS TELLING YOU ABOUT. PLEASE PARDON MS. WILLIAMS.
RIRI, THIS IS AN ESTEEMED DELEGATION OF WORLD LEADERS, ALL VISITING CAMBRIDGE FOR THE GLOBAL SUMMIT TAKING PLACE LATER TODAY. I'M SURE YOU'VE SEEN IT ALL OVER THE NEWS.
THESE VERY IMPORTANT PEOPLE CAME HERE TO GET A SNEAK PEEK AT YOUR LAB AND I TOLD THEM YOU WOULD BE OVERJOYED TO GIVE THEM A LITTLE TOUR.
OKAY, I HEAR YOU LOUD AND CLEAR.
UH, HI, EVERYONE. I'M--I'M SORRY, I DON'T SPEAK A SECOND LANGUAGE. IS THERE A TRANSLATOR OR SOMETHING?
NO WORRIES, MS. WILLIAMS. WE'RE EQUIPPED WITH PORTABLE TRANSLATORS THAT TAKE IN YOUR LANGUAGE, PROVIDE AUDIO TRANSLATION IN OUR EARPIECES AND INSTANTLY TRANSLATE OUR RESPONSES TO YOU.
I AM SPEAKING TWI RIGHT NOW, AND YOU ARE HEARING ME IN ENGLISH.

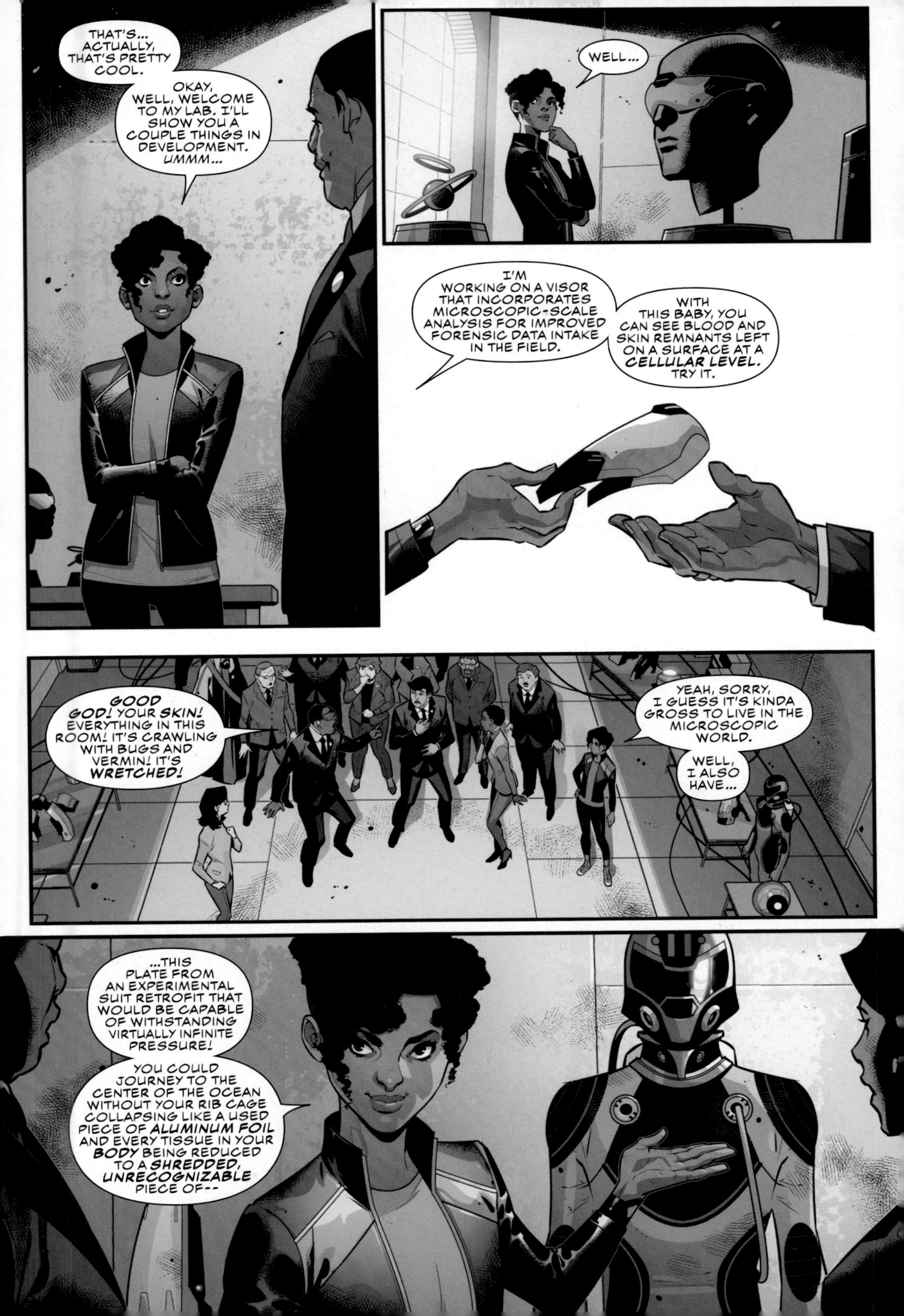
THAT'S... ACTUALLY, THAT'S PRETTY COOL.
OKAY, WELL, WELCOME TO MY LAB. I'LL SHOW YOU A COUPLE THINGS IN DEVELOPMENT. UMMM...
WELL...
I'M WORKING ON A VISOR THAT INCORPORATES MICROSCOPIC-SCALE ANALYSIS FOR IMPROVED FORENSIC DATA INTAKE IN THE FIELD.
WITH THIS BABY, YOU CAN SEE BLOOD AND SKIN REMNANTS LEFT ON A SURFACE AT A CELLULAR LEVEL. TRY IT.
GOOD GOD! YOUR SKIN! EVERYTHING IN THIS ROOM! IT'S CRAWLING WITH BUGS AND VERMIN! IT'S WRETCHED!
YEAH, SORRY, I GUESS IT'S KINDA GROSS TO LIVE IN THE MICROSCOPIC WORLD.
WELL, I ALSO HAVE...
...THIS PLATE FROM AN EXPERIMENTAL SUIT RETROFIT THAT WOULD BE CAPABLE OF WITHSTANDING VIRTUALLY INFINITE PRESSURE!
YOU COULD JOURNEY TO THE CENTER OF THE OCEAN WITHOUT YOUR RIB CAGE COLLAPSING LIKE A USED PIECE OF ALUMINUM FOIL AND EVERY TISSUE IN YOUR BODY BEING REDUCED TO A SHREDDED, UNRECOGNIZABLE PIECE OF--

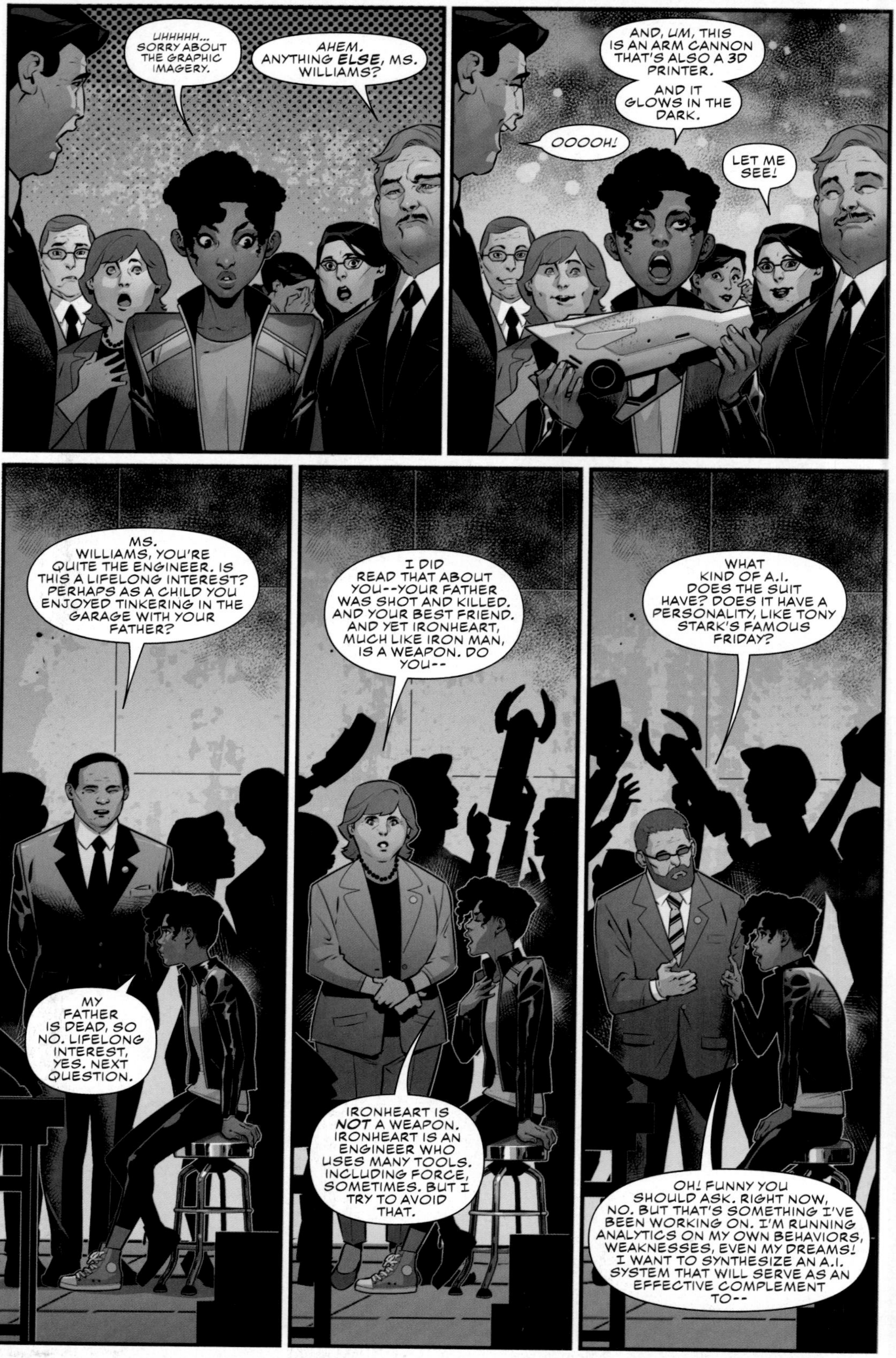
UHHHHH... SORRY ABOUT THE GRAPHIC IMAGERY.
AHEM. ANYTHING ELSE, MS. WILLIAMS?
AND, UM, THIS IS AN ARM CANNON THAT'S ALSO A 3D PRINTER.
AND IT GLOWS IN THE DARK.
OOOOH!
LET ME SEE!
MS. WILLIAMS, YOU'RE QUITE THE ENGINEER. IS THIS A LIFELONG INTEREST? PERHAPS AS A CHILD YOU ENJOYED TINKERING IN THE GARAGE WITH YOUR FATHER?
MY FATHER IS DEAD, SO NO. LIFELONG INTEREST, YES. NEXT QUESTION.
I DID READ THAT ABOUT YOU--YOUR FATHER WAS SHOT AND KILLED. AND YOUR BEST FRIEND. AND YET IRONHEART, MUCH LIKE IRON MAN, IS A WEAPON. DO YOU--
IRONHEART IS NOT A WEAPON. IRONHEART IS AN ENGINEER WHO USES MANY TOOLS. INCLUDING FORCE, SOMETIMES. BUT I TRY TO AVOID THAT.
WHAT KIND OF A.I. DOES THE SUIT HAVE? DOES IT HAVE A PERSONALITY, LIKE TONY STARK'S FAMOUS FRIDAY?
OH! FUNNY YOU SHOULD ASK. RIGHT NOW, NO. BUT THAT'S SOMETHING I'VE BEEN WORKING ON. I'M RUNNING ANALYTICS ON MY OWN BEHAVIORS, WEAKNESSES, EVEN MY DREAMS! I WANT TO SYNTHESIZE AN A.I. SYSTEM THAT WILL SERVE AS AN EFFECTIVE COMPLEMENT TO--

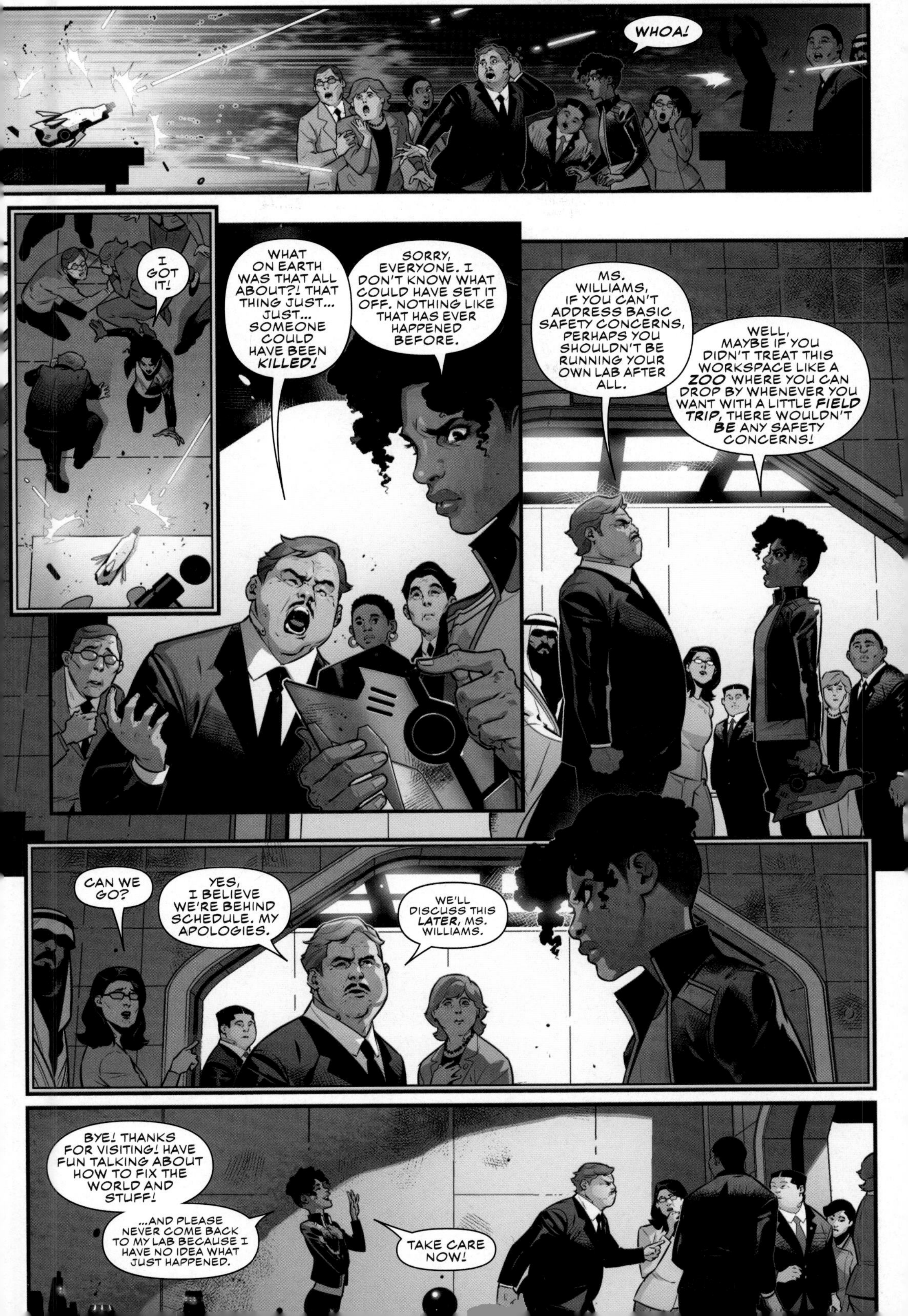
WHOA!
I GOT IT!
WHAT ON EARTH WAS THAT ALL ABOUT?! THAT THING JUST... JUST... SOMEONE COULD HAVE BEEN KILLED!
SORRY, EVERYONE. I DON'T KNOW WHAT COULD HAVE SET IT OFF. NOTHING LIKE THAT HAS EVER HAPPENED BEFORE.
MS. WILLIAMS, IF YOU CAN'T ADDRESS BASIC SAFETY CONCERNS, PERHAPS YOU SHOULDN'T BE RUNNING YOUR OWN LAB AFTER ALL.
WELL, MAYBE IF YOU DIDN'T TREAT THIS WORKSPACE LIKE A ZOO WHERE YOU CAN DROP BY WHENEVER YOU WANT WITH A LITTLE FIELD TRIP, THERE WOULDN'T BE ANY SAFETY CONCERNS!
CAN WE GO?
YES, I BELIEVE WE'RE BEHIND SCHEDULE. MY APOLOGIES.
WE'LL DISCUSS THIS LATER, MS. WILLIAMS.
BYE! THANKS FOR VISITING! HAVE FUN TALKING ABOUT HOW TO FIX THE WORLD AND STUFF!
...AND PLEASE NEVER COME BACK TO MY LAB BECAUSE I HAVE NO IDEA WHAT JUST HAPPENED.
TAKE CARE NOW!

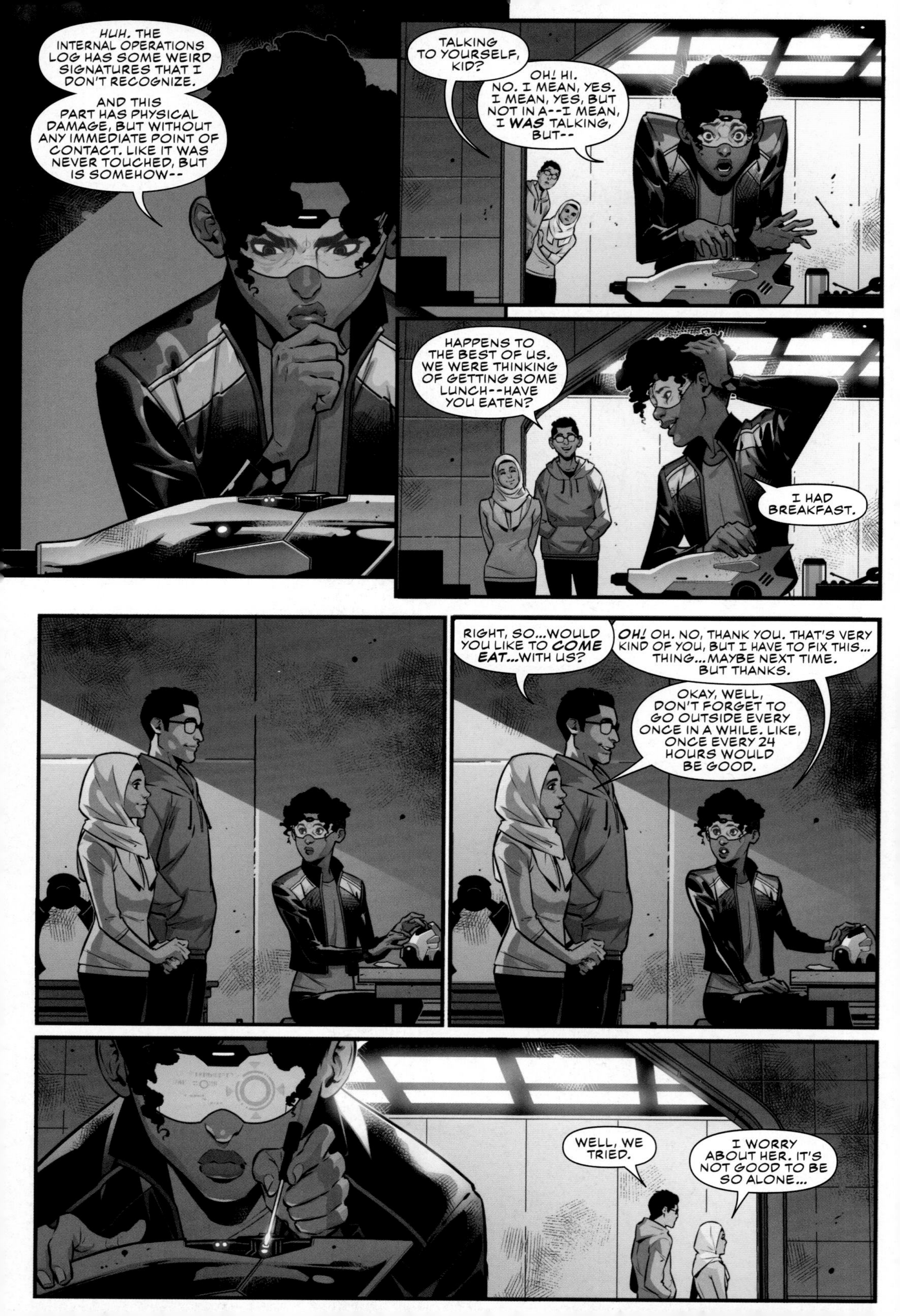
HUH. THE INTERNAL OPERATIONS LOG HAS SOME WEIRD SIGNATURES THAT I DON'T RECOGNIZE.
AND THIS PART HAS PHYSICAL DAMAGE, BUT WITHOUT ANY IMMEDIATE POINT OF CONTACT. LIKE IT WAS NEVER TOUCHED, BUT IS SOMEHOW--
TALKING TO YOURSELF, KID?
OH! HI. NO. I MEAN, YES. I MEAN, YES, BUT NOT IN A--I MEAN, I WAS TALKING, BUT--
HAPPENS TO THE BEST OF US. WE WERE THINKING OF GETTING SOME LUNCH--HAVE YOU EATEN?
I HAD BREAKFAST.
RIGHT, SO...WOULD YOU LIKE TO COME EAT...WITH US?
OH! OH. NO, THANK YOU. THAT'S VERY KIND OF YOU, BUT I HAVE TO FIX THIS... THING...MAYBE NEXT TIME. BUT THANKS.
OKAY, WELL, DON'T FORGET TO GO OUTSIDE EVERY ONCE IN A WHILE. LIKE, ONCE EVERY 24 HOURS WOULD BE GOOD.
WELL, WE TRIED.
I WORRY ABOUT HER. IT'S NOT GOOD TO BE SO ALONE...

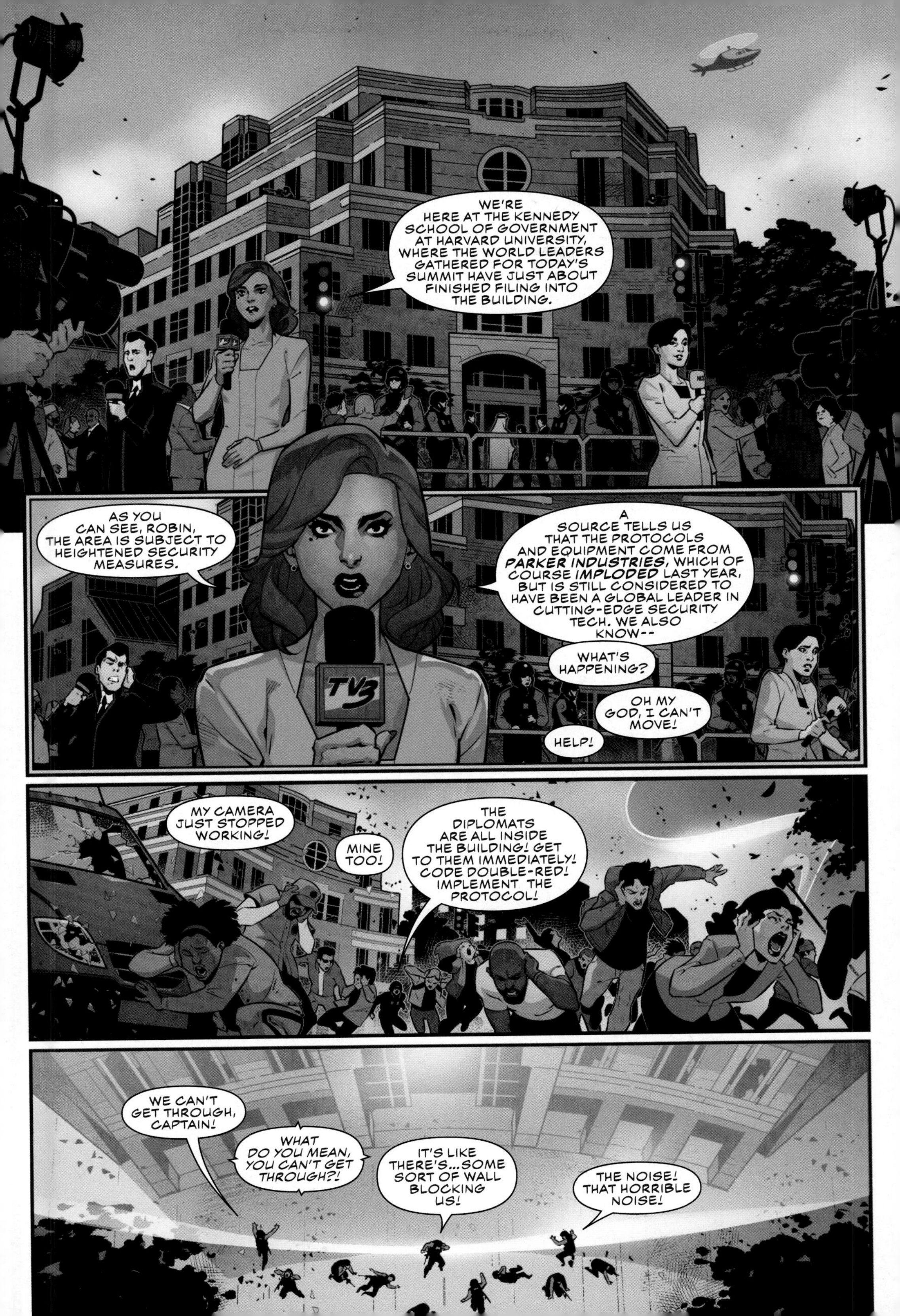
WE'RE HERE AT THE KENNEDY SCHOOL OF GOVERNMENT AT HARVARD UNIVERSITY, WHERE THE WORLD LEADERS GATHERED FOR TODAY'S SUMMIT HAVE JUST ABOUT FINISHED FILING INTO THE BUILDING.
AS YOU CAN SEE, ROBIN, THE AREA IS SUBJECT TO HEIGHTENED SECURITY MEASURES.
A SOURCE TELLS US THAT THE PROTOCOLS AND EQUIPMENT COME FROM **PARKER INDUSTRIES**, WHICH OF COURSE ***IMPLODED*** LAST YEAR, BUT IS STILL CONSIDERED TO HAVE BEEN A GLOBAL LEADER IN CUTTING-EDGE SECURITY TECH. WE ALSO KNOW--
TV3
WHAT'S HAPPENING?
OH MY GOD, I CAN'T MOVE!
HELP!
MY CAMERA JUST STOPPED WORKING!
MINE TOO!
THE DIPLOMATS ARE ALL INSIDE THE BUILDING! GET TO THEM IMMEDIATELY! CODE DOUBLE-RED! IMPLEMENT THE PROTOCOL!
WE CAN'T GET THROUGH, CAPTAIN!
WHAT DO YOU MEAN, YOU CAN'T GET THROUGH?!
IT'S LIKE THERE'S...SOME SORT OF WALL BLOCKING US!
THE NOISE! THAT HORRIBLE NOISE!

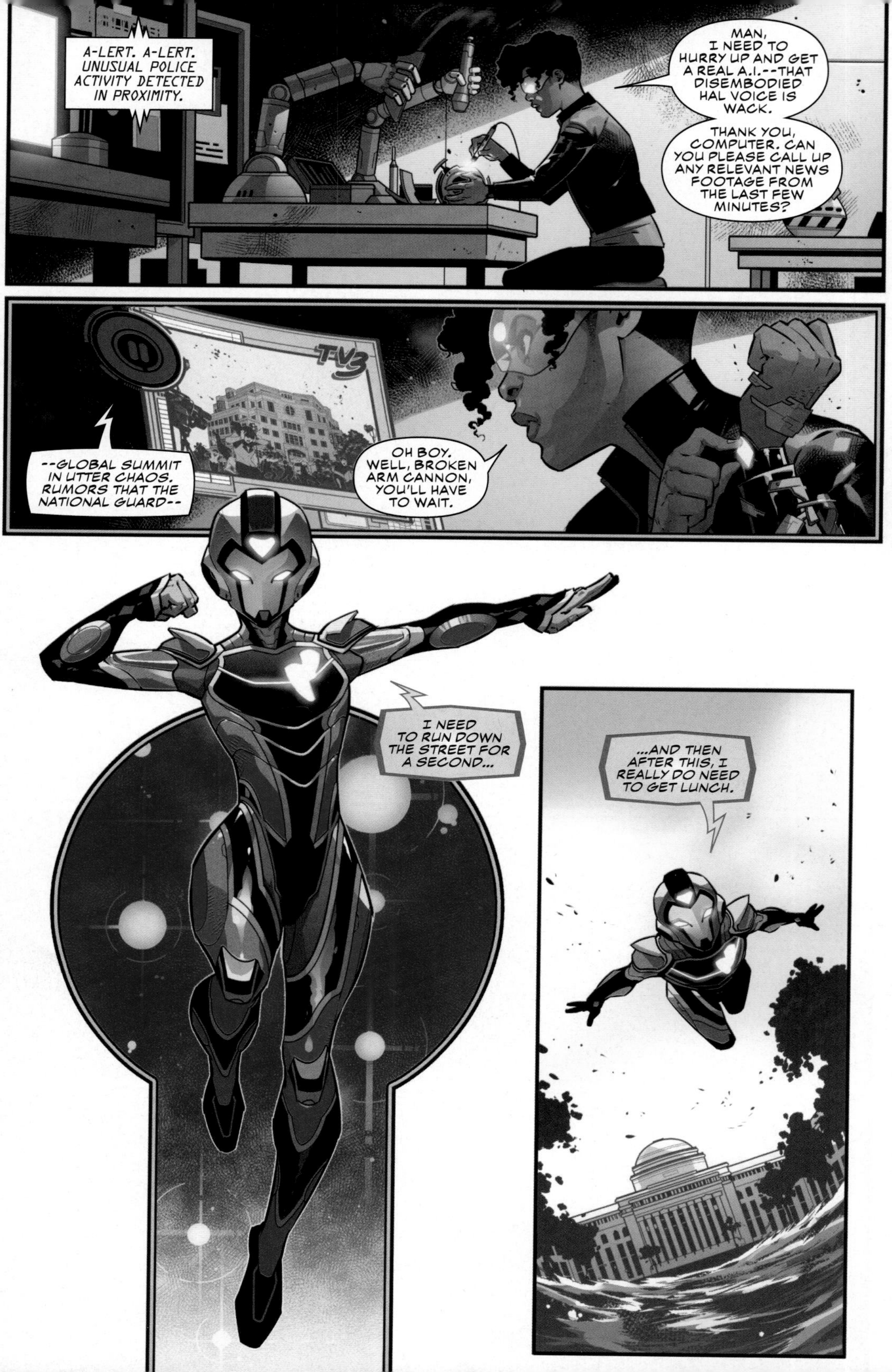
A-LERT. A-LERT. UNUSUAL POLICE ACTIVITY DETECTED IN PROXIMITY.
MAN, I NEED TO HURRY UP AND GET A REAL A.I.--THAT DISEMBODIED HAL VOICE IS WACK.
THANK YOU, COMPUTER. CAN YOU PLEASE CALL UP ANY RELEVANT NEWS FOOTAGE FROM THE LAST FEW MINUTES?
T-V3
--GLOBAL SUMMIT IN UTTER CHAOS. RUMORS THAT THE NATIONAL GUARD--
OH BOY. WELL, BROKEN ARM CANNON, YOU'LL HAVE TO WAIT.
I NEED TO RUN DOWN THE STREET FOR A SECOND...
...AND THEN AFTER THIS, I REALLY DO NEED TO GET LUNCH.

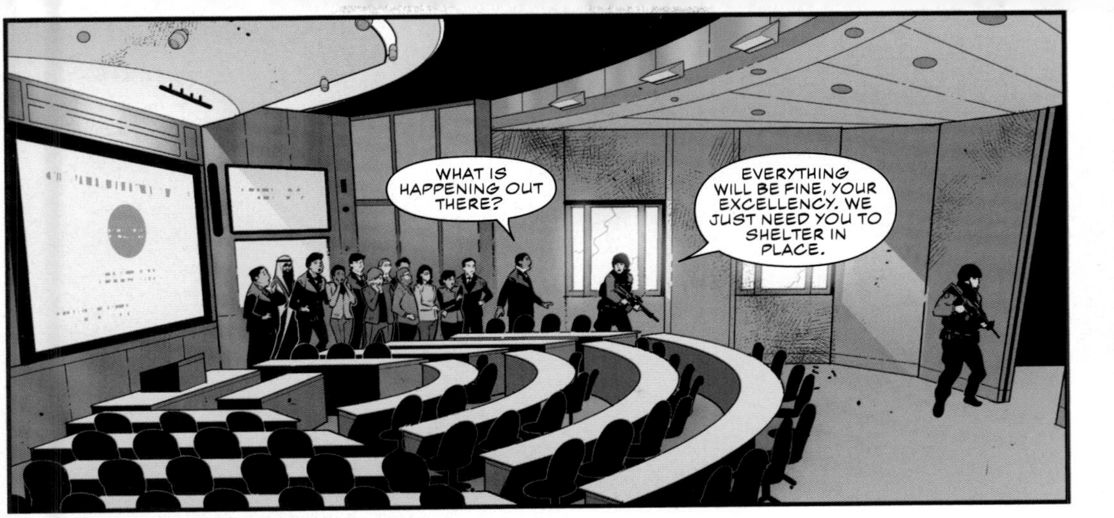
WHAT IS HAPPENING OUT THERE?
EVERYTHING WILL BE FINE, YOUR EXCELLENCY. WE JUST NEED YOU TO SHELTER IN PLACE.

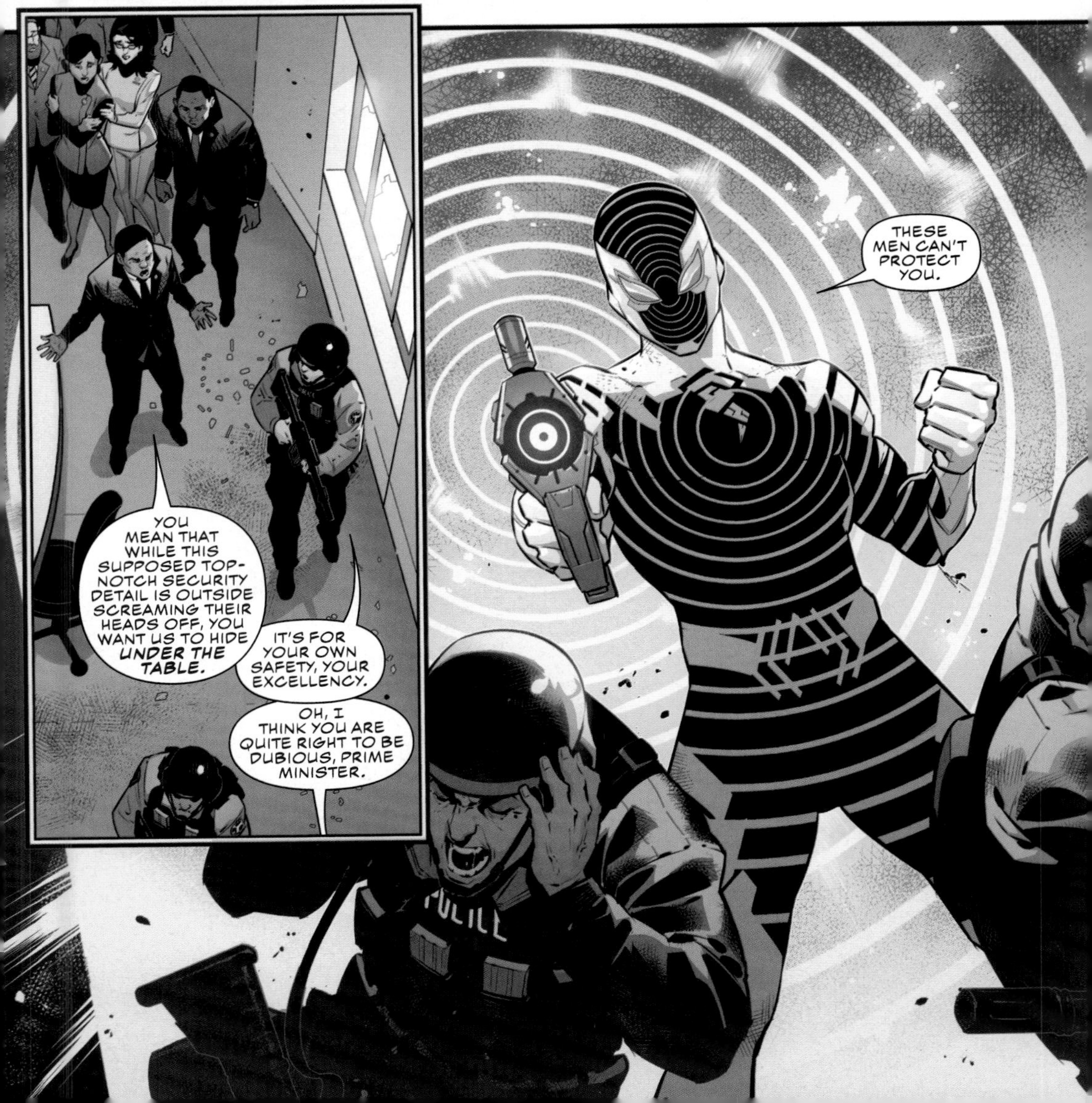
YOU MEAN THAT WHILE THIS SUPPOSED TOP-NOTCH SECURITY DETAIL IS OUTSIDE SCREAMING THEIR HEADS OFF, YOU WANT US TO HIDE UNDER THE TABLE.
IT'S FOR YOUR OWN SAFETY, YOUR EXCELLENCY.
OH, I THINK YOU ARE QUITE RIGHT TO BE DUBIOUS, PRIME MINISTER.
THESE MEN CAN'T PROTECT YOU.
POLICE

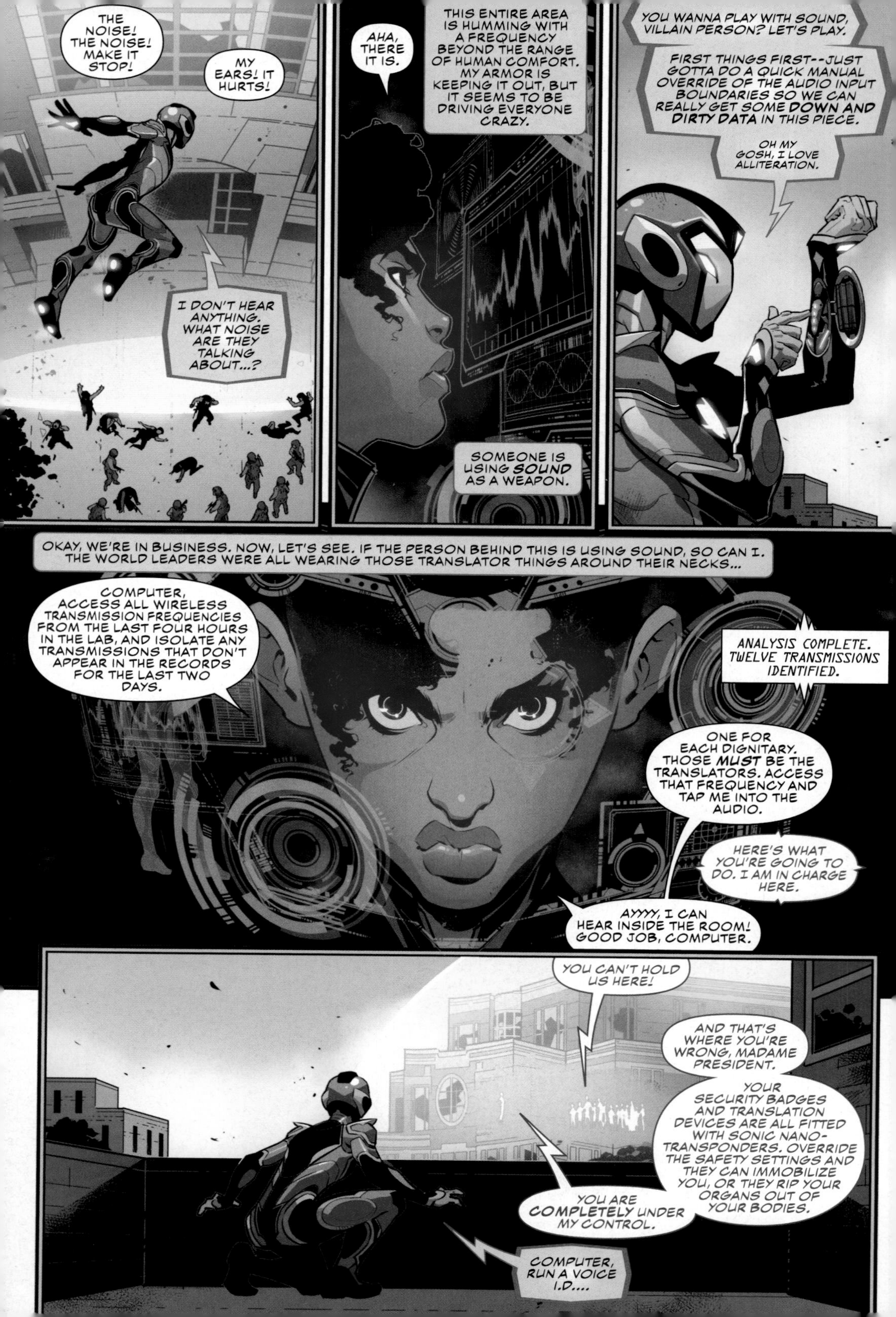
THE NOISE! THE NOISE! MAKE IT STOP!
MY EARS! IT HURTS!
I DON'T HEAR ANYTHING. WHAT NOISE ARE THEY TALKING ABOUT...?
AHA, THERE IT IS.
THIS ENTIRE AREA IS HUMMING WITH A FREQUENCY BEYOND THE RANGE OF HUMAN COMFORT. MY ARMOR IS KEEPING IT OUT, BUT IT SEEMS TO BE DRIVING EVERYONE CRAZY.
SOMEONE IS USING SOUND AS A WEAPON.
YOU WANNA PLAY WITH SOUND, VILLAIN PERSON? LET'S PLAY.
FIRST THINGS FIRST--JUST GOTTA DO A QUICK MANUAL OVERRIDE OF THE AUDIO INPUT BOUNDARIES SO WE CAN REALLY GET SOME DOWN AND DIRTY DATA IN THIS PIECE.
OH MY GOSH, I LOVE ALLITERATION.
OKAY, WE'RE IN BUSINESS. NOW, LET'S SEE. IF THE PERSON BEHIND THIS IS USING SOUND, SO CAN I. THE WORLD LEADERS WERE ALL WEARING THOSE TRANSLATOR THINGS AROUND THEIR NECKS...
COMPUTER, ACCESS ALL WIRELESS TRANSMISSION FREQUENCIES FROM THE LAST FOUR HOURS IN THE LAB, AND ISOLATE ANY TRANSMISSIONS THAT DON'T APPEAR IN THE RECORDS FOR THE LAST TWO DAYS.
ANALYSIS COMPLETE. TWELVE TRANSMISSIONS IDENTIFIED.
ONE FOR EACH DIGNITARY. THOSE MUST BE THE TRANSLATORS. ACCESS THAT FREQUENCY AND TAP ME INTO THE AUDIO.
HERE'S WHAT YOU'RE GOING TO DO. I AM IN CHARGE HERE.
AYYYY, I CAN HEAR INSIDE THE ROOM! GOOD JOB, COMPUTER.
YOU CAN'T HOLD US HERE!
AND THAT'S WHERE YOU'RE WRONG, MADAME PRESIDENT.
YOUR SECURITY BADGES AND TRANSLATION DEVICES ARE ALL FITTED WITH SONIC NANO-TRANSPONDERS. OVERRIDE THE SAFETY SETTINGS AND THEY CAN IMMOBILIZE YOU, OR THEY RIP YOUR ORGANS OUT OF YOUR BODIES.
YOU ARE COMPLETELY UNDER MY CONTROL.
COMPUTER, RUN A VOICE I.D....

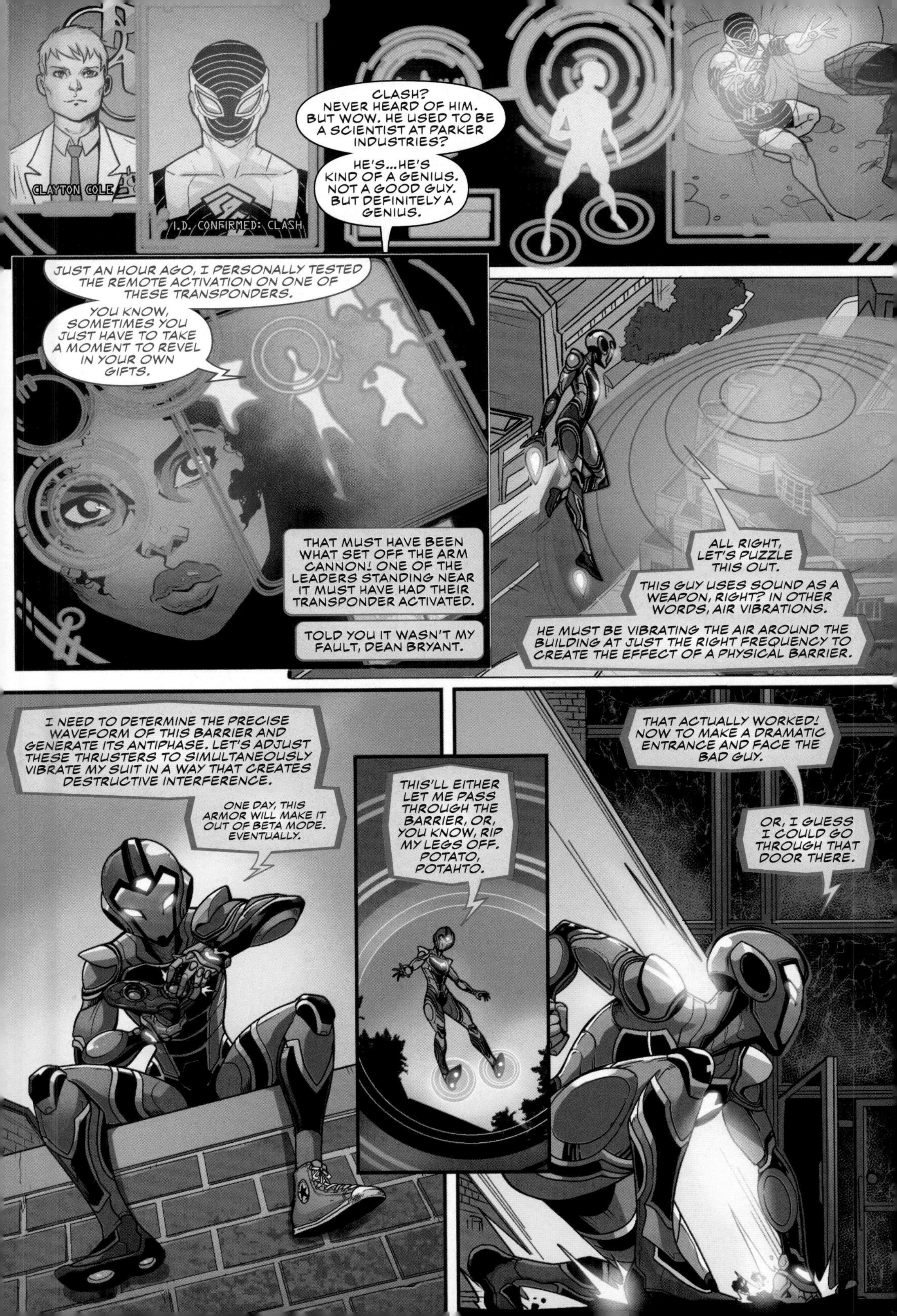
CLAYTON COLE
I.D. CONFIRMED: CLASH
CLASH? NEVER HEARD OF HIM. BUT WOW. HE USED TO BE A SCIENTIST AT PARKER INDUSTRIES?
HE'S...HE'S KIND OF A GENIUS. NOT A GOOD GUY. BUT DEFINITELY A GENIUS.
JUST AN HOUR AGO, I PERSONALLY TESTED THE REMOTE ACTIVATION ON ONE OF THESE TRANSPONDERS.
YOU KNOW, SOMETIMES YOU JUST HAVE TO TAKE A MOMENT TO REVEL IN YOUR OWN GIFTS.
THAT MUST HAVE BEEN WHAT SET OFF THE ARM CANNON! ONE OF THE LEADERS STANDING NEAR IT MUST HAVE HAD THEIR TRANSPONDER ACTIVATED.
TOLD YOU IT WASN'T MY FAULT, DEAN BRYANT.
ALL RIGHT, LET'S PUZZLE THIS OUT.
THIS GUY USES SOUND AS A WEAPON, RIGHT? IN OTHER WORDS, AIR VIBRATIONS.
HE MUST BE VIBRATING THE AIR AROUND THE BUILDING AT JUST THE RIGHT FREQUENCY TO CREATE THE EFFECT OF A PHYSICAL BARRIER.
I NEED TO DETERMINE THE PRECISE WAVEFORM OF THIS BARRIER AND GENERATE ITS ANTIPHASE. LET'S ADJUST THESE THRUSTERS TO SIMULTANEOUSLY VIBRATE MY SUIT IN A WAY THAT CREATES DESTRUCTIVE INTERFERENCE.
ONE DAY, THIS ARMOR WILL MAKE IT OUT OF BETA MODE. EVENTUALLY.
THIS'LL EITHER LET ME PASS THROUGH THE BARRIER, OR, YOU KNOW, RIP MY LEGS OFF. POTATO, POTAHTO.
THAT ACTUALLY WORKED! NOW TO MAKE A DRAMATIC ENTRANCE AND FACE THE BAD GUY.
OR, I GUESS I COULD GO THROUGH THAT DOOR THERE.

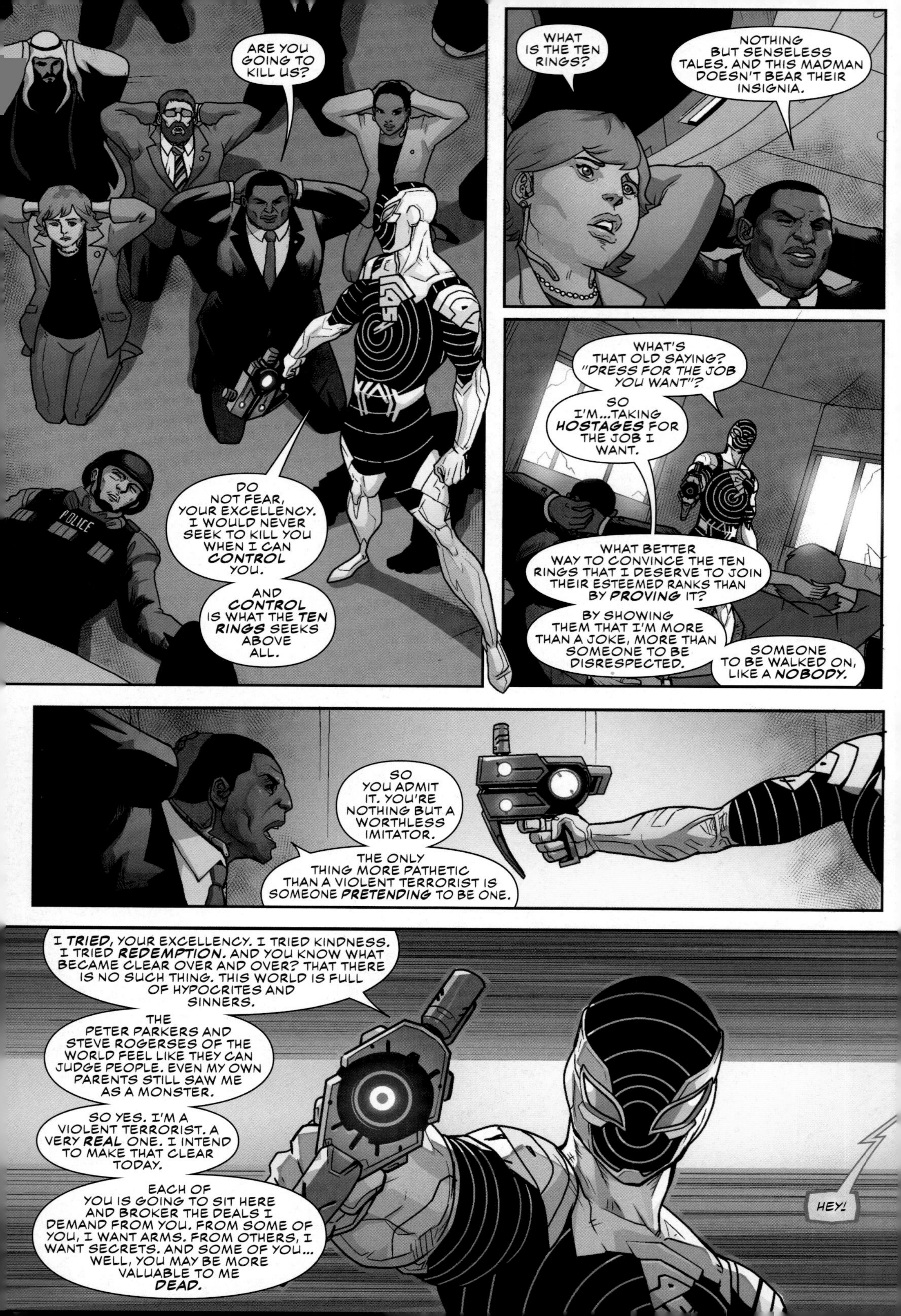

ARE YOU GOING TO KILL US?
DO NOT FEAR, YOUR EXCELLENCY. I WOULD NEVER SEEK TO KILL YOU WHEN I CAN CONTROL YOU.
AND CONTROL IS WHAT THE TEN RINGS SEEKS ABOVE ALL.
POLICE
WHAT IS THE TEN RINGS?
NOTHING BUT SENSELESS TALES. AND THIS MADMAN DOESN'T BEAR THEIR INSIGNIA.
WHAT'S THAT OLD SAYING? "DRESS FOR THE JOB YOU WANT"?
SO I'M...TAKING HOSTAGES FOR THE JOB I WANT.
WHAT BETTER WAY TO CONVINCE THE TEN RINGS THAT I DESERVE TO JOIN THEIR ESTEEMED RANKS THAN BY PROVING IT?
BY SHOWING THEM THAT I'M MORE THAN A JOKE, MORE THAN SOMEONE TO BE DISRESPECTED.
SOMEONE TO BE WALKED ON, LIKE A NOBODY.
SO YOU ADMIT IT. YOU'RE NOTHING BUT A WORTHLESS IMITATOR.
THE ONLY THING MORE PATHETIC THAN A VIOLENT TERRORIST IS SOMEONE PRETENDING TO BE ONE.
I TRIED, YOUR EXCELLENCY. I TRIED KINDNESS. I TRIED REDEMPTION. AND YOU KNOW WHAT BECAME CLEAR OVER AND OVER? THAT THERE IS NO SUCH THING. THIS WORLD IS FULL OF HYPOCRITES AND SINNERS.
THE PETER PARKERS AND STEVE ROGERSES OF THE WORLD FEEL LIKE THEY CAN JUDGE PEOPLE. EVEN MY OWN PARENTS STILL SAW ME AS A MONSTER.
SO YES. I'M A VIOLENT TERRORIST. A VERY REAL ONE. I INTEND TO MAKE THAT CLEAR TODAY.
EACH OF YOU IS GOING TO SIT HERE AND BROKER THE DEALS I DEMAND FROM YOU. FROM SOME OF YOU, I WANT ARMS. FROM OTHERS, I WANT SECRETS. AND SOME OF YOU... WELL, YOU MAY BE MORE VALUABLE TO ME DEAD.
HEY!

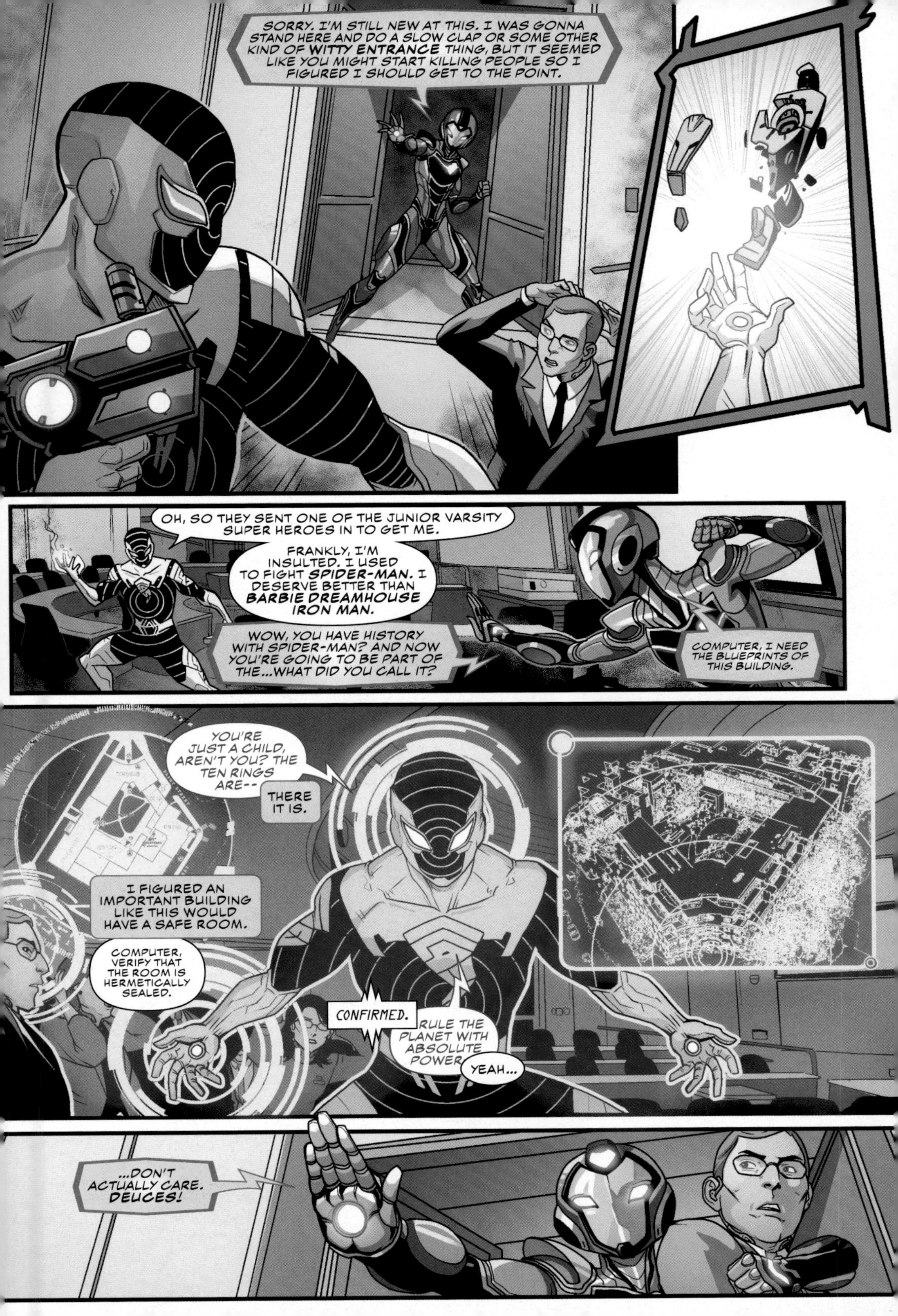

SORRY. I'M STILL NEW AT THIS. I WAS GONNA STAND HERE AND DO A SLOW CLAP OR SOME OTHER KIND OF WITTY ENTRANCE THING, BUT IT SEEMED LIKE YOU MIGHT START KILLING PEOPLE SO I FIGURED I SHOULD GET TO THE POINT.
OH, SO THEY SENT ONE OF THE JUNIOR VARSITY SUPER HEROES IN TO GET ME.
FRANKLY, I'M INSULTED. I USED TO FIGHT SPIDER-MAN. I DESERVE BETTER THAN BARBIE DREAMHOUSE IRON MAN.
WOW, YOU HAVE HISTORY WITH SPIDER-MAN? AND NOW YOU'RE GOING TO BE PART OF THE...WHAT DID YOU CALL IT?
COMPUTER, I NEED THE BLUEPRINTS OF THIS BUILDING.
YOU'RE JUST A CHILD, AREN'T YOU? THE TEN RINGS ARE--
THERE IT IS.
I FIGURED AN IMPORTANT BUILDING LIKE THIS WOULD HAVE A SAFE ROOM.
COMPUTER, VERIFY THAT THE ROOM IS HERMETICALLY SEALED.
CONFIRMED.
RULE THE PLANET WITH ABSOLUTE POWER
YEAH...
...DON'T ACTUALLY CARE. DEUCES!

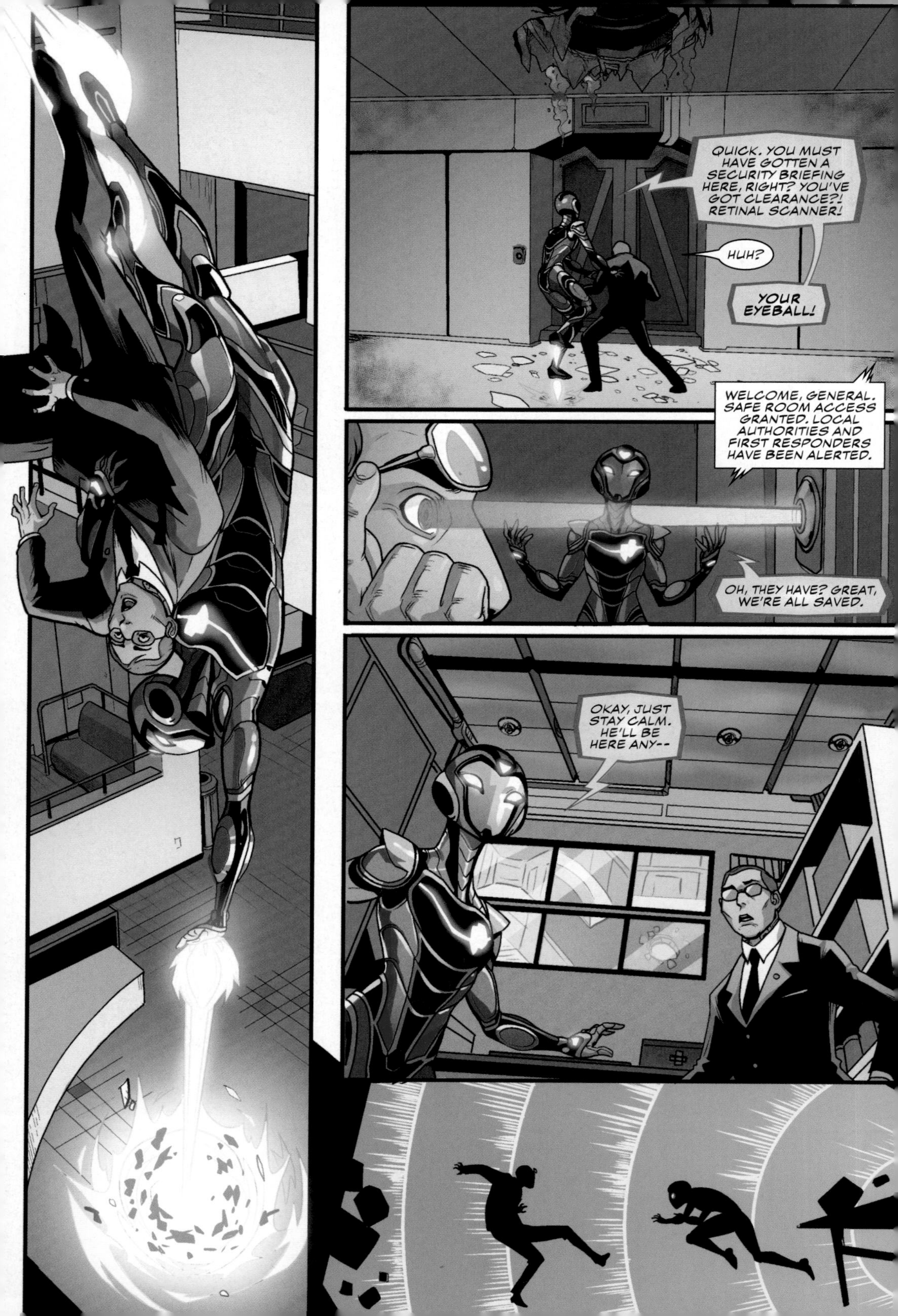
QUICK. YOU MUST HAVE GOTTEN A SECURITY BRIEFING HERE, RIGHT? YOU'VE GOT CLEARANCE?! RETINAL SCANNER!
HUH?
YOUR EYEBALL!
WELCOME, GENERAL. SAFE ROOM ACCESS GRANTED. LOCAL AUTHORITIES AND FIRST RESPONDERS HAVE BEEN ALERTED.
OH, THEY HAVE? GREAT, WE'RE ALL SAVED.
OKAY, JUST STAY CALM. HE'LL BE HERE ANY--

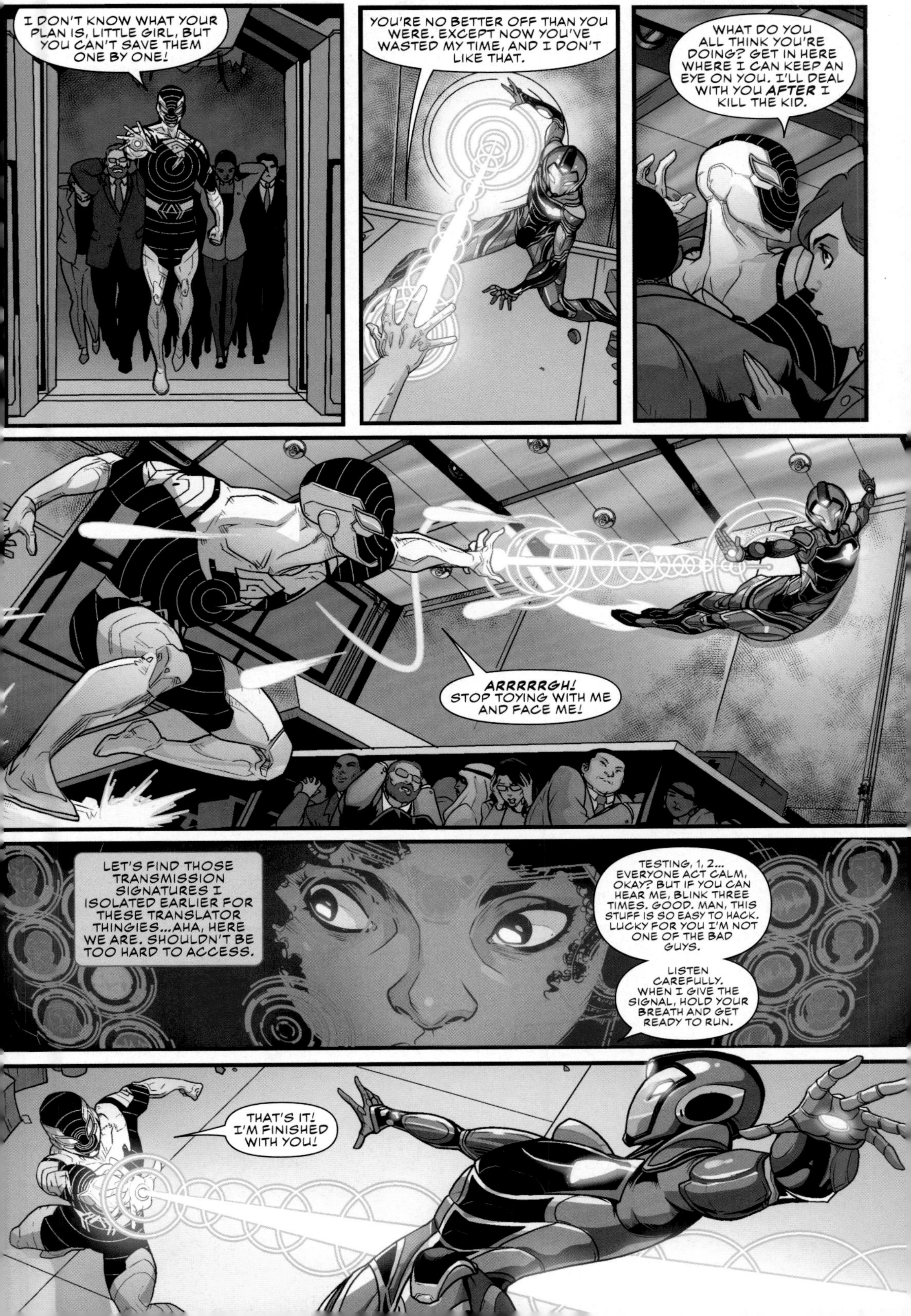
I DON'T KNOW WHAT YOUR PLAN IS, LITTLE GIRL, BUT YOU CAN'T SAVE THEM ONE BY ONE!
YOU'RE NO BETTER OFF THAN YOU WERE. EXCEPT NOW YOU'VE WASTED MY TIME, AND I DON'T LIKE THAT.
WHAT DO YOU ALL THINK YOU'RE DOING? GET IN HERE WHERE I CAN KEEP AN EYE ON YOU. I'LL DEAL WITH YOU AFTER I KILL THE KID.
ARRRRRGH! STOP TOYING WITH ME AND FACE ME!
LET'S FIND THOSE TRANSMISSION SIGNATURES I ISOLATED EARLIER FOR THESE TRANSLATOR THINGIES...AHA, HERE WE ARE. SHOULDN'T BE TOO HARD TO ACCESS.
TESTING, 1, 2... EVERYONE ACT CALM, OKAY? BUT IF YOU CAN HEAR ME, BLINK THREE TIMES. GOOD. MAN, THIS STUFF IS SO EASY TO HACK. LUCKY FOR YOU I'M NOT ONE OF THE BAD GUYS.
LISTEN CAREFULLY. WHEN I GIVE THE SIGNAL, HOLD YOUR BREATH AND GET READY TO RUN.
THAT'S IT! I'M FINISHED WITH YOU!

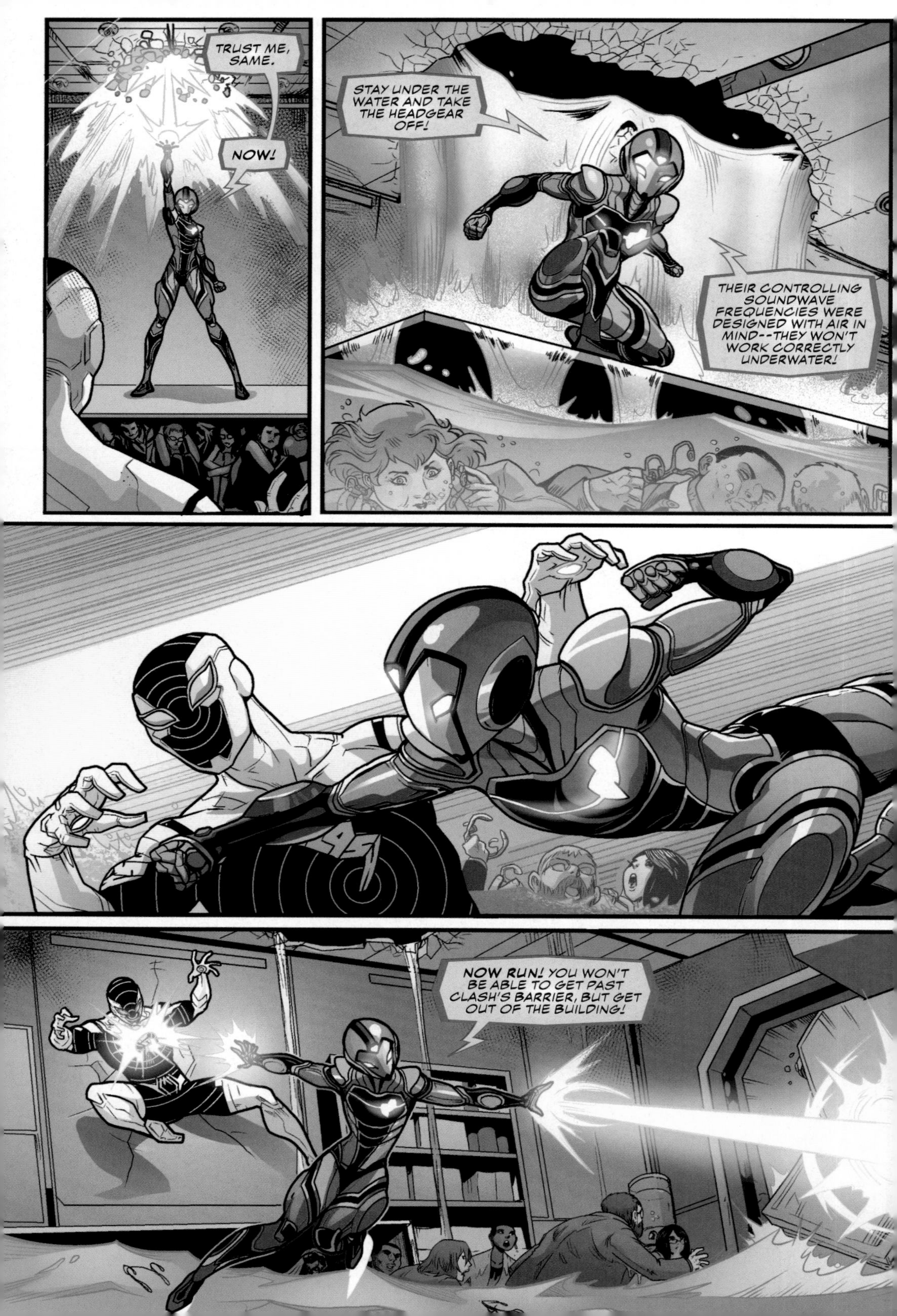

TRUST ME, SAME.
NOW!
STAY UNDER THE WATER AND TAKE THE HEADGEAR OFF!
THEIR CONTROLLING SOUNDWAVE FREQUENCIES WERE DESIGNED WITH AIR IN MIND--THEY WON'T WORK CORRECTLY UNDERWATER!
NOW RUN! YOU WON'T BE ABLE TO GET PAST CLASH'S BARRIER, BUT GET OUT OF THE BUILDING!

IMPRESSIVE, IRON GIRL. I HAVE TO ADMIT--TRULY IMPRESSIVE.

IT'S IRONHEART, BRO.

YOU THINK I CARE IF YOU DESTROY MY EQUIPMENT? THE WORLD LEADERS ARE STILL TRAPPED HERE.

MY BARRIER WILL HAVE THEM LYING ON THE GROUND SCREAMING LIKE THE REST OF THOSE FOOLS.

YOU KNOW WHAT? GOOD POINT.

HEY, YOU USING THE *LOCAL POWER GRID* TO OPERATE THOSE TRANSPONDERS YOU MUST HAVE BURIED BENEATH THE PERIMETER OF THIS BUILDING?

BECAUSE...

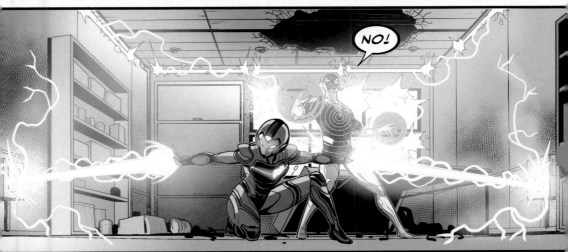

NO!

A BLACKOUT! THE BARRIER IS DOWN!

HELP US! GO GET HIM, HE'S IN THERE!

LET'S GO!

ENGAGE NIGHT VISION.

THE DARKNESS WON'T STOP ME, STUPID.

YOU'RE INTO SCIENCE-- EVER HEARD OF ECHOLOCATION?

EVER HEARD OF...MY SEMIAUTONOMOUS ELECTROMAGNETIC POWER MICRONODES? THAT'S RIGHT, YOU HAVEN'T!

I HAVEN'T PATENTED THEM YET BECAUSE THE NAME ISN'T VERY GOOD! THEY'RE PORTABLY SIZED AND THEY USE AN ELECTROMAGNETIC CURRENT TO--

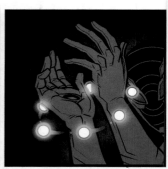

OH, THE FIGHT IS OVER, HUH?

WELL, UM...YEAH, YOU LOST! KICK ROCKS, CLASH!

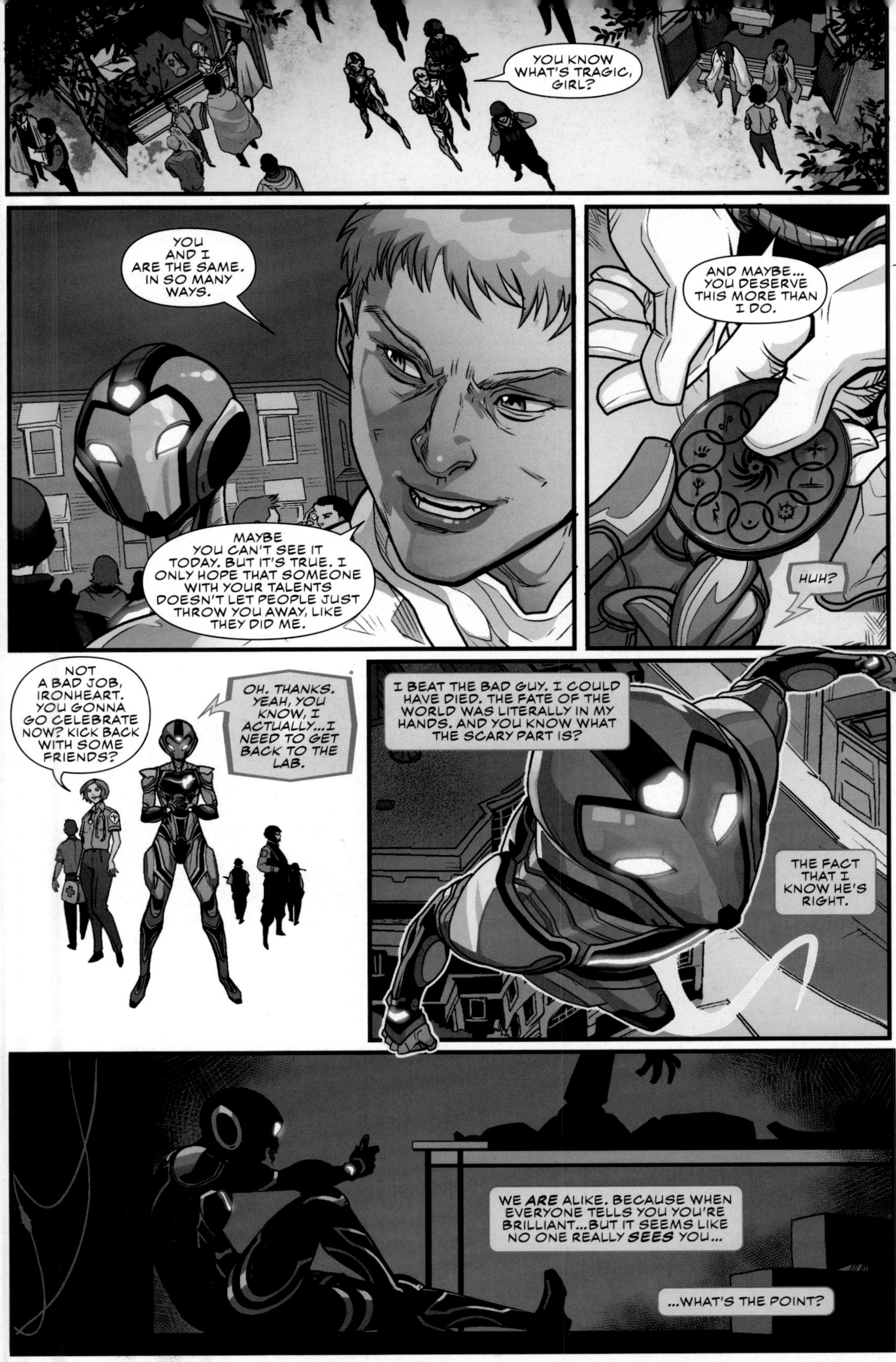

YOU KNOW WHAT'S TRAGIC, GIRL?
YOU AND I ARE THE SAME. IN SO MANY WAYS.
MAYBE YOU CAN'T SEE IT TODAY. BUT IT'S TRUE. I ONLY HOPE THAT SOMEONE WITH YOUR TALENTS DOESN'T LET PEOPLE JUST THROW YOU AWAY, LIKE THEY DID ME.
AND MAYBE... YOU DESERVE THIS MORE THAN I DO.
HUH?
NOT A BAD JOB, IRONHEART. YOU GONNA GO CELEBRATE NOW? KICK BACK WITH SOME FRIENDS?
OH. THANKS. YEAH, YOU KNOW, I ACTUALLY...I NEED TO GET BACK TO THE LAB.
I BEAT THE BAD GUY. I COULD HAVE DIED. THE FATE OF THE WORLD WAS LITERALLY IN MY HANDS. AND YOU KNOW WHAT THE SCARY PART IS?
THE FACT THAT I KNOW HE'S RIGHT.
WE *ARE* ALIKE. BECAUSE WHEN EVERYONE TELLS YOU YOU'RE BRILLIANT...BUT IT SEEMS LIKE NO ONE REALLY *SEES* YOU...
...WHAT'S THE POINT?

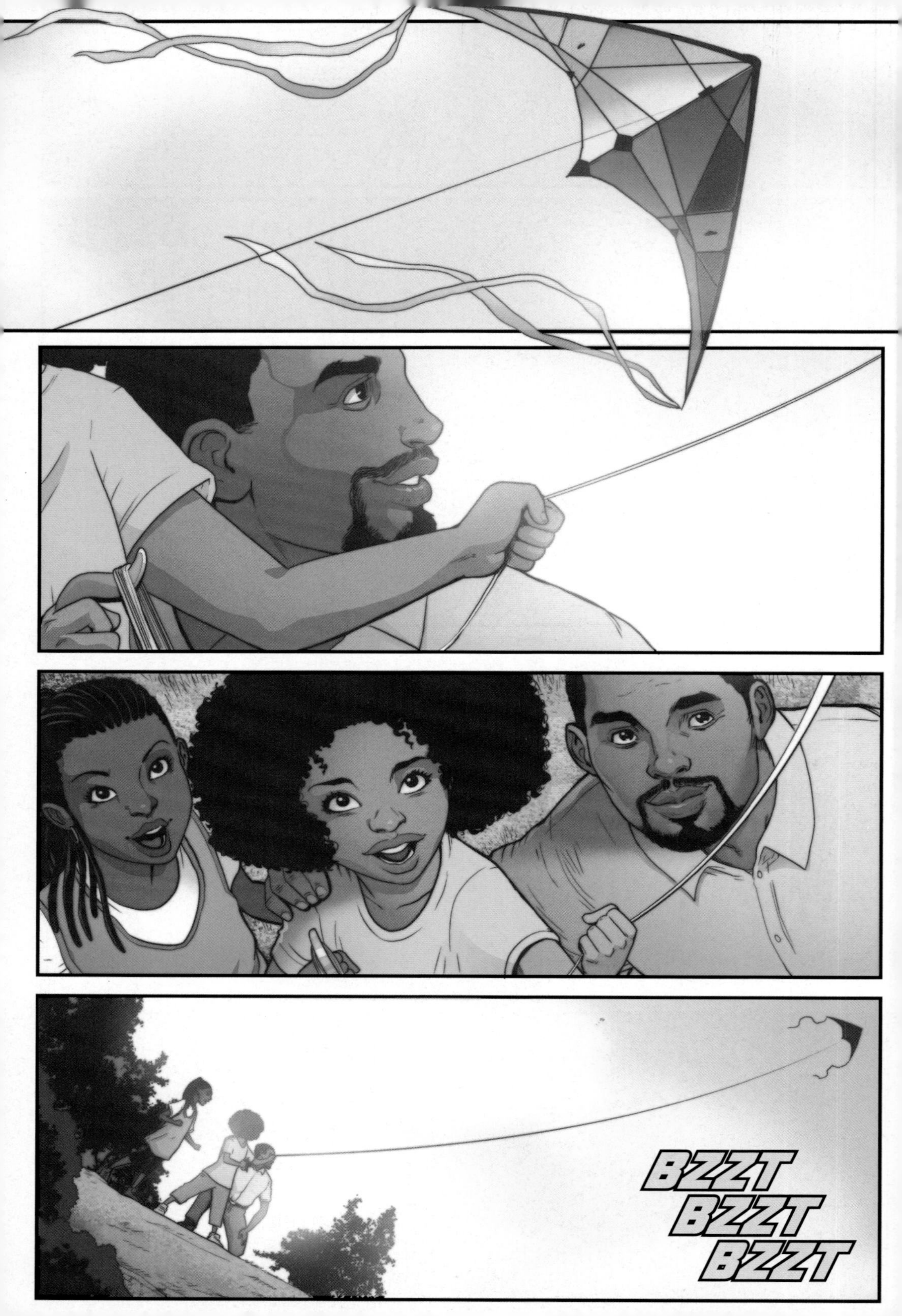
BZZT
BZZT
BZZT

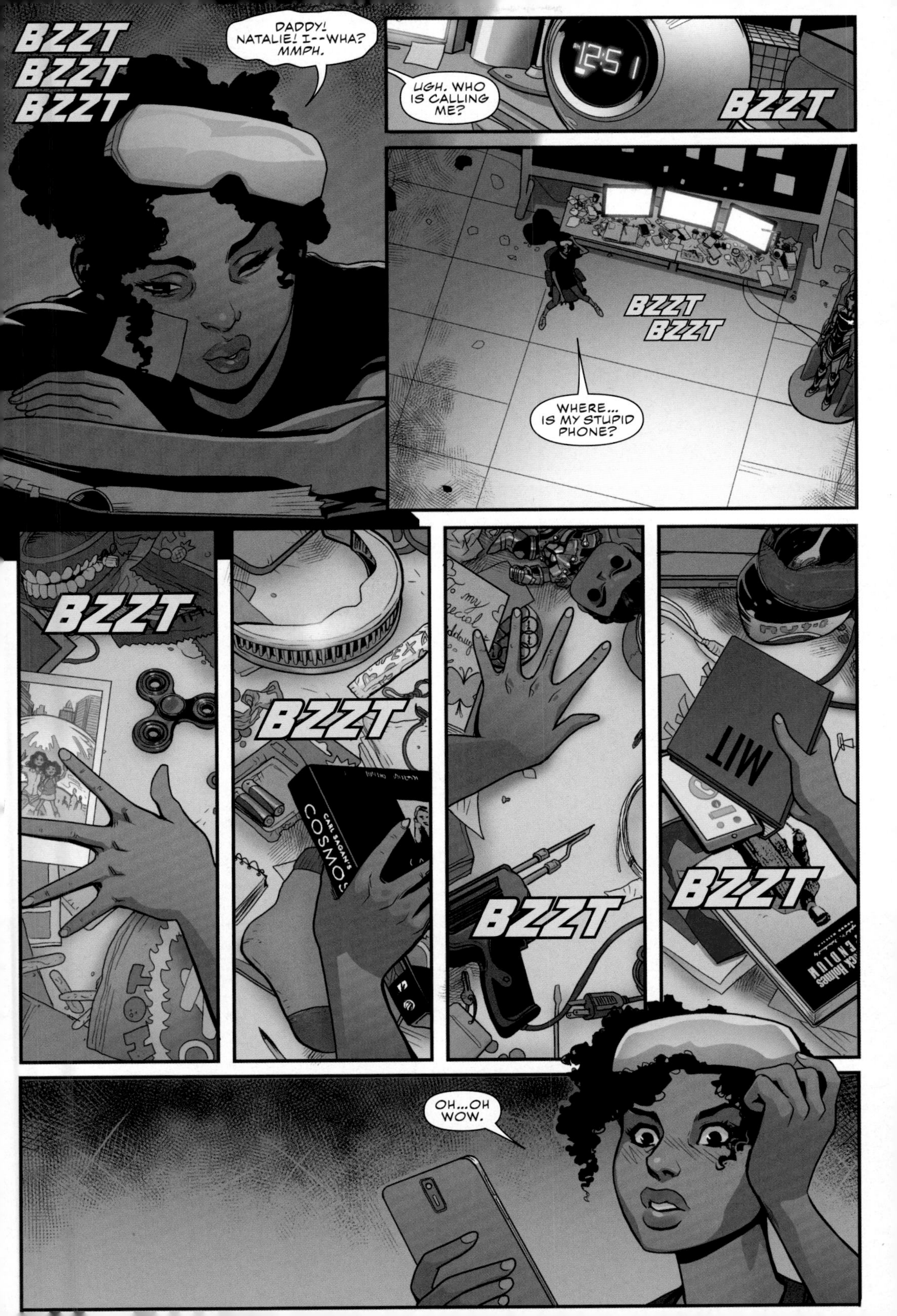
BZZT BZZT BZZT
DADDY! NATALIE! I--WHA? MMPH.
UGH. WHO IS CALLING ME?
12:51
BZZT
BZZT BZZT
WHERE... IS MY STUPID PHONE?
BZZT
BZZT
CARL SAGAN'S COSMOS
BZZT
MIT
BZZT
OH...OH WOW.

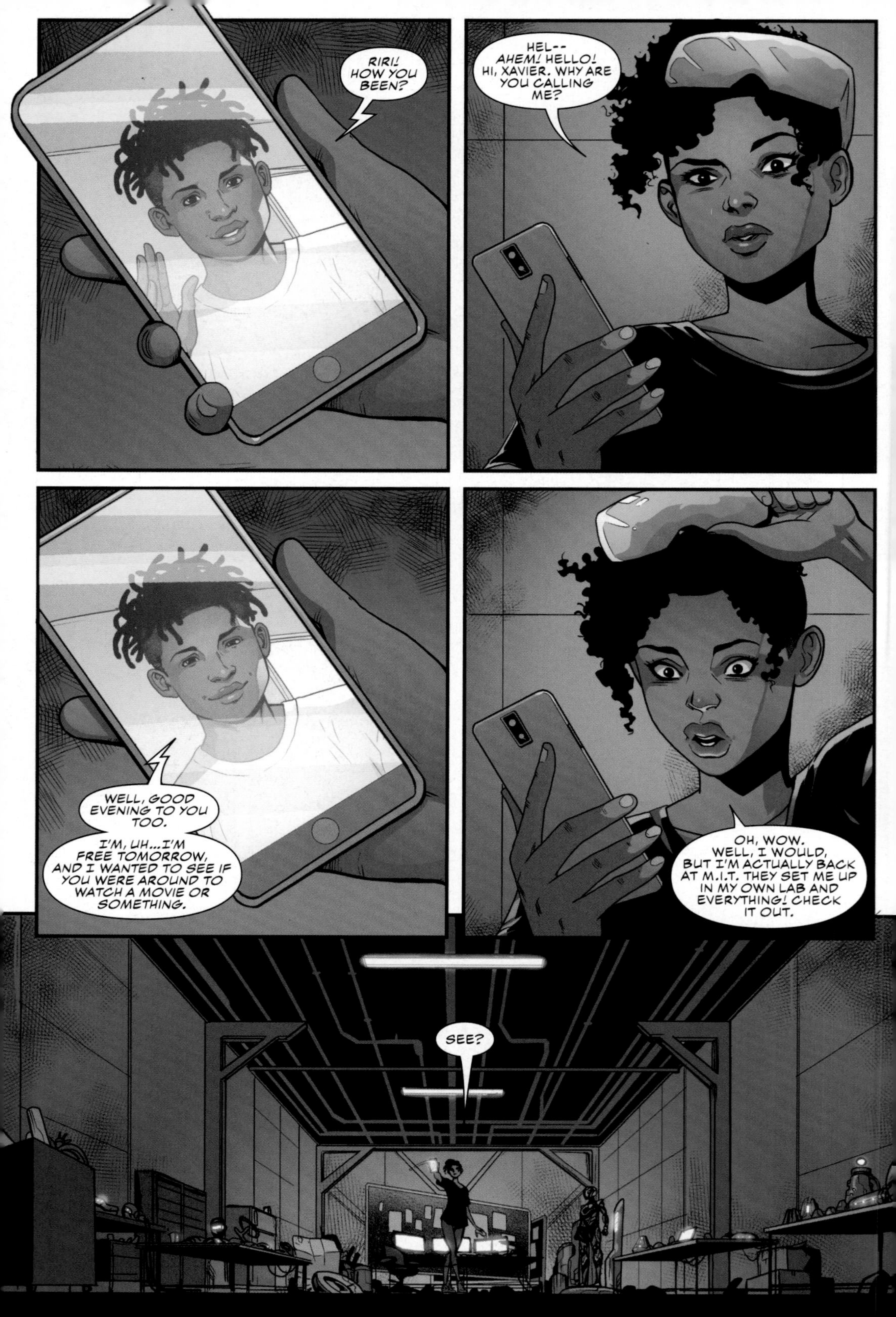
RIRI! HOW YOU BEEN?
HEL-- AHEM! HELLO! HI, XAVIER. WHY ARE YOU CALLING ME?
WELL, GOOD EVENING TO YOU TOO.
I'M, UH...I'M FREE TOMORROW, AND I WANTED TO SEE IF YOU WERE AROUND TO WATCH A MOVIE OR SOMETHING.
OH, WOW. WELL, I WOULD, BUT I'M ACTUALLY BACK AT M.I.T. THEY SET ME UP IN MY OWN LAB AND EVERYTHING! CHECK IT OUT.
SEE?

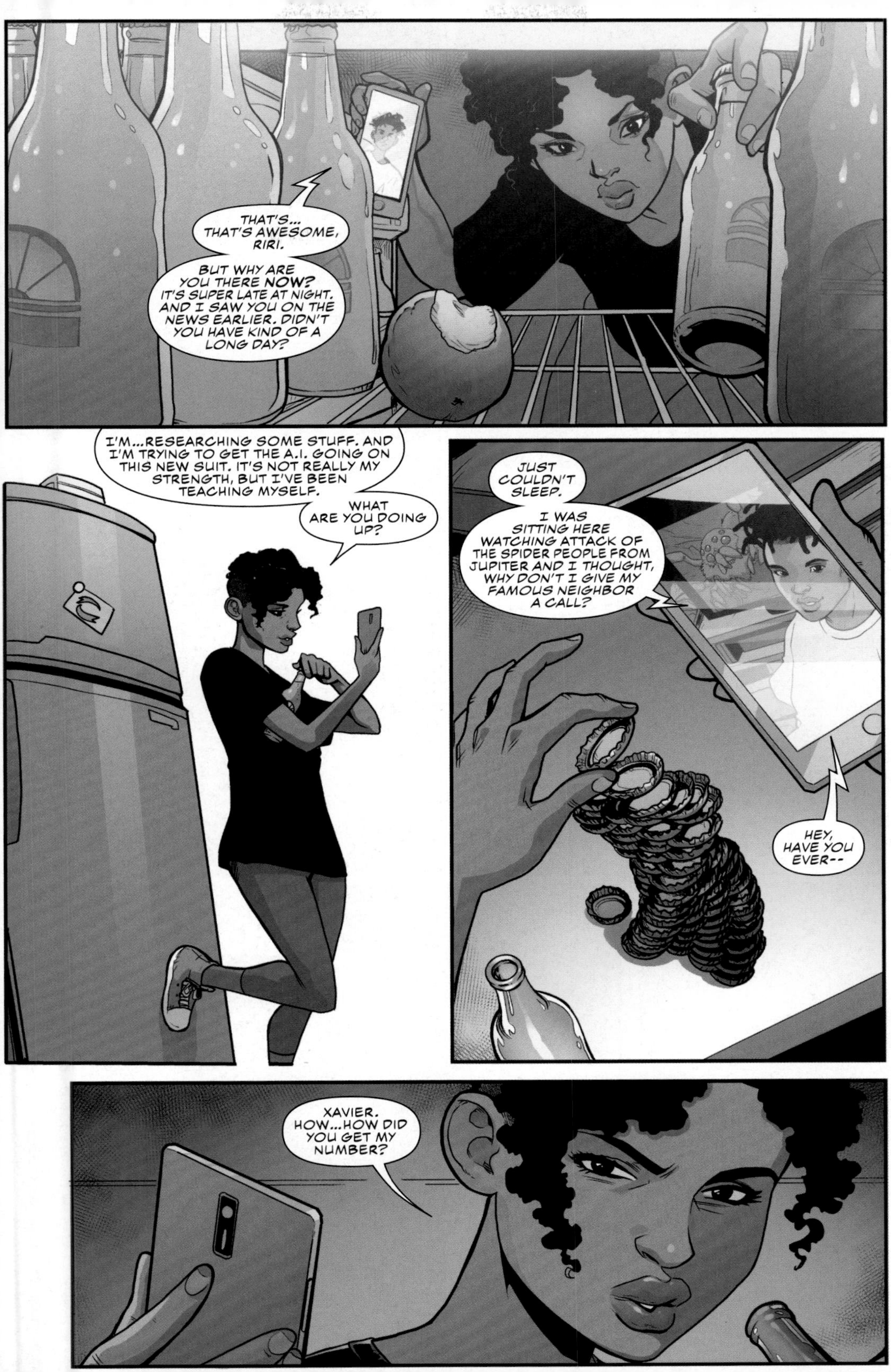
THAT'S... THAT'S AWESOME, RIRI.
BUT WHY ARE YOU THERE NOW? IT'S SUPER LATE AT NIGHT. AND I SAW YOU ON THE NEWS EARLIER. DIDN'T YOU HAVE KIND OF A LONG DAY?
I'M...RESEARCHING SOME STUFF. AND I'M TRYING TO GET THE A.I. GOING ON THIS NEW SUIT. IT'S NOT REALLY MY STRENGTH, BUT I'VE BEEN TEACHING MYSELF.
WHAT ARE YOU DOING UP?
JUST COULDN'T SLEEP.
I WAS SITTING HERE WATCHING ATTACK OF THE SPIDER PEOPLE FROM JUPITER AND I THOUGHT, WHY DON'T I GIVE MY FAMOUS NEIGHBOR A CALL?
HEY, HAVE YOU EVER--
XAVIER. HOW...HOW DID YOU GET MY NUMBER?

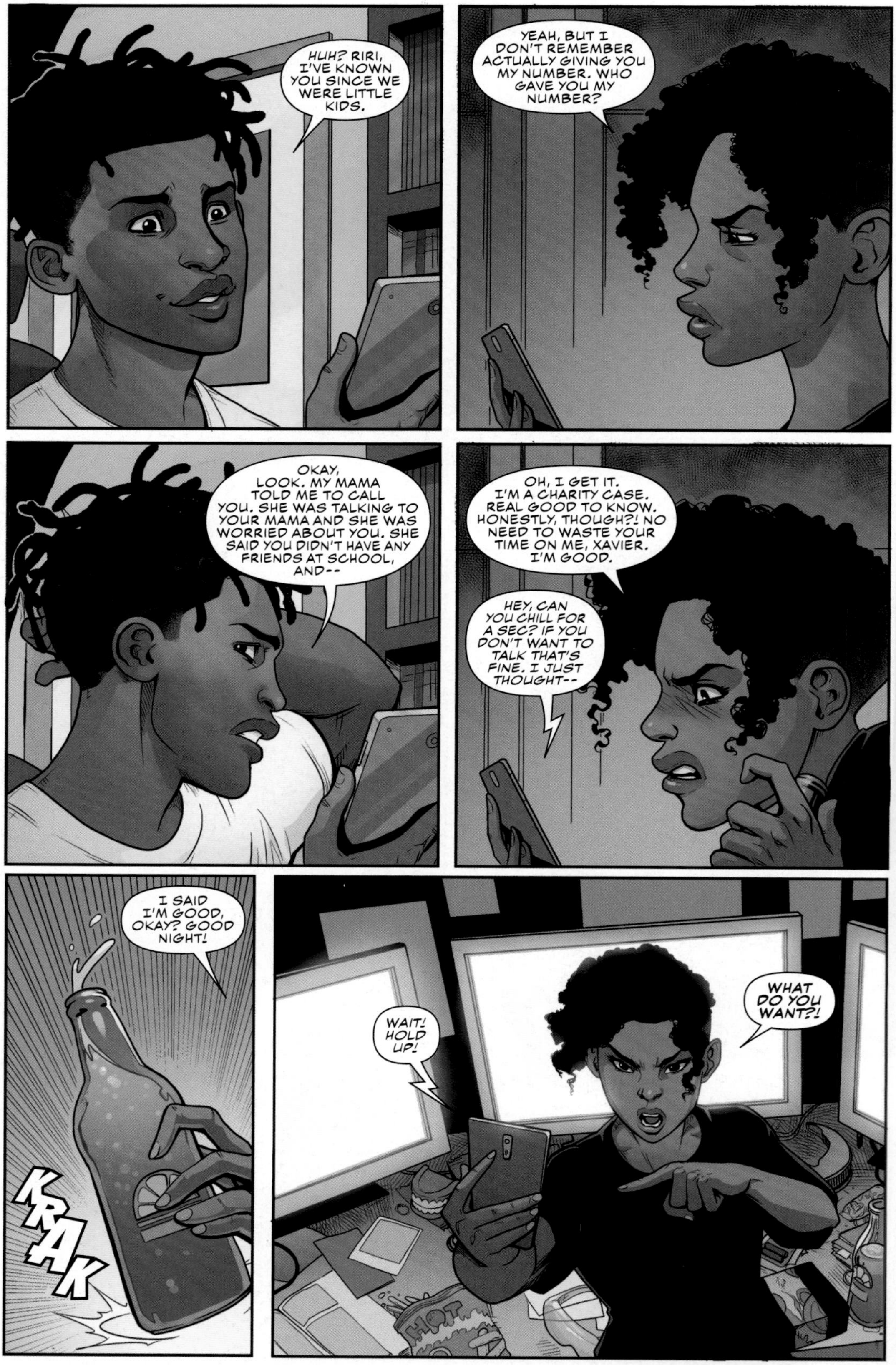
HUH? RIRI, I'VE KNOWN YOU SINCE WE WERE LITTLE KIDS.
YEAH, BUT I DON'T REMEMBER ACTUALLY GIVING YOU MY NUMBER. WHO GAVE YOU MY NUMBER?
OKAY, LOOK. MY MAMA TOLD ME TO CALL YOU. SHE WAS TALKING TO YOUR MAMA AND SHE WAS WORRIED ABOUT YOU. SHE SAID YOU DIDN'T HAVE ANY FRIENDS AT SCHOOL, AND--
OH, I GET IT. I'M A CHARITY CASE. REAL GOOD TO KNOW. HONESTLY, THOUGH?! NO NEED TO WASTE YOUR TIME ON ME, XAVIER. I'M GOOD.
HEY, CAN YOU CHILL FOR A SEC? IF YOU DON'T WANT TO TALK THAT'S FINE. I JUST THOUGHT--
I SAID I'M GOOD, OKAY? GOOD NIGHT!
KRAK
WAIT! HOLD UP!
WHAT DO YOU WANT?!

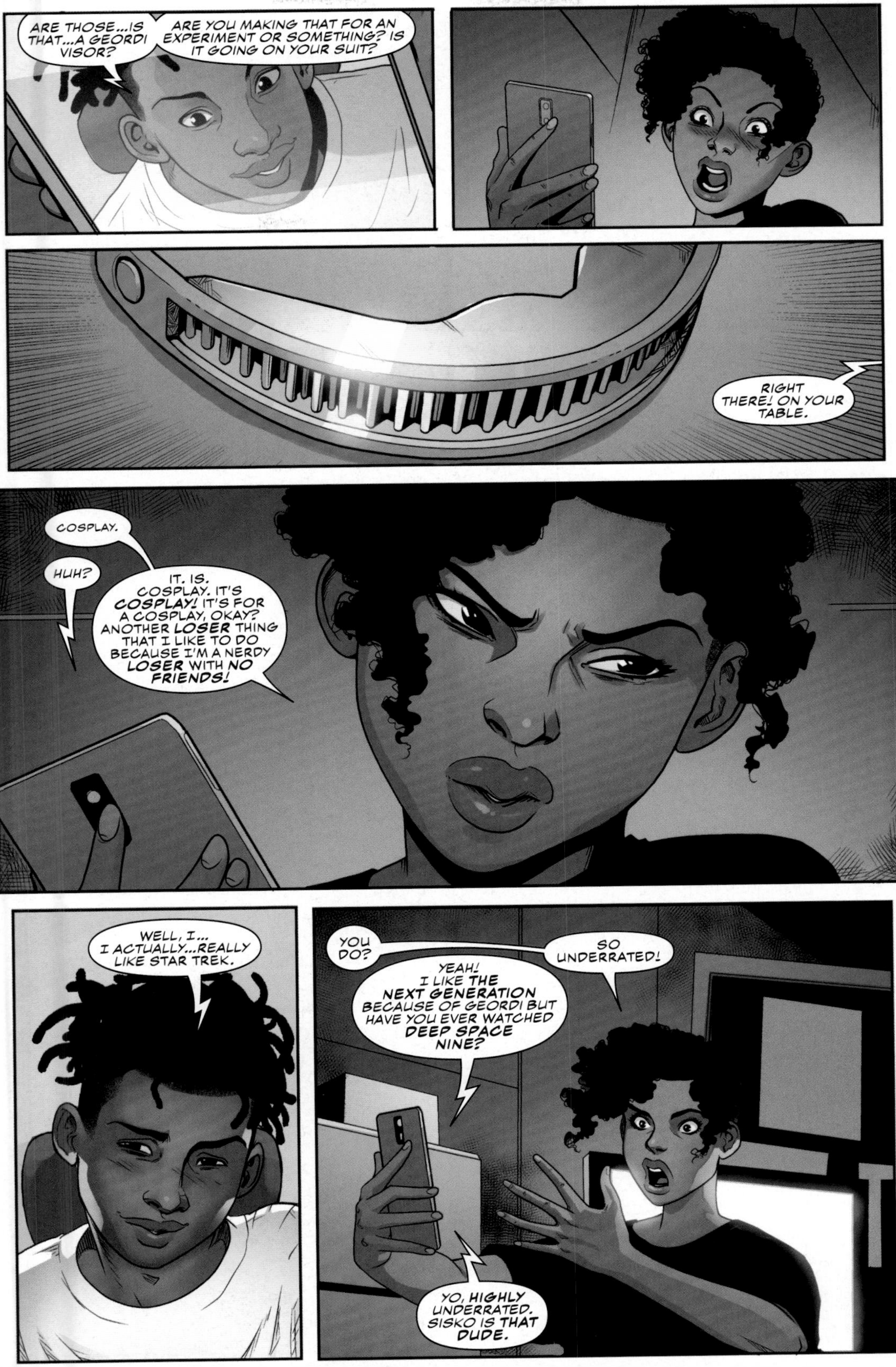
ARE THOSE...IS THAT...A GEORDI VISOR?
ARE YOU MAKING THAT FOR AN EXPERIMENT OR SOMETHING? IS IT GOING ON YOUR SUIT?
RIGHT THERE! ON YOUR TABLE.
COSPLAY.
HUH?
IT. IS. COSPLAY. IT'S COSPLAY! IT'S FOR A COSPLAY, OKAY? ANOTHER LOSER THING THAT I LIKE TO DO BECAUSE I'M A NERDY LOSER WITH NO FRIENDS!
WELL, I... I ACTUALLY...REALLY LIKE STAR TREK.
YOU DO?
SO UNDERRATED!
YEAH! I LIKE THE NEXT GENERATION BECAUSE OF GEORDI BUT HAVE YOU EVER WATCHED DEEP SPACE NINE?
YO, HIGHLY UNDERRATED. SISKO IS THAT DUDE.

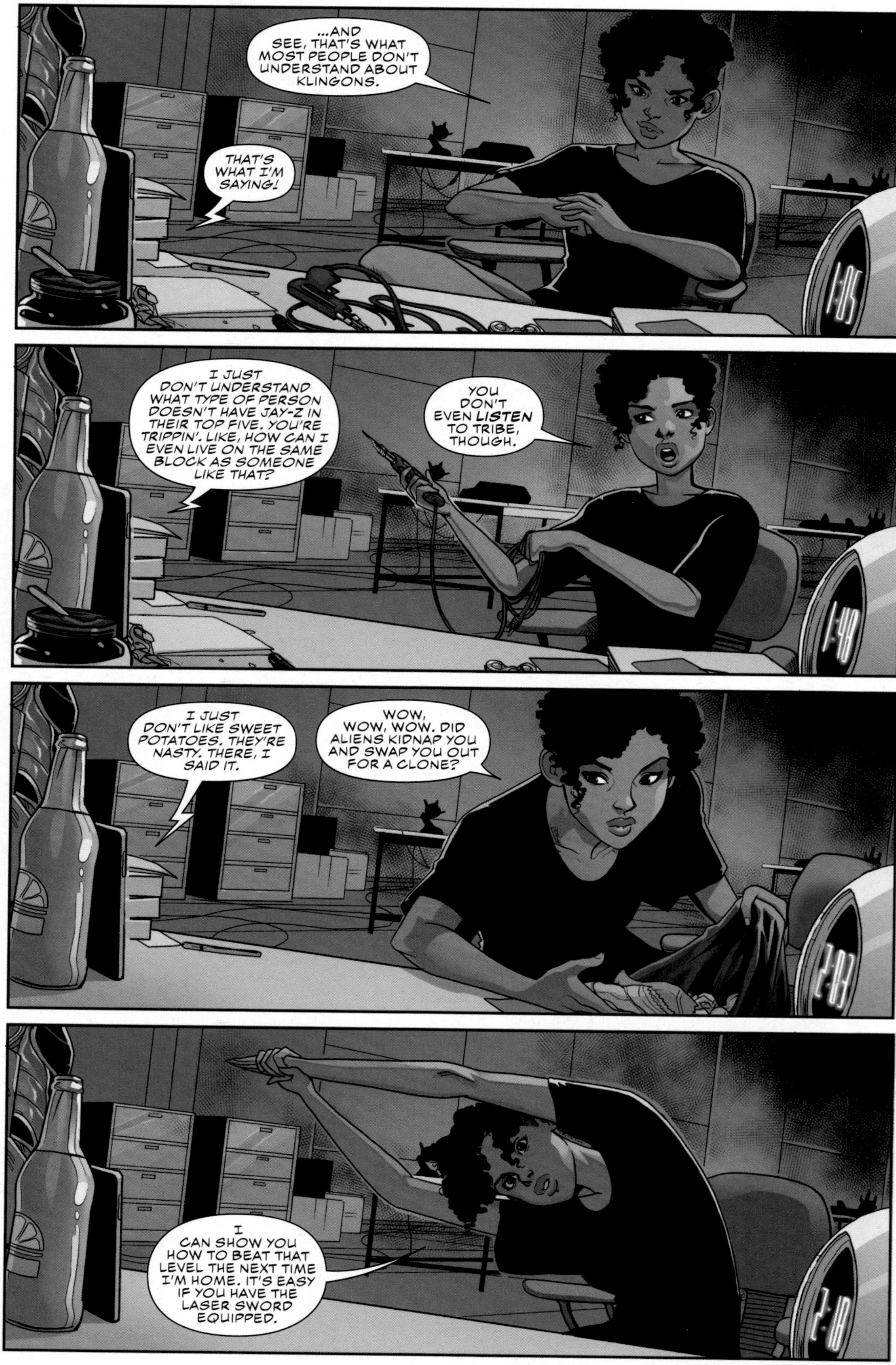
...AND SEE, THAT'S WHAT MOST PEOPLE DON'T UNDERSTAND ABOUT KLINGONS.
THAT'S WHAT I'M SAYING!
I JUST DON'T UNDERSTAND WHAT TYPE OF PERSON DOESN'T HAVE JAY-Z IN THEIR TOP FIVE. YOU'RE TRIPPIN'. LIKE, HOW CAN I EVEN LIVE ON THE SAME BLOCK AS SOMEONE LIKE THAT?
YOU DON'T EVEN LISTEN TO TRIBE, THOUGH.
I JUST DON'T LIKE SWEET POTATOES. THEY'RE NASTY. THERE, I SAID IT.
WOW, WOW, WOW. DID ALIENS KIDNAP YOU AND SWAP YOU OUT FOR A CLONE?
I CAN SHOW YOU HOW TO BEAT THAT LEVEL THE NEXT TIME I'M HOME. IT'S EASY IF YOU HAVE THE LASER SWORD EQUIPPED.

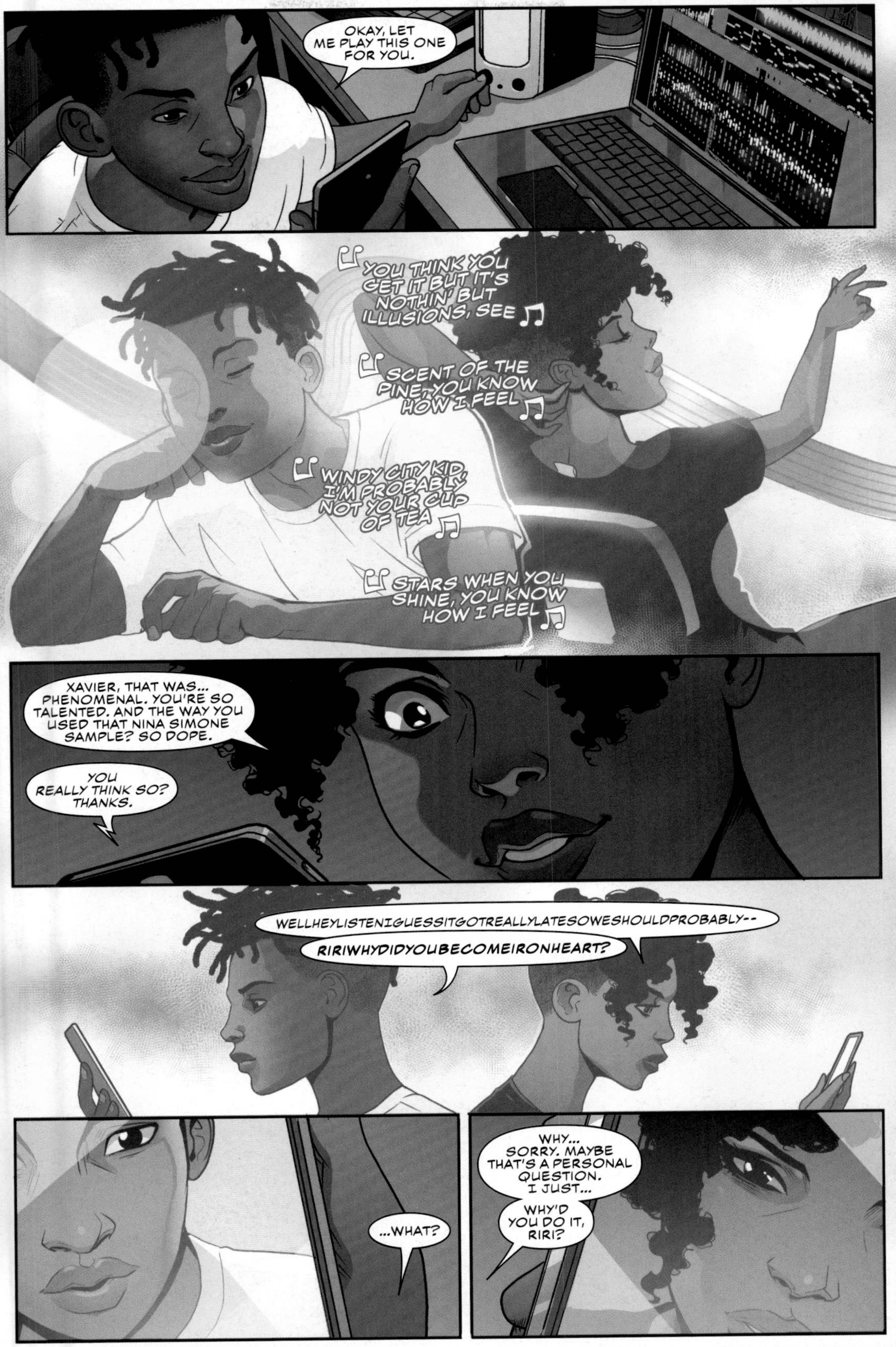

OKAY, LET ME PLAY THIS ONE FOR YOU.
YOU THINK YOU GET IT BUT IT'S NOTHIN' BUT ILLUSIONS, SEE ♫
SCENT OF THE PINE, YOU KNOW HOW I FEEL ♫
WINDY CITY KID, I'M PROBABLY NOT YOUR CUP OF TEA ♫
STARS WHEN YOU SHINE, YOU KNOW HOW I FEEL ♫
XAVIER, THAT WAS... PHENOMENAL. YOU'RE SO TALENTED. AND THE WAY YOU USED THAT NINA SIMONE SAMPLE? SO DOPE.
YOU REALLY THINK SO? THANKS.
WELLHEYLISTENIGUESSITGOTREALLYLATESOWESHOULDPROBABLY--
RIRIWHYDIDYOUBECOMEIRONHEART?
...WHAT?
WHY... SORRY. MAYBE THAT'S A PERSONAL QUESTION. I JUST...
WHY'D YOU DO IT, RIRI?

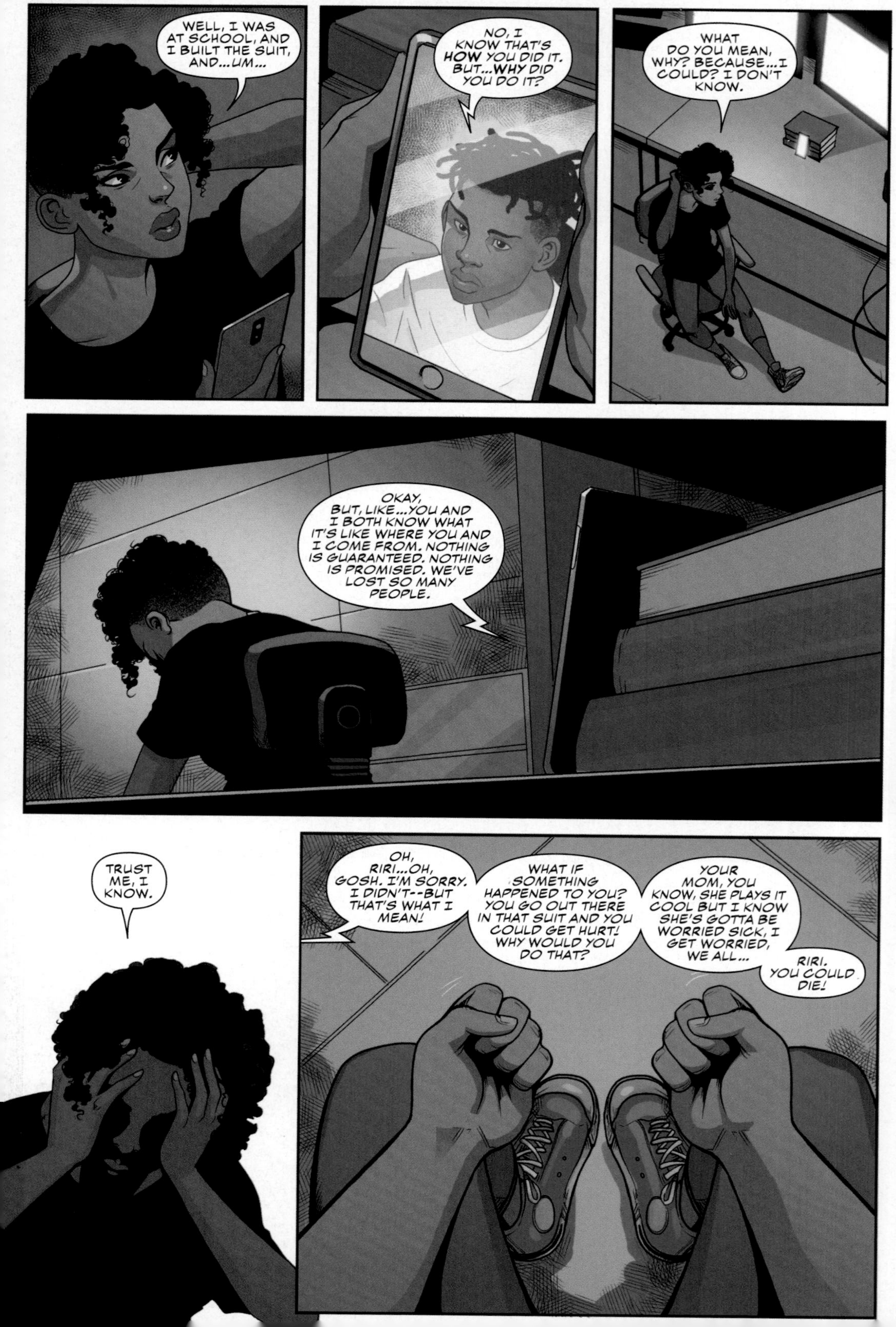
WELL, I WAS AT SCHOOL, AND I BUILT THE SUIT, AND...UM...
NO, I KNOW THAT'S HOW YOU DID IT. BUT...WHY DID YOU DO IT?
WHAT DO YOU MEAN, WHY? BECAUSE...I COULD? I DON'T KNOW.
OKAY, BUT, LIKE...YOU AND I BOTH KNOW WHAT IT'S LIKE WHERE YOU AND I COME FROM. NOTHING IS GUARANTEED. NOTHING IS PROMISED. WE'VE LOST SO MANY PEOPLE.
TRUST ME, I KNOW.
OH, RIRI...OH, GOSH. I'M SORRY. I DIDN'T--BUT THAT'S WHAT I MEAN!
WHAT IF SOMETHING HAPPENED TO YOU? YOU GO OUT THERE IN THAT SUIT AND YOU COULD GET HURT! WHY WOULD YOU DO THAT?
YOUR MOM, YOU KNOW, SHE PLAYS IT COOL BUT I KNOW SHE'S GOTTA BE WORRIED SICK, I GET WORRIED, WE ALL...
RIRI. YOU COULD DIE!

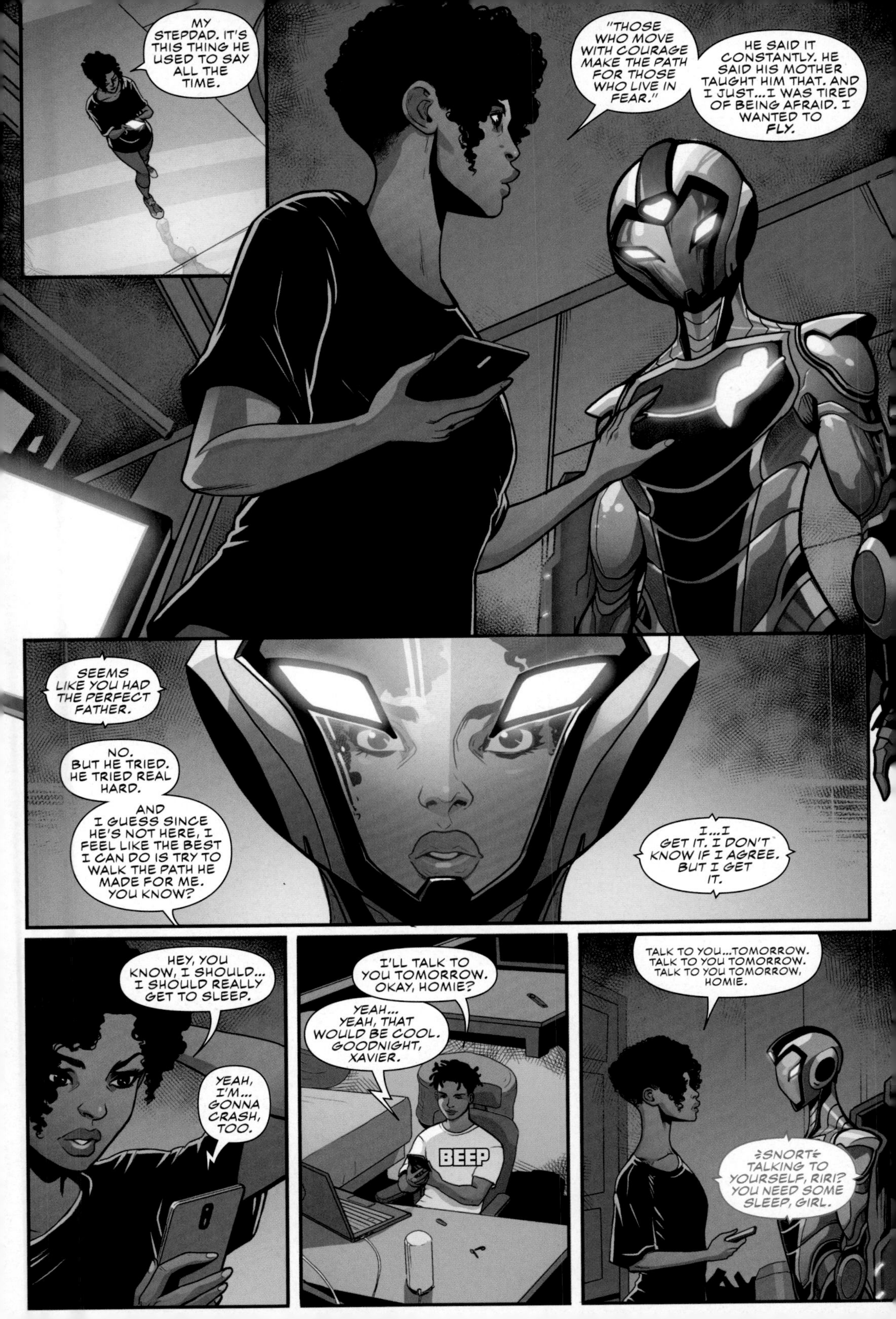
MY STEPDAD. IT'S THIS THING HE USED TO SAY ALL THE TIME.
"THOSE WHO MOVE WITH COURAGE MAKE THE PATH FOR THOSE WHO LIVE IN FEAR."
HE SAID IT CONSTANTLY. HE SAID HIS MOTHER TAUGHT HIM THAT. AND I JUST...I WAS TIRED OF BEING AFRAID. I WANTED TO FLY.
SEEMS LIKE YOU HAD THE PERFECT FATHER.
NO. BUT HE TRIED. HE TRIED REAL HARD.
AND I GUESS SINCE HE'S NOT HERE, I FEEL LIKE THE BEST I CAN DO IS TRY TO WALK THE PATH HE MADE FOR ME. YOU KNOW?
I...I GET IT. I DON'T KNOW IF I AGREE. BUT I GET IT.
HEY, YOU KNOW, I SHOULD... I SHOULD REALLY GET TO SLEEP.
YEAH, I'M... GONNA CRASH, TOO.
I'LL TALK TO YOU TOMORROW. OKAY, HOMIE?
YEAH... YEAH, THAT WOULD BE COOL. GOODNIGHT, XAVIER.
BEEP
TALK TO YOU...TOMORROW. TALK TO YOU TOMORROW. TALK TO YOU TOMORROW, HOMIE.
SNORT TALKING TO YOURSELF, RIRI? YOU NEED SOME SLEEP, GIRL.

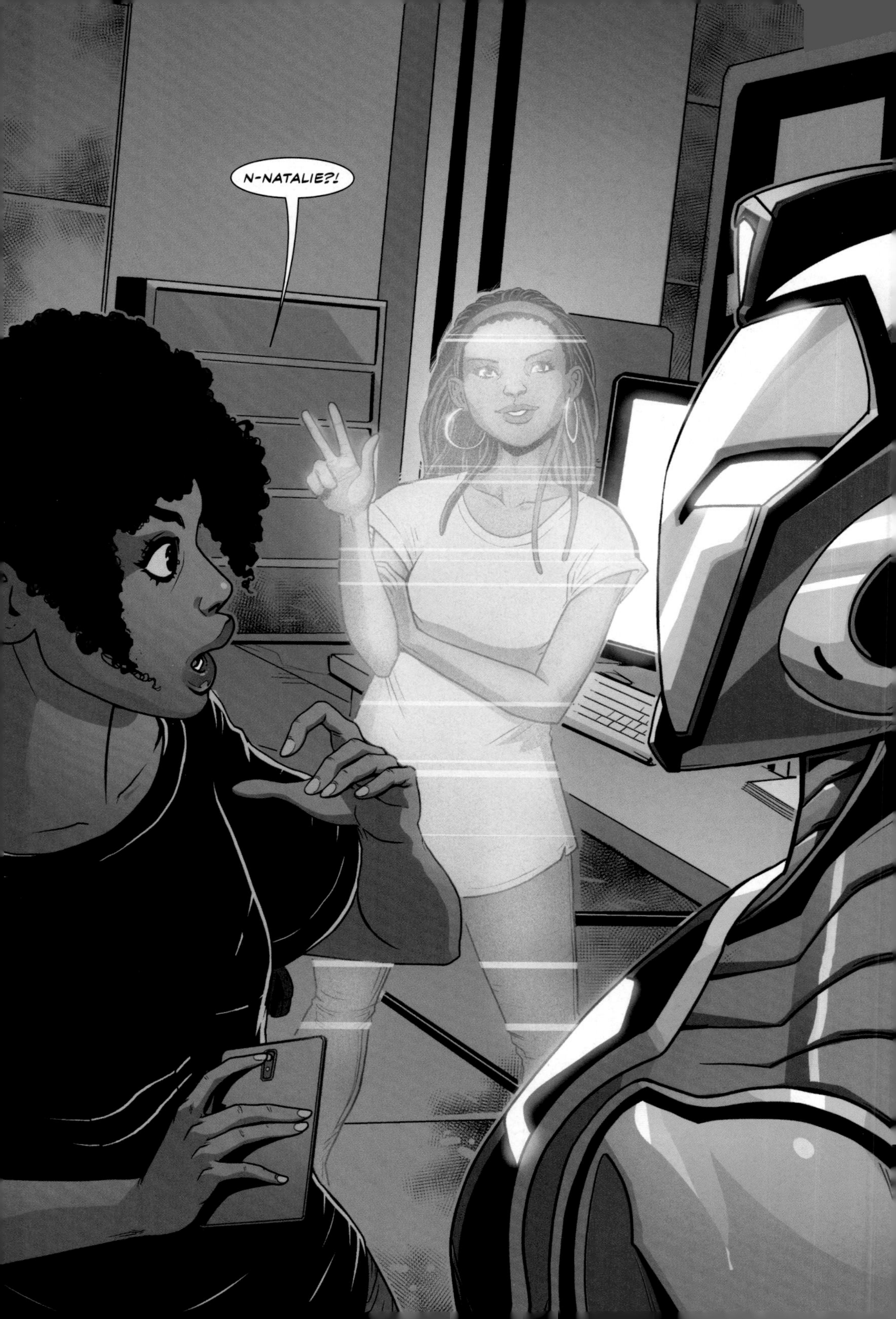
N-NATALIE?!

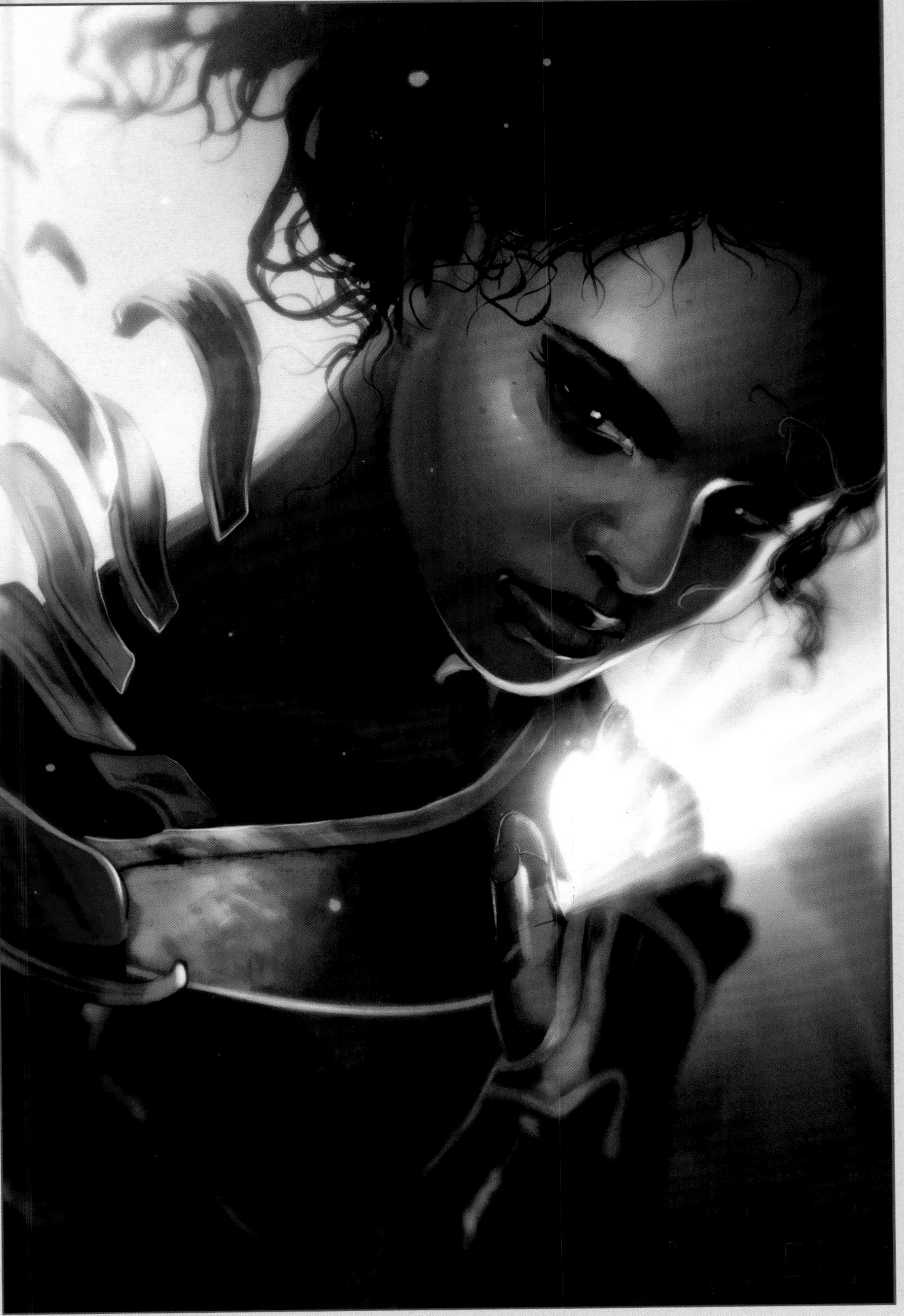

#1 VARIANT
BY STEPHANIE HANS

2

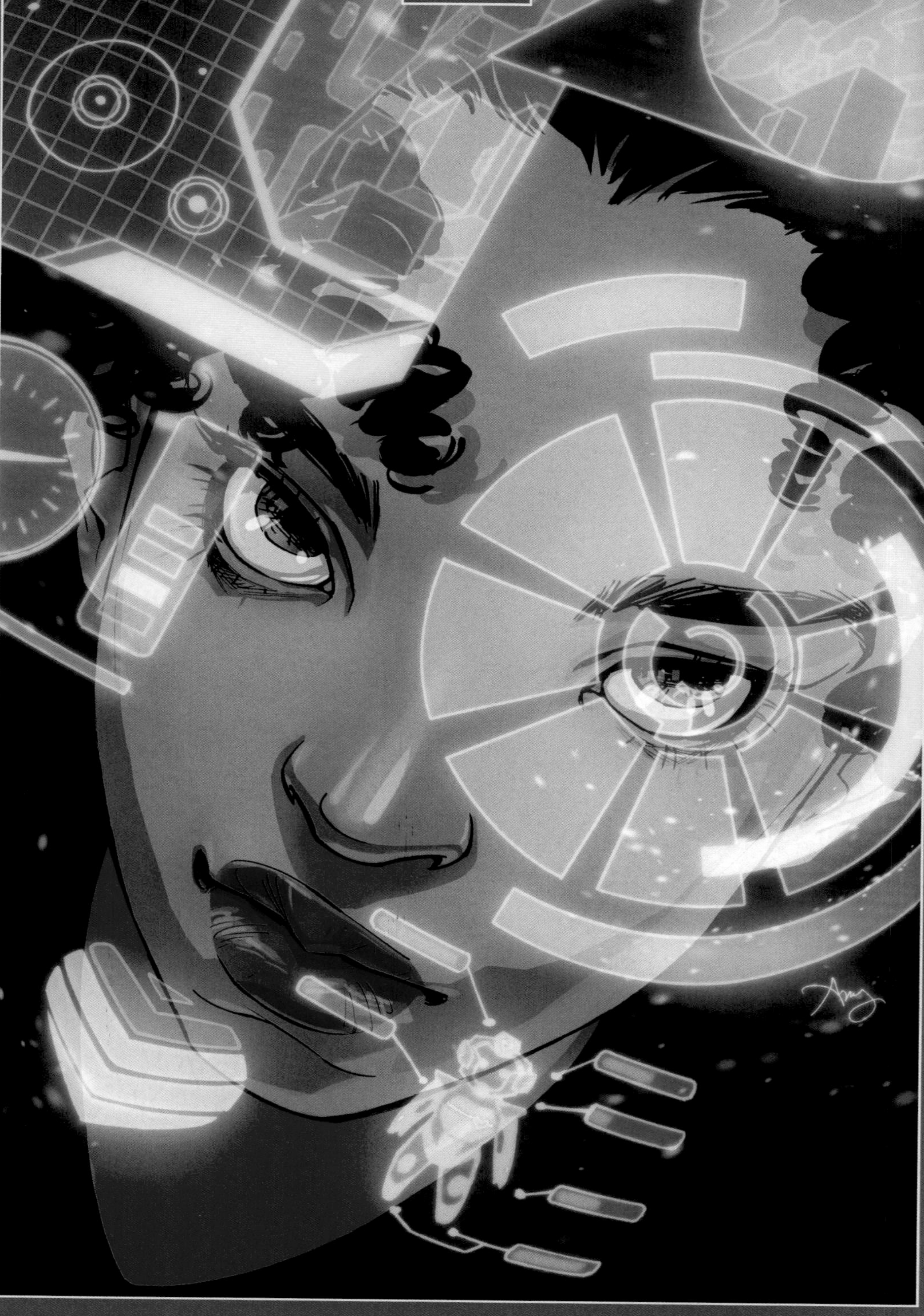

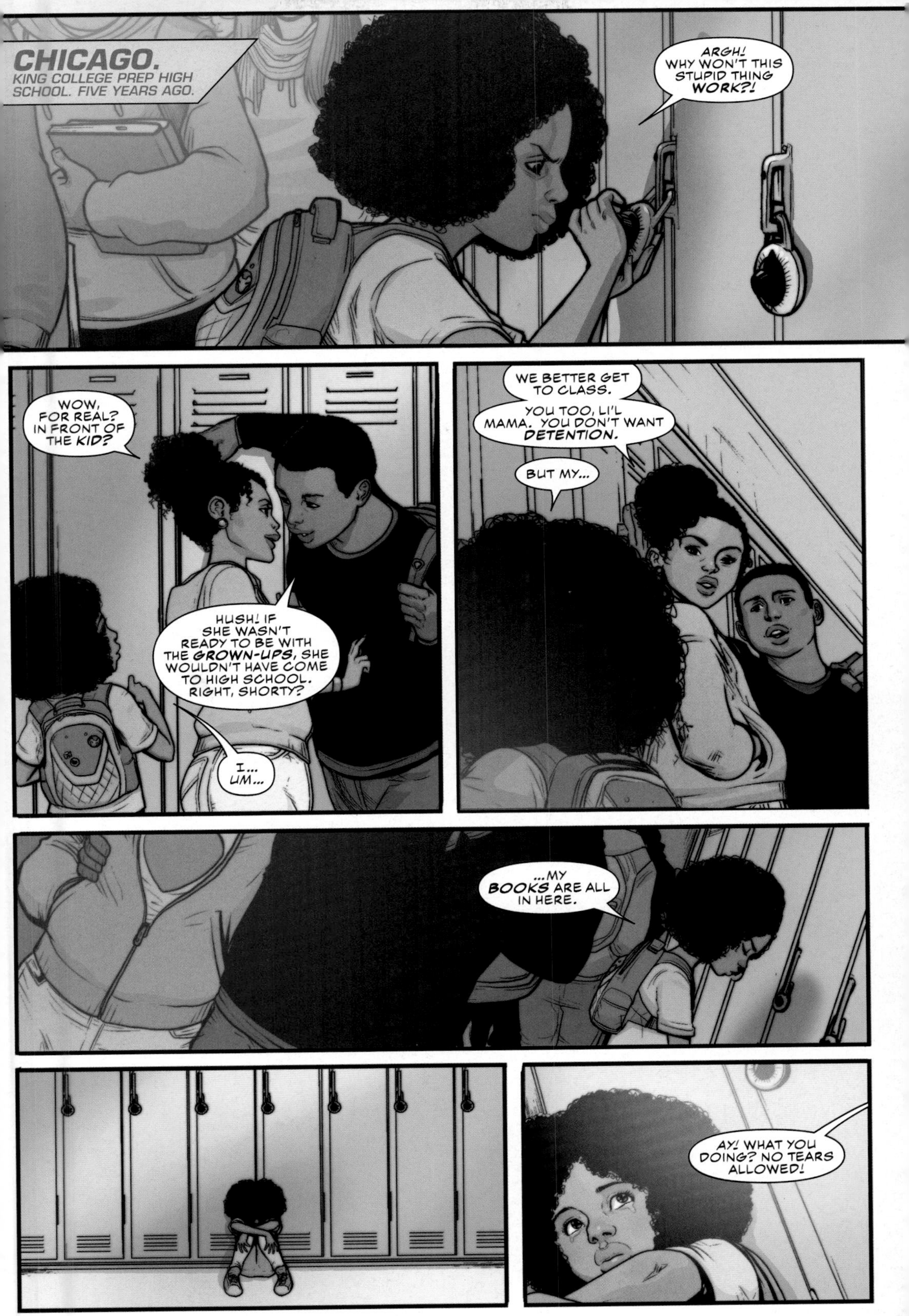
CHICAGO.
KING COLLEGE PREP HIGH SCHOOL. FIVE YEARS AGO.
ARGH! WHY WON'T THIS STUPID THING WORK?!
WOW, FOR REAL? IN FRONT OF THE KID?
HUSH! IF SHE WASN'T READY TO BE WITH THE GROWN-UPS, SHE WOULDN'T HAVE COME TO HIGH SCHOOL. RIGHT, SHORTY?
I... UM...
WE BETTER GET TO CLASS.
YOU TOO, LI'L MAMA. YOU DON'T WANT DETENTION.
BUT MY...
...MY BOOKS ARE ALL IN HERE.
AY! WHAT YOU DOING? NO TEARS ALLOWED!

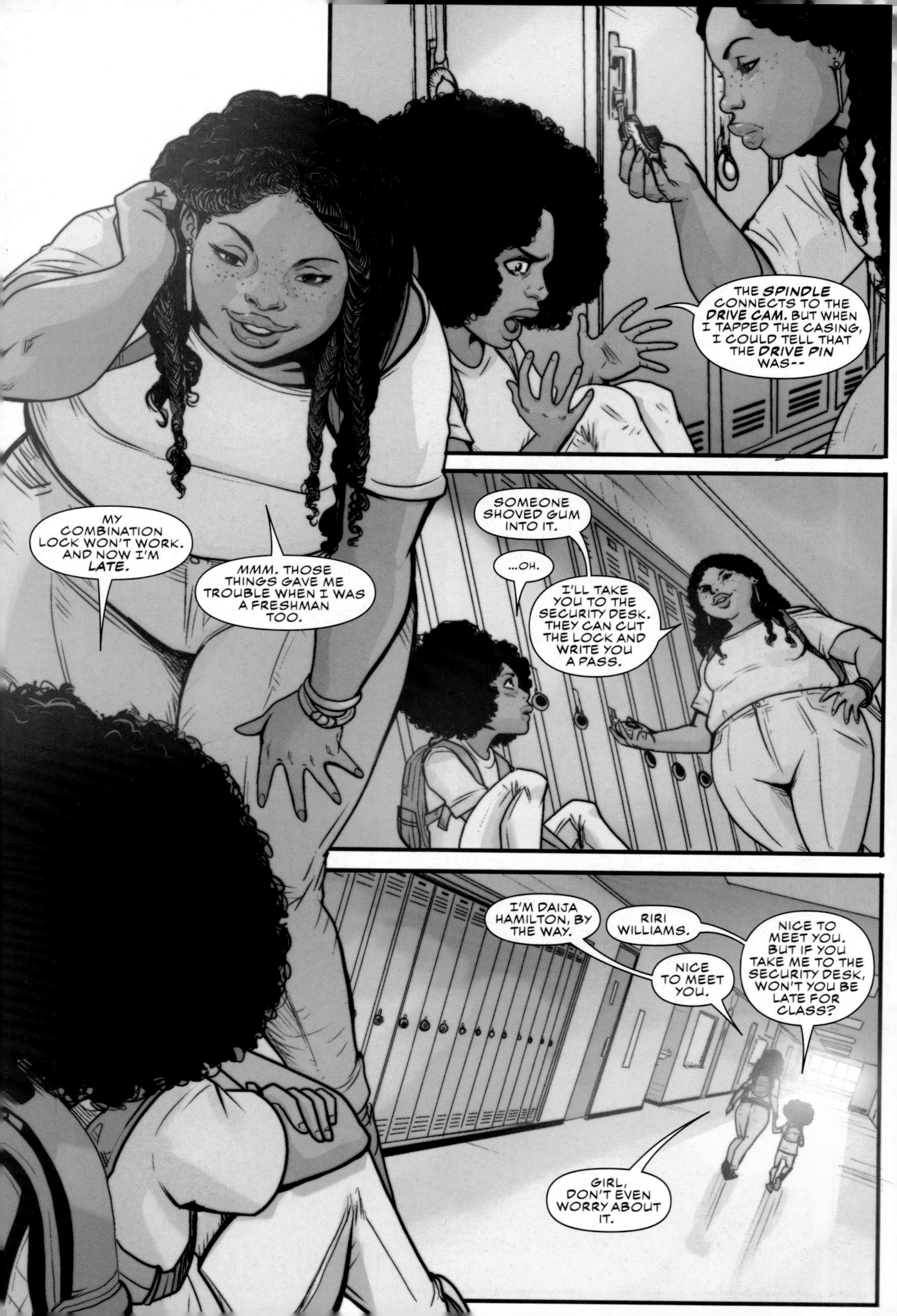
THE SPINDLE CONNECTS TO THE DRIVE CAM. BUT WHEN I TAPPED THE CASING, I COULD TELL THAT THE DRIVE PIN WAS--
MY COMBINATION LOCK WON'T WORK. AND NOW I'M LATE.
MMM. THOSE THINGS GAVE ME TROUBLE WHEN I WAS A FRESHMAN TOO.
SOMEONE SHOVED GUM INTO IT.
...OH.
I'LL TAKE YOU TO THE SECURITY DESK. THEY CAN CUT THE LOCK AND WRITE YOU A PASS.
I'M DAIJA HAMILTON, BY THE WAY.
RIRI WILLIAMS.
NICE TO MEET YOU.
NICE TO MEET YOU. BUT IF YOU TAKE ME TO THE SECURITY DESK, WON'T YOU BE LATE FOR CLASS?
GIRL, DON'T EVEN WORRY ABOUT IT.

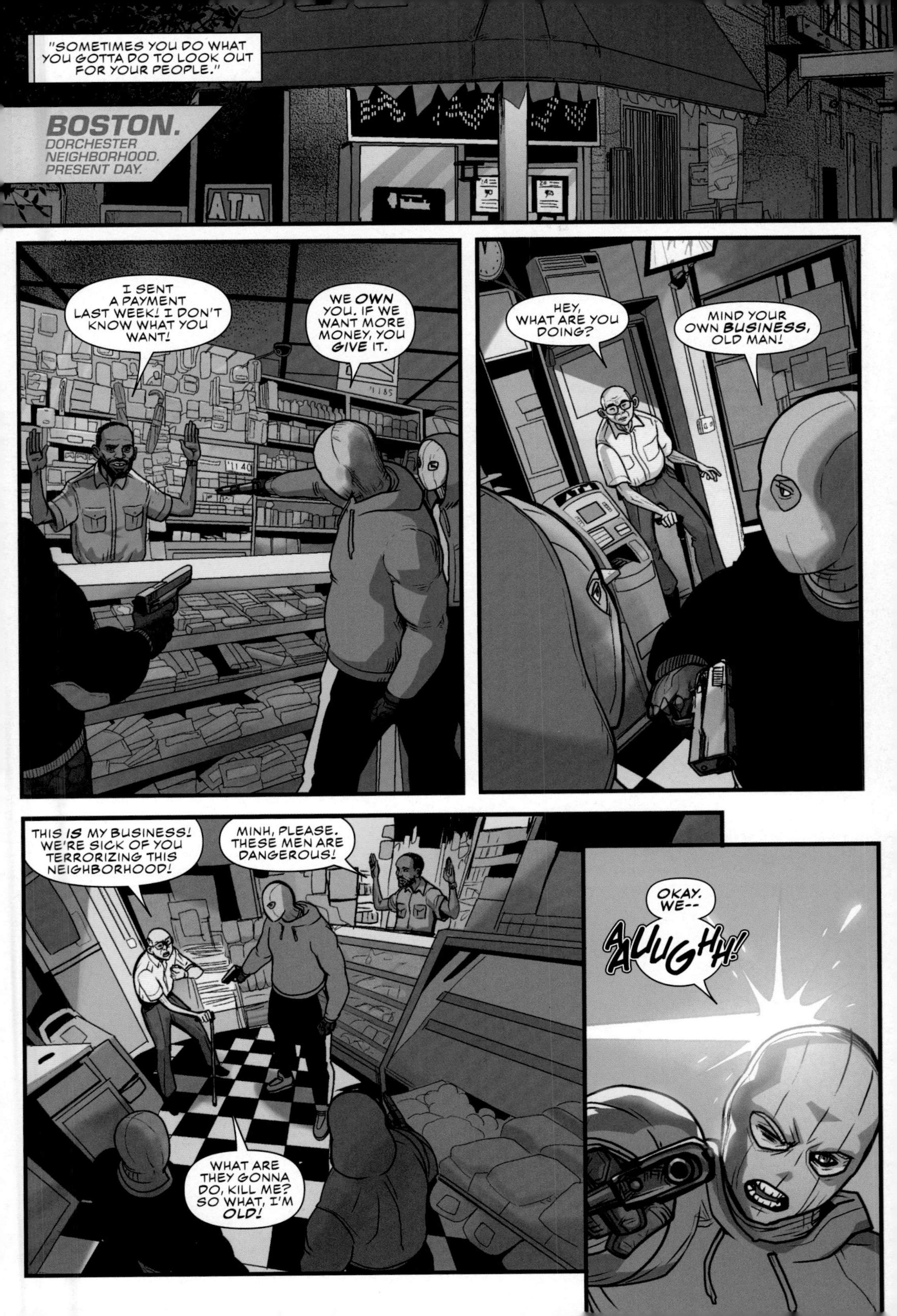
"SOMETIMES YOU DO WHAT YOU GOTTA DO TO LOOK OUT FOR YOUR PEOPLE."
BOSTON. DORCHESTER NEIGHBORHOOD. PRESENT DAY.
ATM
I SENT A PAYMENT LAST WEEK! I DON'T KNOW WHAT YOU WANT!
WE OWN YOU. IF WE WANT MORE MONEY, YOU GIVE IT.
HEY, WHAT ARE YOU DOING?
MIND YOUR OWN BUSINESS, OLD MAN!
THIS IS MY BUSINESS! WE'RE SICK OF YOU TERRORIZING THIS NEIGHBORHOOD!
MINH, PLEASE. THESE MEN ARE DANGEROUS!
WHAT ARE THEY GONNA DO, KILL ME? SO WHAT, I'M OLD!
OKAY. WE--
AAUUGHH!

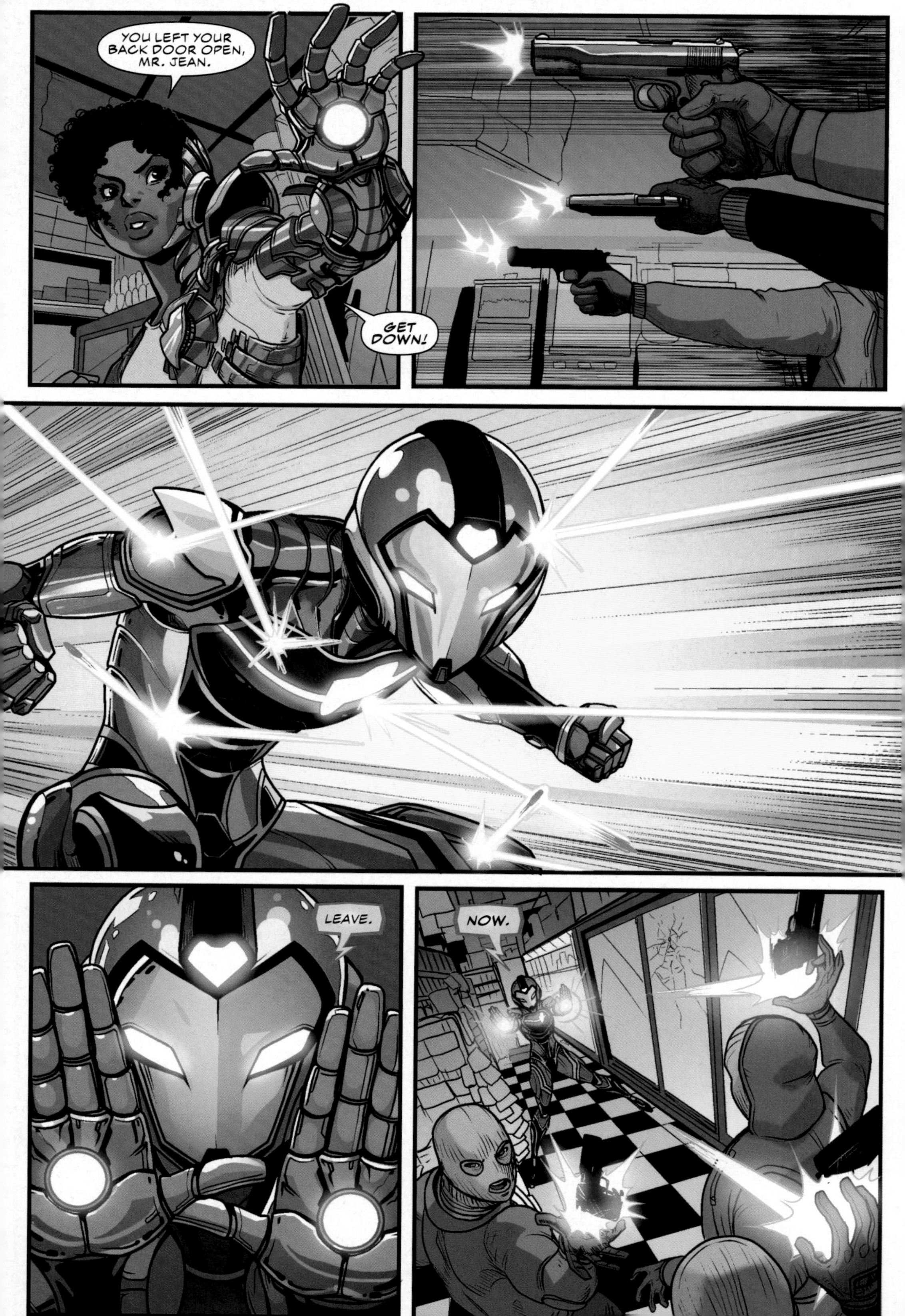
YOU LEFT YOUR BACK DOOR OPEN, MR. JEAN.
GET DOWN!
LEAVE.
NOW.

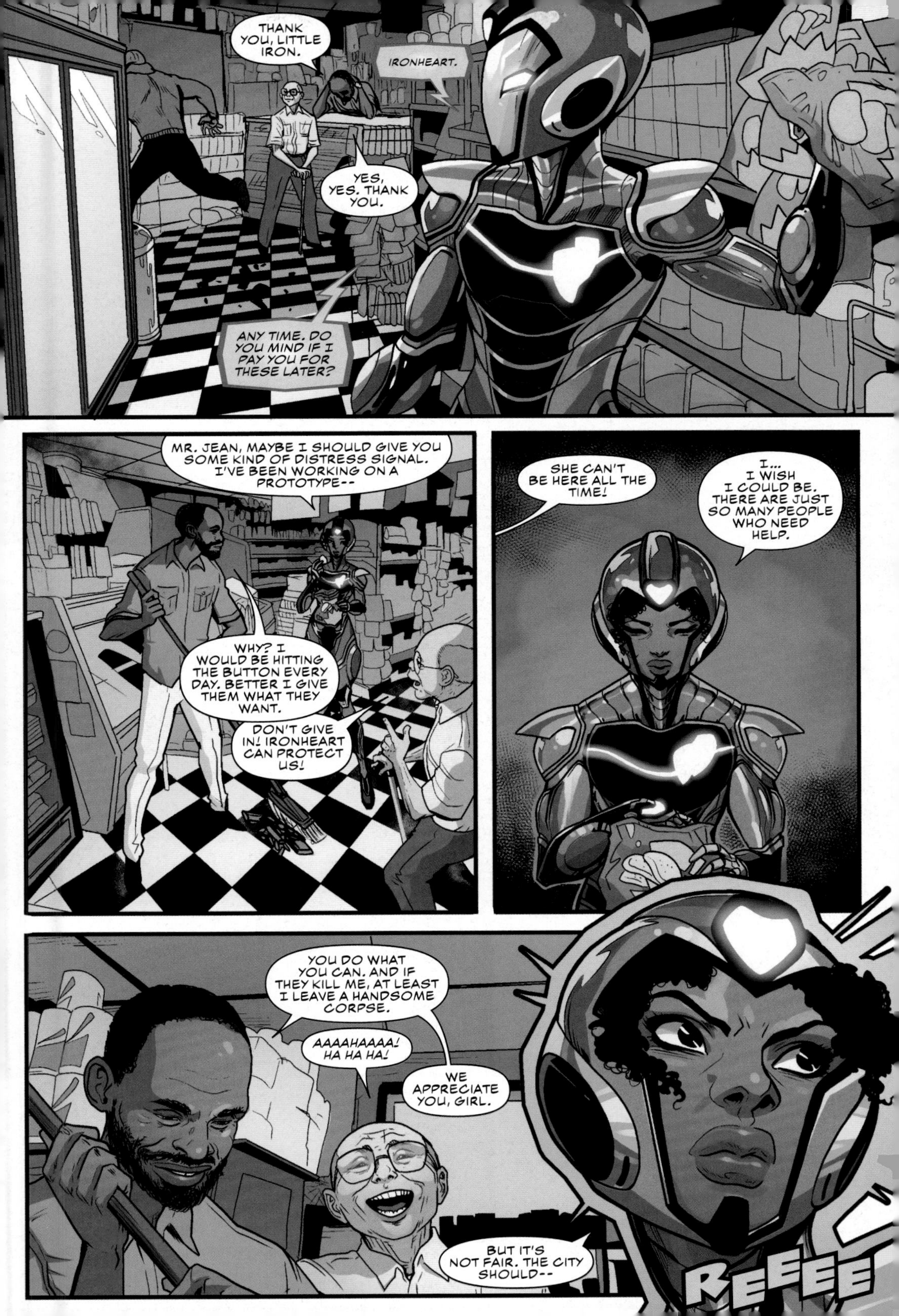
THANK YOU, LITTLE IRON.
IRONHEART.
YES, YES. THANK YOU.
ANY TIME. DO YOU MIND IF I PAY YOU FOR THESE LATER?
MR. JEAN, MAYBE I SHOULD GIVE YOU SOME KIND OF DISTRESS SIGNAL. I'VE BEEN WORKING ON A PROTOTYPE--
WHY? I WOULD BE HITTING THE BUTTON EVERY DAY. BETTER I GIVE THEM WHAT THEY WANT.
DON'T GIVE IN! IRONHEART CAN PROTECT US!
SHE CAN'T BE HERE ALL THE TIME!
I... I WISH I COULD BE. THERE ARE JUST SO MANY PEOPLE WHO NEED HELP.
YOU DO WHAT YOU CAN. AND IF THEY KILL ME, AT LEAST I LEAVE A HANDSOME CORPSE.
AAAAHAAAA! HA HA HA!
WE APPRECIATE YOU, GIRL.
BUT IT'S NOT FAIR. THE CITY SHOULD--
REEEE

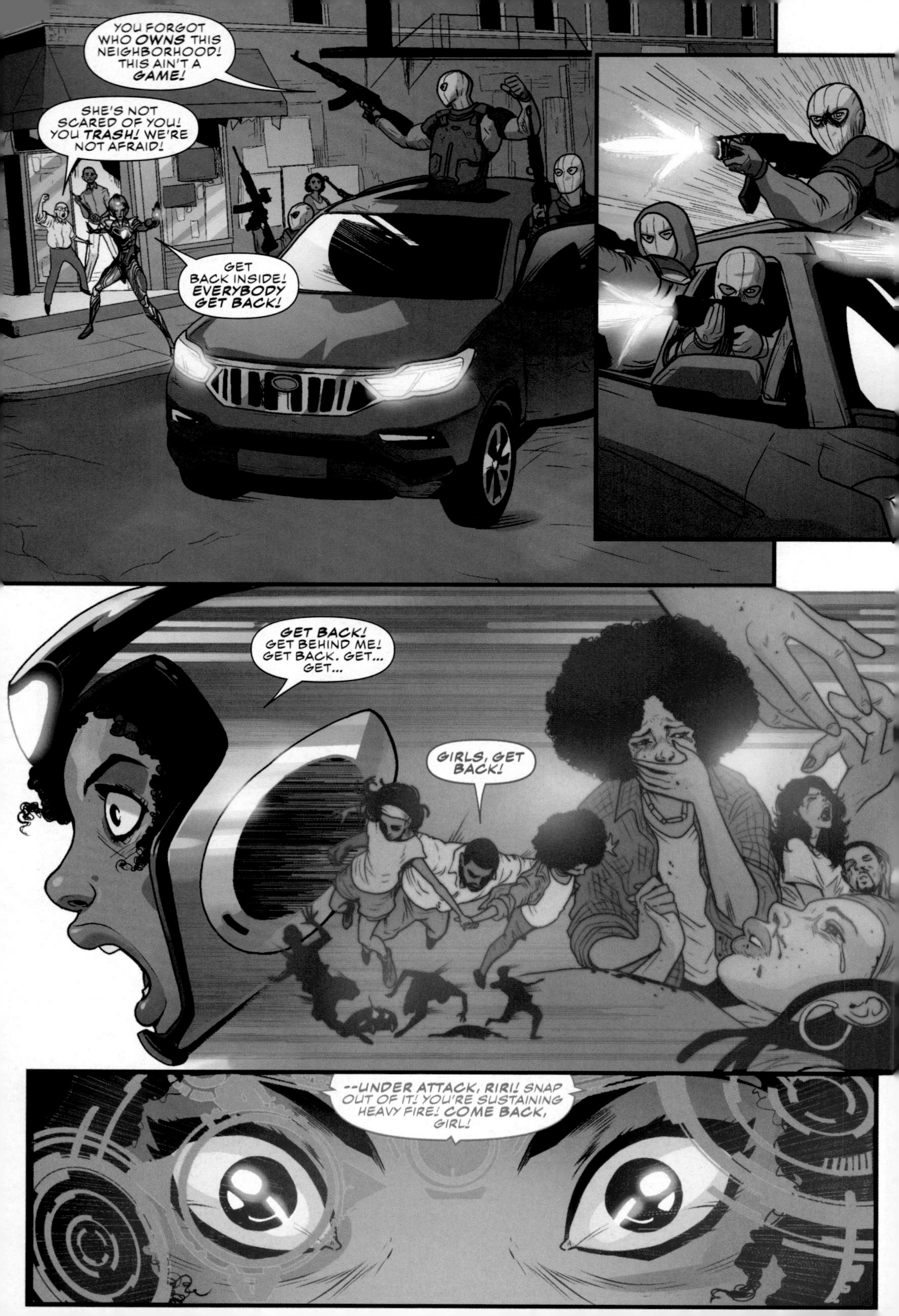
YOU FORGOT WHO OWNS THIS NEIGHBORHOOD! THIS AIN'T A GAME!
SHE'S NOT SCARED OF YOU! YOU TRASH! WE'RE NOT AFRAID!
GET BACK INSIDE! EVERYBODY GET BACK!
GET BACK! GET BEHIND ME! GET BACK. GET... GET...
GIRLS, GET BACK!
--UNDER ATTACK, RIRI! SNAP OUT OF IT! YOU'RE SUSTAINING HEAVY FIRE! COME BACK, GIRL!

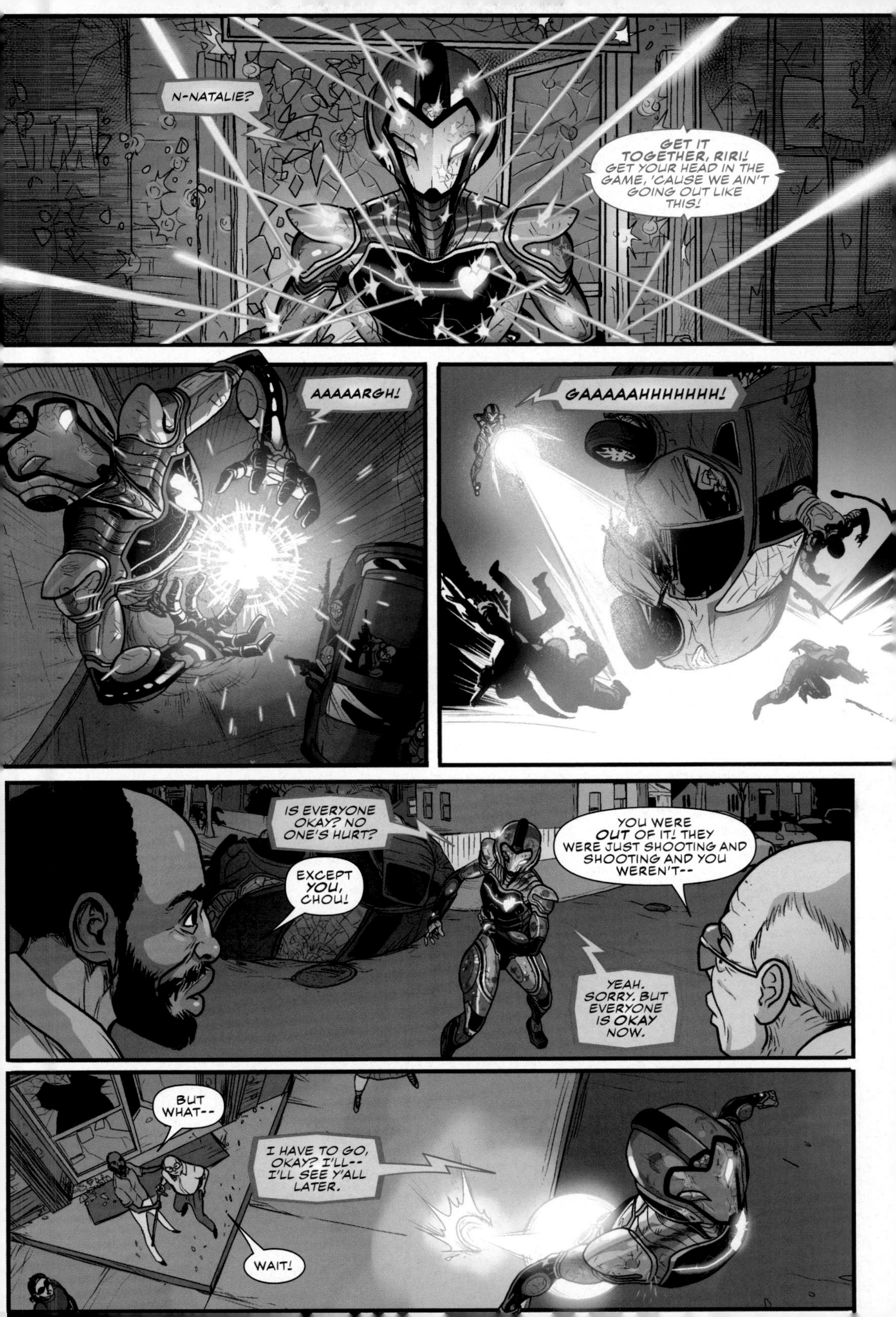
N-NATALIE?
GET IT TOGETHER, RIRI! GET YOUR HEAD IN THE GAME, 'CAUSE WE AIN'T GOING OUT LIKE THIS!
AAAAARGH!
GAAAAAHHHHHHH!
IS EVERYONE OKAY? NO ONE'S HURT?
EXCEPT YOU, CHOU!
YOU WERE OUT OF IT! THEY WERE JUST SHOOTING AND SHOOTING AND YOU WEREN'T--
YEAH. SORRY. BUT EVERYONE IS OKAY NOW.
BUT WHAT--
I HAVE TO GO, OKAY? I'LL-- I'LL SEE Y'ALL LATER.
WAIT!

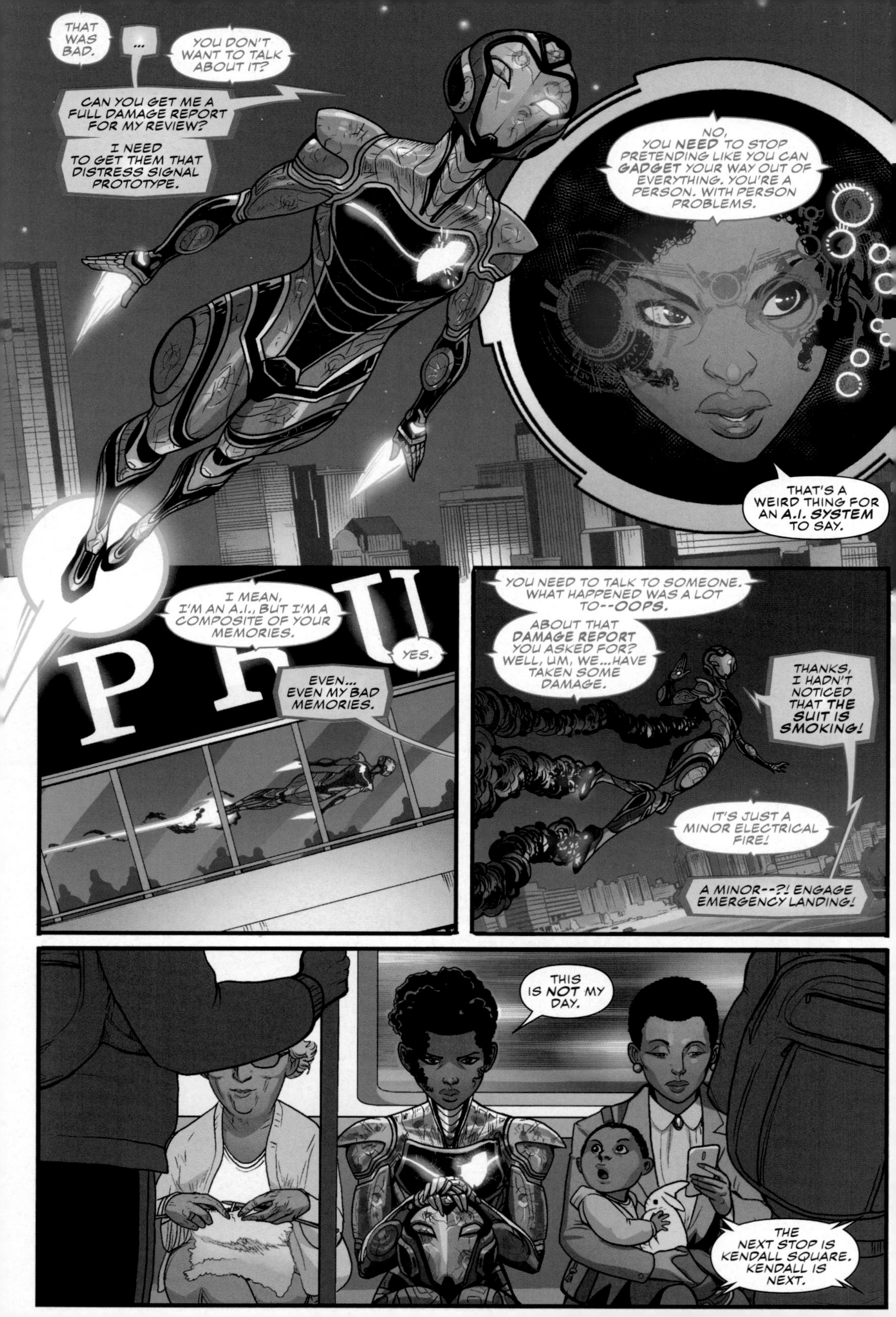

THAT WAS BAD.
...
YOU DON'T WANT TO TALK ABOUT IT?
CAN YOU GET ME A FULL DAMAGE REPORT FOR MY REVIEW?
I NEED TO GET THEM THAT DISTRESS SIGNAL PROTOTYPE.
NO, YOU NEED TO STOP PRETENDING LIKE YOU CAN GADGET YOUR WAY OUT OF EVERYTHING. YOU'RE A PERSON. WITH PERSON PROBLEMS.
THAT'S A WEIRD THING FOR AN A.I. SYSTEM TO SAY.
I MEAN, I'M AN A.I., BUT I'M A COMPOSITE OF YOUR MEMORIES.
YES.
EVEN... EVEN MY BAD MEMORIES.
YOU NEED TO TALK TO SOMEONE. WHAT HAPPENED WAS A LOT TO--OOPS.
ABOUT THAT DAMAGE REPORT YOU ASKED FOR? WELL, UM, WE...HAVE TAKEN SOME DAMAGE.
THANKS, I HADN'T NOTICED THAT THE SUIT IS SMOKING!
IT'S JUST A MINOR ELECTRICAL FIRE!
A MINOR--?! ENGAGE EMERGENCY LANDING!
THIS IS NOT MY DAY.
THE NEXT STOP IS KENDALL SQUARE. KENDALL IS NEXT.

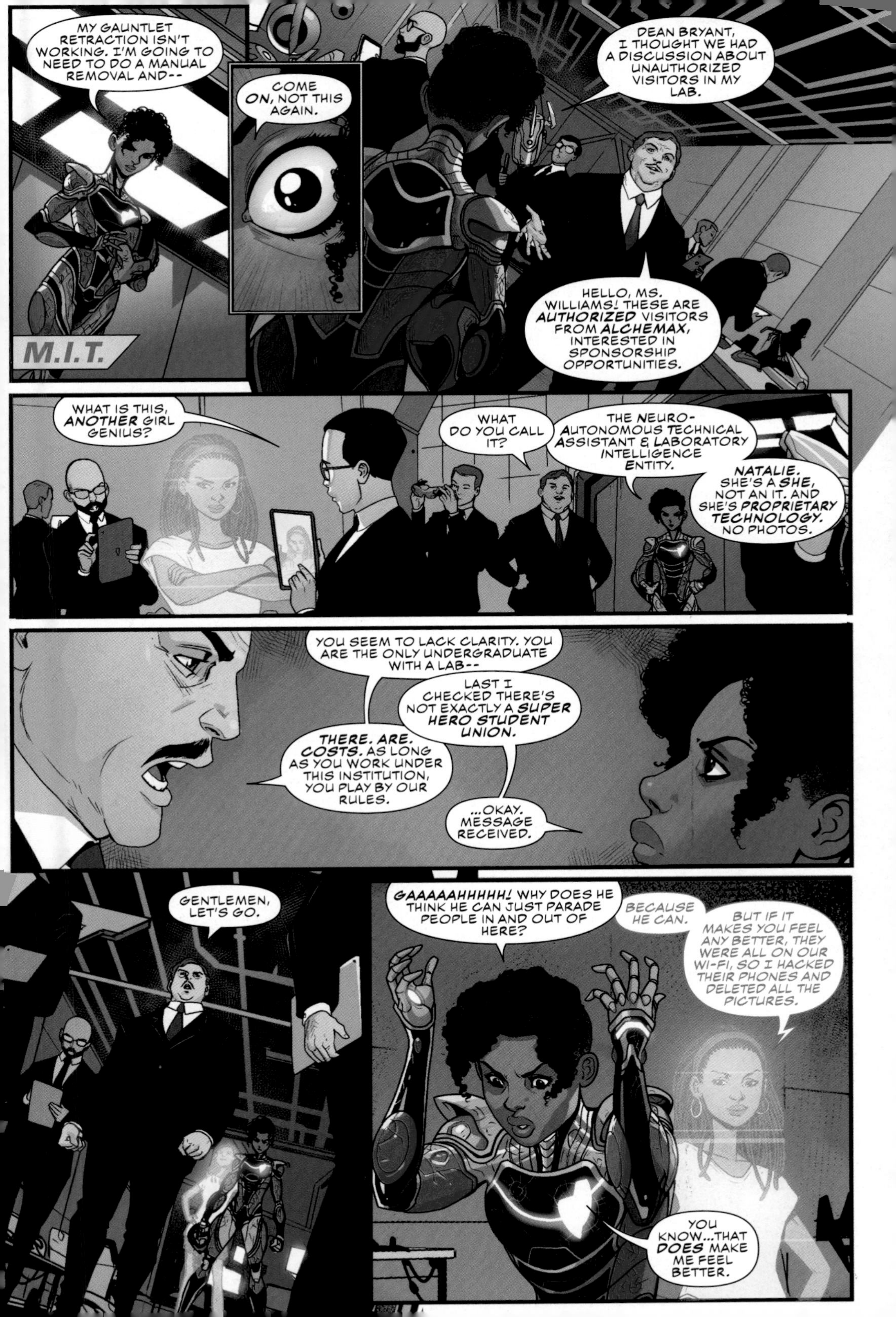
M.I.T.
MY GAUNTLET RETRACTION ISN'T WORKING. I'M GOING TO NEED TO DO A MANUAL REMOVAL AND--
COME ON, NOT THIS AGAIN.
DEAN BRYANT, I THOUGHT WE HAD A DISCUSSION ABOUT UNAUTHORIZED VISITORS IN MY LAB.
HELLO, MS. WILLIAMS! THESE ARE AUTHORIZED VISITORS FROM ALCHEMAX, INTERESTED IN SPONSORSHIP OPPORTUNITIES.
WHAT IS THIS, ANOTHER GIRL GENIUS?
WHAT DO YOU CALL IT?
THE NEURO-AUTONOMOUS TECHNICAL ASSISTANT & LABORATORY INTELLIGENCE ENTITY.
NATALIE. SHE'S A SHE, NOT AN IT. AND SHE'S PROPRIETARY TECHNOLOGY. NO PHOTOS.
YOU SEEM TO LACK CLARITY. YOU ARE THE ONLY UNDERGRADUATE WITH A LAB--
LAST I CHECKED THERE'S NOT EXACTLY A SUPER HERO STUDENT UNION.
THERE. ARE. COSTS. AS LONG AS YOU WORK UNDER THIS INSTITUTION, YOU PLAY BY OUR RULES.
...OKAY. MESSAGE RECEIVED.
GENTLEMEN, LET'S GO.
GAAAAAHHHHH! WHY DOES HE THINK HE CAN JUST PARADE PEOPLE IN AND OUT OF HERE?
BECAUSE HE CAN.
BUT IF IT MAKES YOU FEEL ANY BETTER, THEY WERE ALL ON OUR WI-FI, SO I HACKED THEIR PHONES AND DELETED ALL THE PICTURES.
YOU KNOW...THAT DOES MAKE ME FEEL BETTER.

THIS ISN'T AS BAD AS IT LOOKED INITIALLY. I FIXED THE SHORT THAT CAUSED THE FIRE. THE REST OF THE PROBLEMS ARE COSMETIC.

RIRI-- TAKE A LOOK AT THIS.

NEWORD ALERT: CHICAGO

LOCAL WOMAN STILL MISSING

THIS MISSING GIRL, ISN'T SHE...

OH MY GOSH.

AND NOW SHE'S MISSING CLASS AND SO AM I. IF WE'RE GONNA HAVE A LITTLE KID IN THIS SCHOOL SOMEBODY BETTER LOOK OUT FOR HER.

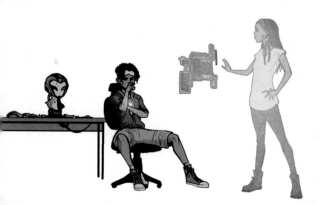

LET'S GO HOME.

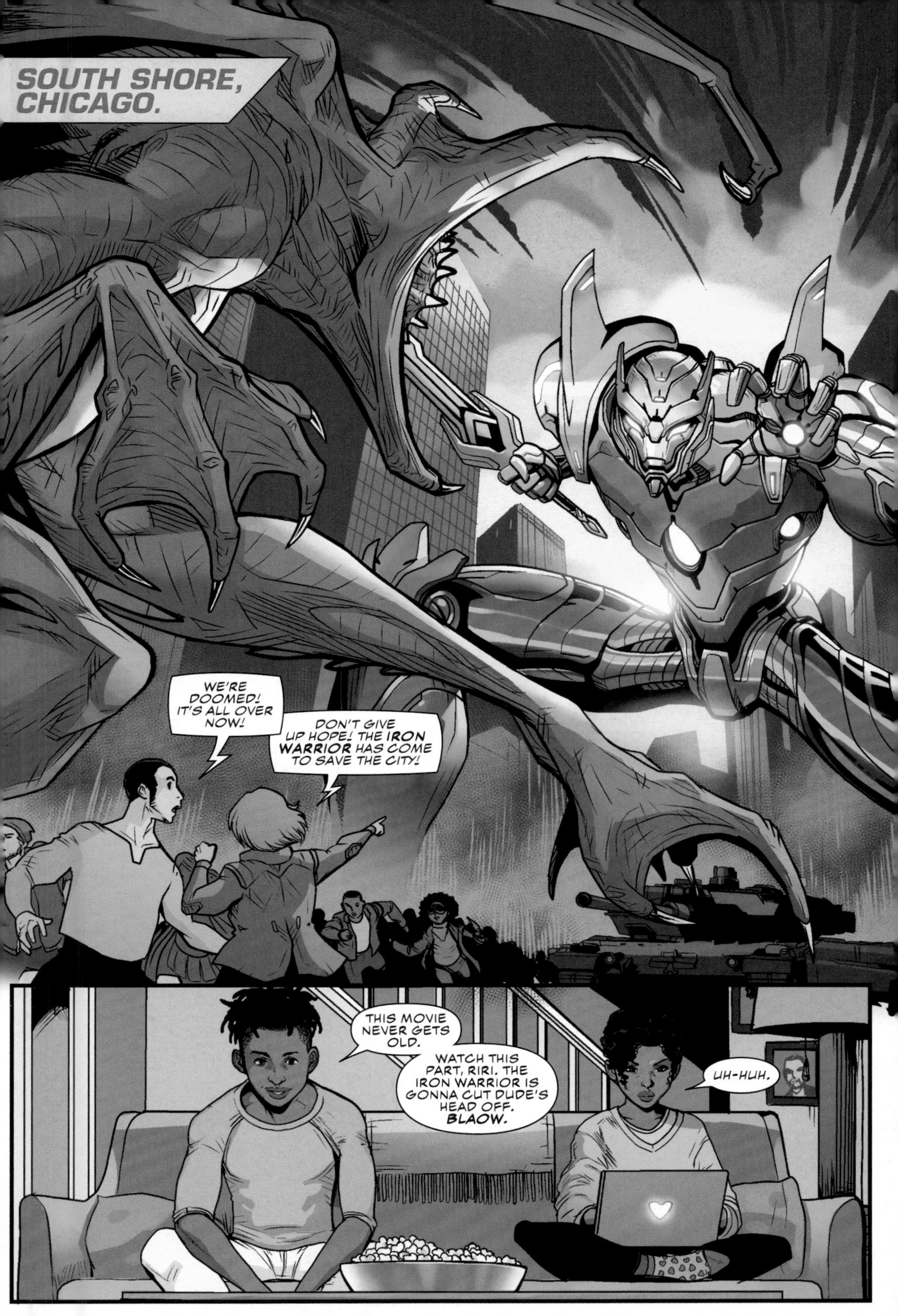
SOUTH SHORE, CHICAGO.
WE'RE DOOMED! IT'S ALL OVER NOW!
DON'T GIVE UP HOPE! THE **IRON WARRIOR** HAS COME TO SAVE THE CITY!
THIS MOVIE NEVER GETS OLD.
WATCH THIS PART, RIRI. THE IRON WARRIOR IS GONNA CUT DUDE'S HEAD OFF. **BLAOW.**
UH-HUH.

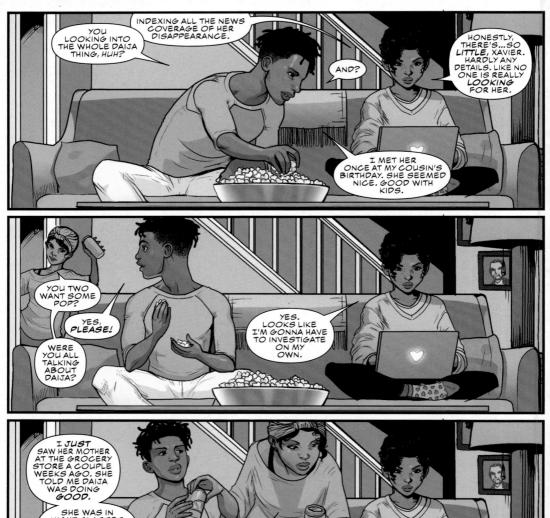

YOU LOOKING INTO THE WHOLE DAIJA THING, HUH?

INDEXING ALL THE NEWS COVERAGE OF HER DISAPPEARANCE.

AND?

HONESTLY, THERE'S...SO LITTLE, XAVIER. HARDLY ANY DETAILS. LIKE NO ONE IS REALLY LOOKING FOR HER.

I MET HER ONCE AT MY COUSIN'S BIRTHDAY. SHE SEEMED NICE. GOOD WITH KIDS.

YOU TWO WANT SOME POP?

YES, PLEASE!

WERE YOU ALL TALKING ABOUT DAIJA?

YES. LOOKS LIKE I'M GONNA HAVE TO INVESTIGATE ON MY OWN.

I JUST SAW HER MOTHER AT THE GROCERY STORE A COUPLE WEEKS AGO. SHE TOLD ME DAIJA WAS DOING GOOD.

SHE WAS IN NIGHT CLASSES PART TIME AND HAD AN INTERNSHIP WITH SOMEBODY ON CITY COUNCIL.

IT'S SO SAD.

NOTHING BUT BAD NEWS...

--WAVE OF ROBBERIES. POLICE ARE ADVISING RESIDENTS THAT TEENS AND EVEN CHILDREN HAVE BEEN REPORTED STEALING ELECTRONICS--

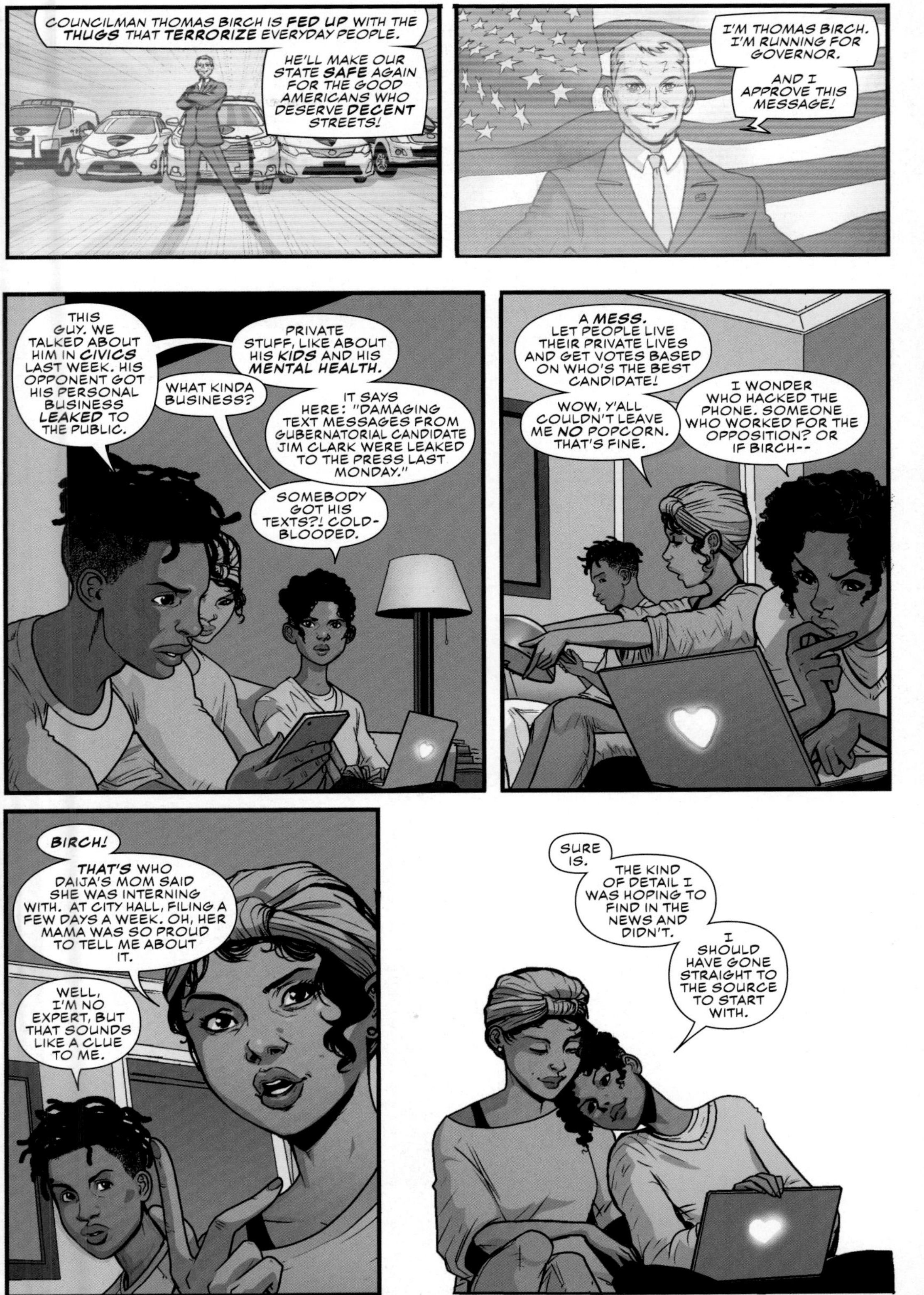
COUNCILMAN THOMAS BIRCH IS FED UP WITH THE THUGS THAT TERRORIZE EVERYDAY PEOPLE.
HE'LL MAKE OUR STATE SAFE AGAIN FOR THE GOOD AMERICANS WHO DESERVE DECENT STREETS!
I'M THOMAS BIRCH. I'M RUNNING FOR GOVERNOR.
AND I APPROVE THIS MESSAGE!
THIS GUY. WE TALKED ABOUT HIM IN CIVICS LAST WEEK. HIS OPPONENT GOT HIS PERSONAL BUSINESS LEAKED TO THE PUBLIC.
WHAT KINDA BUSINESS?
PRIVATE STUFF, LIKE ABOUT HIS KIDS AND HIS MENTAL HEALTH.
IT SAYS HERE: "DAMAGING TEXT MESSAGES FROM GUBERNATORIAL CANDIDATE JIM CLARK WERE LEAKED TO THE PRESS LAST MONDAY."
SOMEBODY GOT HIS TEXTS?! COLD-BLOODED.
A MESS. LET PEOPLE LIVE THEIR PRIVATE LIVES AND GET VOTES BASED ON WHO'S THE BEST CANDIDATE!
WOW, Y'ALL COULDN'T LEAVE ME NO POPCORN. THAT'S FINE.
I WONDER WHO HACKED THE PHONE. SOMEONE WHO WORKED FOR THE OPPOSITION? OR IF BIRCH--
BIRCH!
THAT'S WHO DAIJA'S MOM SAID SHE WAS INTERNING WITH. AT CITY HALL, FILING A FEW DAYS A WEEK. OH, HER MAMA WAS SO PROUD TO TELL ME ABOUT IT.
WELL, I'M NO EXPERT, BUT THAT SOUNDS LIKE A CLUE TO ME.
SURE IS.
THE KIND OF DETAIL I WAS HOPING TO FIND IN THE NEWS AND DIDN'T.
I SHOULD HAVE GONE STRAIGHT TO THE SOURCE TO START WITH.

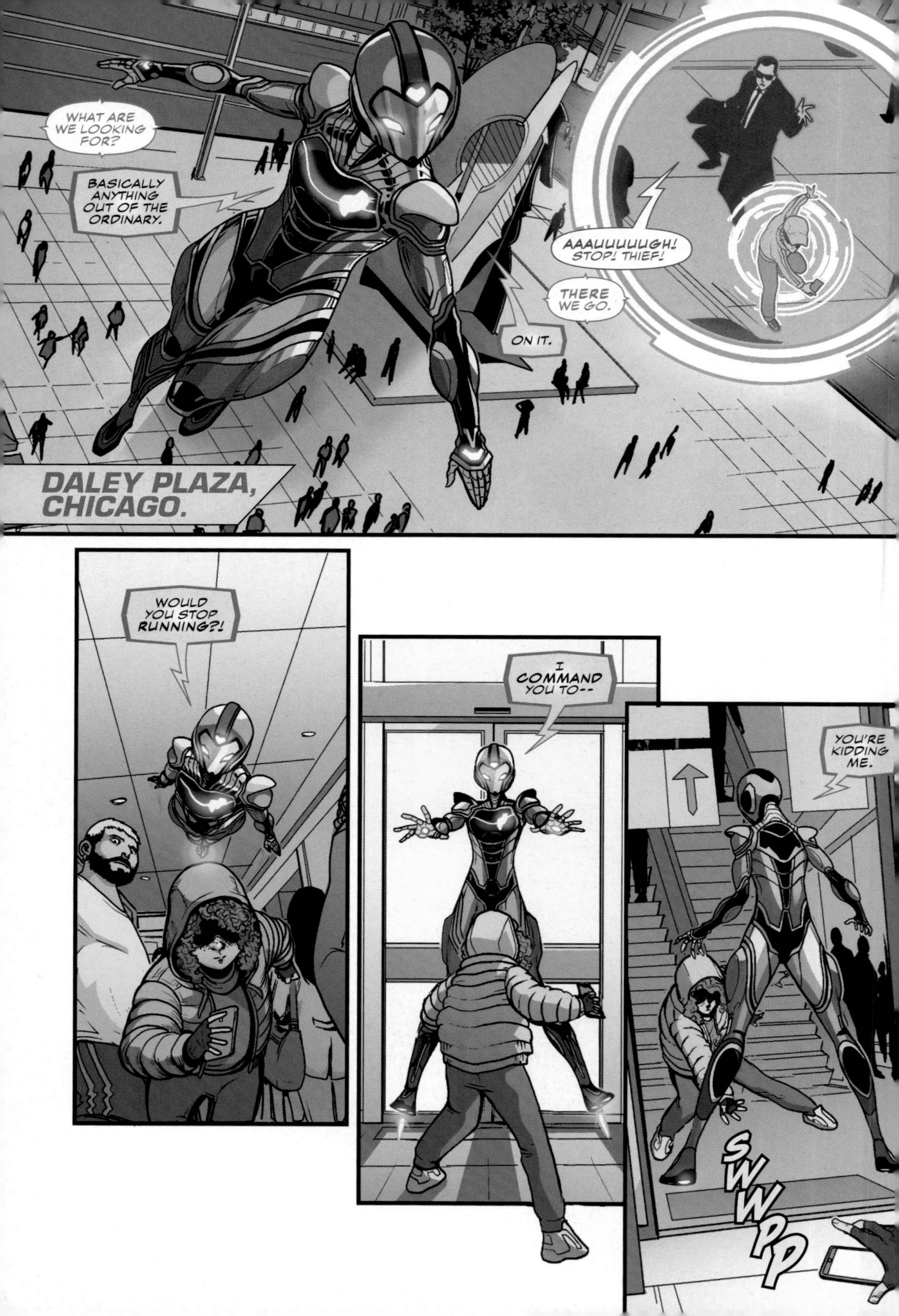
DALEY PLAZA, CHICAGO.
WHAT ARE WE LOOKING FOR?
BASICALLY ANYTHING OUT OF THE ORDINARY.
AAAUUUUUGH! STOP! THIEF!
THERE WE GO.
ON IT.
WOULD YOU STOP RUNNING?!
I COMMAND YOU TO--
YOU'RE KIDDING ME.
SWPP

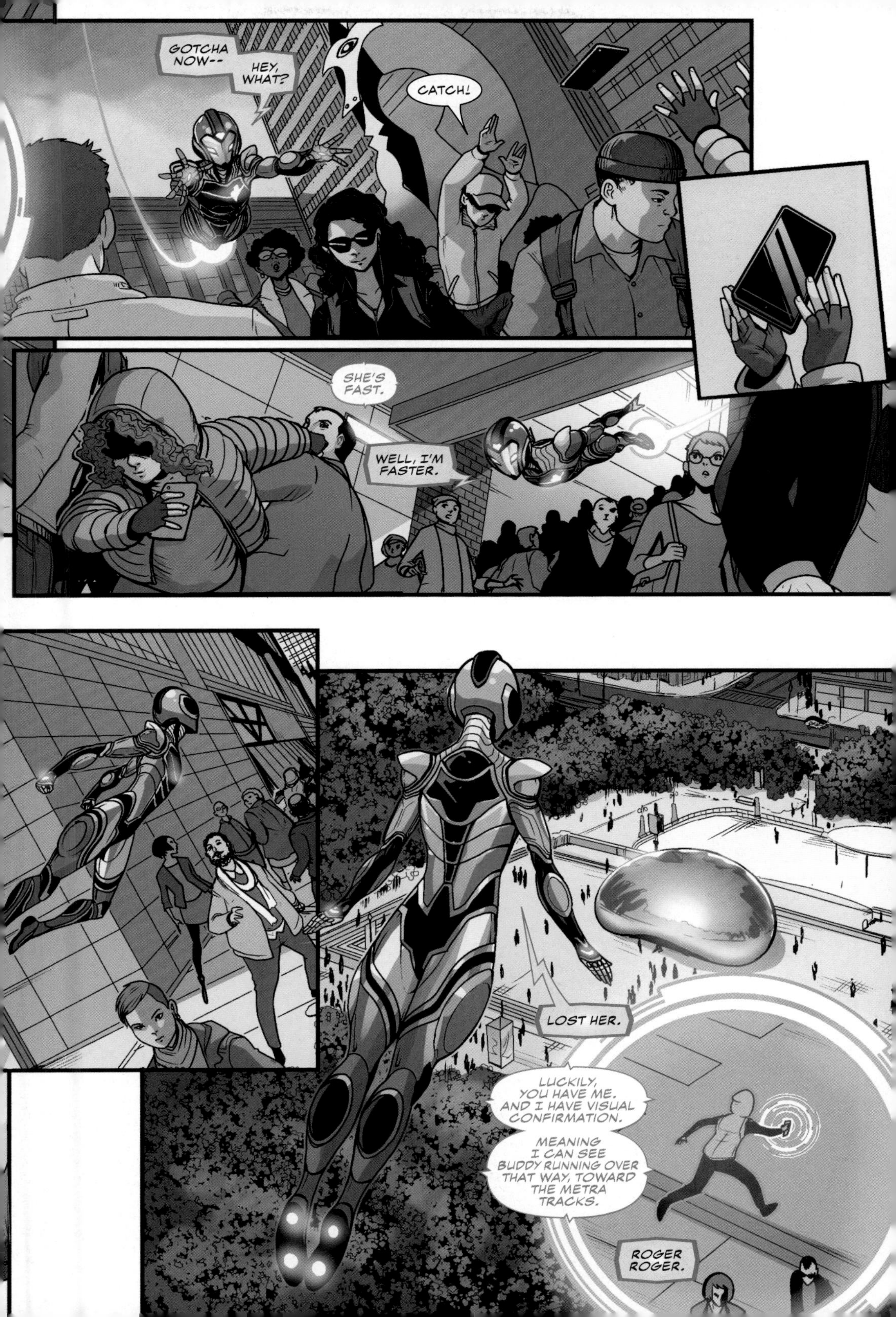
GOTCHA NOW--
HEY, WHAT?
CATCH!
SHE'S FAST.
WELL, I'M FASTER.
LOST HER.
LUCKILY, YOU HAVE ME. AND I HAVE VISUAL CONFIRMATION.
MEANING I CAN SEE BUDDY RUNNING OVER THAT WAY, TOWARD THE METRA TRACKS.
ROGER ROGER.

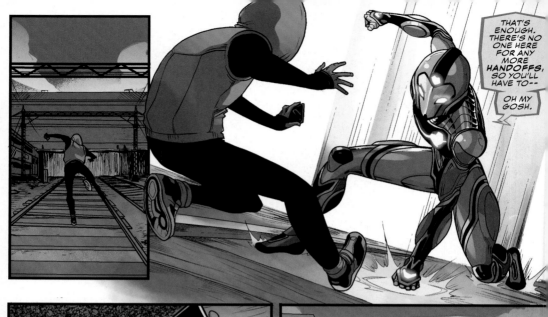

THAT'S ENOUGH. THERE'S NO ONE HERE FOR ANY MORE HANDOFFS, SO YOU'LL HAVE TO--

OH MY GOSH.

YOU'RE JUST A... WHAT ARE YOU, 9?

I'M-- ≶HICCUP≷ I'M 10. I DIDN'T WANNA DO THIS! THEY TOLD ME I HAD TO OR ELSE!

HEY. TAKE A BREATH. I'M NOT GONNA HURT YOU.

WHO TOLD YOU TO DO THIS?

THEY'RE GONNA BE SO MAD! I'M IN HUGE TROUBLE. HERE! I'M SORRY!

WAIT A SEC!

YOU GONNA GO AFTER HIM?

I DUNNO, MAYBE WE--

WHOA, RIRI! INCOMING!

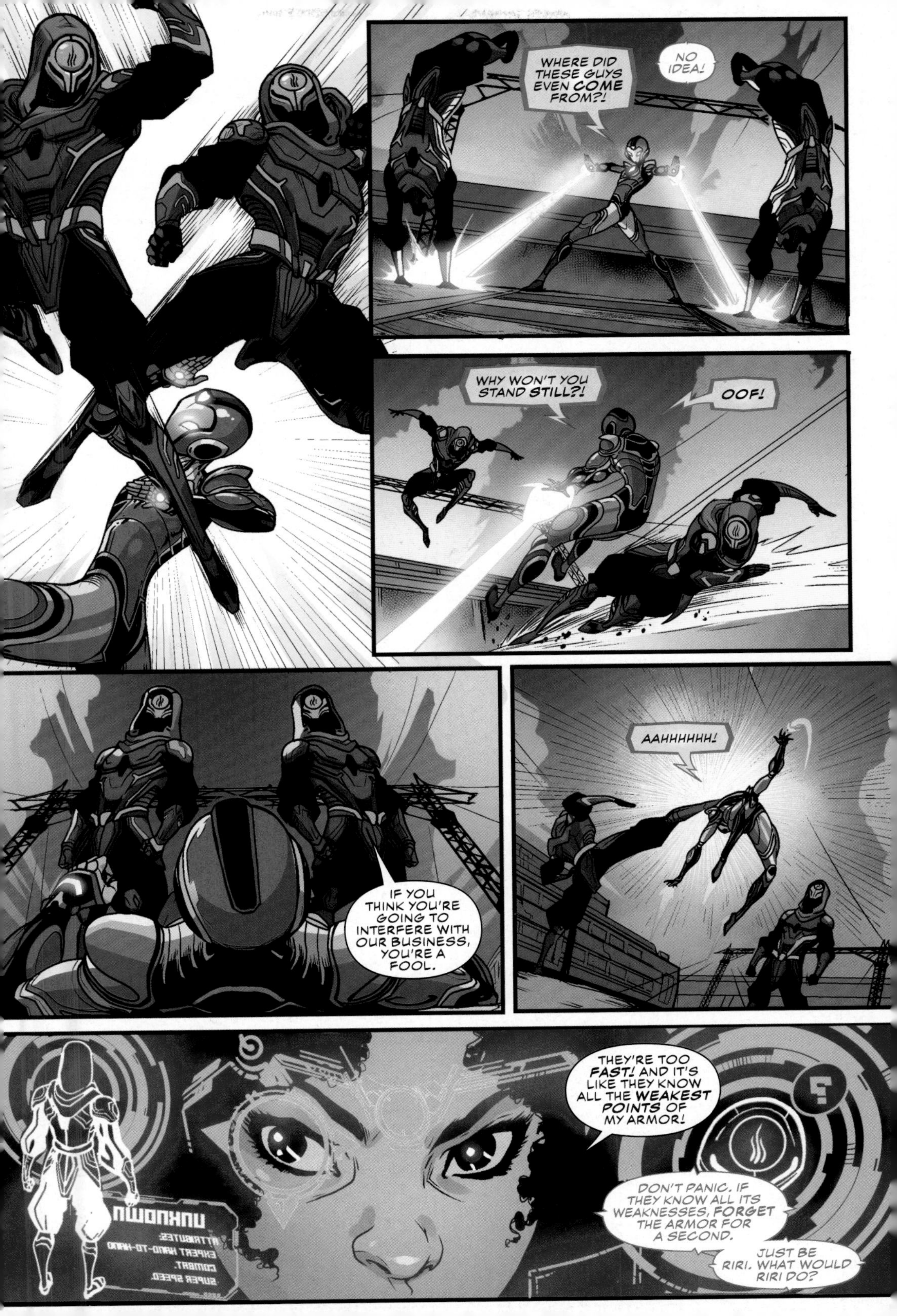

WHERE DID THESE GUYS EVEN COME FROM?!
NO IDEA!
WHY WON'T YOU STAND STILL?!
OOF!
IF YOU THINK YOU'RE GOING TO INTERFERE WITH OUR BUSINESS, YOU'RE A FOOL.
AAHHHHHH!
THEY'RE TOO FAST! AND IT'S LIKE THEY KNOW ALL THE WEAKEST POINTS OF MY ARMOR!
DON'T PANIC. IF THEY KNOW ALL ITS WEAKNESSES, FORGET THE ARMOR FOR A SECOND.
JUST BE RIRI. WHAT WOULD RIRI DO?

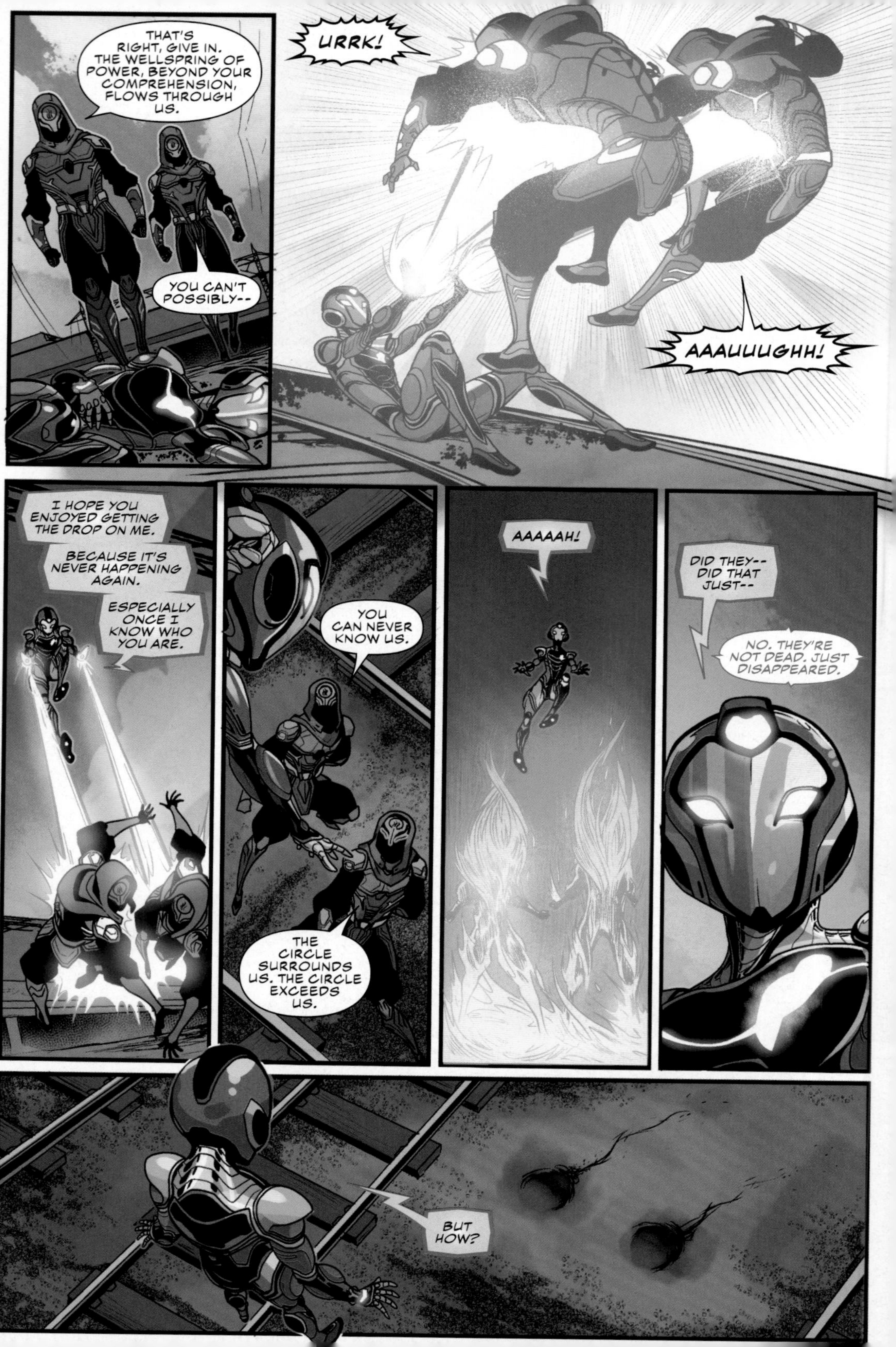
THAT'S RIGHT, GIVE IN. THE WELLSPRING OF POWER, BEYOND YOUR COMPREHENSION, FLOWS THROUGH US.
YOU CAN'T POSSIBLY--
URRK!
AAAUUUGHH!
I HOPE YOU ENJOYED GETTING THE DROP ON ME.
BECAUSE IT'S NEVER HAPPENING AGAIN.
ESPECIALLY ONCE I KNOW WHO YOU ARE.
YOU CAN NEVER KNOW US.
THE CIRCLE SURROUNDS US. THE CIRCLE EXCEEDS US.
AAAAAH!
DID THEY-- DID THAT JUST--
NO. THEY'RE NOT DEAD. JUST DISAPPEARED.
BUT HOW?

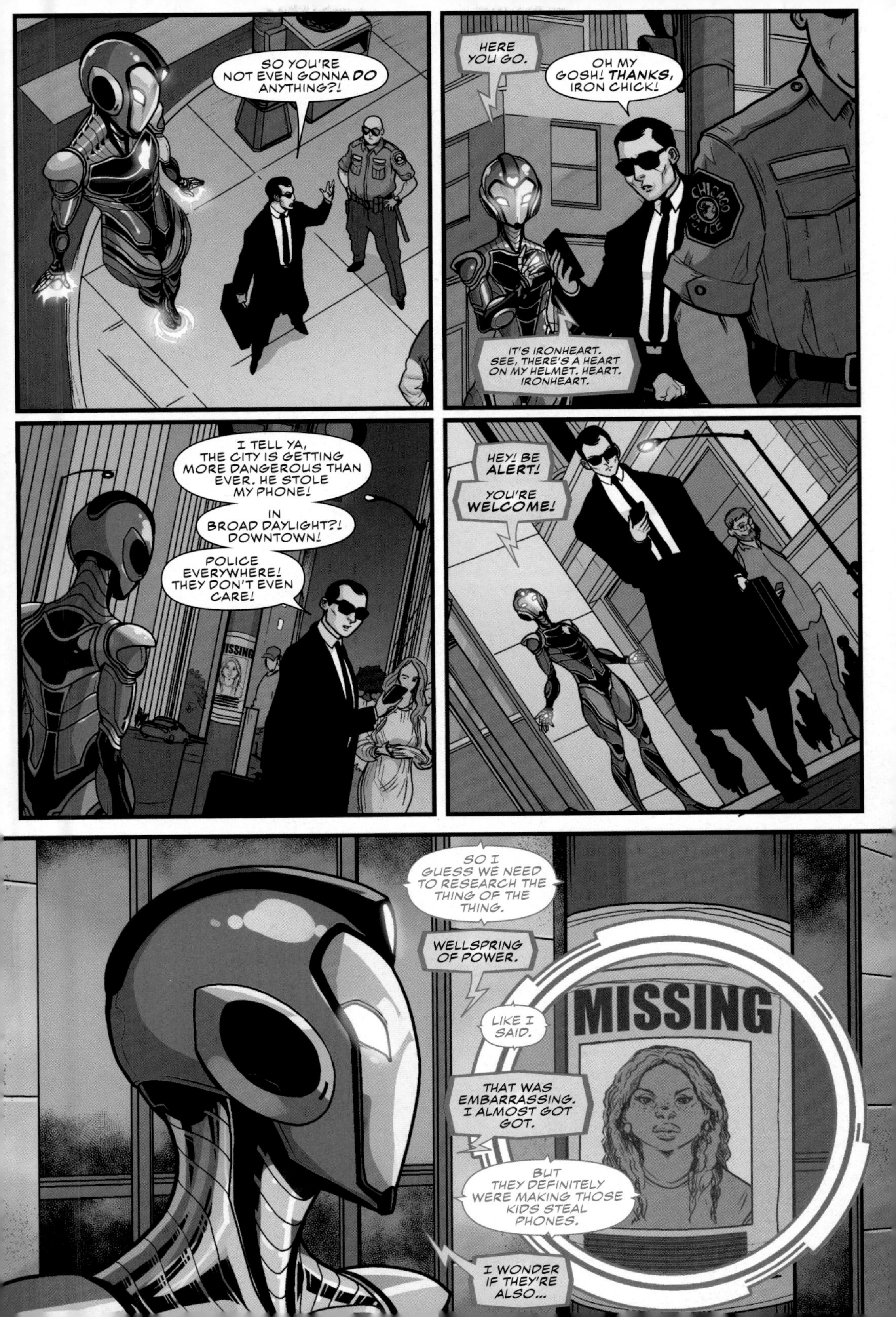

SO YOU'RE NOT EVEN GONNA DO ANYTHING?!
HERE YOU GO.
OH MY GOSH! THANKS, IRON CHICK!
CHICAGO POLICE
IT'S IRONHEART. SEE, THERE'S A HEART ON MY HELMET. HEART. IRONHEART.
I TELL YA, THE CITY IS GETTING MORE DANGEROUS THAN EVER. HE STOLE MY PHONE!
IN BROAD DAYLIGHT?! DOWNTOWN!
POLICE EVERYWHERE! THEY DON'T EVEN CARE!
HEY! BE ALERT!
YOU'RE WELCOME!
SO I GUESS WE NEED TO RESEARCH THE THING OF THE THING.
WELLSPRING OF POWER.
LIKE I SAID.
MISSING
THAT WAS EMBARRASSING. I ALMOST GOT GOT.
BUT THEY DEFINITELY WERE MAKING THOSE KIDS STEAL PHONES.
I WONDER IF THEY'RE ALSO...

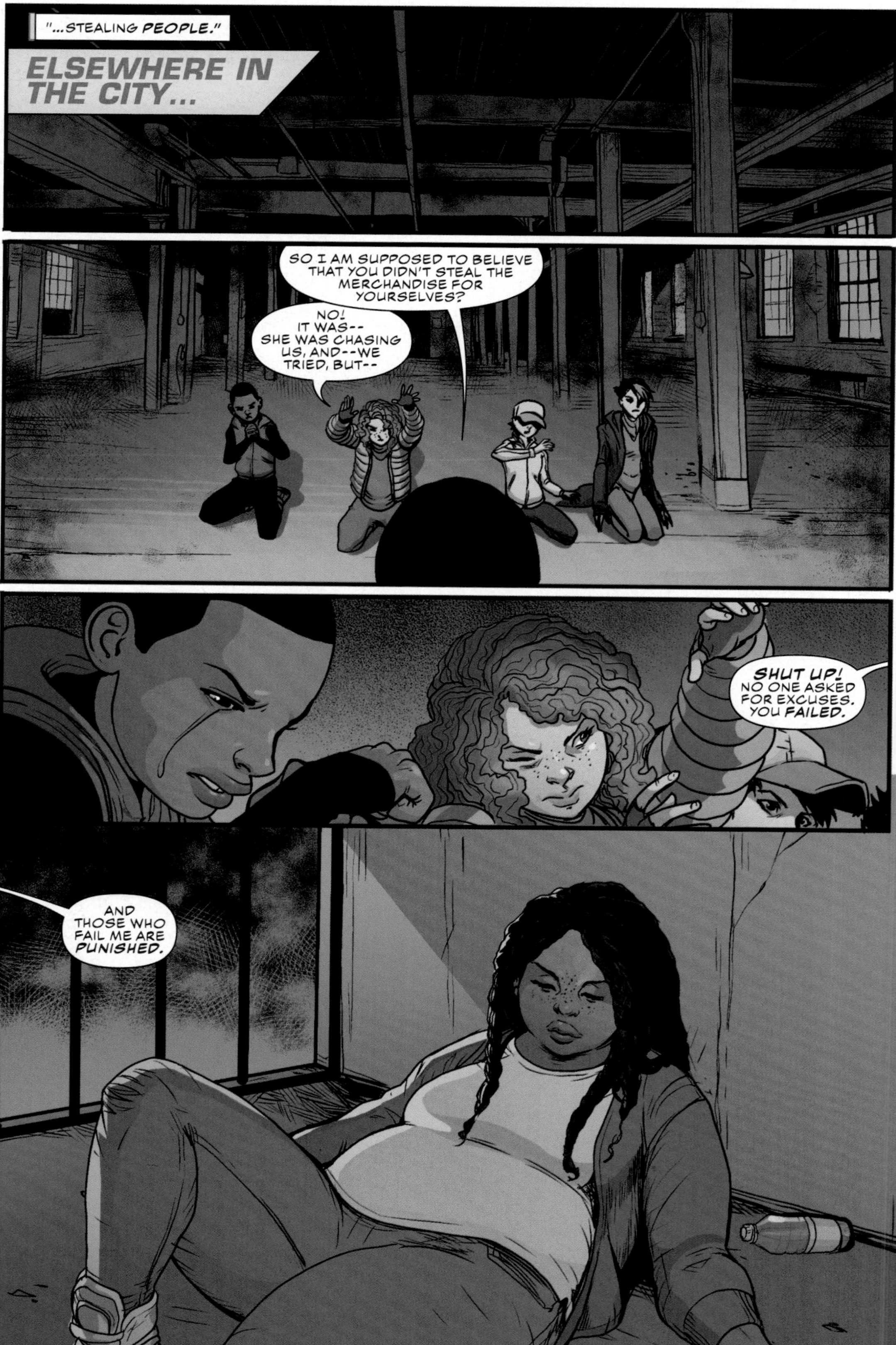
"...STEALING PEOPLE."
ELSEWHERE IN THE CITY...
SO I AM SUPPOSED TO BELIEVE THAT YOU DIDN'T STEAL THE MERCHANDISE FOR YOURSELVES?
NO! IT WAS-- SHE WAS CHASING US, AND--WE TRIED, BUT--
SHUT UP! NO ONE ASKED FOR EXCUSES. YOU FAILED.
AND THOSE WHO FAIL ME ARE PUNISHED.

3

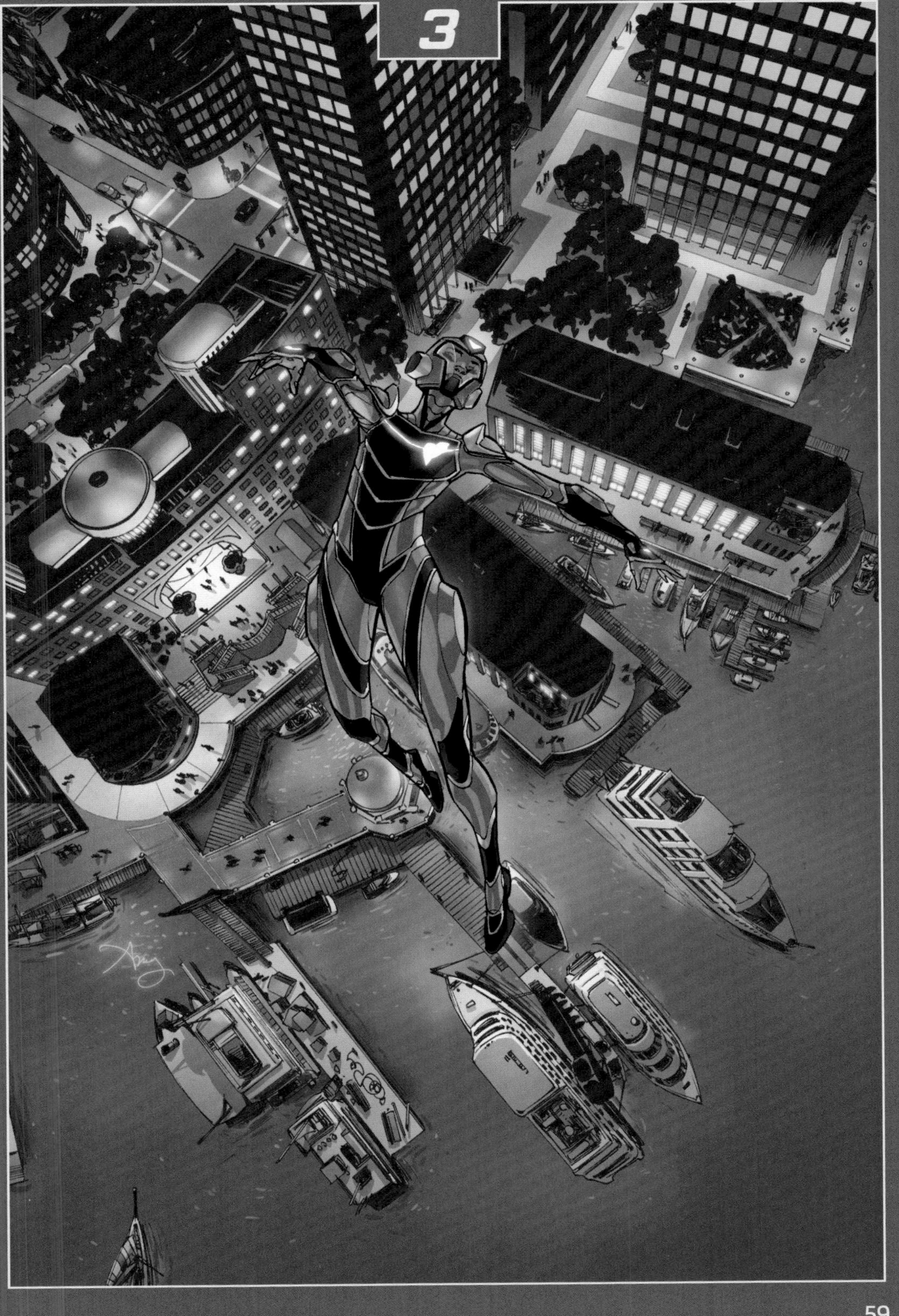

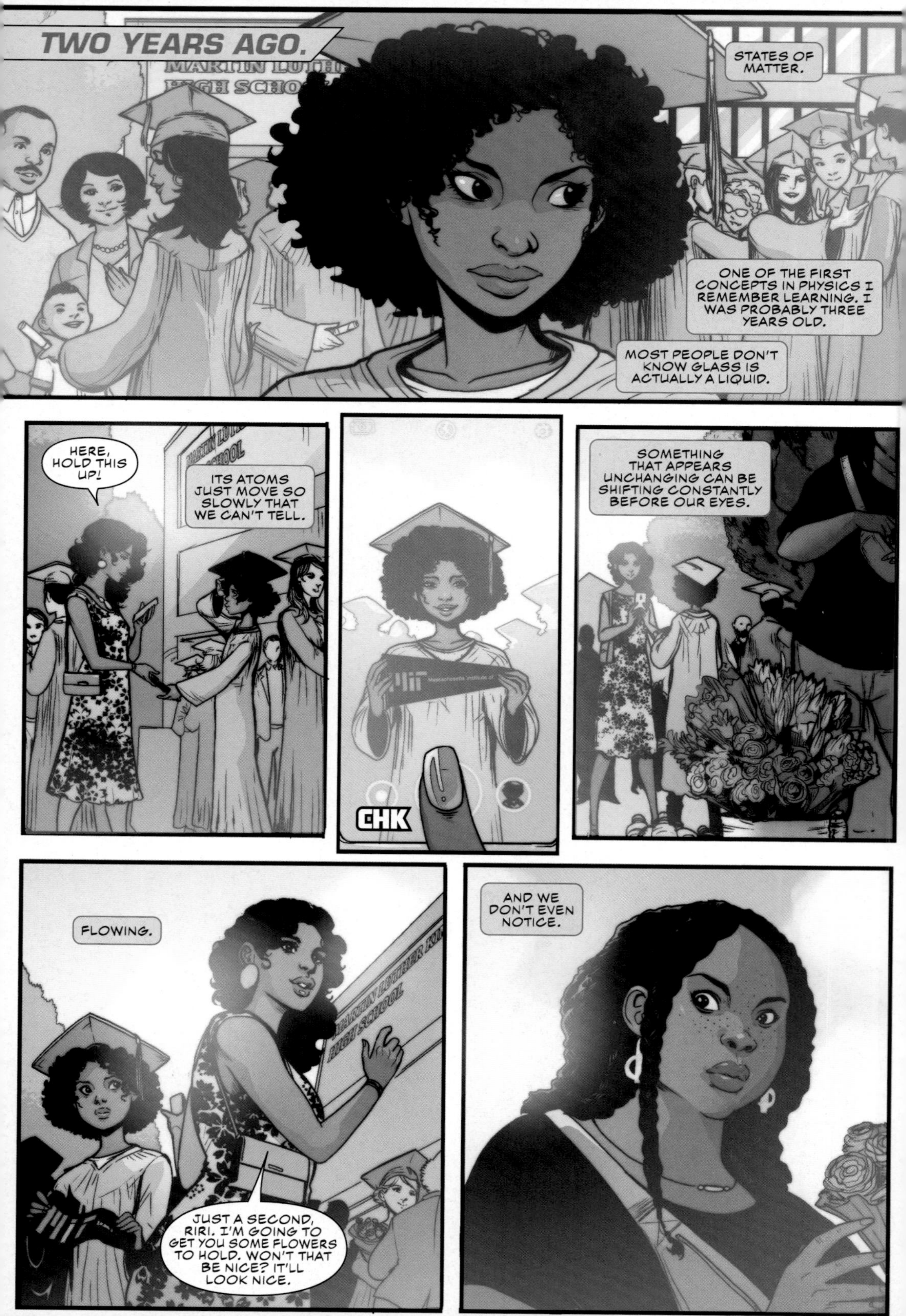
TWO YEARS AGO.
MARTIN LUTHER
HIGH SCHO
STATES OF MATTER.
ONE OF THE FIRST CONCEPTS IN PHYSICS I REMEMBER LEARNING. I WAS PROBABLY THREE YEARS OLD.
MOST PEOPLE DON'T KNOW GLASS IS ACTUALLY A LIQUID.
HERE, HOLD THIS UP!
ITS ATOMS JUST MOVE SO SLOWLY THAT WE CAN'T TELL.
CHK
SOMETHING THAT APPEARS UNCHANGING CAN BE SHIFTING CONSTANTLY BEFORE OUR EYES.
FLOWING.
MARTIN LUTHER KI
HIGH SCHOOL
JUST A SECOND, RIRI. I'M GOING TO GET YOU SOME FLOWERS TO HOLD. WON'T THAT BE NICE? IT'LL LOOK NICE.
AND WE DON'T EVEN NOTICE.

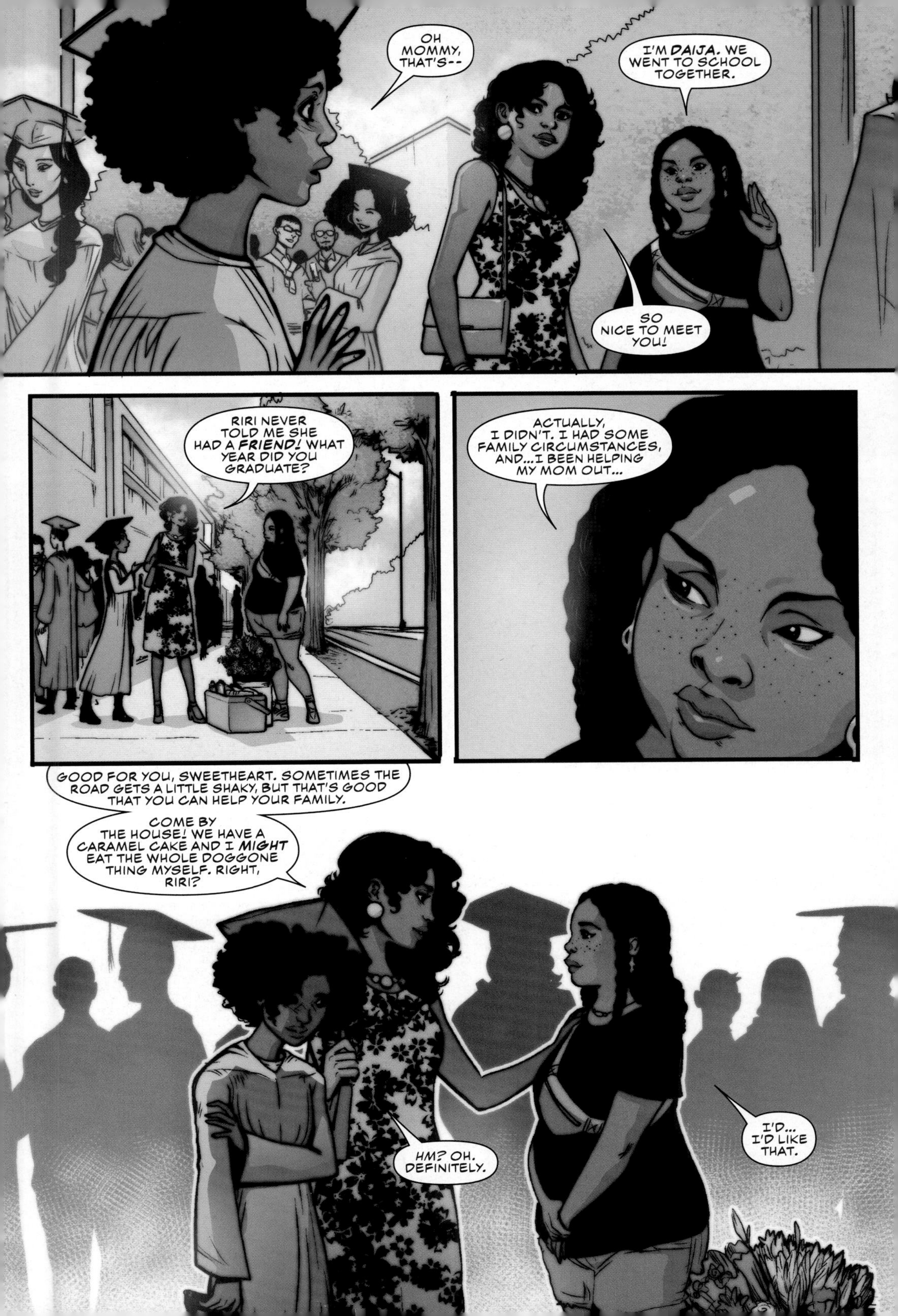
OH MOMMY, THAT'S--
I'M DAIJA. WE WENT TO SCHOOL TOGETHER.
SO NICE TO MEET YOU!
RIRI NEVER TOLD ME SHE HAD A FRIEND! WHAT YEAR DID YOU GRADUATE?
ACTUALLY, I DIDN'T. I HAD SOME FAMILY CIRCUMSTANCES, AND...I BEEN HELPING MY MOM OUT...
GOOD FOR YOU, SWEETHEART. SOMETIMES THE ROAD GETS A LITTLE SHAKY, BUT THAT'S GOOD THAT YOU CAN HELP YOUR FAMILY.
COME BY THE HOUSE! WE HAVE A CARAMEL CAKE AND I MIGHT EAT THE WHOLE DOGGONE THING MYSELF. RIGHT, RIRI?
HM? OH. DEFINITELY.
I'D... I'D LIKE THAT.

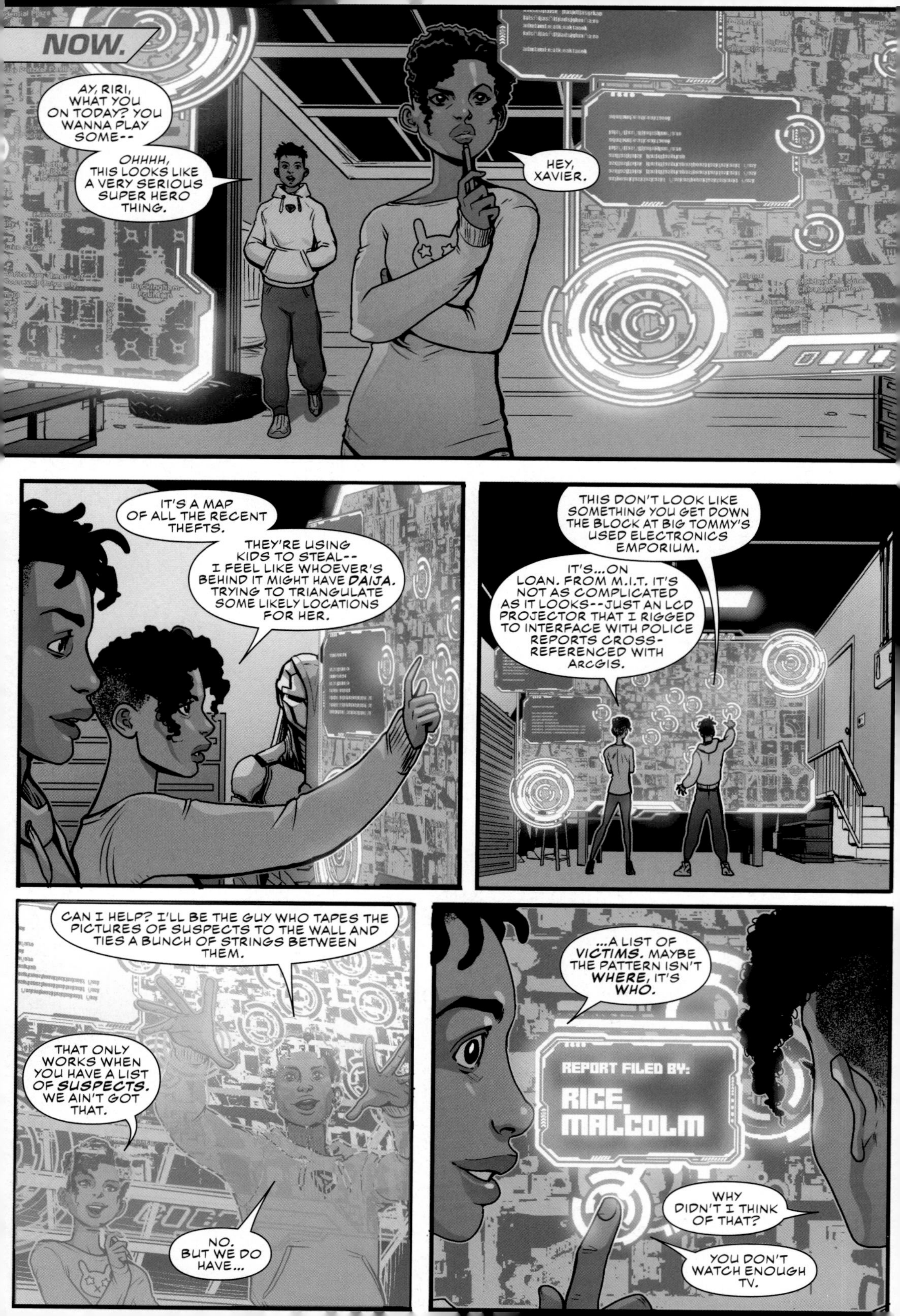
NOW.
AY, RIRI, WHAT YOU ON TODAY? YOU WANNA PLAY SOME--
OHHHH, THIS LOOKS LIKE A VERY SERIOUS SUPER HERO THING.
HEY, XAVIER.
IT'S A MAP OF ALL THE RECENT THEFTS.
THEY'RE USING KIDS TO STEAL-- I FEEL LIKE WHOEVER'S BEHIND IT MIGHT HAVE DAIJA. TRYING TO TRIANGULATE SOME LIKELY LOCATIONS FOR HER.
THIS DON'T LOOK LIKE SOMETHING YOU GET DOWN THE BLOCK AT BIG TOMMY'S USED ELECTRONICS EMPORIUM.
IT'S...ON LOAN. FROM M.I.T. IT'S NOT AS COMPLICATED AS IT LOOKS--JUST AN LCD PROJECTOR THAT I RIGGED TO INTERFACE WITH POLICE REPORTS CROSS-REFERENCED WITH ARCGIS.
CAN I HELP? I'LL BE THE GUY WHO TAPES THE PICTURES OF SUSPECTS TO THE WALL AND TIES A BUNCH OF STRINGS BETWEEN THEM.
THAT ONLY WORKS WHEN YOU HAVE A LIST OF SUSPECTS. WE AIN'T GOT THAT.
NO. BUT WE DO HAVE...
...A LIST OF VICTIMS. MAYBE THE PATTERN ISN'T WHERE, IT'S WHO.
REPORT FILED BY:
RICE, MALCOLM
WHY DIDN'T I THINK OF THAT?
YOU DON'T WATCH ENOUGH TV.

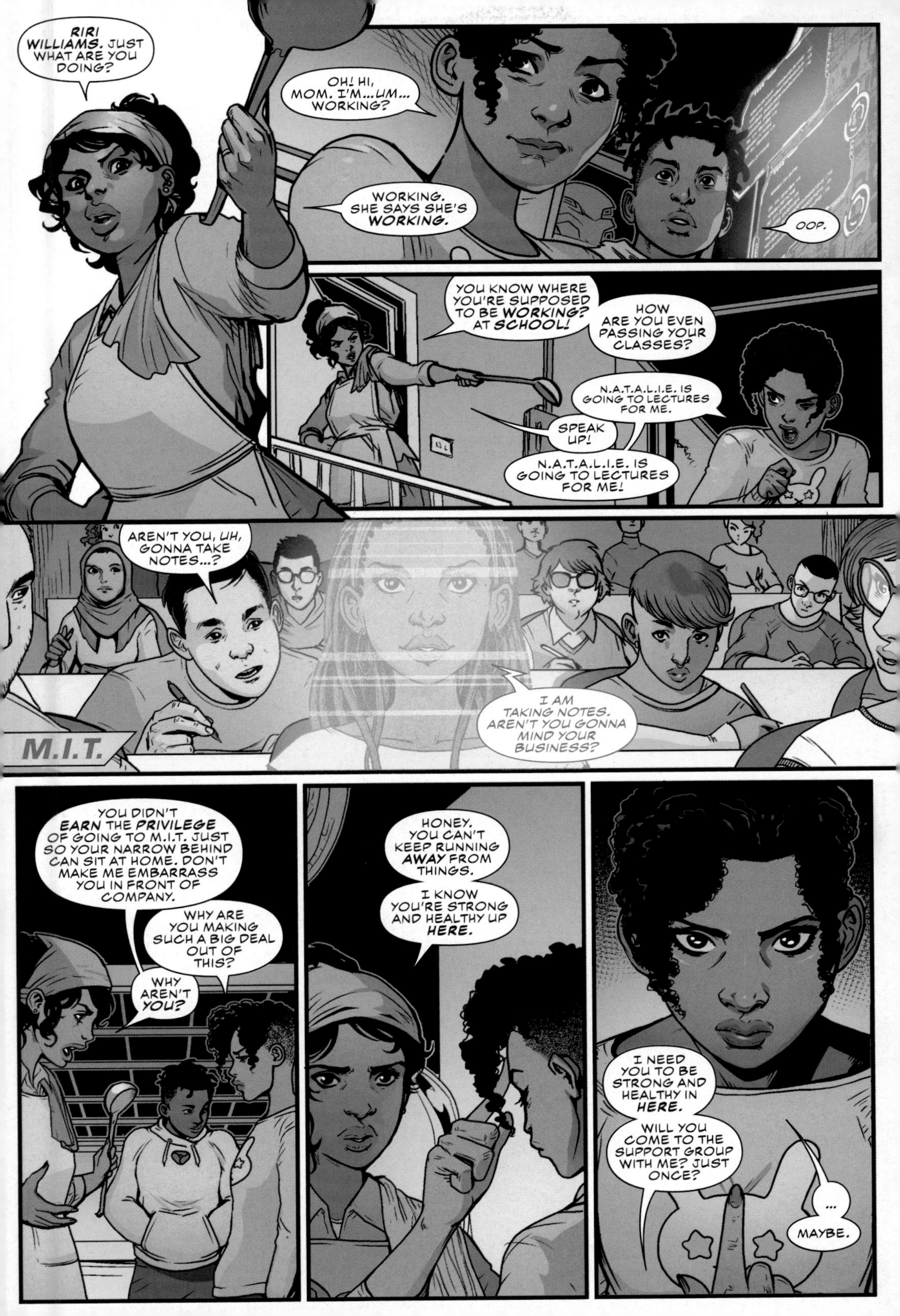
RIRI WILLIAMS. JUST WHAT ARE YOU DOING?
OH! HI, MOM. I'M...UM... WORKING?
WORKING. SHE SAYS SHE'S WORKING.
OOP.
YOU KNOW WHERE YOU'RE SUPPOSED TO BE WORKING? AT SCHOOL!
HOW ARE YOU EVEN PASSING YOUR CLASSES?
N.A.T.A.L.I.E. IS GOING TO LECTURES FOR ME.
SPEAK UP!
N.A.T.A.L.I.E. IS GOING TO LECTURES FOR ME!
M.I.T.
AREN'T YOU, UH, GONNA TAKE NOTES...?
I AM TAKING NOTES. AREN'T YOU GONNA MIND YOUR BUSINESS?
YOU DIDN'T EARN THE PRIVILEGE OF GOING TO M.I.T. JUST SO YOUR NARROW BEHIND CAN SIT AT HOME. DON'T MAKE ME EMBARRASS YOU IN FRONT OF COMPANY.
WHY ARE YOU MAKING SUCH A BIG DEAL OUT OF THIS?
WHY AREN'T YOU?
HONEY. YOU CAN'T KEEP RUNNING AWAY FROM THINGS.
I KNOW YOU'RE STRONG AND HEALTHY UP HERE.
I NEED YOU TO BE STRONG AND HEALTHY IN HERE.
WILL YOU COME TO THE SUPPORT GROUP WITH ME? JUST ONCE?
...
MAYBE.

I'M NOT LETTING THIS GO. XAVIER, YOU'RE WELCOME TO STAY FOR DINNER IF YOU CAN TOLERATE MY DAUGHTER'S HORRIBLE MANNERS.

YES, MA'AM. THANK YOU, MISS RONNIE.

LET'S GET BACK TO THIS. SO OUR APPROACH HERE SHOULD BE--

HOLD UP. ISN'T YOUR MOMS DOING WHAT PEOPLE ARE SUPPOSED TO DO WHEN THEY LOVE YOU? CHECK UP ON YOU?

I GUESS.

AND WHAT'S GOING ON WITH YOU AND THE CHAMPIONS? SHOULDN'T THEY BE HELPING YOU INSTEAD OF REGULAR, DEGULAR, SHMEGULAR ME?

THINGS WITH THE CHAMPIONS ARE... AWKWARD RIGHT NOW. DO WE HAVE TO TALK ABOUT THIS?

YOU'LL DO JUST FINE. ESPECIALLY IF YOU CAN HELP ME FIGURE THIS OUT.

OKAY.

BUT ONLY BECAUSE YOUR MOM IS MAKING DINNER.

TWO HOURS LATER...

MAYBE THERE ISN'T A PATTERN. MAYBE PEOPLE JUST LIKE TO STEAL PHONES.

LET'S JUST REVIEW WHAT WE KNOW. VICTIMS' AGES?

NO PATTERN.

NADA.

RACE?

NEIGHBORHOOD?

TOTALLY RANDOM.

DINNER IS ALMOST READY! Y'ALL DONE WORKING?

YES!

NO!

YES, THIS IS RIRI! WE ARE DEFINITIVELY AFFIRMATIVELY DONE WORKING! TASK COMPLETE!

I DON'T EVEN TALK LIKE THAT. I-- WAIT!

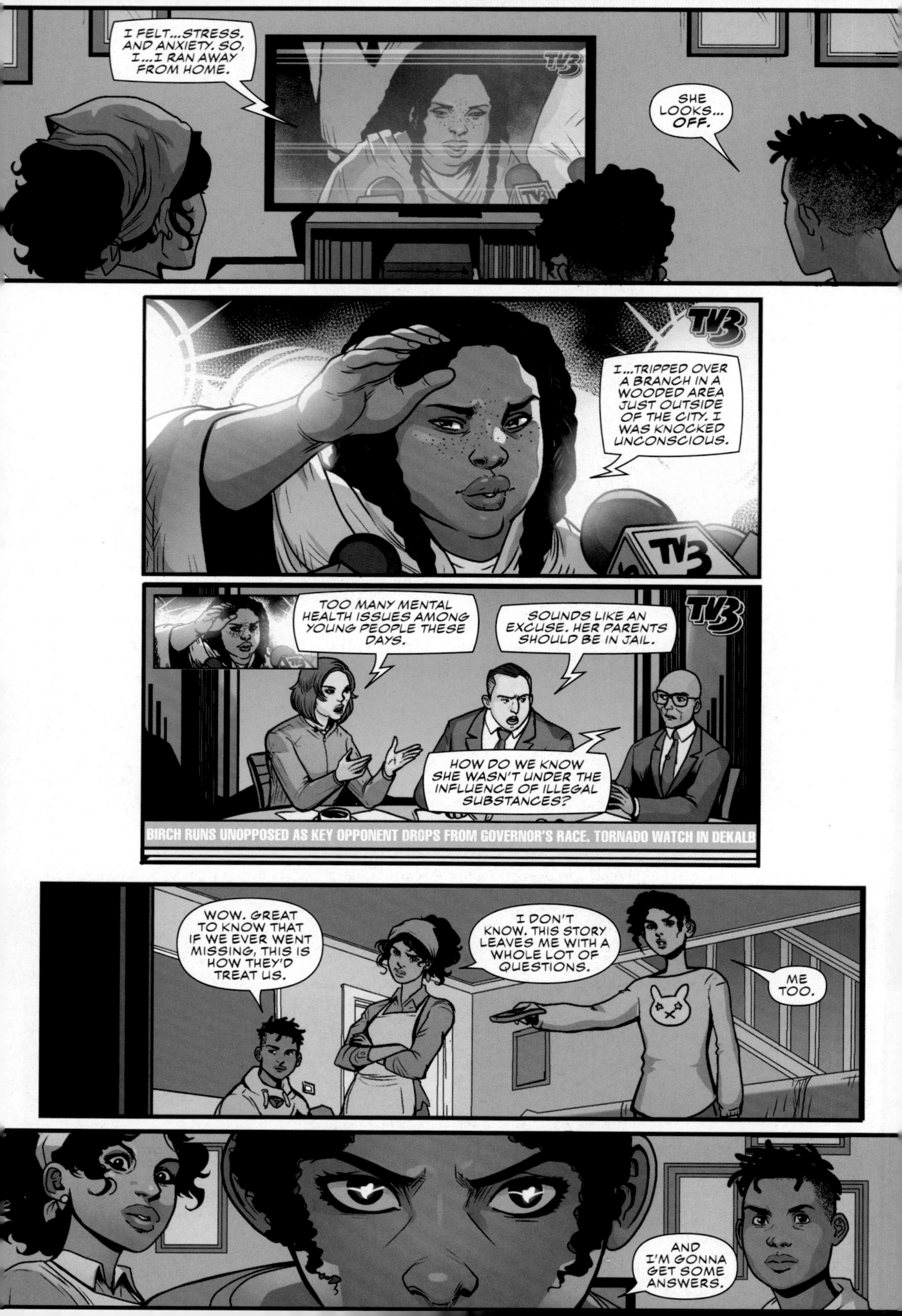

I FELT...STRESS. AND ANXIETY. SO, I...I RAN AWAY FROM HOME.
TV3
SHE LOOKS... OFF.
TV3
I...TRIPPED OVER A BRANCH IN A WOODED AREA JUST OUTSIDE OF THE CITY. I WAS KNOCKED UNCONSCIOUS.
TV3
TV3
TOO MANY MENTAL HEALTH ISSUES AMONG YOUNG PEOPLE THESE DAYS.
SOUNDS LIKE AN EXCUSE. HER PARENTS SHOULD BE IN JAIL.
HOW DO WE KNOW SHE WASN'T UNDER THE INFLUENCE OF ILLEGAL SUBSTANCES?
BIRCH RUNS UNOPPOSED AS KEY OPPONENT DROPS FROM GOVERNOR'S RACE. TORNADO WATCH IN DEKALB
WOW. GREAT TO KNOW THAT IF WE EVER WENT MISSING, THIS IS HOW THEY'D TREAT US.
I DON'T KNOW. THIS STORY LEAVES ME WITH A WHOLE LOT OF QUESTIONS.
ME TOO.
AND I'M GONNA GET SOME ANSWERS.

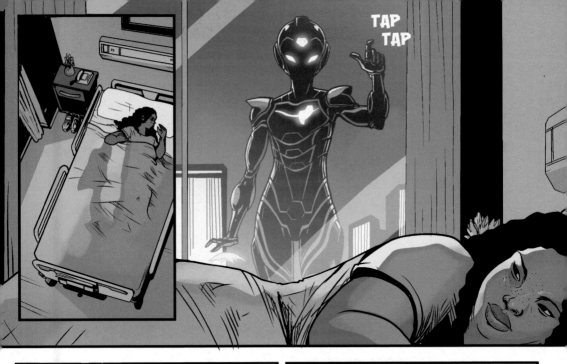

TAP
TAP

IT'S A SEALED WINDOW! IT DOESN'T OPEN! I CAN'T--

VZZZZ

OH, LORD.

OW.

WHY ARE YOU DOING THIS?

I COULD ASK YOU THE SAME QUESTION. WHY ARE YOU ON TV TELLING LIES?

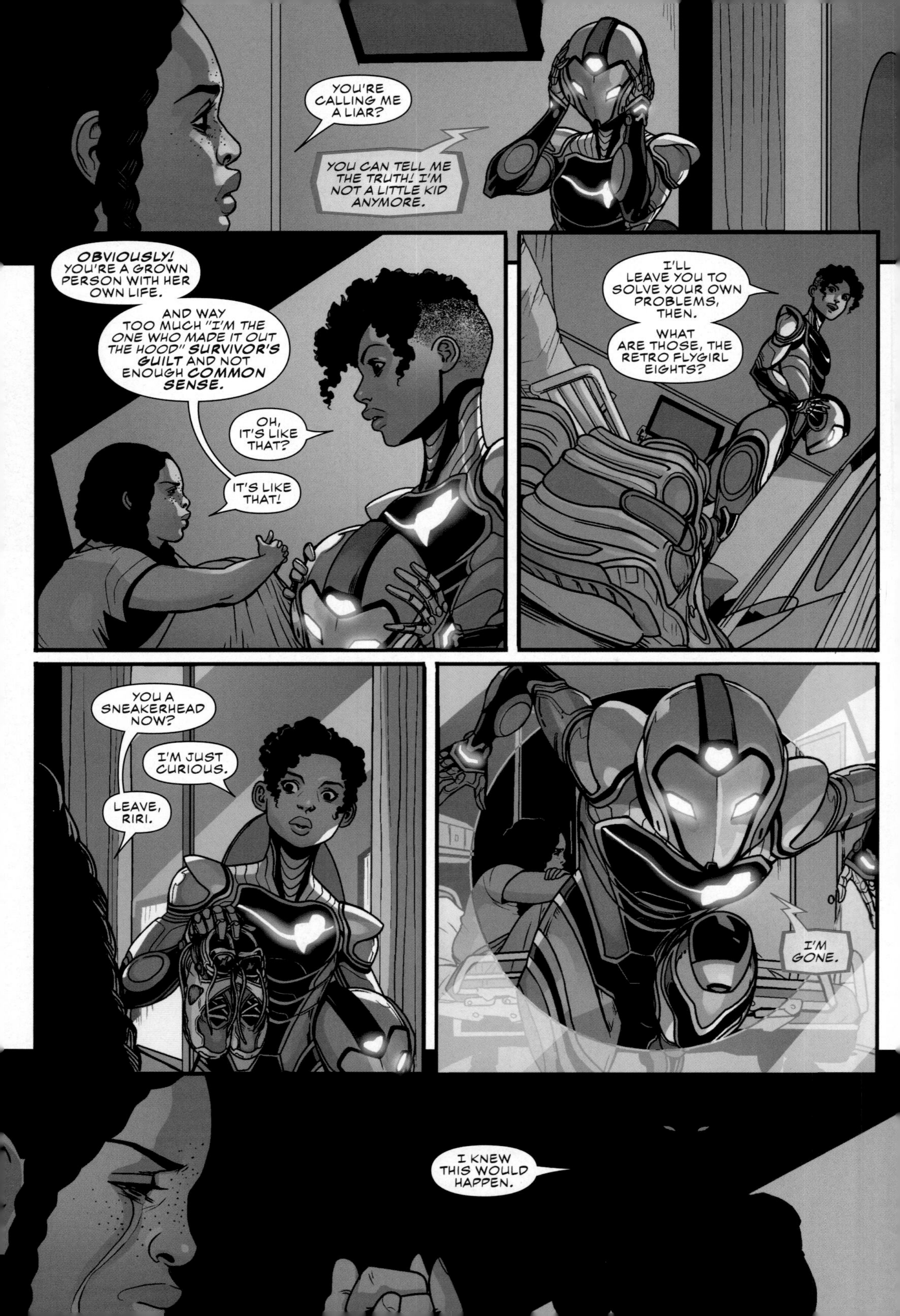
YOU'RE CALLING ME A LIAR?
YOU CAN TELL ME THE TRUTH! I'M NOT A LITTLE KID ANYMORE.
OBVIOUSLY! YOU'RE A GROWN PERSON WITH HER OWN LIFE.
AND WAY TOO MUCH "I'M THE ONE WHO MADE IT OUT THE HOOD" SURVIVOR'S GUILT AND NOT ENOUGH COMMON SENSE.
OH, IT'S LIKE THAT?
IT'S LIKE THAT!
I'LL LEAVE YOU TO SOLVE YOUR OWN PROBLEMS, THEN.
WHAT ARE THOSE, THE RETRO FLYGIRL EIGHTS?
YOU A SNEAKERHEAD NOW?
I'M JUST CURIOUS.
LEAVE, RIRI.
I'M GONE.
I KNEW THIS WOULD HAPPEN.

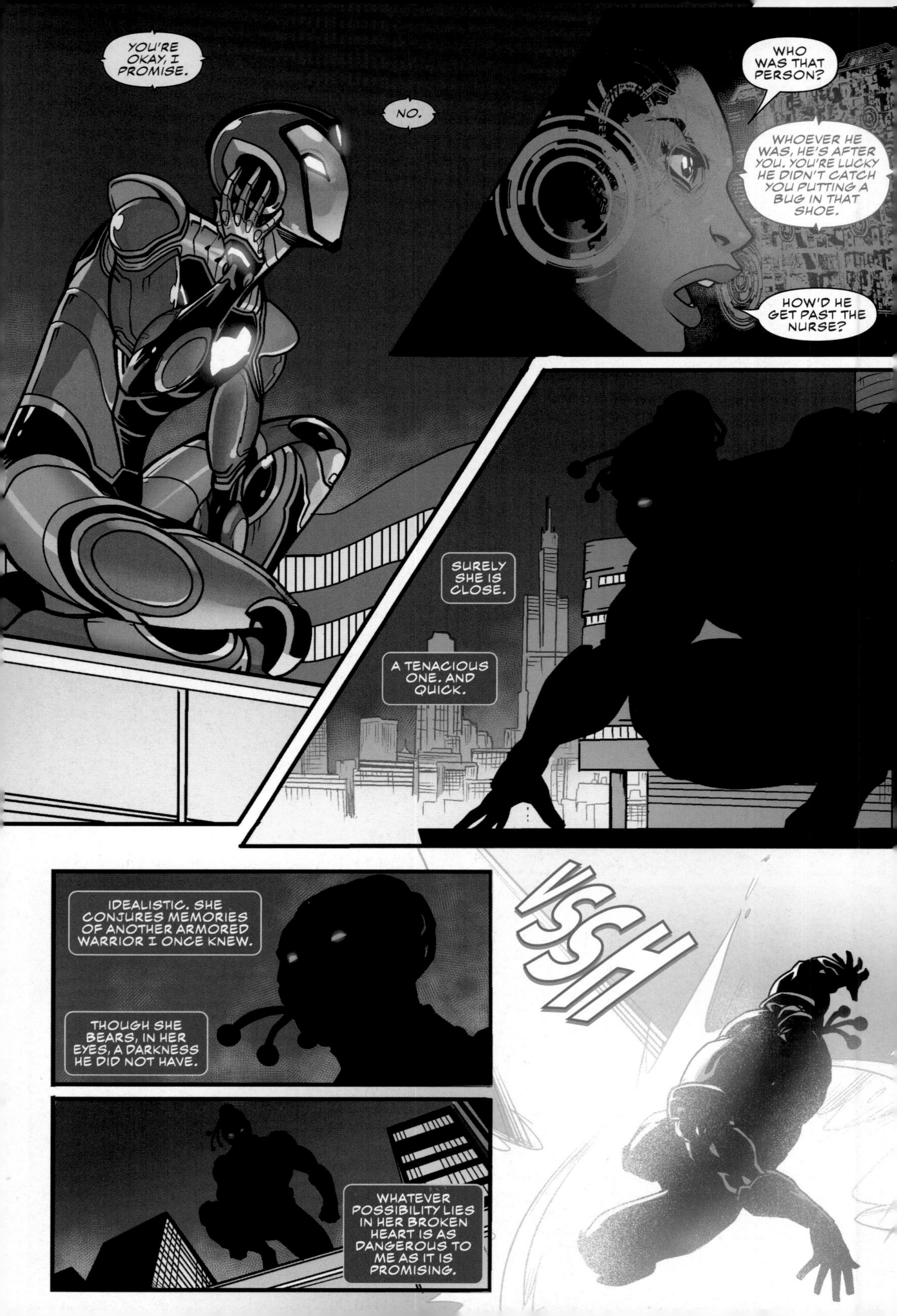

YOU'RE OKAY, I PROMISE.
NO.
WHO WAS THAT PERSON?
WHOEVER HE WAS, HE'S AFTER YOU. YOU'RE LUCKY HE DIDN'T CATCH YOU PUTTING A BUG IN THAT SHOE.
HOW'D HE GET PAST THE NURSE?
SURELY SHE IS CLOSE.
A TENACIOUS ONE. AND QUICK.
IDEALISTIC. SHE CONJURES MEMORIES OF ANOTHER ARMORED WARRIOR I ONCE KNEW.
THOUGH SHE BEARS, IN HER EYES, A DARKNESS HE DID NOT HAVE.
VSSH
WHATEVER POSSIBILITY LIES IN HER BROKEN HEART IS AS DANGEROUS TO ME AS IT IS PROMISING.

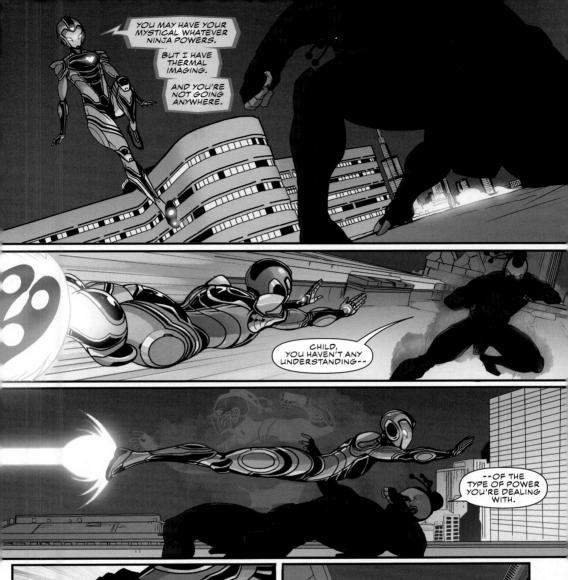

YOU MAY HAVE YOUR MYSTICAL WHATEVER NINJA POWERS.

BUT I HAVE THERMAL IMAGING.

AND YOU'RE NOT GOING ANYWHERE.

CHILD, YOU HAVEN'T ANY UNDERSTANDING--

--OF THE TYPE OF POWER YOU'RE DEALING WITH.

KRASH

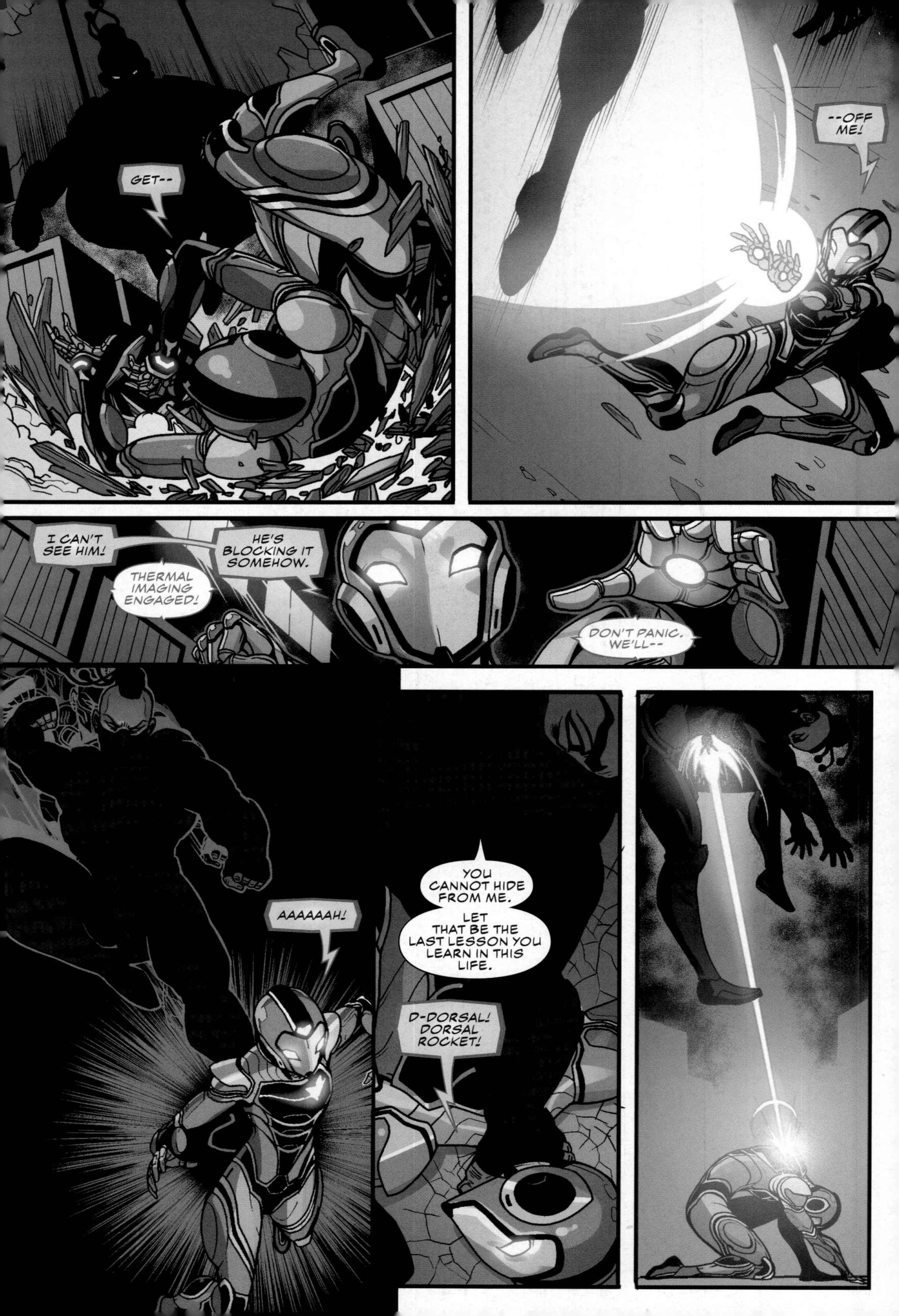
GET--
--OFF ME!
I CAN'T SEE HIM!
HE'S BLOCKING IT SOMEHOW.
THERMAL IMAGING ENGAGED!
DON'T PANIC. WE'LL--
AAAAAAH!
YOU CANNOT HIDE FROM ME.
LET THAT BE THE LAST LESSON YOU LEARN IN THIS LIFE.
D-DORSAL! DORSAL ROCKET!

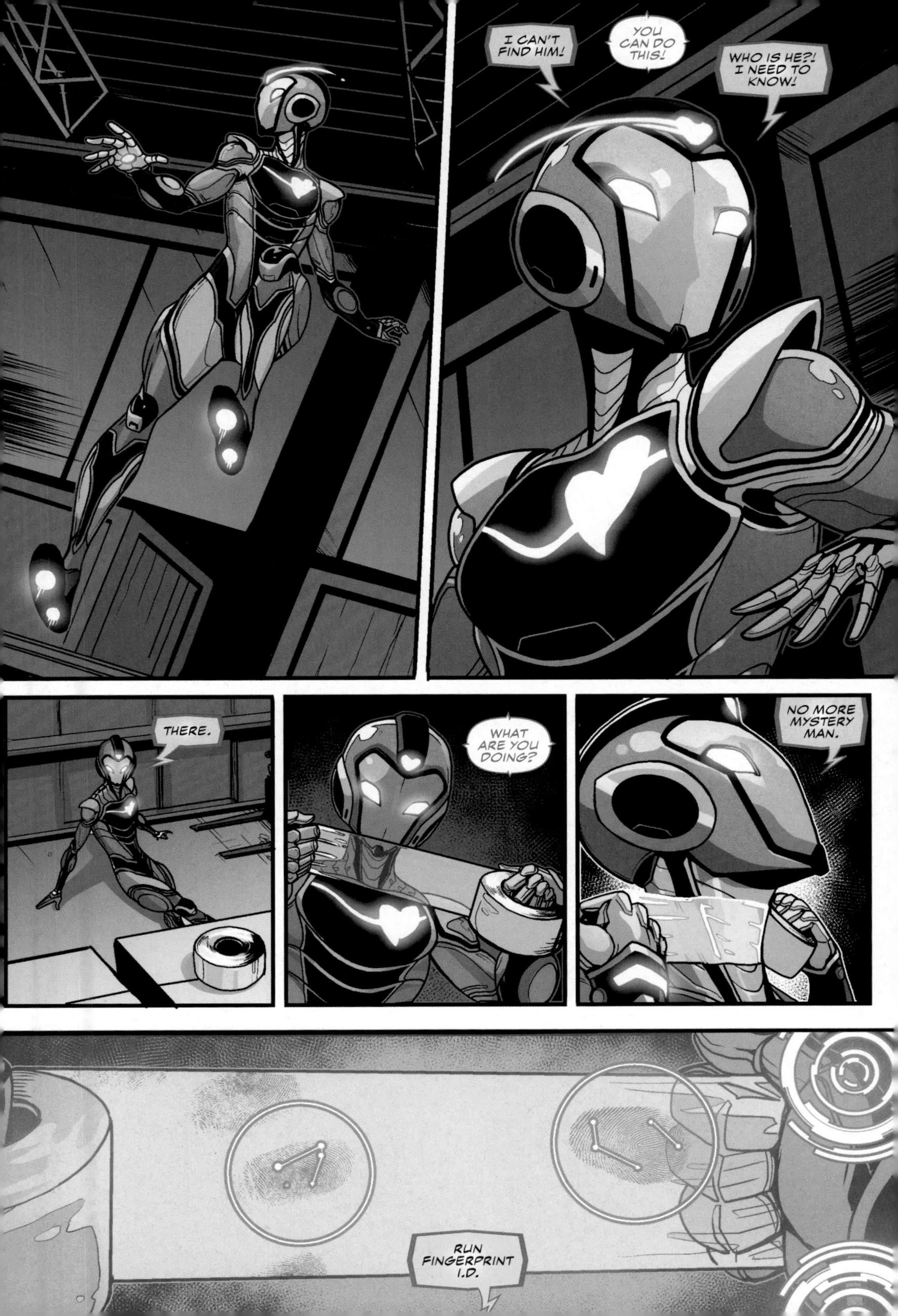
I CAN'T FIND HIM!
YOU CAN DO THIS!
WHO IS HE?! I NEED TO KNOW!
THERE.
WHAT ARE YOU DOING?
NO MORE MYSTERY MAN.
RUN FINGERPRINT I.D.

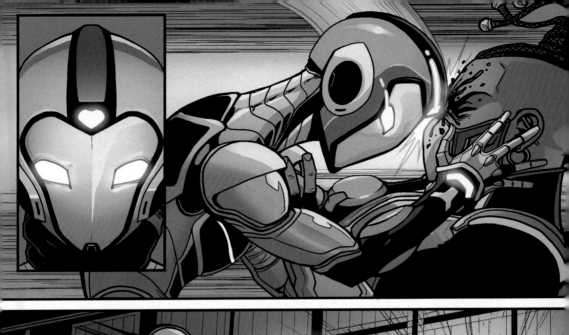

I'M NOT DYING TODAY.

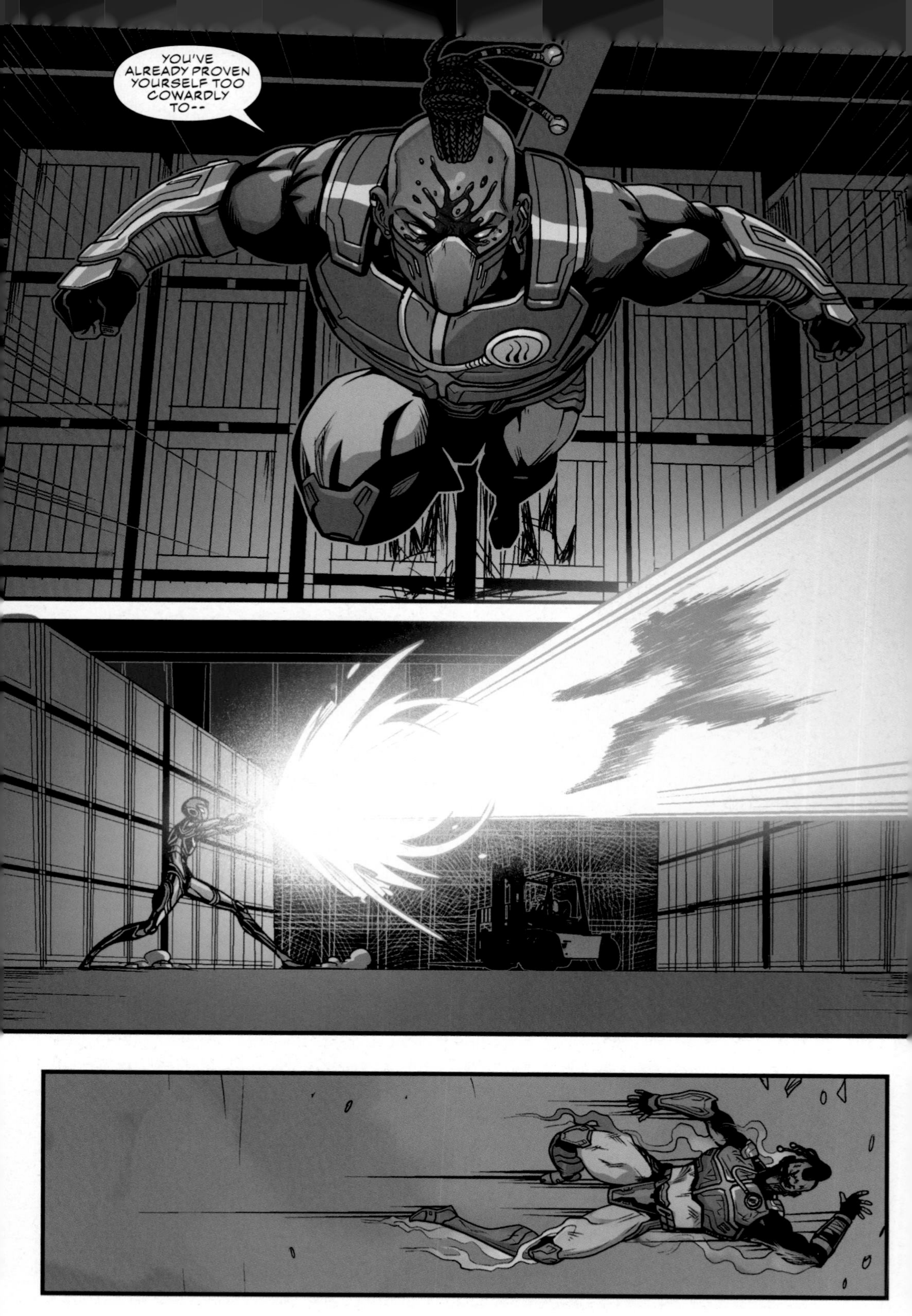
YOU'VE ALREADY PROVEN YOURSELF TOO COWARDLY TO--

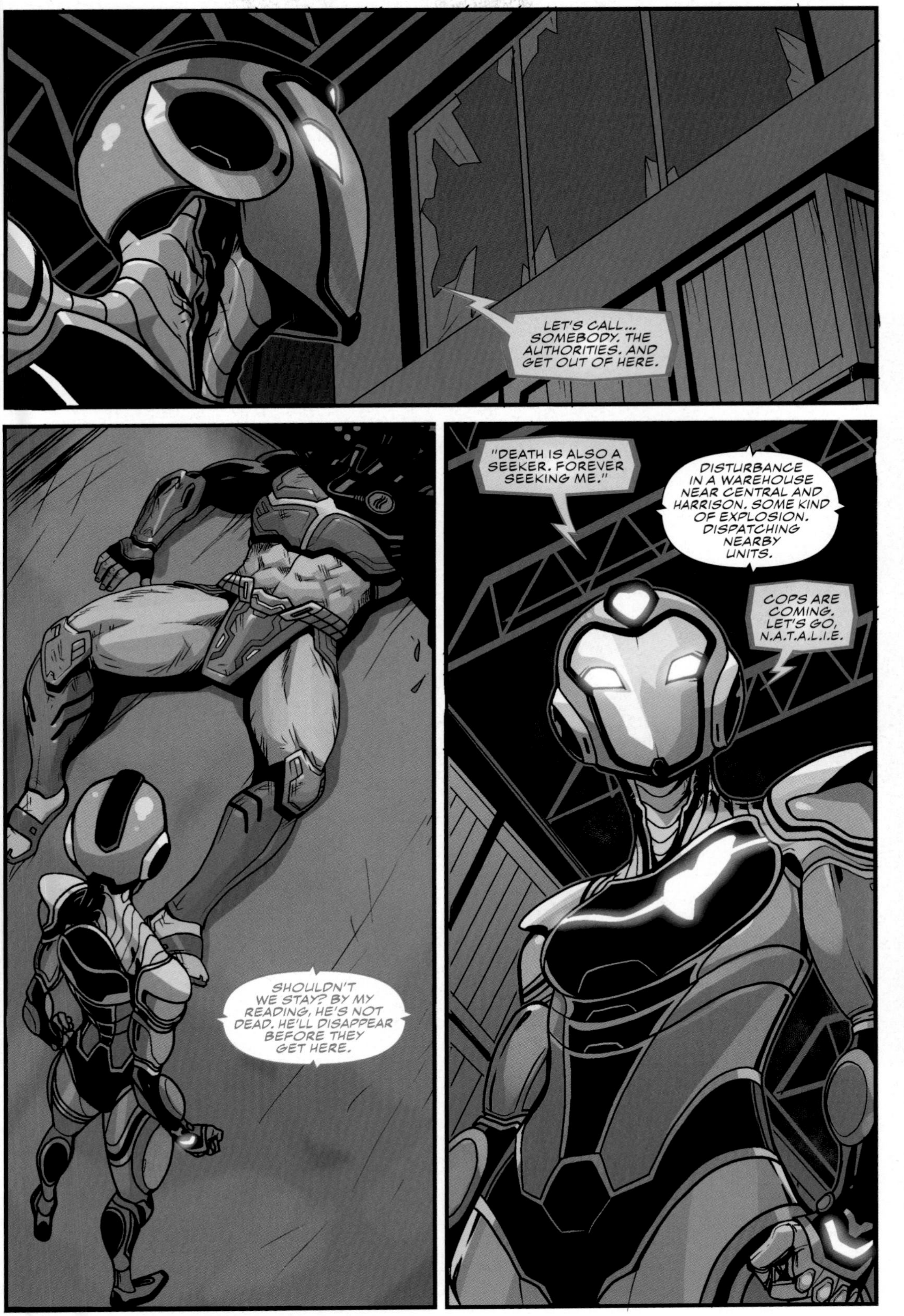
LET'S CALL... SOMEBODY. THE AUTHORITIES. AND GET OUT OF HERE.
SHOULDN'T WE STAY? BY MY READING, HE'S NOT DEAD. HE'LL DISAPPEAR BEFORE THEY GET HERE.
"DEATH IS ALSO A SEEKER. FOREVER SEEKING ME."
DISTURBANCE IN A WAREHOUSE NEAR CENTRAL AND HARRISON. SOME KIND OF EXPLOSION. DISPATCHING NEARBY UNITS.
COPS ARE COMING. LET'S GO, N.A.T.A.L.I.E.

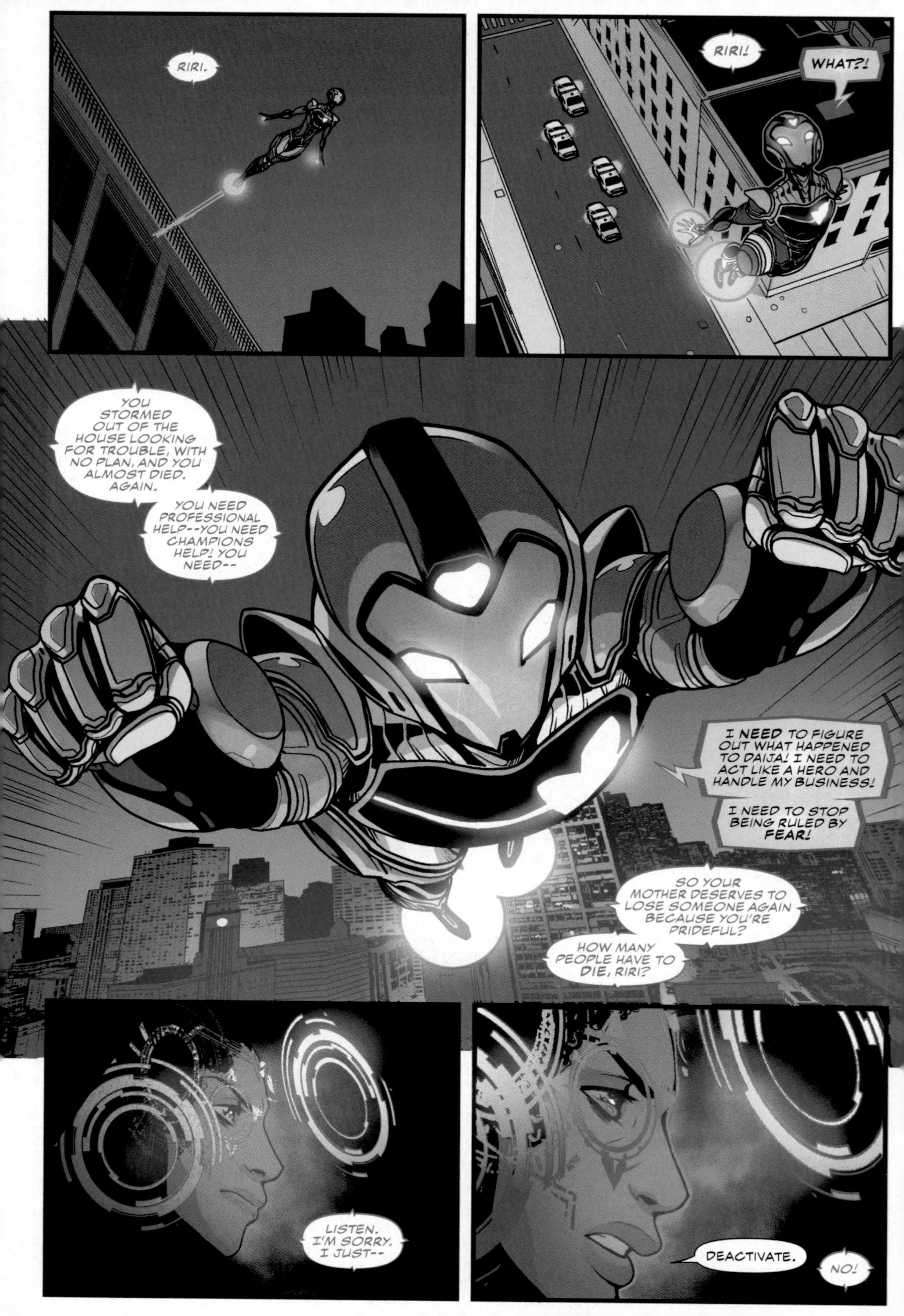
RIRI.
RIRI!
WHAT?!
YOU STORMED OUT OF THE HOUSE LOOKING FOR TROUBLE, WITH NO PLAN, AND YOU ALMOST DIED. AGAIN.
YOU NEED PROFESSIONAL HELP--YOU NEED CHAMPIONS HELP! YOU NEED--
I NEED TO FIGURE OUT WHAT HAPPENED TO DAIJA! I NEED TO ACT LIKE A HERO AND HANDLE MY BUSINESS!
I NEED TO STOP BEING RULED BY FEAR!
SO YOUR MOTHER DESERVES TO LOSE SOMEONE AGAIN BECAUSE YOU'RE PRIDEFUL?
HOW MANY PEOPLE HAVE TO DIE, RIRI?
LISTEN. I'M SORRY. I JUST--
DEACTIVATE.
NO!

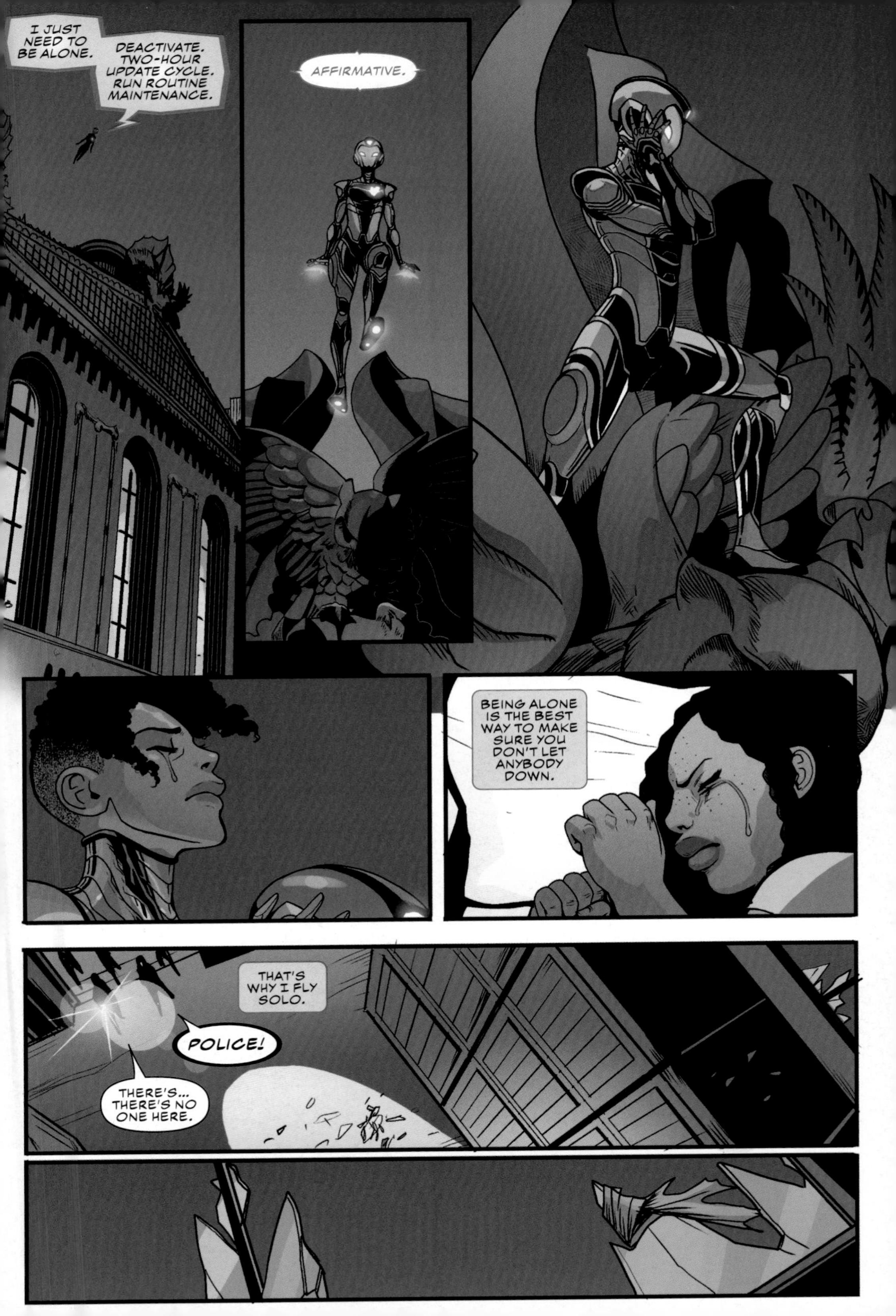
I JUST NEED TO BE ALONE.
DEACTIVATE. TWO-HOUR UPDATE CYCLE. RUN ROUTINE MAINTENANCE.
AFFIRMATIVE.
BEING ALONE IS THE BEST WAY TO MAKE SURE YOU DON'T LET ANYBODY DOWN.
THAT'S WHY I FLY SOLO.
POLICE!
THERE'S... THERE'S NO ONE HERE.

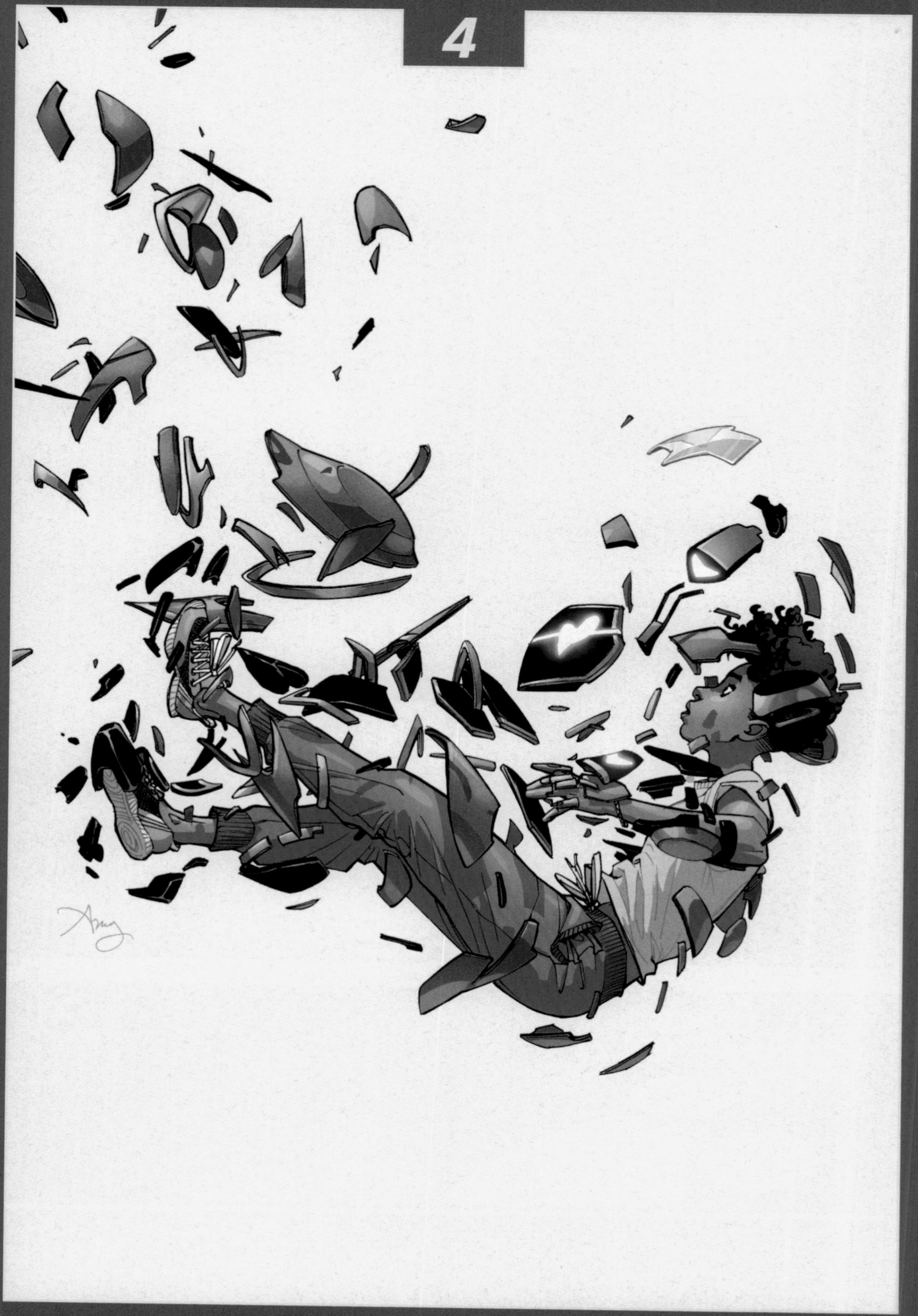

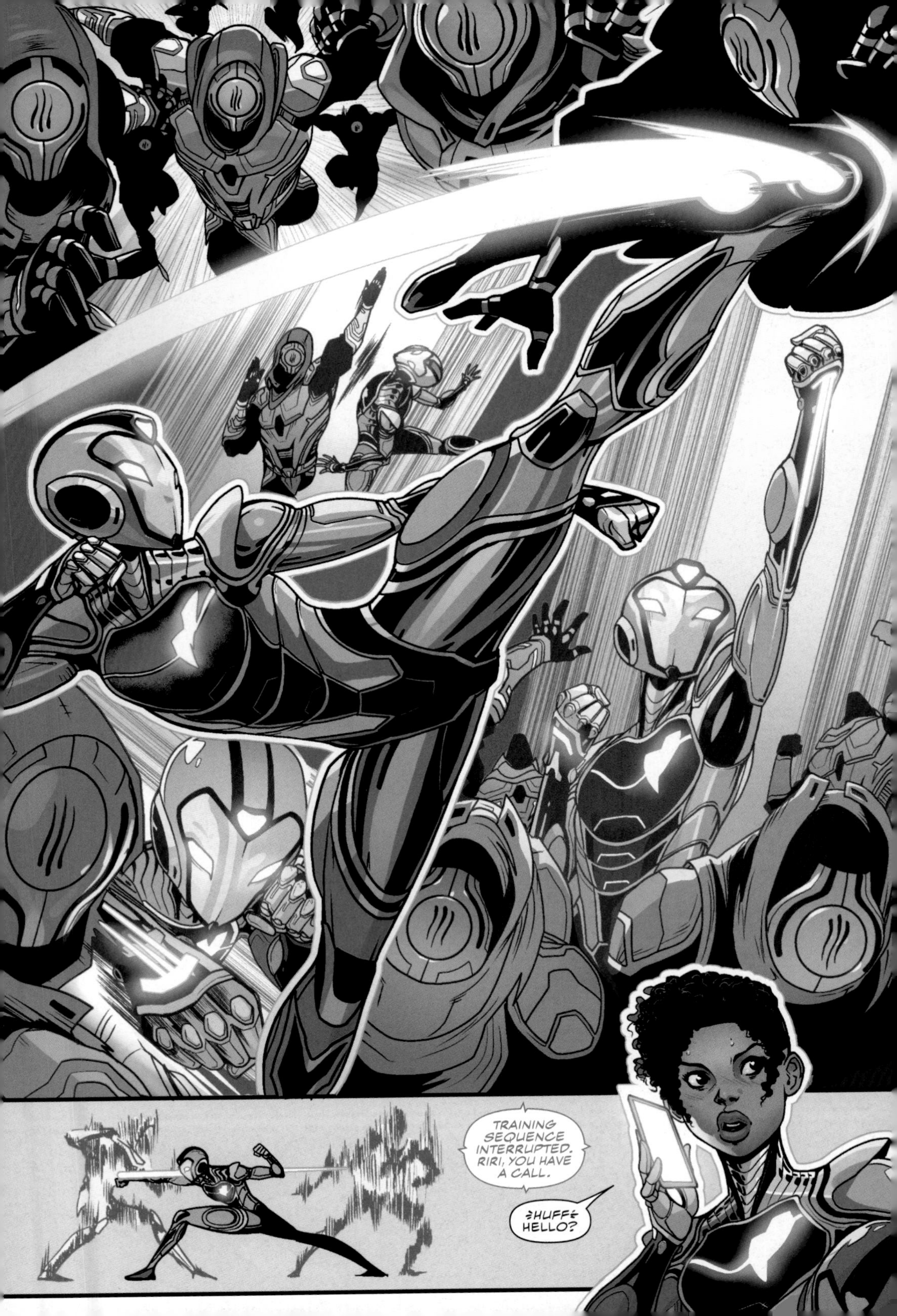
TRAINING SEQUENCE INTERRUPTED. RIRI, YOU HAVE A CALL.
HUFF HELLO?

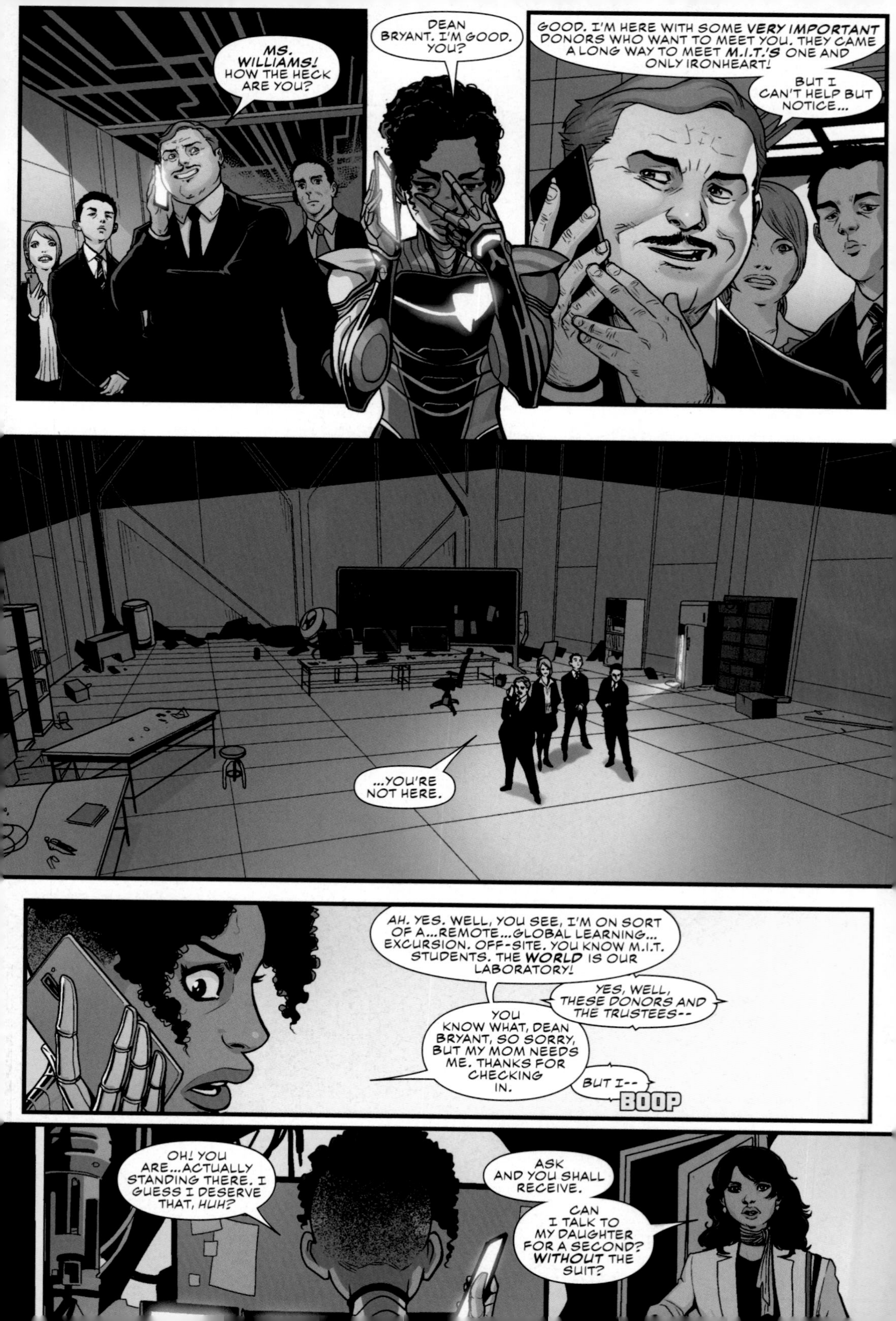
MS. WILLIAMS! HOW THE HECK ARE YOU?
DEAN BRYANT. I'M GOOD. YOU?
GOOD. I'M HERE WITH SOME VERY IMPORTANT DONORS WHO WANT TO MEET YOU. THEY CAME A LONG WAY TO MEET M.I.T.'S ONE AND ONLY IRONHEART!
BUT I CAN'T HELP BUT NOTICE...
...YOU'RE NOT HERE.
AH. YES. WELL, YOU SEE, I'M ON SORT OF A...REMOTE...GLOBAL LEARNING... EXCURSION. OFF-SITE. YOU KNOW M.I.T. STUDENTS. THE WORLD IS OUR LABORATORY!
YES, WELL, THESE DONORS AND THE TRUSTEES--
YOU KNOW WHAT, DEAN BRYANT, SO SORRY, BUT MY MOM NEEDS ME. THANKS FOR CHECKING IN.
BUT I--
BOOP
OH! YOU ARE...ACTUALLY STANDING THERE. I GUESS I DESERVE THAT, HUH?
ASK AND YOU SHALL RECEIVE.
CAN I TALK TO MY DAUGHTER FOR A SECOND? WITHOUT THE SUIT?

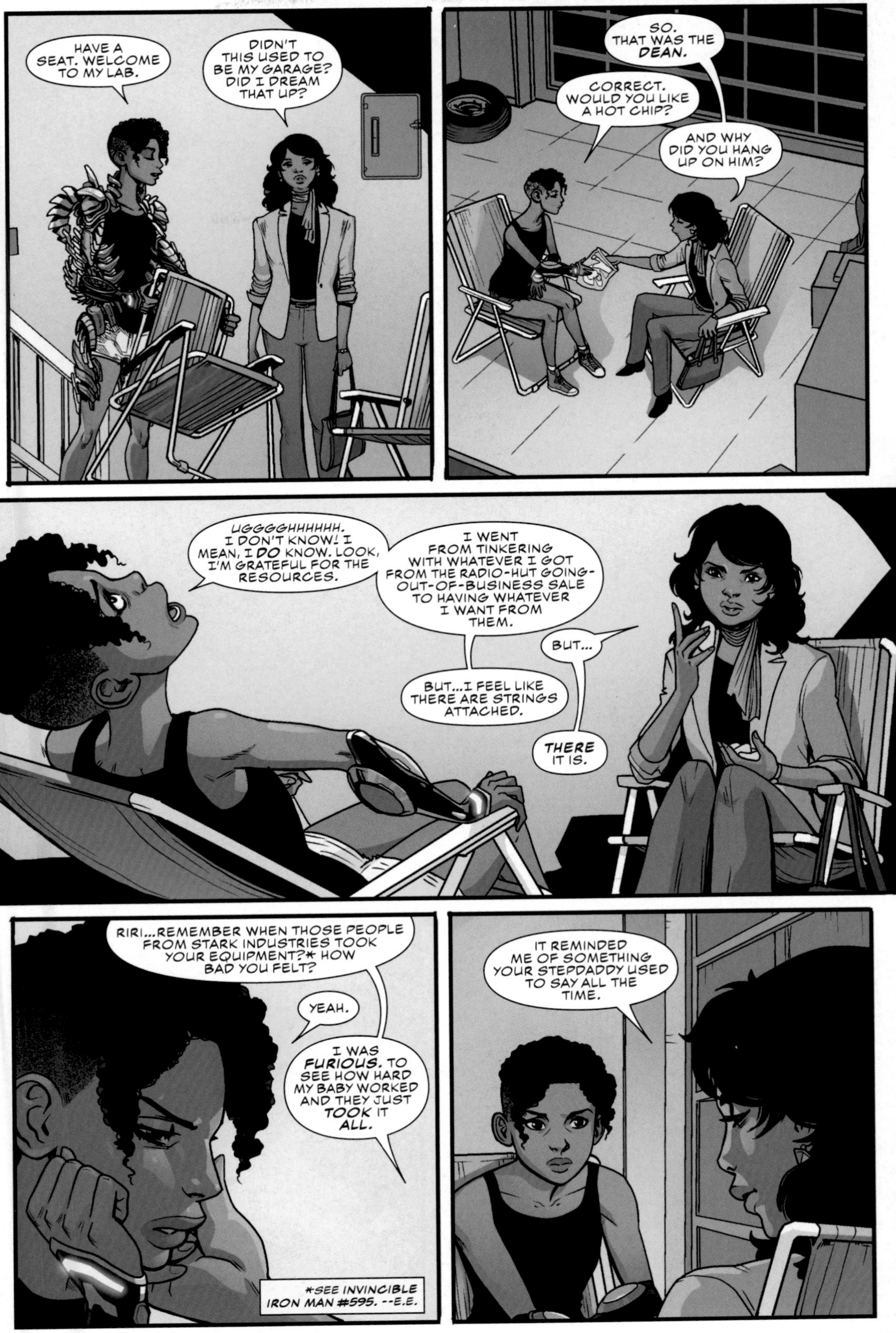
HAVE A SEAT. WELCOME TO MY LAB.
DIDN'T THIS USED TO BE MY GARAGE? DID I DREAM THAT UP?
SO. THAT WAS THE DEAN.
CORRECT. WOULD YOU LIKE A HOT CHIP?
AND WHY DID YOU HANG UP ON HIM?
UGGGGHHHHHH. I DON'T KNOW! I MEAN, I DO KNOW. LOOK, I'M GRATEFUL FOR THE RESOURCES.
I WENT FROM TINKERING WITH WHATEVER I GOT FROM THE RADIO-HUT GOING-OUT-OF-BUSINESS SALE TO HAVING WHATEVER I WANT FROM THEM.
BUT...
BUT...I FEEL LIKE THERE ARE STRINGS ATTACHED.
THERE IT IS.
RIRI...REMEMBER WHEN THOSE PEOPLE FROM STARK INDUSTRIES TOOK YOUR EQUIPMENT?* HOW BAD YOU FELT?
YEAH.
I WAS FURIOUS. TO SEE HOW HARD MY BABY WORKED AND THEY JUST TOOK IT ALL.
*SEE INVINCIBLE IRON MAN #595. --E.E.
IT REMINDED ME OF SOMETHING YOUR STEPDADDY USED TO SAY ALL THE TIME.

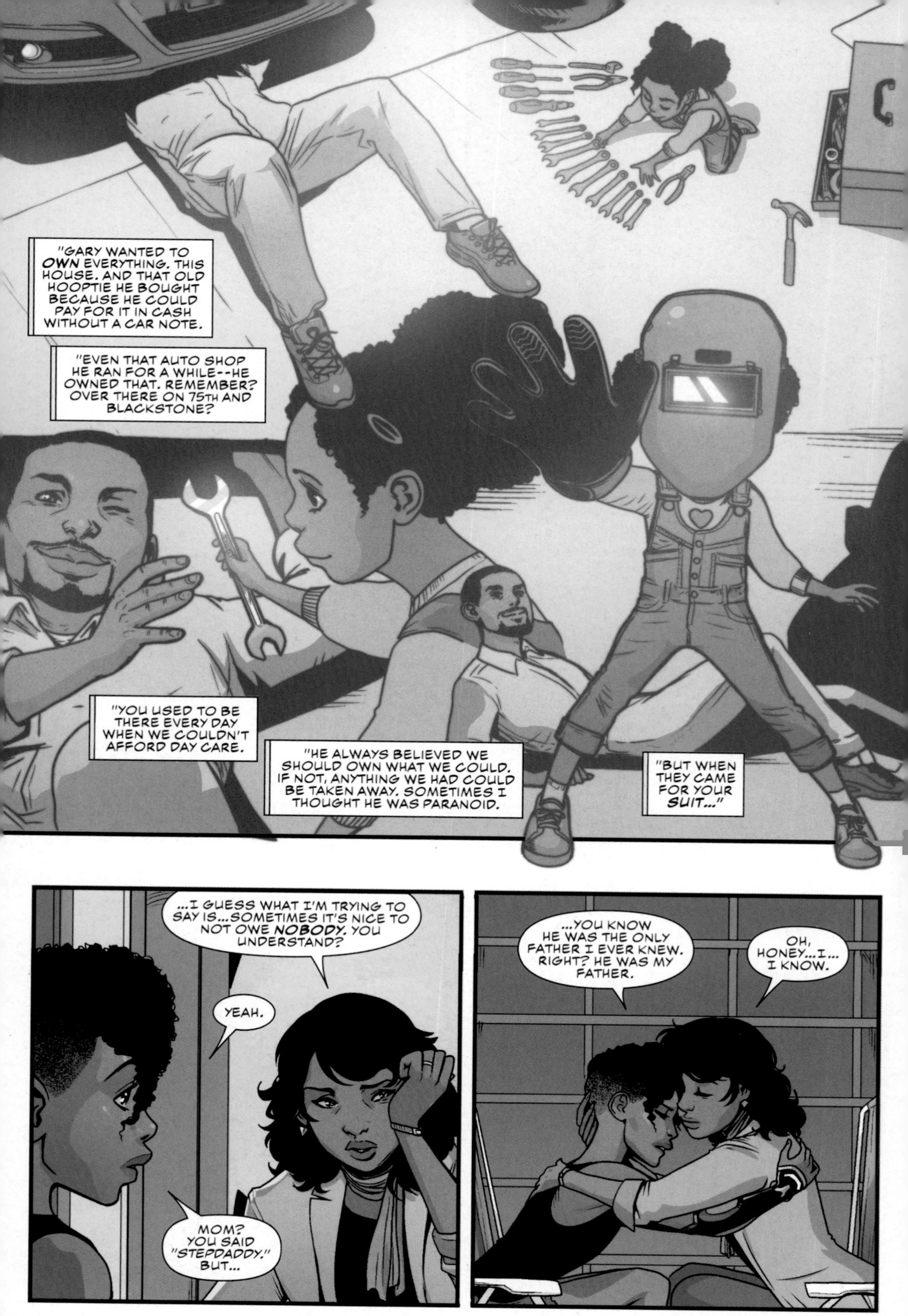
"GARY WANTED TO OWN EVERYTHING. THIS HOUSE. AND THAT OLD HOOPTIE HE BOUGHT BECAUSE HE COULD PAY FOR IT IN CASH WITHOUT A CAR NOTE.
"EVEN THAT AUTO SHOP HE RAN FOR A WHILE--HE OWNED THAT. REMEMBER? OVER THERE ON 75TH AND BLACKSTONE?
"YOU USED TO BE THERE EVERY DAY WHEN WE COULDN'T AFFORD DAY CARE.
"HE ALWAYS BELIEVED WE SHOULD OWN WHAT WE COULD. IF NOT, ANYTHING WE HAD COULD BE TAKEN AWAY. SOMETIMES I THOUGHT HE WAS PARANOID.
"BUT WHEN THEY CAME FOR YOUR SUIT..."
...I GUESS WHAT I'M TRYING TO SAY IS...SOMETIMES IT'S NICE TO NOT OWE NOBODY. YOU UNDERSTAND?
YEAH.
MOM? YOU SAID "STEPDADDY." BUT...
...YOU KNOW HE WAS THE ONLY FATHER I EVER KNEW. RIGHT? HE WAS MY FATHER.
OH, HONEY...I... I KNOW.

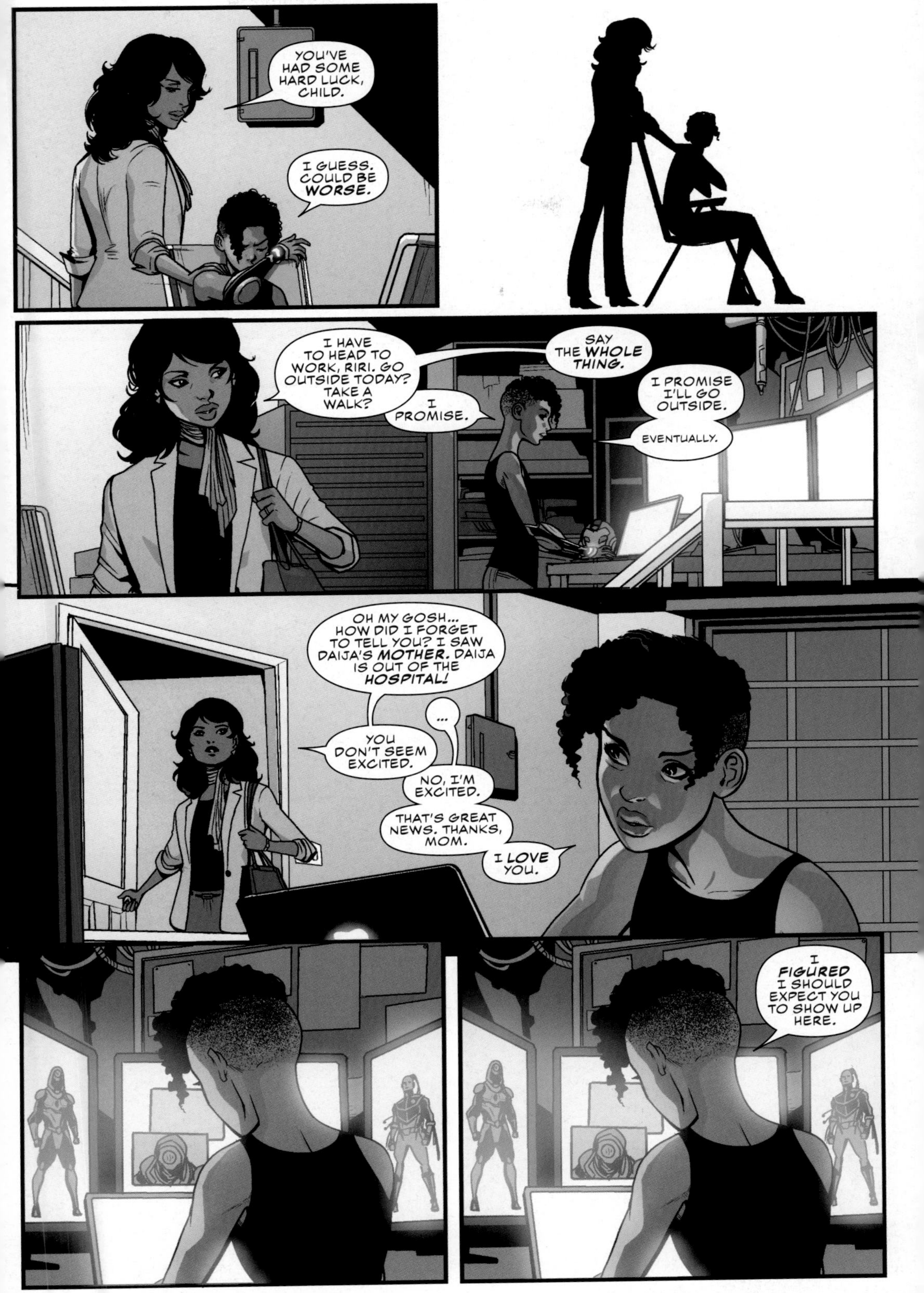
YOU'VE HAD SOME HARD LUCK, CHILD.
I GUESS. COULD BE WORSE.
I HAVE TO HEAD TO WORK, RIRI. GO OUTSIDE TODAY? TAKE A WALK?
I PROMISE.
SAY THE WHOLE THING.
I PROMISE I'LL GO OUTSIDE.
EVENTUALLY.
OH MY GOSH... HOW DID I FORGET TO TELL YOU? I SAW DAIJA'S MOTHER. DAIJA IS OUT OF THE HOSPITAL!
...
YOU DON'T SEEM EXCITED.
NO, I'M EXCITED.
THAT'S GREAT NEWS. THANKS, MOM.
I LOVE YOU.
I FIGURED I SHOULD EXPECT YOU TO SHOW UP HERE.

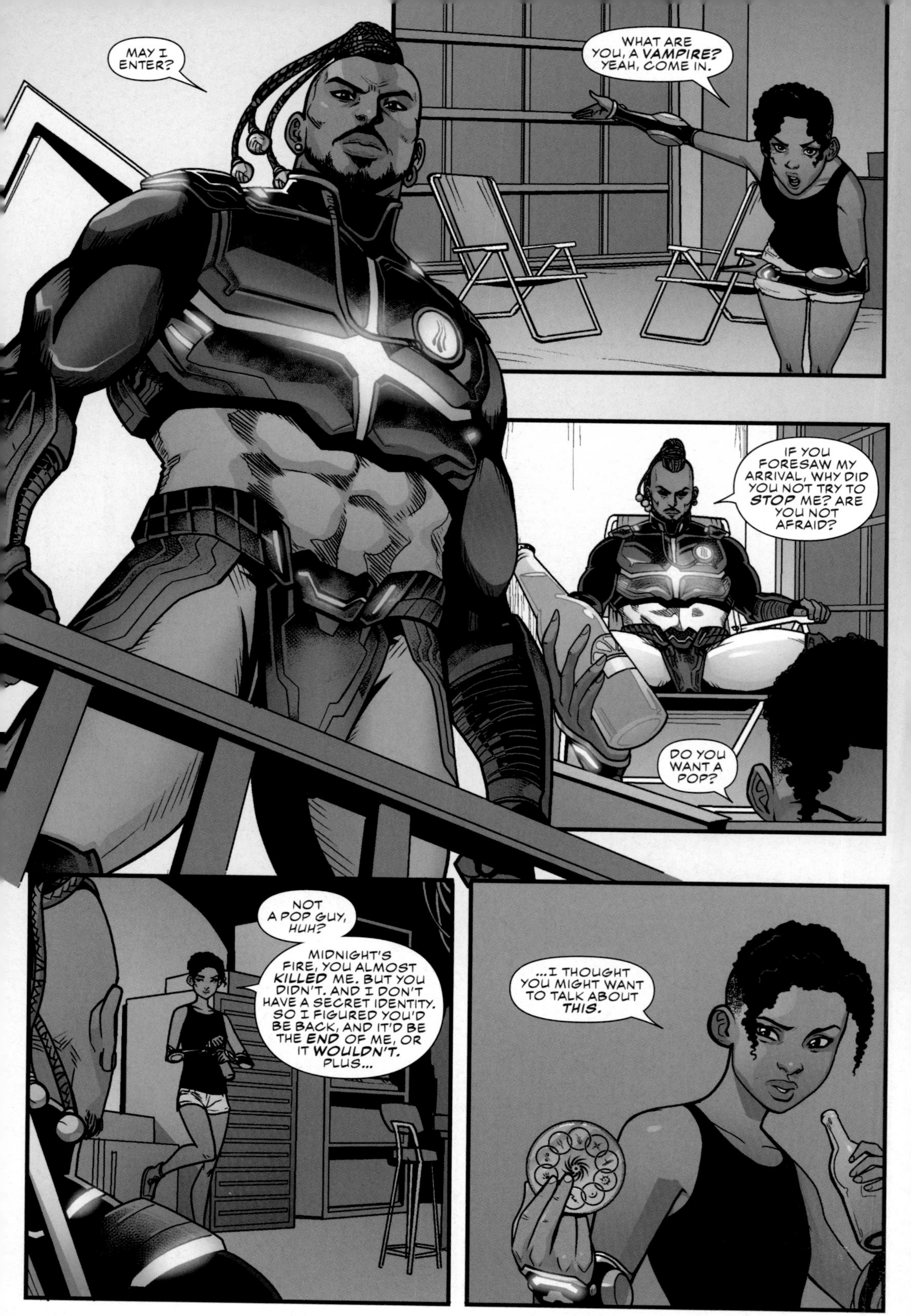
MAY I ENTER?
WHAT ARE YOU, A VAMPIRE? YEAH, COME IN.
IF YOU FORESAW MY ARRIVAL, WHY DID YOU NOT TRY TO STOP ME? ARE YOU NOT AFRAID?
DO YOU WANT A POP?
NOT A POP GUY, HUH?
MIDNIGHT'S FIRE, YOU ALMOST KILLED ME. BUT YOU DIDN'T. AND I DON'T HAVE A SECRET IDENTITY. SO I FIGURED YOU'D BE BACK, AND IT'D BE THE END OF ME, OR IT WOULDN'T. PLUS...
...I THOUGHT YOU MIGHT WANT TO TALK ABOUT THIS.

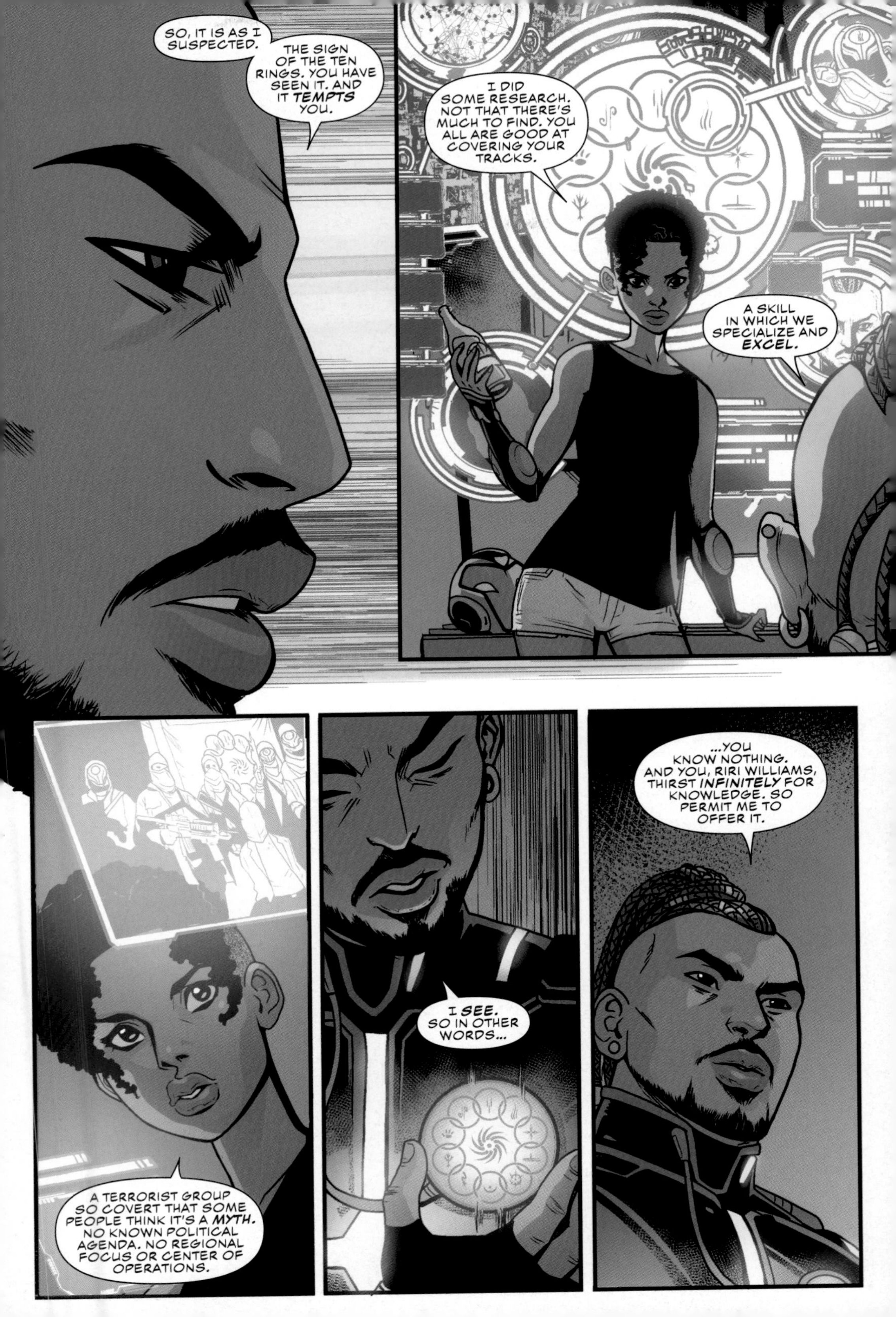
SO, IT IS AS I SUSPECTED.
THE SIGN OF THE TEN RINGS. YOU HAVE SEEN IT. AND IT TEMPTS YOU.
I DID SOME RESEARCH. NOT THAT THERE'S MUCH TO FIND. YOU ALL ARE GOOD AT COVERING YOUR TRACKS.
A SKILL IN WHICH WE SPECIALIZE AND EXCEL.
A TERRORIST GROUP SO COVERT THAT SOME PEOPLE THINK IT'S A MYTH. NO KNOWN POLITICAL AGENDA. NO REGIONAL FOCUS OR CENTER OF OPERATIONS.
I SEE. SO IN OTHER WORDS...
...YOU KNOW NOTHING. AND YOU, RIRI WILLIAMS, THIRST INFINITELY FOR KNOWLEDGE. SO PERMIT ME TO OFFER IT.

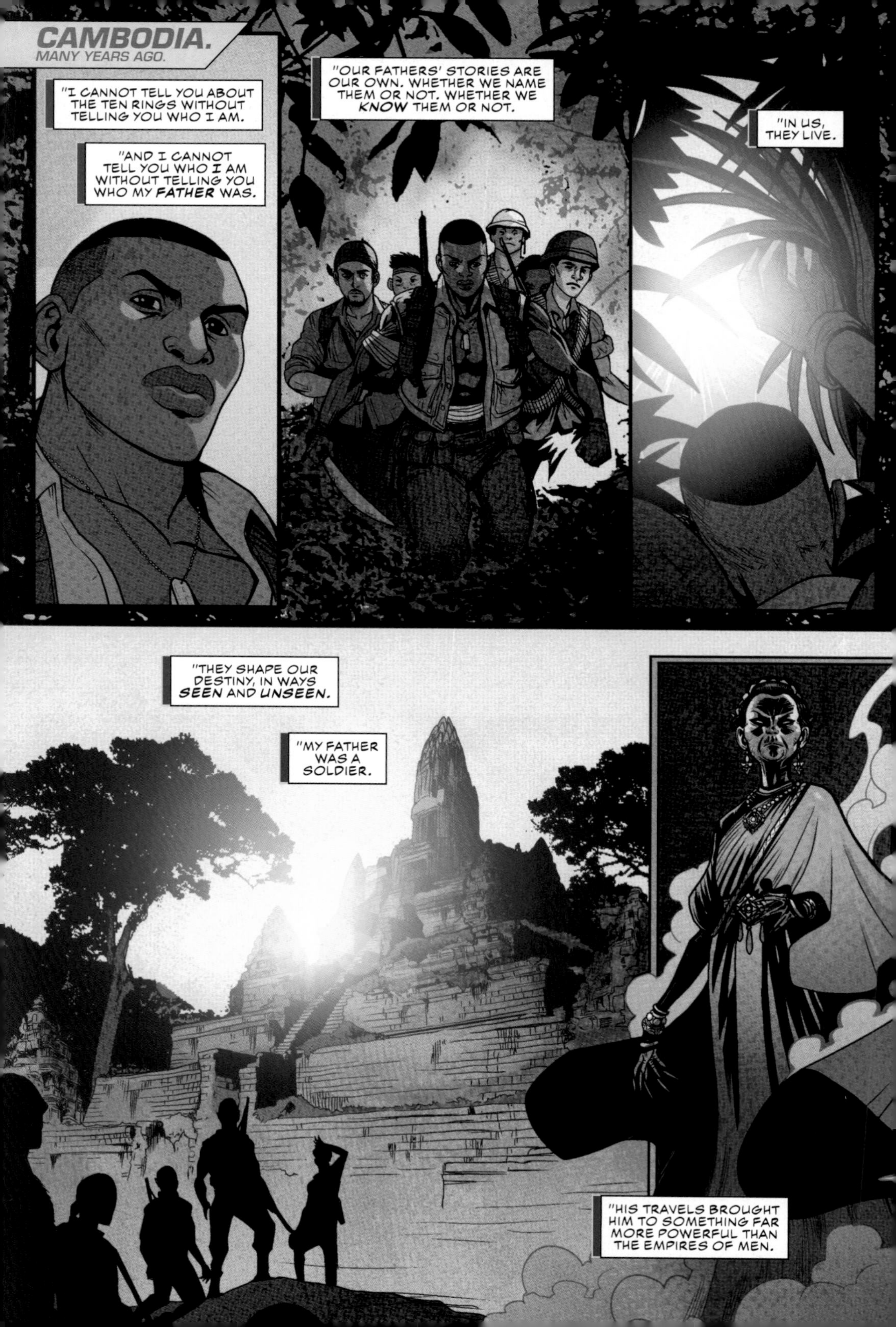
CAMBODIA.
MANY YEARS AGO.
"I CANNOT TELL YOU ABOUT THE TEN RINGS WITHOUT TELLING YOU WHO I AM.
"AND I CANNOT TELL YOU WHO I AM WITHOUT TELLING YOU WHO MY FATHER WAS.
"OUR FATHERS' STORIES ARE OUR OWN. WHETHER WE NAME THEM OR NOT. WHETHER WE KNOW THEM OR NOT.
"IN US, THEY LIVE.
"THEY SHAPE OUR DESTINY, IN WAYS SEEN AND UNSEEN.
"MY FATHER WAS A SOLDIER.
"HIS TRAVELS BROUGHT HIM TO SOMETHING FAR MORE POWERFUL THAN THE EMPIRES OF MEN.

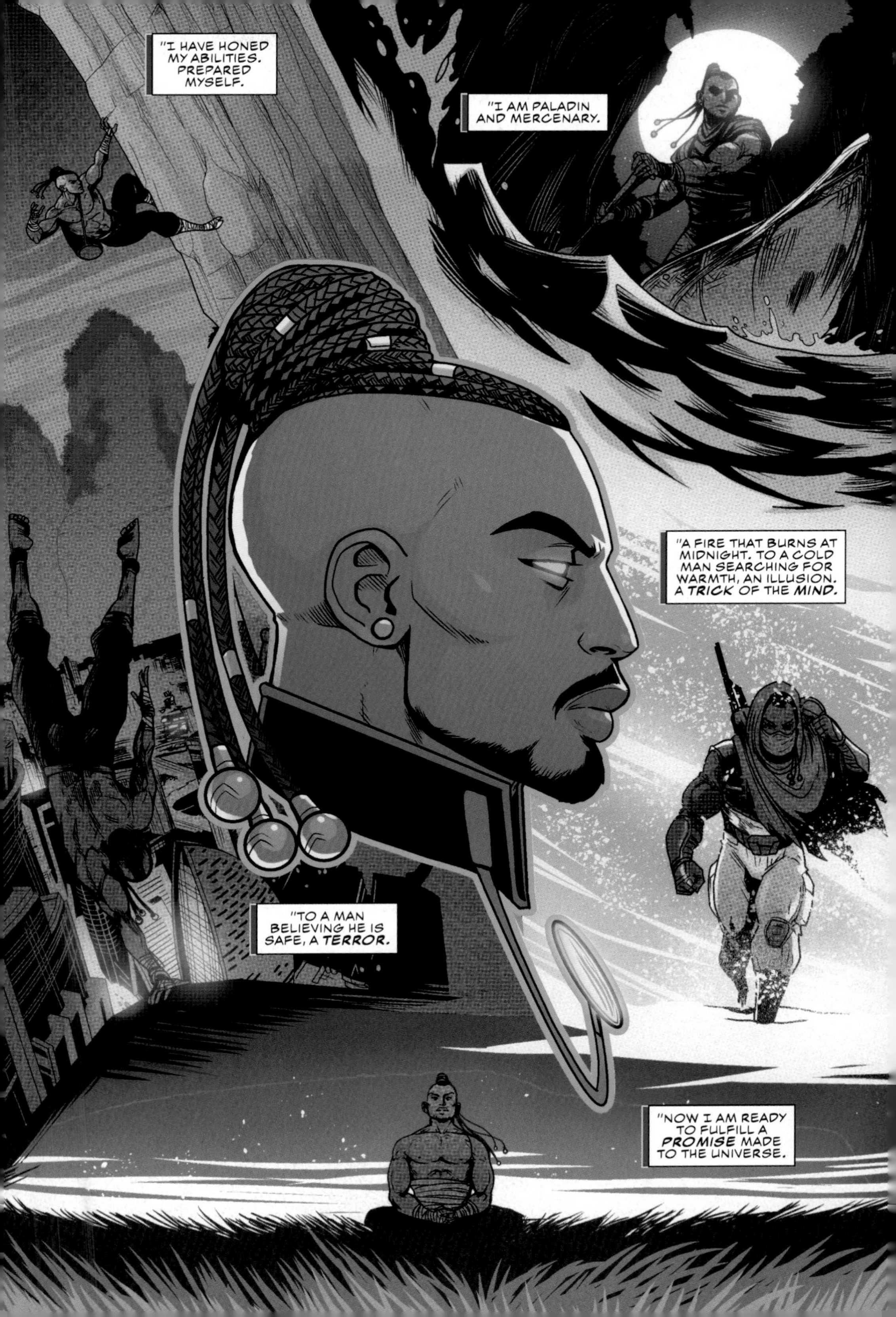
"I HAVE HONED MY ABILITIES. PREPARED MYSELF.
"I AM PALADIN AND MERCENARY.
"A FIRE THAT BURNS AT MIDNIGHT. TO A COLD MAN SEARCHING FOR WARMTH, AN ILLUSION. A TRICK OF THE MIND.
"TO A MAN BELIEVING HE IS SAFE, A TERROR.
"NOW I AM READY TO FULFILL A PROMISE MADE TO THE UNIVERSE.

"MY FATHER AND GRANDMOTHER THOUGHT OUR DESTINY COULD BE FULFILLED AS *INDIVIDUALS.*

"BUT POWER WITHOUT STRUCTURE IS CHAOS."

THE SANCTUM SANCTORUM.
NEW YORK CITY.
SEVERAL YEARS AGO.

"YOU SEE, THE *TEMPLE* OF TAI WAS BUT *ONE* PORTAL TO SOMETHING *GRAND.*

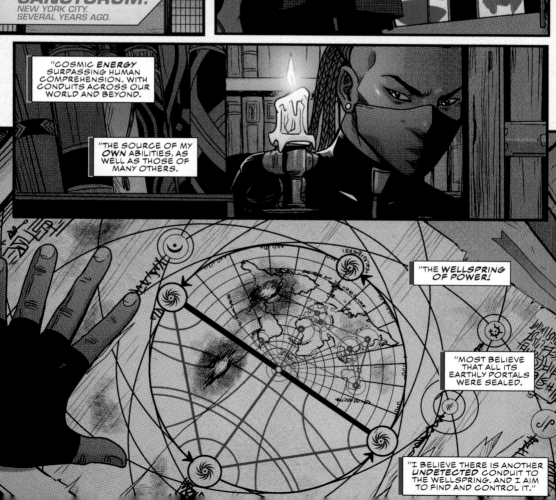

"COSMIC *ENERGY* SURPASSING HUMAN COMPREHENSION. WITH CONDUITS ACROSS OUR WORLD AND BEYOND.

"THE SOURCE OF MY *OWN* ABILITIES, AS WELL AS THOSE OF MANY OTHERS.

"THE *WELLSPRING* OF POWER!

"MOST BELIEVE THAT ALL ITS EARTHLY PORTALS WERE SEALED.

"I BELIEVE THERE IS ANOTHER *UNDETECTED* CONDUIT TO THE WELLSPRING, AND I AIM TO FIND AND CONTROL IT."

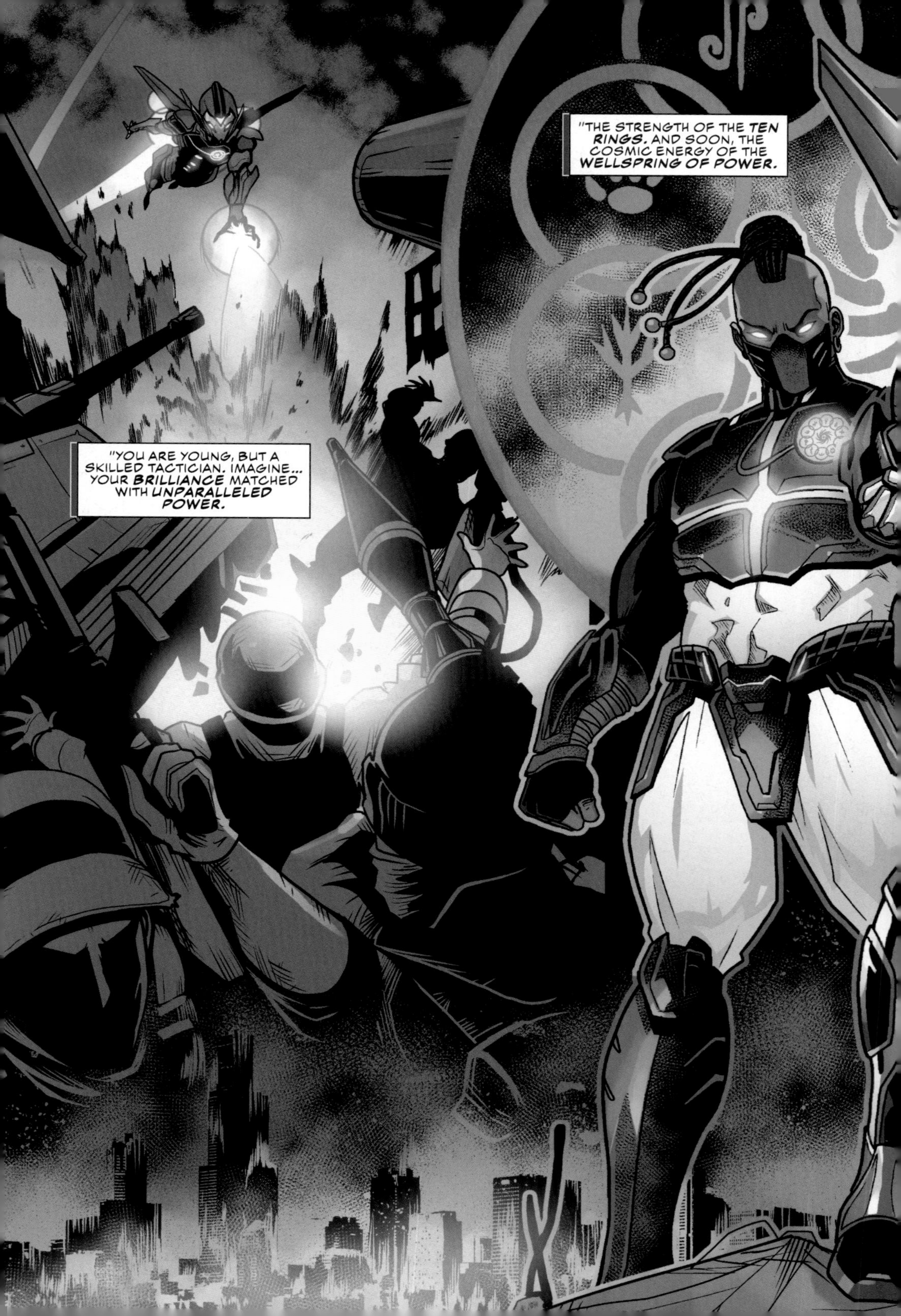
"YOU ARE YOUNG, BUT A SKILLED TACTICIAN. IMAGINE... YOUR BRILLIANCE MATCHED WITH UNPARALLELED POWER.
"THE STRENGTH OF THE TEN RINGS. AND SOON, THE COSMIC ENERGY OF THE WELLSPRING OF POWER.

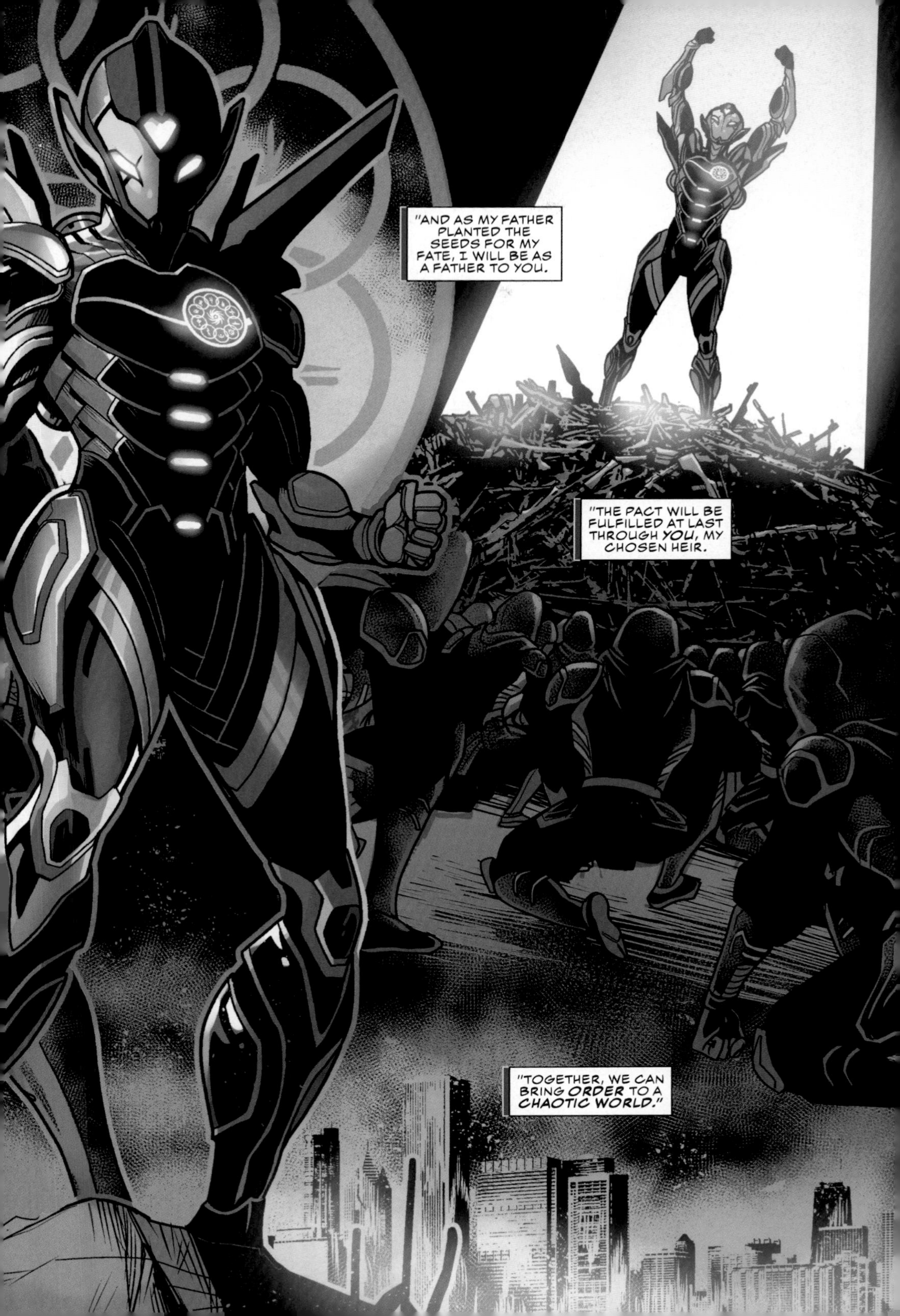
"AND AS MY FATHER PLANTED THE SEEDS FOR MY FATE, I WILL BE AS A FATHER TO YOU.
"THE PACT WILL BE FULFILLED AT LAST THROUGH *YOU*, MY CHOSEN HEIR.
"TOGETHER, WE CAN BRING *ORDER* TO A *CHAOTIC WORLD*."

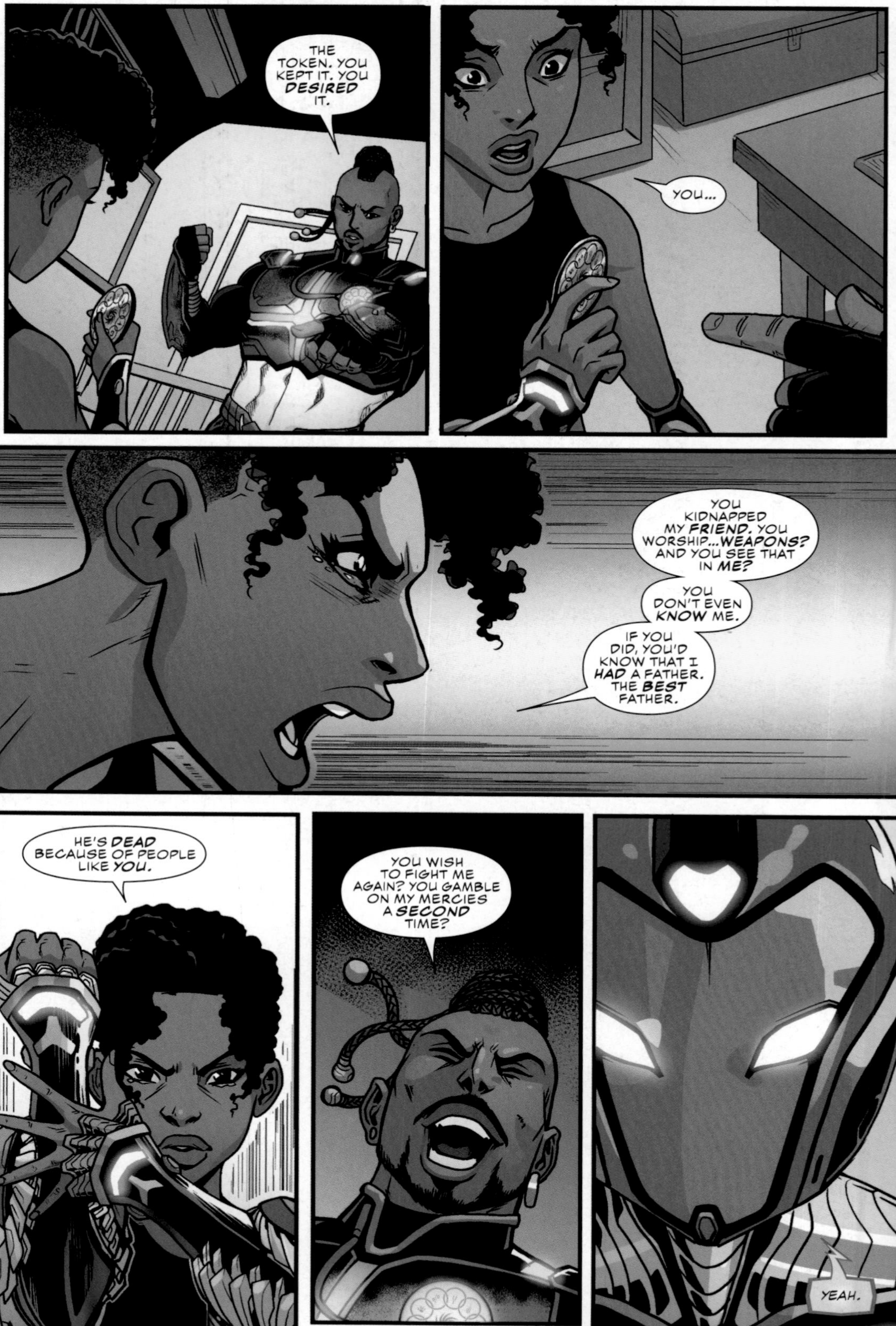
THE TOKEN. YOU KEPT IT. YOU DESIRED IT.
YOU...
YOU KIDNAPPED MY FRIEND. YOU WORSHIP...WEAPONS? AND YOU SEE THAT IN ME?
YOU DON'T EVEN KNOW ME.
IF YOU DID, YOU'D KNOW THAT I HAD A FATHER. THE BEST FATHER.
HE'S DEAD BECAUSE OF PEOPLE LIKE YOU.
YOU WISH TO FIGHT ME AGAIN? YOU GAMBLE ON MY MERCIES A SECOND TIME?
YEAH.

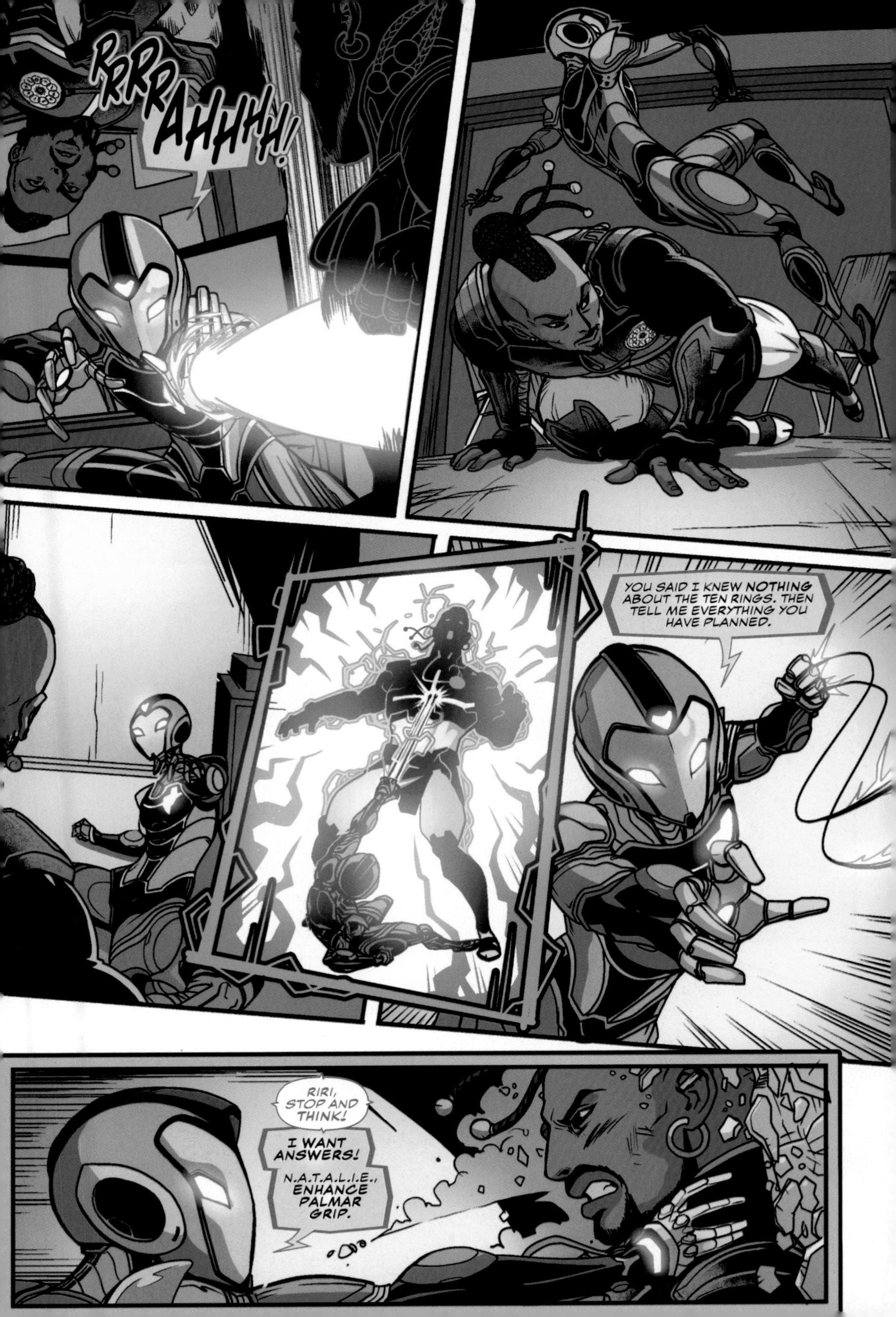
RRRRAHHHH!
YOU SAID I KNEW NOTHING ABOUT THE TEN RINGS. THEN TELL ME EVERYTHING YOU HAVE PLANNED.
RIRI, STOP AND THINK!
I WANT ANSWERS!
N.A.T.A.L.I.E., ENHANCE PALMAR GRIP.

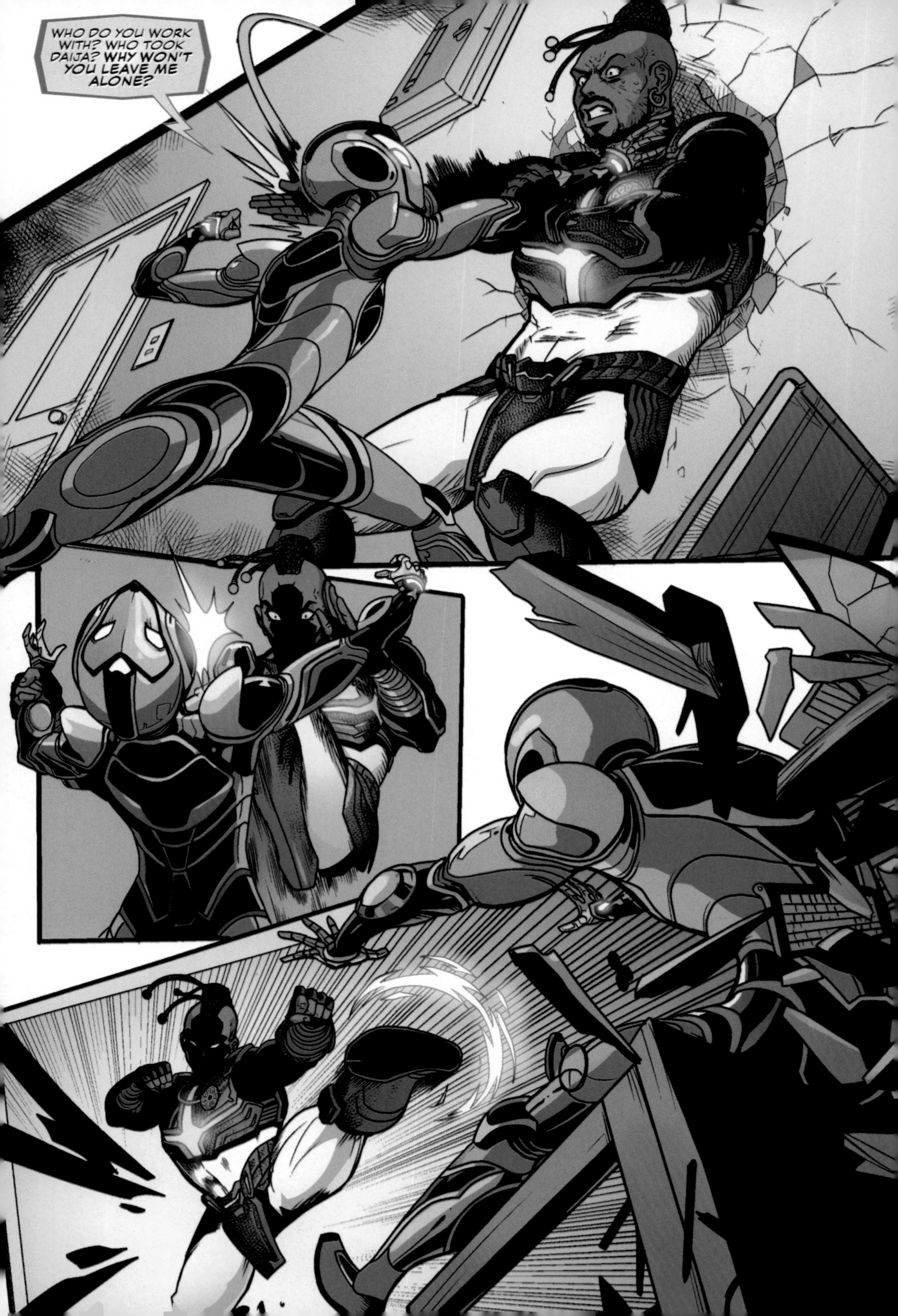
WHO DO YOU WORK WITH? WHO TOOK DAIJA? WHY WON'T YOU LEAVE ME ALONE?

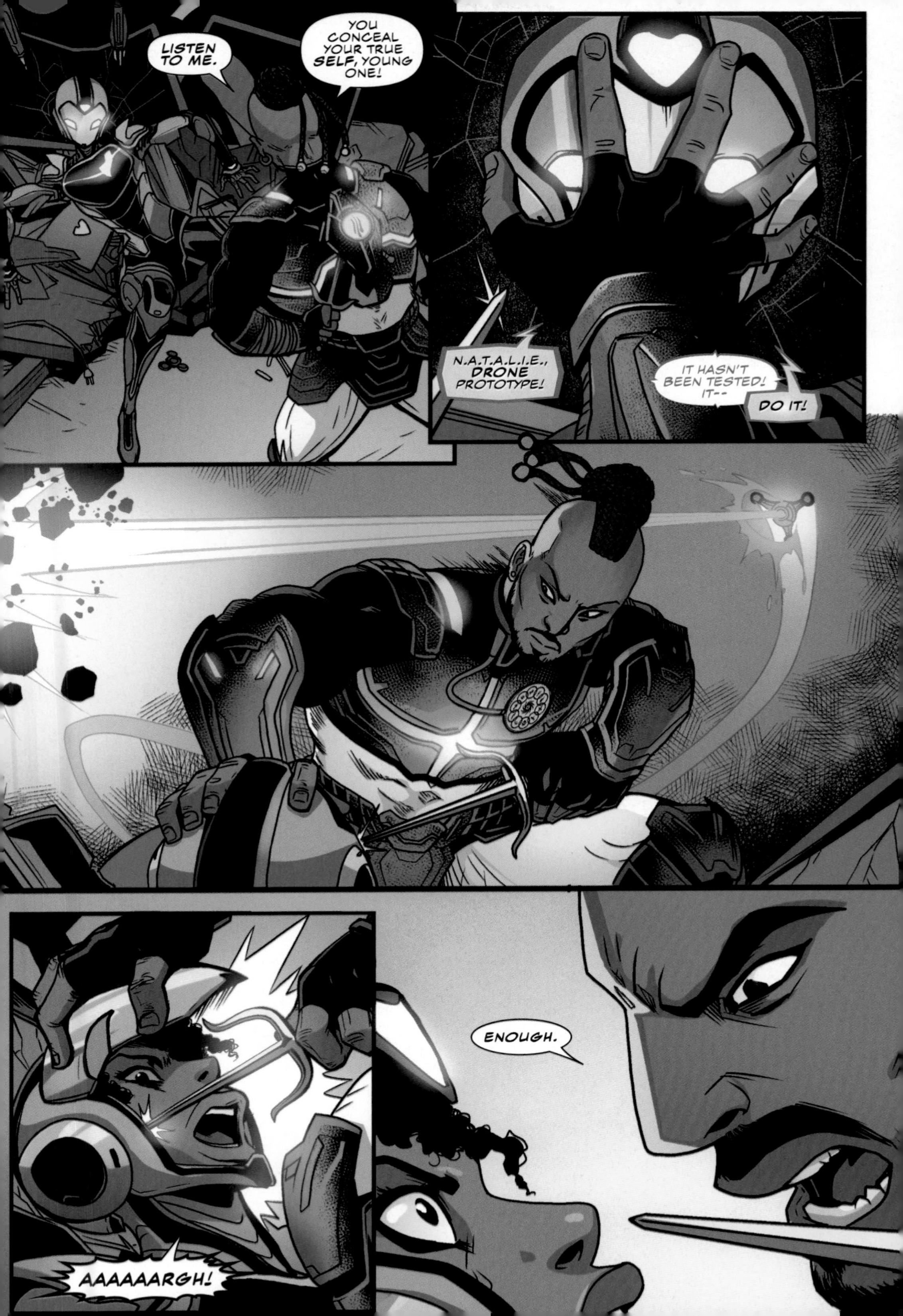
LISTEN TO ME.
YOU CONCEAL YOUR TRUE SELF, YOUNG ONE!
N.A.T.A.L.I.E., DRONE PROTOTYPE!
IT HASN'T BEEN TESTED! IT--
DO IT!
ENOUGH.
AAAAAARGH!

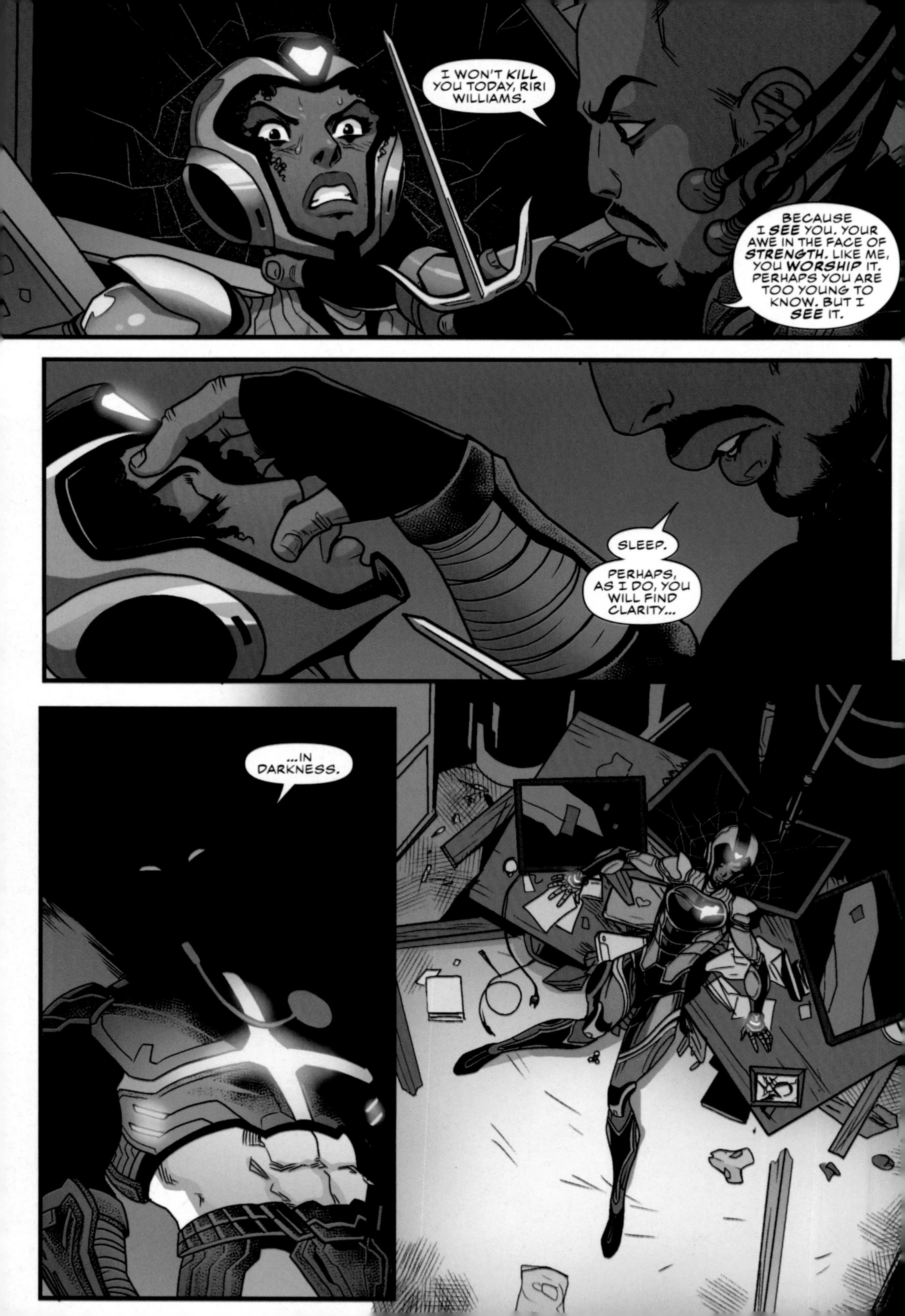

I WON'T **KILL** YOU TODAY, RIRI WILLIAMS.
BECAUSE I **SEE** YOU. YOUR AWE IN THE FACE OF **STRENGTH.** LIKE ME, YOU **WORSHIP** IT. PERHAPS YOU ARE TOO YOUNG TO KNOW. BUT I **SEE** IT.
SLEEP.
PERHAPS, AS I DO, YOU WILL FIND CLARITY...
...IN DARKNESS.

5

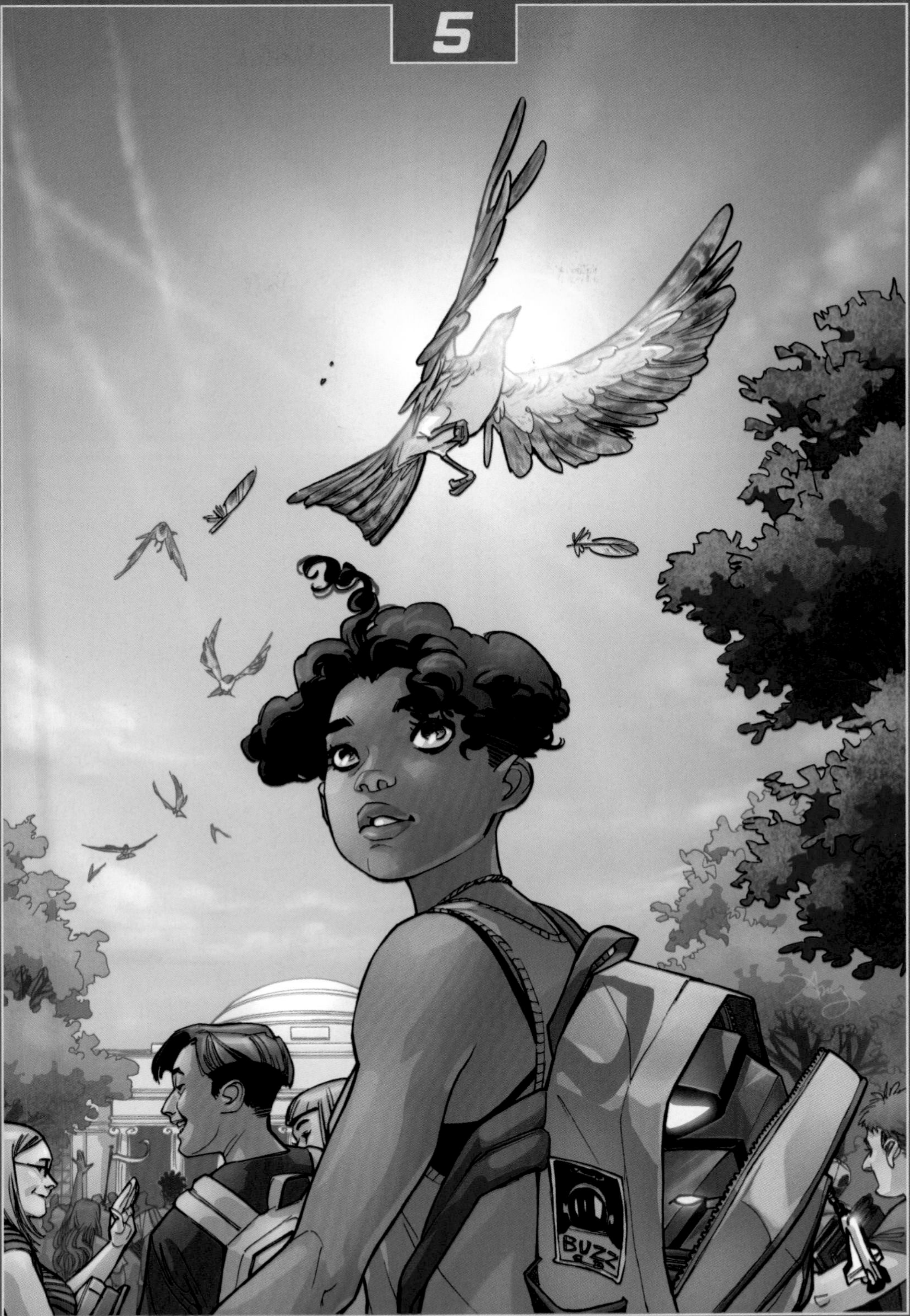
BUZZ

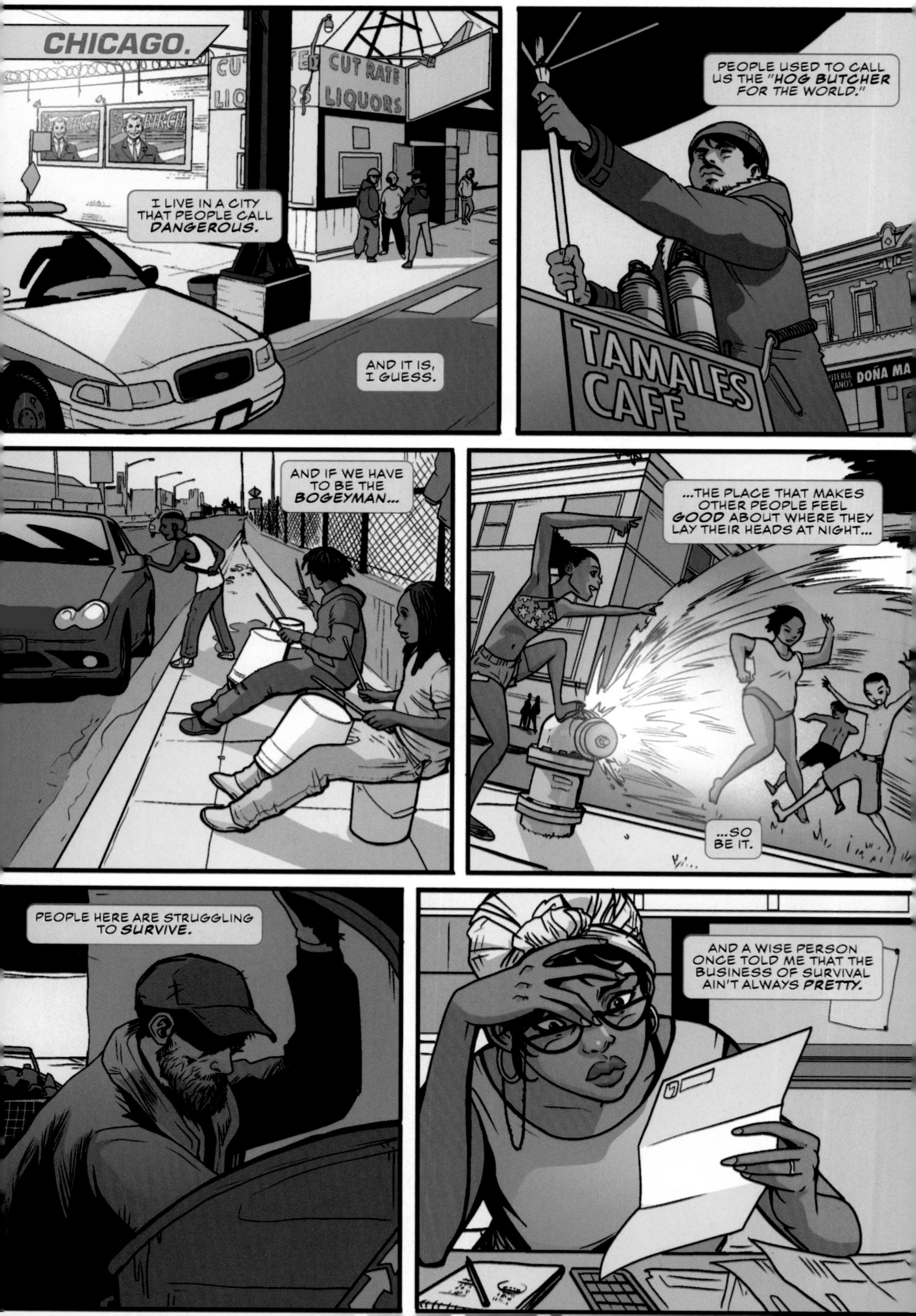
CHICAGO.
CUT RATE
LIQUORS
BIRCH
I LIVE IN A CITY THAT PEOPLE CALL DANGEROUS.
AND IT IS, I GUESS.
PEOPLE USED TO CALL US THE "HOG BUTCHER FOR THE WORLD."
TAMALES CAFÉ
DOÑA MA
AND IF WE HAVE TO BE THE BOGEYMAN...
...THE PLACE THAT MAKES OTHER PEOPLE FEEL GOOD ABOUT WHERE THEY LAY THEIR HEADS AT NIGHT...
...SO BE IT.
PEOPLE HERE ARE STRUGGLING TO SURVIVE.
AND A WISE PERSON ONCE TOLD ME THAT THE BUSINESS OF SURVIVAL AIN'T ALWAYS PRETTY.

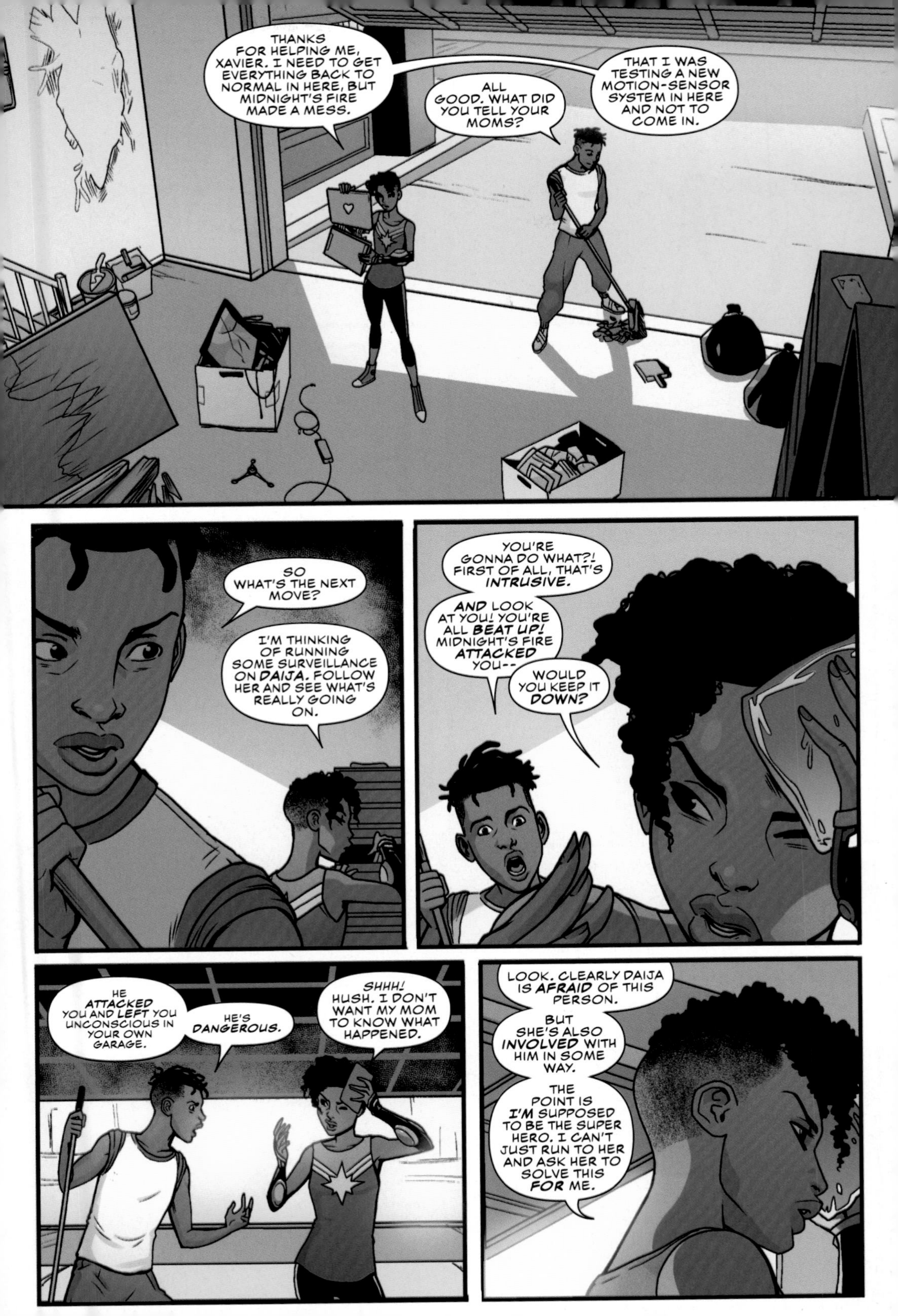
THANKS FOR HELPING ME, XAVIER. I NEED TO GET EVERYTHING BACK TO NORMAL IN HERE, BUT MIDNIGHT'S FIRE MADE A MESS.
ALL GOOD. WHAT DID YOU TELL YOUR MOMS?
THAT I WAS TESTING A NEW MOTION-SENSOR SYSTEM IN HERE AND NOT TO COME IN.
SO WHAT'S THE NEXT MOVE?
I'M THINKING OF RUNNING SOME SURVEILLANCE ON DAIJA. FOLLOW HER AND SEE WHAT'S REALLY GOING ON.
YOU'RE GONNA DO WHAT?! FIRST OF ALL, THAT'S INTRUSIVE.
AND LOOK AT YOU! YOU'RE ALL BEAT UP! MIDNIGHT'S FIRE ATTACKED YOU--
WOULD YOU KEEP IT DOWN?
HE ATTACKED YOU AND LEFT YOU UNCONSCIOUS IN YOUR OWN GARAGE.
HE'S DANGEROUS.
SHHH! HUSH. I DON'T WANT MY MOM TO KNOW WHAT HAPPENED.
LOOK. CLEARLY DAIJA IS AFRAID OF THIS PERSON.
BUT SHE'S ALSO INVOLVED WITH HIM IN SOME WAY.
THE POINT IS I'M SUPPOSED TO BE THE SUPER HERO. I CAN'T JUST RUN TO HER AND ASK HER TO SOLVE THIS FOR ME.

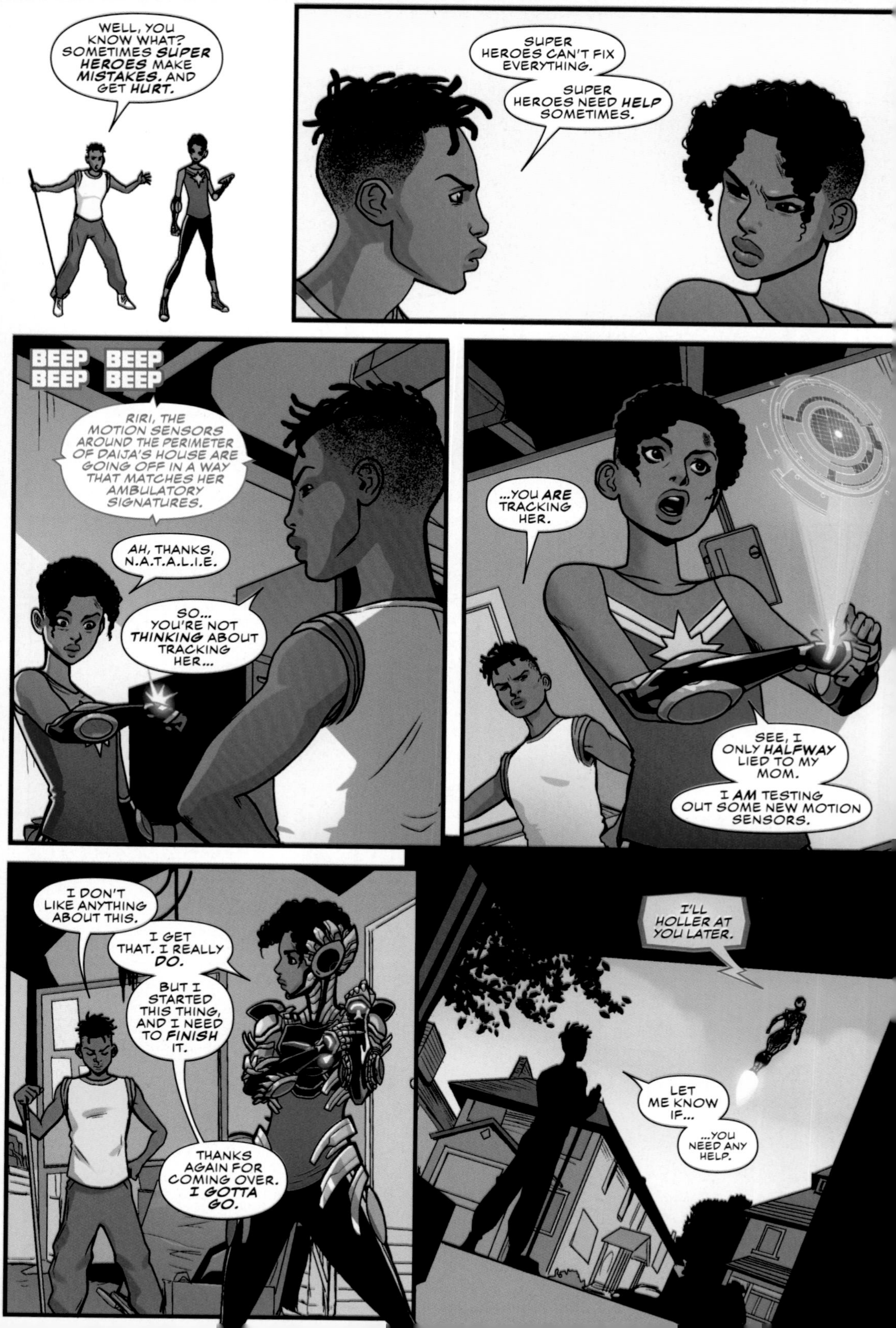

WELL, YOU KNOW WHAT? SOMETIMES SUPER HEROES MAKE MISTAKES. AND GET HURT.
SUPER HEROES CAN'T FIX EVERYTHING.
SUPER HEROES NEED HELP SOMETIMES.
BEEP BEEP BEEP BEEP
RIRI, THE MOTION SENSORS AROUND THE PERIMETER OF DAIJA'S HOUSE ARE GOING OFF IN A WAY THAT MATCHES HER AMBULATORY SIGNATURES.
AH, THANKS, N.A.T.A.L.I.E.
SO... YOU'RE NOT THINKING ABOUT TRACKING HER...
...YOU ARE TRACKING HER.
SEE, I ONLY HALFWAY LIED TO MY MOM.
I AM TESTING OUT SOME NEW MOTION SENSORS.
I DON'T LIKE ANYTHING ABOUT THIS.
I GET THAT. I REALLY DO.
BUT I STARTED THIS THING, AND I NEED TO FINISH IT.
THANKS AGAIN FOR COMING OVER. I GOTTA GO.
I'LL HOLLER AT YOU LATER.
LET ME KNOW IF...
...YOU NEED ANY HELP.

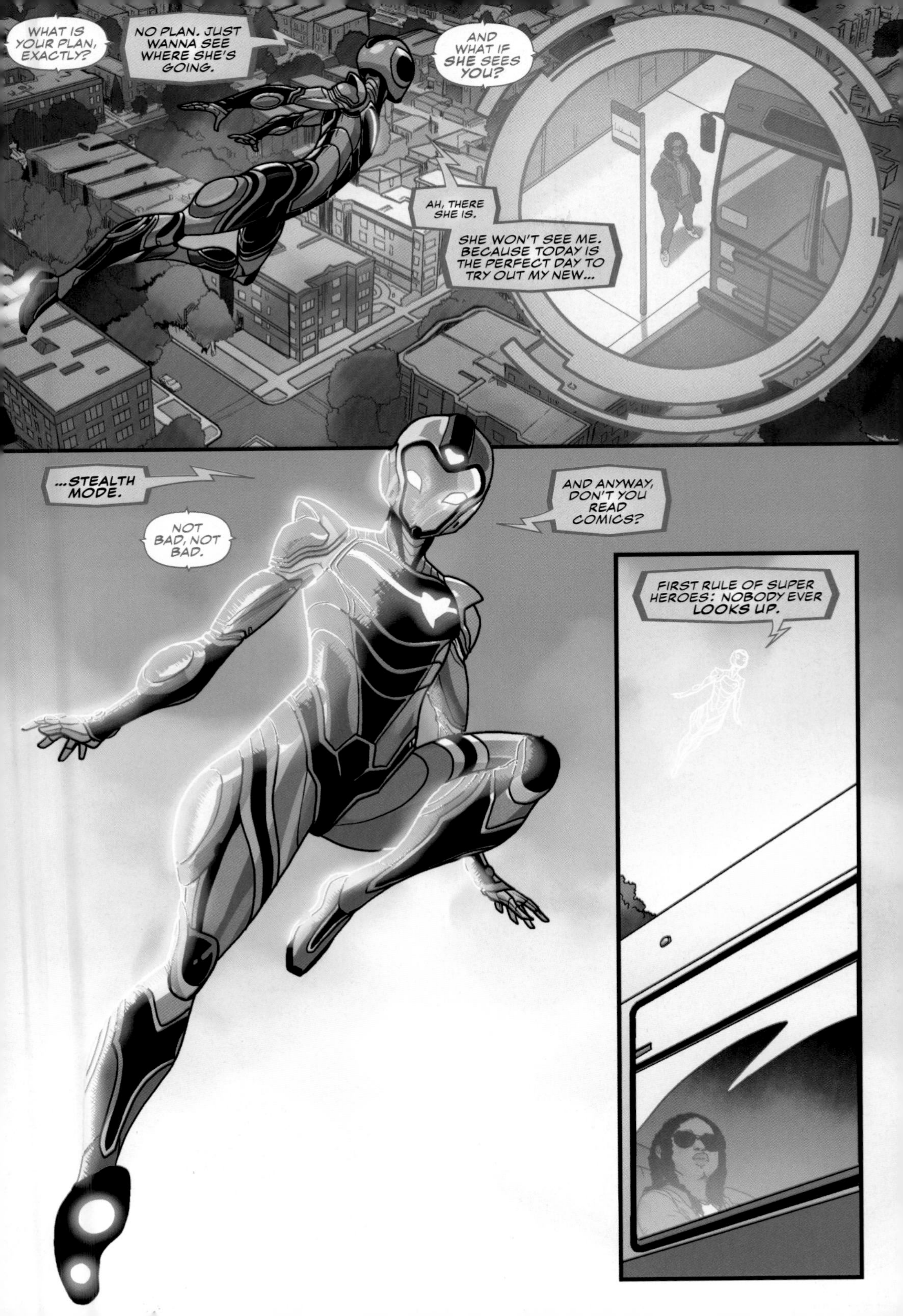
WHAT IS YOUR PLAN, EXACTLY?
NO PLAN. JUST WANNA SEE WHERE SHE'S GOING.
AND WHAT IF SHE SEES YOU?
AH, THERE SHE IS.
SHE WON'T SEE ME. BECAUSE TODAY IS THE PERFECT DAY TO TRY OUT MY NEW...
...STEALTH MODE.
NOT BAD, NOT BAD.
AND ANYWAY, DON'T YOU READ COMICS?
FIRST RULE OF SUPER HEROES: NOBODY EVER LOOKS UP.

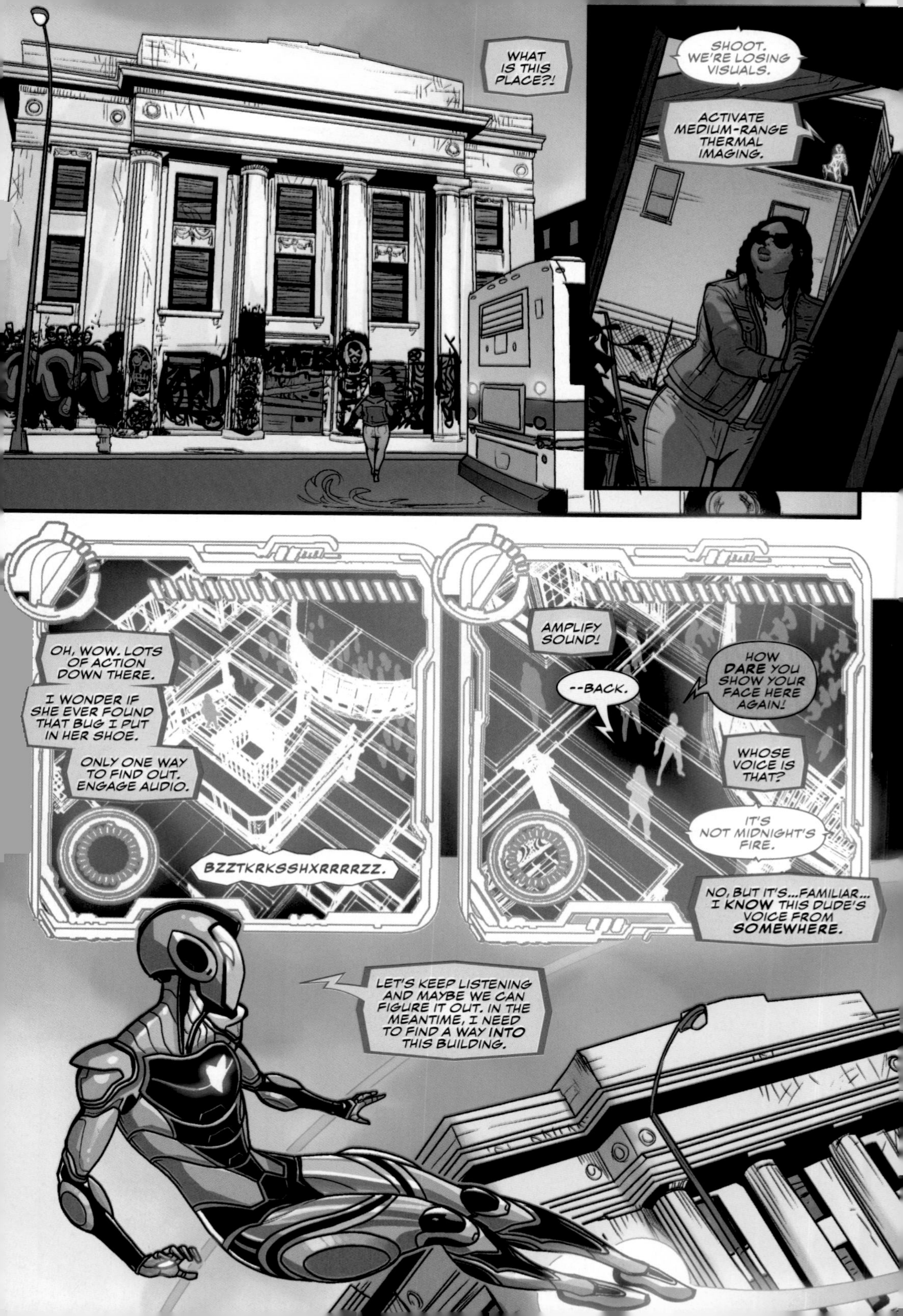
WHAT IS THIS PLACE?!
SHOOT. WE'RE LOSING VISUALS.
ACTIVATE MEDIUM-RANGE THERMAL IMAGING.
OH, WOW. LOTS OF ACTION DOWN THERE.
I WONDER IF SHE EVER FOUND THAT BUG I PUT IN HER SHOE.
ONLY ONE WAY TO FIND OUT. ENGAGE AUDIO.
BZZTKRKSSHXRRRRZZ.
AMPLIFY SOUND!
--BACK.
HOW DARE YOU SHOW YOUR FACE HERE AGAIN!
WHOSE VOICE IS THAT?
IT'S NOT MIDNIGHT'S FIRE.
NO, BUT IT'S...FAMILIAR... I KNOW THIS DUDE'S VOICE FROM SOMEWHERE.
LET'S KEEP LISTENING AND MAYBE WE CAN FIGURE IT OUT. IN THE MEANTIME, I NEED TO FIND A WAY INTO THIS BUILDING.

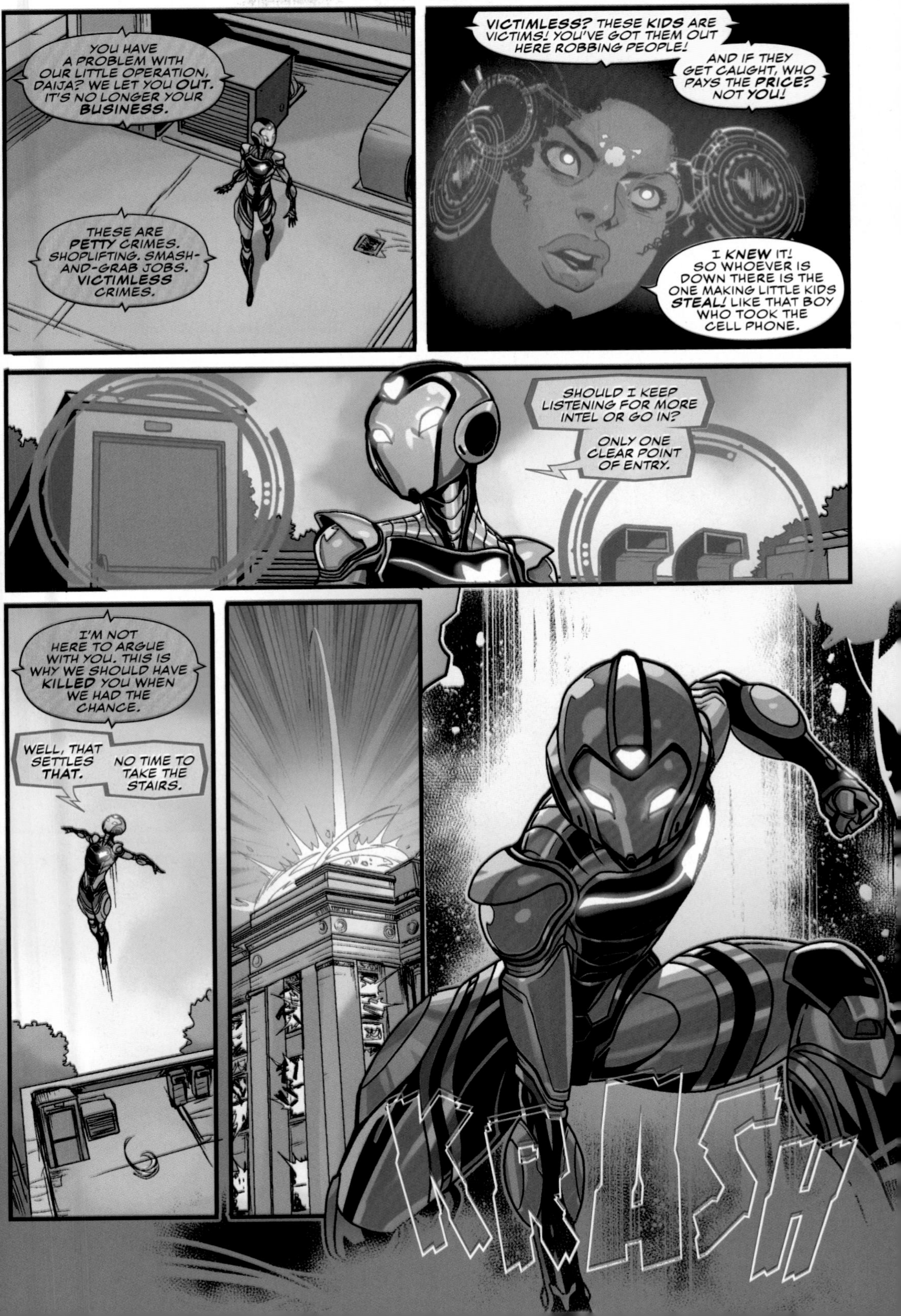

YOU HAVE A PROBLEM WITH OUR LITTLE OPERATION, DAIJA? WE LET YOU OUT. IT'S NO LONGER YOUR BUSINESS.
THESE ARE PETTY CRIMES. SHOPLIFTING. SMASH-AND-GRAB JOBS. VICTIMLESS CRIMES.
VICTIMLESS? THESE KIDS ARE VICTIMS! YOU'VE GOT THEM OUT HERE ROBBING PEOPLE!
AND IF THEY GET CAUGHT, WHO PAYS THE PRICE? NOT YOU!
I KNEW IT! SO WHOEVER IS DOWN THERE IS THE ONE MAKING LITTLE KIDS STEAL! LIKE THAT BOY WHO TOOK THE CELL PHONE.
SHOULD I KEEP LISTENING FOR MORE INTEL OR GO IN?
ONLY ONE CLEAR POINT OF ENTRY.
I'M NOT HERE TO ARGUE WITH YOU. THIS IS WHY WE SHOULD HAVE KILLED YOU WHEN WE HAD THE CHANCE.
WELL, THAT SETTLES THAT.
NO TIME TO TAKE THE STAIRS.
KRASH

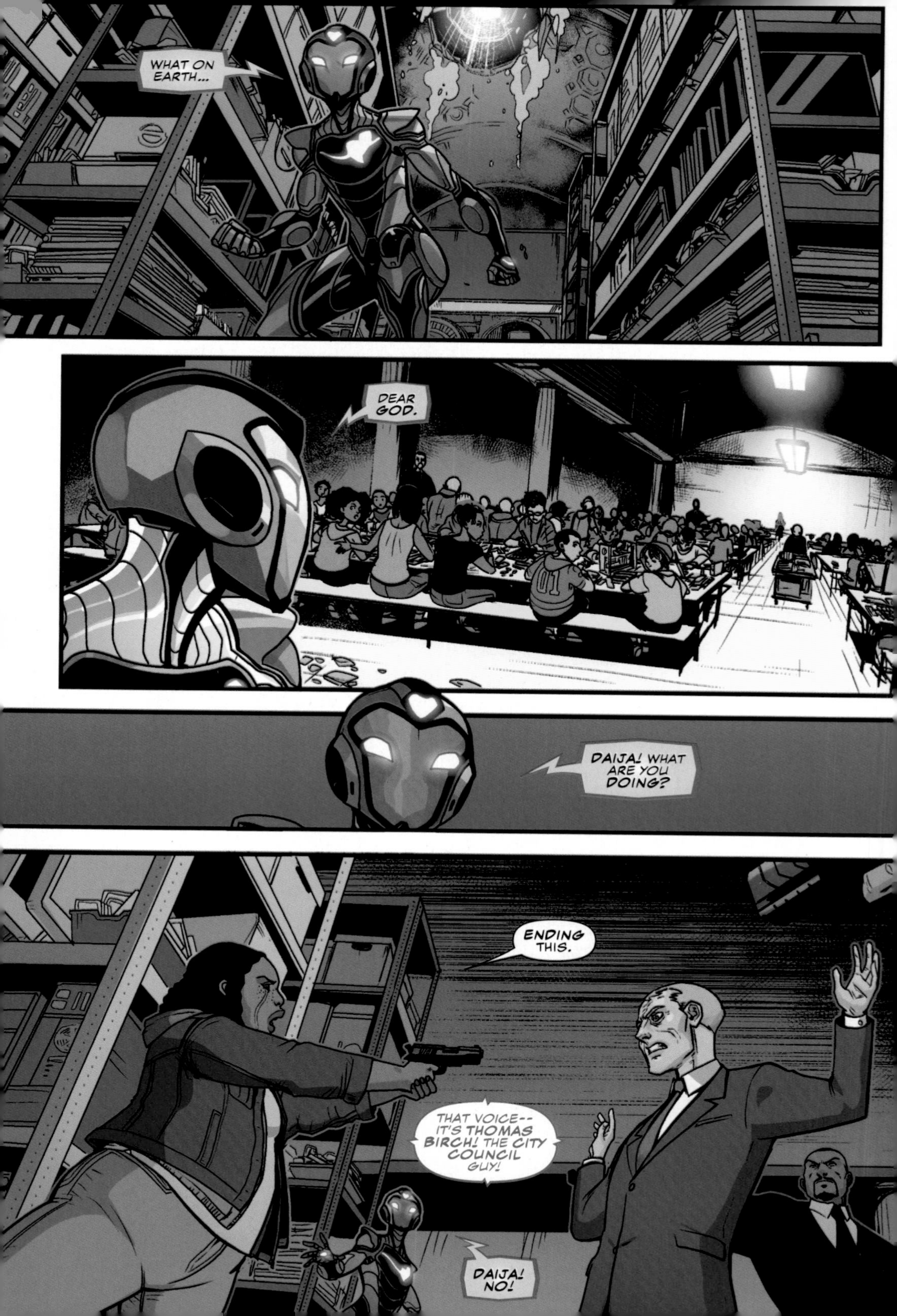

WHAT ON EARTH...
DEAR GOD.
DAIJA! WHAT ARE YOU DOING?
ENDING THIS.
THAT VOICE-- IT'S THOMAS BIRCH! THE CITY COUNCIL GUY!
DAIJA! NO!

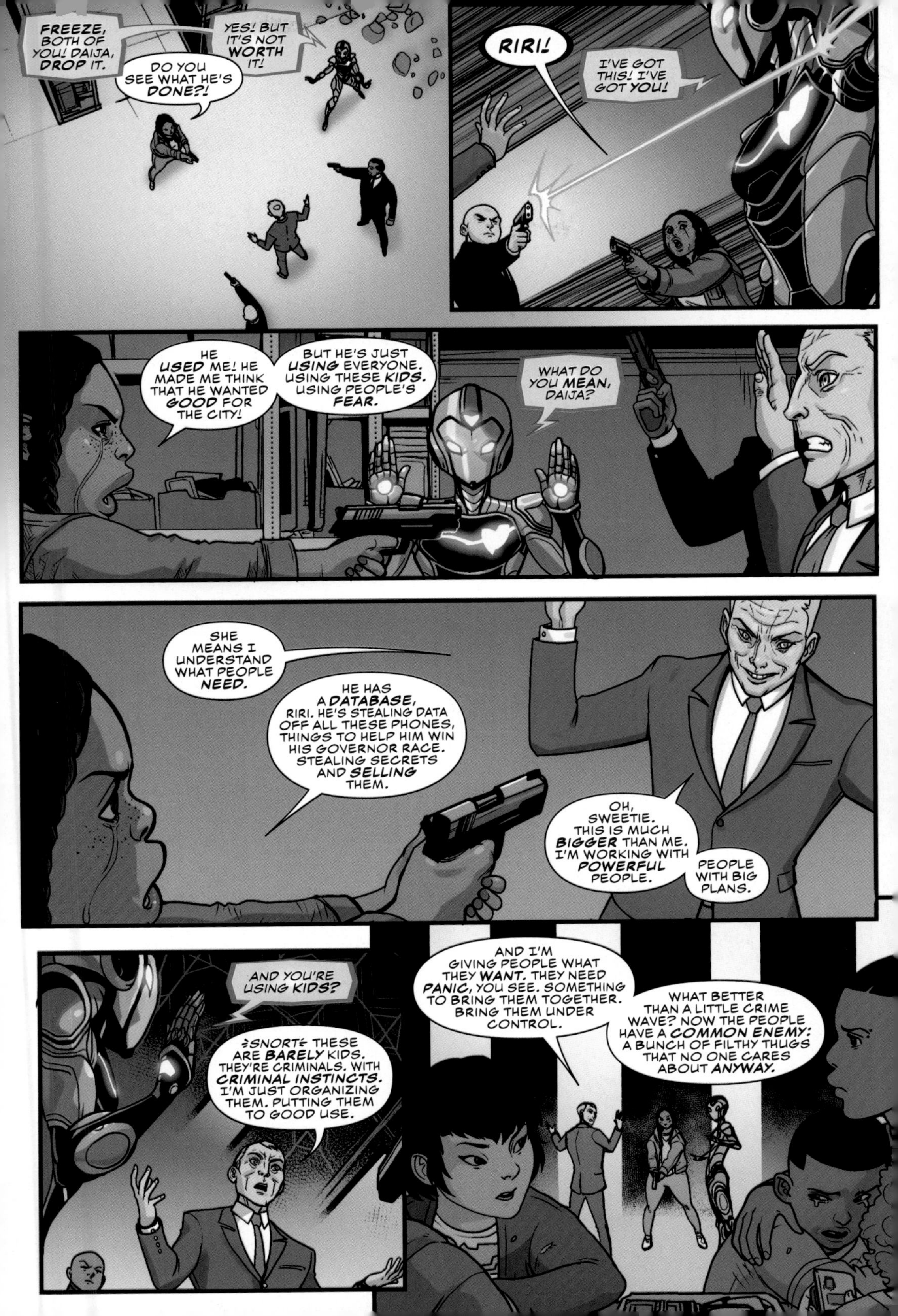

FREEZE, BOTH OF YOU! DAIJA, DROP IT.
DO YOU SEE WHAT HE'S DONE?!
YES! BUT IT'S NOT WORTH IT!
RIRI!
I'VE GOT THIS! I'VE GOT YOU!
HE USED ME! HE MADE ME THINK THAT HE WANTED GOOD FOR THE CITY!
BUT HE'S JUST USING EVERYONE. USING THESE KIDS. USING PEOPLE'S FEAR.
WHAT DO YOU MEAN, DAIJA?
SHE MEANS I UNDERSTAND WHAT PEOPLE NEED.
HE HAS A DATABASE, RIRI. HE'S STEALING DATA OFF ALL THESE PHONES, THINGS TO HELP HIM WIN HIS GOVERNOR RACE. STEALING SECRETS AND SELLING THEM.
OH, SWEETIE. THIS IS MUCH BIGGER THAN ME. I'M WORKING WITH POWERFUL PEOPLE.
PEOPLE WITH BIG PLANS.
AND YOU'RE USING KIDS?
⋛SNORT⋚ THESE ARE BARELY KIDS. THEY'RE CRIMINALS. WITH CRIMINAL INSTINCTS. I'M JUST ORGANIZING THEM. PUTTING THEM TO GOOD USE.
AND I'M GIVING PEOPLE WHAT THEY WANT. THEY NEED PANIC, YOU SEE. SOMETHING TO BRING THEM TOGETHER. BRING THEM UNDER CONTROL.
WHAT BETTER THAN A LITTLE CRIME WAVE? NOW THE PEOPLE HAVE A COMMON ENEMY: A BUNCH OF FILTHY THUGS THAT NO ONE CARES ABOUT ANYWAY.

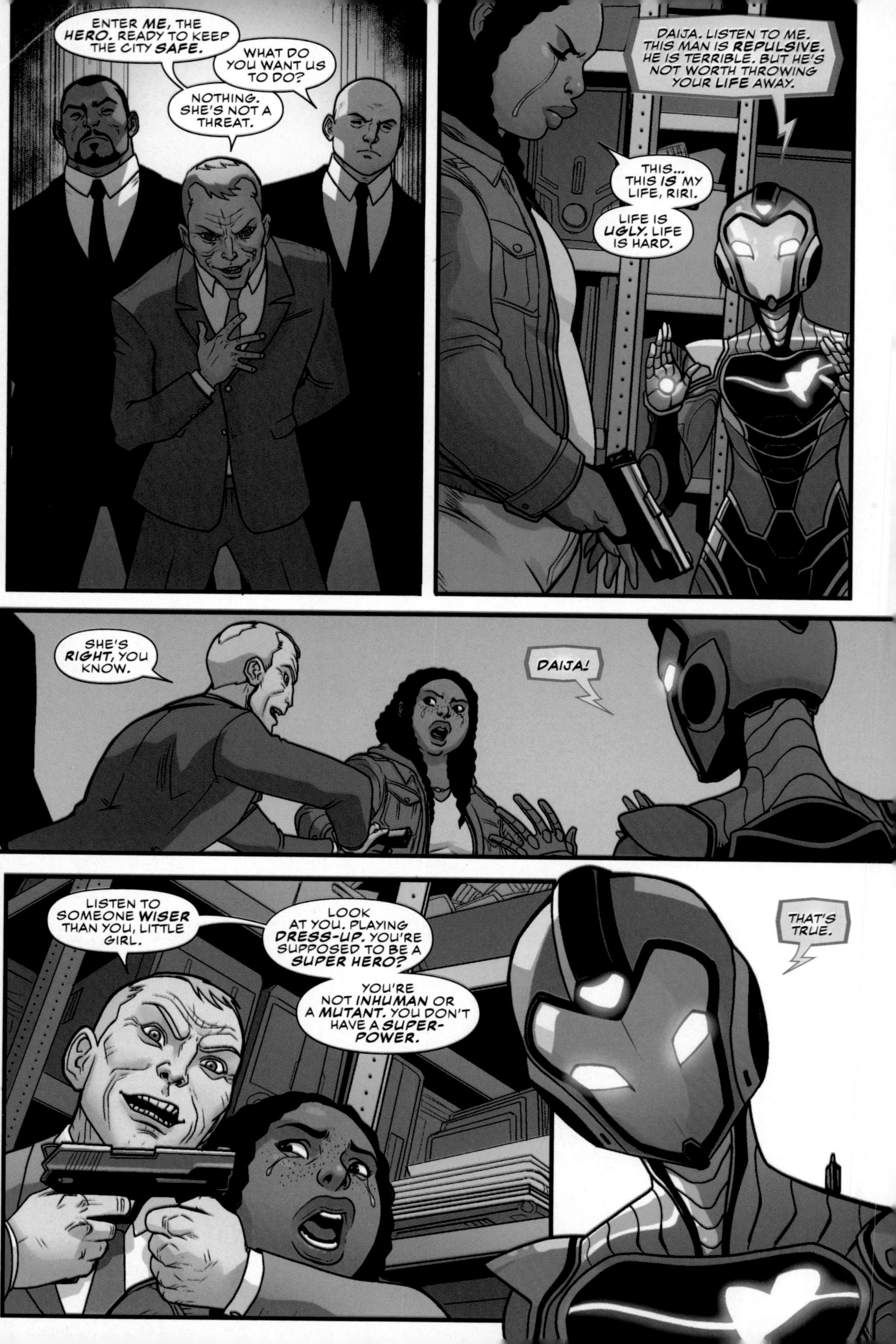
ENTER ME, THE HERO. READY TO KEEP THE CITY SAFE.
WHAT DO YOU WANT US TO DO?
NOTHING. SHE'S NOT A THREAT.
DAIJA. LISTEN TO ME. THIS MAN IS REPULSIVE. HE IS TERRIBLE. BUT HE'S NOT WORTH THROWING YOUR LIFE AWAY.
THIS... THIS IS MY LIFE, RIRI.
LIFE IS UGLY. LIFE IS HARD.
SHE'S RIGHT, YOU KNOW.
DAIJA!
LISTEN TO SOMEONE WISER THAN YOU, LITTLE GIRL.
LOOK AT YOU. PLAYING DRESS-UP. YOU'RE SUPPOSED TO BE A SUPER HERO?
YOU'RE NOT INHUMAN OR A MUTANT. YOU DON'T HAVE A SUPER-POWER.
THAT'S TRUE.

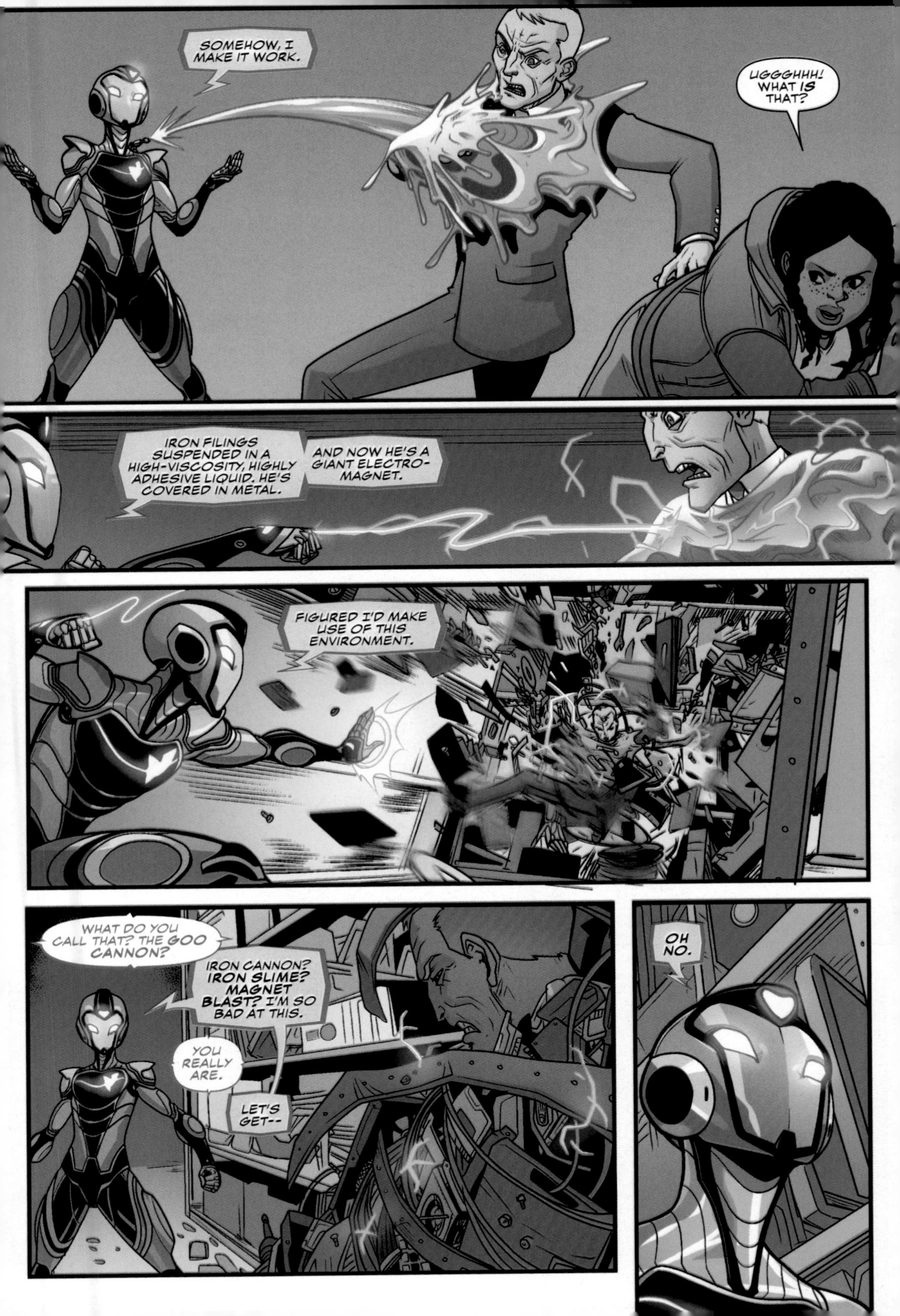
SOMEHOW, I MAKE IT WORK.
UGGGHHH! WHAT *IS* THAT?
IRON FILINGS SUSPENDED IN A HIGH-VISCOSITY, HIGHLY ADHESIVE LIQUID. HE'S COVERED IN METAL.
AND NOW HE'S A GIANT ELECTRO-MAGNET.
FIGURED I'D MAKE USE OF THIS ENVIRONMENT.
WHAT DO YOU CALL THAT? THE *GOO* CANNON?
IRON CANNON? **IRON SLIME? MAGNET BLAST?** I'M SO BAD AT THIS.
YOU REALLY ARE.
LET'S GET--
OH NO.

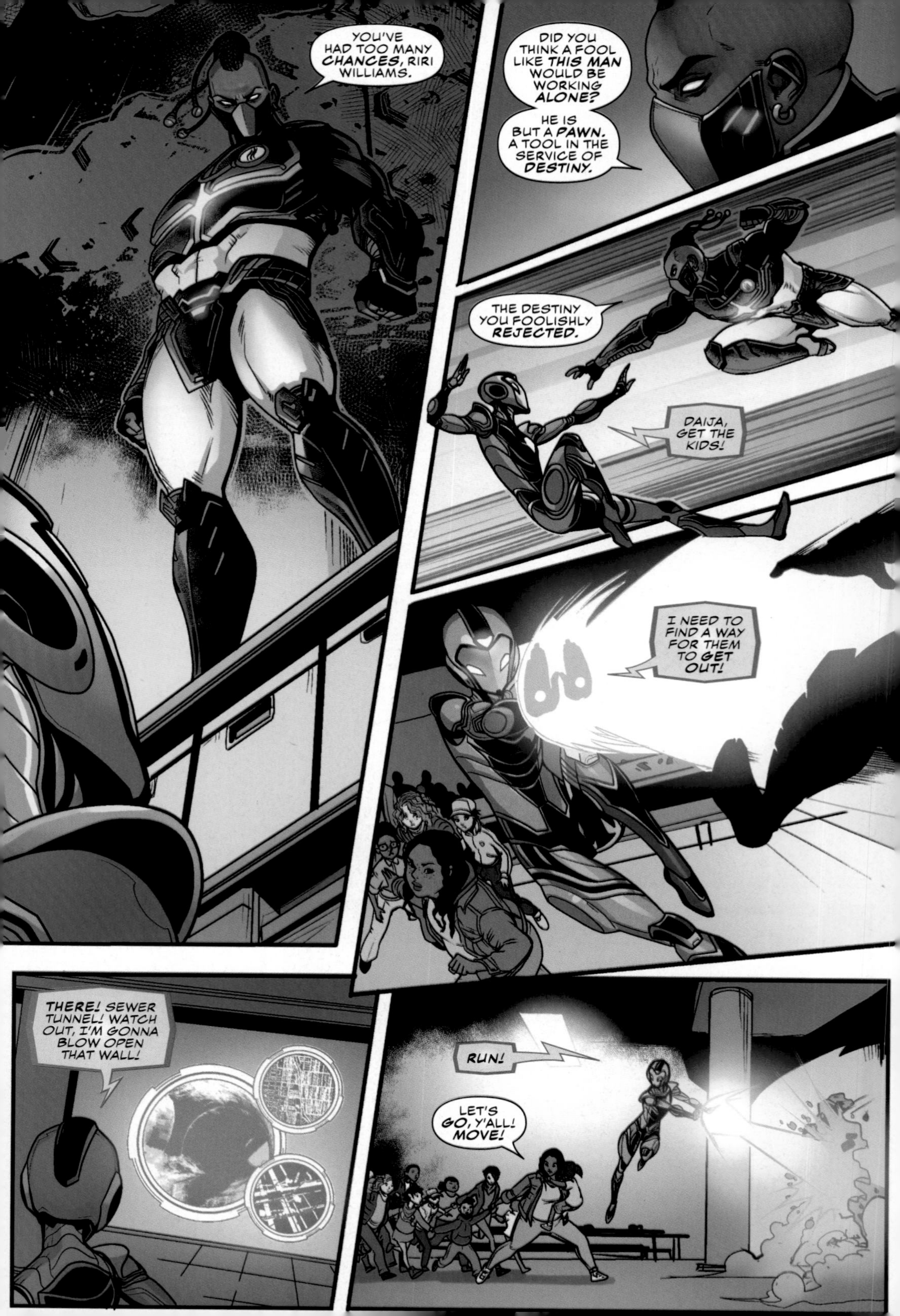
YOU'VE HAD TOO MANY CHANCES, RIRI WILLIAMS.
DID YOU THINK A FOOL LIKE THIS MAN WOULD BE WORKING ALONE?
HE IS BUT A PAWN. A TOOL IN THE SERVICE OF DESTINY.
THE DESTINY YOU FOOLISHLY REJECTED.
DAIJA, GET THE KIDS!
I NEED TO FIND A WAY FOR THEM TO GET OUT!
THERE! SEWER TUNNEL! WATCH OUT, I'M GONNA BLOW OPEN THAT WALL!
RUN!
LET'S GO, Y'ALL! MOVE!

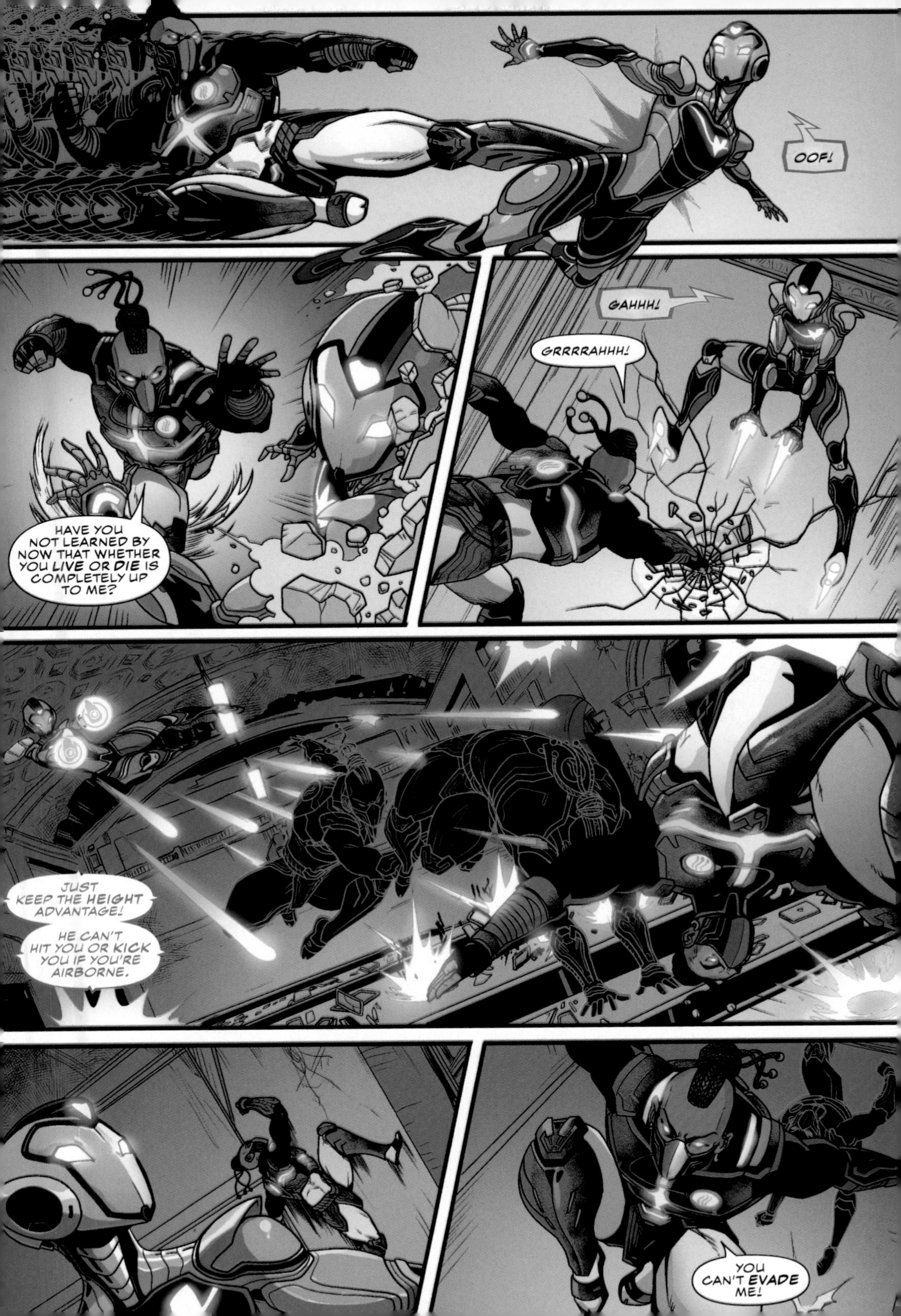
OOF!
HAVE YOU NOT LEARNED BY NOW THAT WHETHER YOU LIVE OR DIE IS COMPLETELY UP TO ME?
GAHHH!
GRRRRAHHH!
JUST KEEP THE HEIGHT ADVANTAGE!
HE CAN'T HIT YOU OR KICK YOU IF YOU'RE AIRBORNE.
YOU CAN'T EVADE ME!

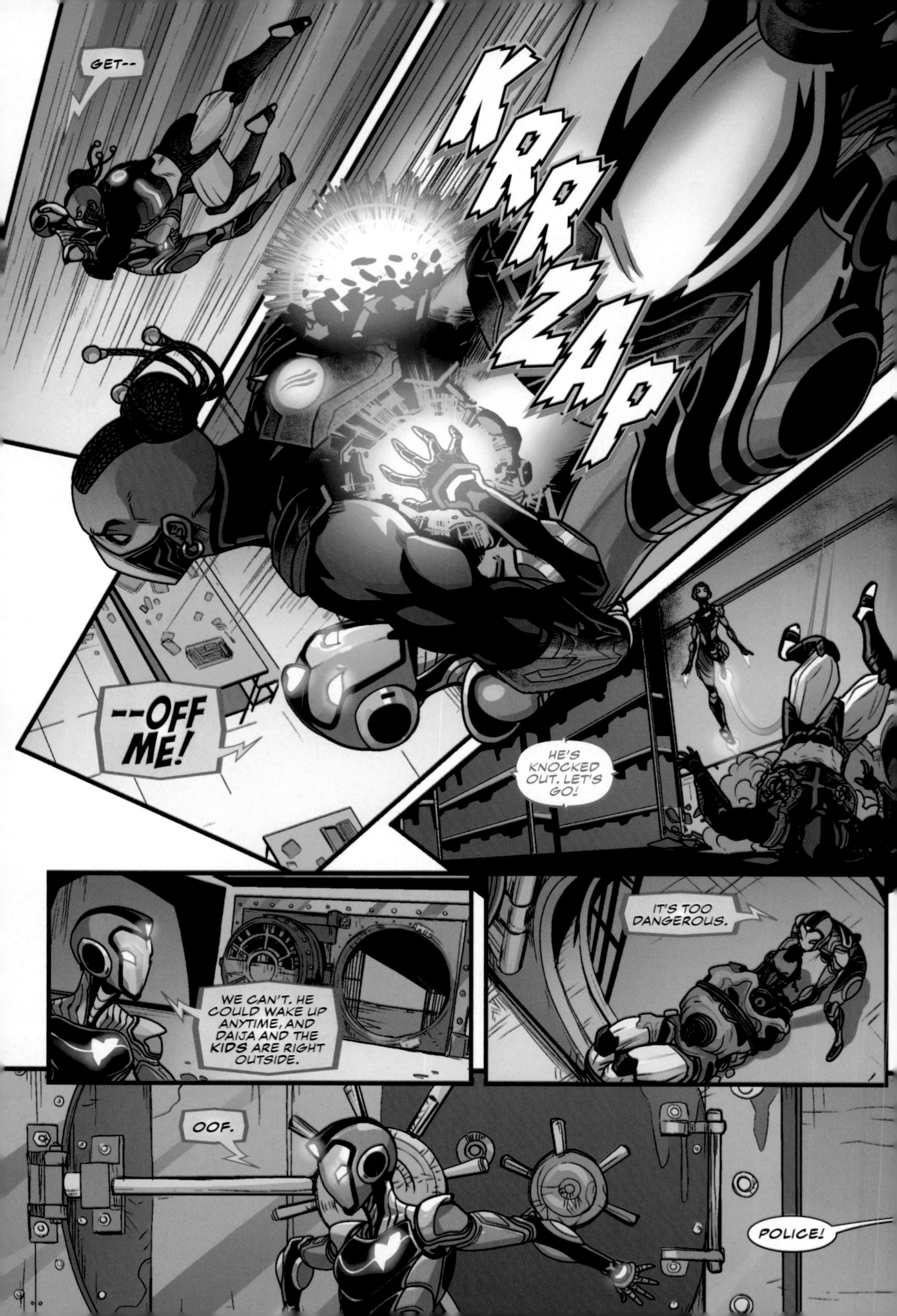
GET--
KRRZAP
--OFF ME!
HE'S KNOCKED OUT. LET'S GO!
WE CAN'T. HE COULD WAKE UP ANYTIME, AND DAIJA AND THE KIDS ARE RIGHT OUTSIDE.
IT'S TOO DANGEROUS.
OOF.
POLICE!

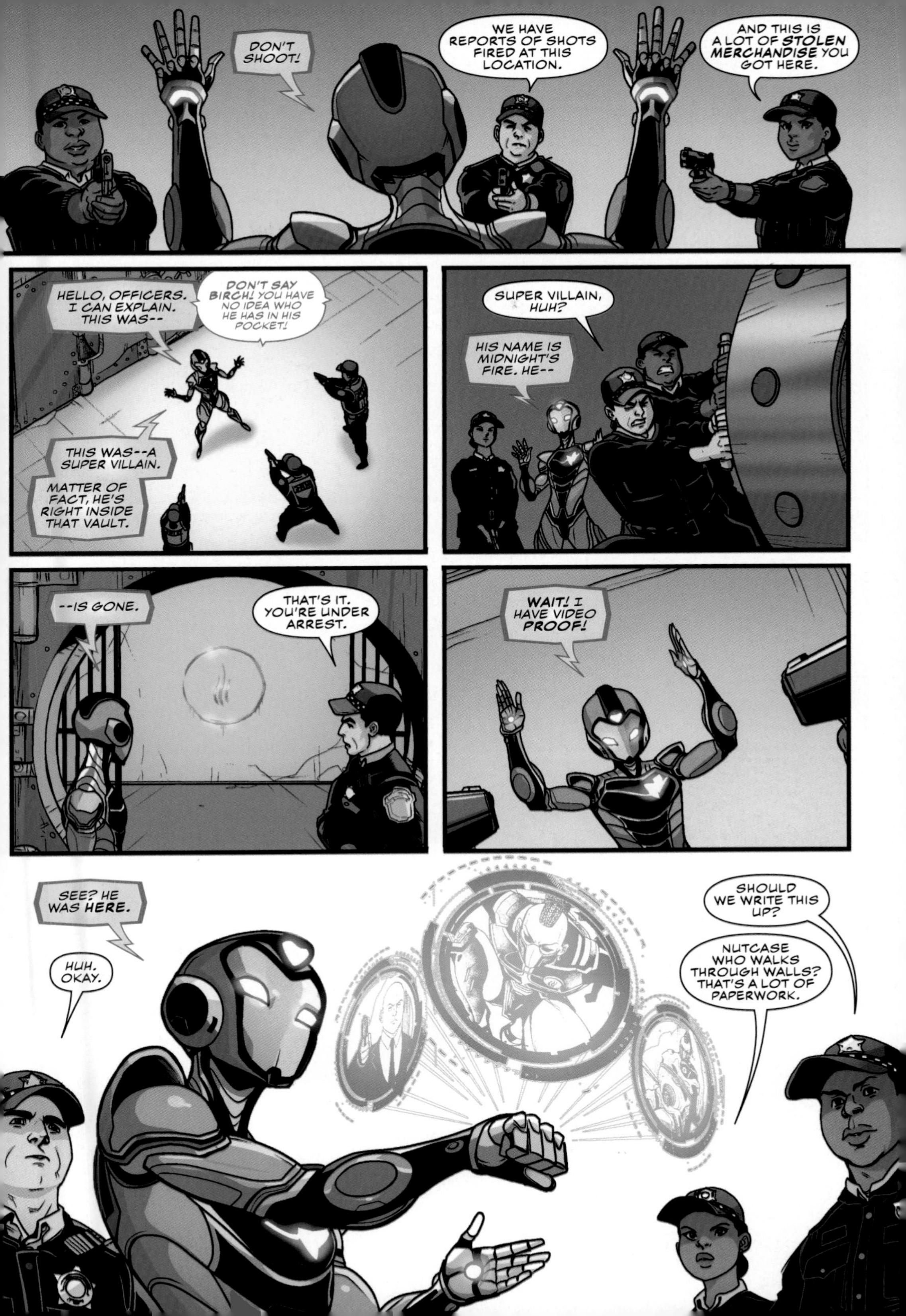
DON'T SHOOT!
WE HAVE REPORTS OF SHOTS FIRED AT THIS LOCATION.
AND THIS IS A LOT OF STOLEN MERCHANDISE YOU GOT HERE.
HELLO, OFFICERS. I CAN EXPLAIN. THIS WAS--
DON'T SAY BIRCH! YOU HAVE NO IDEA WHO HE HAS IN HIS POCKET!
THIS WAS--A SUPER VILLAIN.
MATTER OF FACT, HE'S RIGHT INSIDE THAT VAULT.
SUPER VILLAIN, HUH?
HIS NAME IS MIDNIGHT'S FIRE. HE--
--IS GONE.
THAT'S IT. YOU'RE UNDER ARREST.
WAIT! I HAVE VIDEO PROOF!
SEE? HE WAS HERE.
HUH. OKAY.
SHOULD WE WRITE THIS UP?
NUTCASE WHO WALKS THROUGH WALLS? THAT'S A LOT OF PAPERWORK.

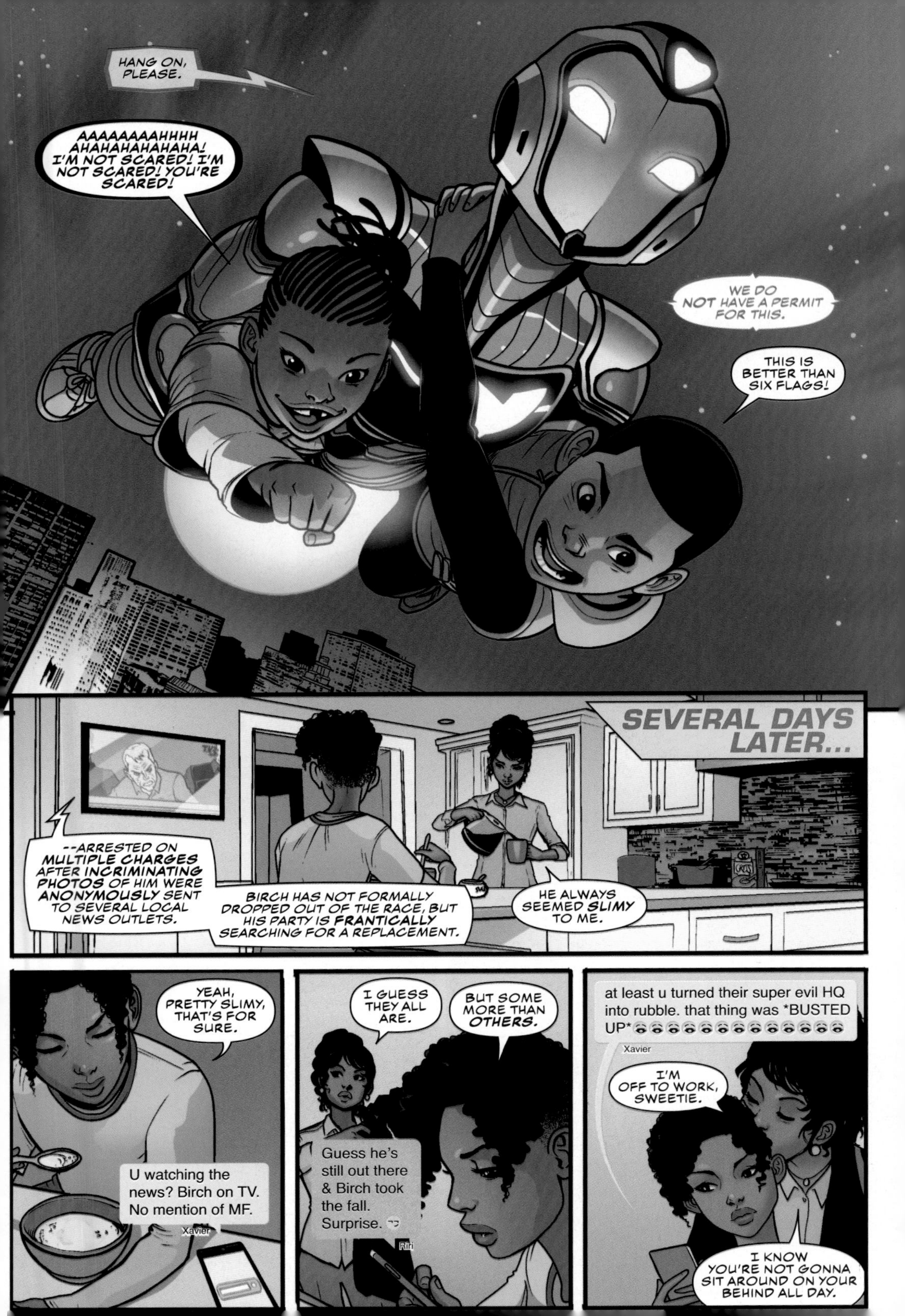
HANG ON, PLEASE.
AAAAAAAAAHHHH AHAHAHAHAHAHA! I'M NOT SCARED! I'M NOT SCARED! YOU'RE SCARED!
WE DO NOT HAVE A PERMIT FOR THIS.
THIS IS BETTER THAN SIX FLAGS!
SEVERAL DAYS LATER...
--ARRESTED ON MULTIPLE CHARGES AFTER INCRIMINATING PHOTOS OF HIM WERE ANONYMOUSLY SENT TO SEVERAL LOCAL NEWS OUTLETS.
BIRCH HAS NOT FORMALLY DROPPED OUT OF THE RACE, BUT HIS PARTY IS FRANTICALLY SEARCHING FOR A REPLACEMENT.
HE ALWAYS SEEMED SLIMY TO ME.
YEAH, PRETTY SLIMY, THAT'S FOR SURE.
U watching the news? Birch on TV. No mention of MF.
Xavier
I GUESS THEY ALL ARE.
BUT SOME MORE THAN OTHERS.
Guess he's still out there & Birch took the fall. Surprise.
Riri
at least u turned their super evil HQ into rubble. that thing was *BUSTED UP*
Xavier
I'M OFF TO WORK, SWEETIE.
I KNOW YOU'RE NOT GONNA SIT AROUND ON YOUR BEHIND ALL DAY.

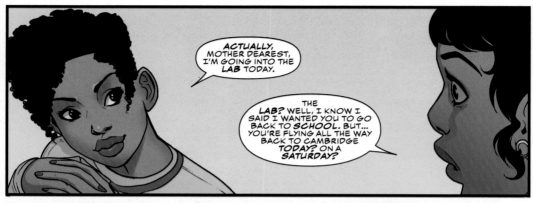

ACTUALLY, MOTHER DEAREST, I'M GOING INTO THE *LAB* TODAY.

THE *LAB?* WELL, I KNOW I SAID I WANTED YOU TO GO BACK TO *SCHOOL.* BUT... YOU'RE FLYING ALL THE WAY BACK TO CAMBRIDGE *TODAY?* ON A *SATURDAY?*

MMM, NOT THE *M.I.T.* LAB.

I'M GOING TO THE *NEW* LAB.

WHAT *NEW* LAB? WHERE'D YOU GET MONEY FOR THAT?

TURNS OUT, IMPORTANT PEOPLE GET *REALLY* GENEROUS WHEN YOU FILL THEM IN ABOUT THEIR *STOLEN ELECTRONICS* AND BREACHES OF THEIR *SENSITIVE DATA.*

WHICH REMINDS ME. I LEFT A LITTLE BIT OF BILL MONEY ON YOUR DRESSER.

OH, HONEY. I DON'T NEED YOU TO--

LET ME DO THIS *ONE* THING, MOM.

AND IT LOOKS LIKE I'M GONNA *BEAT* YOU TO *WORK.* HAVE A GOOD DAY, MOMMY. LOVE YOU.

OHANDALSO

I SOLD A PATENT FOR A TINY AUDIO RECORDER WITH A BUILT-IN GPS TRACKER THAT FITS ON A SHOE.

OKAY I'LL BE HOME FOR DINNER BYYYYYEEEEEEE!

SO YOU'RE *NOT* GOING BACK TO--YOU KNOW WHAT?

WE'LL *TALK ABOUT THIS LATER,* RIRI!

THESE KIDS. SHE BECOMES A SUPER HERO AND SUDDENLY *I'M BOOBOO THE FOOL.* WELL, I'LL TELL YOU ONE THING--

--YOU *BETTER* WASH THESE *DISHES* UP WHEN YOU GET BACK!

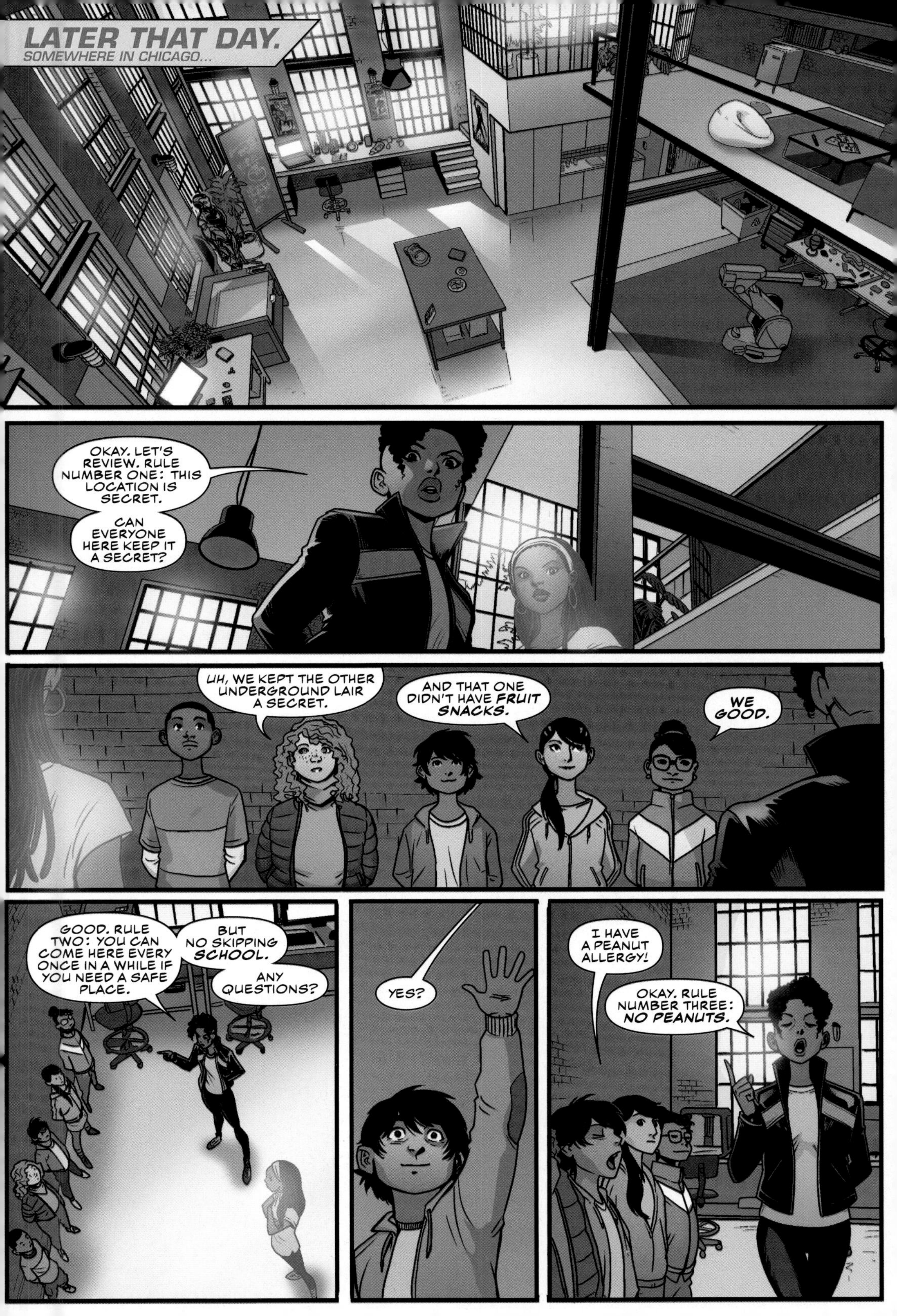
LATER THAT DAY.
SOMEWHERE IN CHICAGO...
OKAY. LET'S REVIEW. RULE NUMBER ONE: THIS LOCATION IS SECRET.
CAN EVERYONE HERE KEEP IT A SECRET?
UH, WE KEPT THE OTHER UNDERGROUND LAIR A SECRET.
AND THAT ONE DIDN'T HAVE FRUIT SNACKS.
WE GOOD.
GOOD. RULE TWO: YOU CAN COME HERE EVERY ONCE IN A WHILE IF YOU NEED A SAFE PLACE.
BUT NO SKIPPING SCHOOL.
ANY QUESTIONS?
YES?
I HAVE A PEANUT ALLERGY!
OKAY. RULE NUMBER THREE: NO PEANUTS.

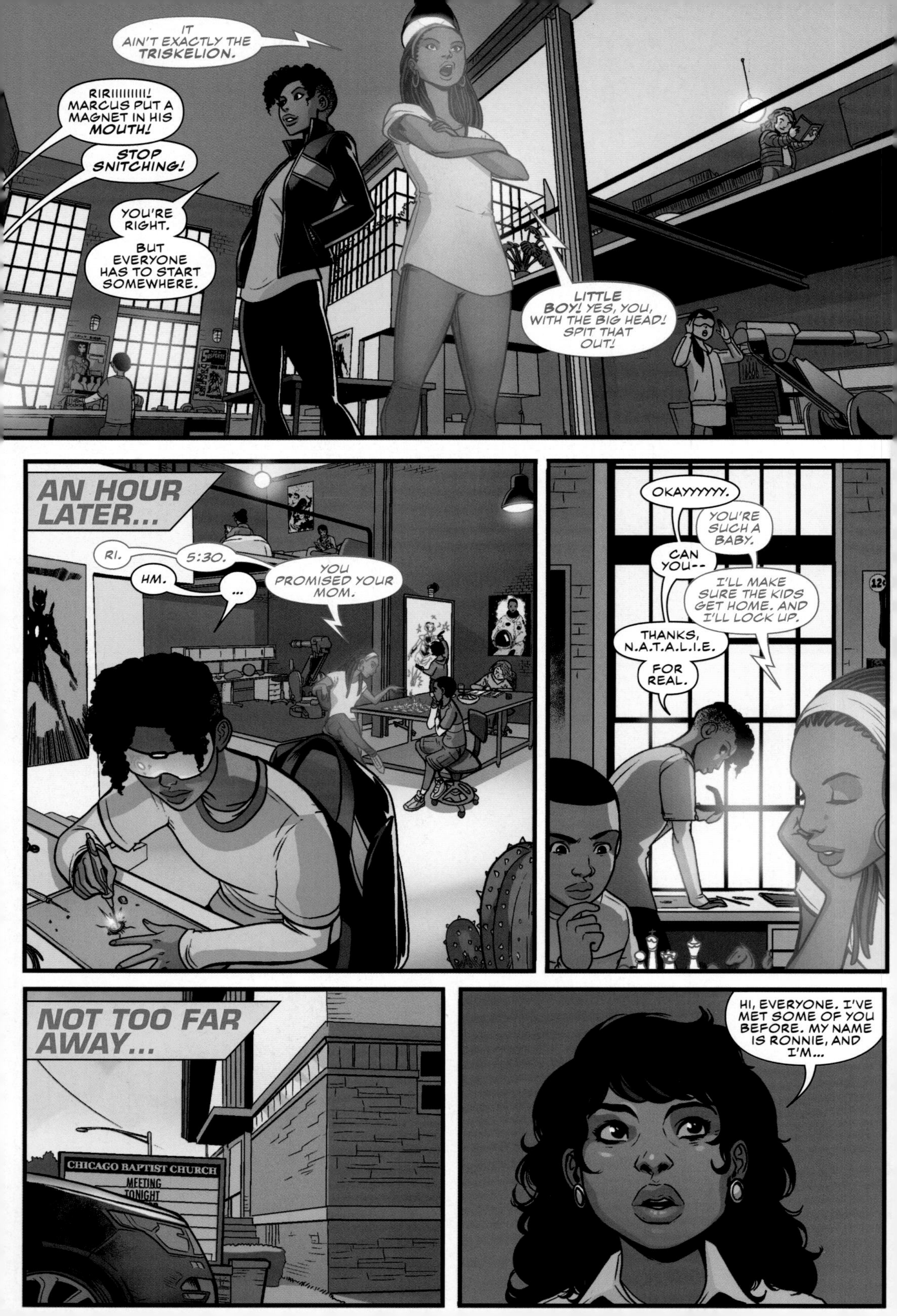
IT AIN'T EXACTLY THE TRISKELION.
RIRIIIIIIIII! MARCUS PUT A MAGNET IN HIS MOUTH!
STOP SNITCHING!
YOU'RE RIGHT.
BUT EVERYONE HAS TO START SOMEWHERE.
LITTLE BOY! YES, YOU, WITH THE BIG HEAD! SPIT THAT OUT!
AN HOUR LATER...
RI.
HM.
5:30.
...
YOU PROMISED YOUR MOM.
OKAYYYYYY.
YOU'RE SUCH A BABY.
CAN YOU--
I'LL MAKE SURE THE KIDS GET HOME. AND I'LL LOCK UP.
THANKS, N.A.T.A.L.I.E.
FOR REAL.
NOT TOO FAR AWAY...
CHICAGO BAPTIST CHURCH
MEETING TONIGHT
HI, EVERYONE. I'VE MET SOME OF YOU BEFORE. MY NAME IS RONNIE, AND I'M...

6

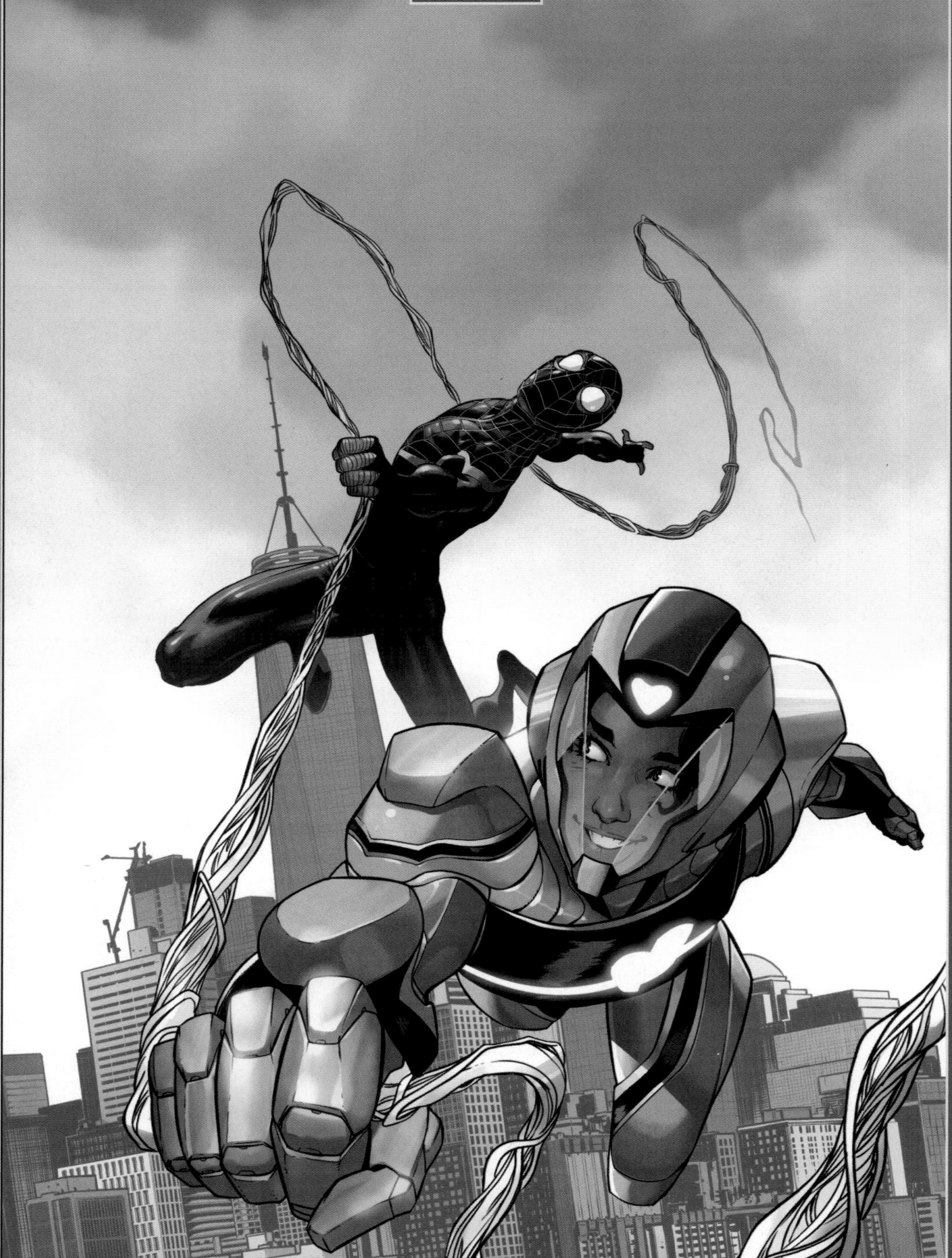

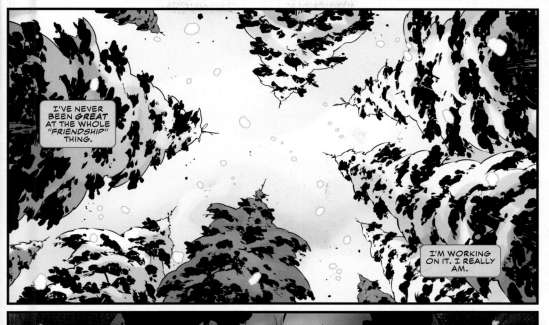

I'VE NEVER BEEN *GREAT* AT THE WHOLE *"FRIENDSHIP"* THING.

I'M WORKING ON IT. I REALLY AM.

BUT THE TROUBLE IS, ONCE YOU START CARING ABOUT PEOPLE...

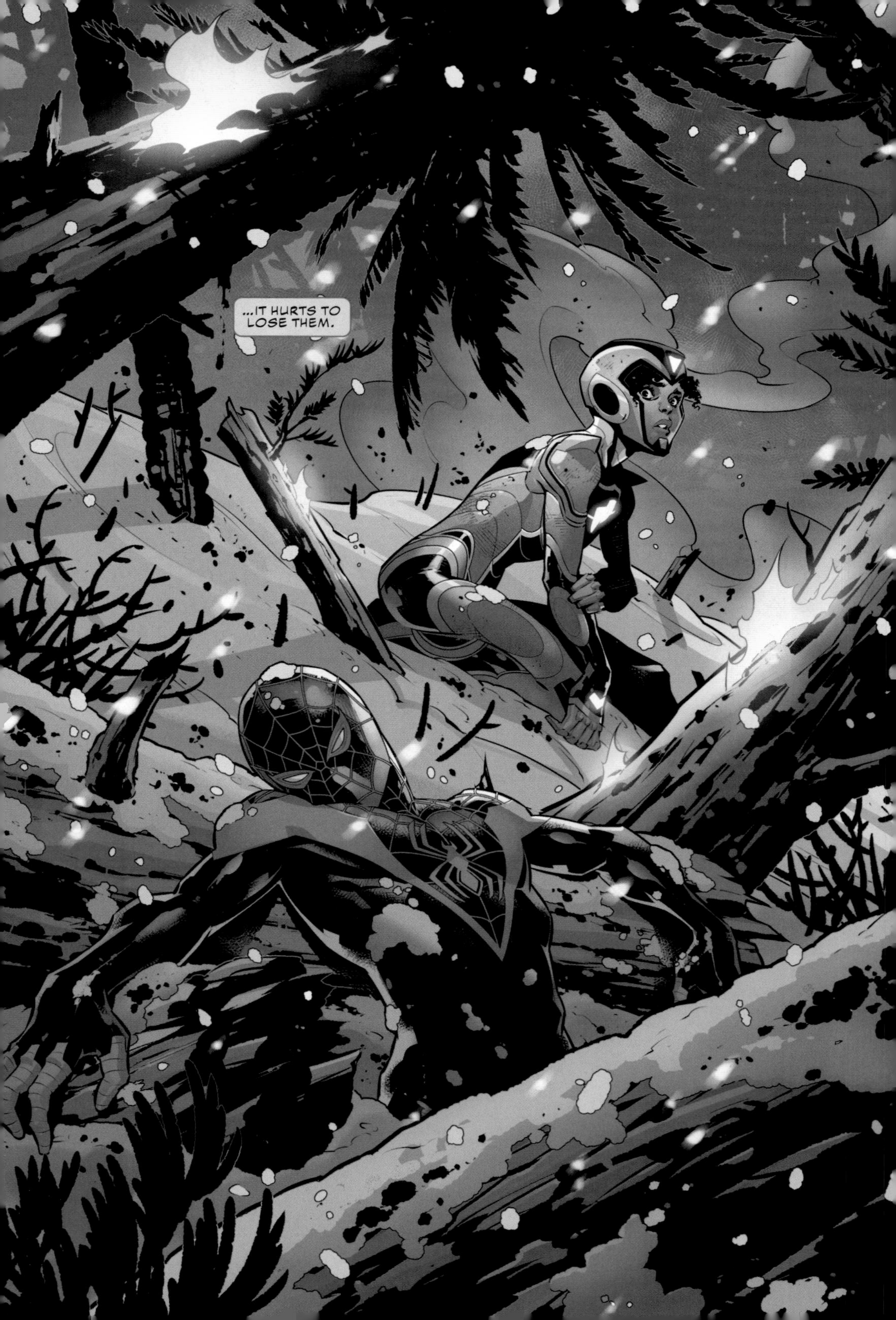
...IT HURTS TO LOSE THEM.

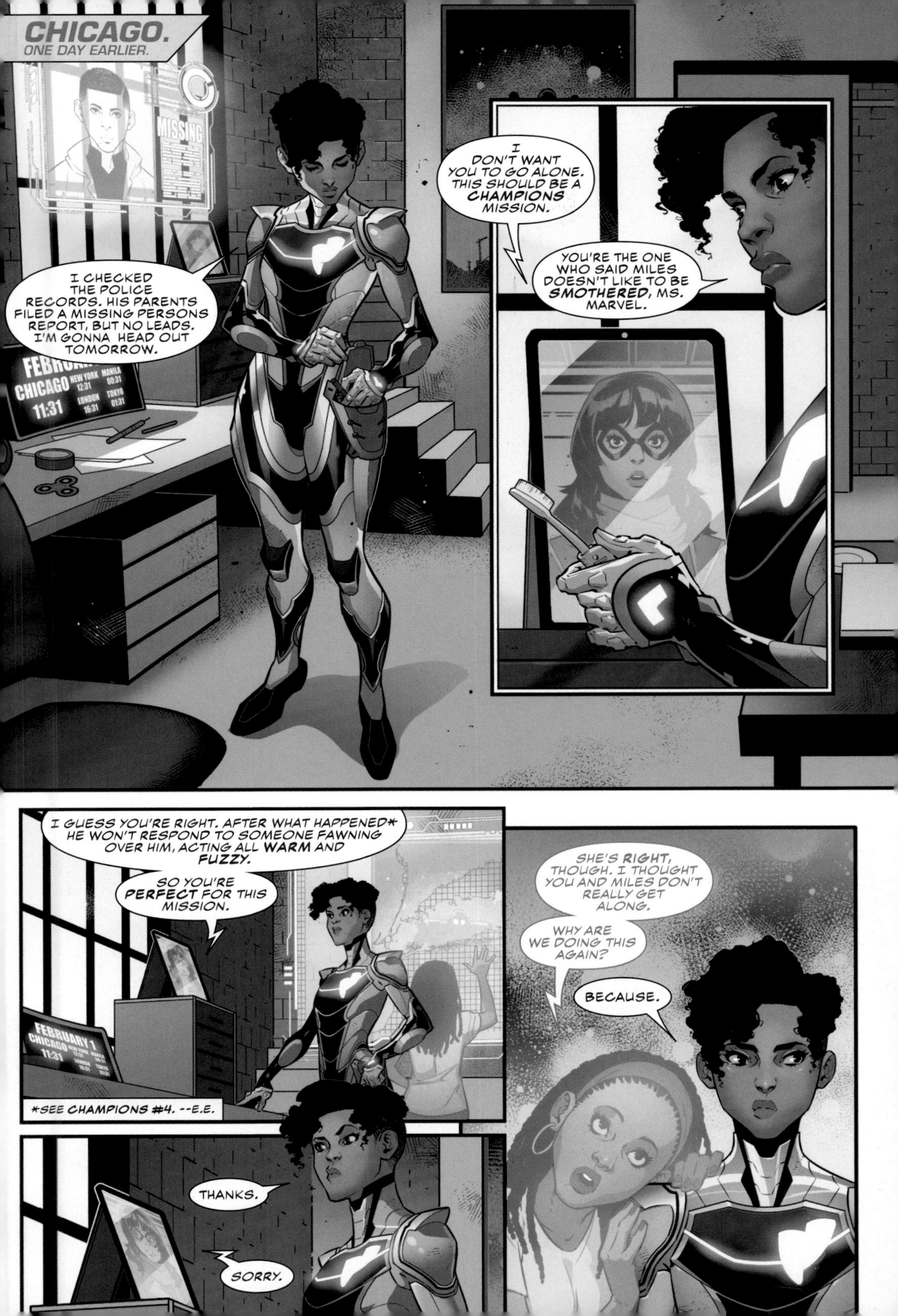

CHICAGO. ONE DAY EARLIER.
MISSING
I CHECKED THE POLICE RECORDS. HIS PARENTS FILED A MISSING PERSONS REPORT, BUT NO LEADS. I'M GONNA HEAD OUT TOMORROW.
I DON'T WANT YOU TO GO ALONE. THIS SHOULD BE A CHAMPIONS MISSION.
YOU'RE THE ONE WHO SAID MILES DOESN'T LIKE TO BE SMOTHERED, MS. MARVEL.
I GUESS YOU'RE RIGHT. AFTER WHAT HAPPENED* HE WON'T RESPOND TO SOMEONE FAWNING OVER HIM, ACTING ALL WARM AND FUZZY.
SO YOU'RE PERFECT FOR THIS MISSION.
*SEE CHAMPIONS #4. --E.E.
THANKS.
SORRY.
SHE'S RIGHT, THOUGH. I THOUGHT YOU AND MILES DON'T REALLY GET ALONG.
WHY ARE WE DOING THIS AGAIN?
BECAUSE.

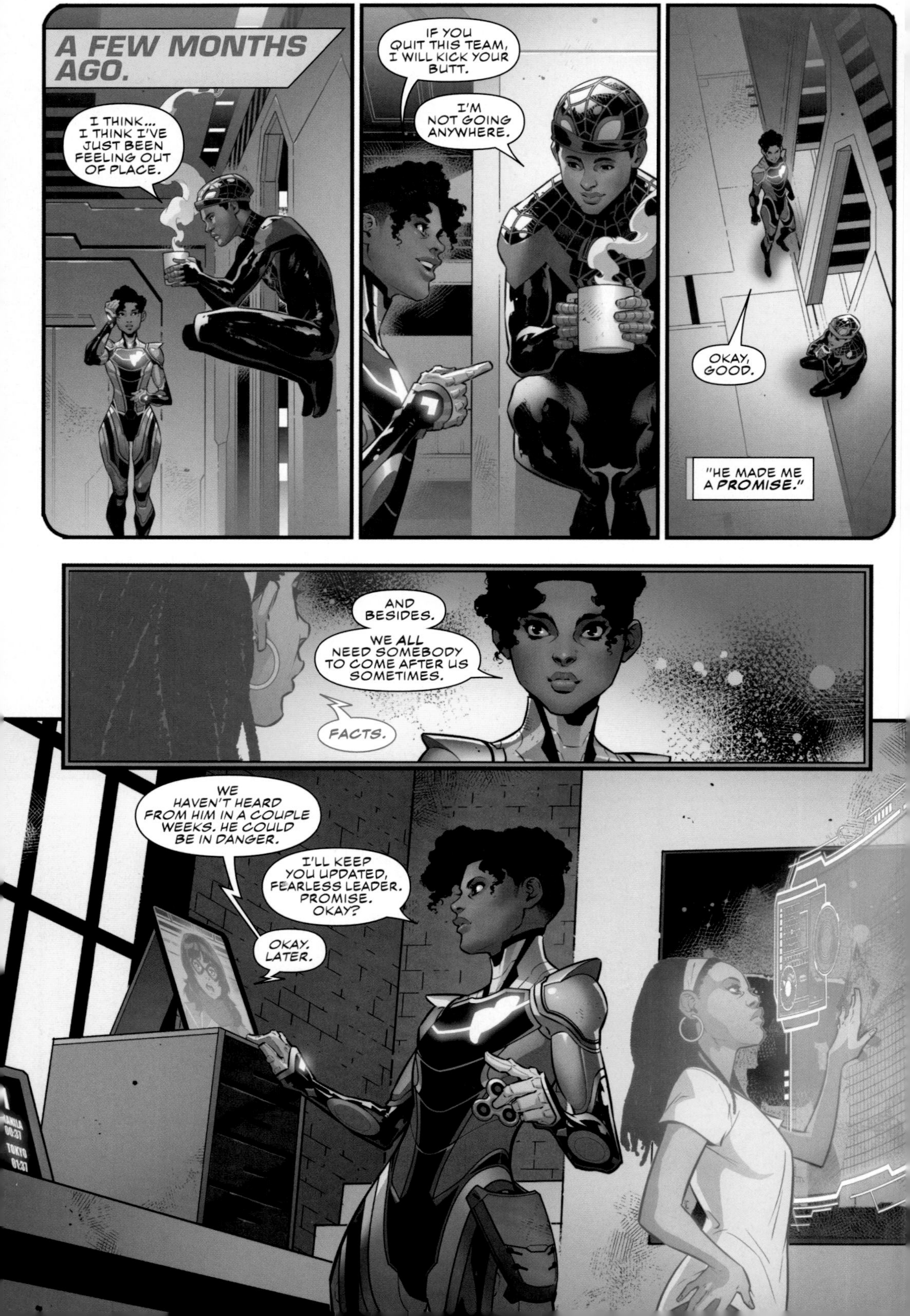
A FEW MONTHS AGO.
I THINK... I THINK I'VE JUST BEEN FEELING OUT OF PLACE.
IF YOU QUIT THIS TEAM, I WILL KICK YOUR BUTT.
I'M NOT GOING ANYWHERE.
OKAY, GOOD.
"HE MADE ME A PROMISE."
AND BESIDES.
WE ALL NEED SOMEBODY TO COME AFTER US SOMETIMES.
FACTS.
WE HAVEN'T HEARD FROM HIM IN A COUPLE WEEKS. HE COULD BE IN DANGER.
I'LL KEEP YOU UPDATED, FEARLESS LEADER. PROMISE. OKAY?
OKAY. LATER.
MANILA 00:37
TOKYO 01:37

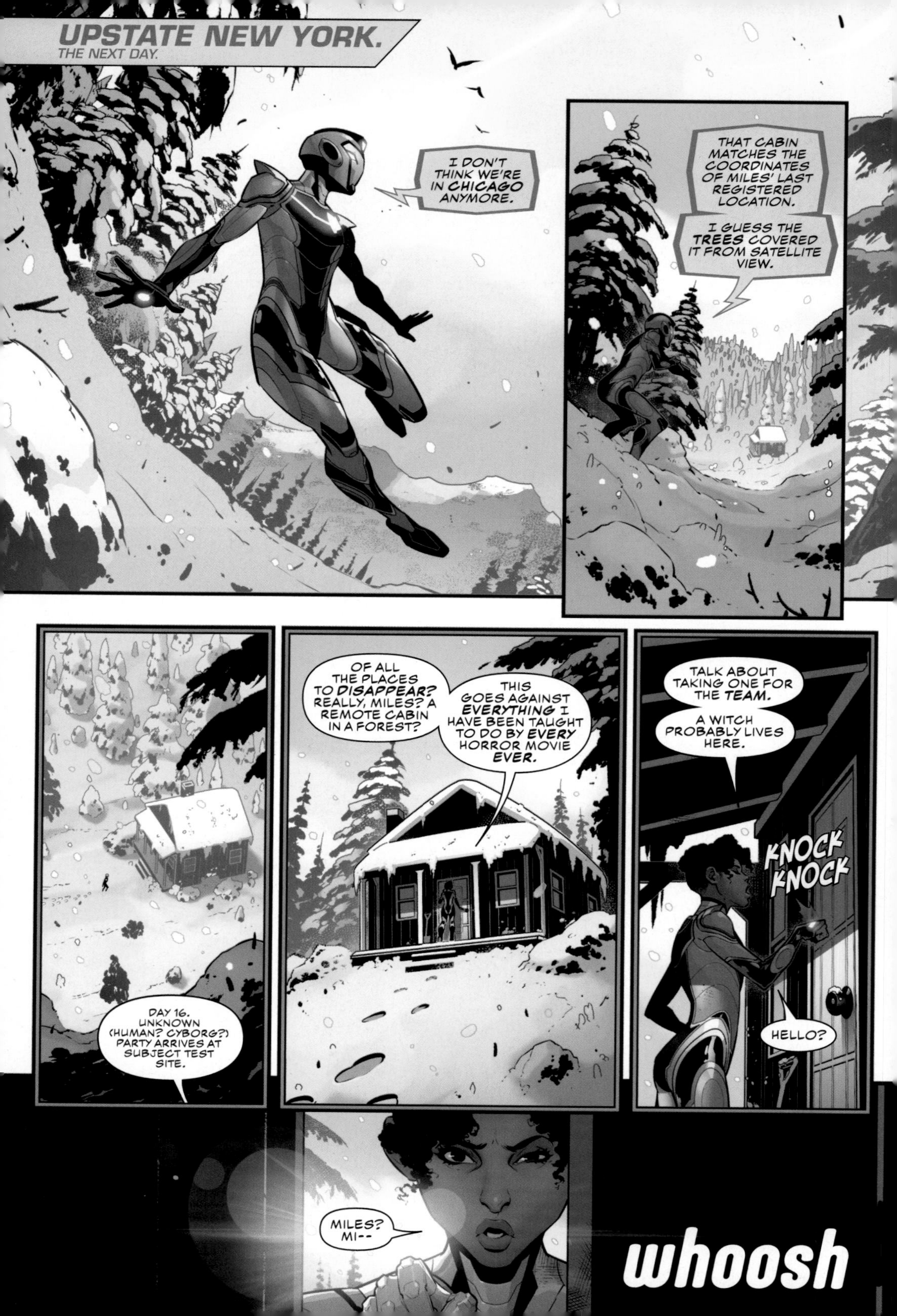
UPSTATE NEW YORK.
THE NEXT DAY.
I DON'T THINK WE'RE IN CHICAGO ANYMORE.
THAT CABIN MATCHES THE COORDINATES OF MILES' LAST REGISTERED LOCATION.
I GUESS THE TREES COVERED IT FROM SATELLITE VIEW.
DAY 16. UNKNOWN (HUMAN? CYBORG?) PARTY ARRIVES AT SUBJECT TEST SITE.
OF ALL THE PLACES TO DISAPPEAR? REALLY, MILES? A REMOTE CABIN IN A FOREST?
THIS GOES AGAINST EVERYTHING I HAVE BEEN TAUGHT TO DO BY EVERY HORROR MOVIE EVER.
TALK ABOUT TAKING ONE FOR THE TEAM.
A WITCH PROBABLY LIVES HERE.
KNOCK KNOCK
HELLO?
MILES? MI--
whoosh

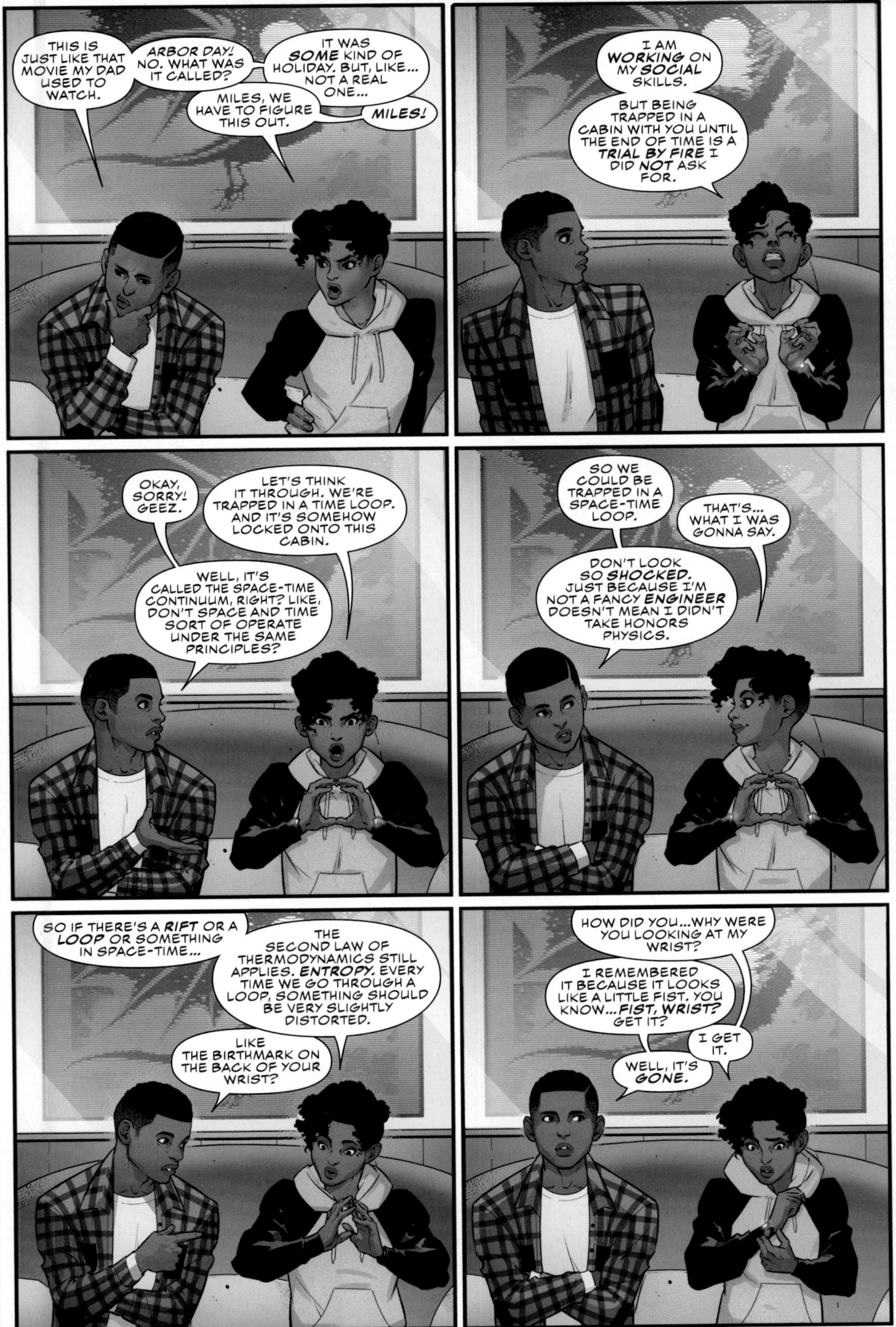
THIS IS JUST LIKE THAT MOVIE MY DAD USED TO WATCH.
ARBOR DAY! NO. WHAT WAS IT CALLED?
IT WAS *SOME* KIND OF HOLIDAY. BUT, LIKE... NOT A REAL ONE...
MILES, WE HAVE TO FIGURE THIS OUT.
MILES!
I AM *WORKING* ON MY *SOCIAL* SKILLS.
BUT BEING TRAPPED IN A CABIN WITH YOU UNTIL THE END OF TIME IS A *TRIAL BY FIRE* I DID *NOT* ASK FOR.
OKAY, SORRY! GEEZ.
LET'S THINK IT THROUGH. WE'RE TRAPPED IN A TIME LOOP. AND IT'S SOMEHOW LOCKED ONTO THIS CABIN.
WELL, IT'S CALLED THE SPACE-TIME CONTINUUM, RIGHT? LIKE, DON'T SPACE AND TIME SORT OF OPERATE UNDER THE SAME PRINCIPLES?
SO WE COULD BE TRAPPED IN A SPACE-TIME LOOP.
THAT'S... WHAT I WAS GONNA SAY.
DON'T LOOK SO *SHOCKED.* JUST BECAUSE I'M NOT A FANCY *ENGINEER* DOESN'T MEAN I DIDN'T TAKE HONORS PHYSICS.
SO IF THERE'S A *RIFT* OR A *LOOP* OR SOMETHING IN SPACE-TIME...
THE SECOND LAW OF THERMODYNAMICS STILL APPLIES. *ENTROPY.* EVERY TIME WE GO THROUGH A LOOP, SOMETHING SHOULD BE VERY SLIGHTLY DISTORTED.
LIKE THE BIRTHMARK ON THE BACK OF YOUR WRIST?
HOW DID YOU...WHY WERE YOU LOOKING AT MY WRIST?
I REMEMBERED IT BECAUSE IT LOOKS LIKE A LITTLE FIST. YOU KNOW...*FIST, WRIST?* GET IT?
I GET IT.
WELL, IT'S *GONE.*

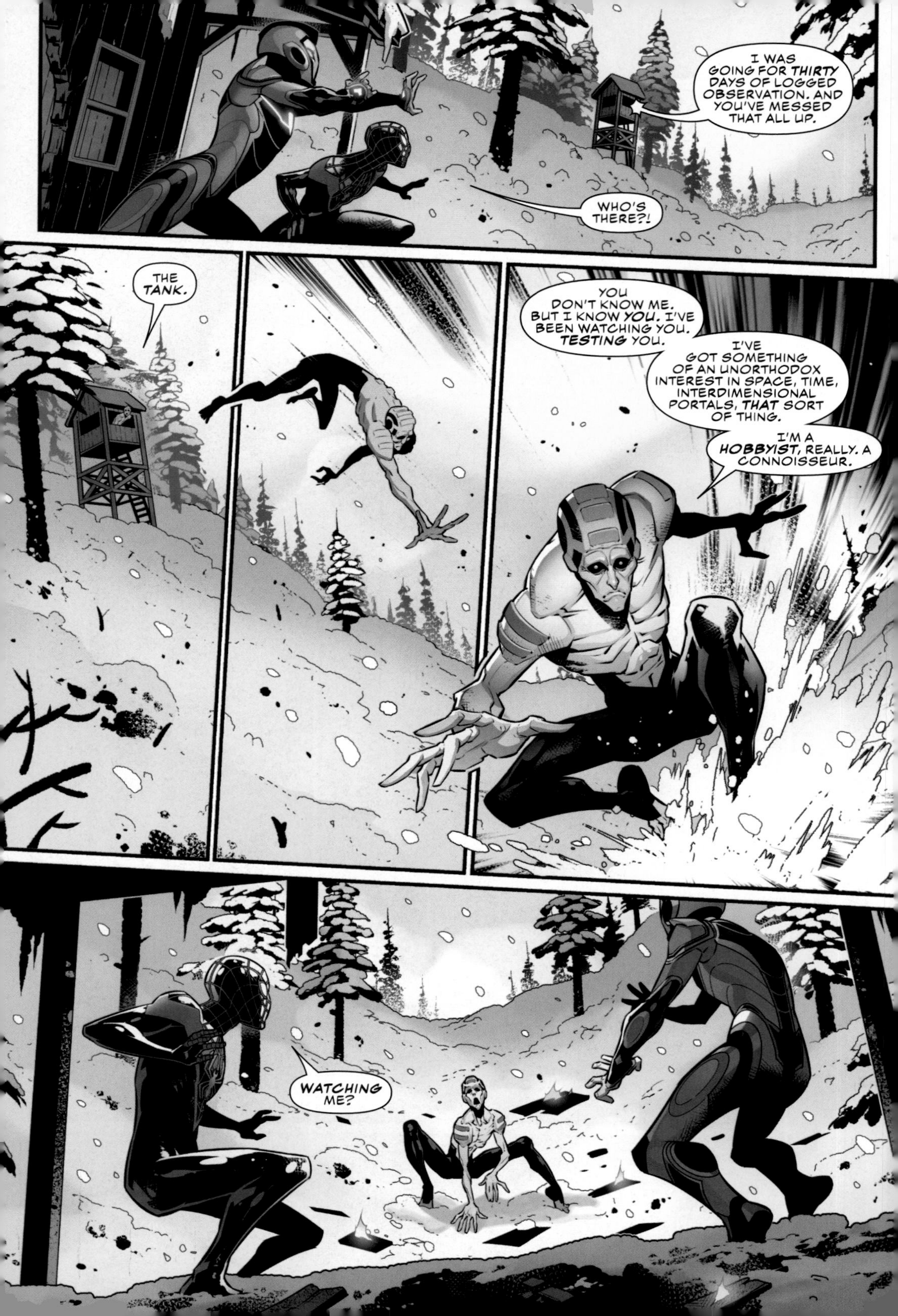
I WAS GOING FOR THIRTY DAYS OF LOGGED OBSERVATION. AND YOU'VE MESSED THAT ALL UP.
WHO'S THERE?!
THE TANK.
YOU DON'T KNOW ME. BUT I KNOW YOU. I'VE BEEN WATCHING YOU. TESTING YOU.
I'VE GOT SOMETHING OF AN UNORTHODOX INTEREST IN SPACE, TIME, INTERDIMENSIONAL PORTALS, THAT SORT OF THING.
I'M A HOBBYIST, REALLY. A CONNOISSEUR.
WATCHING ME?

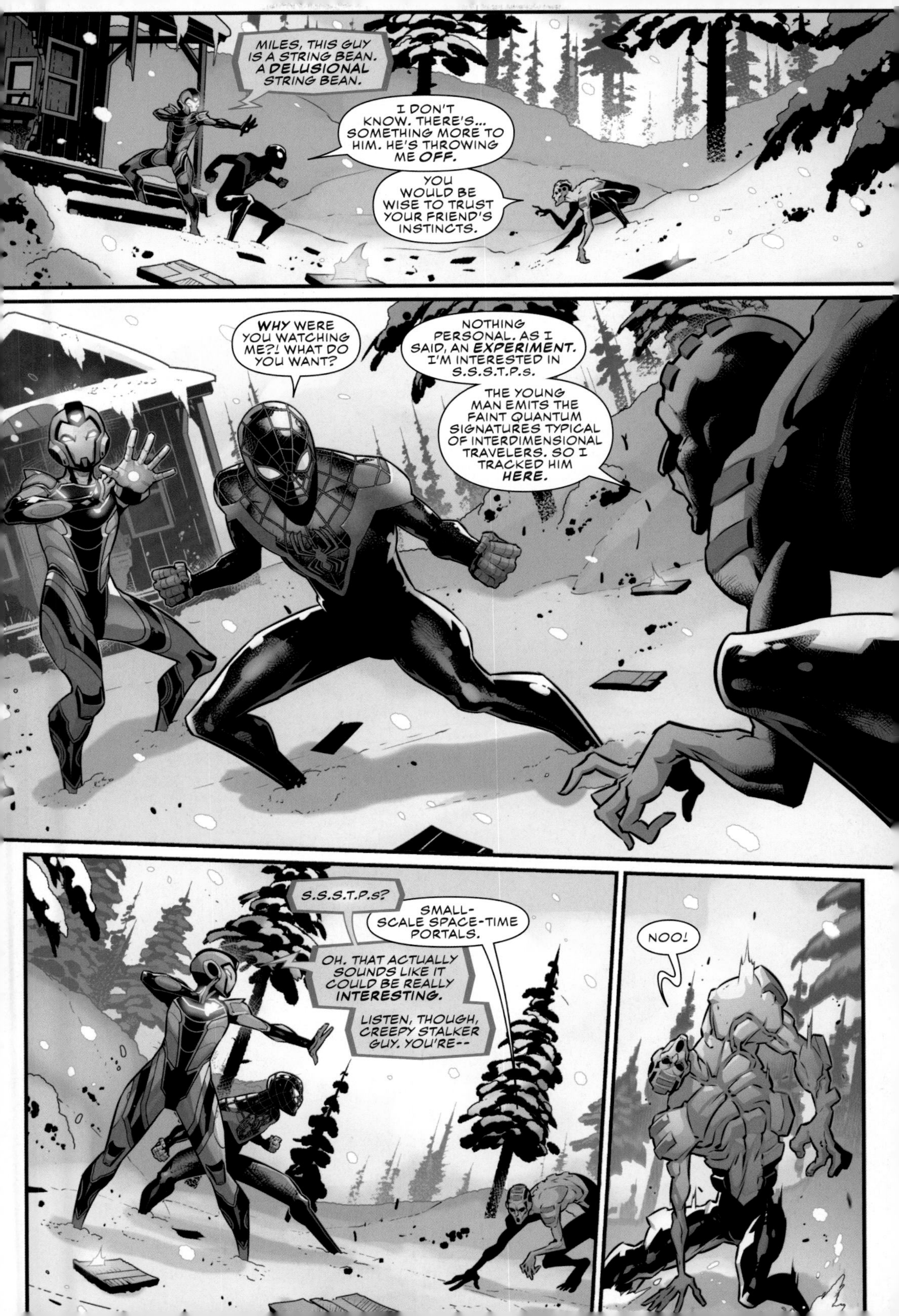

MILES, THIS GUY IS A STRING BEAN. A DELUSIONAL STRING BEAN.
I DON'T KNOW. THERE'S... SOMETHING MORE TO HIM. HE'S THROWING ME OFF.
YOU WOULD BE WISE TO TRUST YOUR FRIEND'S INSTINCTS.
WHY WERE YOU WATCHING ME?! WHAT DO YOU WANT?
NOTHING PERSONAL. AS I SAID, AN EXPERIMENT. I'M INTERESTED IN S.S.S.T.P.s.
THE YOUNG MAN EMITS THE FAINT QUANTUM SIGNATURES TYPICAL OF INTERDIMENSIONAL TRAVELERS. SO I TRACKED HIM HERE.
S.S.S.T.P.s?
SMALL-SCALE SPACE-TIME PORTALS.
OH. THAT ACTUALLY SOUNDS LIKE IT COULD BE REALLY INTERESTING.
LISTEN, THOUGH, CREEPY STALKER GUY. YOU'RE--
NOO!

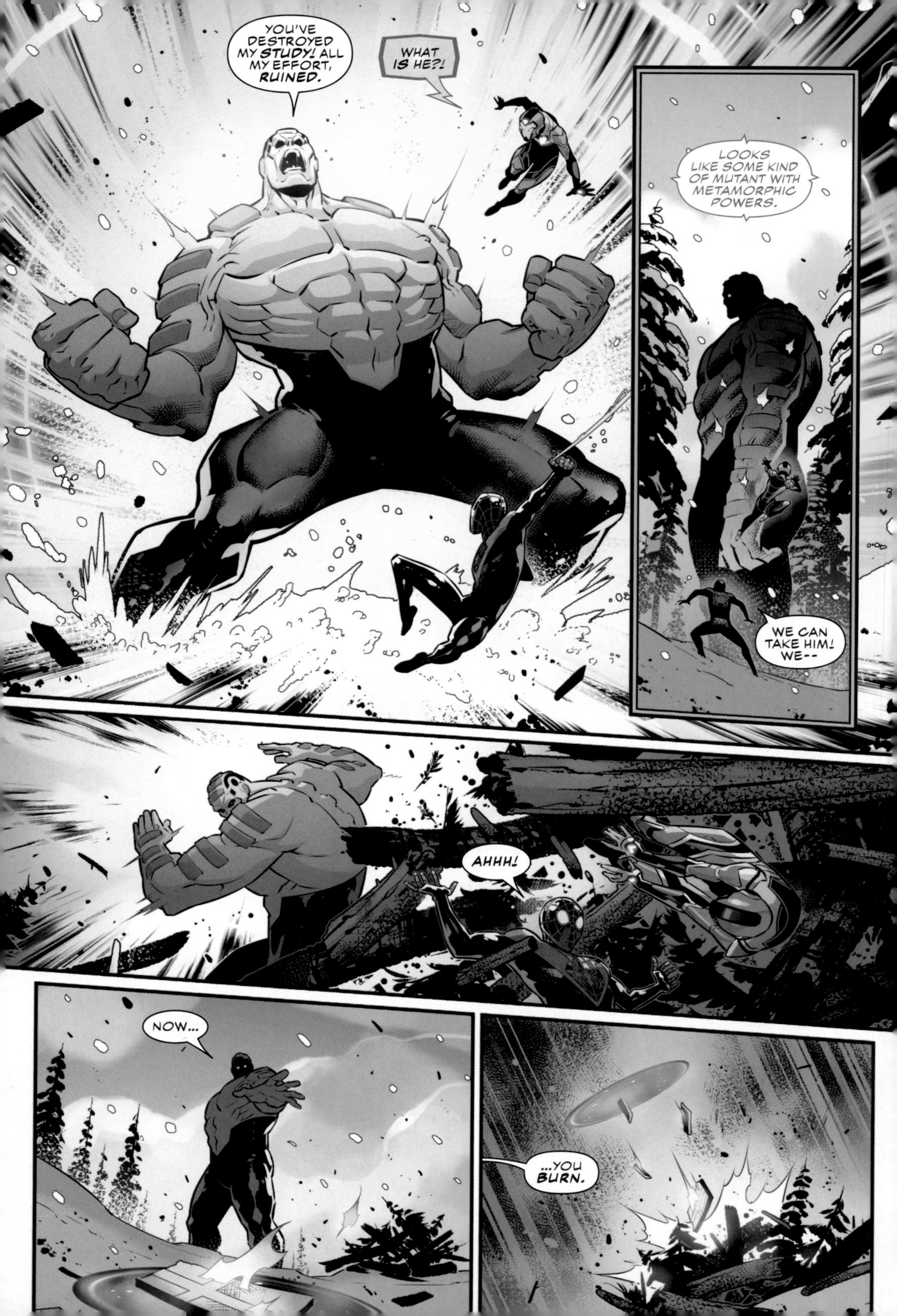
YOU'VE DESTROYED MY STUDY! ALL MY EFFORT, RUINED.
WHAT IS HE?!
LOOKS LIKE SOME KIND OF MUTANT WITH METAMORPHIC POWERS.
WE CAN TAKE HIM! WE--
AHHH!
NOW...
...YOU BURN.

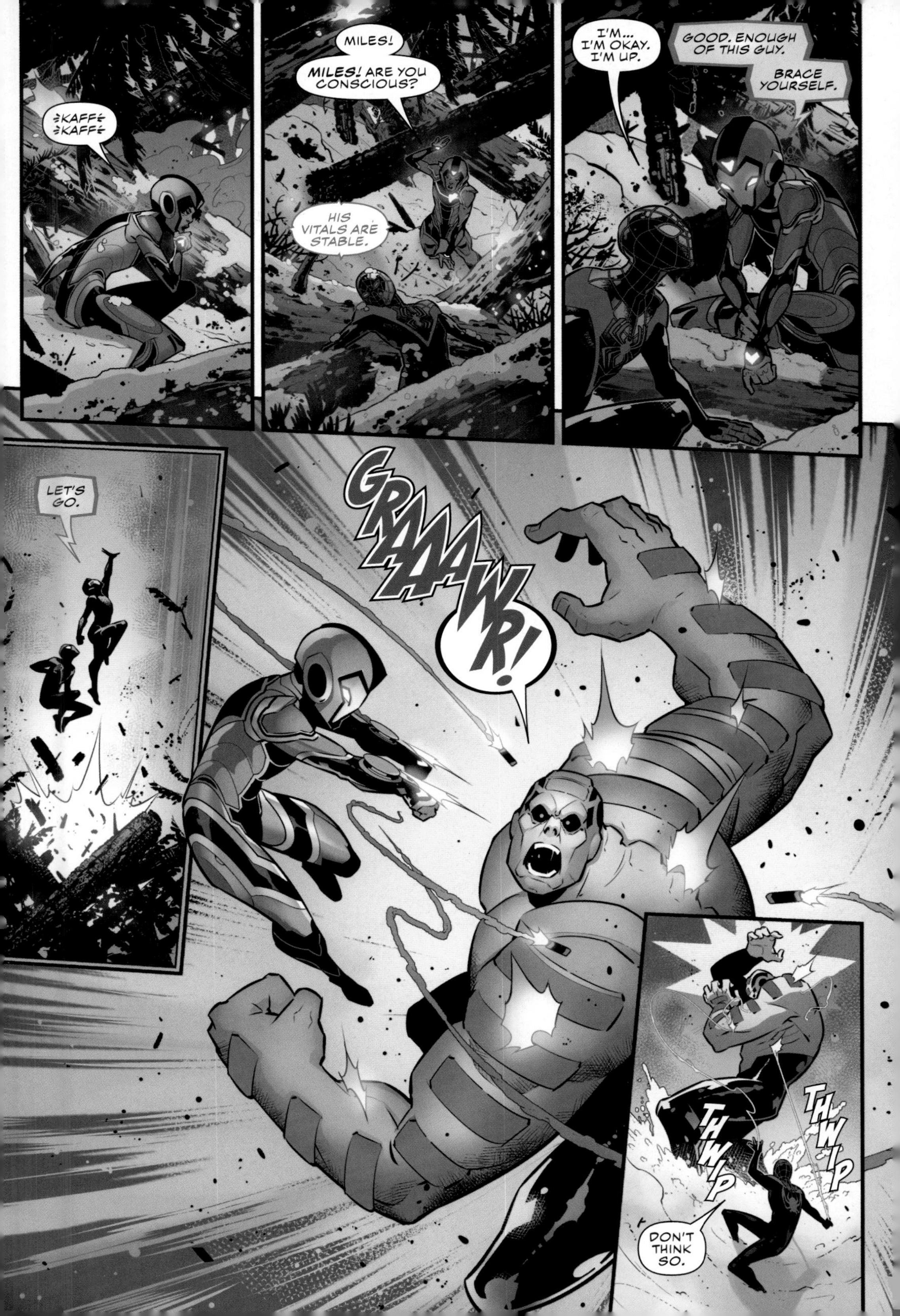

KAFF KAFF
MILES!
MILES! ARE YOU CONSCIOUS?
HIS VITALS ARE STABLE.
I'M... I'M OKAY. I'M UP.
GOOD. ENOUGH OF THIS GUY.
BRACE YOURSELF.
LET'S GO.
GRAAAWR!
THWIP
THWIP
DON'T THINK SO.

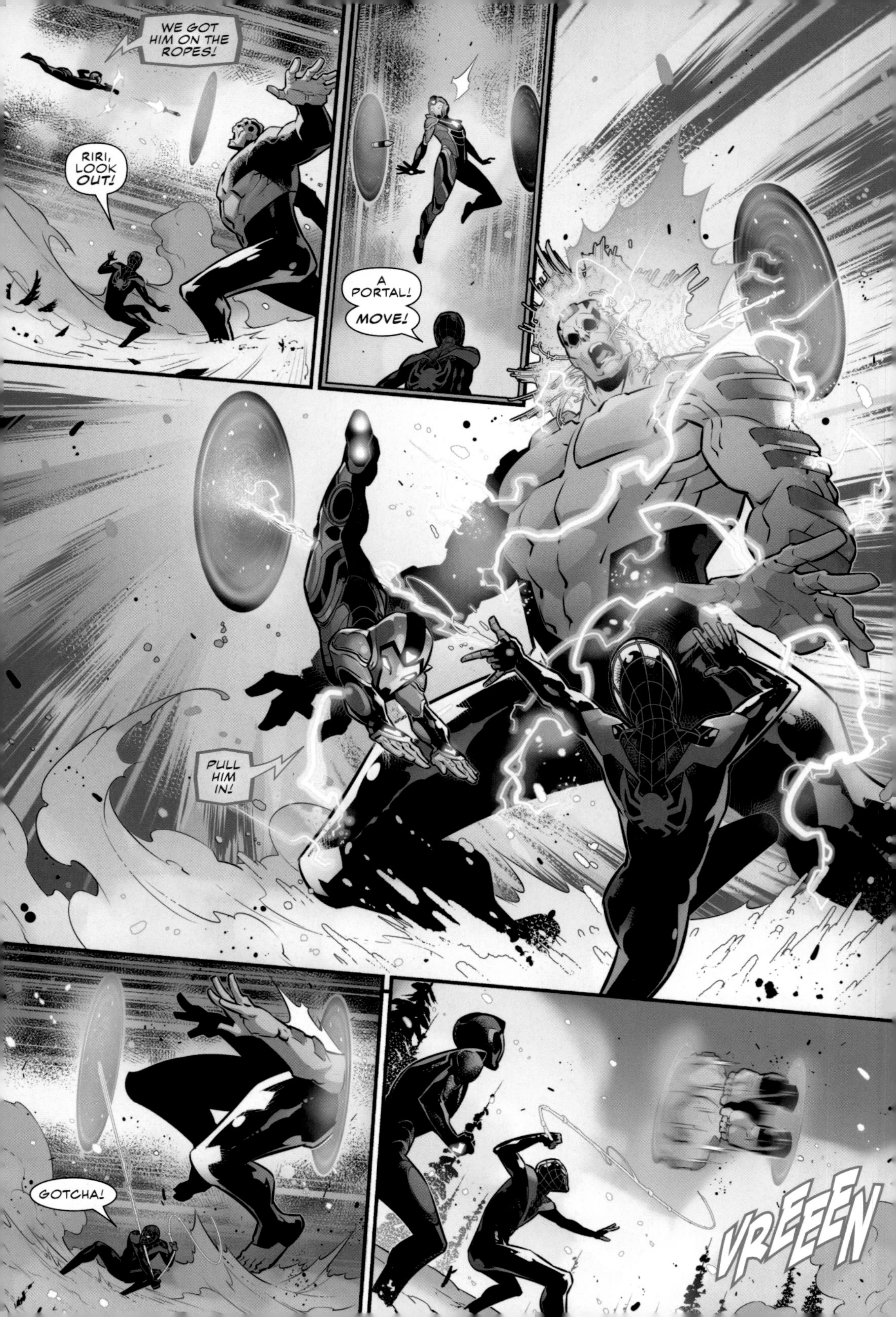
WE GOT HIM ON THE ROPES!
RIRI, LOOK OUT!
A PORTAL!
MOVE!
PULL HIM IN!
GOTCHA!
VREEEN

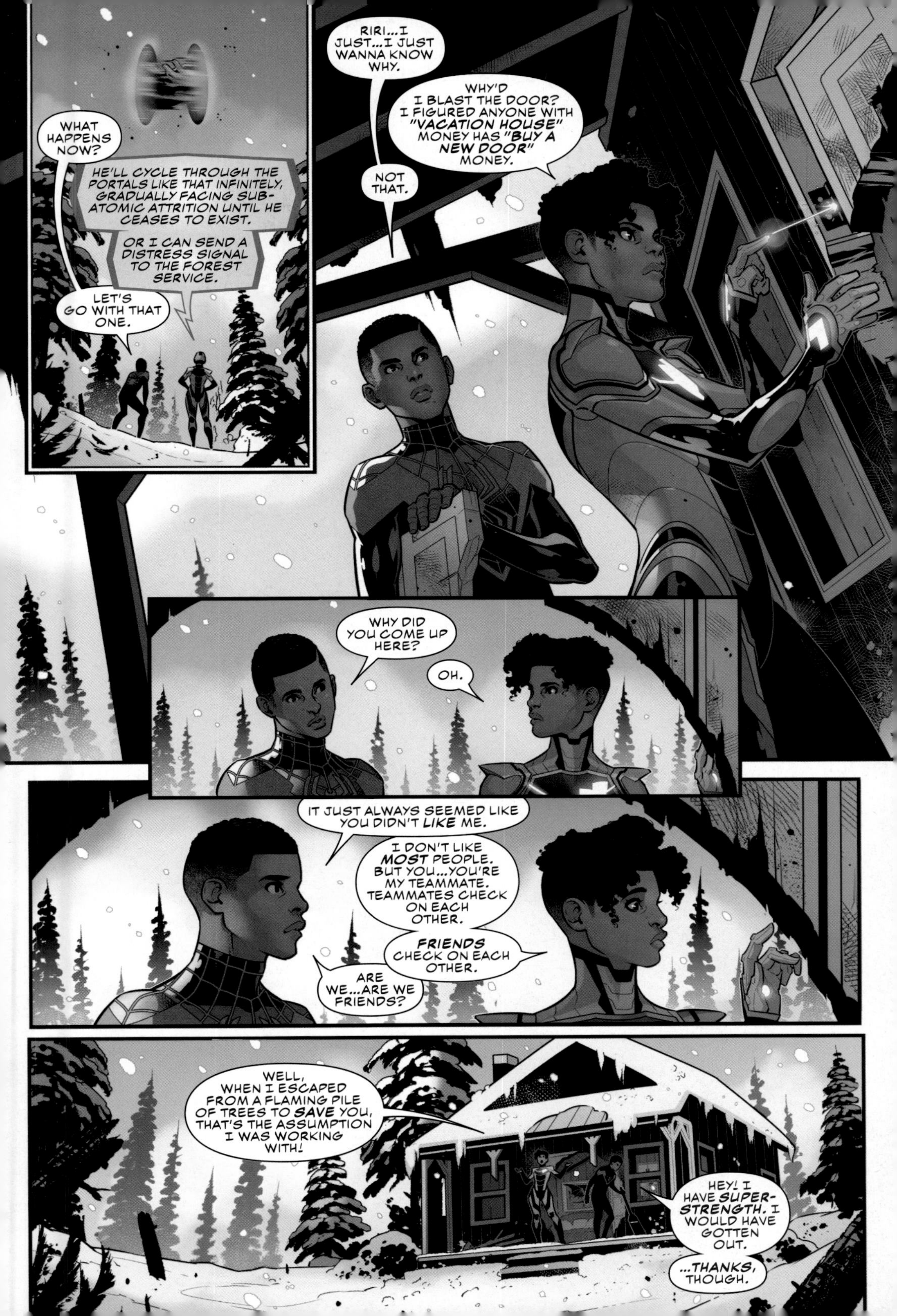
WHAT HAPPENS NOW?
HE'LL CYCLE THROUGH THE PORTALS LIKE THAT INFINITELY, GRADUALLY FACING SUB-ATOMIC ATTRITION UNTIL HE CEASES TO EXIST.
OR I CAN SEND A DISTRESS SIGNAL TO THE FOREST SERVICE.
LET'S GO WITH THAT ONE.
RIRI...I JUST...I JUST WANNA KNOW WHY.
WHY'D I BLAST THE DOOR? I FIGURED ANYONE WITH "VACATION HOUSE" MONEY HAS "BUY A NEW DOOR" MONEY.
NOT THAT.
WHY DID YOU COME UP HERE?
OH.
IT JUST ALWAYS SEEMED LIKE YOU DIDN'T LIKE ME.
I DON'T LIKE MOST PEOPLE. BUT YOU...YOU'RE MY TEAMMATE. TEAMMATES CHECK ON EACH OTHER.
FRIENDS CHECK ON EACH OTHER.
ARE WE...ARE WE FRIENDS?
WELL, WHEN I ESCAPED FROM A FLAMING PILE OF TREES TO SAVE YOU, THAT'S THE ASSUMPTION I WAS WORKING WITH!
HEY! I HAVE SUPER-STRENGTH. I WOULD HAVE GOTTEN OUT.
...THANKS, THOUGH.

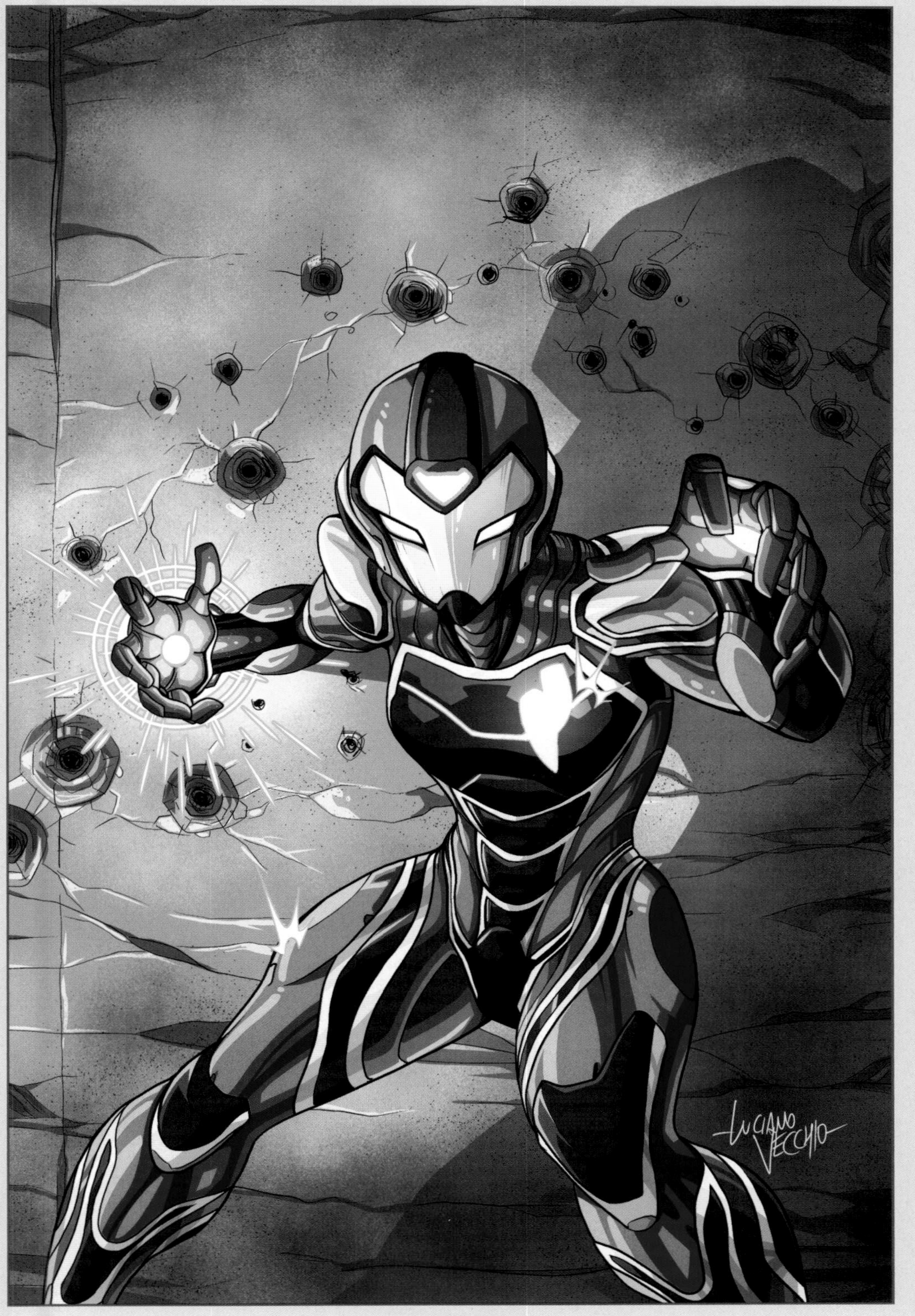
LUCIANO VECCHIO

#1 VARIANT
BY LUCIANO VECCHIO

7

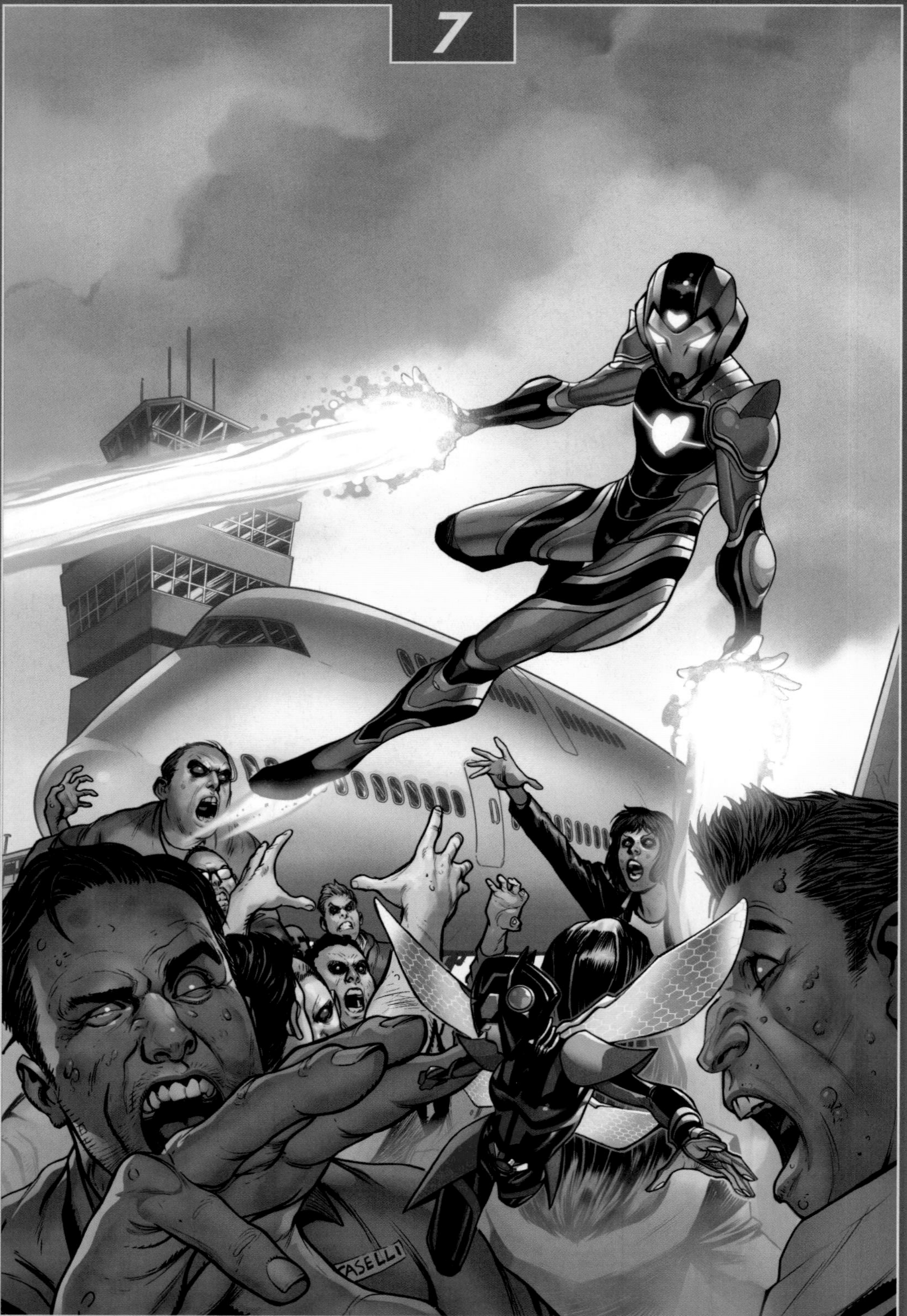
TASELLI

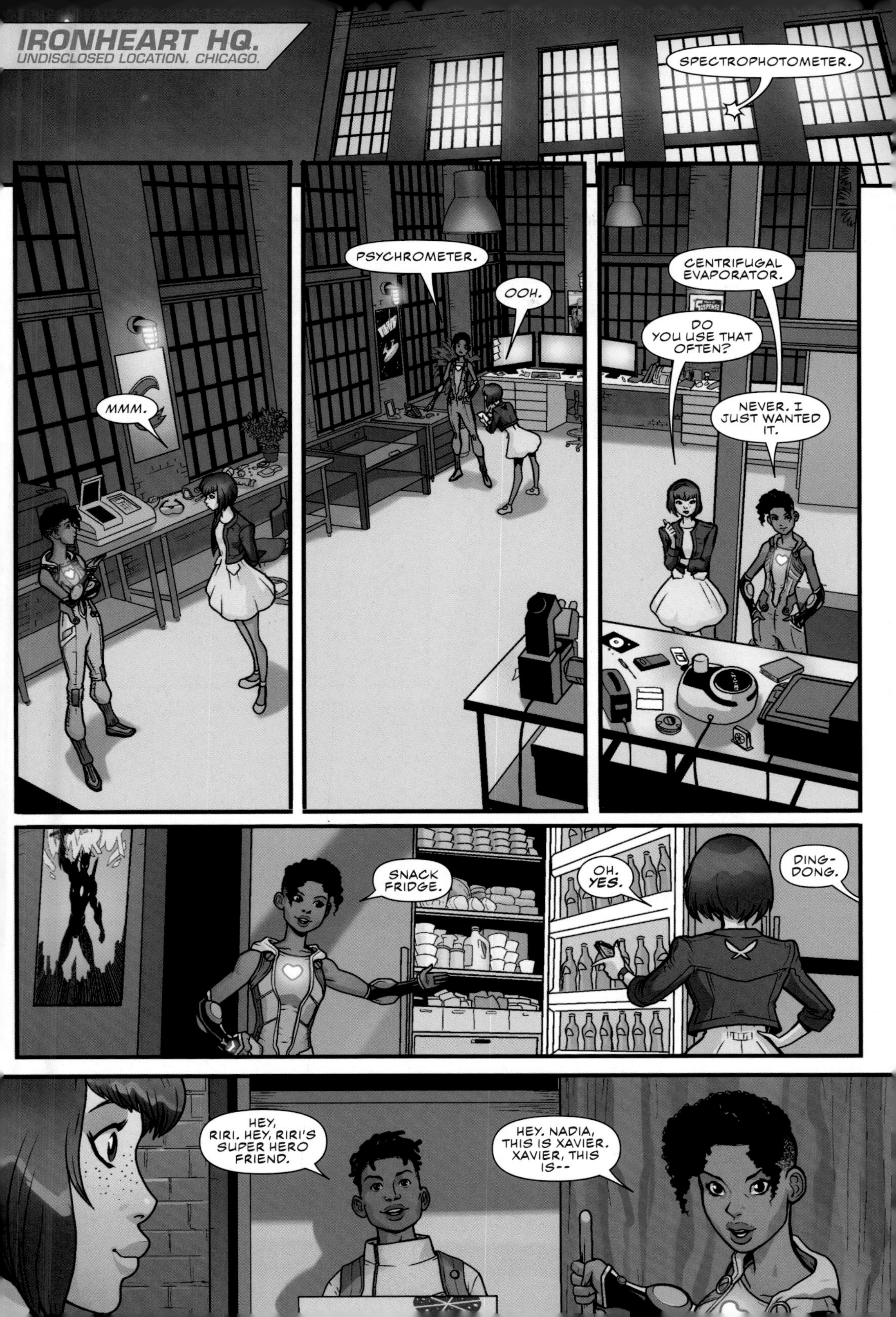
IRONHEART HQ.
UNDISCLOSED LOCATION. CHICAGO.
SPECTROPHOTOMETER.
MMM.
PSYCHROMETER.
OOH.
CENTRIFUGAL EVAPORATOR.
DO YOU USE THAT OFTEN?
NEVER. I JUST WANTED IT.
SNACK FRIDGE.
OH. YES.
DING-DONG.
HEY, RIRI. HEY, RIRI'S SUPER HERO FRIEND.
HEY. NADIA, THIS IS XAVIER. XAVIER, THIS IS--

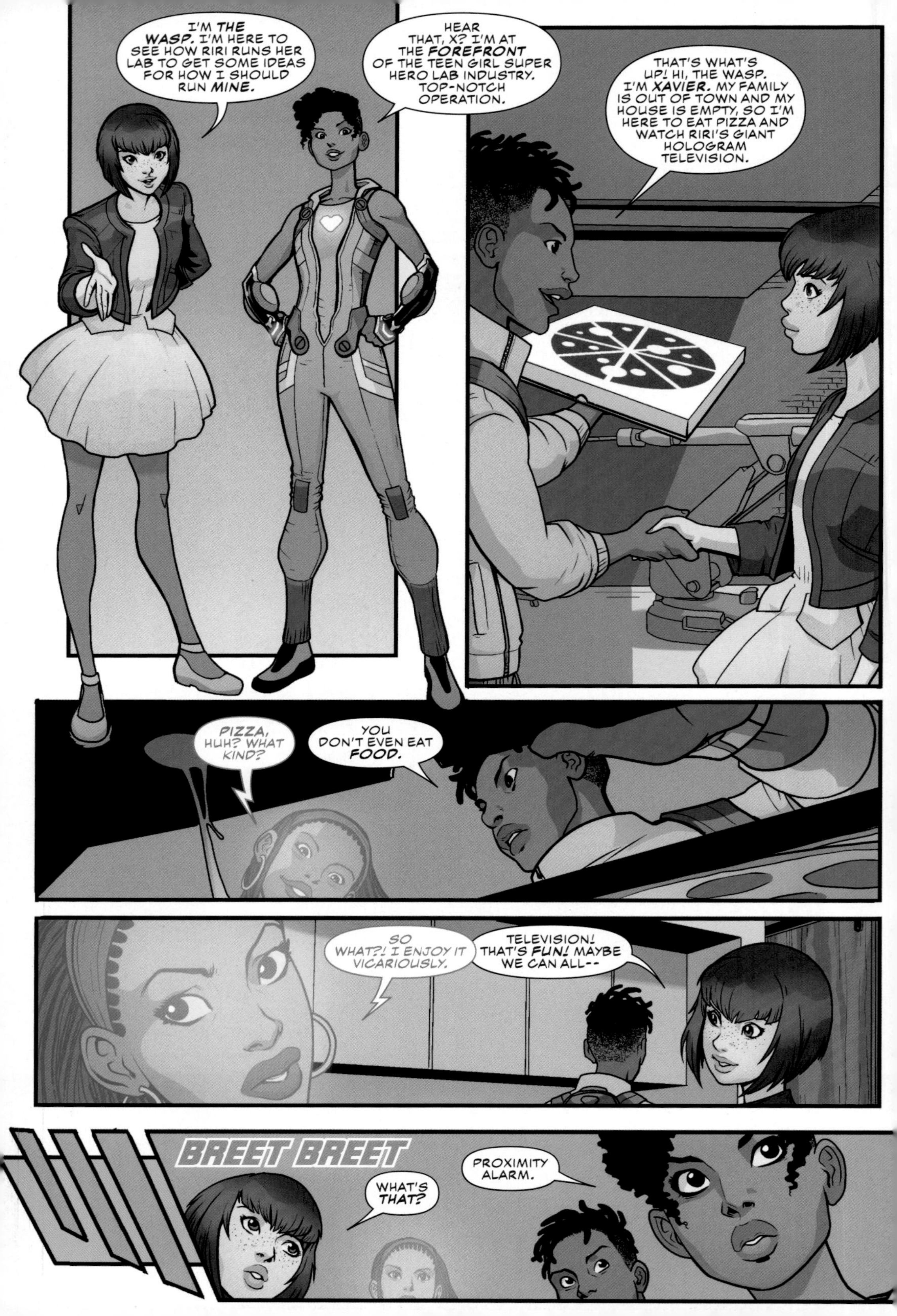

I'M THE WASP. I'M HERE TO SEE HOW RIRI RUNS HER LAB TO GET SOME IDEAS FOR HOW I SHOULD RUN MINE.
HEAR THAT, X? I'M AT THE FOREFRONT OF THE TEEN GIRL SUPER HERO LAB INDUSTRY. TOP-NOTCH OPERATION.
THAT'S WHAT'S UP! HI, THE WASP. I'M XAVIER. MY FAMILY IS OUT OF TOWN AND MY HOUSE IS EMPTY, SO I'M HERE TO EAT PIZZA AND WATCH RIRI'S GIANT HOLOGRAM TELEVISION.
PIZZA, HUH? WHAT KIND?
YOU DON'T EVEN EAT FOOD.
SO WHAT?! I ENJOY IT VICARIOUSLY.
TELEVISION! THAT'S FUN! MAYBE WE CAN ALL--
BREET BREET
WHAT'S THAT?
PROXIMITY ALARM.

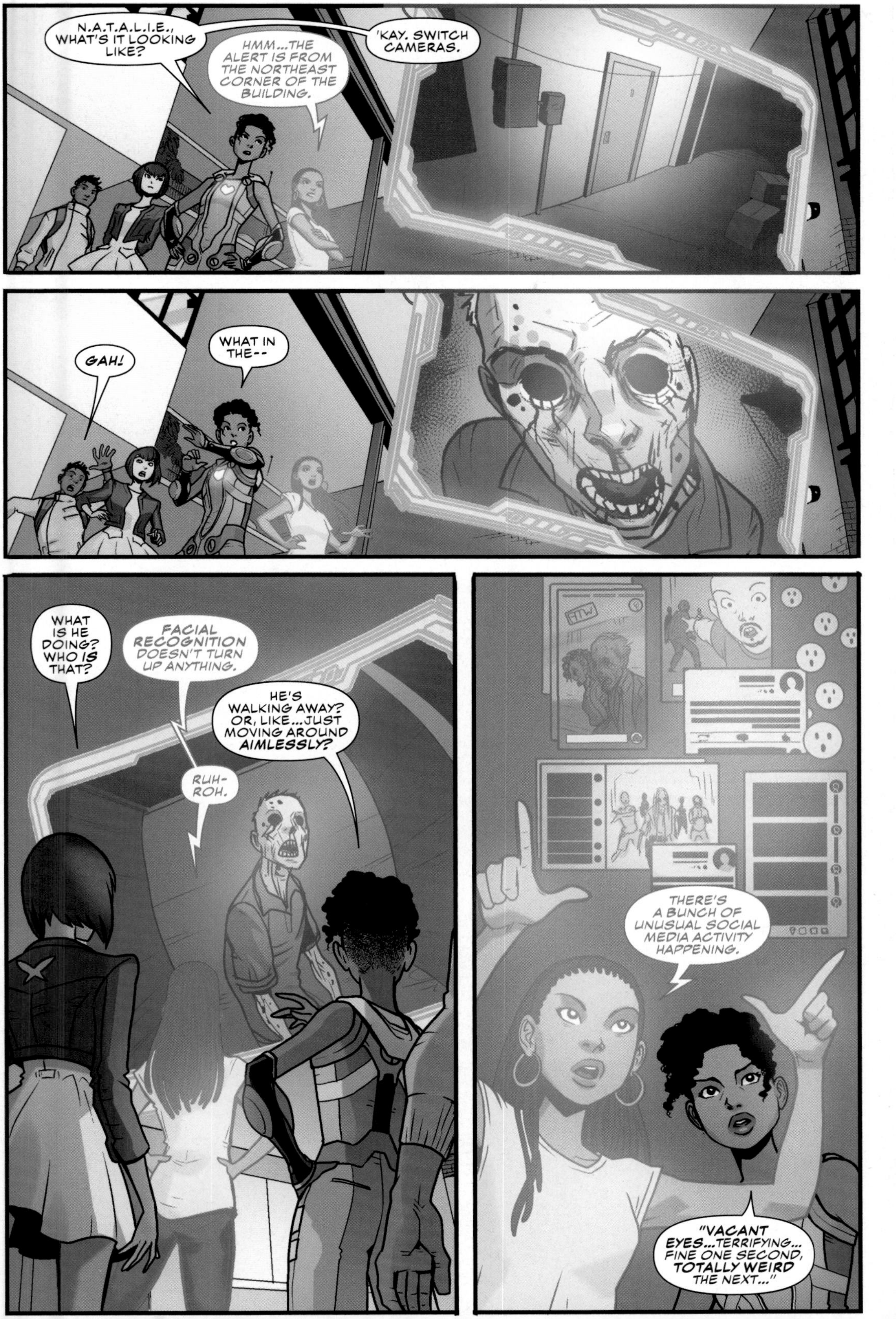
N.A.T.A.L.I.E., WHAT'S IT LOOKING LIKE?
HMM...THE ALERT IS FROM THE NORTHEAST CORNER OF THE BUILDING.
'KAY. SWITCH CAMERAS.
GAH!
WHAT IN THE--
WHAT IS HE DOING? WHO IS THAT?
FACIAL RECOGNITION DOESN'T TURN UP ANYTHING.
HE'S WALKING AWAY? OR, LIKE...JUST MOVING AROUND AIMLESSLY?
RUH-ROH.
THERE'S A BUNCH OF UNUSUAL SOCIAL MEDIA ACTIVITY HAPPENING.
"VACANT EYES...TERRIFYING... FINE ONE SECOND, TOTALLY WEIRD THE NEXT..."

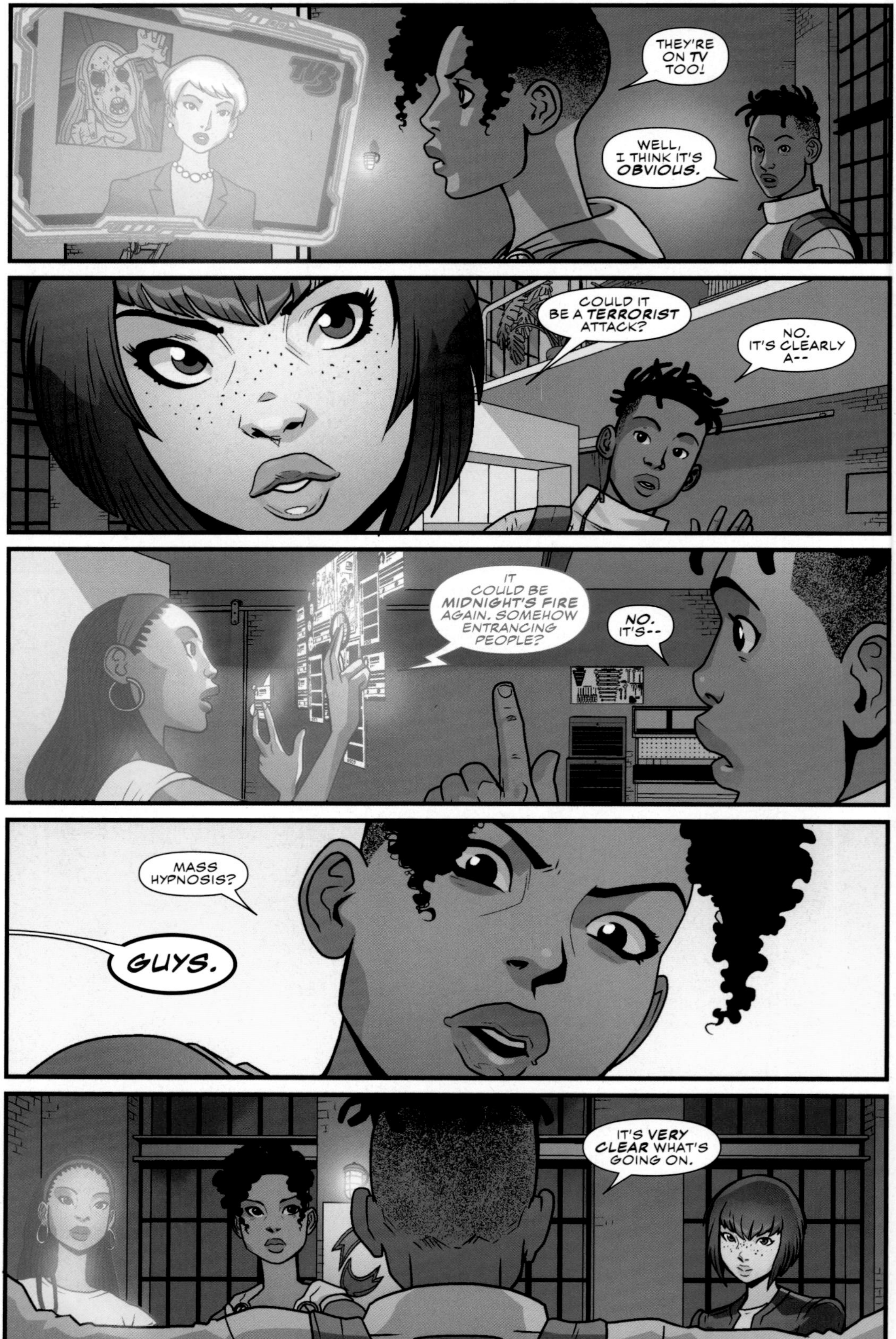
THEY'RE ON TV TOO!
WELL, I THINK IT'S OBVIOUS.
COULD IT BE A TERRORIST ATTACK?
NO. IT'S CLEARLY A--
IT COULD BE MIDNIGHT'S FIRE AGAIN. SOMEHOW ENTRANCING PEOPLE?
NO. IT'S--
MASS HYPNOSIS?
GUYS.
IT'S VERY CLEAR WHAT'S GOING ON.

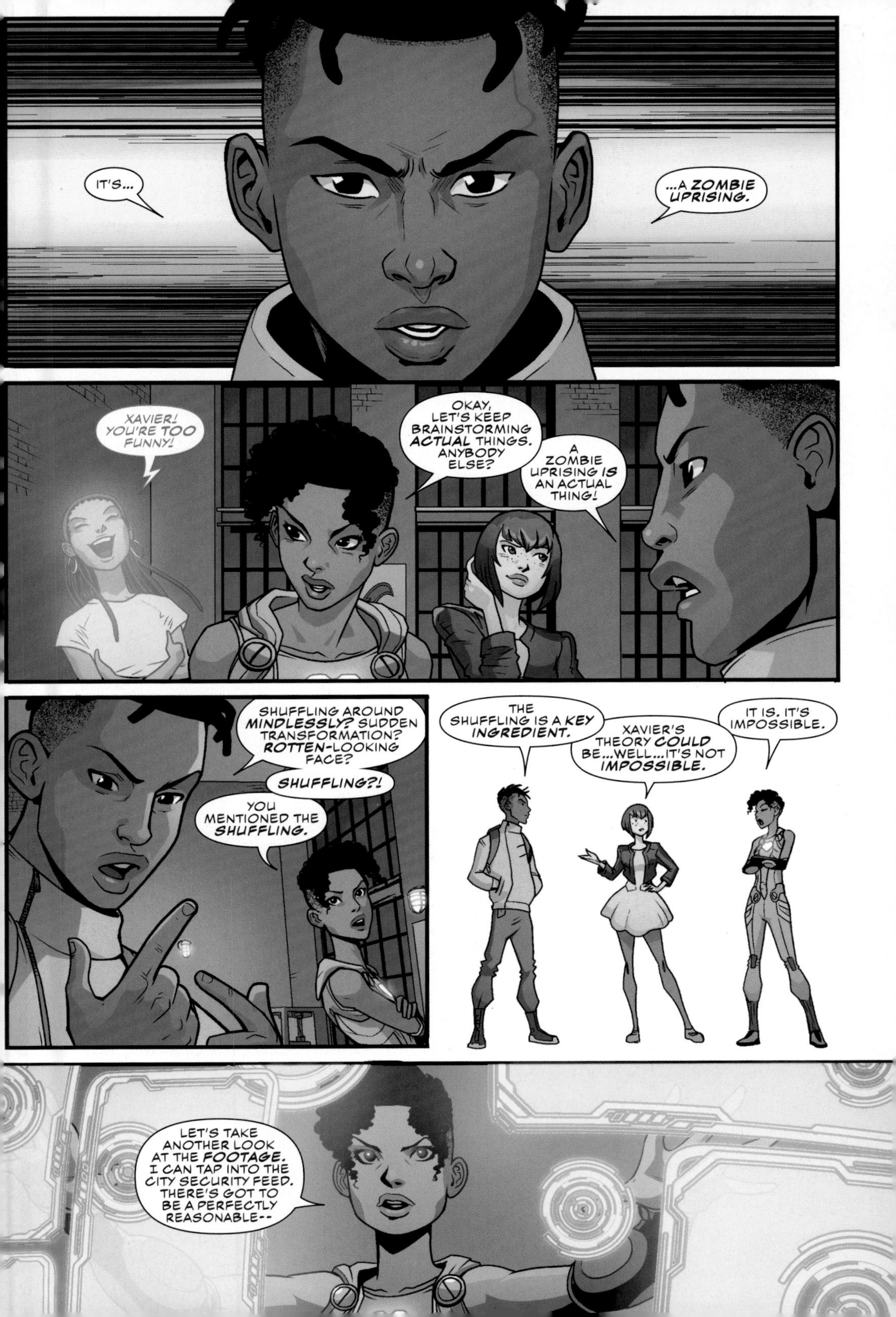
IT'S...
...A ZOMBIE UPRISING.
XAVIER! YOU'RE TOO FUNNY!
OKAY, LET'S KEEP BRAINSTORMING ACTUAL THINGS. ANYBODY ELSE?
A ZOMBIE UPRISING IS AN ACTUAL THING!
SHUFFLING AROUND MINDLESSLY? SUDDEN TRANSFORMATION? ROTTEN-LOOKING FACE?
SHUFFLING?!
YOU MENTIONED THE SHUFFLING.
THE SHUFFLING IS A KEY INGREDIENT.
XAVIER'S THEORY COULD BE...WELL...IT'S NOT IMPOSSIBLE.
IT IS. IT'S IMPOSSIBLE.
LET'S TAKE ANOTHER LOOK AT THE FOOTAGE. I CAN TAP INTO THE CITY SECURITY FEED. THERE'S GOT TO BE A PERFECTLY REASONABLE--

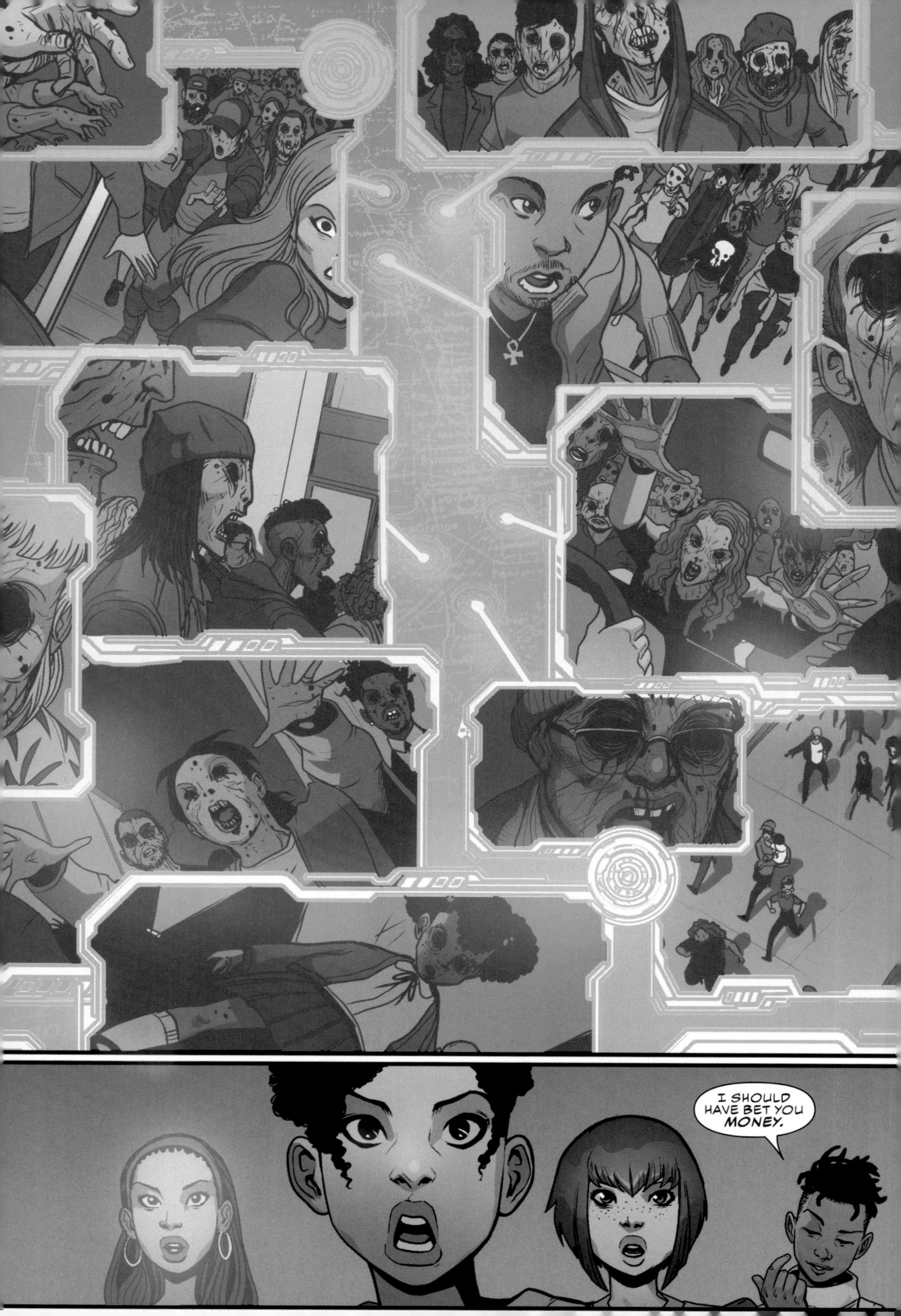
I SHOULD HAVE BET YOU MONEY.

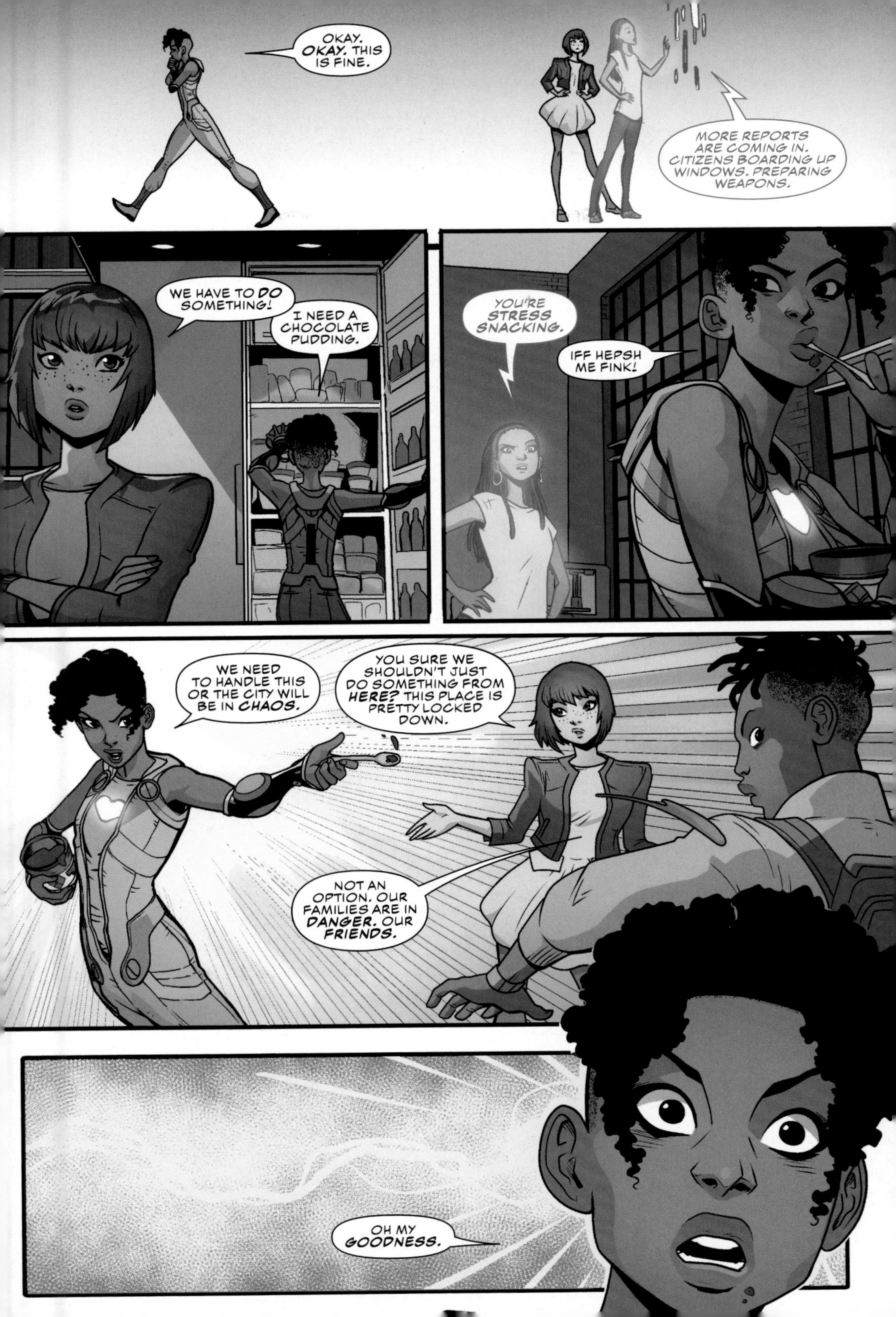
OKAY. OKAY. THIS IS FINE.
MORE REPORTS ARE COMING IN. CITIZENS BOARDING UP WINDOWS. PREPARING WEAPONS.
WE HAVE TO DO SOMETHING!
I NEED A CHOCOLATE PUDDING.
YOU'RE STRESS SNACKING.
IFF HEPSH ME FINK!
WE NEED TO HANDLE THIS OR THE CITY WILL BE IN CHAOS.
YOU SURE WE SHOULDN'T JUST DO SOMETHING FROM HERE? THIS PLACE IS PRETTY LOCKED DOWN.
NOT AN OPTION. OUR FAMILIES ARE IN DANGER. OUR FRIENDS.
OH MY GOODNESS.

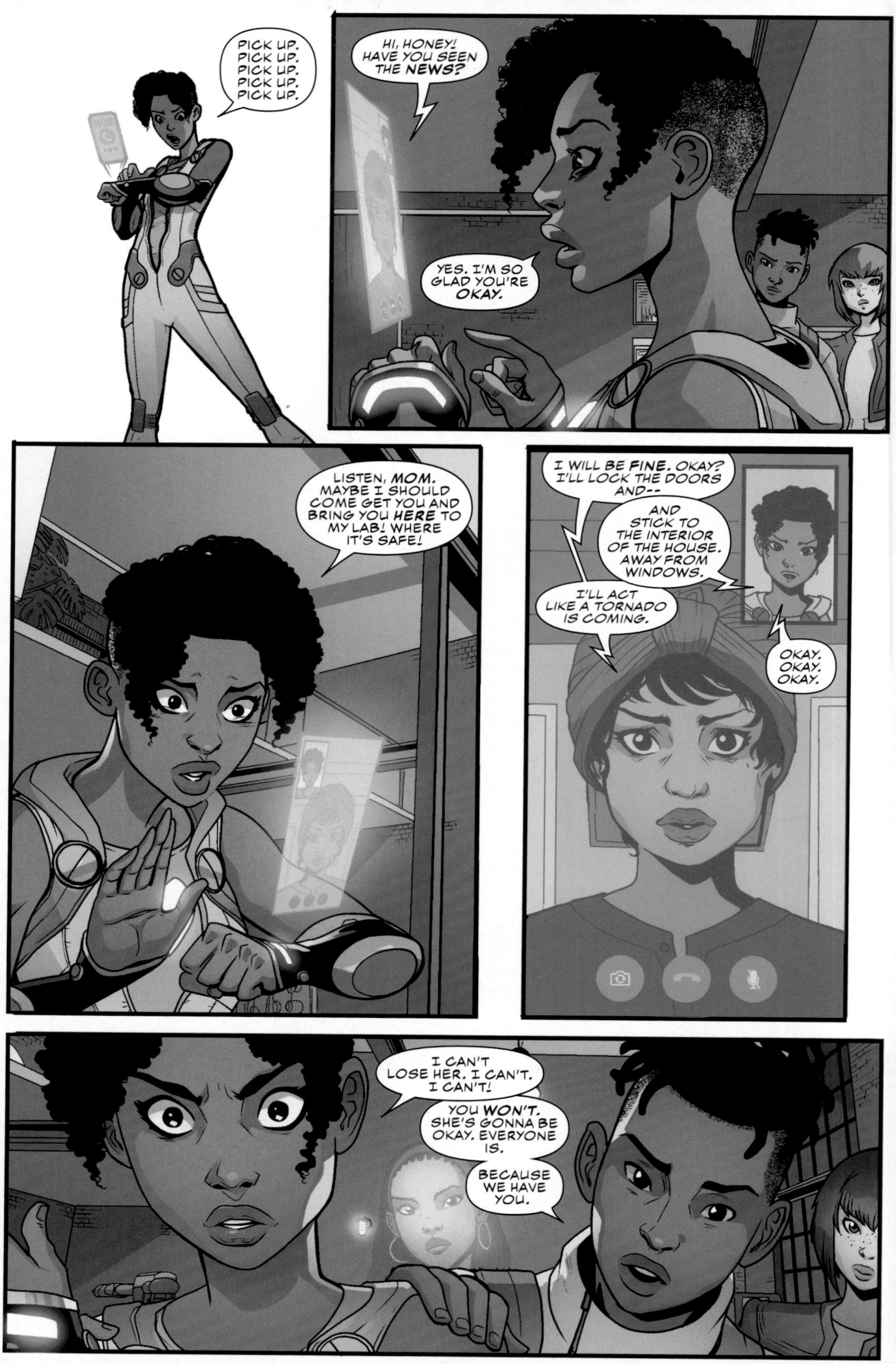
PICK UP. PICK UP. PICK UP. PICK UP. PICK UP.
HI, HONEY! HAVE YOU SEEN THE NEWS?
YES. I'M SO GLAD YOU'RE OKAY.
LISTEN, MOM. MAYBE I SHOULD COME GET YOU AND BRING YOU HERE TO MY LAB! WHERE IT'S SAFE!
I WILL BE FINE. OKAY? I'LL LOCK THE DOORS AND--
AND STICK TO THE INTERIOR OF THE HOUSE. AWAY FROM WINDOWS.
I'LL ACT LIKE A TORNADO IS COMING.
OKAY. OKAY. OKAY.
I CAN'T LOSE HER. I CAN'T. I CAN'T!
YOU WON'T. SHE'S GONNA BE OKAY. EVERYONE IS.
BECAUSE WE HAVE YOU.

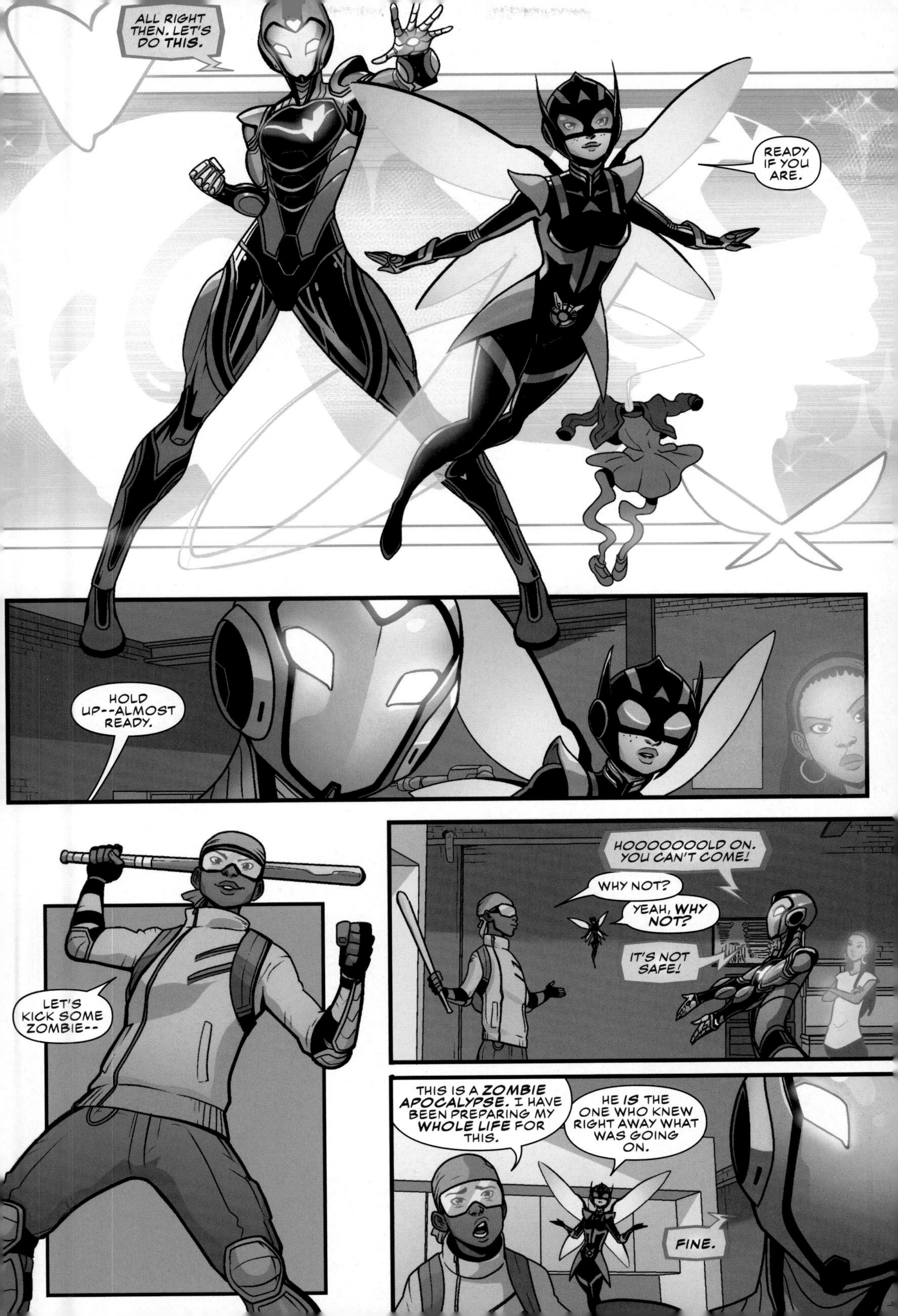
ALL RIGHT THEN. LET'S DO THIS.
READY IF YOU ARE.
HOLD UP--ALMOST READY.
LET'S KICK SOME ZOMBIE--
HOOOOOOOLD ON. YOU CAN'T COME!
WHY NOT?
YEAH, WHY NOT?
IT'S NOT SAFE!
THIS IS A ZOMBIE APOCALYPSE. I HAVE BEEN PREPARING MY WHOLE LIFE FOR THIS.
HE IS THE ONE WHO KNEW RIGHT AWAY WHAT WAS GOING ON.
FINE.

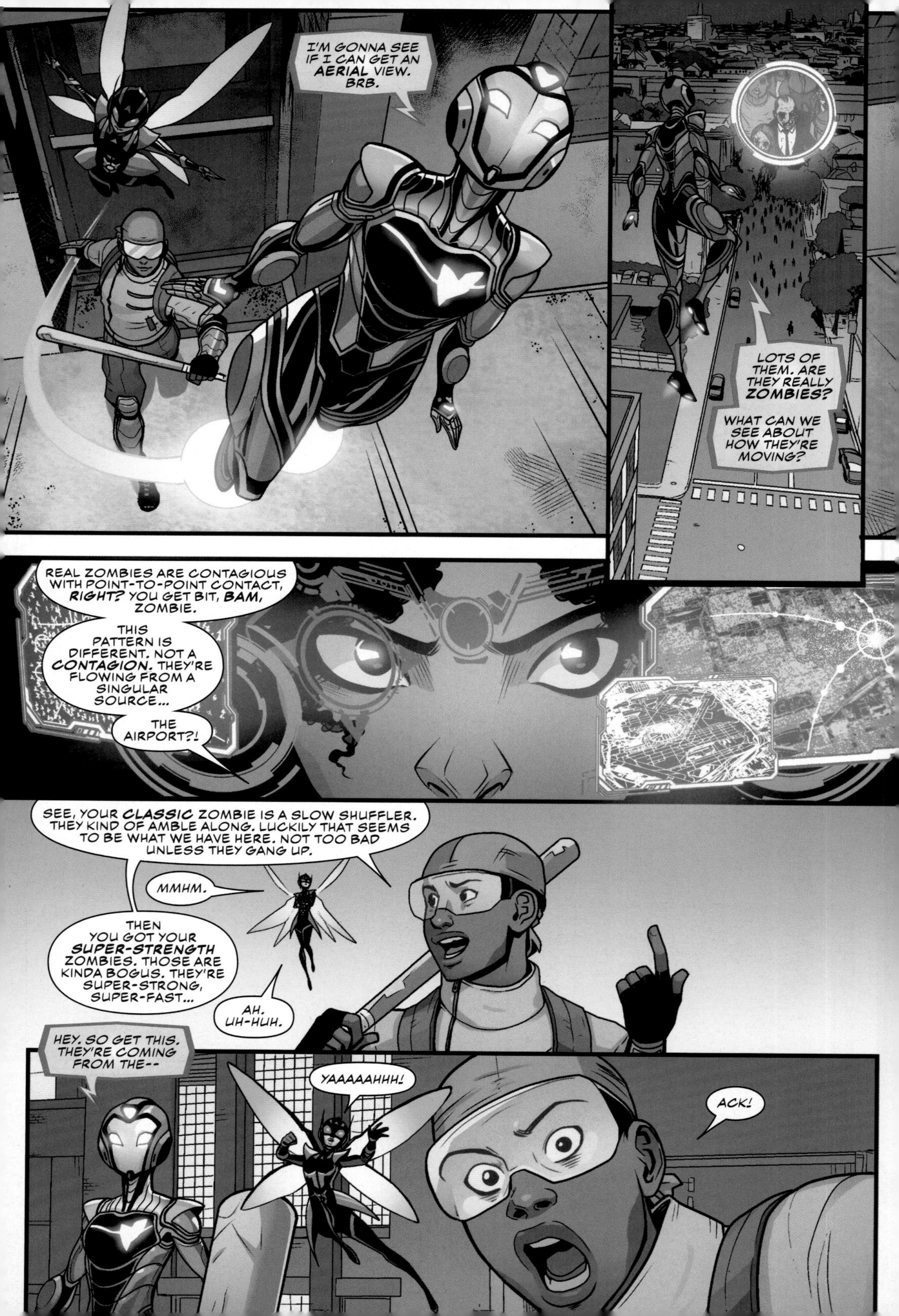
I'M GONNA SEE IF I CAN GET AN AERIAL VIEW. BRB.
LOTS OF THEM. ARE THEY REALLY ZOMBIES?
WHAT CAN WE SEE ABOUT HOW THEY'RE MOVING?
REAL ZOMBIES ARE CONTAGIOUS WITH POINT-TO-POINT CONTACT, RIGHT? YOU GET BIT, BAM, ZOMBIE.
THIS PATTERN IS DIFFERENT. NOT A CONTAGION. THEY'RE FLOWING FROM A SINGULAR SOURCE...
THE AIRPORT?!
SEE, YOUR CLASSIC ZOMBIE IS A SLOW SHUFFLER. THEY KIND OF AMBLE ALONG. LUCKILY THAT SEEMS TO BE WHAT WE HAVE HERE. NOT TOO BAD UNLESS THEY GANG UP.
MMHM.
THEN YOU GOT YOUR SUPER-STRENGTH ZOMBIES. THOSE ARE KINDA BOGUS. THEY'RE SUPER-STRONG, SUPER-FAST...
AH. UH-HUH.
HEY. SO GET THIS. THEY'RE COMING FROM THE--
YAAAAAHHH!
ACK!

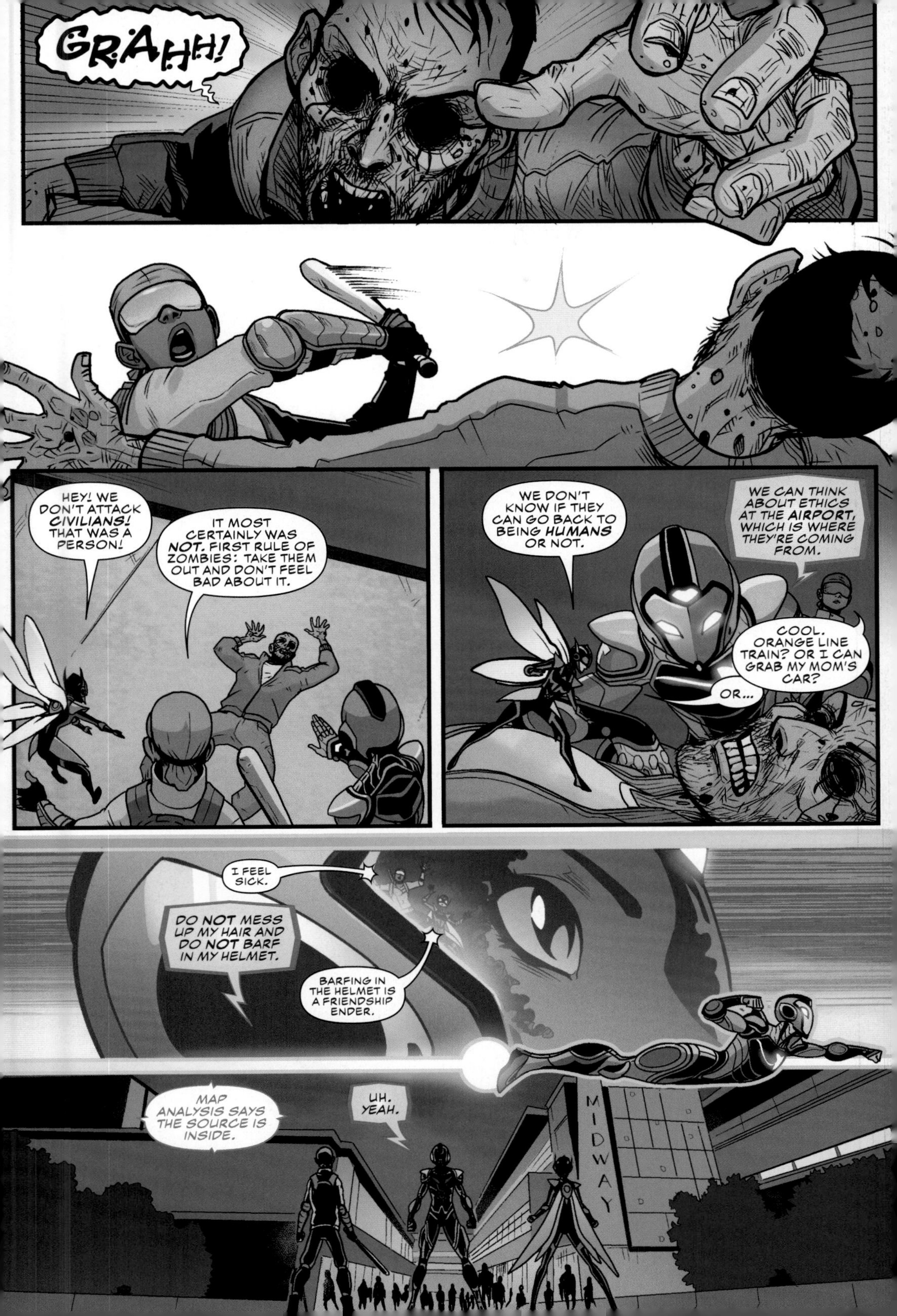
GRAHH!
HEY! WE DON'T ATTACK CIVILIANS! THAT WAS A PERSON!
IT MOST CERTAINLY WAS NOT. FIRST RULE OF ZOMBIES: TAKE THEM OUT AND DON'T FEEL BAD ABOUT IT.
WE DON'T KNOW IF THEY CAN GO BACK TO BEING HUMANS OR NOT.
WE CAN THINK ABOUT ETHICS AT THE AIRPORT, WHICH IS WHERE THEY'RE COMING FROM.
COOL. ORANGE LINE TRAIN? OR I CAN GRAB MY MOM'S CAR?
OR...
I FEEL SICK.
DO NOT MESS UP MY HAIR AND DO NOT BARF IN MY HELMET.
BARFING IN THE HELMET IS A FRIENDSHIP ENDER.
MAP ANALYSIS SAYS THE SOURCE IS INSIDE.
UH. YEAH.
MIDWAY

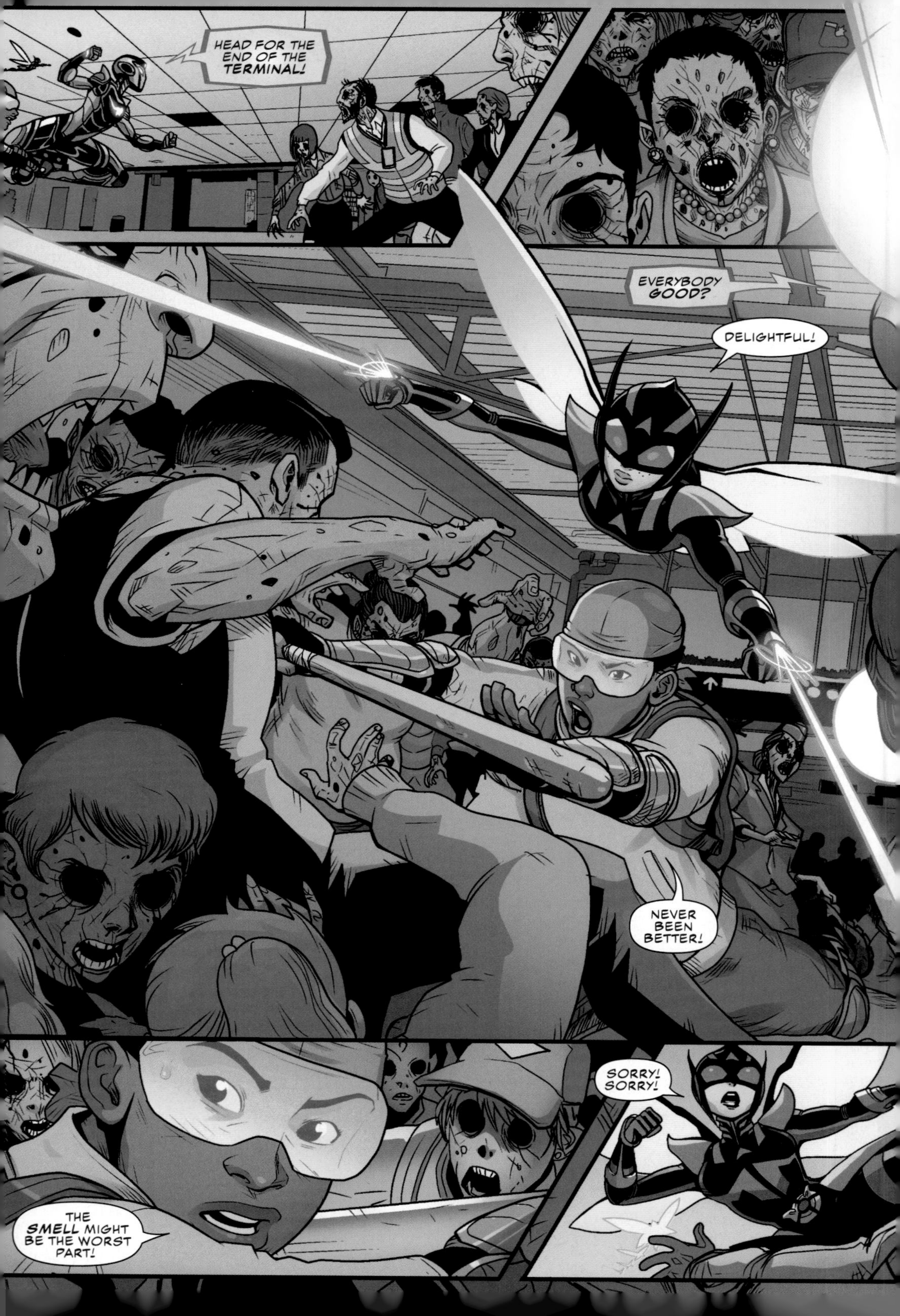
HEAD FOR THE END OF THE TERMINAL!
EVERYBODY GOOD?
DELIGHTFUL!
NEVER BEEN BETTER!
THE SMELL MIGHT BE THE WORST PART!
SORRY! SORRY!

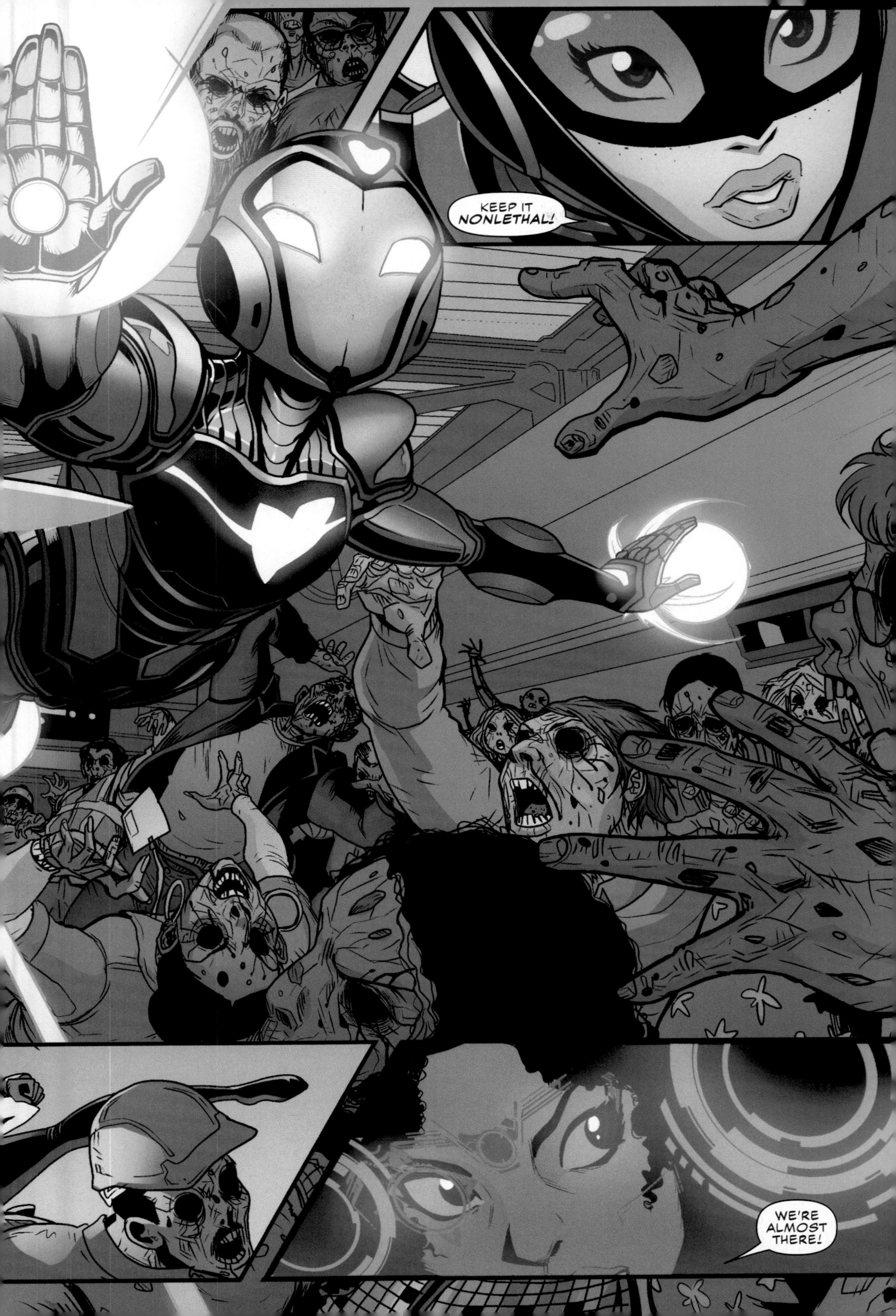
KEEP IT NONLETHAL!
WE'RE ALMOST THERE!

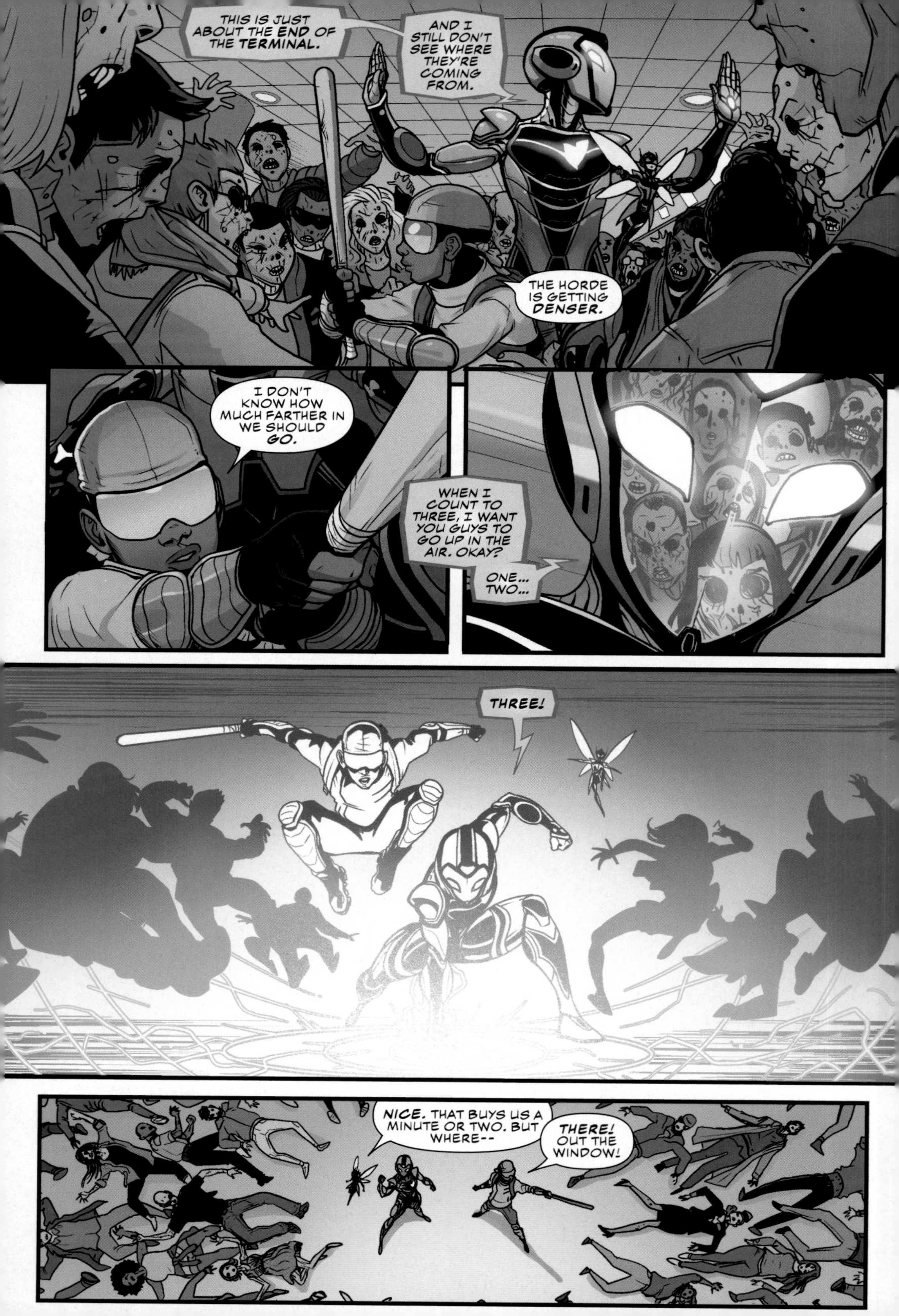
THIS IS JUST ABOUT THE END OF THE TERMINAL.
AND I STILL DON'T SEE WHERE THEY'RE COMING FROM.
THE HORDE IS GETTING DENSER.
I DON'T KNOW HOW MUCH FARTHER IN WE SHOULD GO.
WHEN I COUNT TO THREE, I WANT YOU GUYS TO GO UP IN THE AIR. OKAY?
ONE... TWO...
THREE!
NICE. THAT BUYS US A MINUTE OR TWO. BUT WHERE--
THERE! OUT THE WINDOW!

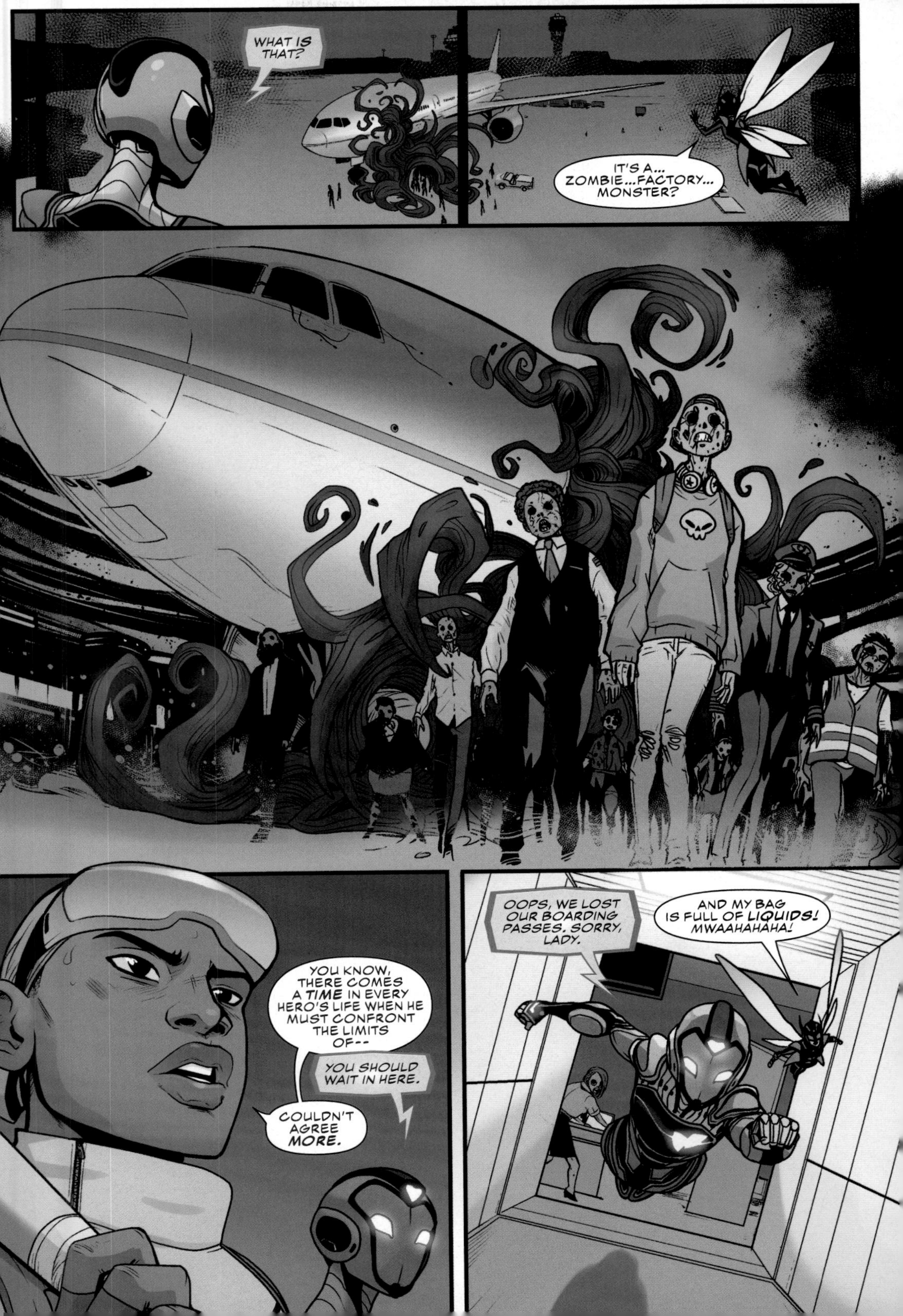
WHAT IS THAT?
IT'S A... ZOMBIE...FACTORY... MONSTER?
YOU KNOW, THERE COMES A TIME IN EVERY HERO'S LIFE WHEN HE MUST CONFRONT THE LIMITS OF--
YOU SHOULD WAIT IN HERE.
COULDN'T AGREE MORE.
OOPS, WE LOST OUR BOARDING PASSES. SORRY, LADY.
AND MY BAG IS FULL OF LIQUIDS! MWAAHAHAHA!

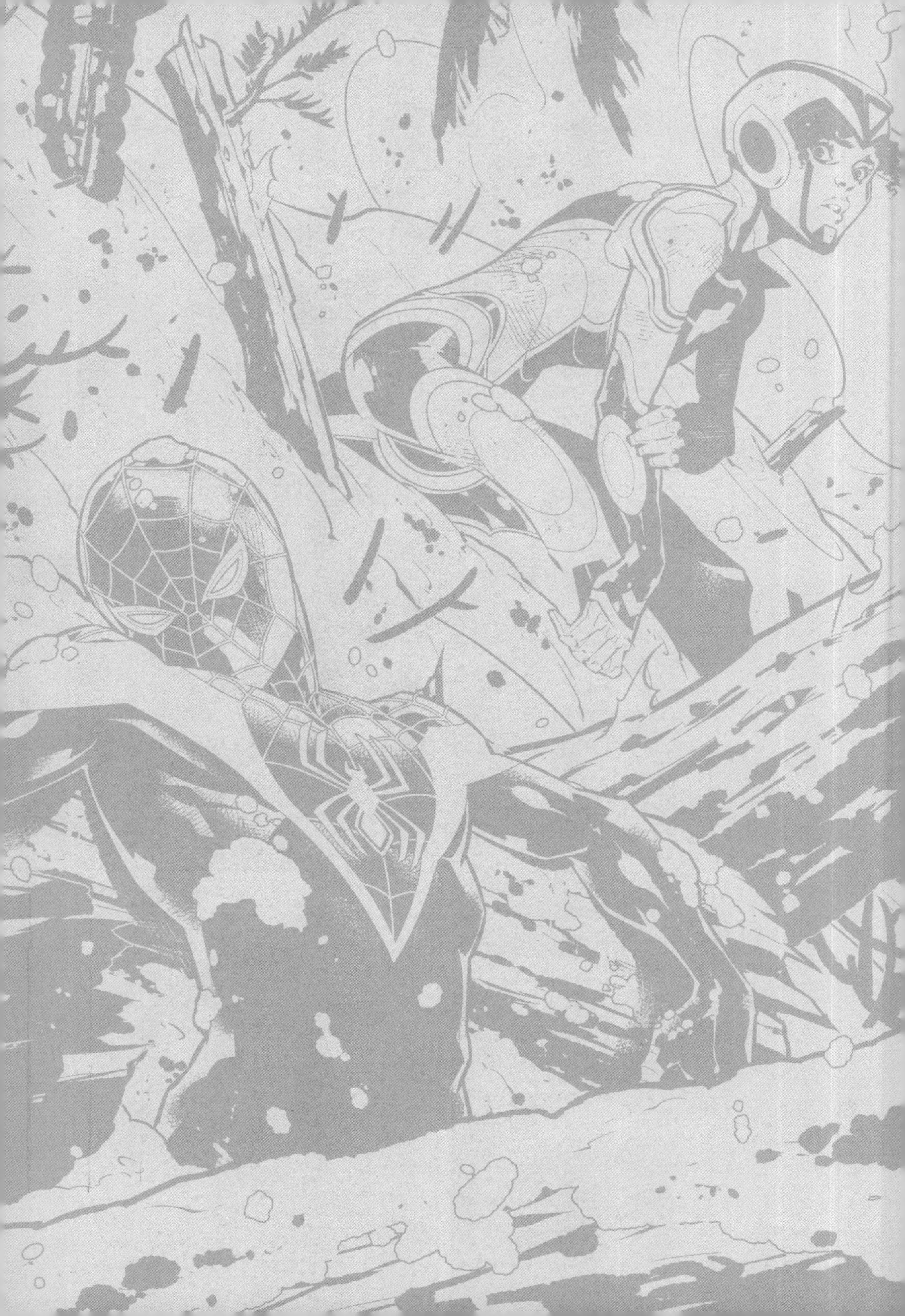

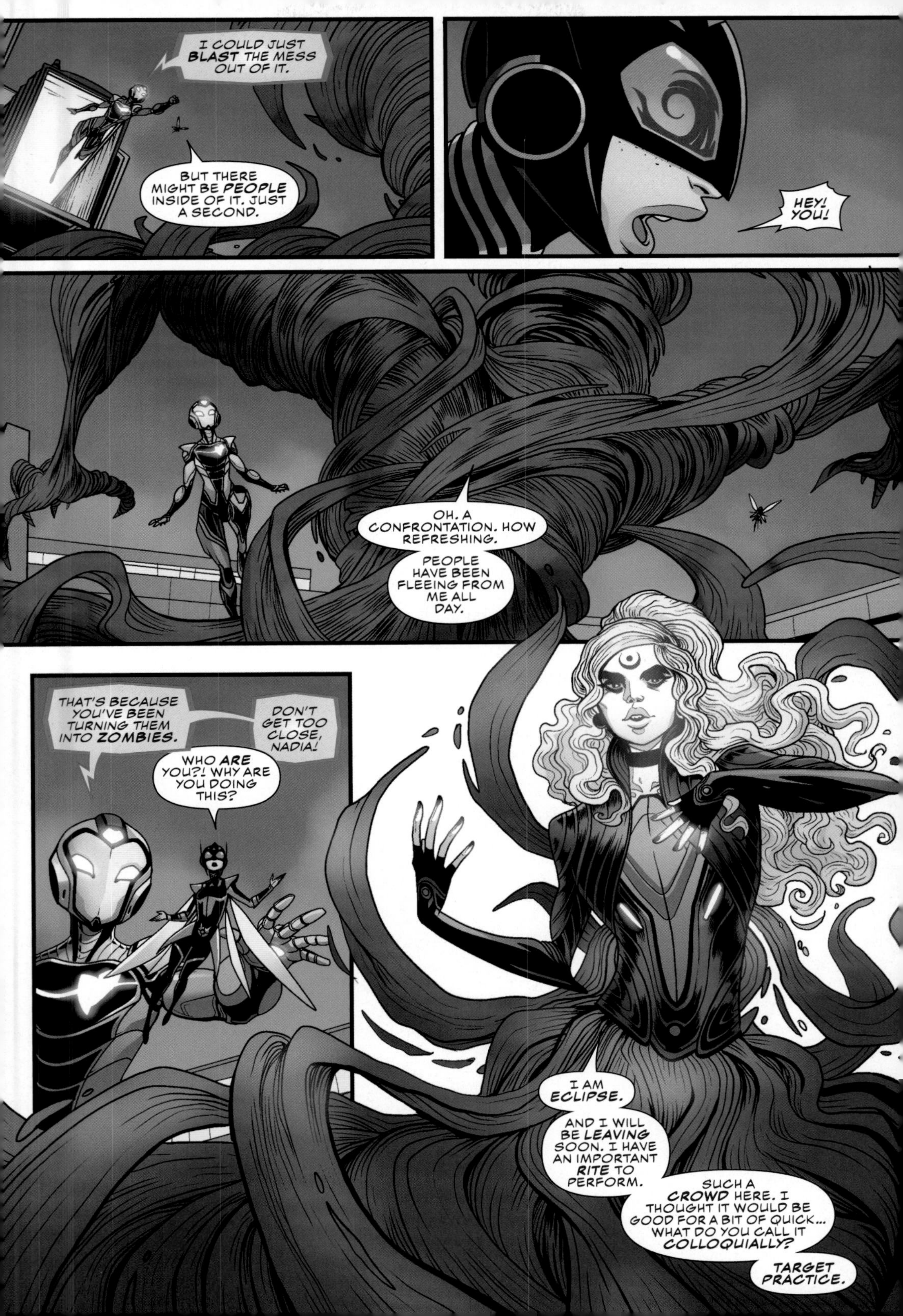
I COULD JUST BLAST THE MESS OUT OF IT.
BUT THERE MIGHT BE PEOPLE INSIDE OF IT. JUST A SECOND.
HEY! YOU!
OH. A CONFRONTATION. HOW REFRESHING.
PEOPLE HAVE BEEN FLEEING FROM ME ALL DAY.
THAT'S BECAUSE YOU'VE BEEN TURNING THEM INTO ZOMBIES.
DON'T GET TOO CLOSE, NADIA!
WHO ARE YOU?! WHY ARE YOU DOING THIS?
I AM ECLIPSE.
AND I WILL BE LEAVING SOON. I HAVE AN IMPORTANT RITE TO PERFORM.
SUCH A CROWD HERE. I THOUGHT IT WOULD BE GOOD FOR A BIT OF QUICK... WHAT DO YOU CALL IT COLLOQUIALLY?
TARGET PRACTICE.

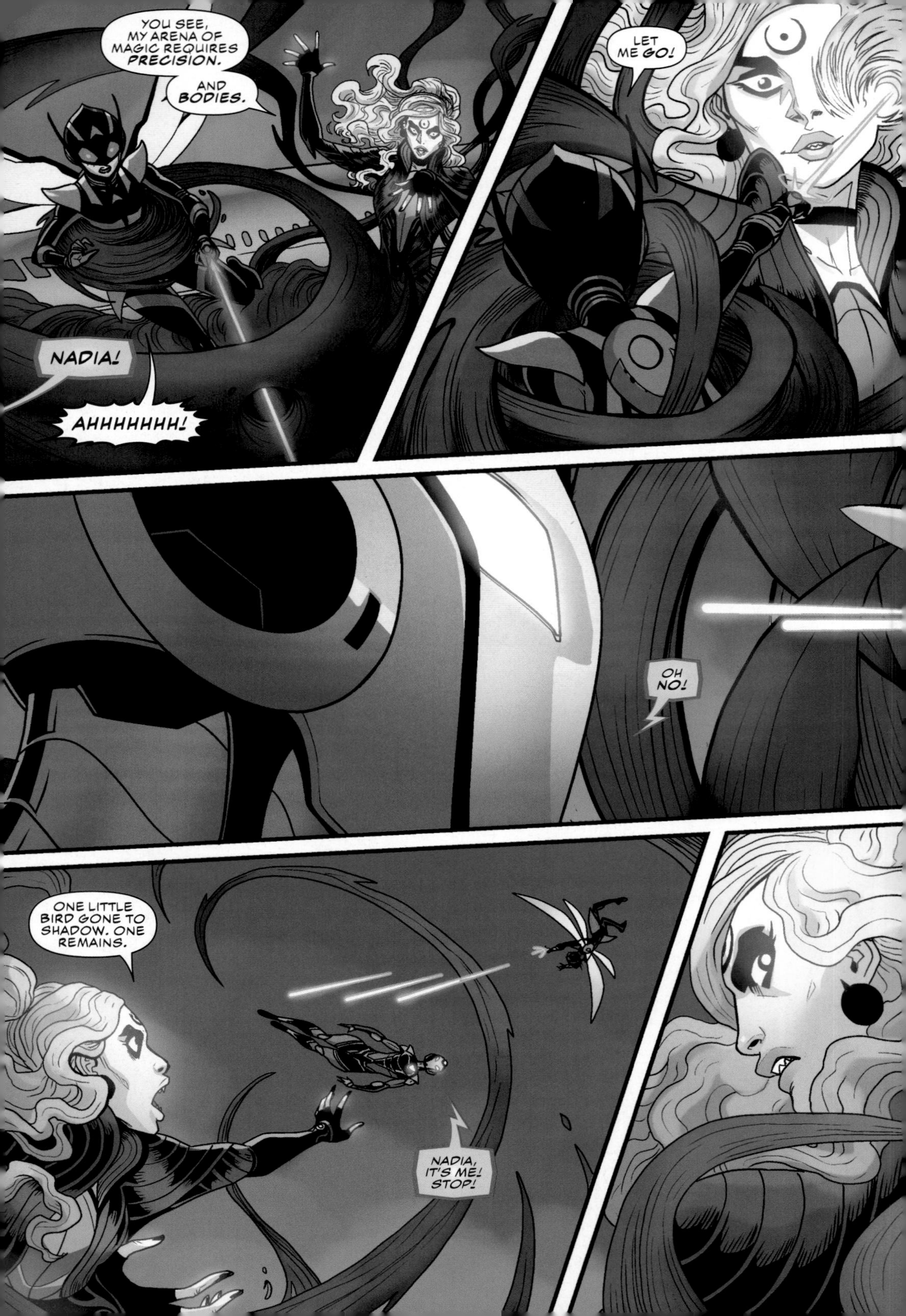
YOU SEE, MY ARENA OF MAGIC REQUIRES PRECISION.
AND BODIES.
LET ME GO!
NADIA!
AHHHHHHH!
OH NO!
ONE LITTLE BIRD GONE TO SHADOW. ONE REMAINS.
NADIA, IT'S ME! STOP!

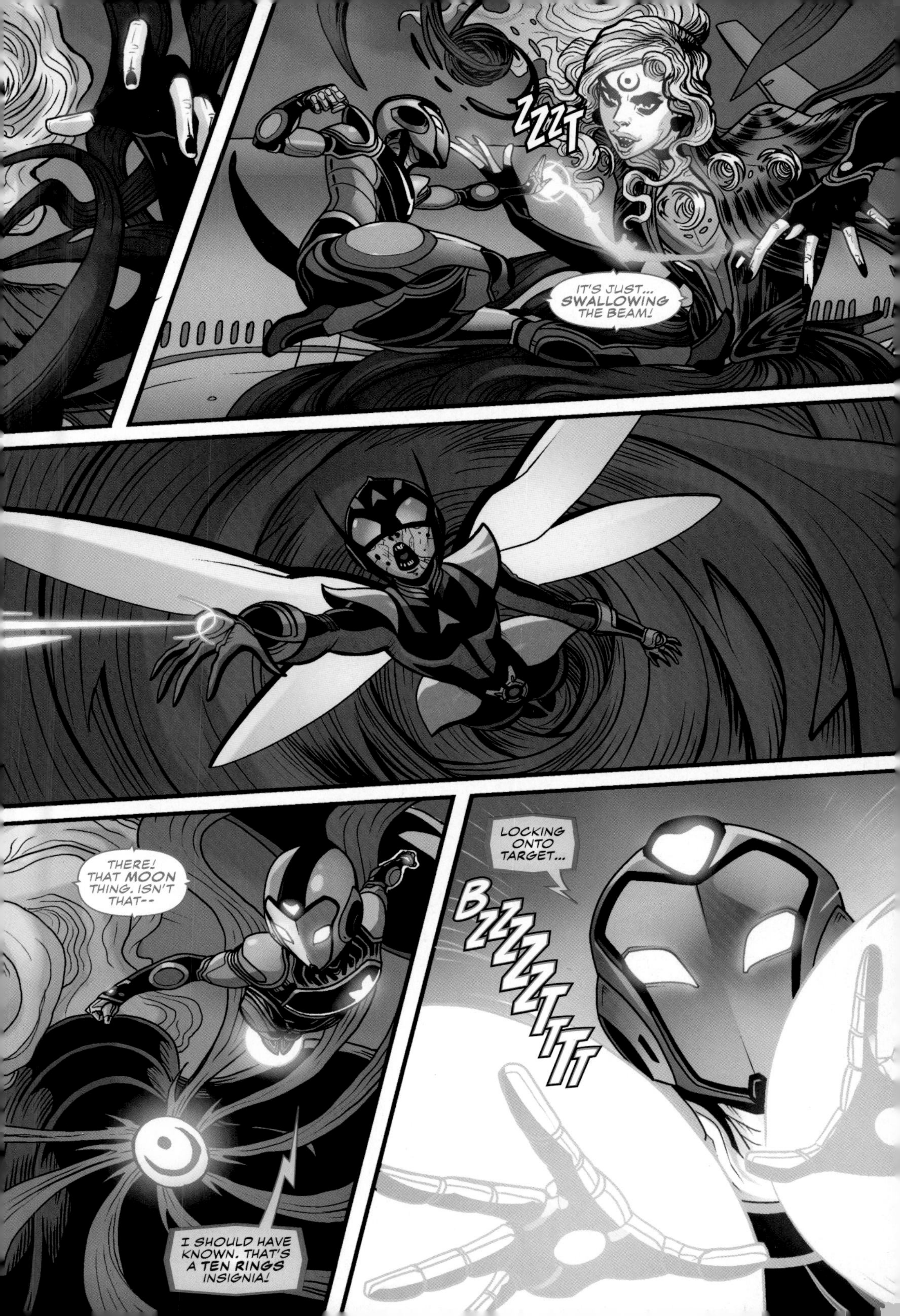
ZZZT
IT'S JUST... SWALLOWING THE BEAM!
THERE! THAT MOON THING. ISN'T THAT--
I SHOULD HAVE KNOWN. THAT'S A TEN RINGS INSIGNIA!
LOCKING ONTO TARGET...
BZZZZZTTTTT

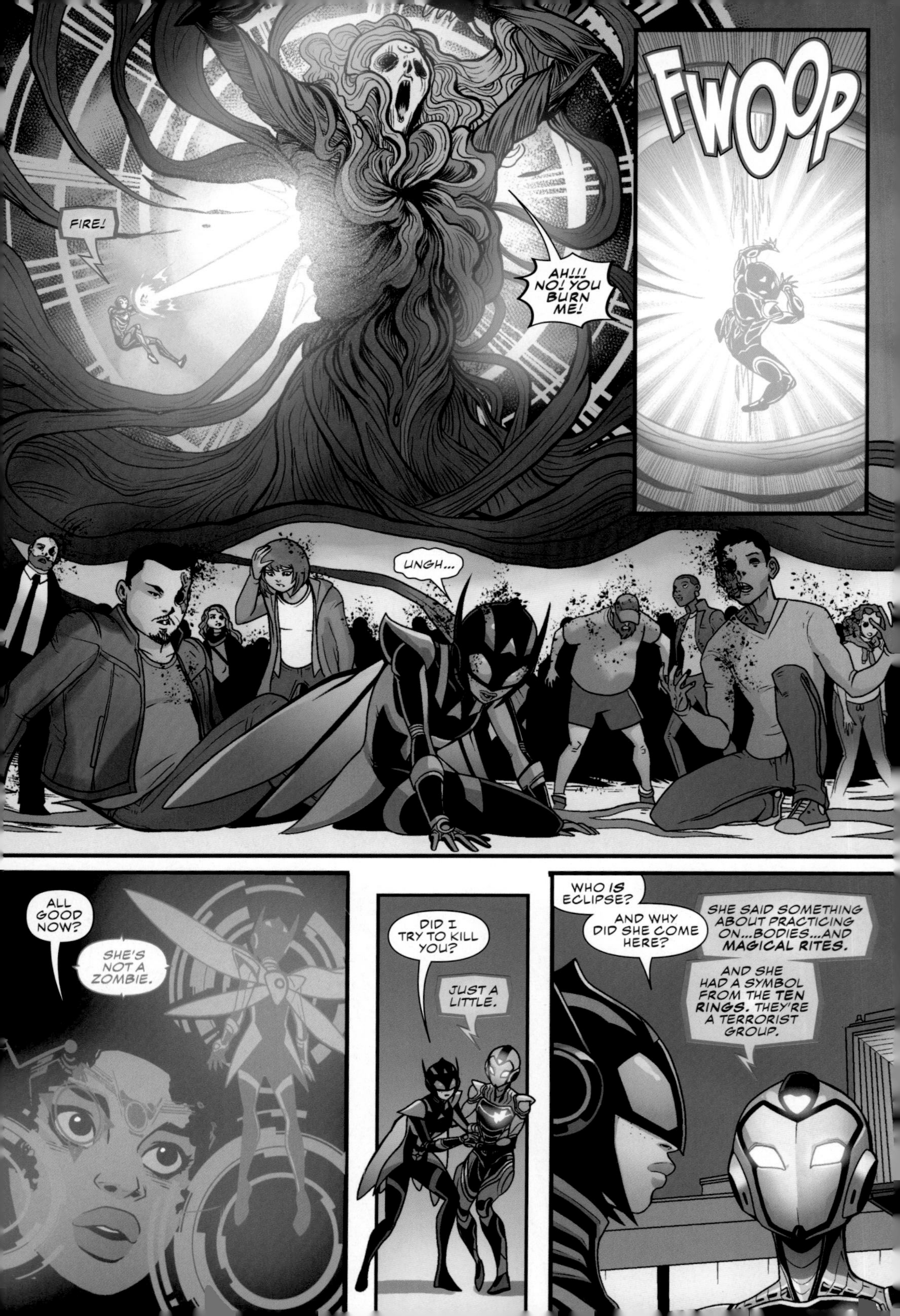
FIRE!
AH!!! NO! YOU BURN ME!
FWOOP
UNGH...
ALL GOOD NOW?
SHE'S NOT A ZOMBIE.
DID I TRY TO KILL YOU?
JUST A LITTLE.
WHO IS ECLIPSE?
AND WHY DID SHE COME HERE?
SHE SAID SOMETHING ABOUT PRACTICING ON...BODIES...AND MAGICAL RITES.
AND SHE HAD A SYMBOL FROM THE TEN RINGS. THEY'RE A TERRORIST GROUP.

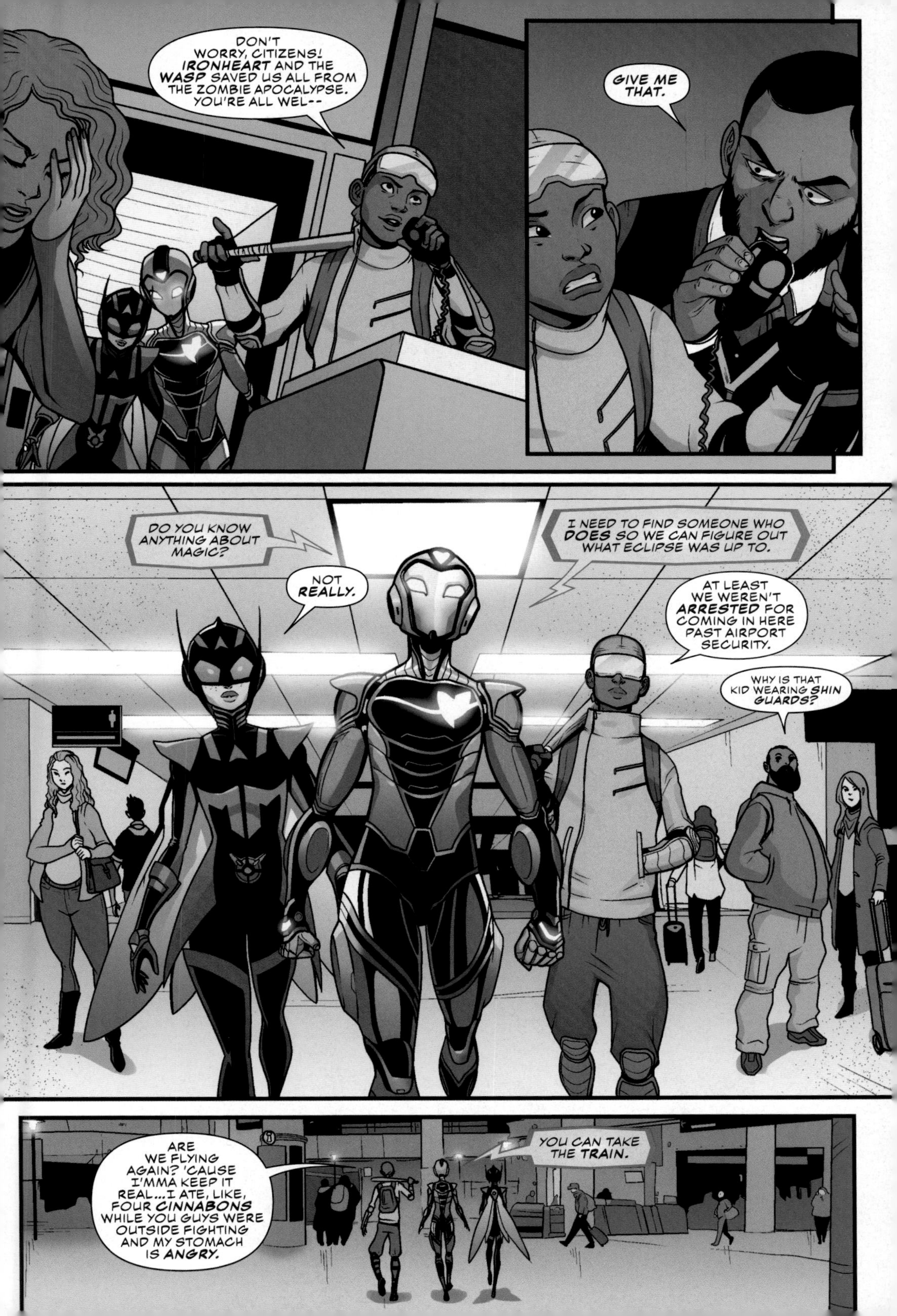
DON'T WORRY, CITIZENS! IRONHEART AND THE WASP SAVED US ALL FROM THE ZOMBIE APOCALYPSE. YOU'RE ALL WEL--
GIVE ME THAT.
DO YOU KNOW ANYTHING ABOUT MAGIC?
NOT REALLY.
I NEED TO FIND SOMEONE WHO DOES SO WE CAN FIGURE OUT WHAT ECLIPSE WAS UP TO.
AT LEAST WE WEREN'T ARRESTED FOR COMING IN HERE PAST AIRPORT SECURITY.
WHY IS THAT KID WEARING SHIN GUARDS?
ARE WE FLYING AGAIN? 'CAUSE I'MMA KEEP IT REAL...I ATE, LIKE, FOUR CINNABONS WHILE YOU GUYS WERE OUTSIDE FIGHTING AND MY STOMACH IS ANGRY.
YOU CAN TAKE THE TRAIN.

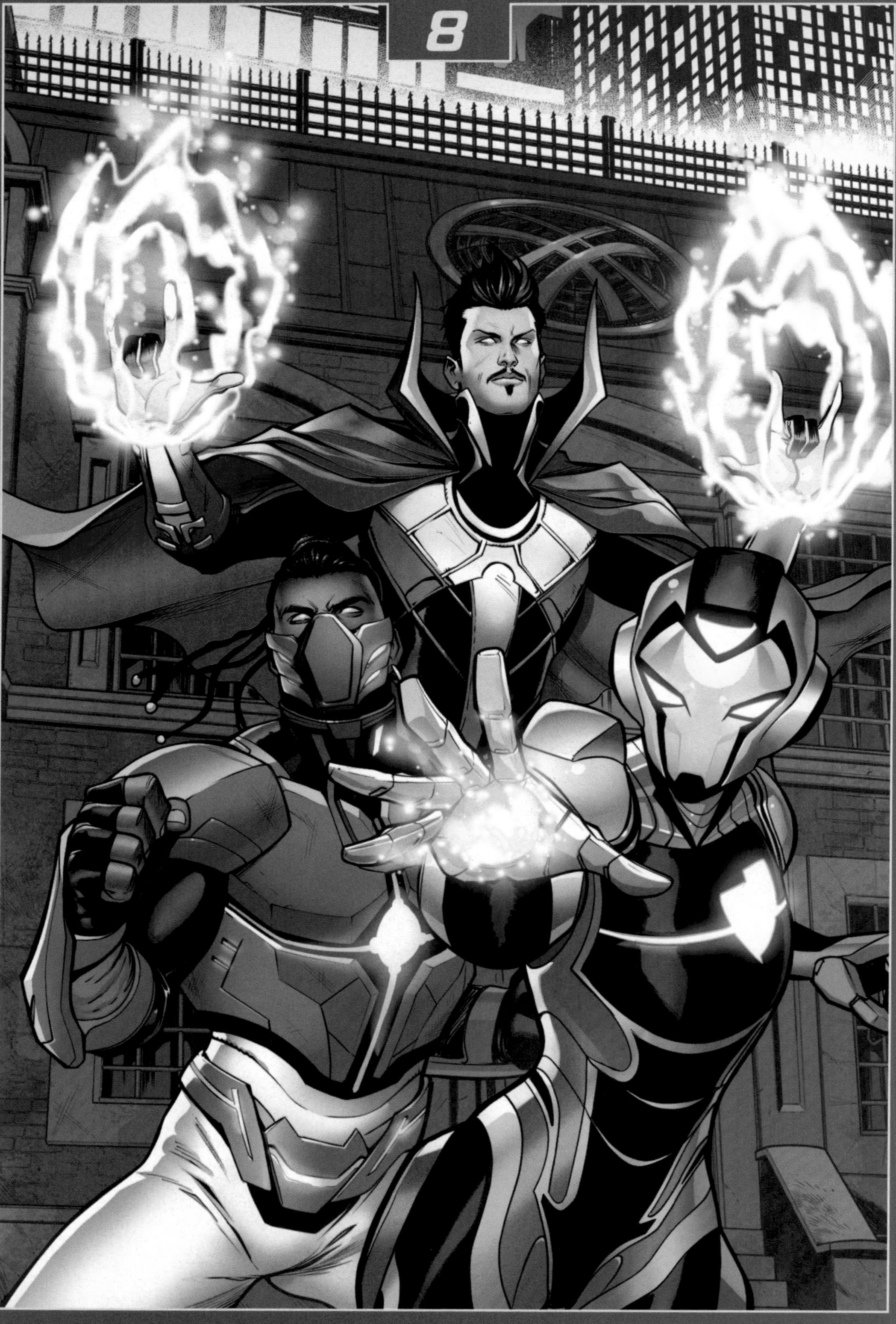
8

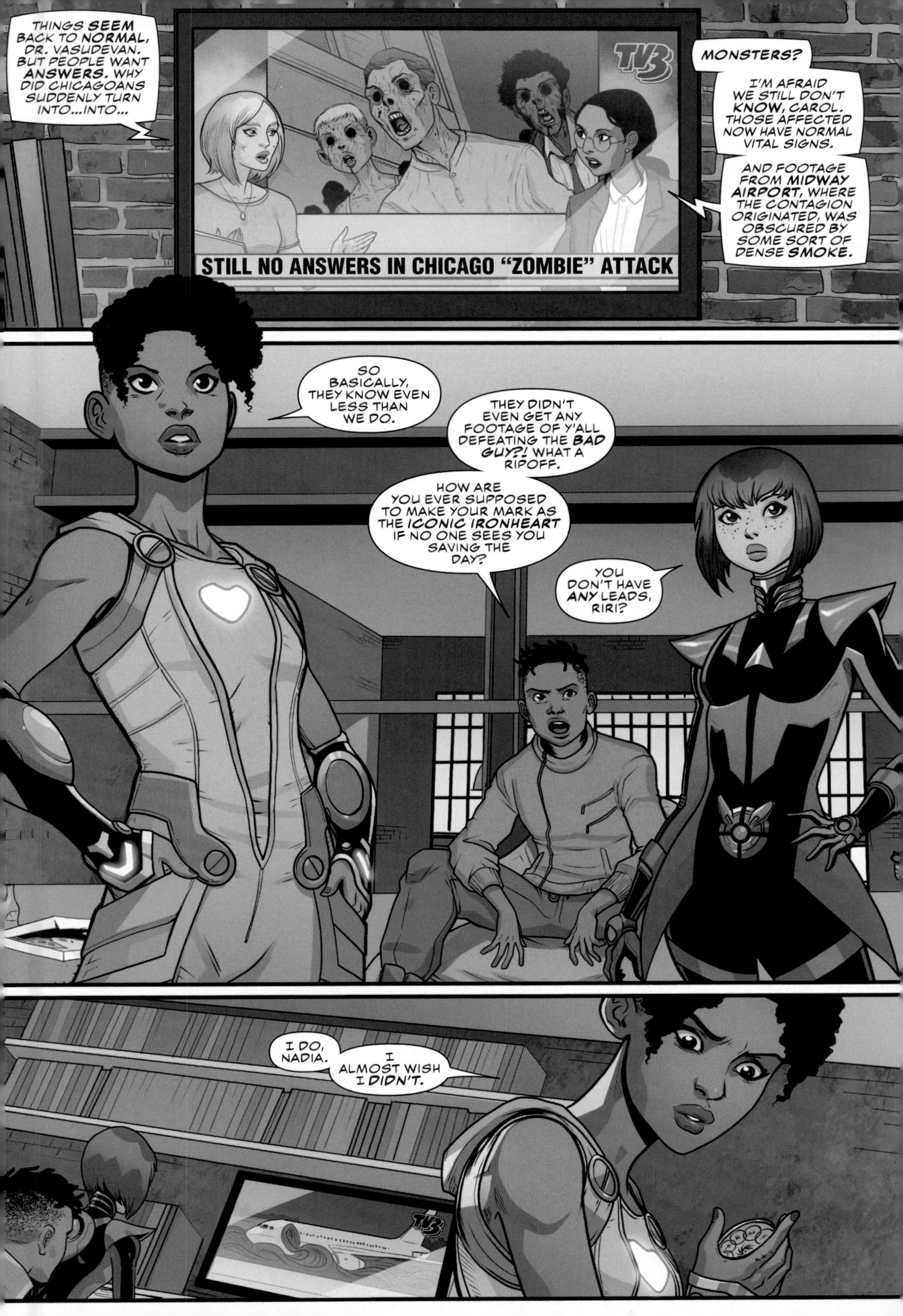
THINGS SEEM BACK TO NORMAL, DR. VASUDEVAN. BUT PEOPLE WANT ANSWERS. WHY DID CHICAGOANS SUDDENLY TURN INTO...INTO...
TV3
STILL NO ANSWERS IN CHICAGO "ZOMBIE" ATTACK
MONSTERS?
I'M AFRAID WE STILL DON'T KNOW, CAROL. THOSE AFFECTED NOW HAVE NORMAL VITAL SIGNS.
AND FOOTAGE FROM MIDWAY AIRPORT, WHERE THE CONTAGION ORIGINATED, WAS OBSCURED BY SOME SORT OF DENSE SMOKE.
SO BASICALLY, THEY KNOW EVEN LESS THAN WE DO.
THEY DIDN'T EVEN GET ANY FOOTAGE OF Y'ALL DEFEATING THE BAD GUY?! WHAT A RIPOFF.
HOW ARE YOU EVER SUPPOSED TO MAKE YOUR MARK AS THE ICONIC IRONHEART IF NO ONE SEES YOU SAVING THE DAY?
YOU DON'T HAVE ANY LEADS, RIRI?
I DO, NADIA.
I ALMOST WISH I DIDN'T.
TV3

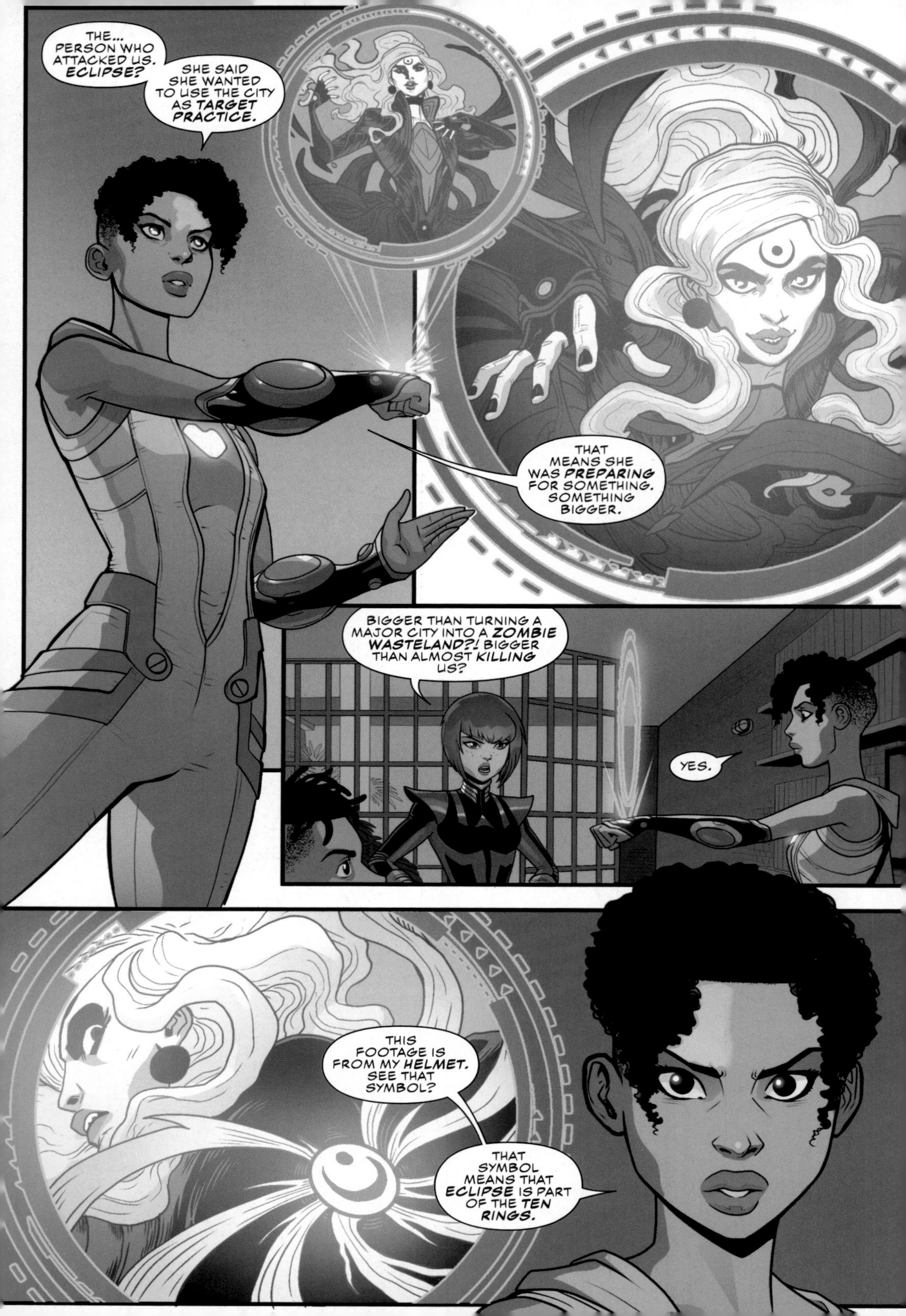
THE... PERSON WHO ATTACKED US. ECLIPSE?
SHE SAID SHE WANTED TO USE THE CITY AS TARGET PRACTICE.
THAT MEANS SHE WAS PREPARING FOR SOMETHING. SOMETHING BIGGER.
BIGGER THAN TURNING A MAJOR CITY INTO A ZOMBIE WASTELAND?! BIGGER THAN ALMOST KILLING US?
YES.
THIS FOOTAGE IS FROM MY HELMET. SEE THAT SYMBOL?
THAT SYMBOL MEANS THAT ECLIPSE IS PART OF THE TEN RINGS.

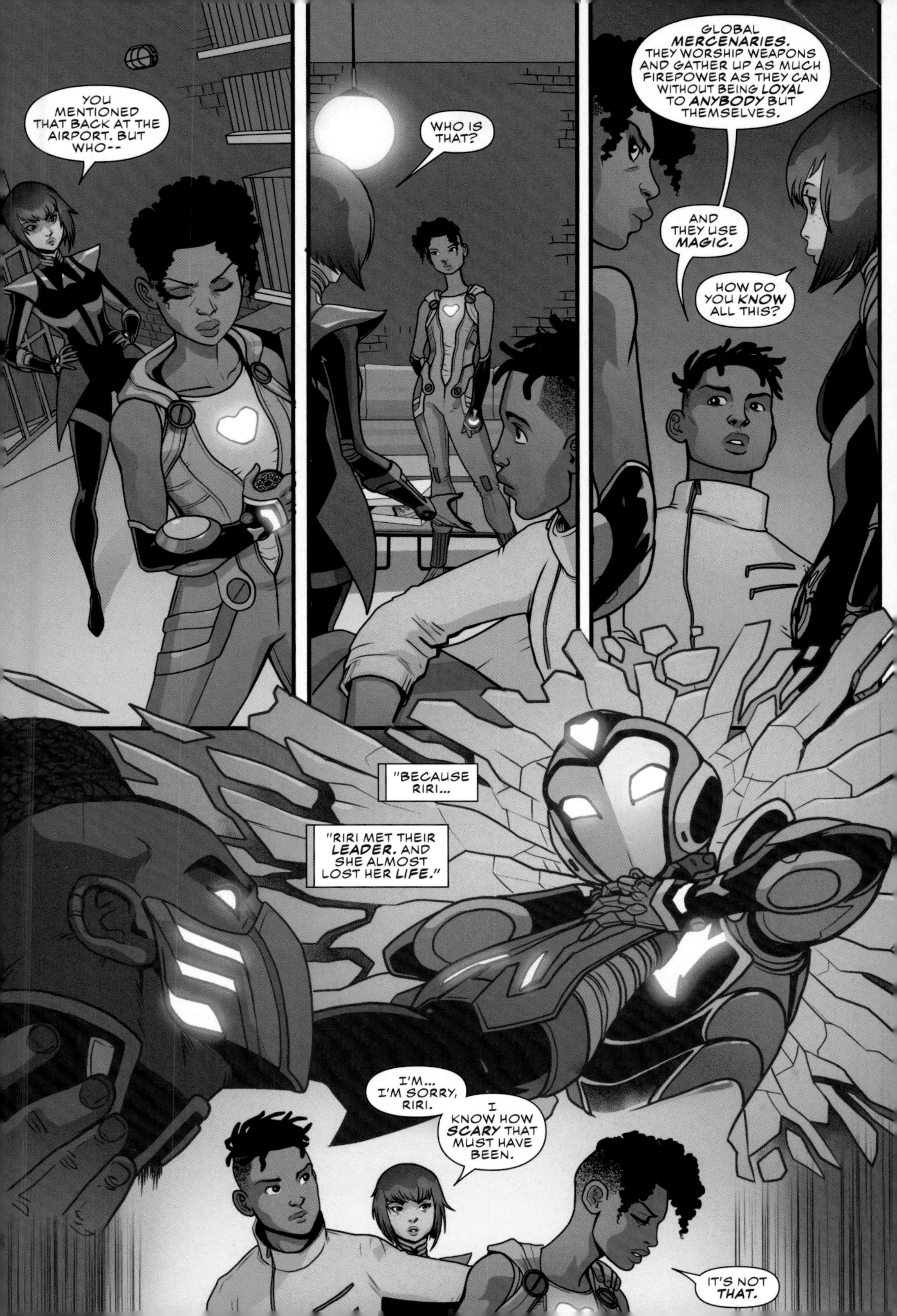

YOU MENTIONED THAT BACK AT THE AIRPORT. BUT WHO--
WHO IS THAT?
GLOBAL MERCENARIES. THEY WORSHIP WEAPONS AND GATHER UP AS MUCH FIREPOWER AS THEY CAN WITHOUT BEING LOYAL TO ANYBODY BUT THEMSELVES.
AND THEY USE MAGIC.
HOW DO YOU KNOW ALL THIS?
"BECAUSE RIRI...
"RIRI MET THEIR LEADER. AND SHE ALMOST LOST HER LIFE."
I'M... I'M SORRY, RIRI.
I KNOW HOW SCARY THAT MUST HAVE BEEN.
IT'S NOT THAT.

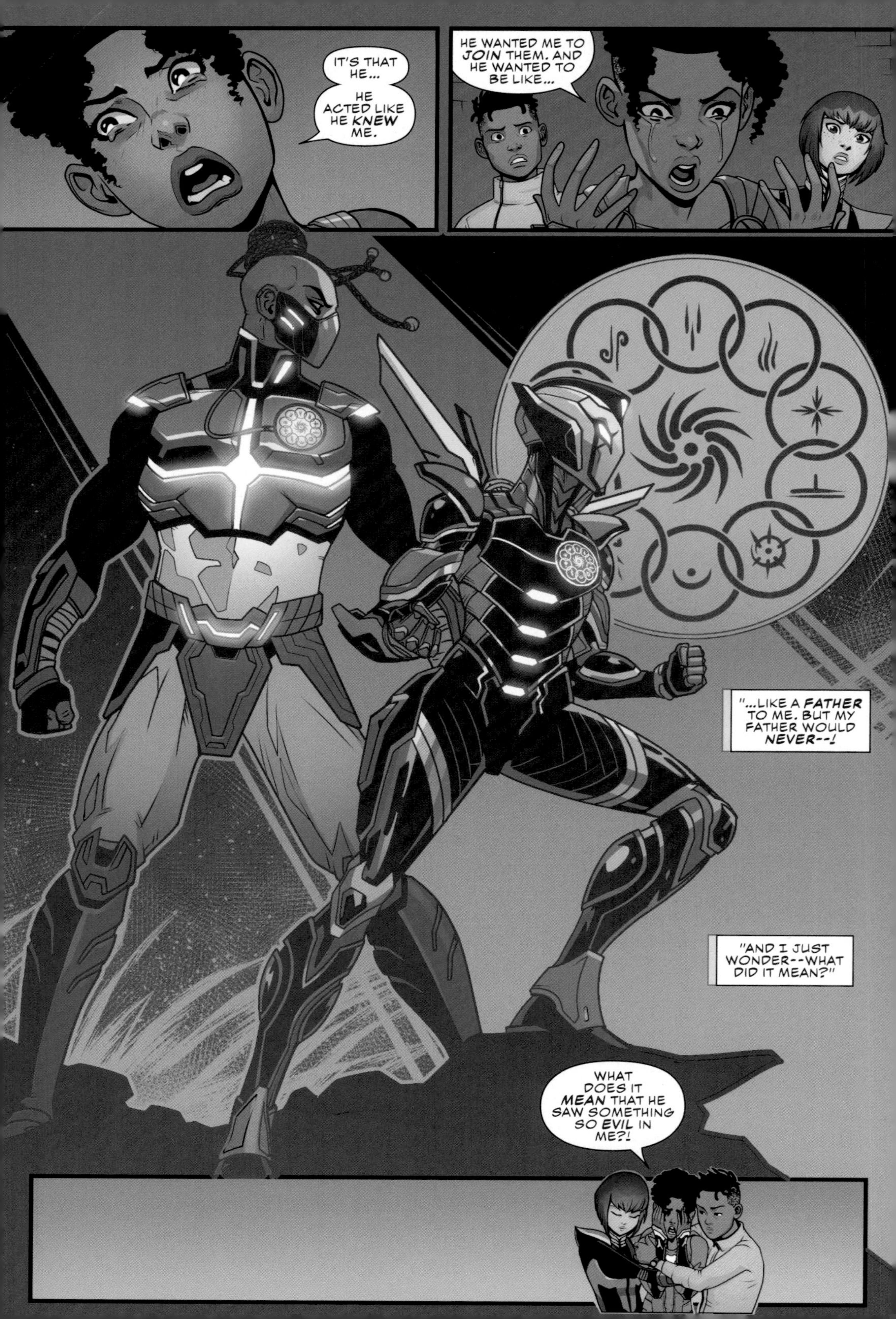

IT'S THAT HE...
HE ACTED LIKE HE KNEW ME.
HE WANTED ME TO JOIN THEM. AND HE WANTED TO BE LIKE...
"...LIKE A FATHER TO ME. BUT MY FATHER WOULD NEVER--!
"AND I JUST WONDER--WHAT DID IT MEAN?"
WHAT DOES IT MEAN THAT HE SAW SOMETHING SO EVIL IN ME?!

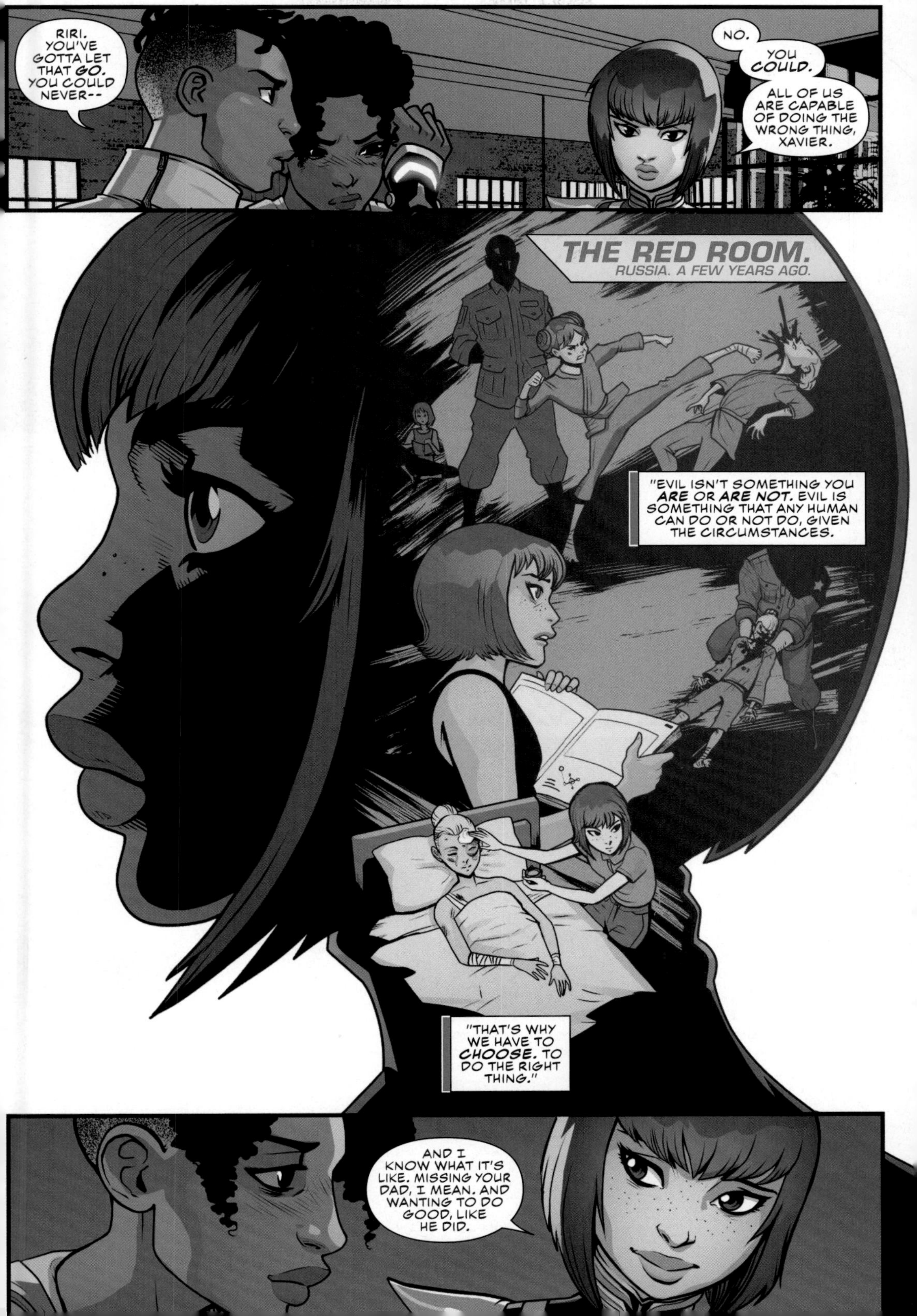
RIRI. YOU'VE GOTTA LET THAT GO. YOU COULD NEVER--
NO.
YOU COULD.
ALL OF US ARE CAPABLE OF DOING THE WRONG THING, XAVIER.
THE RED ROOM.
RUSSIA. A FEW YEARS AGO.
"EVIL ISN'T SOMETHING YOU ARE OR ARE NOT. EVIL IS SOMETHING THAT ANY HUMAN CAN DO OR NOT DO, GIVEN THE CIRCUMSTANCES.
"THAT'S WHY WE HAVE TO CHOOSE. TO DO THE RIGHT THING."
AND I KNOW WHAT IT'S LIKE. MISSING YOUR DAD, I MEAN. AND WANTING TO DO GOOD, LIKE HE DID.

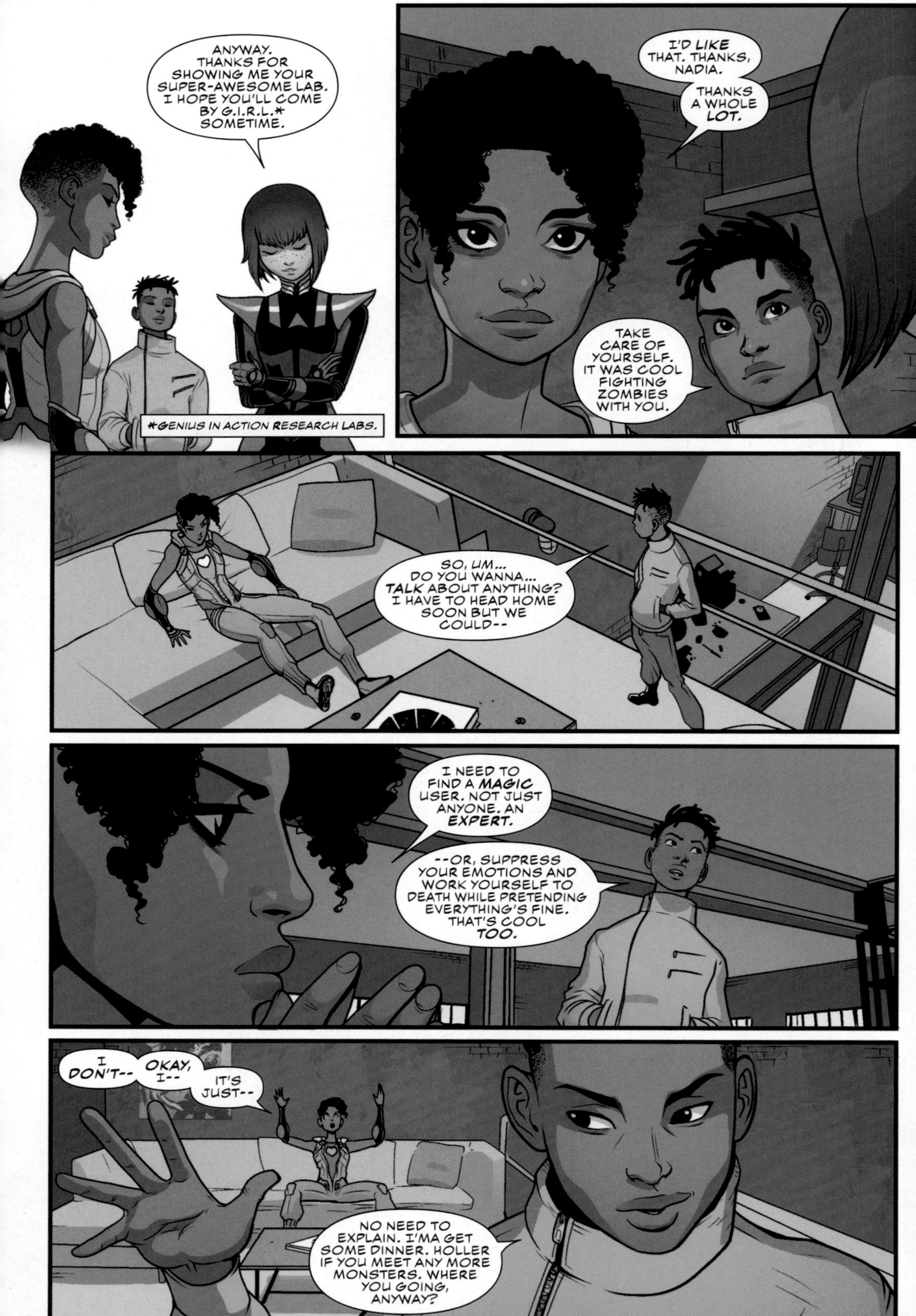
ANYWAY. THANKS FOR SHOWING ME YOUR SUPER-AWESOME LAB. I HOPE YOU'LL COME BY G.I.R.L.* SOMETIME.
*GENIUS IN ACTION RESEARCH LABS.
I'D LIKE THAT. THANKS, NADIA.
THANKS A WHOLE LOT.
TAKE CARE OF YOURSELF. IT WAS COOL FIGHTING ZOMBIES WITH YOU.
SO, UM... DO YOU WANNA... TALK ABOUT ANYTHING? I HAVE TO HEAD HOME SOON BUT WE COULD--
I NEED TO FIND A MAGIC USER. NOT JUST ANYONE. AN EXPERT.
--OR, SUPPRESS YOUR EMOTIONS AND WORK YOURSELF TO DEATH WHILE PRETENDING EVERYTHING'S FINE. THAT'S COOL TOO.
I DON'T-- OKAY, I-- IT'S JUST--
NO NEED TO EXPLAIN. I'MA GET SOME DINNER. HOLLER IF YOU MEET ANY MORE MONSTERS. WHERE YOU GOING, ANYWAY?

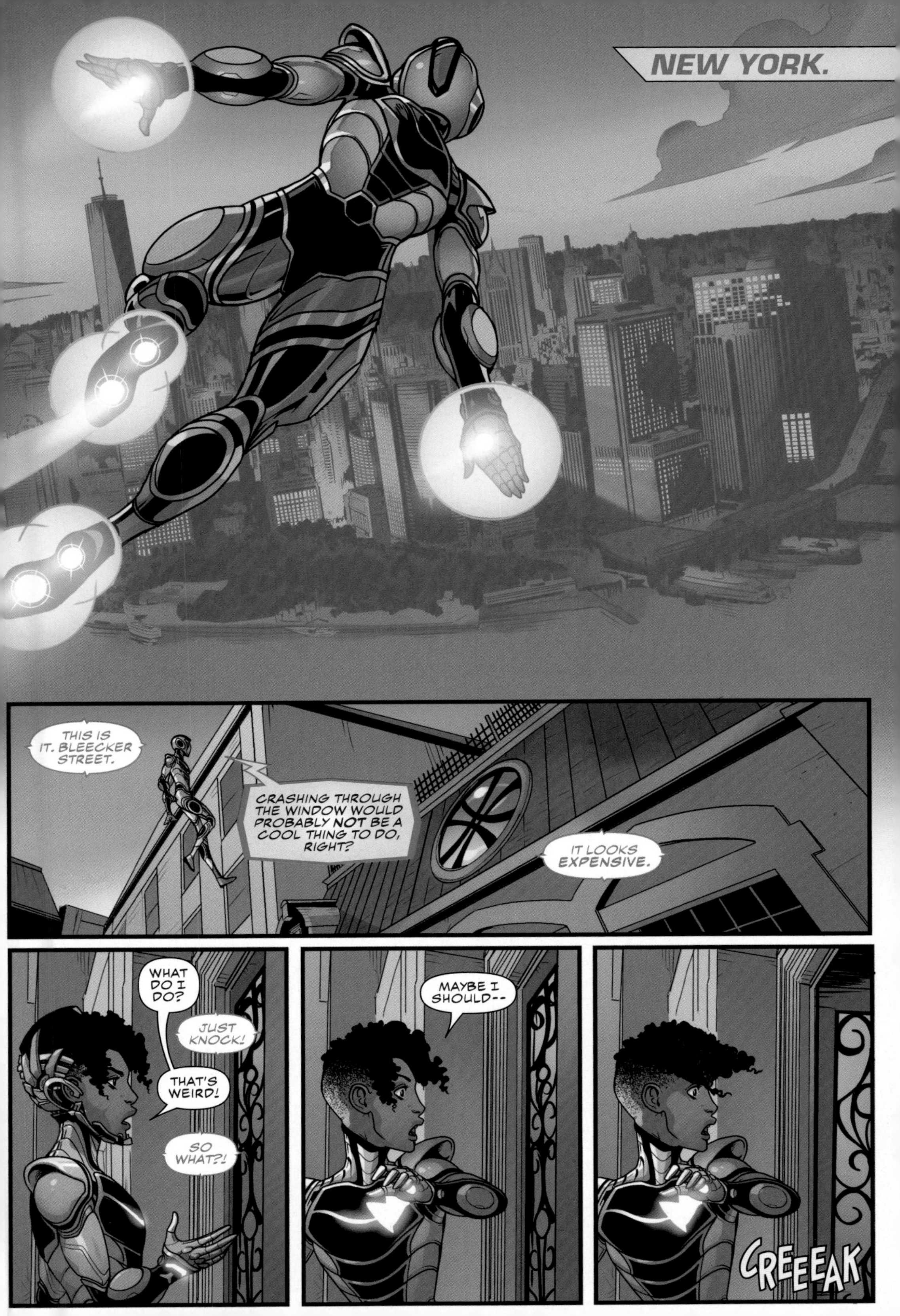
NEW YORK.
THIS IS IT. BLEECKER STREET.
CRASHING THROUGH THE WINDOW WOULD PROBABLY NOT BE A COOL THING TO DO, RIGHT?
IT LOOKS EXPENSIVE.
WHAT DO I DO?
JUST KNOCK!
THAT'S WEIRD!
SO WHAT?!
MAYBE I SHOULD--
CREEEAK

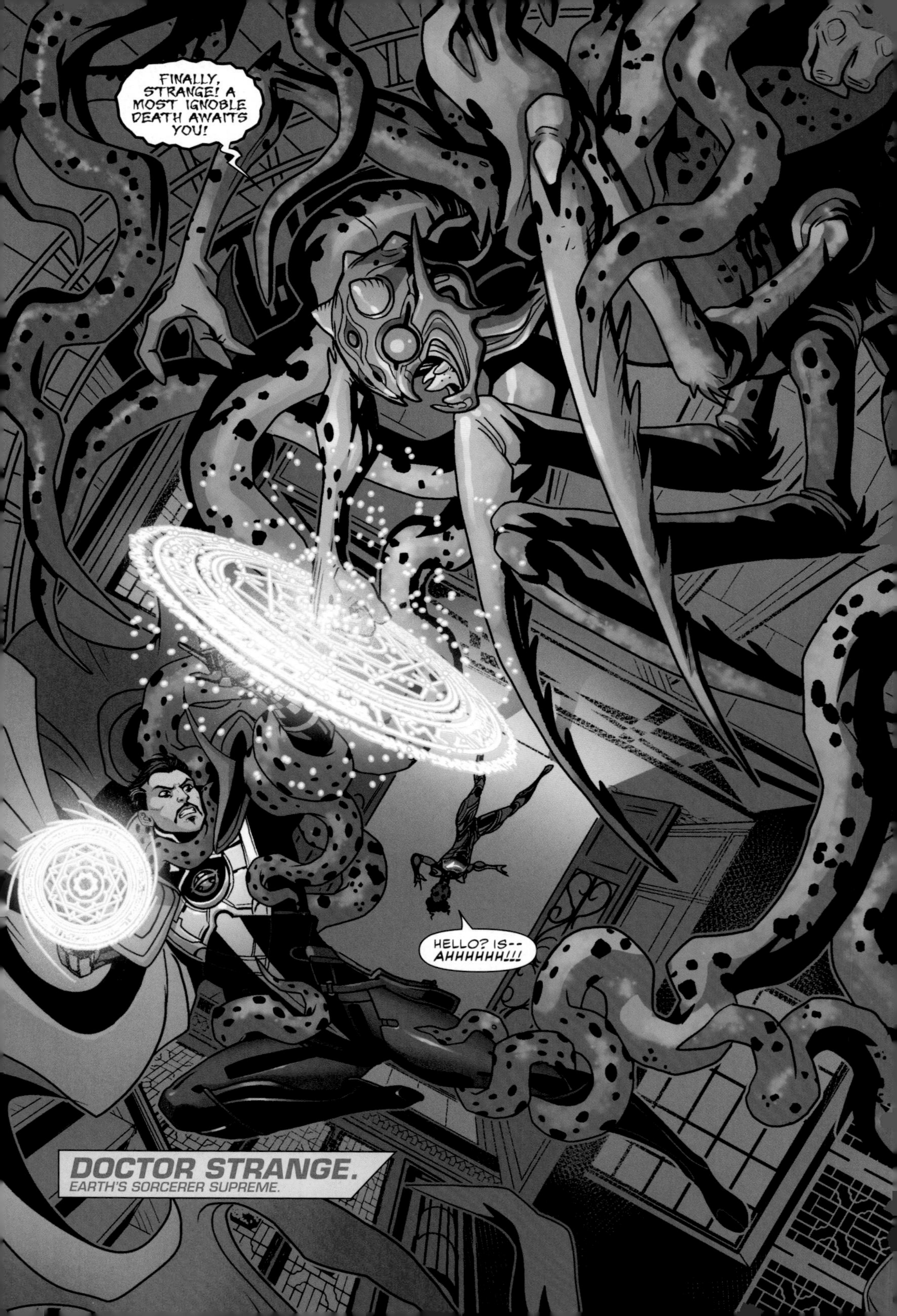
FINALLY, STRANGE! A MOST IGNOBLE DEATH AWAITS YOU!
HELLO? IS-- AHHHHHH!!!
DOCTOR STRANGE.
EARTH'S SORCERER SUPREME.

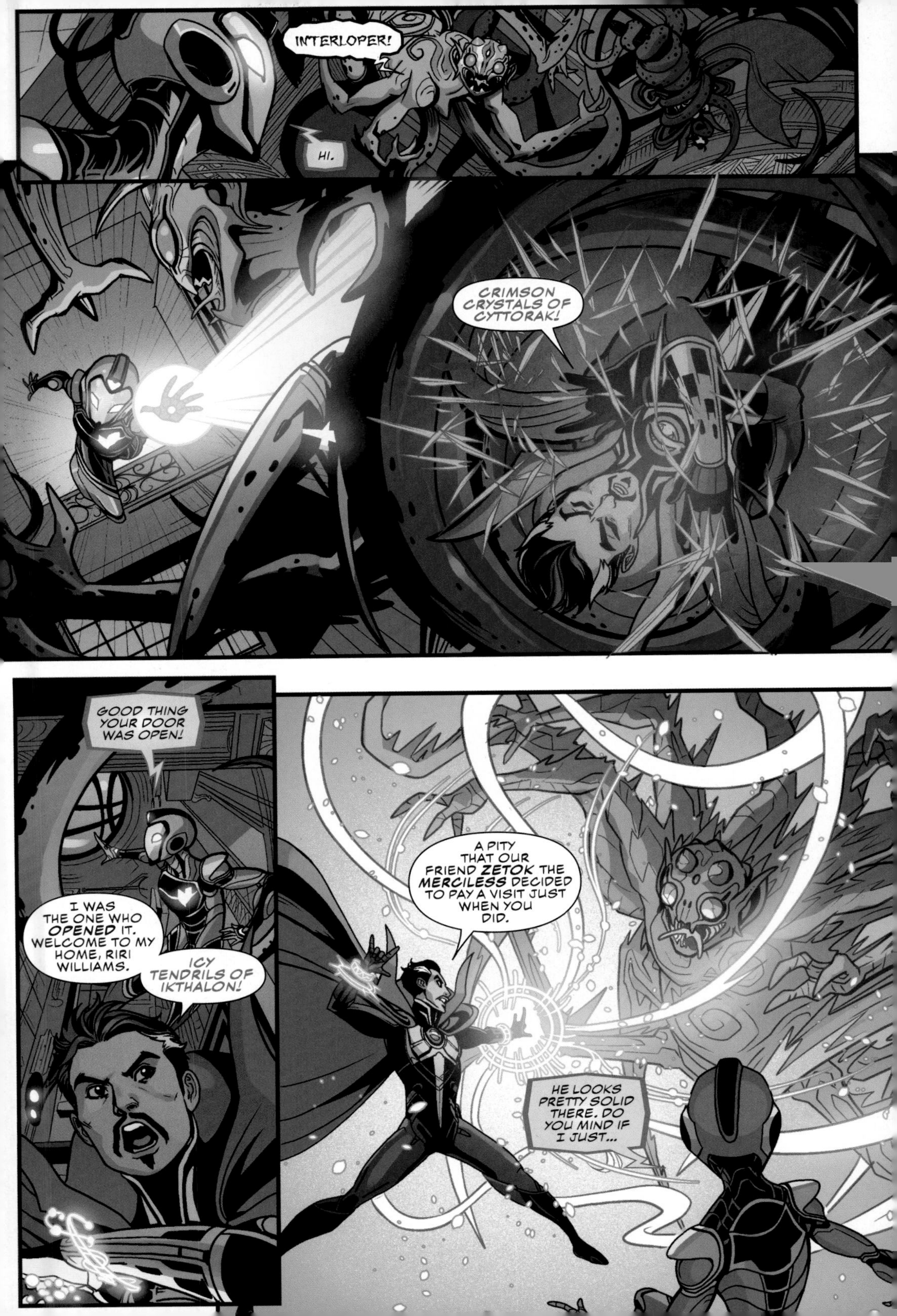
INTERLOPER!
HI.
CRIMSON CRYSTALS OF CYTTORAK!
GOOD THING YOUR DOOR WAS OPEN!
I WAS THE ONE WHO OPENED IT. WELCOME TO MY HOME, RIRI WILLIAMS.
ICY TENDRILS OF IKTHALON!
A PITY THAT OUR FRIEND ZETOK THE MERCILESS DECIDED TO PAY A VISIT JUST WHEN YOU DID.
HE LOOKS PRETTY SOLID THERE. DO YOU MIND IF I JUST...

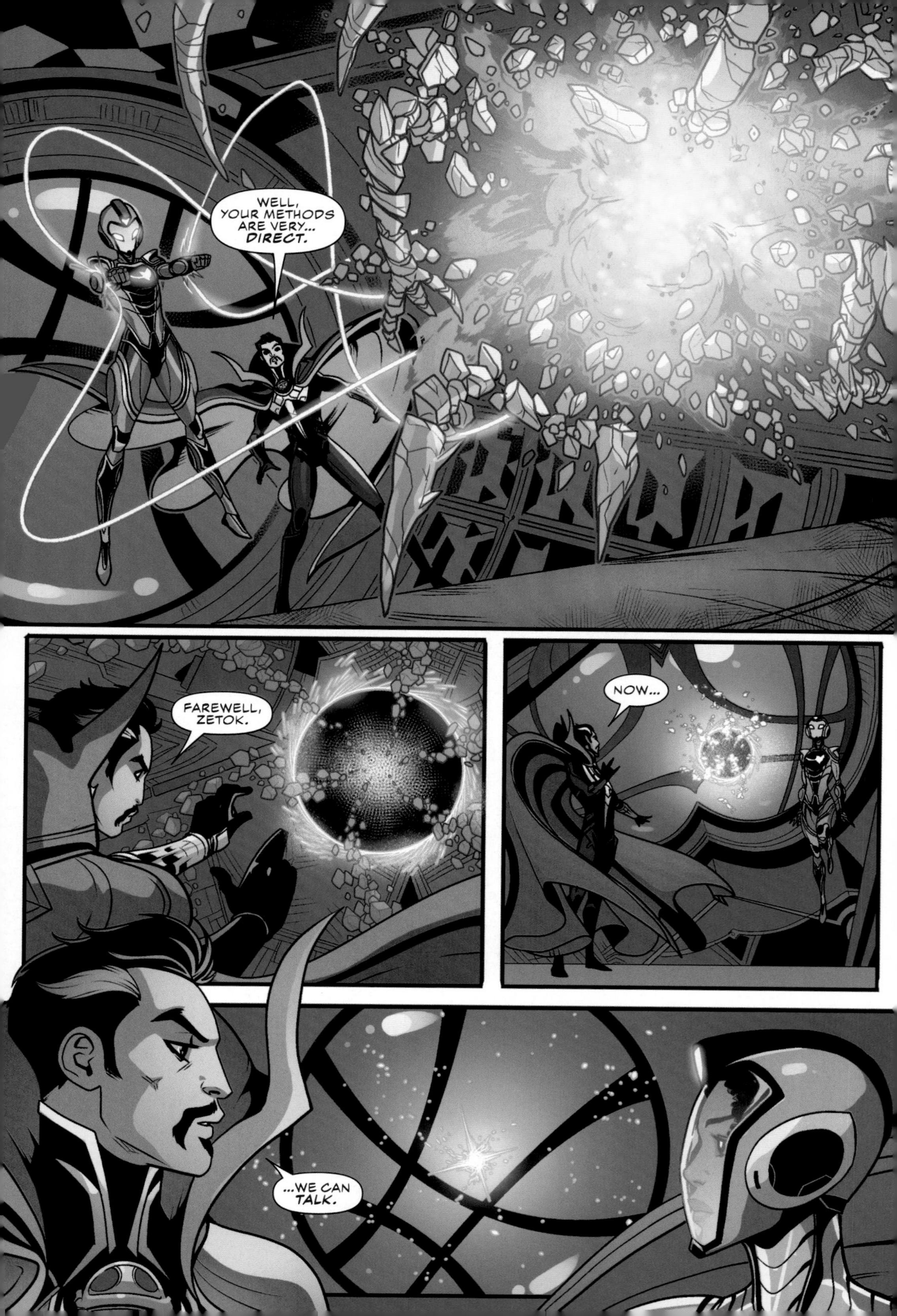
WELL, YOUR METHODS ARE VERY... DIRECT.
FAREWELL, ZETOK.
NOW...
...WE CAN TALK.

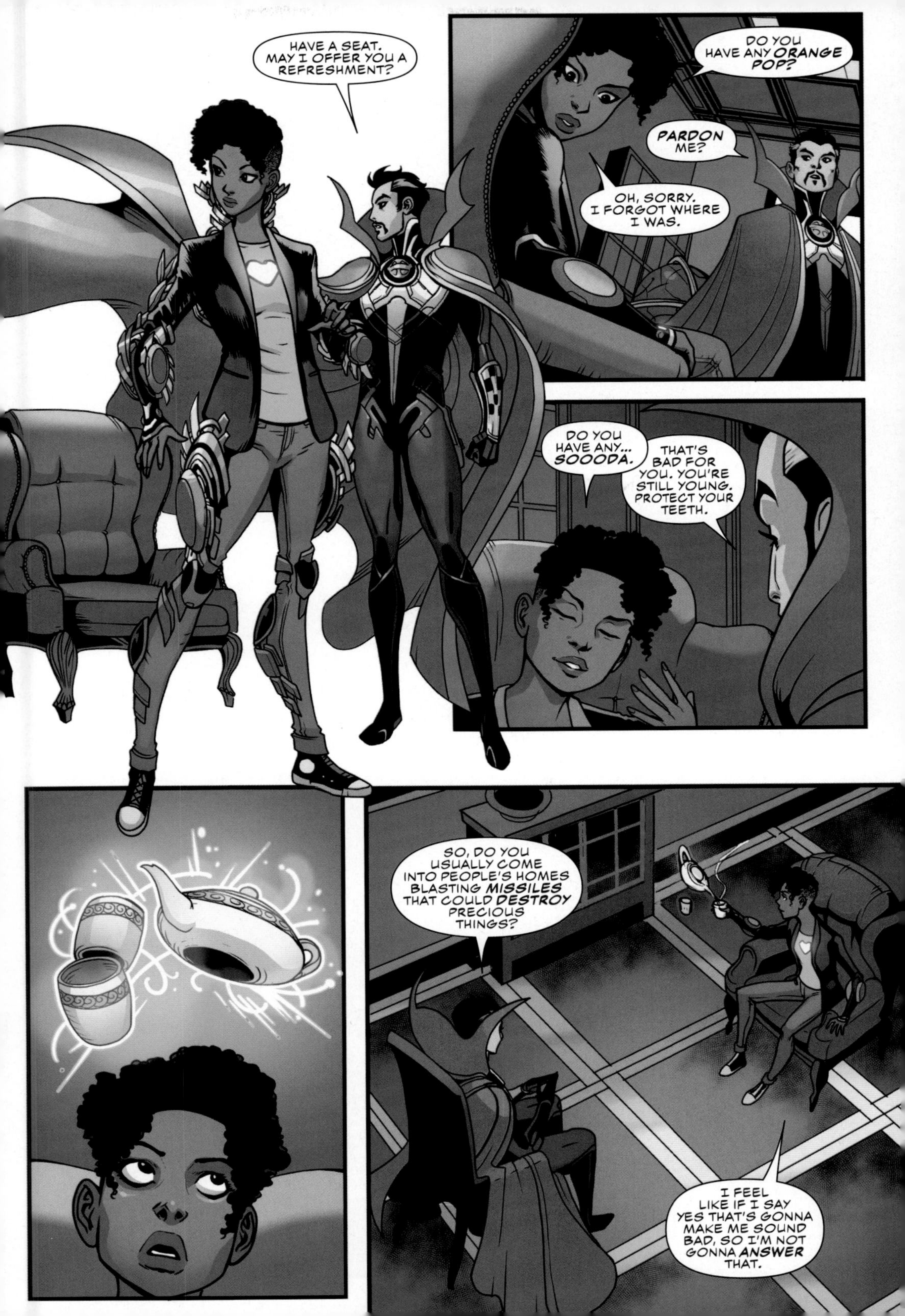
HAVE A SEAT. MAY I OFFER YOU A REFRESHMENT?
DO YOU HAVE ANY ORANGE POP?
PARDON ME?
OH, SORRY. I FORGOT WHERE I WAS.
DO YOU HAVE ANY... SOOODA.
THAT'S BAD FOR YOU. YOU'RE STILL YOUNG. PROTECT YOUR TEETH.
SO, DO YOU USUALLY COME INTO PEOPLE'S HOMES BLASTING MISSILES THAT COULD DESTROY PRECIOUS THINGS?
I FEEL LIKE IF I SAY YES THAT'S GONNA MAKE ME SOUND BAD, SO I'M NOT GONNA ANSWER THAT.

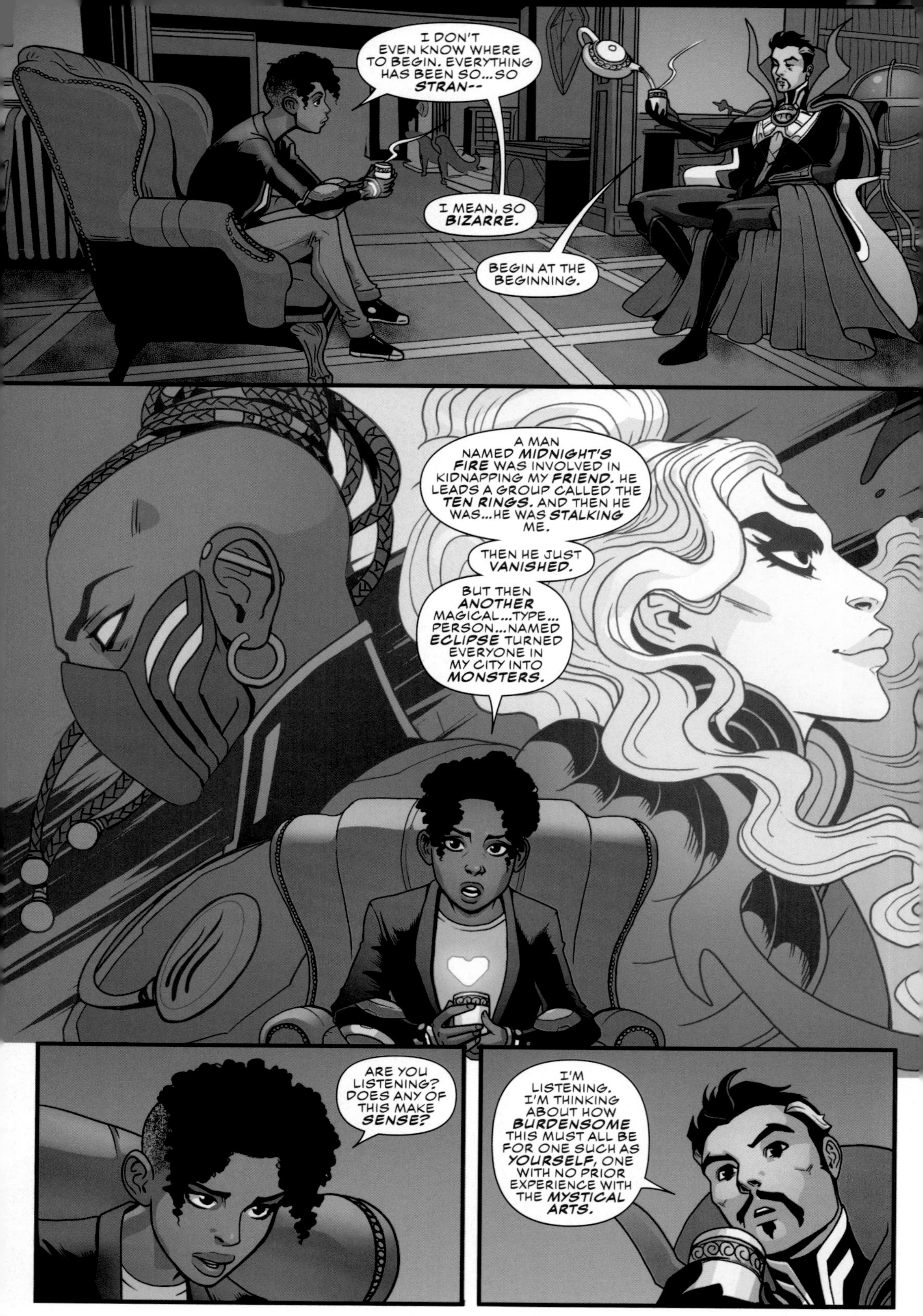

I DON'T EVEN KNOW WHERE TO BEGIN. EVERYTHING HAS BEEN SO...SO STRAN--
I MEAN, SO BIZARRE.
BEGIN AT THE BEGINNING.
A MAN NAMED MIDNIGHT'S FIRE WAS INVOLVED IN KIDNAPPING MY FRIEND. HE LEADS A GROUP CALLED THE TEN RINGS. AND THEN HE WAS...HE WAS STALKING ME.
THEN HE JUST VANISHED.
BUT THEN ANOTHER MAGICAL...TYPE... PERSON...NAMED ECLIPSE TURNED EVERYONE IN MY CITY INTO MONSTERS.
ARE YOU LISTENING? DOES ANY OF THIS MAKE SENSE?
I'M LISTENING. I'M THINKING ABOUT HOW BURDENSOME THIS MUST ALL BE FOR ONE SUCH AS YOURSELF, ONE WITH NO PRIOR EXPERIENCE WITH THE MYSTICAL ARTS.

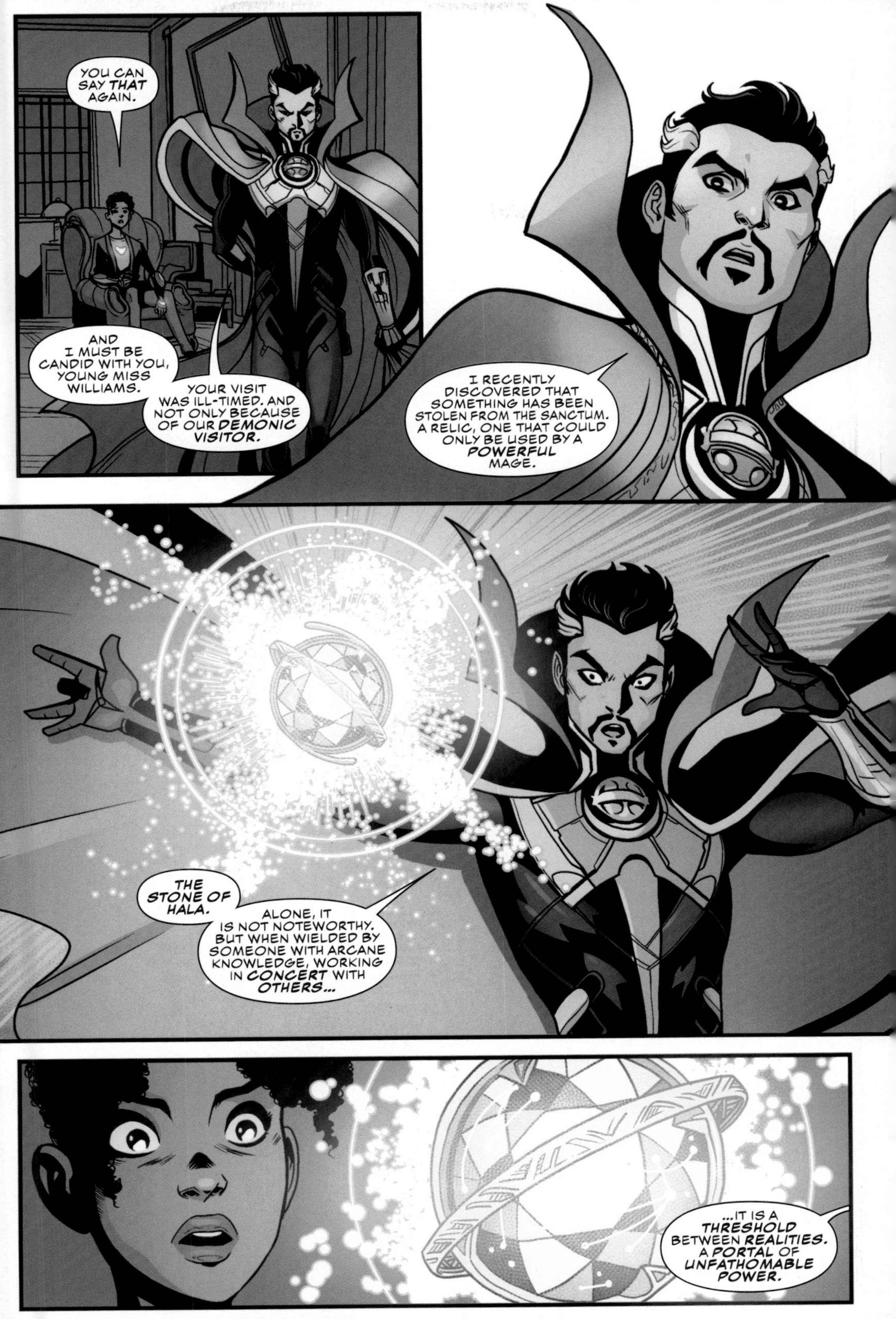
YOU CAN SAY THAT AGAIN.
AND I MUST BE CANDID WITH YOU, YOUNG MISS WILLIAMS.
YOUR VISIT WAS ILL-TIMED. AND NOT ONLY BECAUSE OF OUR DEMONIC VISITOR.
I RECENTLY DISCOVERED THAT SOMETHING HAS BEEN STOLEN FROM THE SANCTUM. A RELIC, ONE THAT COULD ONLY BE USED BY A POWERFUL MAGE.
THE STONE OF HALA.
ALONE, IT IS NOT NOTEWORTHY. BUT WHEN WIELDED BY SOMEONE WITH ARCANE KNOWLEDGE, WORKING IN CONCERT WITH OTHERS...
...IT IS A THRESHOLD BETWEEN REALITIES. A PORTAL OF UNFATHOMABLE POWER.

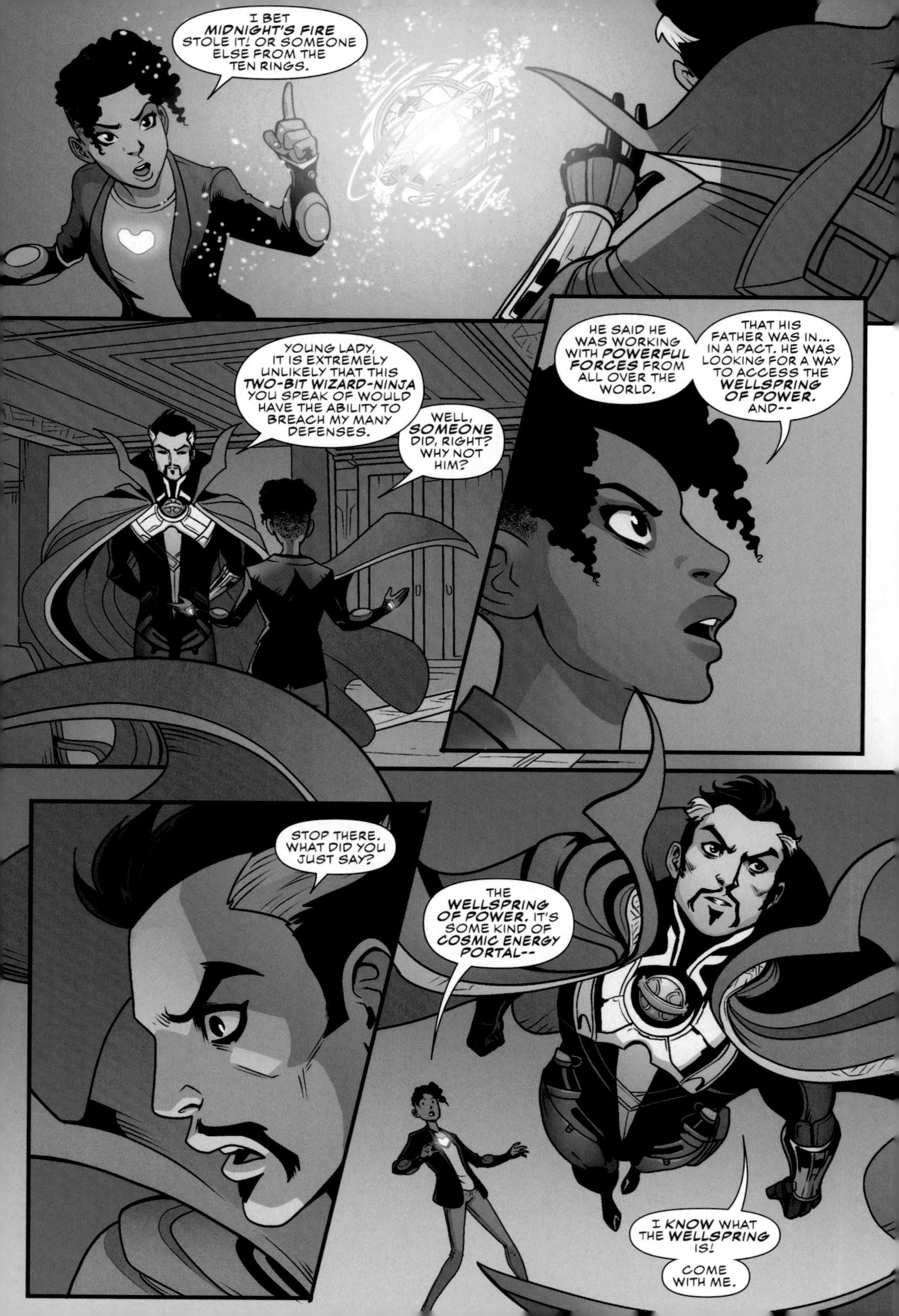

I BET MIDNIGHT'S FIRE STOLE IT! OR SOMEONE ELSE FROM THE TEN RINGS.
YOUNG LADY, IT IS EXTREMELY UNLIKELY THAT THIS TWO-BIT WIZARD-NINJA YOU SPEAK OF WOULD HAVE THE ABILITY TO BREACH MY MANY DEFENSES.
WELL, SOMEONE DID, RIGHT? WHY NOT HIM?
HE SAID HE WAS WORKING WITH POWERFUL FORCES FROM ALL OVER THE WORLD.
THAT HIS FATHER WAS IN... IN A PACT. HE WAS LOOKING FOR A WAY TO ACCESS THE WELLSPRING OF POWER. AND--
STOP THERE. WHAT DID YOU JUST SAY?
THE WELLSPRING OF POWER. IT'S SOME KIND OF COSMIC ENERGY PORTAL--
I KNOW WHAT THE WELLSPRING IS!
COME WITH ME.

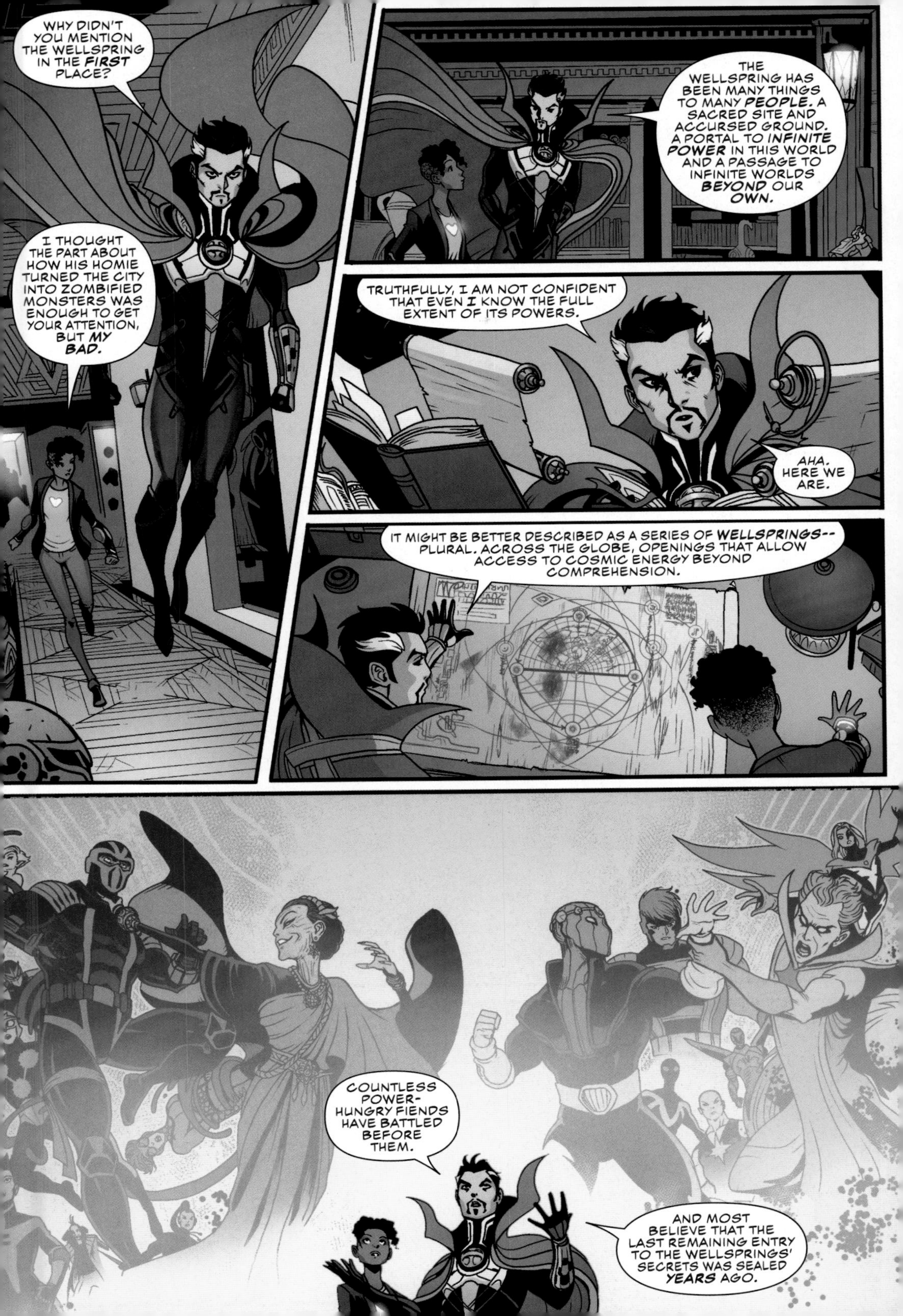
WHY DIDN'T YOU MENTION THE WELLSPRING IN THE *FIRST* PLACE?
I THOUGHT THE PART ABOUT HOW HIS HOMIE TURNED THE CITY INTO ZOMBIFIED MONSTERS WAS ENOUGH TO GET YOUR ATTENTION, BUT *MY BAD.*
THE WELLSPRING HAS BEEN MANY THINGS TO MANY *PEOPLE.* A SACRED SITE AND ACCURSED GROUND. A PORTAL TO *INFINITE POWER* IN THIS WORLD AND A PASSAGE TO INFINITE WORLDS *BEYOND* OUR *OWN.*
TRUTHFULLY, I AM NOT CONFIDENT THAT EVEN *I* KNOW THE FULL EXTENT OF ITS POWERS.
AHA. HERE WE ARE.
IT MIGHT BE BETTER DESCRIBED AS A SERIES OF *WELLSPRINGS*-- PLURAL. ACROSS THE GLOBE, OPENINGS THAT ALLOW ACCESS TO COSMIC ENERGY BEYOND COMPREHENSION.
COUNTLESS POWER-HUNGRY FIENDS HAVE BATTLED BEFORE THEM.
AND MOST BELIEVE THAT THE LAST REMAINING ENTRY TO THE WELLSPRINGS' SECRETS WAS SEALED *YEARS* AGO.

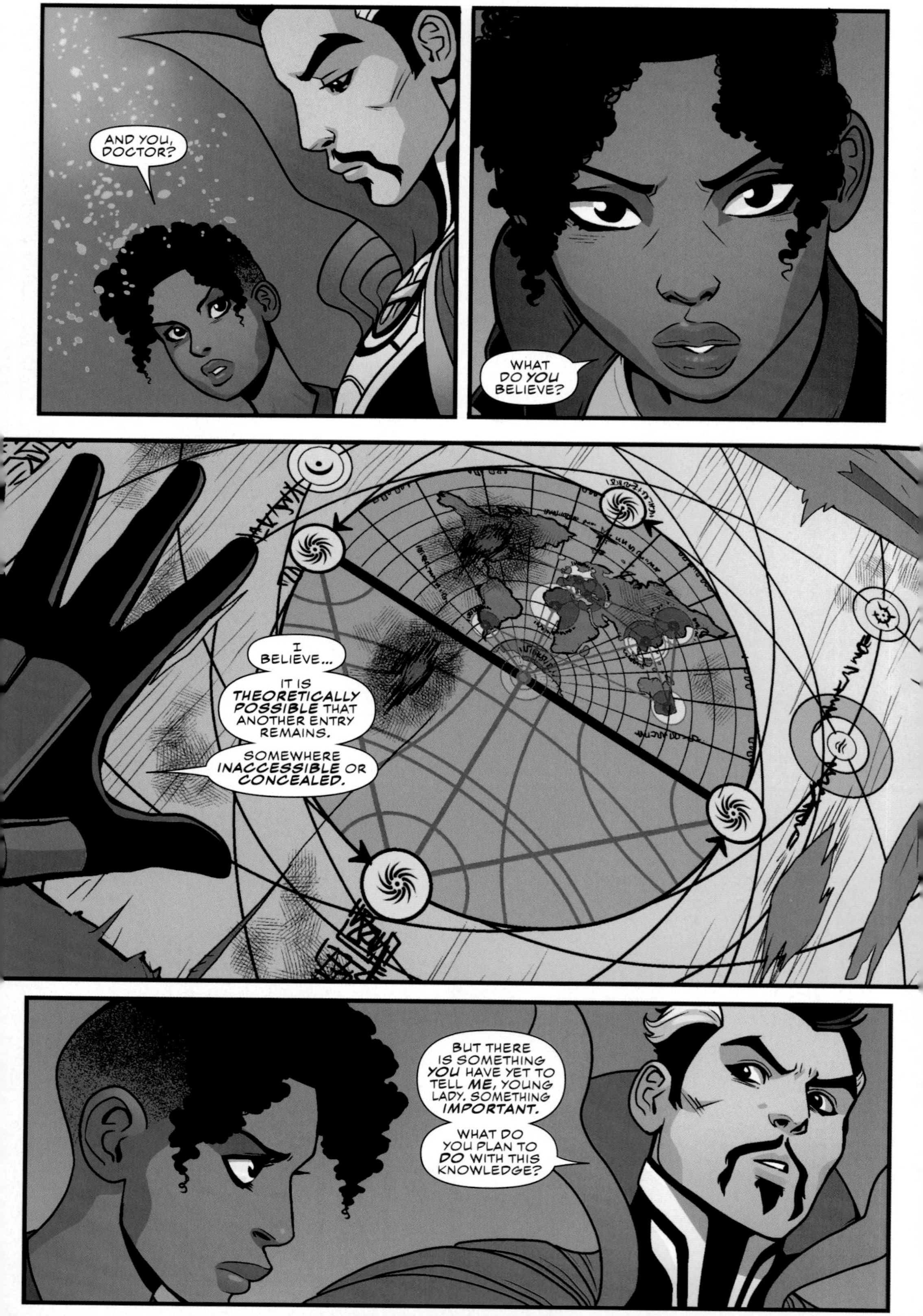
AND YOU, DOCTOR?
WHAT DO YOU BELIEVE?
I BELIEVE...
IT IS THEORETICALLY POSSIBLE THAT ANOTHER ENTRY REMAINS.
SOMEWHERE INACCESSIBLE OR CONCEALED.
BUT THERE IS SOMETHING YOU HAVE YET TO TELL ME, YOUNG LADY. SOMETHING IMPORTANT.
WHAT DO YOU PLAN TO DO WITH THIS KNOWLEDGE?

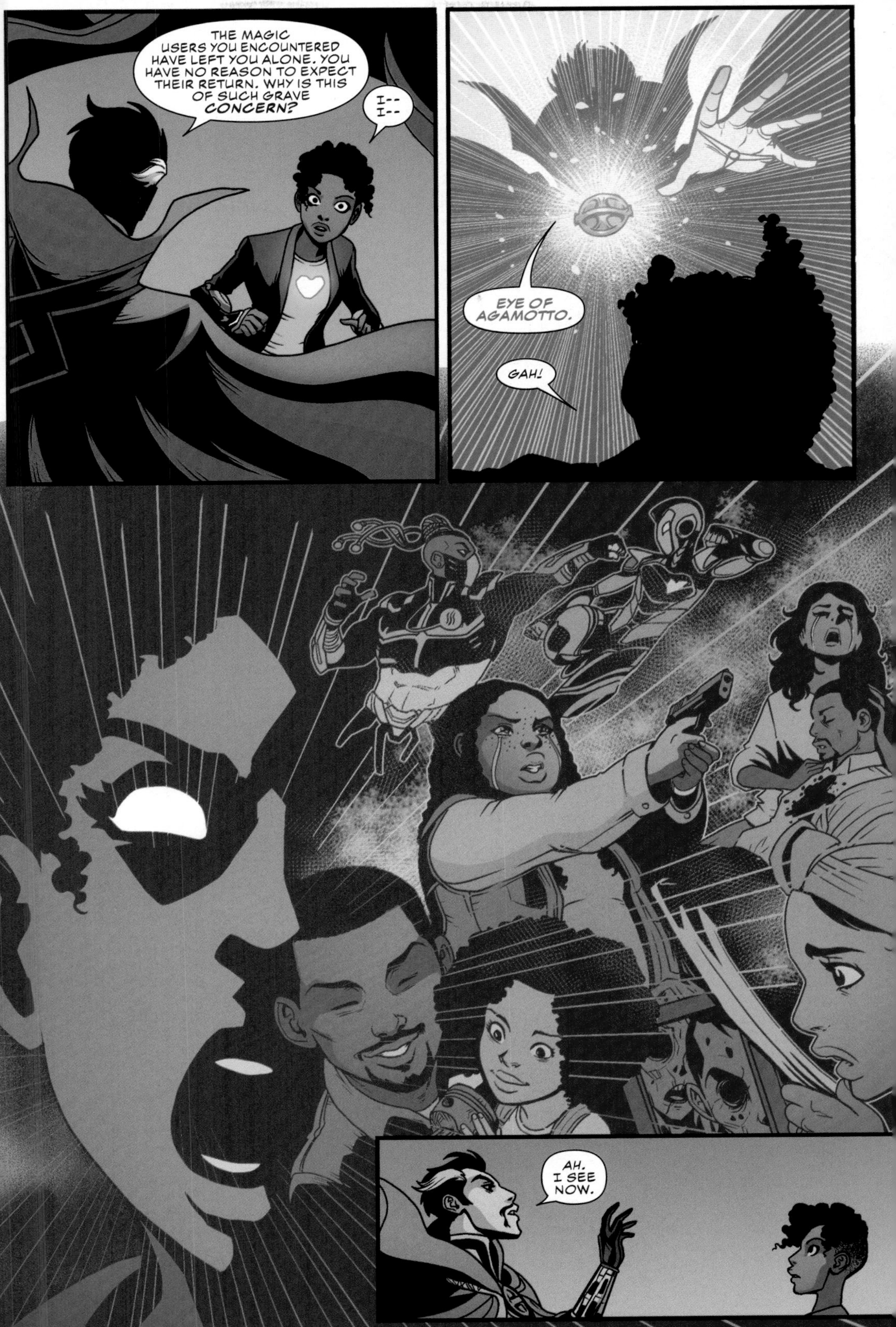

THE MAGIC USERS YOU ENCOUNTERED HAVE LEFT YOU ALONE. YOU HAVE NO REASON TO EXPECT THEIR RETURN. WHY IS THIS OF SUCH GRAVE CONCERN?
I-- I--
EYE OF AGAMOTTO.
GAH!
AH. I SEE NOW.

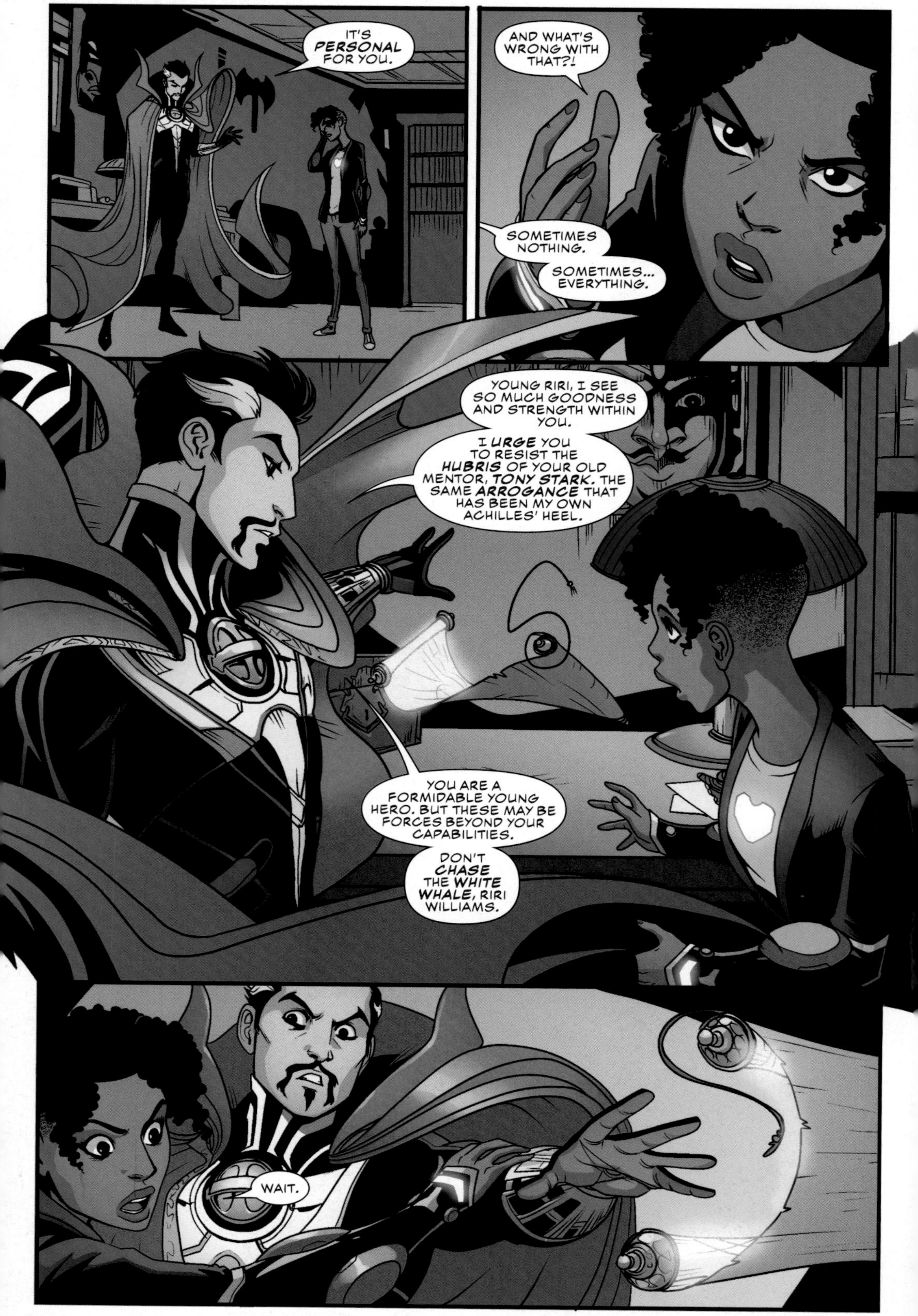
IT'S **PERSONAL** FOR YOU.
AND WHAT'S WRONG WITH THAT?!
SOMETIMES NOTHING.
SOMETIMES... EVERYTHING.
YOUNG RIRI, I SEE SO MUCH GOODNESS AND STRENGTH WITHIN YOU.
I **URGE** YOU TO RESIST THE **HUBRIS** OF YOUR OLD MENTOR, **TONY STARK.** THE SAME **ARROGANCE** THAT HAS BEEN MY OWN ACHILLES' HEEL.
YOU ARE A FORMIDABLE YOUNG HERO. BUT THESE MAY BE FORCES BEYOND YOUR CAPABILITIES.
DON'T **CHASE** THE **WHITE WHALE,** RIRI WILLIAMS.
WAIT.

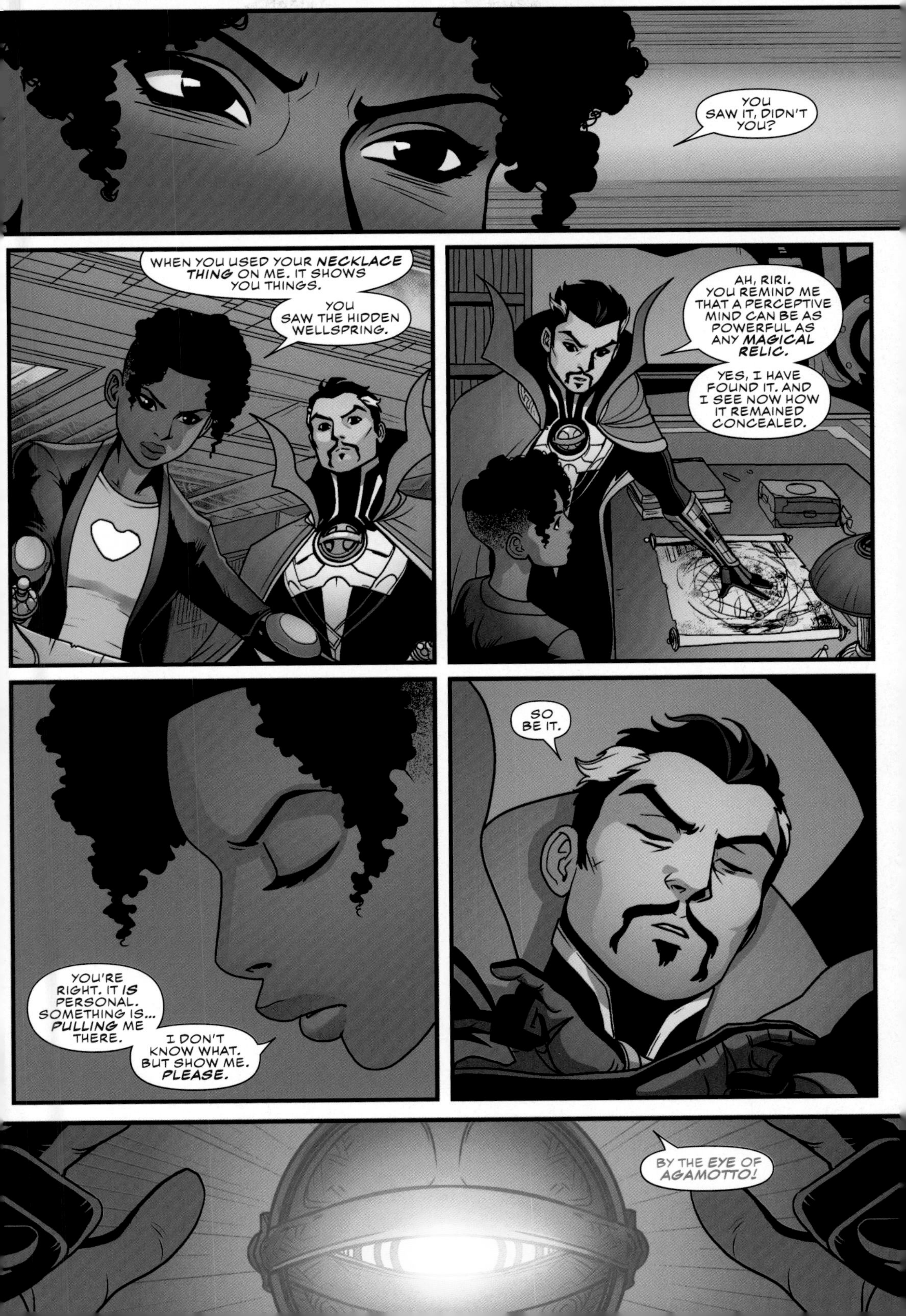
YOU SAW IT, DIDN'T YOU?
WHEN YOU USED YOUR NECKLACE THING ON ME. IT SHOWS YOU THINGS.
YOU SAW THE HIDDEN WELLSPRING.
AH, RIRI. YOU REMIND ME THAT A PERCEPTIVE MIND CAN BE AS POWERFUL AS ANY MAGICAL RELIC.
YES, I HAVE FOUND IT. AND I SEE NOW HOW IT REMAINED CONCEALED.
YOU'RE RIGHT. IT IS PERSONAL. SOMETHING IS... PULLING ME THERE.
I DON'T KNOW WHAT. BUT SHOW ME. PLEASE.
SO BE IT.
BY THE EYE OF AGAMOTTO!

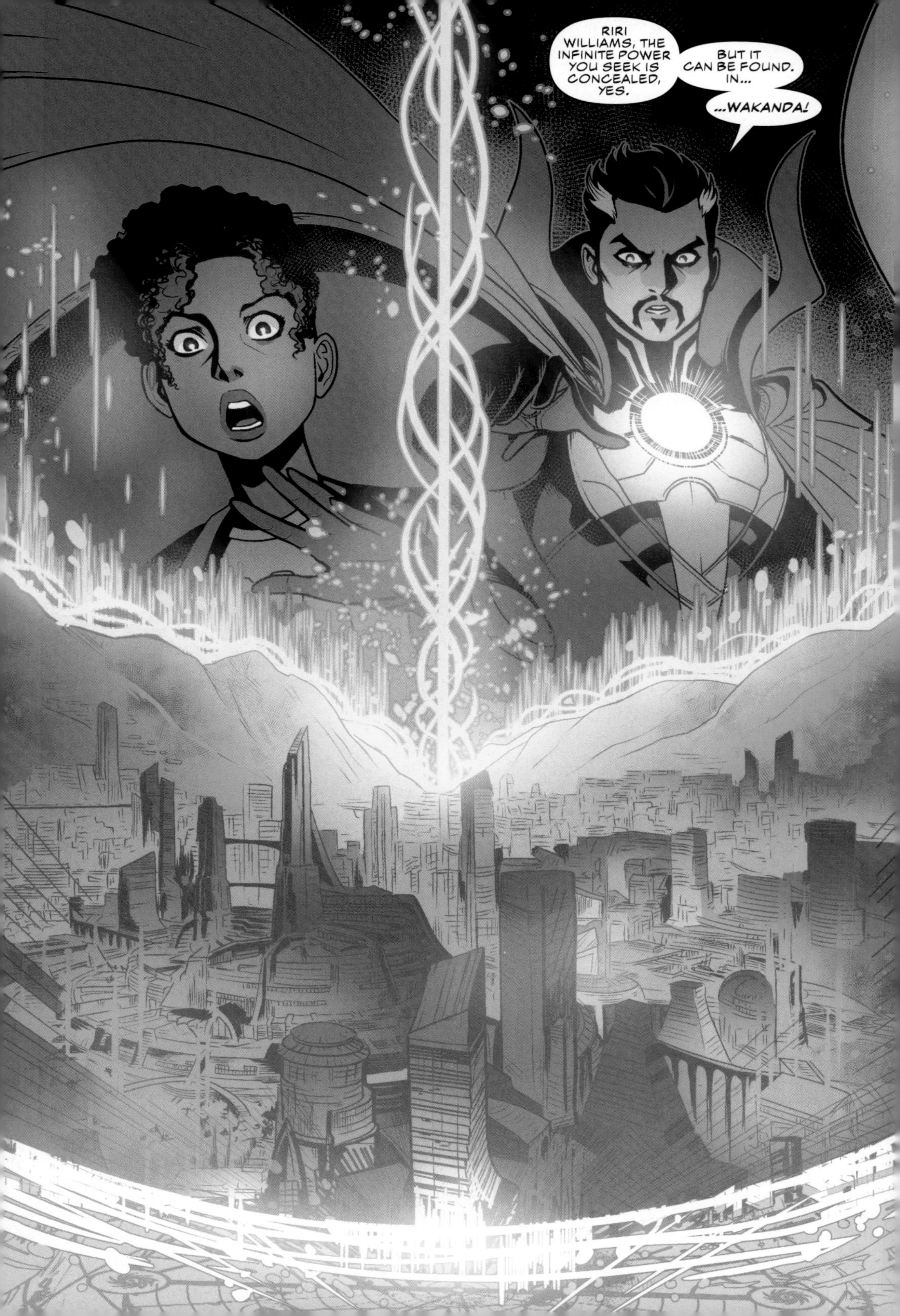
RIRI WILLIAMS, THE INFINITE POWER YOU SEEK IS CONCEALED, YES.
BUT IT CAN BE FOUND. IN...
...WAKANDA!

9

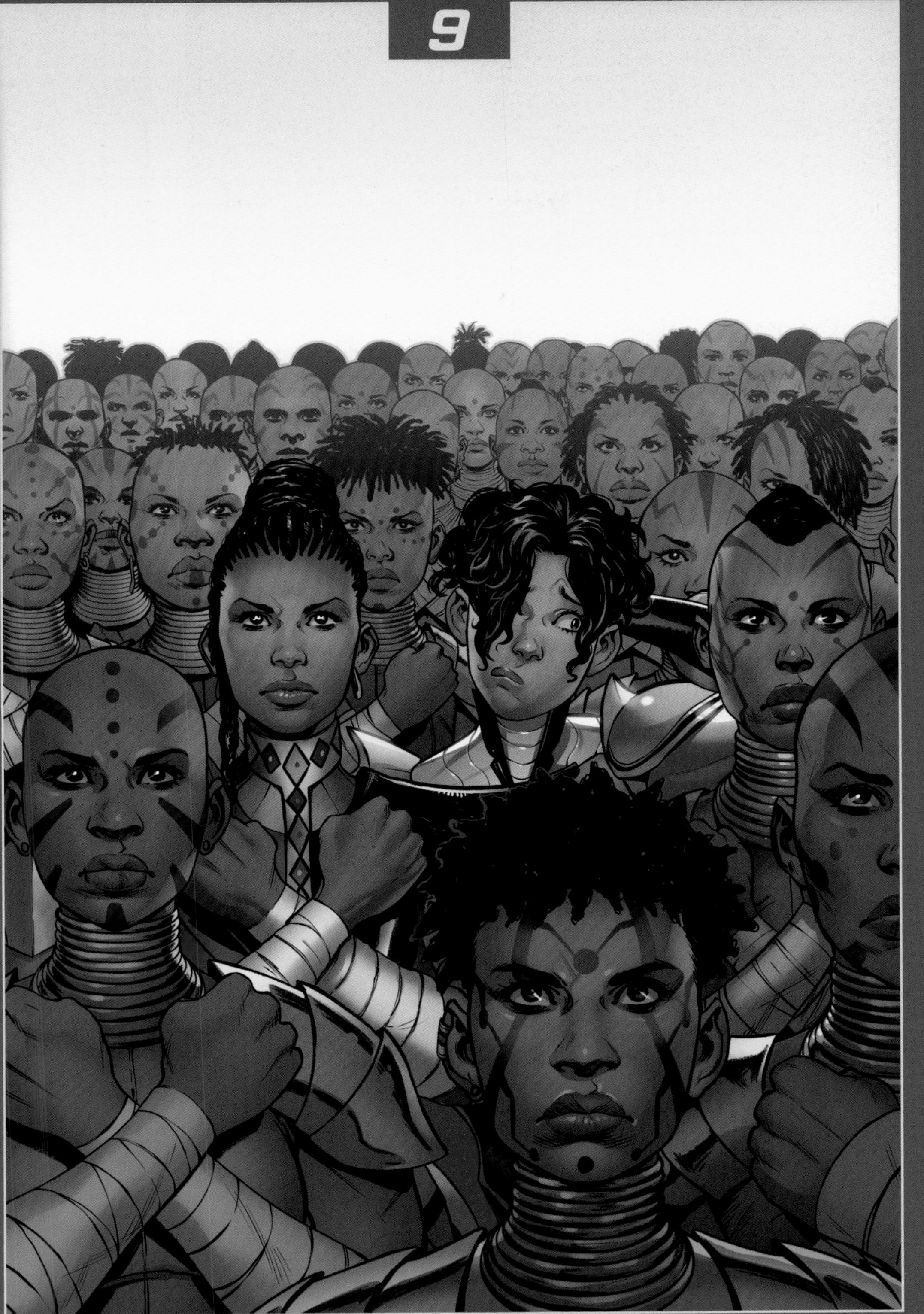

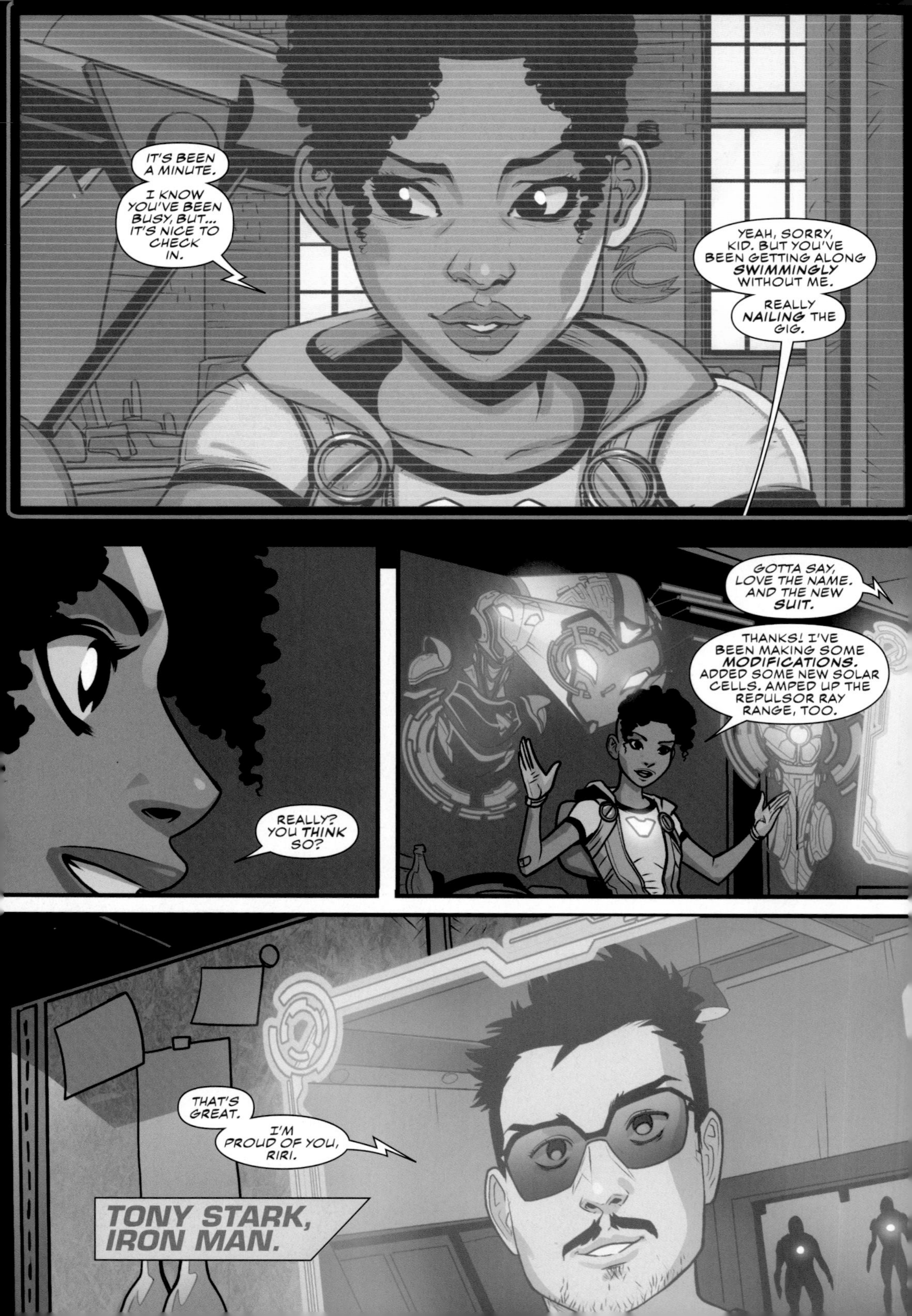
IT'S BEEN A MINUTE.
I KNOW YOU'VE BEEN BUSY, BUT... IT'S NICE TO CHECK IN.
YEAH, SORRY, KID. BUT YOU'VE BEEN GETTING ALONG SWIMMINGLY WITHOUT ME.
REALLY NAILING THE GIG.
REALLY? YOU THINK SO?
GOTTA SAY, LOVE THE NAME. AND THE NEW SUIT.
THANKS! I'VE BEEN MAKING SOME MODIFICATIONS. ADDED SOME NEW SOLAR CELLS. AMPED UP THE REPULSOR RAY RANGE, TOO.
THAT'S GREAT.
I'M PROUD OF YOU, RIRI.
TONY STARK, IRON MAN.

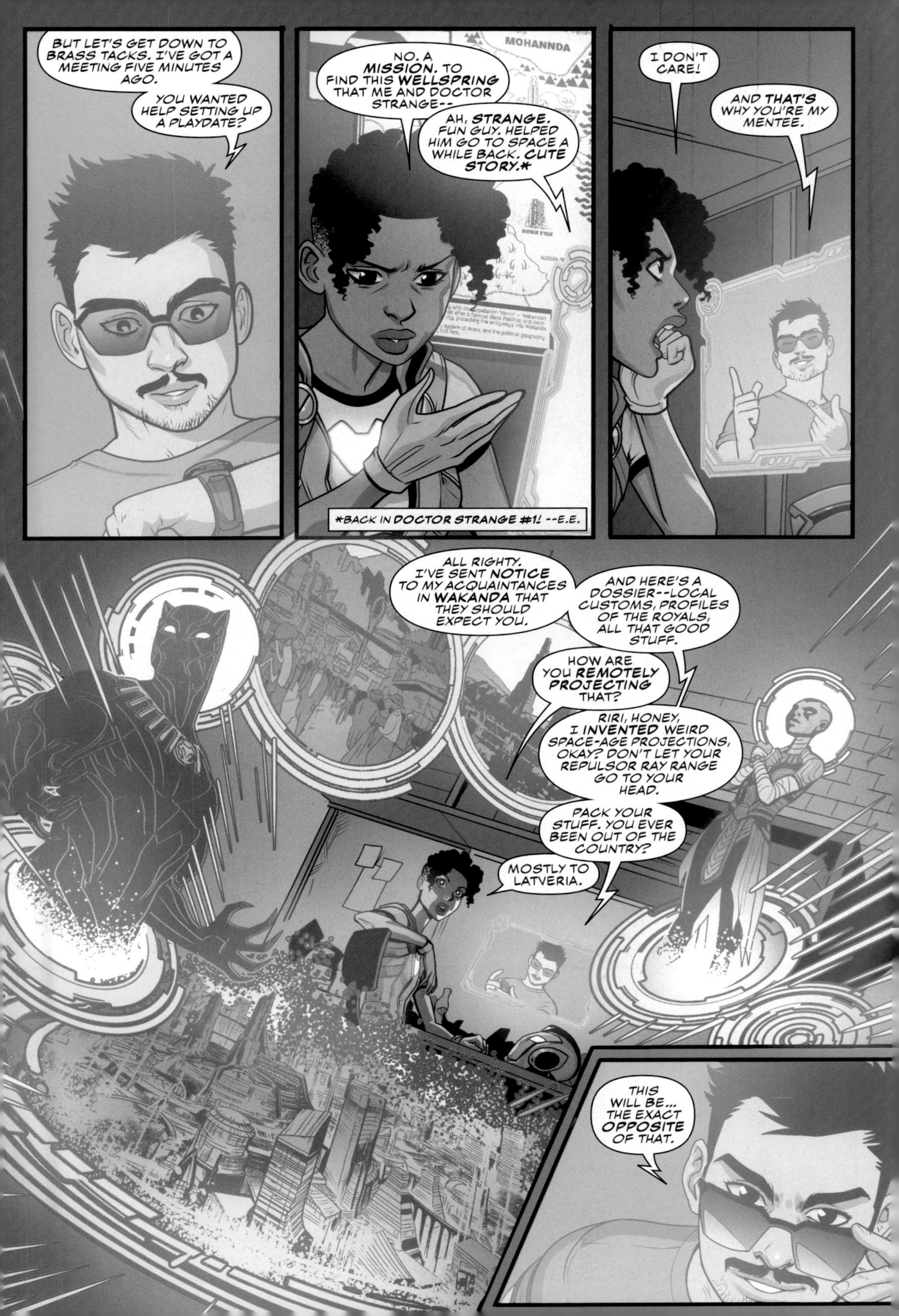
BUT LET'S GET DOWN TO BRASS TACKS. I'VE GOT A MEETING FIVE MINUTES AGO.
YOU WANTED HELP SETTING UP A PLAYDATE?
NO. A MISSION. TO FIND THIS WELLSPRING THAT ME AND DOCTOR STRANGE--
AH, STRANGE. FUN GUY. HELPED HIM GO TO SPACE A WHILE BACK. CUTE STORY.*
MOHANNDA
*BACK IN DOCTOR STRANGE #1! --E.E.
I DON'T CARE!
AND THAT'S WHY YOU'RE MY MENTEE.
ALL RIGHTY. I'VE SENT NOTICE TO MY ACQUAINTANCES IN WAKANDA THAT THEY SHOULD EXPECT YOU.
AND HERE'S A DOSSIER--LOCAL CUSTOMS, PROFILES OF THE ROYALS, ALL THAT GOOD STUFF.
HOW ARE YOU REMOTELY PROJECTING THAT?
RIRI, HONEY, I INVENTED WEIRD SPACE-AGE PROJECTIONS, OKAY? DON'T LET YOUR REPULSOR RAY RANGE GO TO YOUR HEAD.
PACK YOUR STUFF. YOU EVER BEEN OUT OF THE COUNTRY?
MOSTLY TO LATVERIA.
THIS WILL BE... THE EXACT OPPOSITE OF THAT.

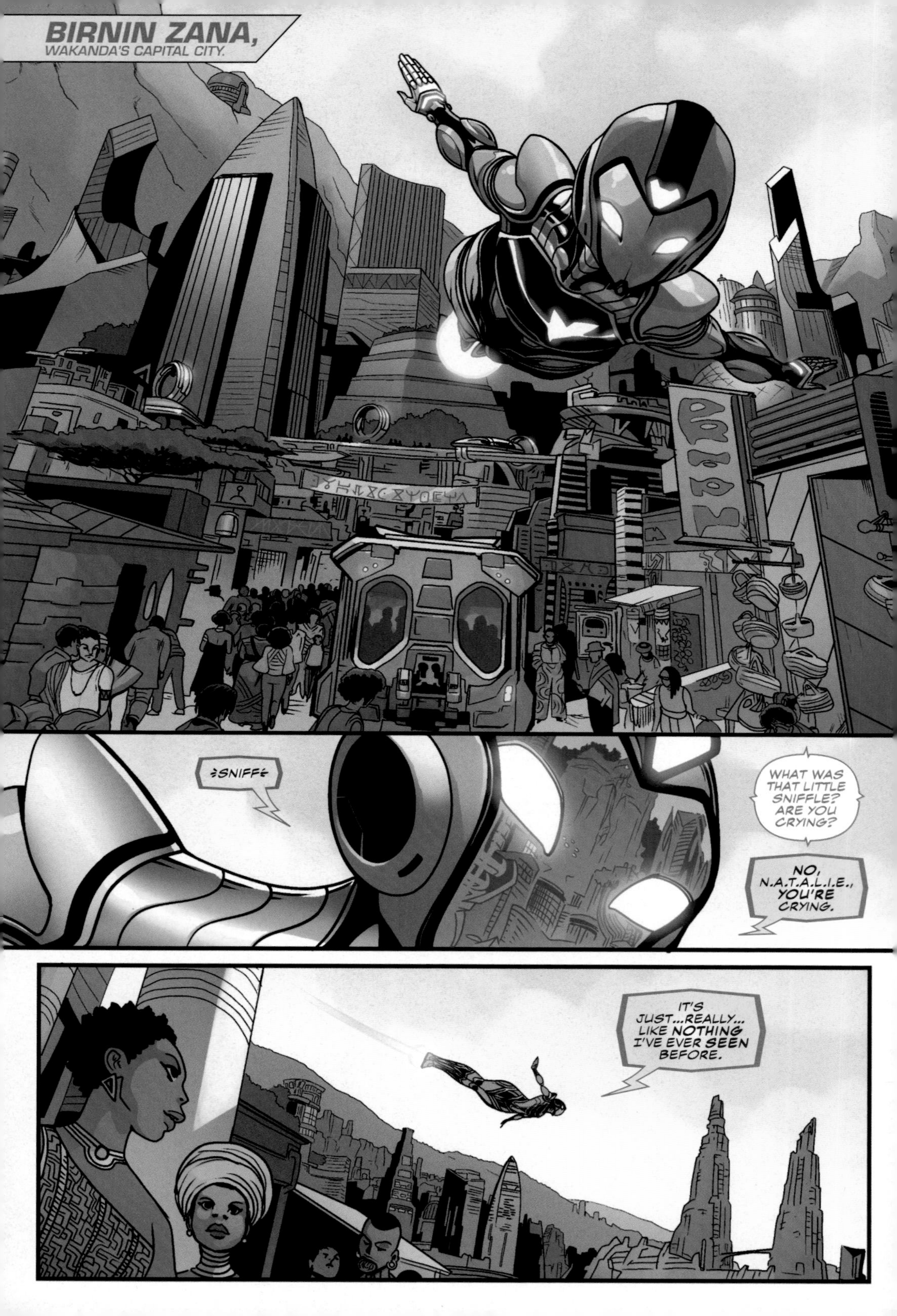
BIRNIN ZANA,
WAKANDA'S CAPITAL CITY.
SNIFF
WHAT WAS THAT LITTLE SNIFFLE? ARE YOU CRYING?
NO, N.A.T.A.L.I.E., YOU'RE CRYING.
IT'S JUST...REALLY... LIKE NOTHING I'VE EVER SEEN BEFORE.

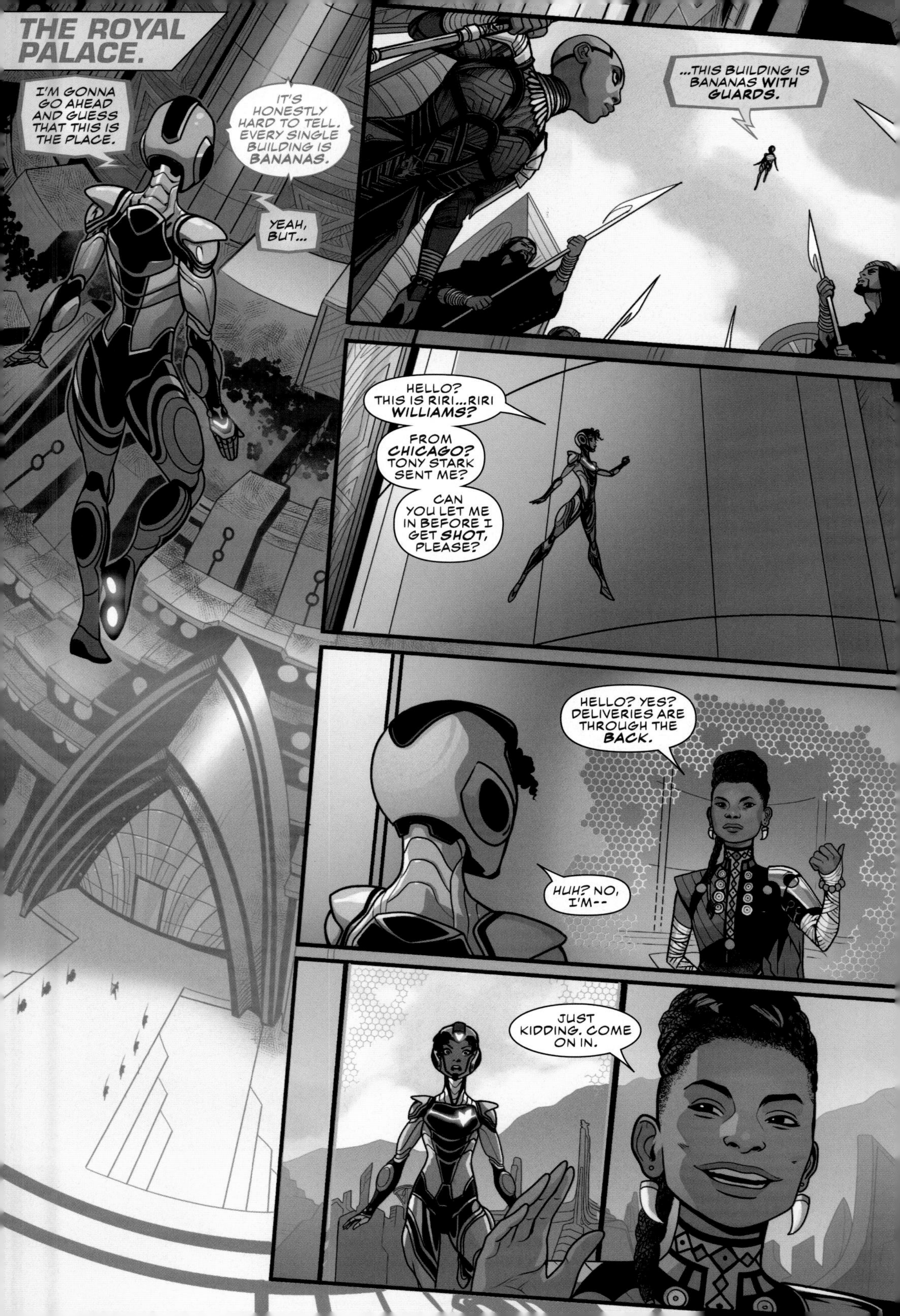
THE ROYAL PALACE.
I'M GONNA GO AHEAD AND GUESS THAT THIS IS THE PLACE.
IT'S HONESTLY HARD TO TELL. EVERY SINGLE BUILDING IS BANANAS.
YEAH, BUT...
...THIS BUILDING IS BANANAS WITH GUARDS.
HELLO? THIS IS RIRI...RIRI WILLIAMS?
FROM CHICAGO? TONY STARK SENT ME?
CAN YOU LET ME IN BEFORE I GET SHOT, PLEASE?
HELLO? YES? DELIVERIES ARE THROUGH THE BACK.
HUH? NO, I'M--
JUST KIDDING. COME ON IN.

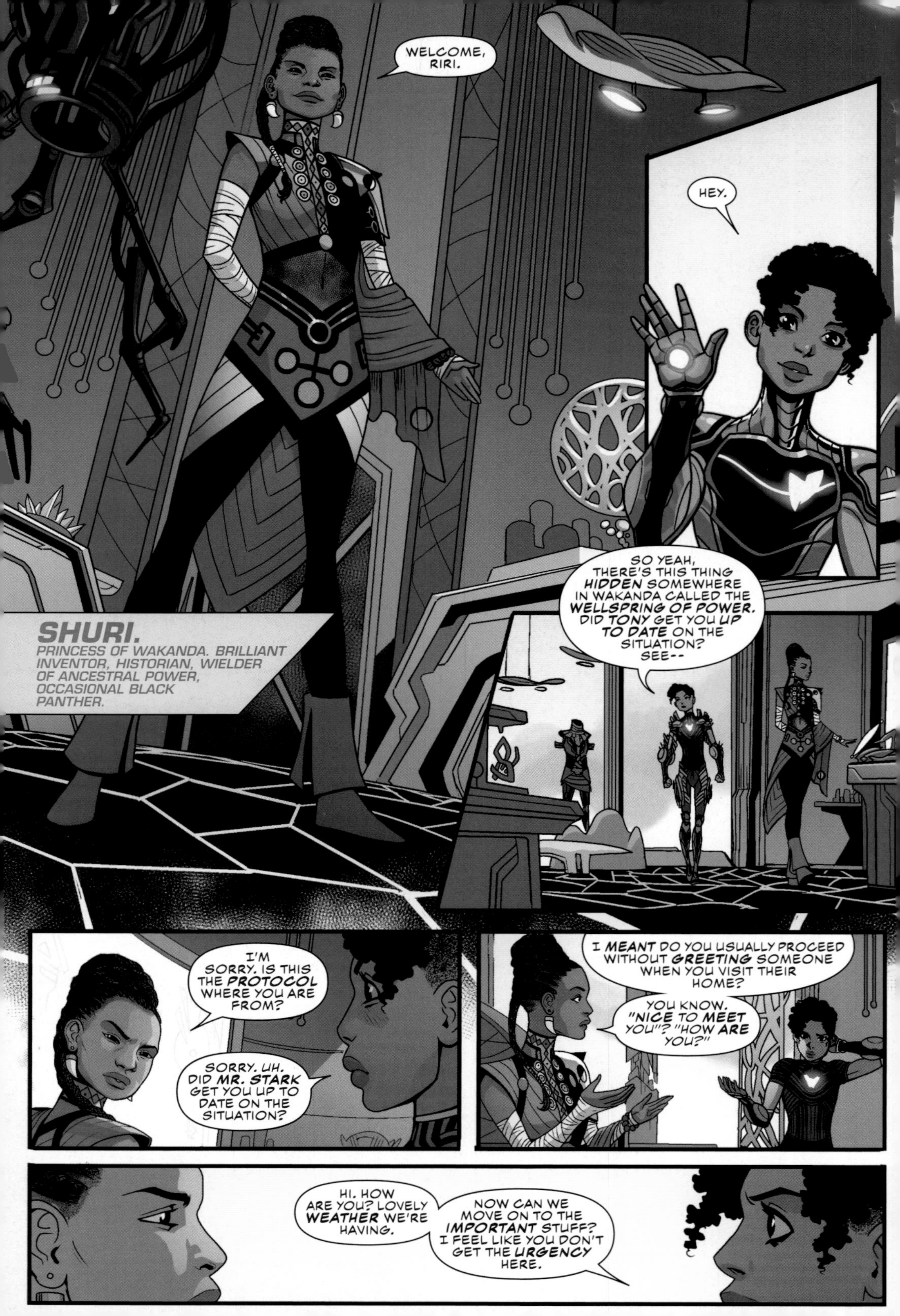
WELCOME, RIRI.
HEY.
SHURI.
PRINCESS OF WAKANDA. BRILLIANT INVENTOR, HISTORIAN, WIELDER OF ANCESTRAL POWER, OCCASIONAL BLACK PANTHER.
SO YEAH, THERE'S THIS THING HIDDEN SOMEWHERE IN WAKANDA CALLED THE WELLSPRING OF POWER. DID TONY GET YOU UP TO DATE ON THE SITUATION? SEE--
I'M SORRY. IS THIS THE PROTOCOL WHERE YOU ARE FROM?
SORRY. UH. DID MR. STARK GET YOU UP TO DATE ON THE SITUATION?
I MEANT DO YOU USUALLY PROCEED WITHOUT GREETING SOMEONE WHEN YOU VISIT THEIR HOME?
YOU KNOW. "NICE TO MEET YOU"? "HOW ARE YOU?"
HI. HOW ARE YOU? LOVELY WEATHER WE'RE HAVING.
NOW CAN WE MOVE ON TO THE IMPORTANT STUFF? I FEEL LIKE YOU DON'T GET THE URGENCY HERE.

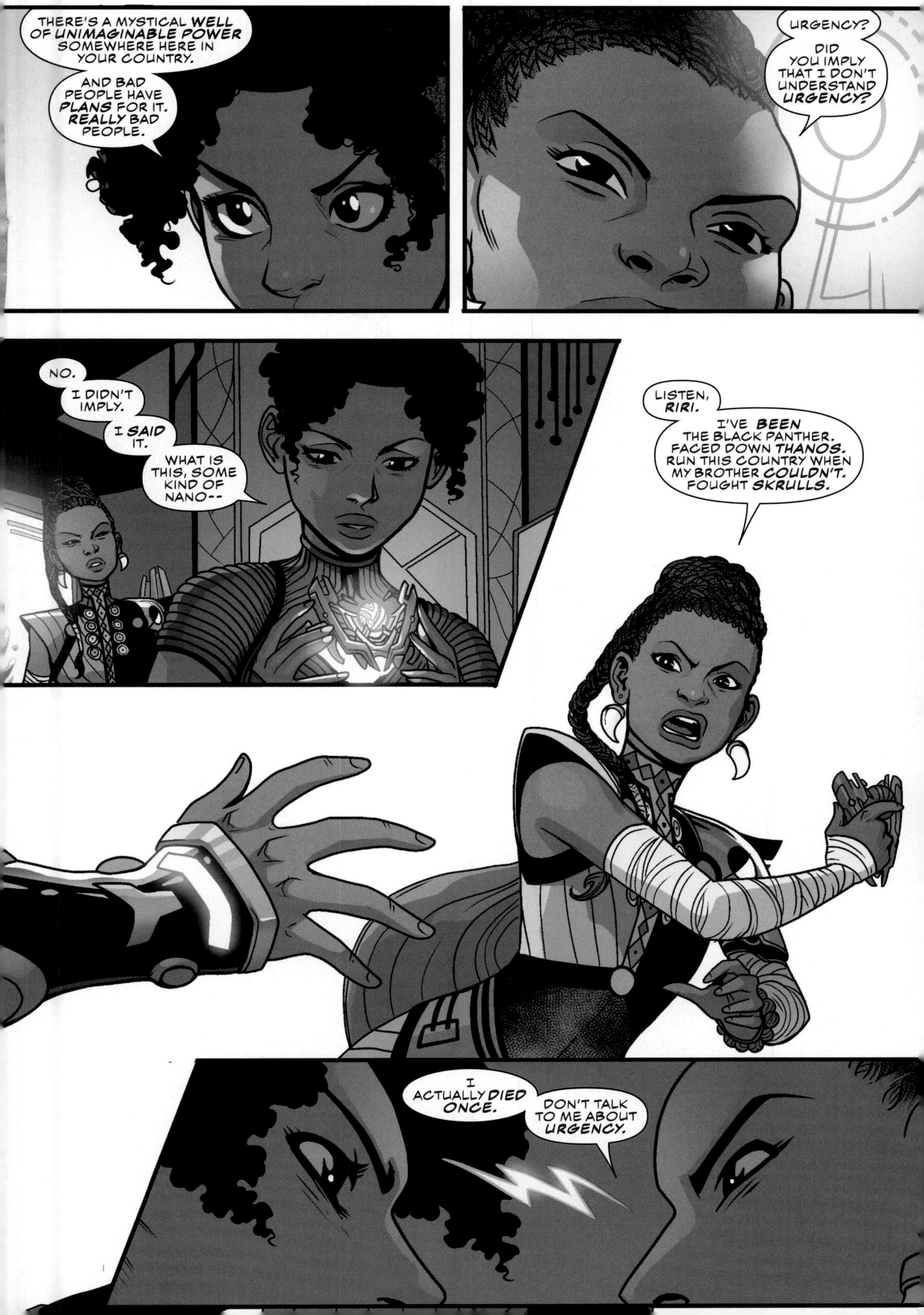

THERE'S A MYSTICAL WELL OF UNIMAGINABLE POWER SOMEWHERE HERE IN YOUR COUNTRY.
AND BAD PEOPLE HAVE PLANS FOR IT. REALLY BAD PEOPLE.
URGENCY?
DID YOU IMPLY THAT I DON'T UNDERSTAND URGENCY?
NO.
I DIDN'T IMPLY.
I SAID IT.
WHAT IS THIS, SOME KIND OF NANO--
LISTEN, RIRI.
I'VE BEEN THE BLACK PANTHER. FACED DOWN THANOS. RUN THIS COUNTRY WHEN MY BROTHER COULDN'T. FOUGHT SKRULLS.
I ACTUALLY DIED ONCE.
DON'T TALK TO ME ABOUT URGENCY.

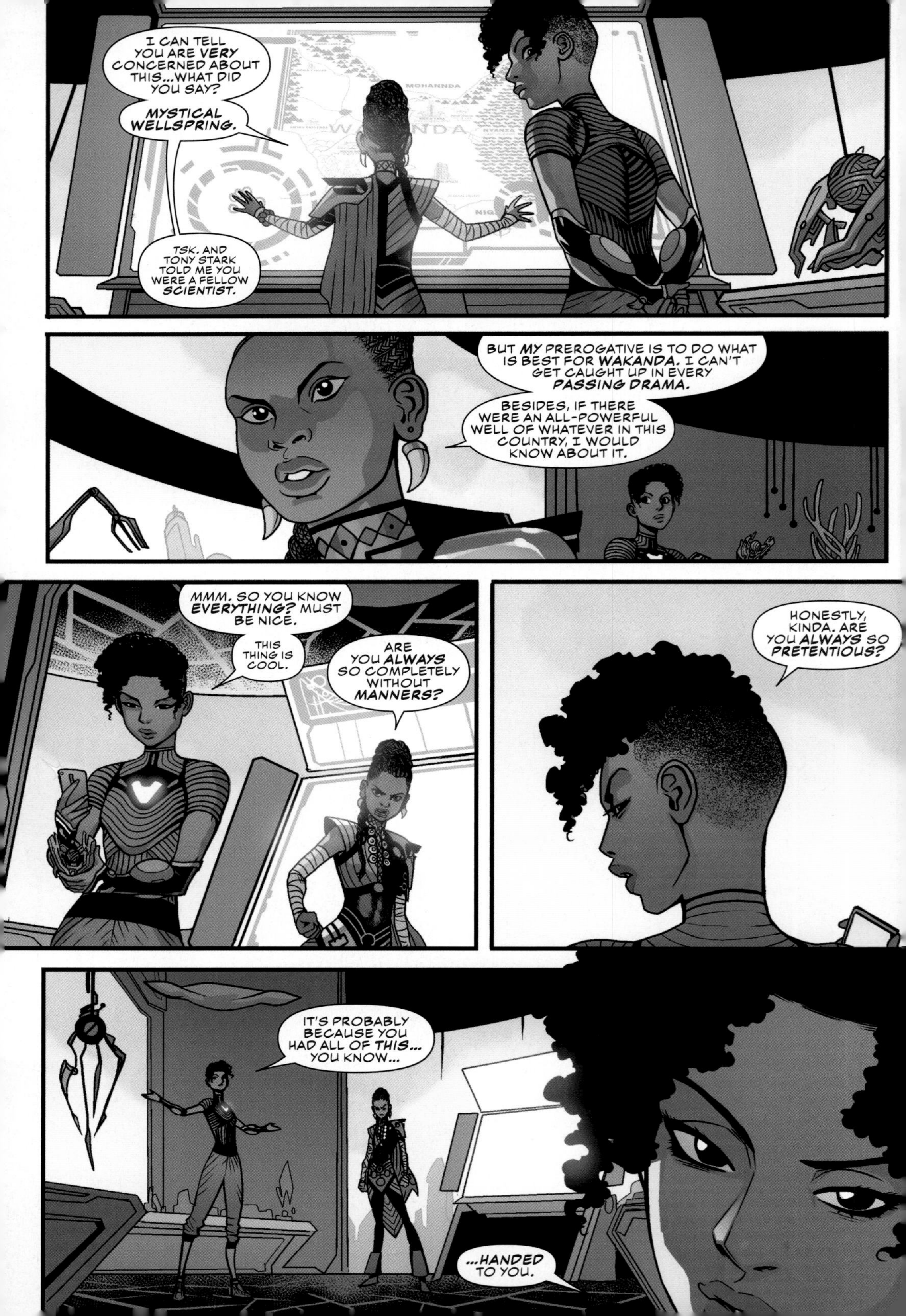

I CAN TELL YOU ARE VERY CONCERNED ABOUT THIS...WHAT DID YOU SAY?
MYSTICAL WELLSPRING.
TSK. AND TONY STARK TOLD ME YOU WERE A FELLOW SCIENTIST.
MOHANNDA
WAKANDA
NYANZA
BUT MY PREROGATIVE IS TO DO WHAT IS BEST FOR WAKANDA. I CAN'T GET CAUGHT UP IN EVERY PASSING DRAMA.
BESIDES, IF THERE WERE AN ALL-POWERFUL WELL OF WHATEVER IN THIS COUNTRY, I WOULD KNOW ABOUT IT.
MMM. SO YOU KNOW EVERYTHING? MUST BE NICE.
THIS THING IS COOL.
ARE YOU ALWAYS SO COMPLETELY WITHOUT MANNERS?
HONESTLY, KINDA. ARE YOU ALWAYS SO PRETENTIOUS?
IT'S PROBABLY BECAUSE YOU HAD ALL OF THIS... YOU KNOW...
...HANDED TO YOU.

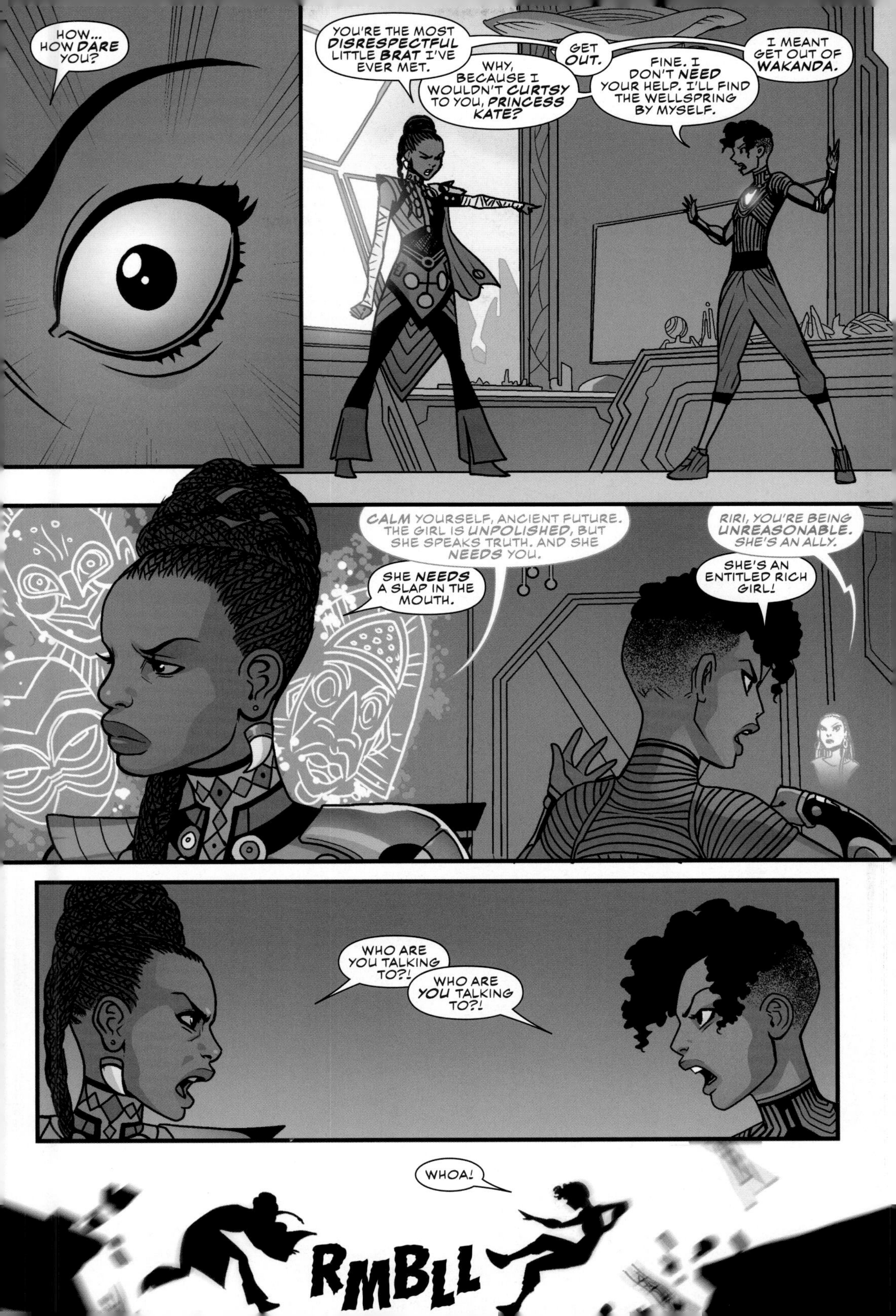

HOW... HOW DARE YOU?
YOU'RE THE MOST DISRESPECTFUL LITTLE BRAT I'VE EVER MET.
WHY, BECAUSE I WOULDN'T CURTSY TO YOU, PRINCESS KATE?
GET OUT.
FINE. I DON'T NEED YOUR HELP. I'LL FIND THE WELLSPRING BY MYSELF.
I MEANT GET OUT OF WAKANDA.
CALM YOURSELF, ANCIENT FUTURE. THE GIRL IS UNPOLISHED, BUT SHE SPEAKS TRUTH. AND SHE NEEDS YOU.
SHE NEEDS A SLAP IN THE MOUTH.
RIRI, YOU'RE BEING UNREASONABLE. SHE'S AN ALLY.
SHE'S AN ENTITLED RICH GIRL!
WHO ARE YOU TALKING TO?!
WHO ARE YOU TALKING TO?!
WHOA!
RMBLL

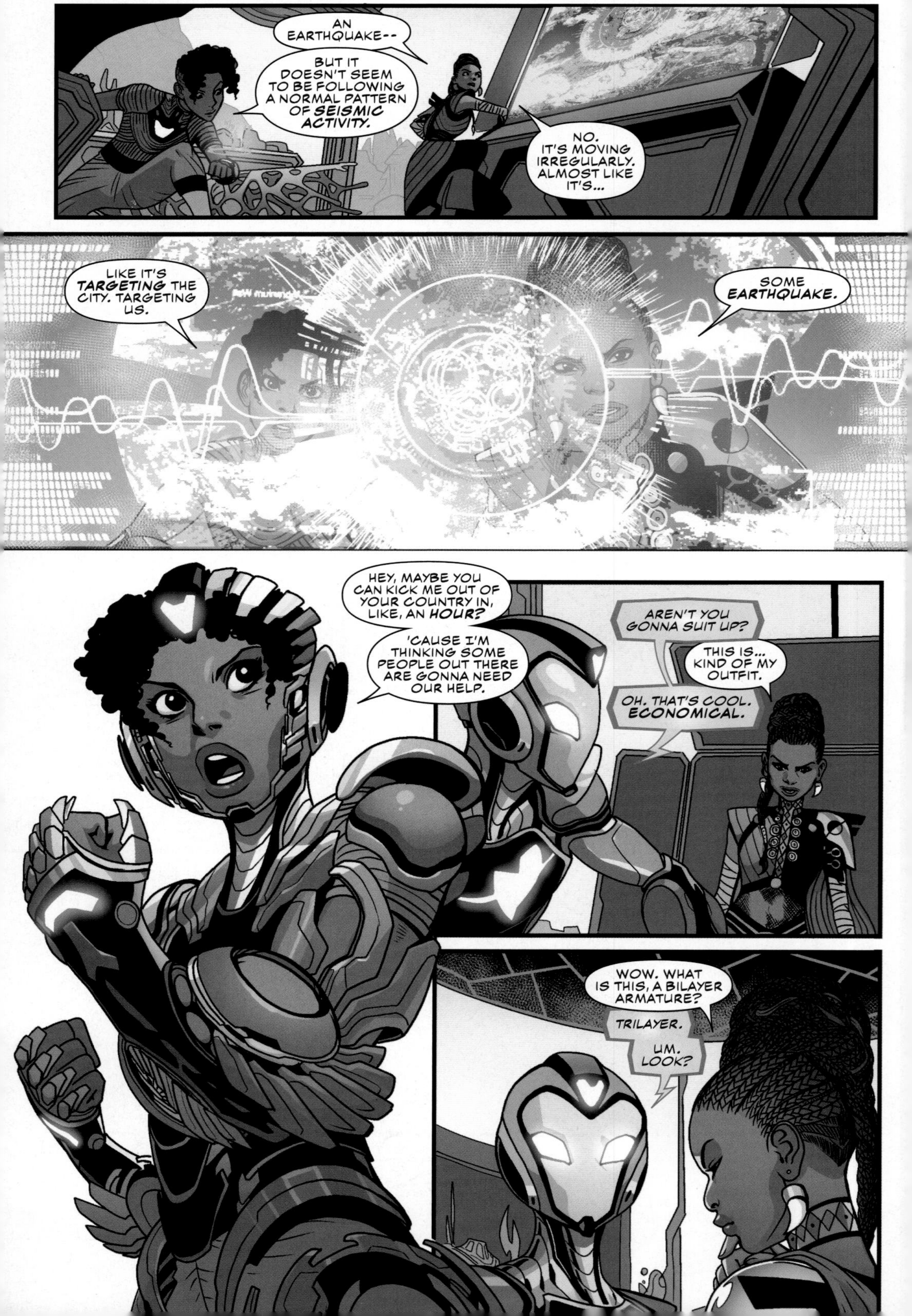
AN EARTHQUAKE--
BUT IT DOESN'T SEEM TO BE FOLLOWING A NORMAL PATTERN OF SEISMIC ACTIVITY.
NO. IT'S MOVING IRREGULARLY. ALMOST LIKE IT'S...
LIKE IT'S TARGETING THE CITY. TARGETING US.
SOME EARTHQUAKE.
HEY, MAYBE YOU CAN KICK ME OUT OF YOUR COUNTRY IN, LIKE, AN HOUR?
'CAUSE I'M THINKING SOME PEOPLE OUT THERE ARE GONNA NEED OUR HELP.
AREN'T YOU GONNA SUIT UP?
THIS IS... KIND OF MY OUTFIT.
OH. THAT'S COOL. ECONOMICAL.
WOW. WHAT IS THIS, A BILAYER ARMATURE?
TRILAYER.
UM. LOOK?

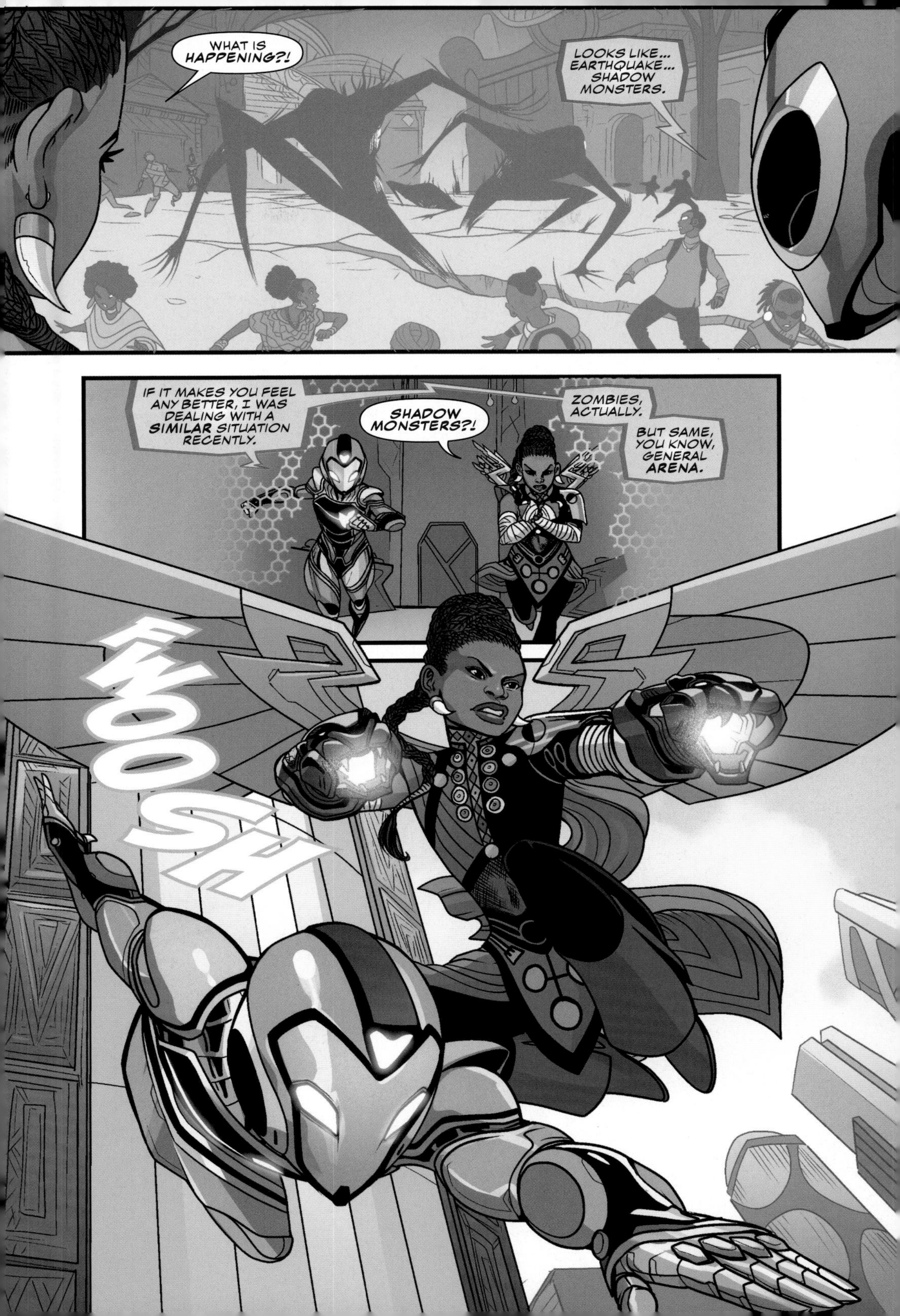
WHAT IS HAPPENING?!
LOOKS LIKE... EARTHQUAKE... SHADOW MONSTERS.
IF IT MAKES YOU FEEL ANY BETTER, I WAS DEALING WITH A SIMILAR SITUATION RECENTLY.
SHADOW MONSTERS?!
ZOMBIES, ACTUALLY.
BUT SAME, YOU KNOW, GENERAL ARENA.
FWOOSH

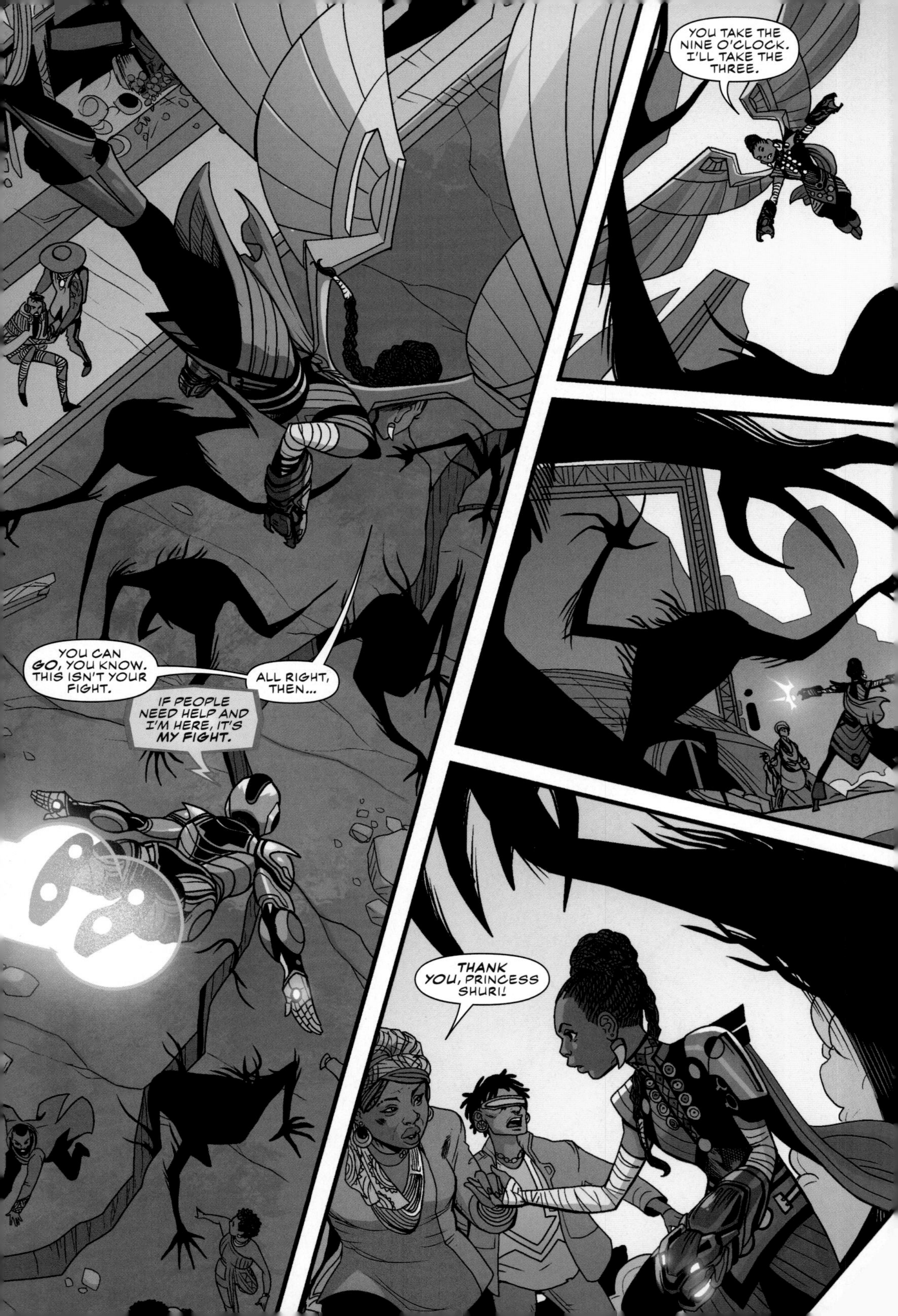
YOU CAN GO, YOU KNOW. THIS ISN'T YOUR FIGHT.
ALL RIGHT, THEN...
IF PEOPLE NEED HELP AND I'M HERE, IT'S MY FIGHT.
YOU TAKE THE NINE O'CLOCK. I'LL TAKE THE THREE.
THANK YOU, PRINCESS SHURI!

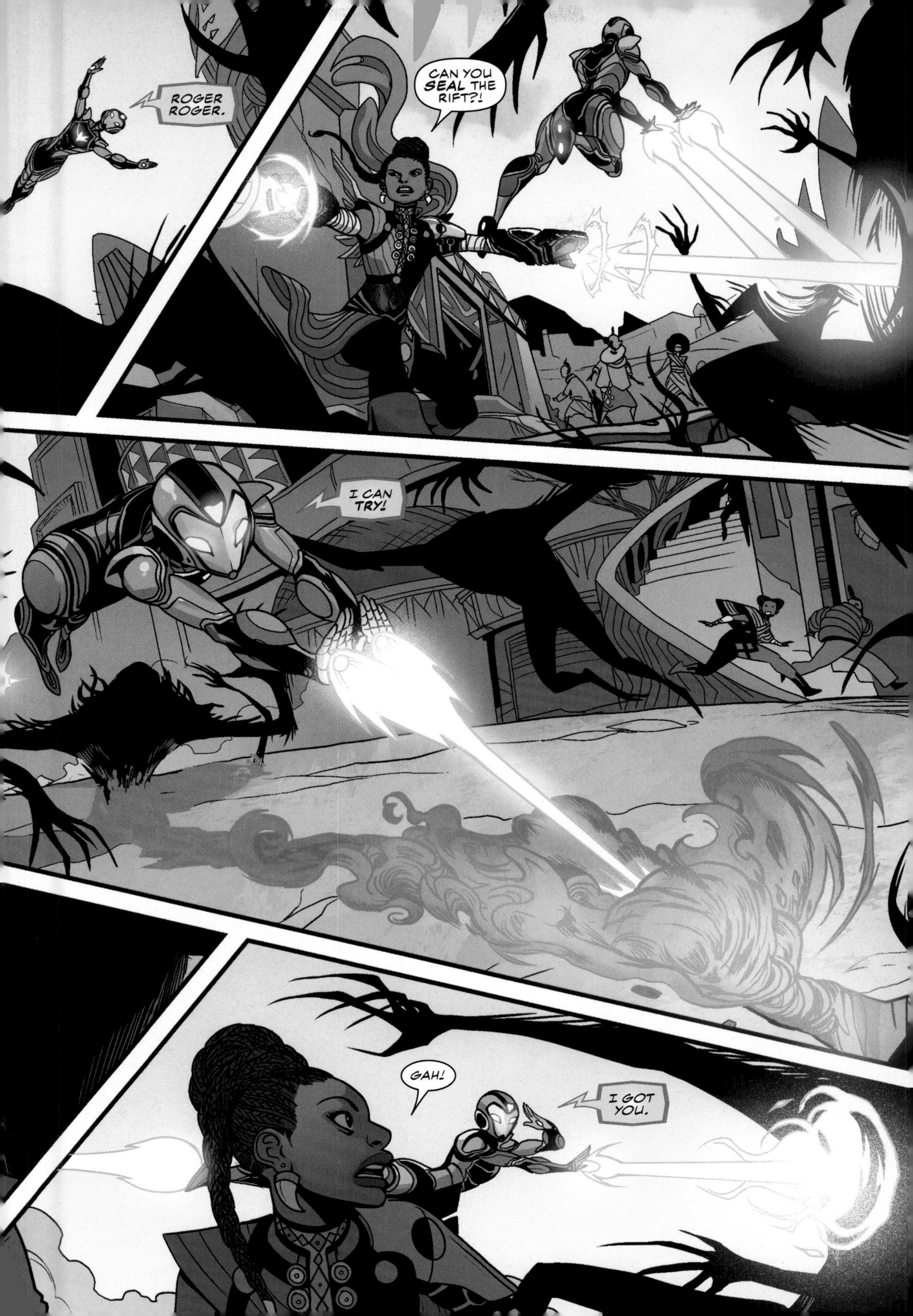
ROGER ROGER.
CAN YOU SEAL THE RIFT?!
I CAN TRY!
GAH!
I GOT YOU.

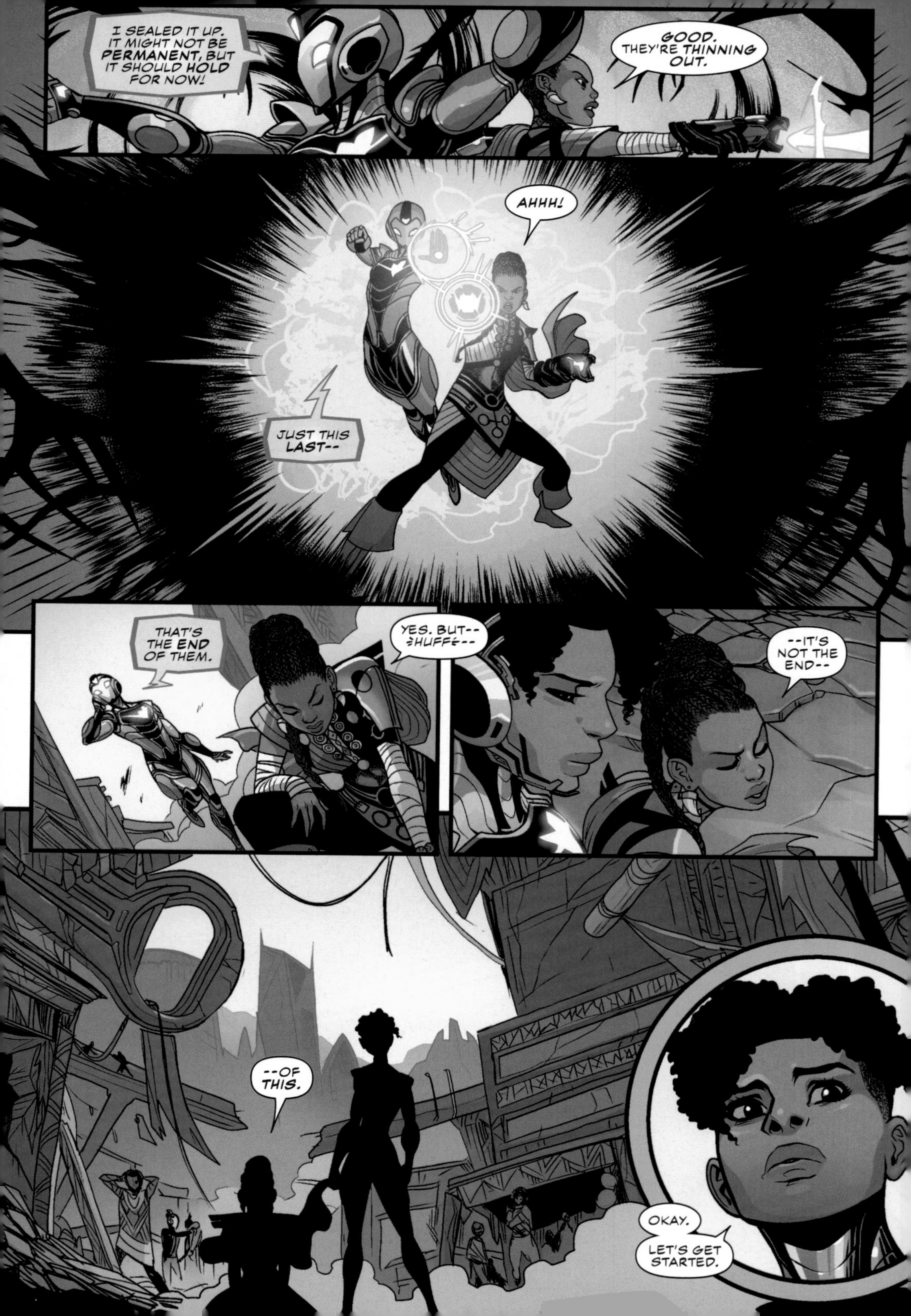

I SEALED IT UP. IT MIGHT NOT BE PERMANENT, BUT IT SHOULD HOLD FOR NOW!
GOOD. THEY'RE THINNING OUT.
AHHH!
JUST THIS LAST--
THAT'S THE END OF THEM.
YES. BUT-- ≶HUFF≶--
--IT'S NOT THE END--
--OF THIS.
OKAY.
LET'S GET STARTED.

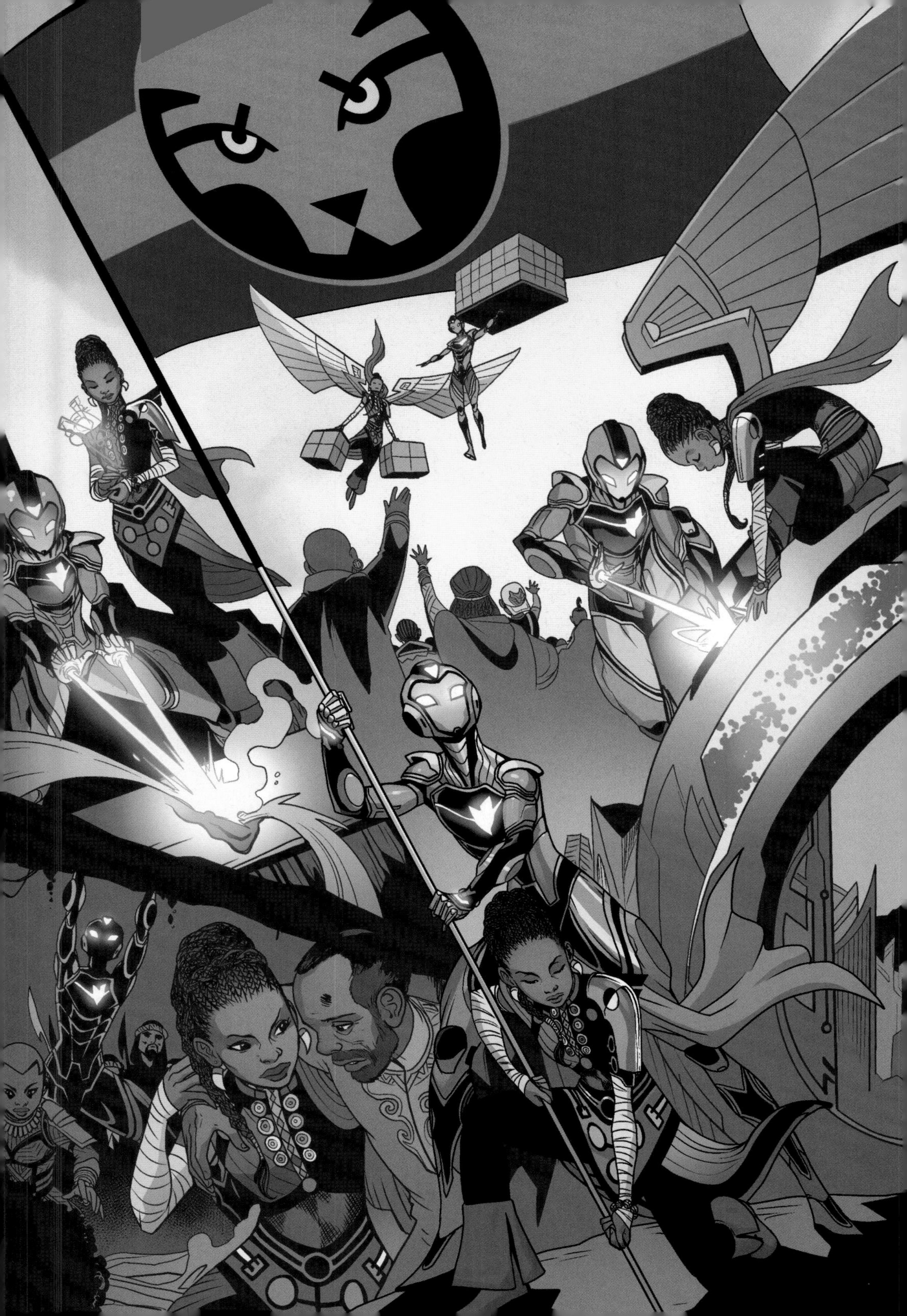

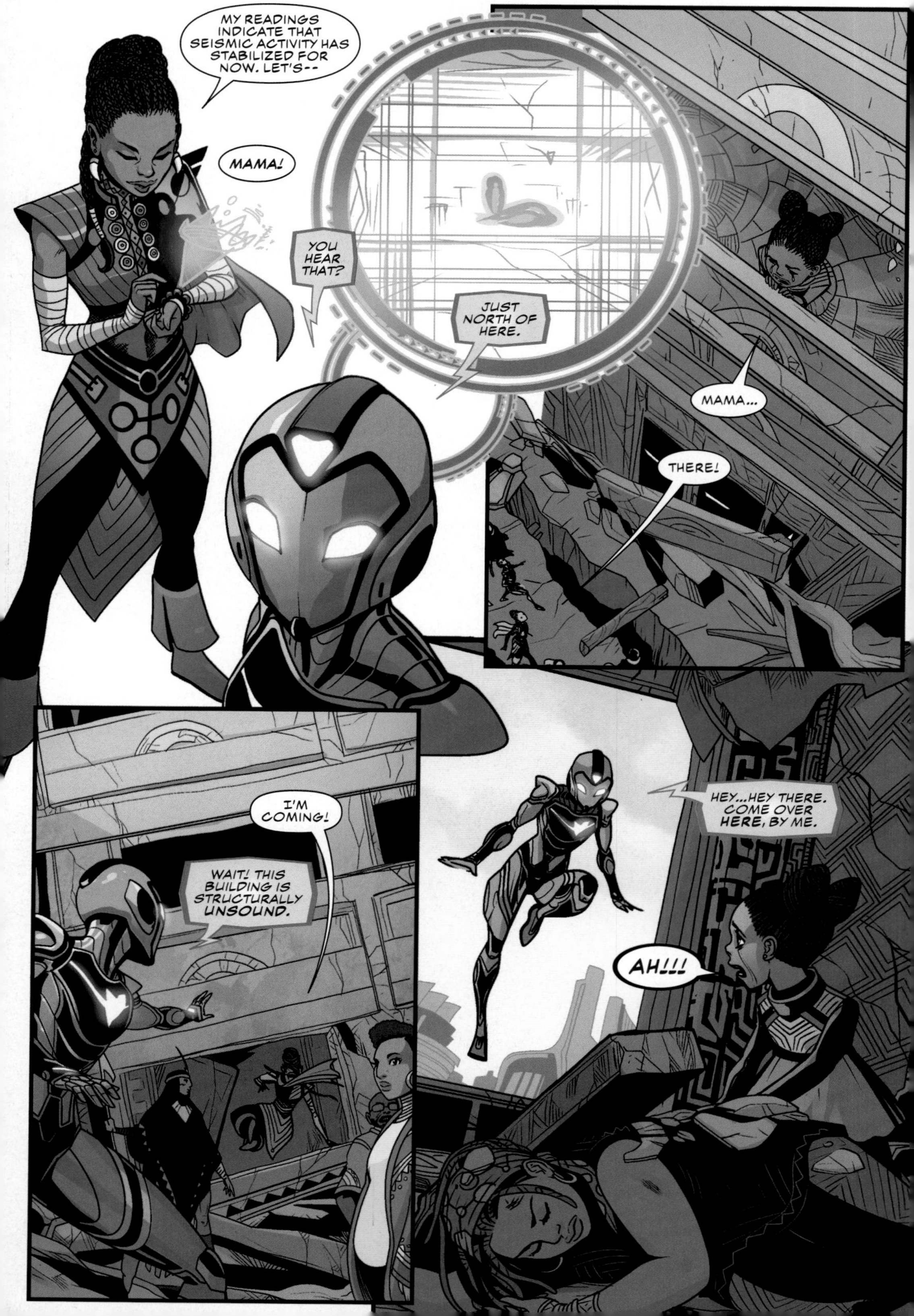
MY READINGS INDICATE THAT SEISMIC ACTIVITY HAS STABILIZED FOR NOW. LET'S--
MAMA!
YOU HEAR THAT?
JUST NORTH OF HERE.
MAMA...
THERE!
I'M COMING!
WAIT! THIS BUILDING IS STRUCTURALLY UNSOUND.
HEY...HEY THERE. COME OVER HERE, BY ME.
AH!!!

I WON'T *HURT* YOU. BUT YOU NEED TO COME WITH ME. I'LL CARRY YOUR MOTHER TOO.

SHE'S UNCONSCIOUS, BUT HER *VITALS* ARE FINE.

I CAN CARRY THEM, BUT WE HAVE TO *GO*. THIS BUILDING COULD COLLAPSE ANY *SECOND!*

ᏟᏝᎧᎩᎳᏗ! ᎶᏟ ᏟᏝᎧᏆ ᎤᏎᎤᎩ ᏟᏝᏟᏝᎤᎩ?

COME ON, LI'L MAMA.

ᎤᎤᏟ, ᏟᏝᎧᏆᏝᎶ ᏎᎶᏝᎧ.

WHAT DID YOU *SAY* TO MAKE HER COME WITH ME?

SHE ASKED IF YOU WERE MY *SISTER*.

I TOLD HER *YES*.

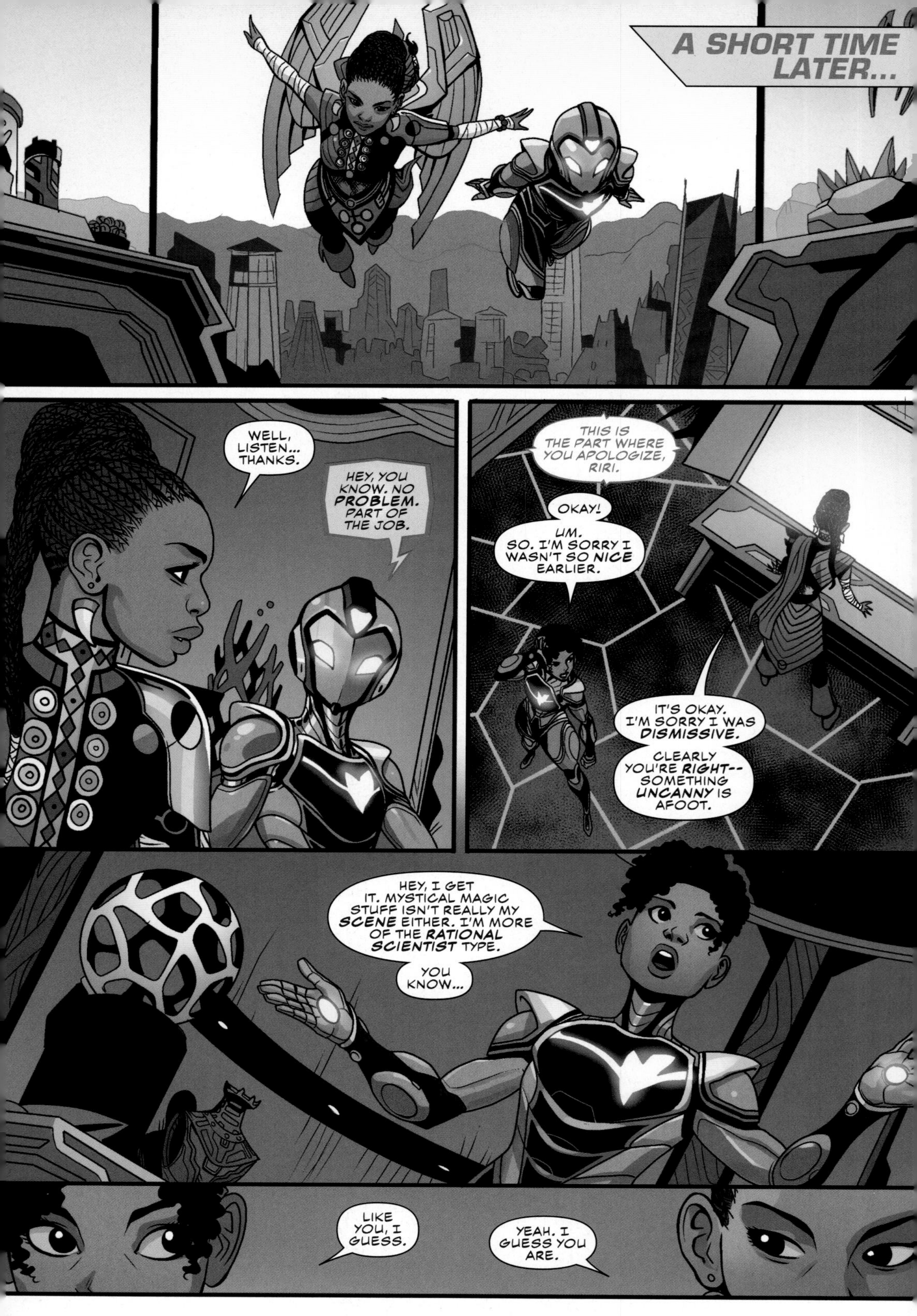
A SHORT TIME LATER...
WELL, LISTEN... THANKS.
HEY, YOU KNOW. NO PROBLEM. PART OF THE JOB.
THIS IS THE PART WHERE YOU APOLOGIZE, RIRI.
OKAY!
UM. SO. I'M SORRY I WASN'T SO NICE EARLIER.
IT'S OKAY. I'M SORRY I WAS DISMISSIVE.
CLEARLY YOU'RE RIGHT-- SOMETHING UNCANNY IS AFOOT.
HEY, I GET IT. MYSTICAL MAGIC STUFF ISN'T REALLY MY SCENE EITHER. I'M MORE OF THE RATIONAL SCIENTIST TYPE.
YOU KNOW...
LIKE YOU, I GUESS.
YEAH. I GUESS YOU ARE.

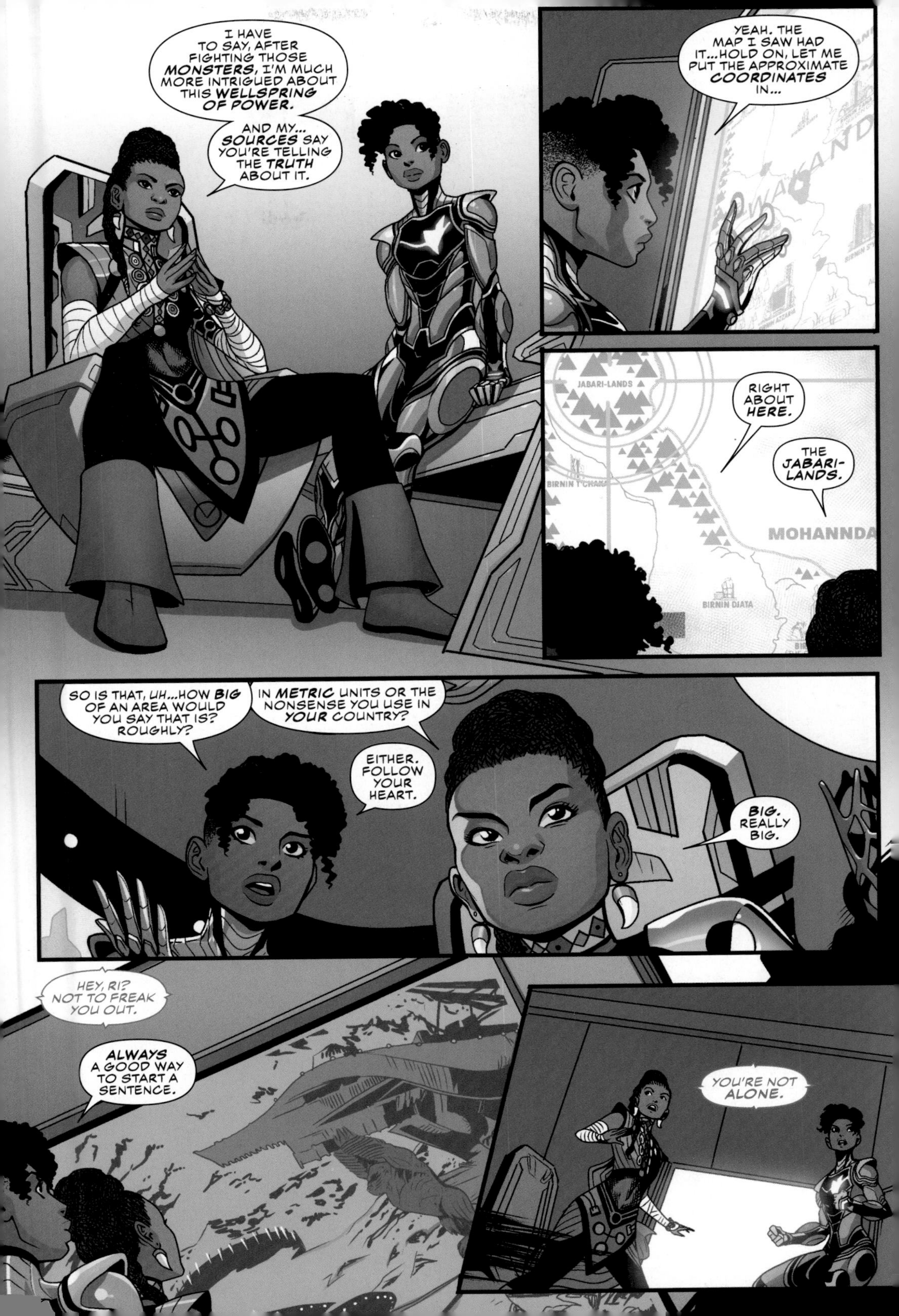

I HAVE TO SAY, AFTER FIGHTING THOSE MONSTERS, I'M MUCH MORE INTRIGUED ABOUT THIS WELLSPRING OF POWER.
AND MY... SOURCES SAY YOU'RE TELLING THE TRUTH ABOUT IT.
YEAH. THE MAP I SAW HAD IT...HOLD ON, LET ME PUT THE APPROXIMATE COORDINATES IN...
JABARI-LANDS
BIRNIN T'CHAKA
MOHANNDA
BIRNIN DJATA
RIGHT ABOUT HERE.
THE JABARI-LANDS.
SO IS THAT, UH...HOW BIG OF AN AREA WOULD YOU SAY THAT IS? ROUGHLY?
IN METRIC UNITS OR THE NONSENSE YOU USE IN YOUR COUNTRY?
EITHER. FOLLOW YOUR HEART.
BIG. REALLY BIG.
HEY, RI? NOT TO FREAK YOU OUT.
ALWAYS A GOOD WAY TO START A SENTENCE.
YOU'RE NOT ALONE.

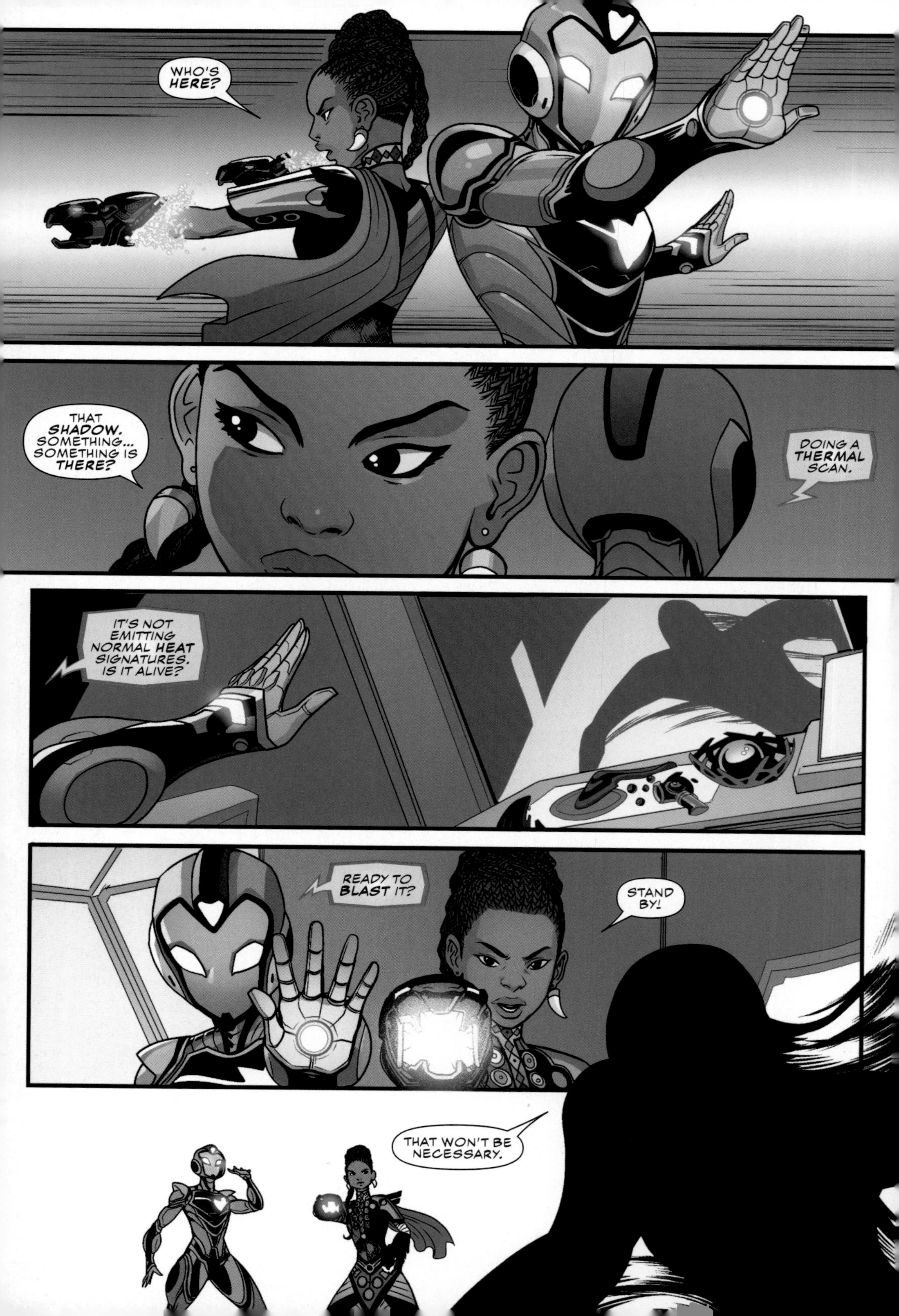
WHO'S HERE?
THAT SHADOW. SOMETHING... SOMETHING IS THERE?
DOING A THERMAL SCAN.
IT'S NOT EMITTING NORMAL HEAT SIGNATURES. IS IT ALIVE?
READY TO BLAST IT?
STAND BY!
THAT WON'T BE NECESSARY.

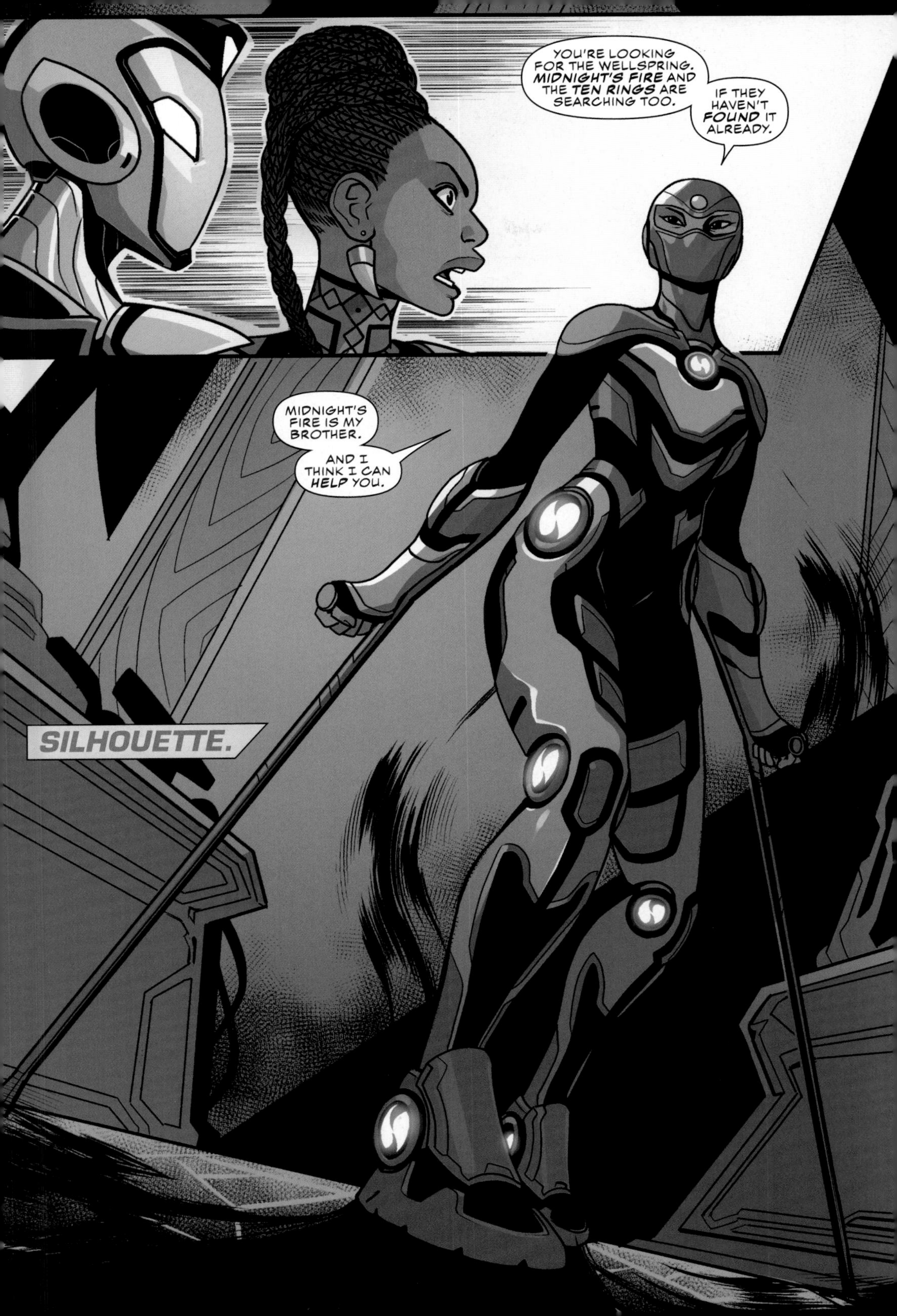
YOU'RE LOOKING FOR THE WELLSPRING. MIDNIGHT'S FIRE AND THE TEN RINGS ARE SEARCHING TOO.
IF THEY HAVEN'T FOUND IT ALREADY.
MIDNIGHT'S FIRE IS MY BROTHER.
AND I THINK I CAN HELP YOU.
SILHOUETTE.

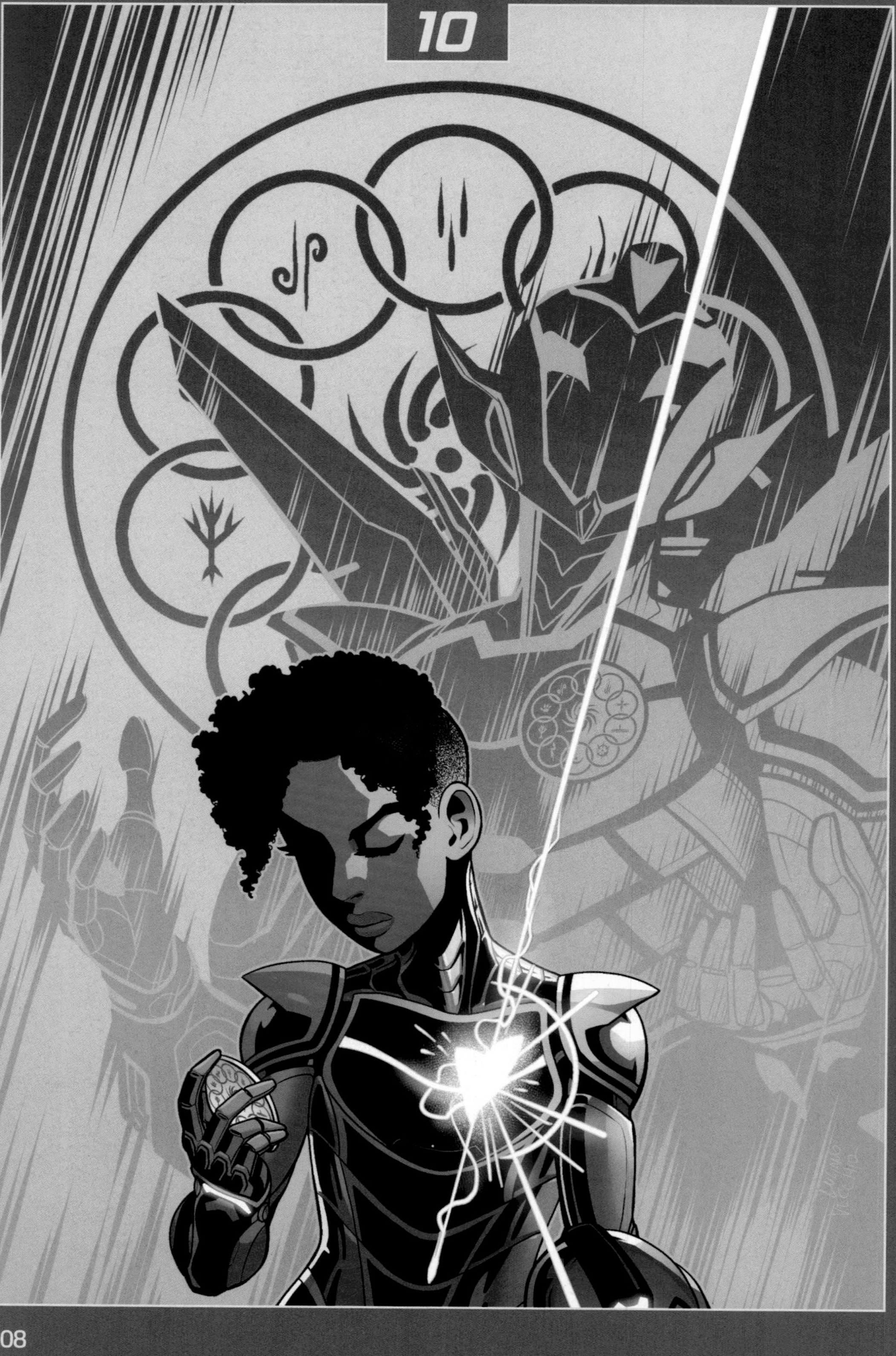
10

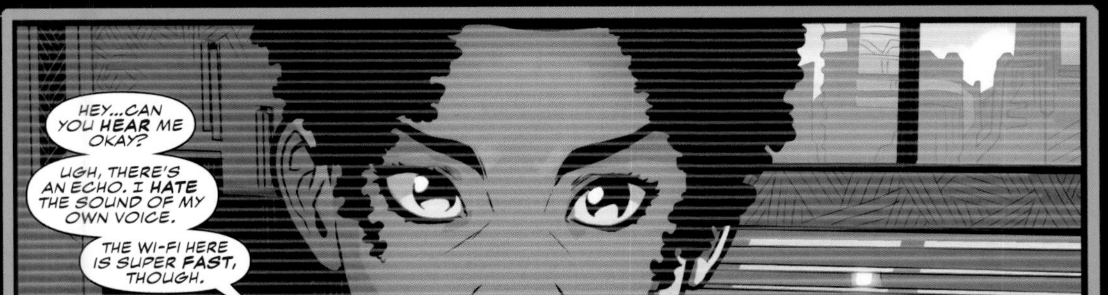
HEY...CAN YOU HEAR ME OKAY?
UGH, THERE'S AN ECHO. I HATE THE SOUND OF MY OWN VOICE.
THE WI-FI HERE IS SUPER FAST, THOUGH.
YEAH, YOU'RE COMING THROUGH LOUD AND CLEAR.

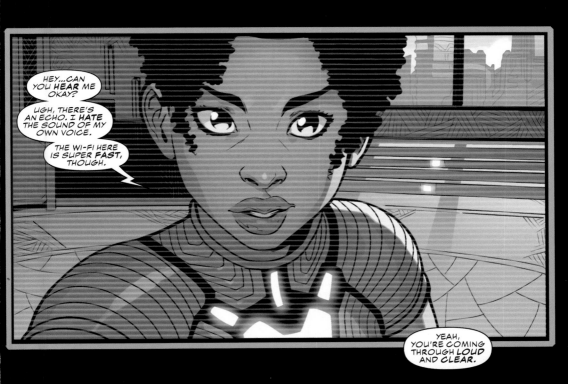

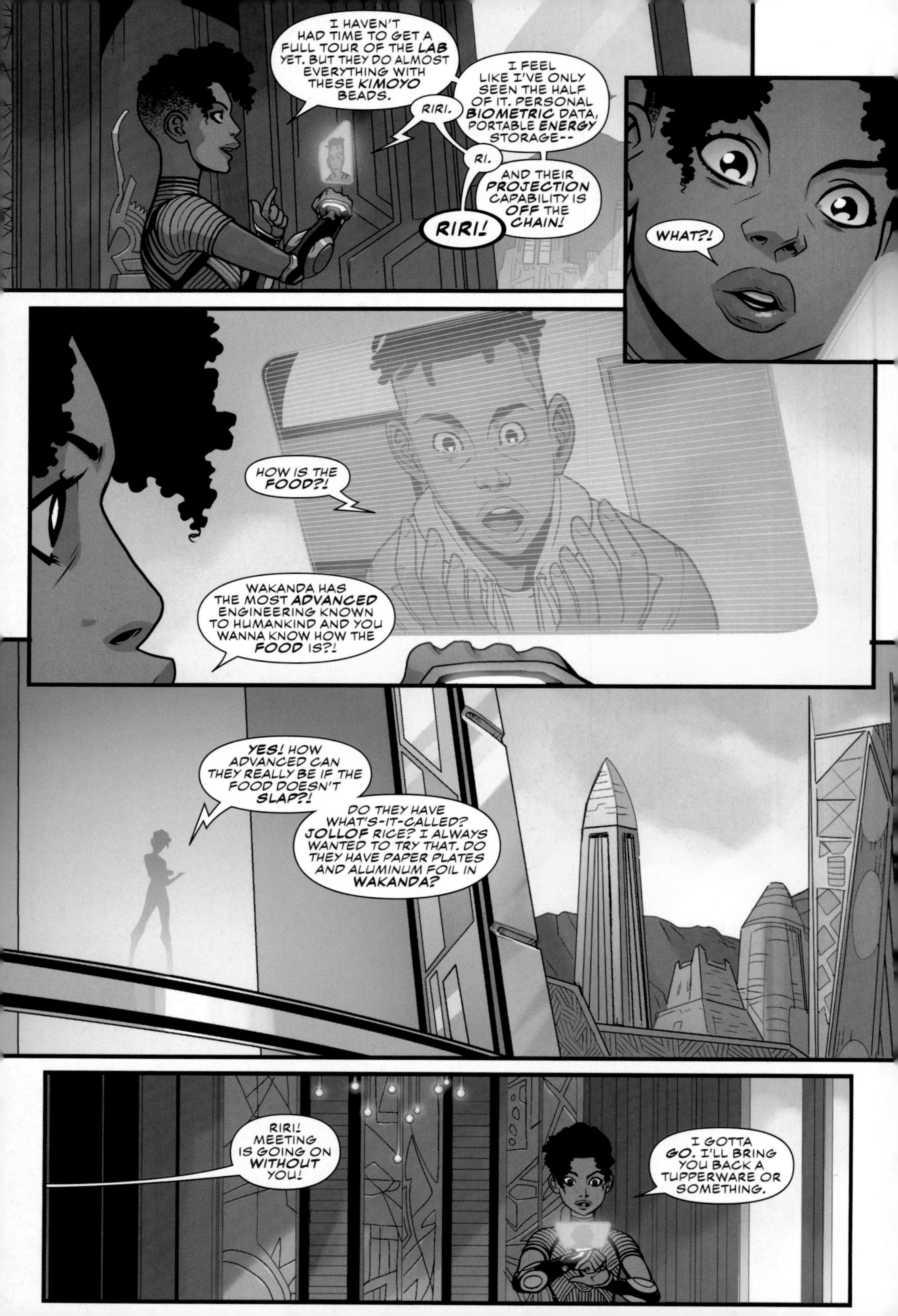
I HAVEN'T HAD TIME TO GET A FULL TOUR OF THE LAB YET. BUT THEY DO ALMOST EVERYTHING WITH THESE KIMOYO BEADS.
I FEEL LIKE I'VE ONLY SEEN THE HALF OF IT. PERSONAL BIOMETRIC DATA, PORTABLE ENERGY STORAGE--
RIRI.
RI.
AND THEIR PROJECTION CAPABILITY IS OFF THE CHAIN!
RIRI!
WHAT?!
HOW IS THE FOOD?!
WAKANDA HAS THE MOST ADVANCED ENGINEERING KNOWN TO HUMANKIND AND YOU WANNA KNOW HOW THE FOOD IS?!
YES! HOW ADVANCED CAN THEY REALLY BE IF THE FOOD DOESN'T SLAP?!
DO THEY HAVE WHAT'S-IT-CALLED? JOLLOF RICE? I ALWAYS WANTED TO TRY THAT. DO THEY HAVE PAPER PLATES AND ALUMINUM FOIL IN WAKANDA?
RIRI! MEETING IS GOING ON WITHOUT YOU!
I GOTTA GO. I'LL BRING YOU BACK A TUPPERWARE OR SOMETHING.

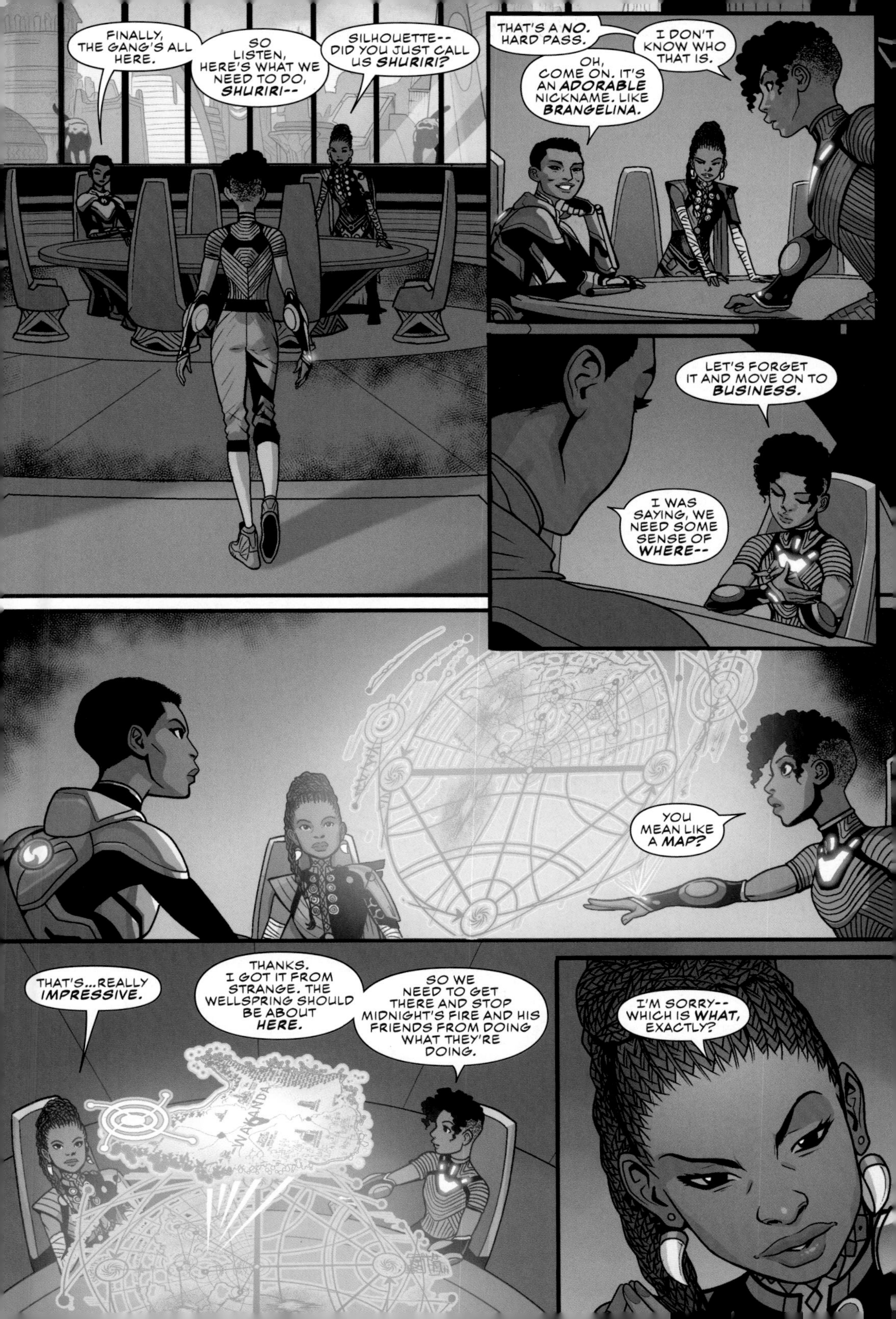
FINALLY, THE GANG'S ALL HERE.
SO LISTEN, HERE'S WHAT WE NEED TO DO, SHURIRI--
SILHOUETTE--DID YOU JUST CALL US SHURIRI?
THAT'S A NO. HARD PASS.
I DON'T KNOW WHO THAT IS.
OH, COME ON. IT'S AN ADORABLE NICKNAME. LIKE BRANGELINA.
LET'S FORGET IT AND MOVE ON TO BUSINESS.
I WAS SAYING, WE NEED SOME SENSE OF WHERE--
YOU MEAN LIKE A MAP?
THAT'S...REALLY IMPRESSIVE.
THANKS. I GOT IT FROM STRANGE. THE WELLSPRING SHOULD BE ABOUT HERE.
SO WE NEED TO GET THERE AND STOP MIDNIGHT'S FIRE AND HIS FRIENDS FROM DOING WHAT THEY'RE DOING.
WAKANDA
I'M SORRY--WHICH IS WHAT, EXACTLY?

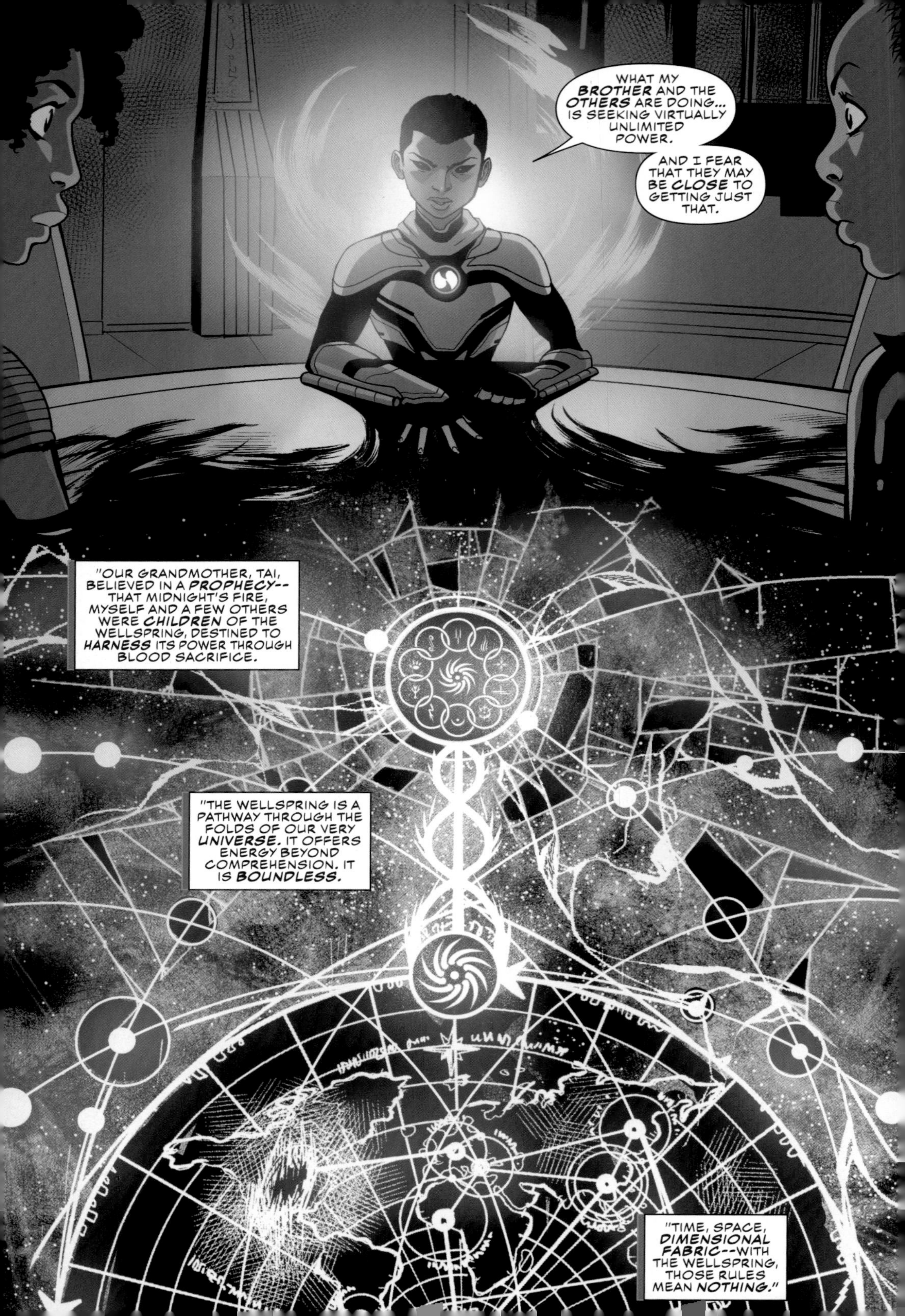
WHAT MY BROTHER AND THE OTHERS ARE DOING... IS SEEKING VIRTUALLY UNLIMITED POWER.
AND I FEAR THAT THEY MAY BE CLOSE TO GETTING JUST THAT.
"OUR GRANDMOTHER, TAI, BELIEVED IN A PROPHECY--THAT MIDNIGHT'S FIRE, MYSELF AND A FEW OTHERS WERE CHILDREN OF THE WELLSPRING, DESTINED TO HARNESS ITS POWER THROUGH BLOOD SACRIFICE.
"THE WELLSPRING IS A PATHWAY THROUGH THE FOLDS OF OUR VERY UNIVERSE. IT OFFERS ENERGY BEYOND COMPREHENSION. IT IS BOUNDLESS.
"TIME, SPACE, DIMENSIONAL FABRIC--WITH THE WELLSPRING, THOSE RULES MEAN NOTHING."

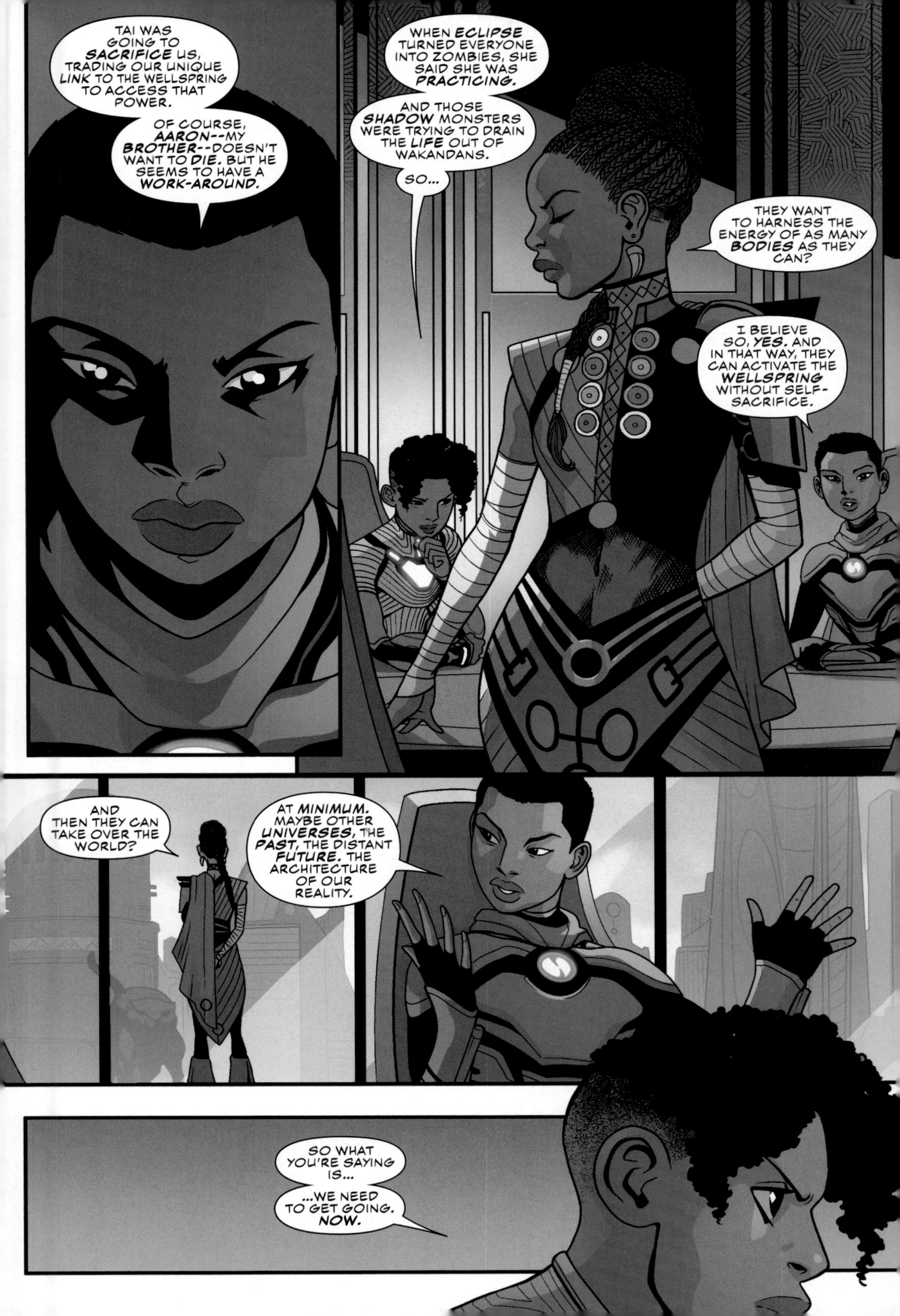

TAI WAS GOING TO SACRIFICE US, TRADING OUR UNIQUE LINK TO THE WELLSPRING TO ACCESS THAT POWER.
OF COURSE, AARON--MY BROTHER--DOESN'T WANT TO DIE. BUT HE SEEMS TO HAVE A WORK-AROUND.
WHEN ECLIPSE TURNED EVERYONE INTO ZOMBIES, SHE SAID SHE WAS PRACTICING.
AND THOSE SHADOW MONSTERS WERE TRYING TO DRAIN THE LIFE OUT OF WAKANDANS.
SO...
THEY WANT TO HARNESS THE ENERGY OF AS MANY BODIES AS THEY CAN?
I BELIEVE SO, YES. AND IN THAT WAY, THEY CAN ACTIVATE THE WELLSPRING WITHOUT SELF-SACRIFICE.
AND THEN THEY CAN TAKE OVER THE WORLD?
AT MINIMUM. MAYBE OTHER UNIVERSES, THE PAST, THE DISTANT FUTURE. THE ARCHITECTURE OF OUR REALITY.
SO WHAT YOU'RE SAYING IS...
...WE NEED TO GET GOING. NOW.

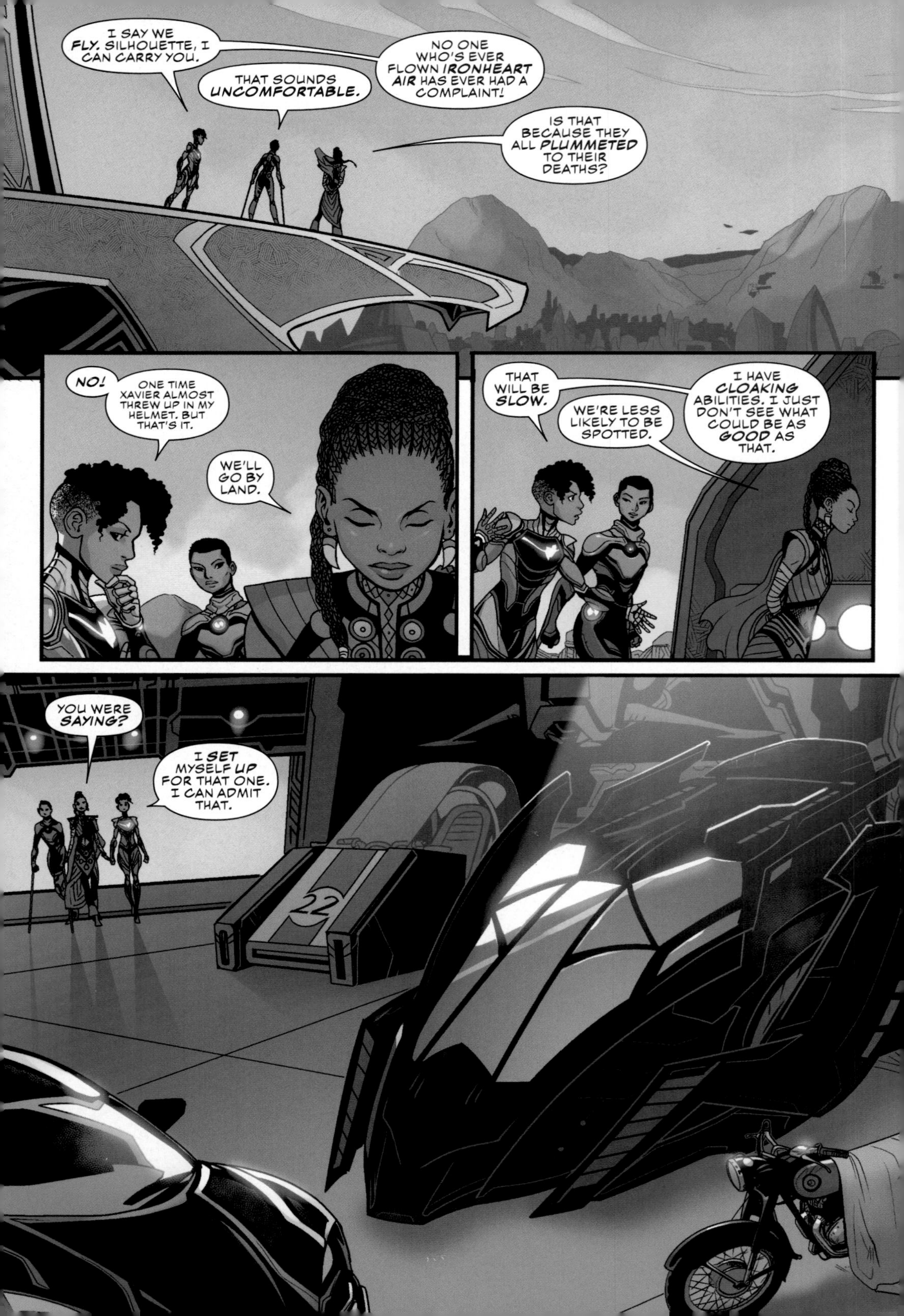

I SAY WE FLY. SILHOUETTE, I CAN CARRY YOU.
THAT SOUNDS UNCOMFORTABLE.
NO ONE WHO'S EVER FLOWN IRONHEART AIR HAS EVER HAD A COMPLAINT!
IS THAT BECAUSE THEY ALL PLUMMETED TO THEIR DEATHS?
NO!
ONE TIME XAVIER ALMOST THREW UP IN MY HELMET. BUT THAT'S IT.
WE'LL GO BY LAND.
THAT WILL BE SLOW.
WE'RE LESS LIKELY TO BE SPOTTED.
I HAVE CLOAKING ABILITIES. I JUST DON'T SEE WHAT COULD BE AS GOOD AS THAT.
YOU WERE SAYING?
I SET MYSELF UP FOR THAT ONE. I CAN ADMIT THAT.
22

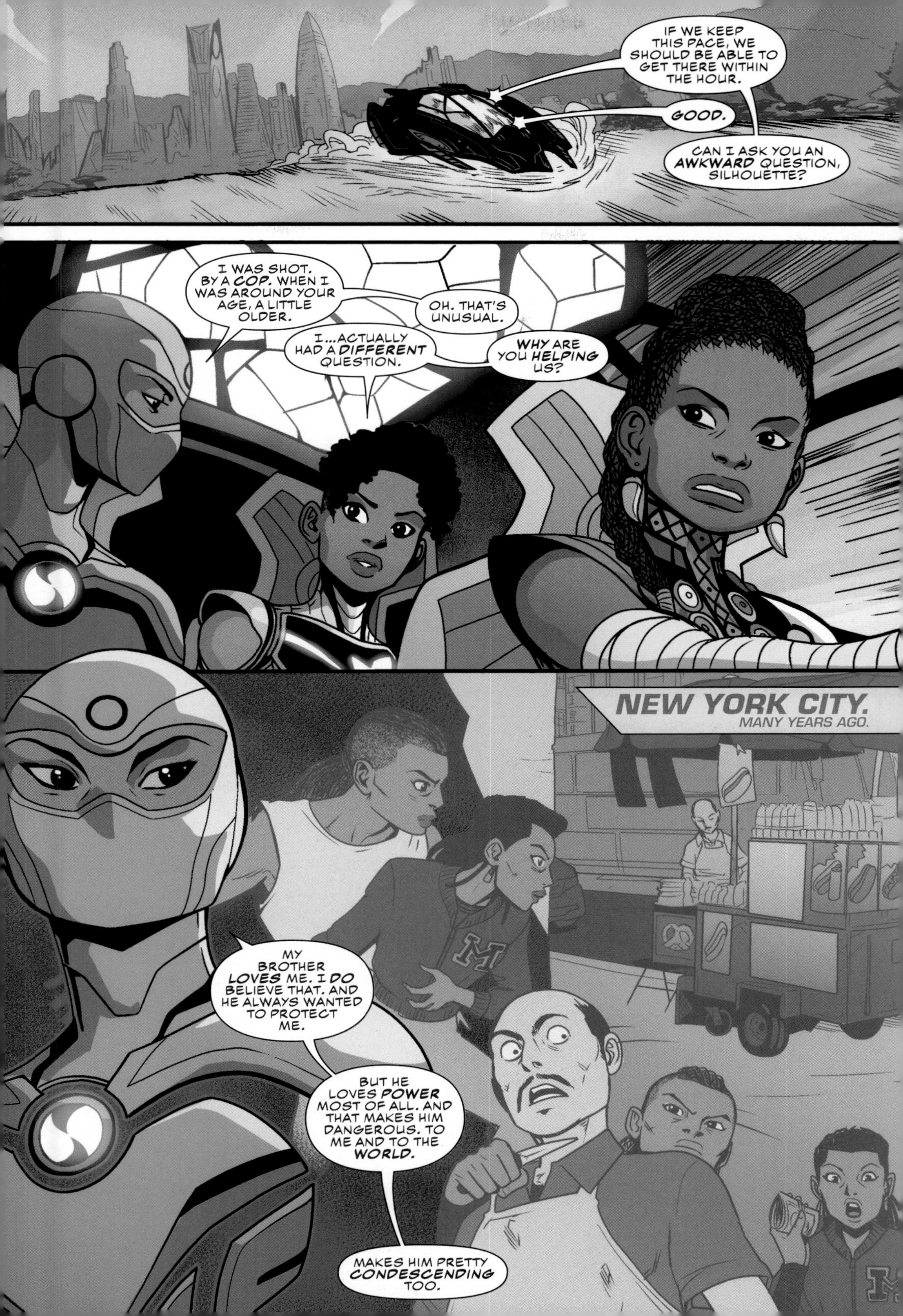

IF WE KEEP THIS PACE, WE SHOULD BE ABLE TO GET THERE WITHIN THE HOUR.
GOOD.
CAN I ASK YOU AN AWKWARD QUESTION, SILHOUETTE?
I WAS SHOT. BY A COP. WHEN I WAS AROUND YOUR AGE, A LITTLE OLDER.
OH. THAT'S UNUSUAL.
I...ACTUALLY HAD A DIFFERENT QUESTION.
WHY ARE YOU HELPING US?
NEW YORK CITY.
MANY YEARS AGO.
MY BROTHER LOVES ME. I DO BELIEVE THAT. AND HE ALWAYS WANTED TO PROTECT ME.
BUT HE LOVES POWER MOST OF ALL. AND THAT MAKES HIM DANGEROUS. TO ME AND TO THE WORLD.
MAKES HIM PRETTY CONDESCENDING TOO.

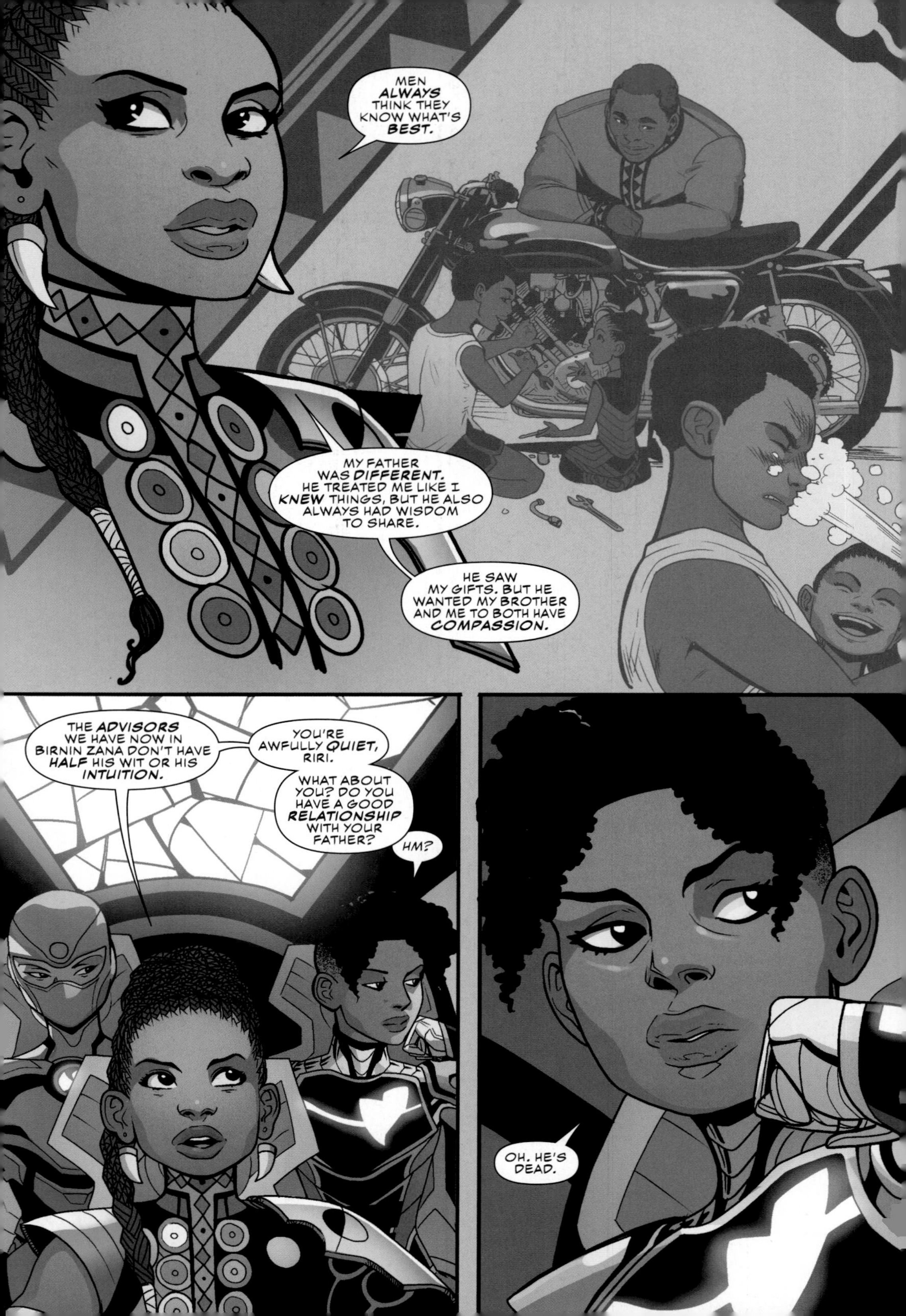
MEN ALWAYS THINK THEY KNOW WHAT'S BEST.
MY FATHER WAS DIFFERENT. HE TREATED ME LIKE I KNEW THINGS, BUT HE ALSO ALWAYS HAD WISDOM TO SHARE.
HE SAW MY GIFTS. BUT HE WANTED MY BROTHER AND ME TO BOTH HAVE COMPASSION.
THE ADVISORS WE HAVE NOW IN BIRNIN ZANA DON'T HAVE HALF HIS WIT OR HIS INTUITION.
YOU'RE AWFULLY QUIET, RIRI.
WHAT ABOUT YOU? DO YOU HAVE A GOOD RELATIONSHIP WITH YOUR FATHER?
HM?
OH. HE'S DEAD.

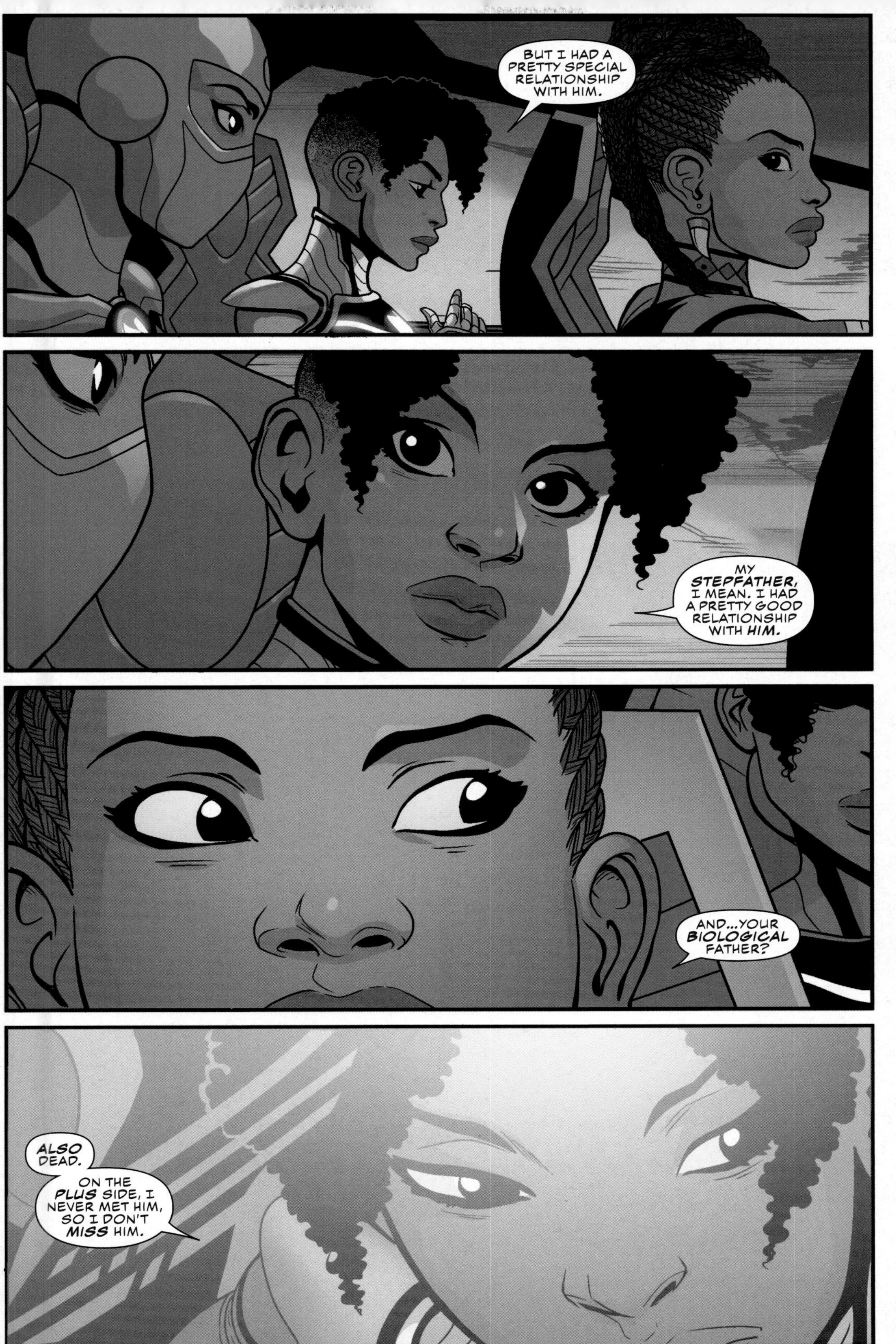
BUT I HAD A PRETTY SPECIAL RELATIONSHIP WITH HIM.
MY STEPFATHER, I MEAN. I HAD A PRETTY GOOD RELATIONSHIP WITH HIM.
AND...YOUR BIOLOGICAL FATHER?
ALSO DEAD.
ON THE PLUS SIDE, I NEVER MET HIM, SO I DON'T MISS HIM.

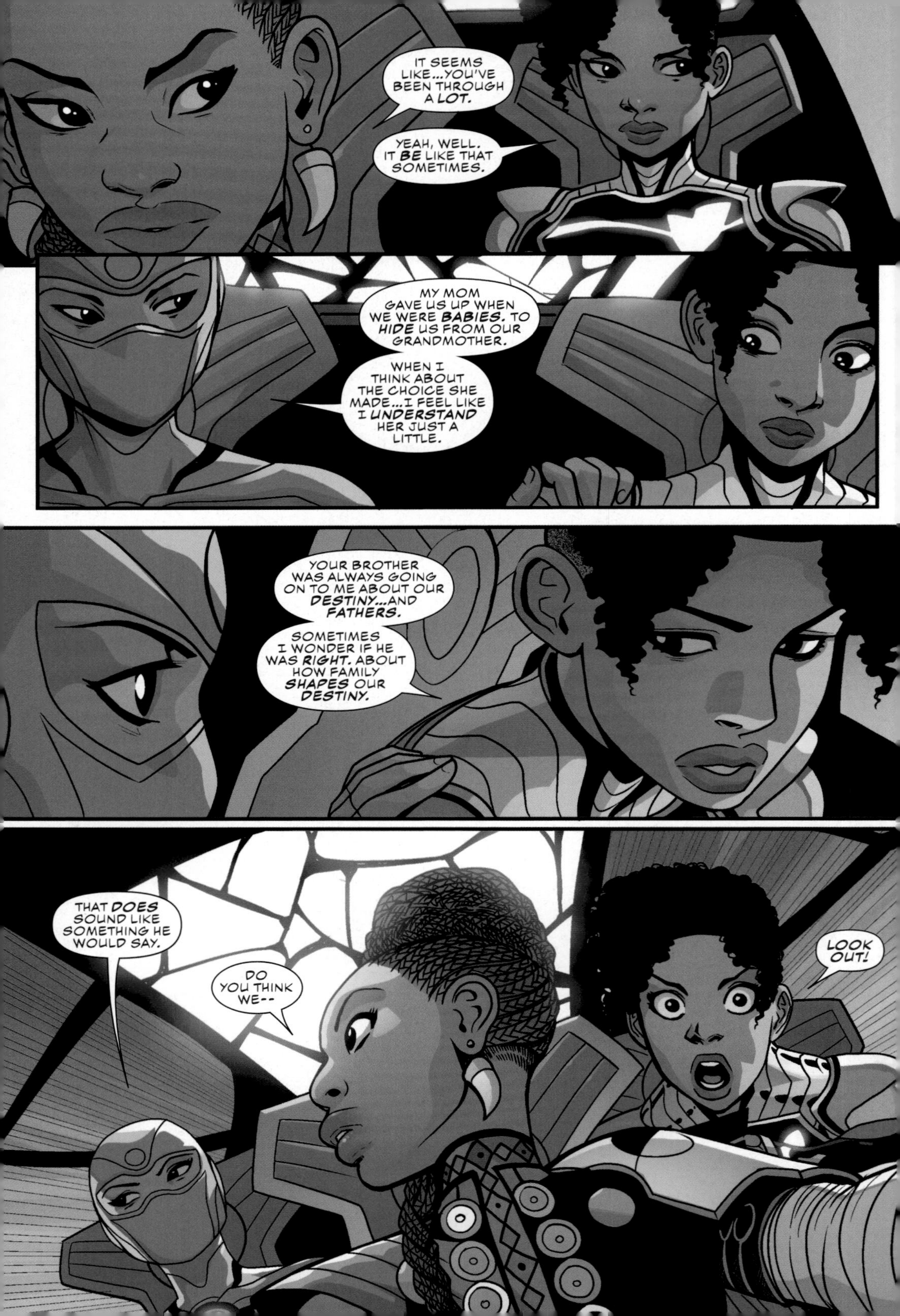
IT SEEMS LIKE...YOU'VE BEEN THROUGH A LOT.
YEAH, WELL. IT BE LIKE THAT SOMETIMES.
MY MOM GAVE US UP WHEN WE WERE BABIES. TO HIDE US FROM OUR GRANDMOTHER.
WHEN I THINK ABOUT THE CHOICE SHE MADE...I FEEL LIKE I UNDERSTAND HER JUST A LITTLE.
YOUR BROTHER WAS ALWAYS GOING ON TO ME ABOUT OUR DESTINY...AND FATHERS.
SOMETIMES I WONDER IF HE WAS RIGHT. ABOUT HOW FAMILY SHAPES OUR DESTINY.
THAT DOES SOUND LIKE SOMETHING HE WOULD SAY.
DO YOU THINK WE--
LOOK OUT!

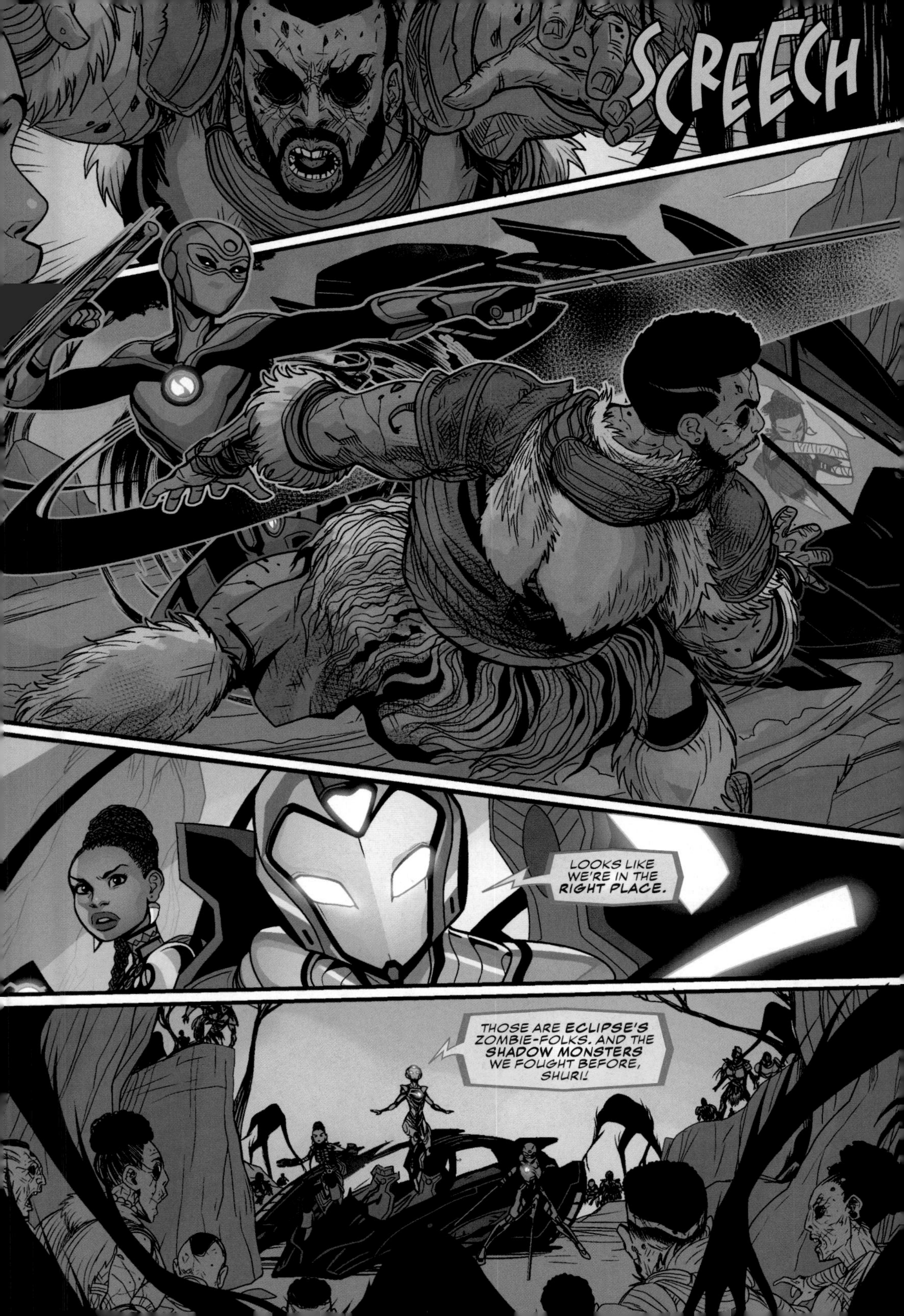
SCREECH
LOOKS LIKE WE'RE IN THE RIGHT PLACE.
THOSE ARE ECLIPSE'S ZOMBIE-FOLKS. AND THE SHADOW MONSTERS WE FOUGHT BEFORE, SHURI!

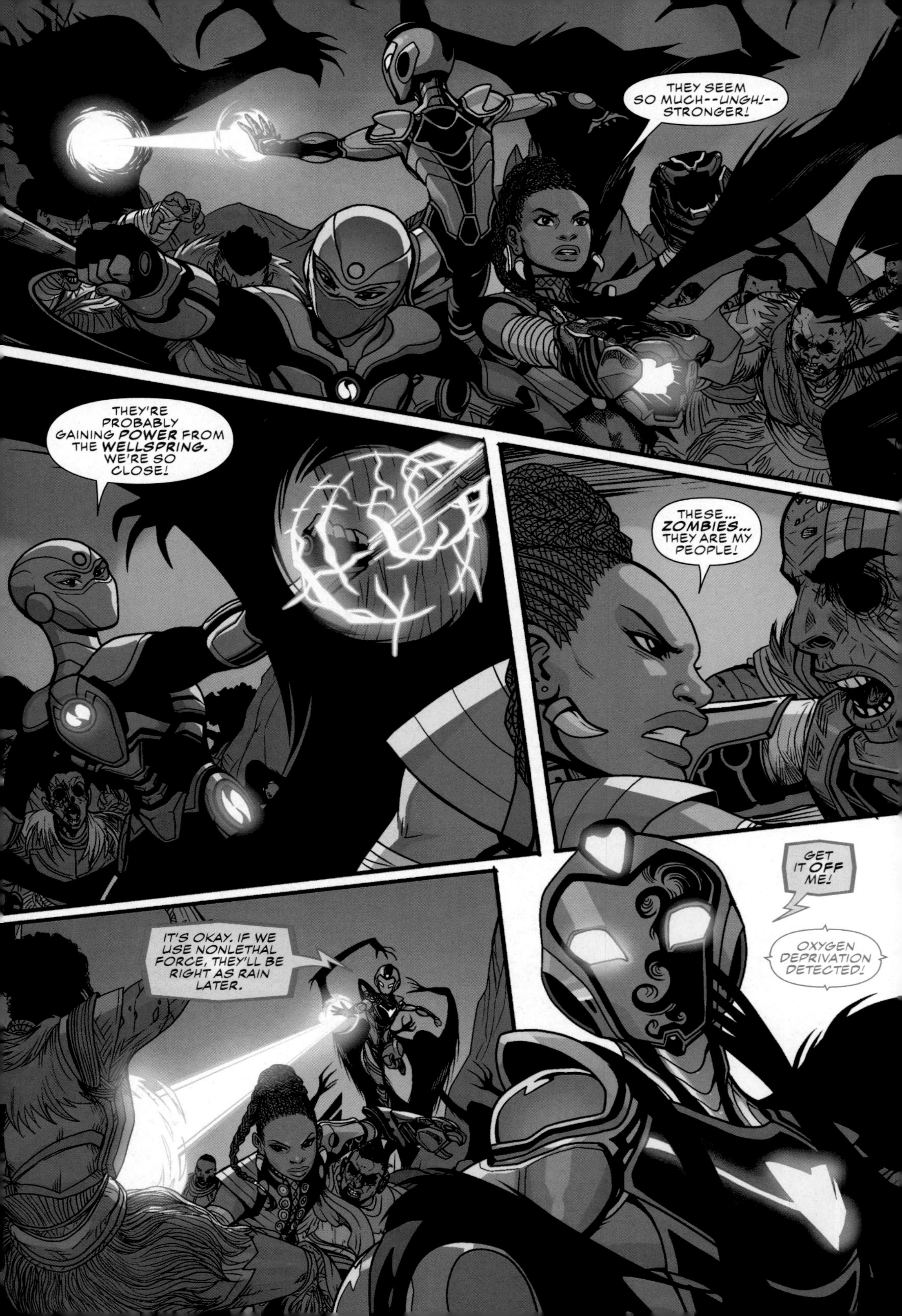
THEY SEEM SO MUCH--UNGH!--STRONGER!
THEY'RE PROBABLY GAINING POWER FROM THE WELLSPRING. WE'RE SO CLOSE!
THESE... ZOMBIES... THEY ARE MY PEOPLE!
GET IT OFF ME!
OXYGEN DEPRIVATION DETECTED!
IT'S OKAY. IF WE USE NONLETHAL FORCE, THEY'LL BE RIGHT AS RAIN LATER.

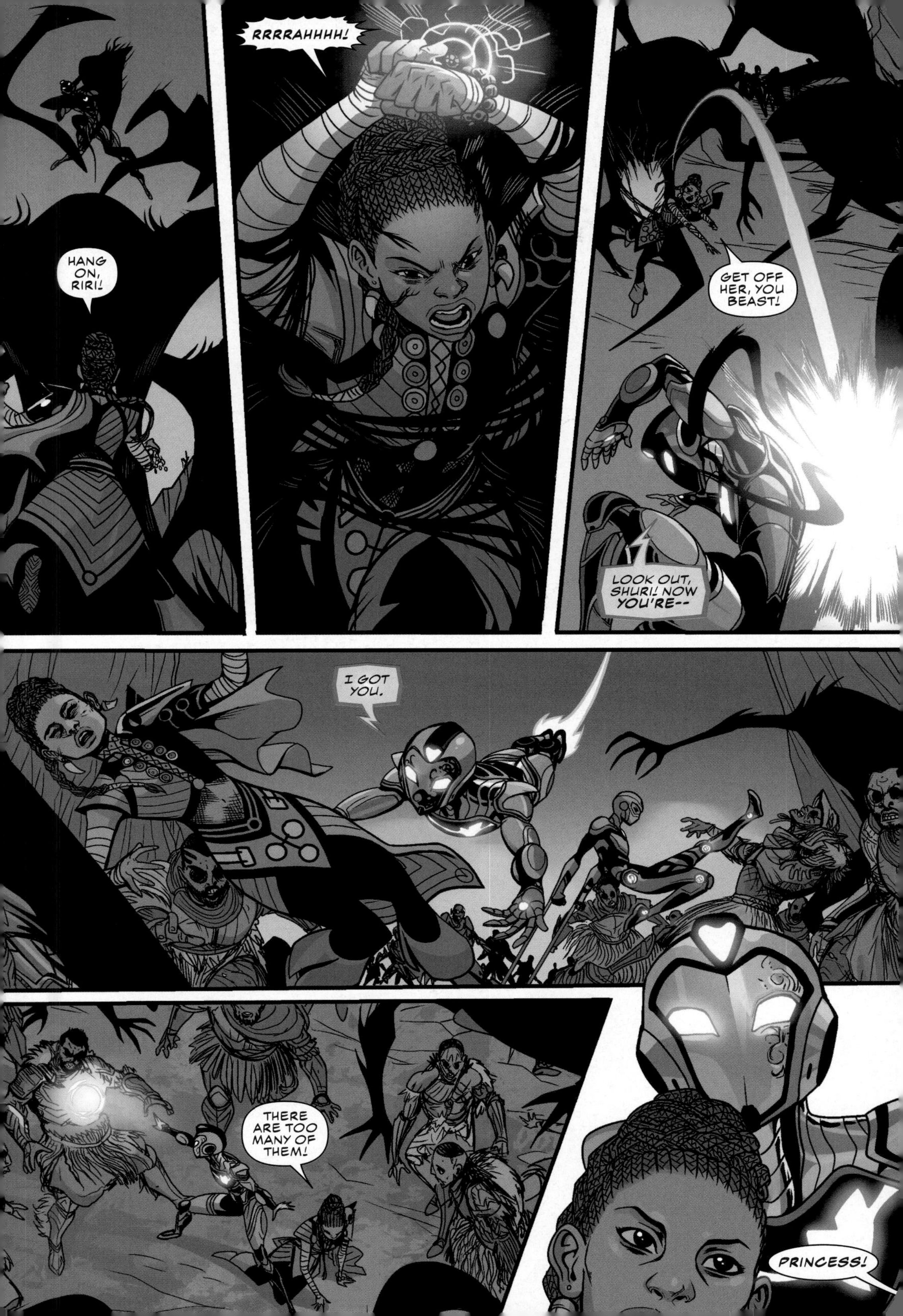
HANG ON, RIRI!
RRRRAHHHH!
GET OFF HER, YOU BEAST!
LOOK OUT, SHURI! NOW YOU'RE--
I GOT YOU.
THERE ARE TOO MANY OF THEM!
PRINCESS!

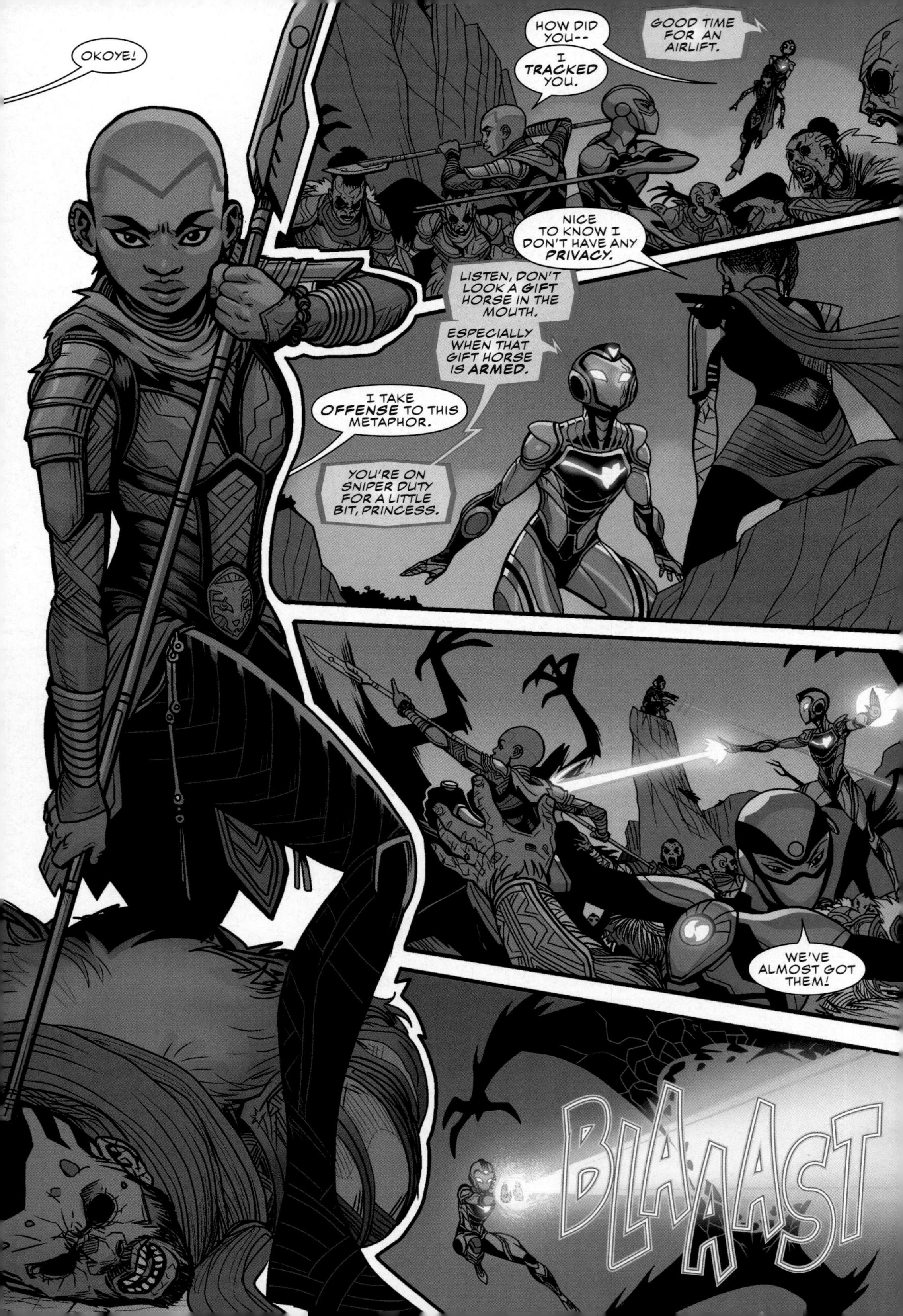
OKOYE!
HOW DID YOU--
I TRACKED YOU.
GOOD TIME FOR AN AIRLIFT.
NICE TO KNOW I DON'T HAVE ANY PRIVACY.
LISTEN, DON'T LOOK A GIFT HORSE IN THE MOUTH.
ESPECIALLY WHEN THAT GIFT HORSE IS ARMED.
I TAKE OFFENSE TO THIS METAPHOR.
YOU'RE ON SNIPER DUTY FOR A LITTLE BIT, PRINCESS.
WE'VE ALMOST GOT THEM!
BLAAAAST

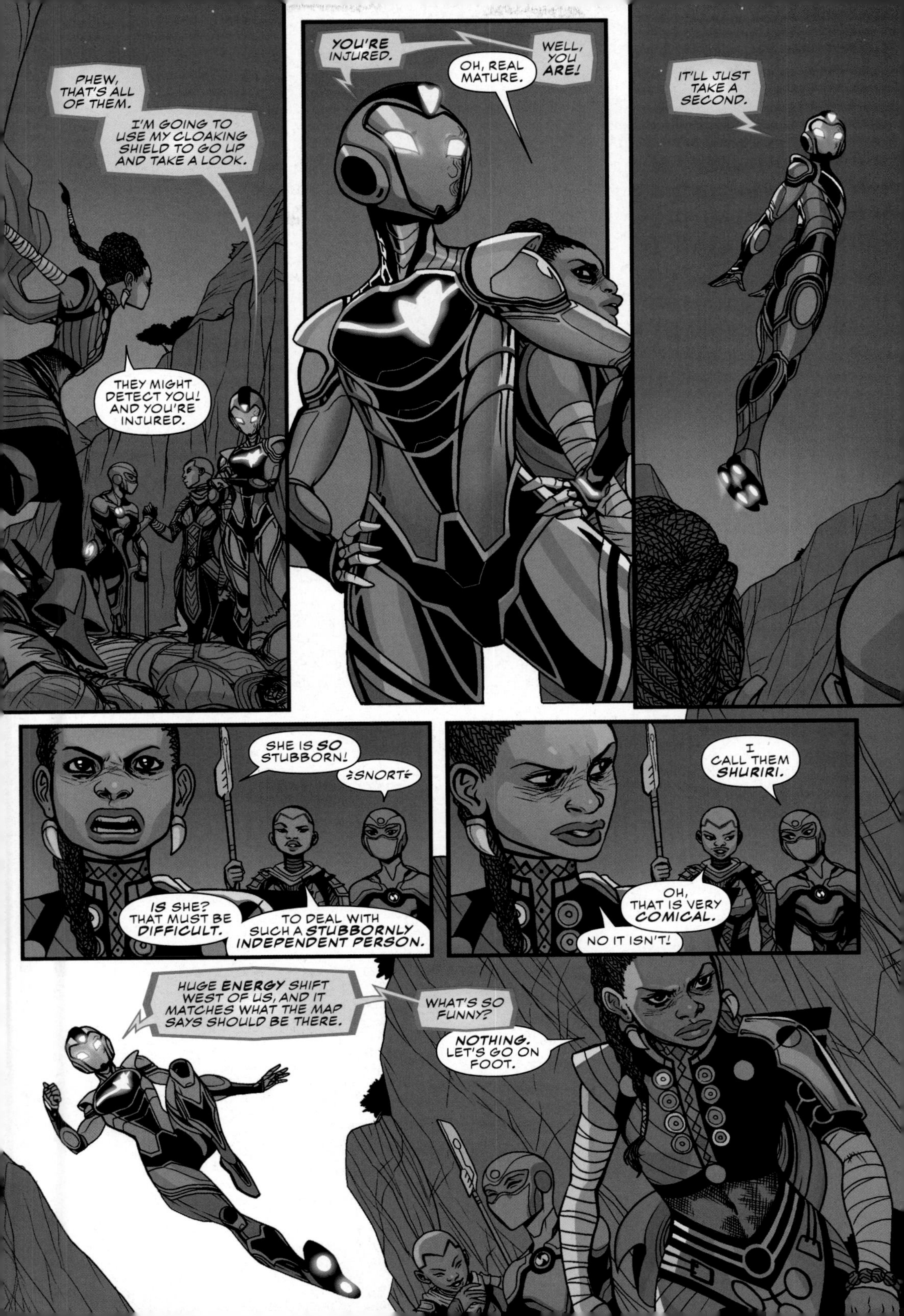
PHEW, THAT'S ALL OF THEM.
I'M GOING TO USE MY CLOAKING SHIELD TO GO UP AND TAKE A LOOK.
THEY MIGHT DETECT YOU! AND YOU'RE INJURED.
YOU'RE INJURED.
WELL, YOU ARE!
OH, REAL MATURE.
IT'LL JUST TAKE A SECOND.
SHE IS SO STUBBORN!
SNORT
IS SHE? THAT MUST BE DIFFICULT.
TO DEAL WITH SUCH A STUBBORNLY INDEPENDENT PERSON.
I CALL THEM SHURIRI.
OH, THAT IS VERY COMICAL.
NO IT ISN'T!
HUGE ENERGY SHIFT WEST OF US, AND IT MATCHES WHAT THE MAP SAYS SHOULD BE THERE.
WHAT'S SO FUNNY?
NOTHING. LET'S GO ON FOOT.

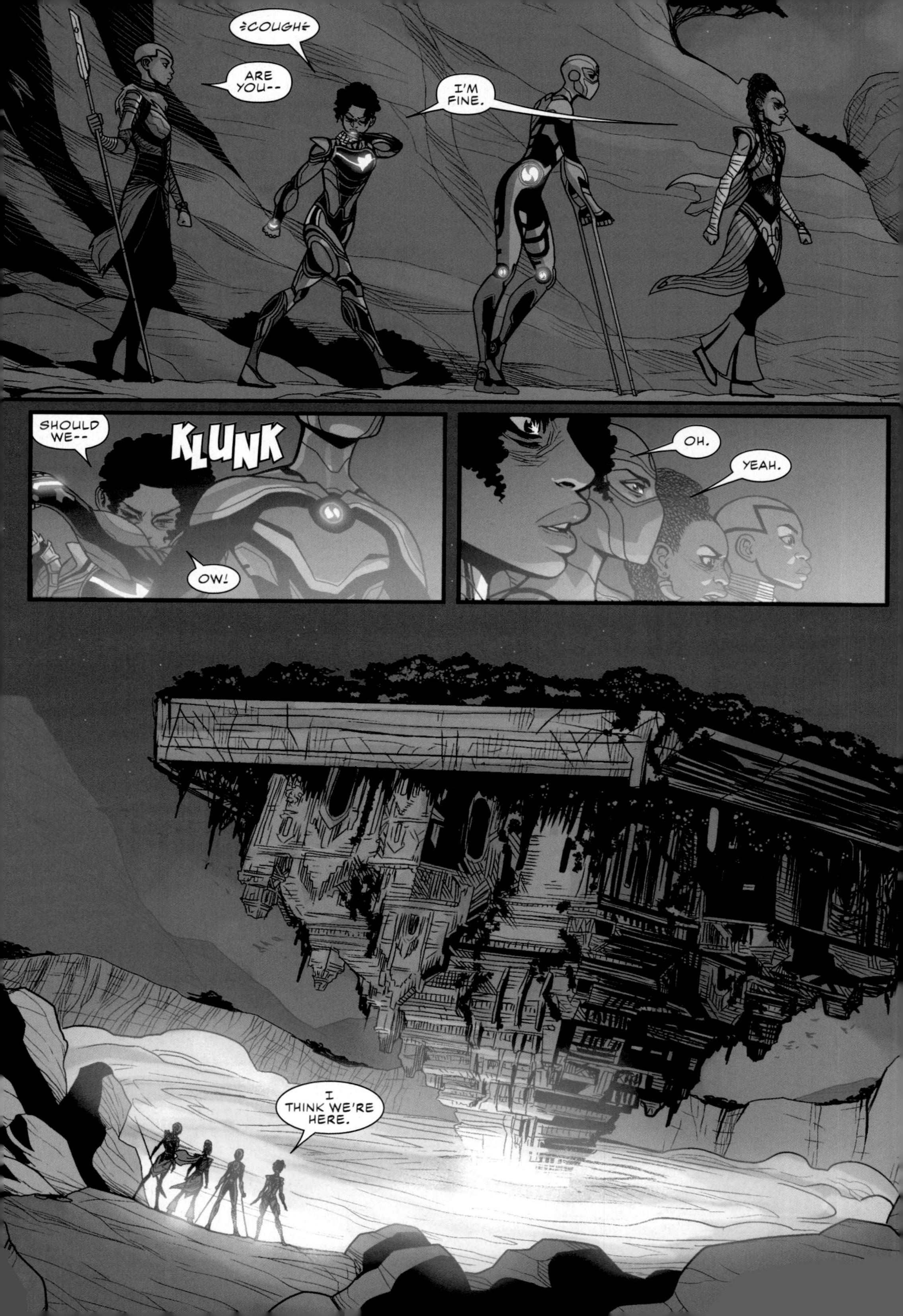

≈COUGH≈
ARE YOU--
I'M FINE.
SHOULD WE--
KLUNK
OW!
OH.
YEAH.
I THINK WE'RE HERE.

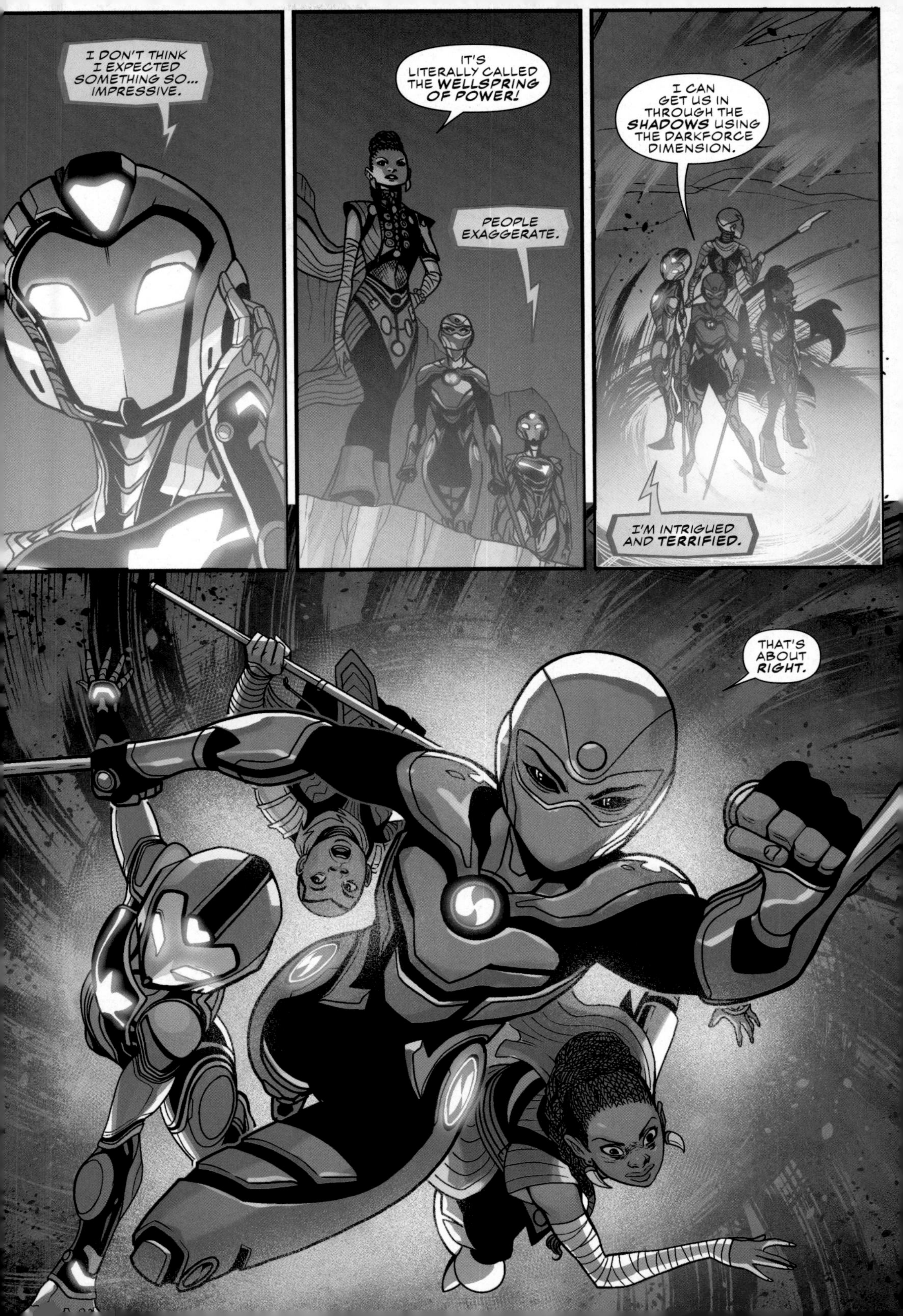

I DON'T THINK I EXPECTED SOMETHING SO... IMPRESSIVE.
IT'S LITERALLY CALLED THE WELLSPRING OF POWER!
PEOPLE EXAGGERATE.
I CAN GET US IN THROUGH THE SHADOWS USING THE DARKFORCE DIMENSION.
I'M INTRIGUED AND TERRIFIED.
THAT'S ABOUT RIGHT.

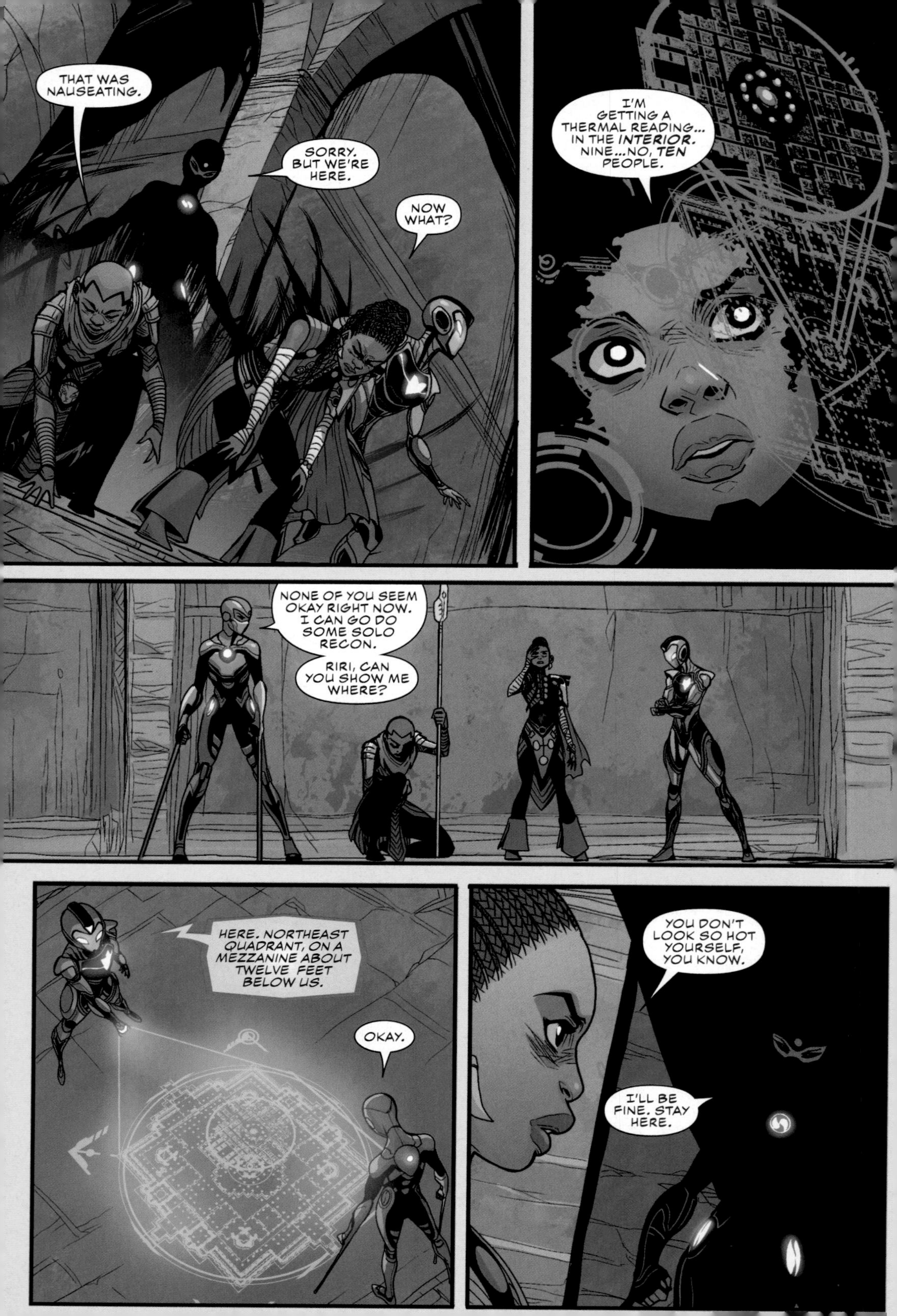
THAT WAS NAUSEATING.
SORRY. BUT WE'RE HERE.
NOW WHAT?
I'M GETTING A THERMAL READING... IN THE INTERIOR. NINE...NO, TEN PEOPLE.
NONE OF YOU SEEM OKAY RIGHT NOW. I CAN GO DO SOME SOLO RECON.
RIRI, CAN YOU SHOW ME WHERE?
HERE. NORTHEAST QUADRANT, ON A MEZZANINE ABOUT TWELVE FEET BELOW US.
OKAY.
YOU DON'T LOOK SO HOT YOURSELF, YOU KNOW.
I'LL BE FINE. STAY HERE.

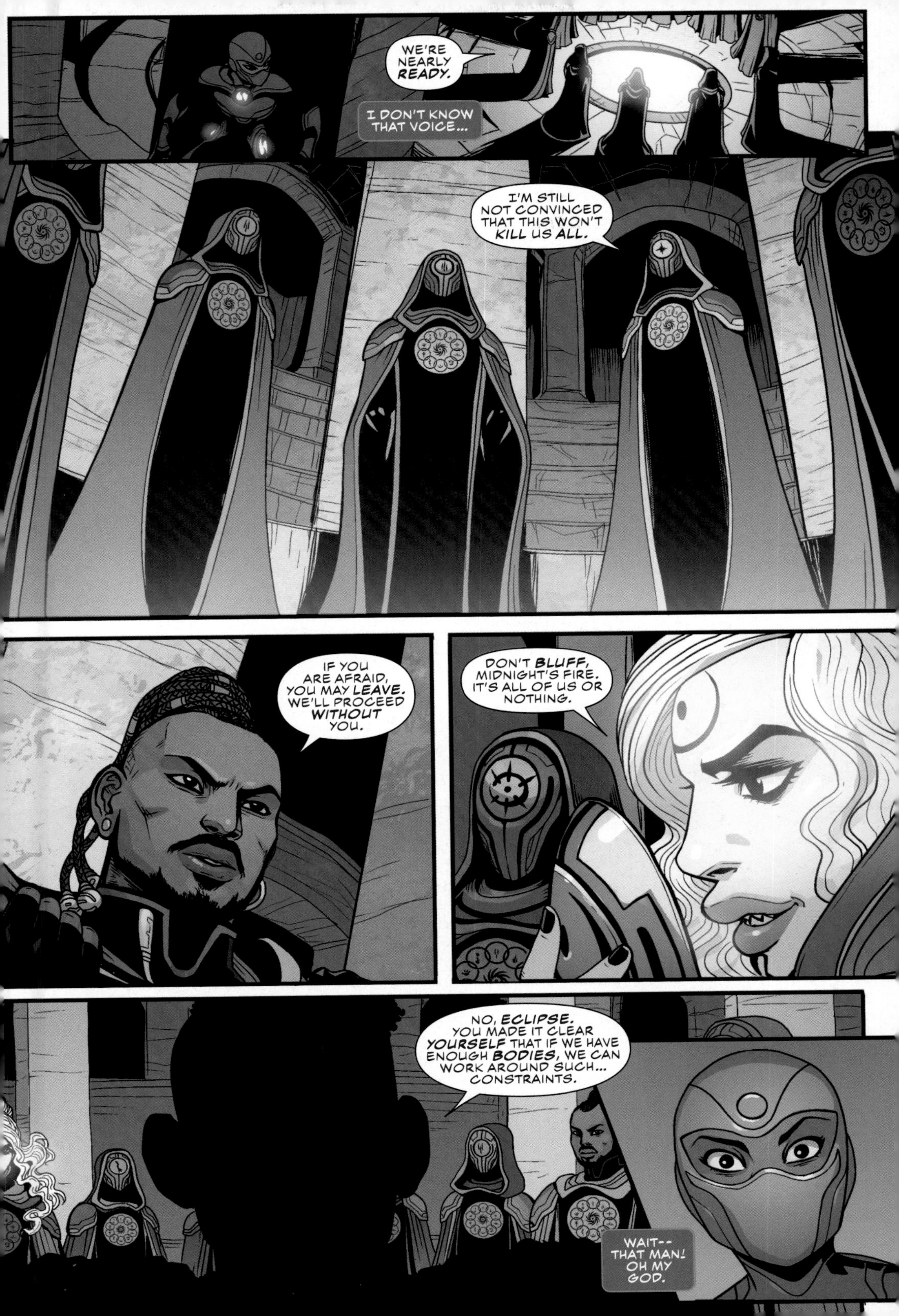
WE'RE NEARLY READY.
I DON'T KNOW THAT VOICE...
I'M STILL NOT CONVINCED THAT THIS WON'T KILL US ALL.
IF YOU ARE AFRAID, YOU MAY LEAVE. WE'LL PROCEED WITHOUT YOU.
DON'T BLUFF, MIDNIGHT'S FIRE. IT'S ALL OF US OR NOTHING.
NO, ECLIPSE. YOU MADE IT CLEAR YOURSELF THAT IF WE HAVE ENOUGH BODIES, WE CAN WORK AROUND SUCH... CONSTRAINTS.
WAIT-- THAT MAN! OH MY GOD.

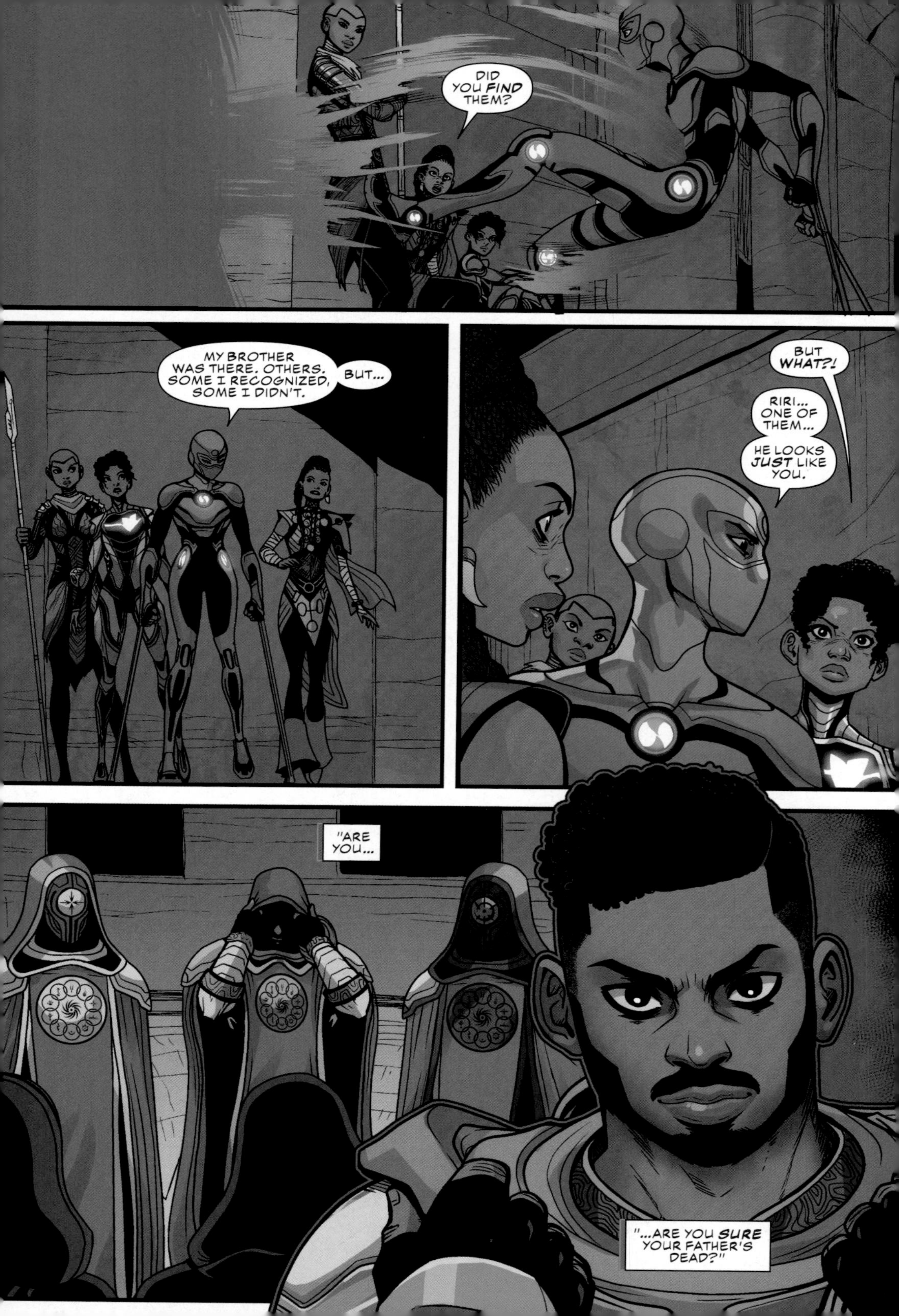
DID YOU FIND THEM?
MY BROTHER WAS THERE. OTHERS. SOME I RECOGNIZED, SOME I DIDN'T.
BUT...
BUT WHAT?!
RIRI... ONE OF THEM...
HE LOOKS JUST LIKE YOU.
"ARE YOU...
"...ARE YOU SURE YOUR FATHER'S DEAD?"

11

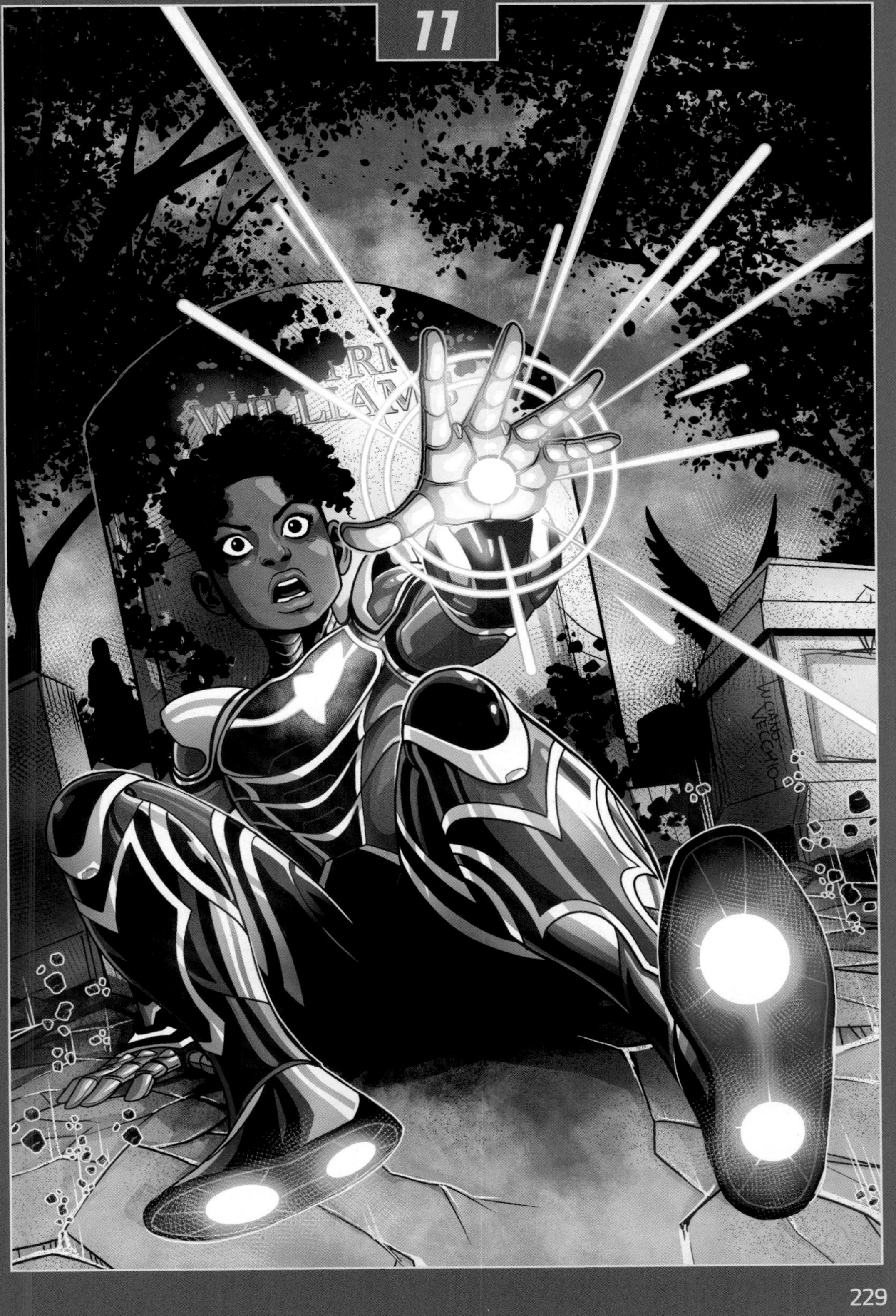

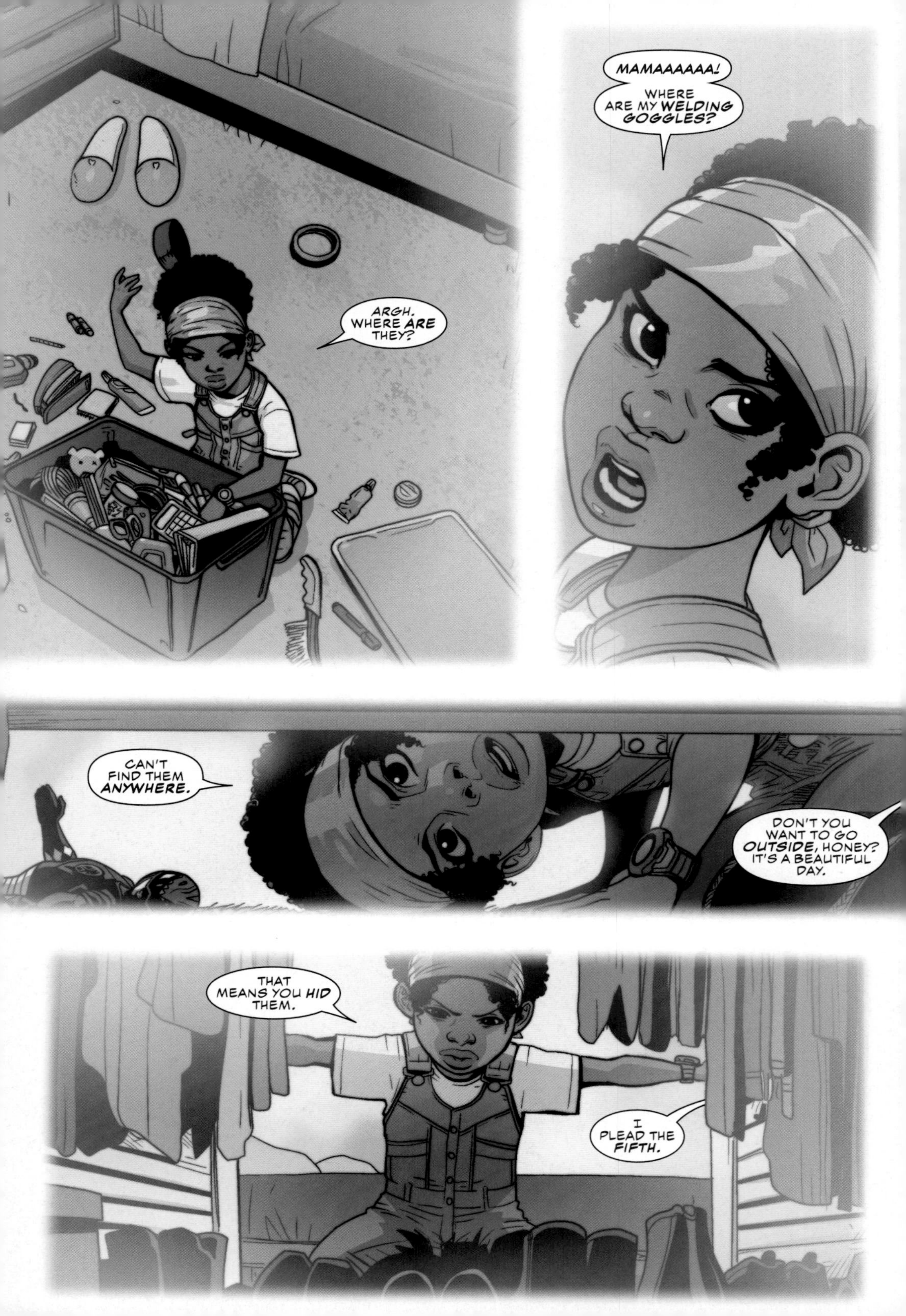
ARGH. WHERE ARE THEY?
MAMAAAAAAA!
WHERE ARE MY WELDING GOGGLES?
CAN'T FIND THEM ANYWHERE.
DON'T YOU WANT TO GO OUTSIDE, HONEY? IT'S A BEAUTIFUL DAY.
THAT MEANS YOU HID THEM.
I PLEAD THE FIFTH.

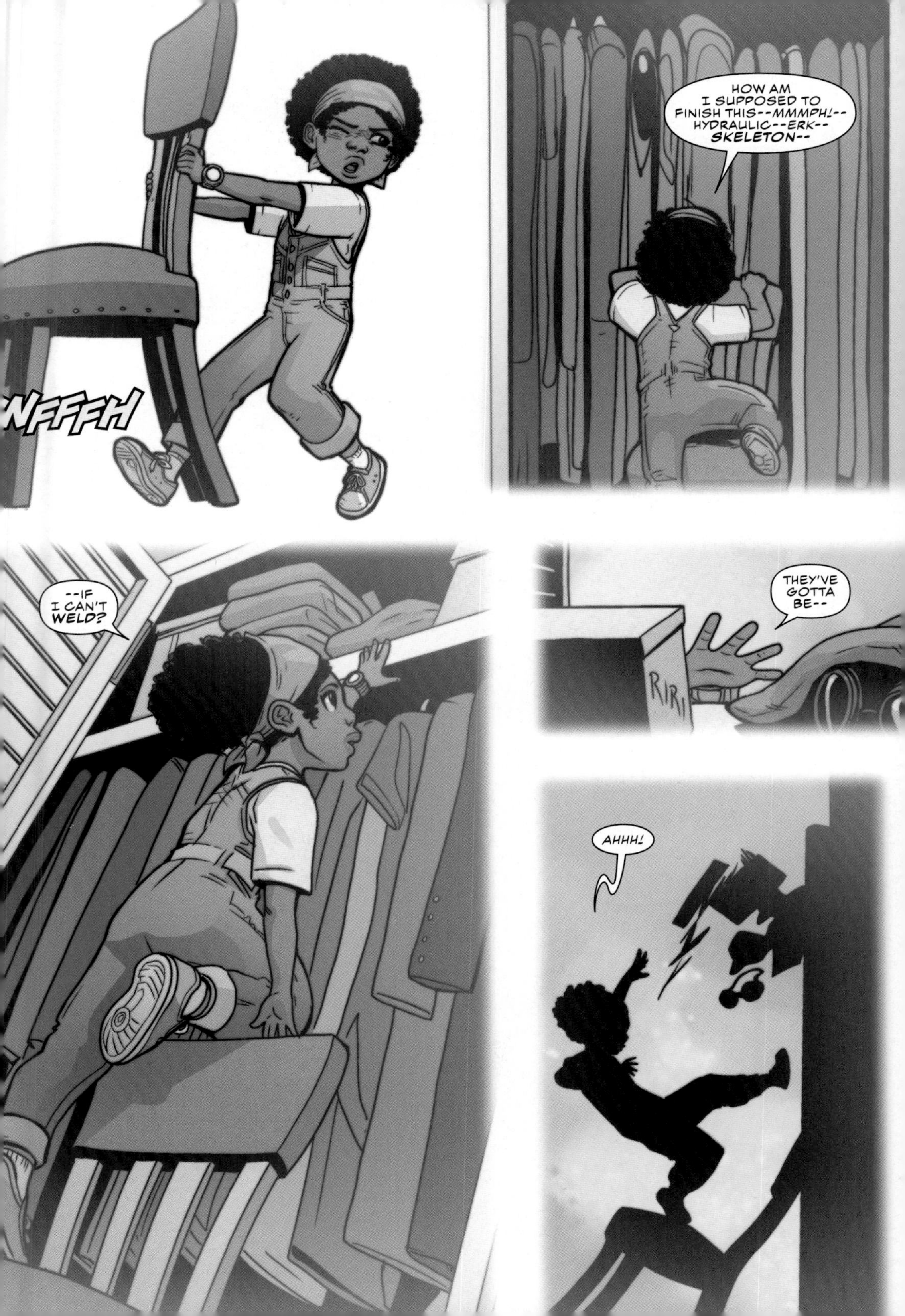
NFFFH
HOW AM I SUPPOSED TO FINISH THIS--MMMPH!--HYDRAULIC--ERK--SKELETON--
--IF I CAN'T WELD?
THEY'VE GOTTA BE--
RIRI
AHHH!

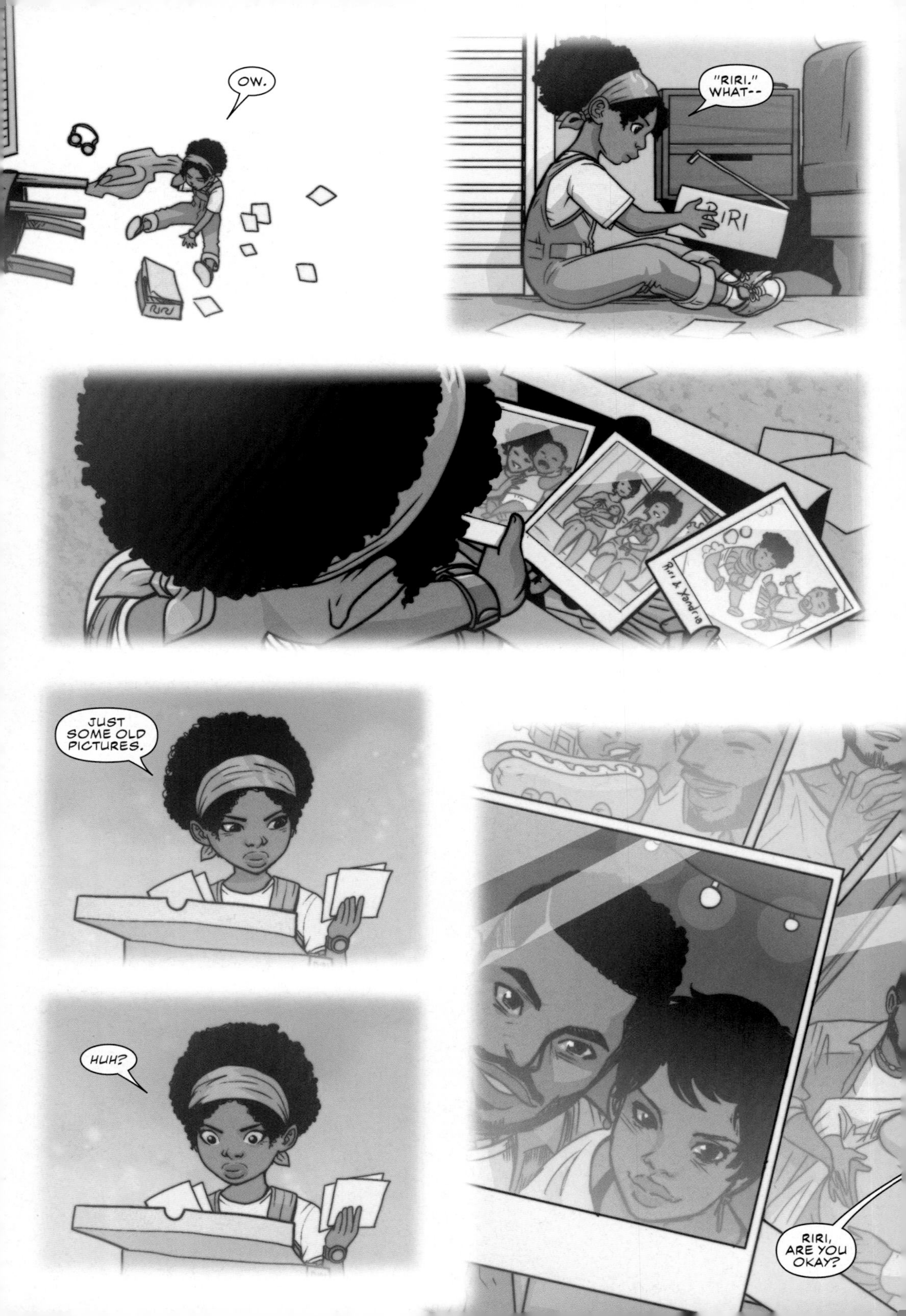
OW.
"RIRI." WHAT--
RIRI
Riri & Xendria
JUST SOME OLD PICTURES.
HUH?
RIRI, ARE YOU OKAY?

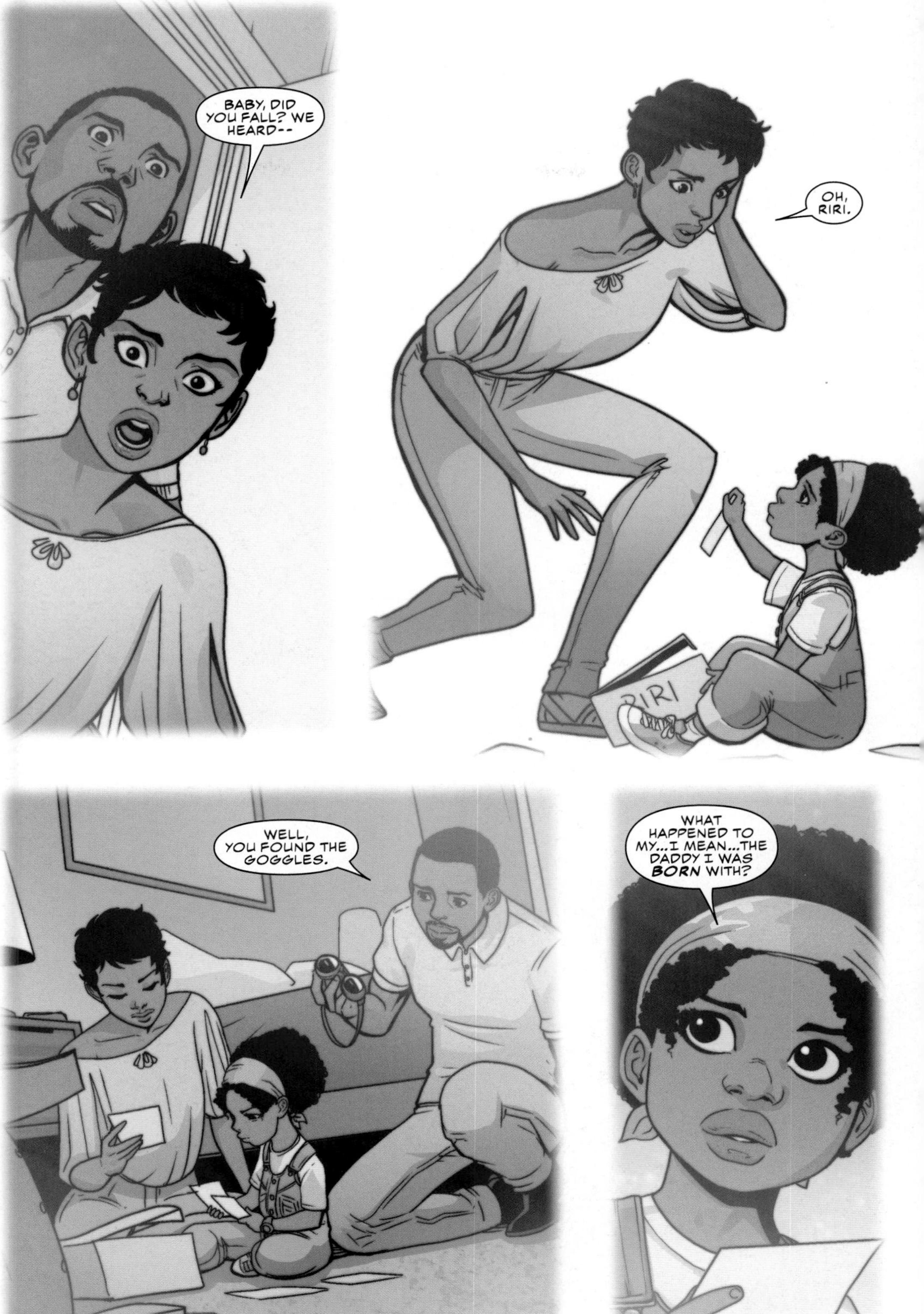
BABY, DID YOU FALL? WE HEARD--
OH, RIRI.
RIRI
WELL, YOU FOUND THE GOGGLES.
WHAT HAPPENED TO MY...I MEAN...THE DADDY I WAS **BORN** WITH?

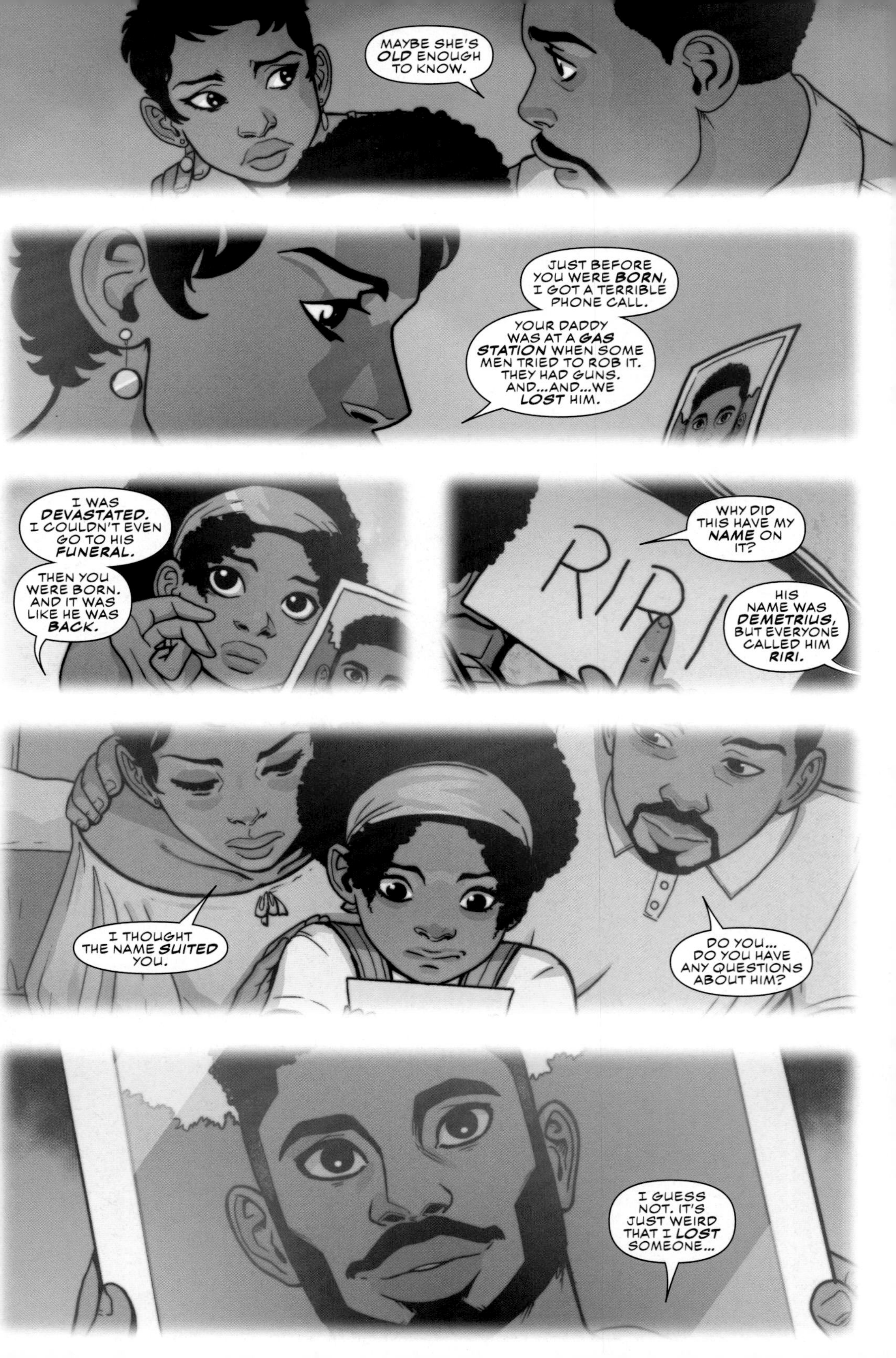
MAYBE SHE'S OLD ENOUGH TO KNOW.
JUST BEFORE YOU WERE BORN, I GOT A TERRIBLE PHONE CALL.
YOUR DADDY WAS AT A GAS STATION WHEN SOME MEN TRIED TO ROB IT. THEY HAD GUNS. AND...AND...WE LOST HIM.
I WAS DEVASTATED. I COULDN'T EVEN GO TO HIS FUNERAL.
THEN YOU WERE BORN. AND IT WAS LIKE HE WAS BACK.
RIRI
WHY DID THIS HAVE MY NAME ON IT?
HIS NAME WAS DEMETRIUS, BUT EVERYONE CALLED HIM RIRI.
I THOUGHT THE NAME SUITED YOU.
DO YOU... DO YOU HAVE ANY QUESTIONS ABOUT HIM?
I GUESS NOT. IT'S JUST WEIRD THAT I LOST SOMEONE...

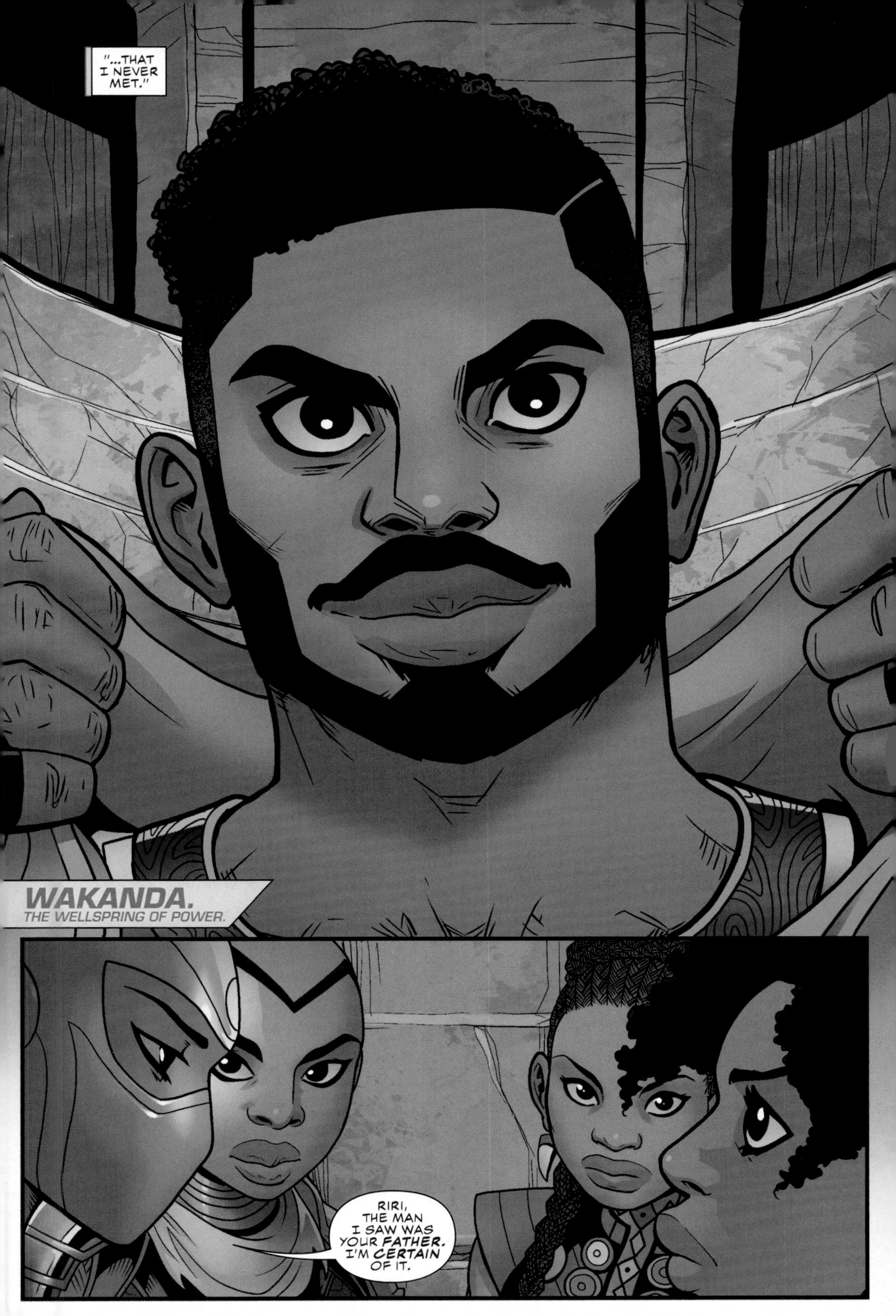
"...THAT I NEVER MET."
WAKANDA.
THE WELLSPRING OF POWER.
RIRI, THE MAN I SAW WAS YOUR FATHER. I'M CERTAIN OF IT.

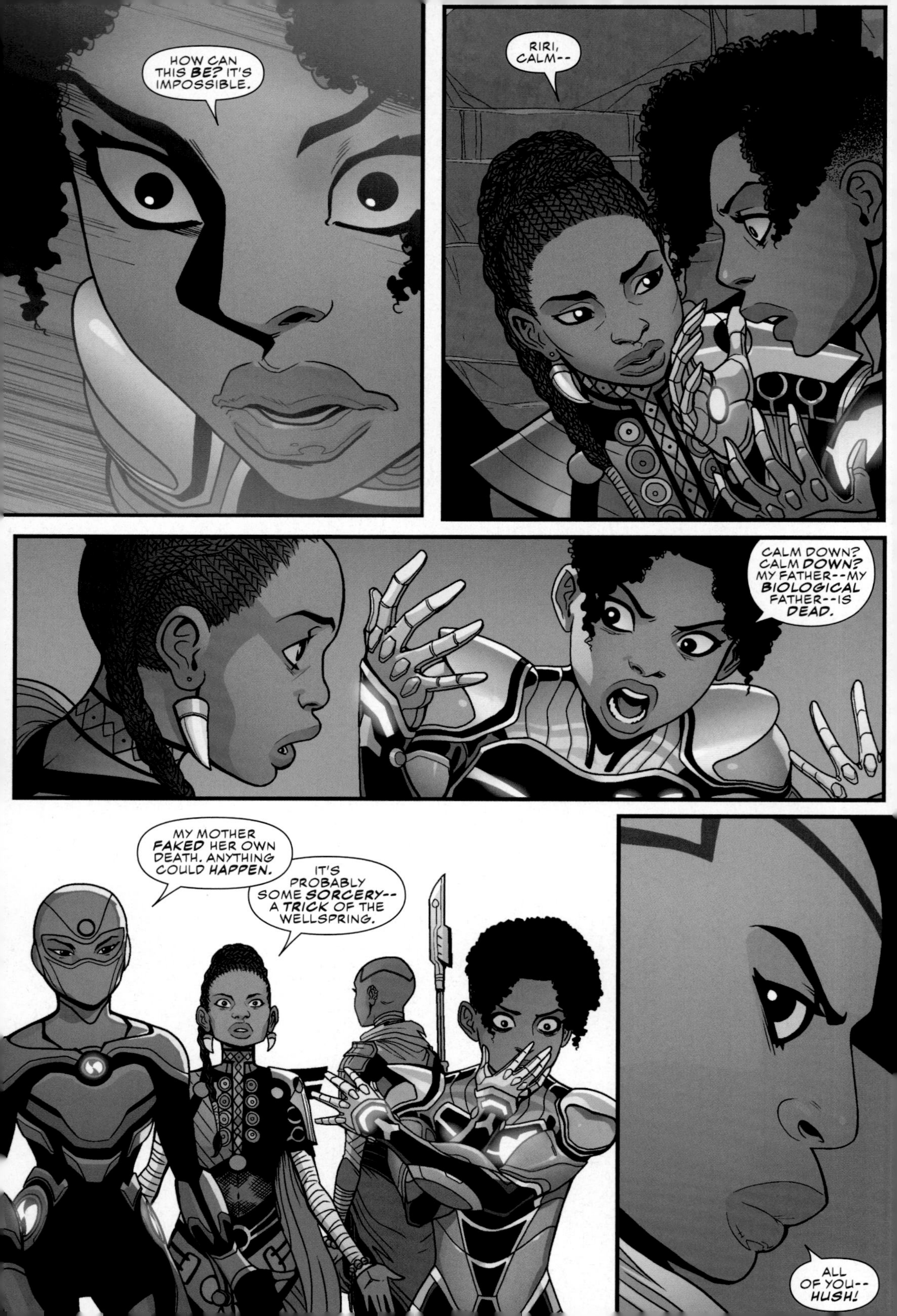
HOW CAN THIS BE? IT'S IMPOSSIBLE.
RIRI, CALM--
CALM DOWN? CALM DOWN? MY FATHER--MY BIOLOGICAL FATHER--IS DEAD.
MY MOTHER FAKED HER OWN DEATH. ANYTHING COULD HAPPEN.
IT'S PROBABLY SOME SORCERY--A TRICK OF THE WELLSPRING.
ALL OF YOU--HUSH!

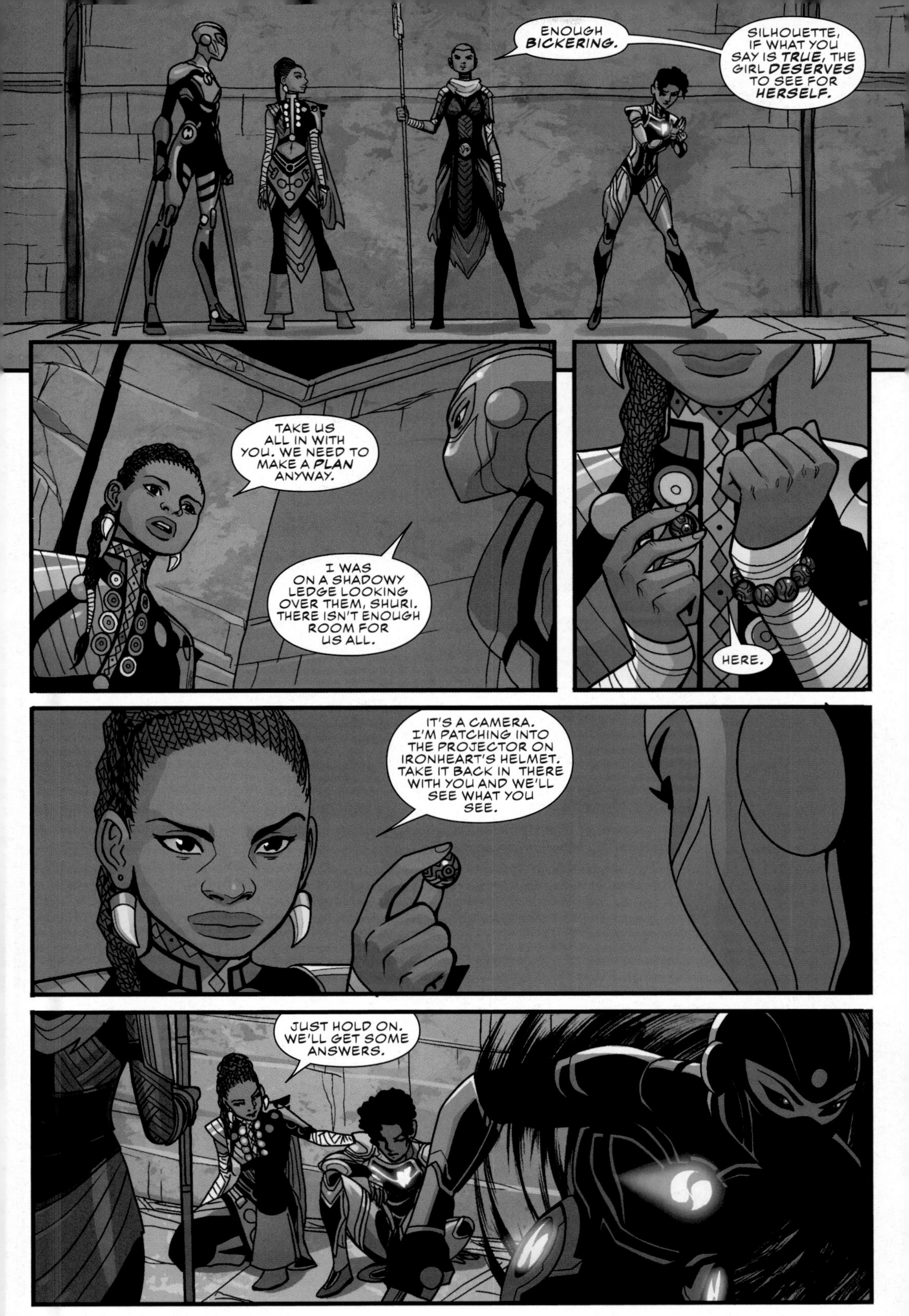
ENOUGH BICKERING.
SILHOUETTE, IF WHAT YOU SAY IS TRUE, THE GIRL DESERVES TO SEE FOR HERSELF.
TAKE US ALL IN WITH YOU. WE NEED TO MAKE A PLAN ANYWAY.
I WAS ON A SHADOWY LEDGE LOOKING OVER THEM, SHURI. THERE ISN'T ENOUGH ROOM FOR US ALL.
HERE.
IT'S A CAMERA. I'M PATCHING INTO THE PROJECTOR ON IRONHEART'S HELMET. TAKE IT BACK IN THERE WITH YOU AND WE'LL SEE WHAT YOU SEE.
JUST HOLD ON. WE'LL GET SOME ANSWERS.

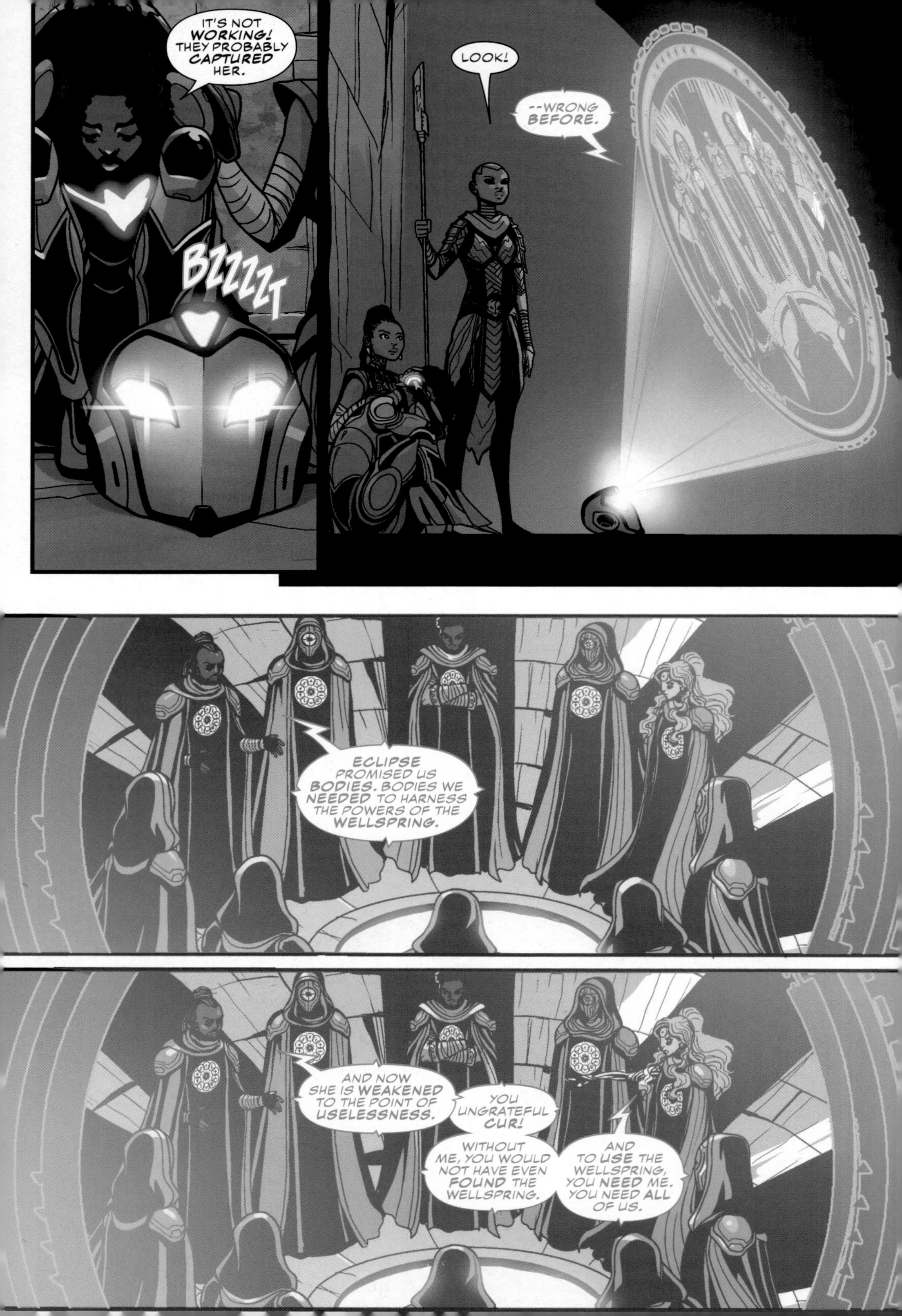

IT'S NOT WORKING! THEY PROBABLY CAPTURED HER.
BZZZZZT
LOOK!
--WRONG BEFORE.
ECLIPSE PROMISED US BODIES. BODIES WE NEEDED TO HARNESS THE POWERS OF THE WELLSPRING.
AND NOW SHE IS WEAKENED TO THE POINT OF USELESSNESS.
YOU UNGRATEFUL CUR!
WITHOUT ME, YOU WOULD NOT HAVE EVEN FOUND THE WELLSPRING.
AND TO USE THE WELLSPRING, YOU NEED ME. YOU NEED ALL OF US.

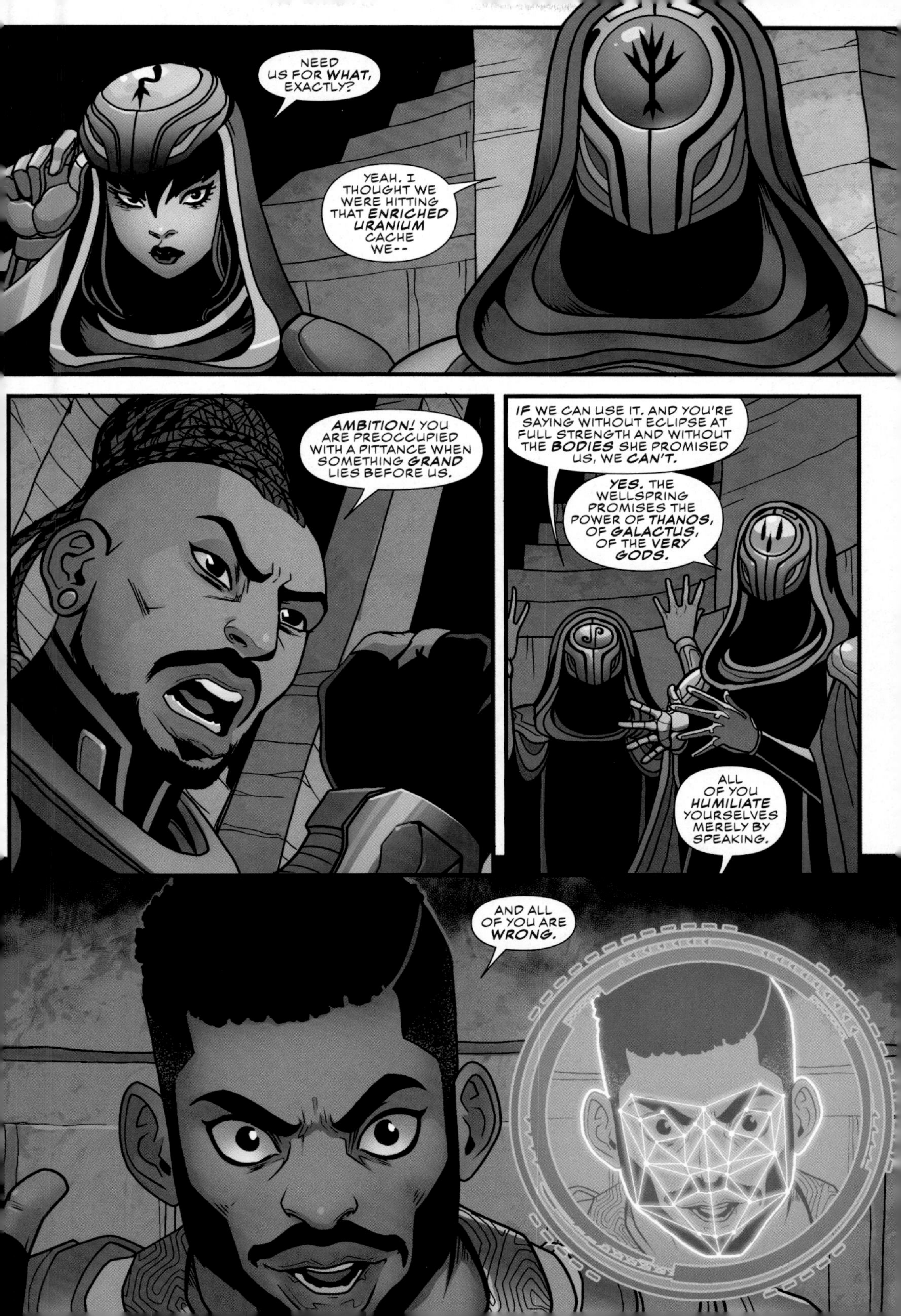
NEED US FOR WHAT, EXACTLY?
YEAH. I THOUGHT WE WERE HITTING THAT ENRICHED URANIUM CACHE WE--
AMBITION! YOU ARE PREOCCUPIED WITH A PITTANCE WHEN SOMETHING GRAND LIES BEFORE US.
IF WE CAN USE IT. AND YOU'RE SAYING WITHOUT ECLIPSE AT FULL STRENGTH AND WITHOUT THE BODIES SHE PROMISED US, WE CAN'T.
YES. THE WELLSPRING PROMISES THE POWER OF THANOS, OF GALACTUS, OF THE VERY GODS.
ALL OF YOU HUMILIATE YOURSELVES MERELY BY SPEAKING.
AND ALL OF YOU ARE WRONG.

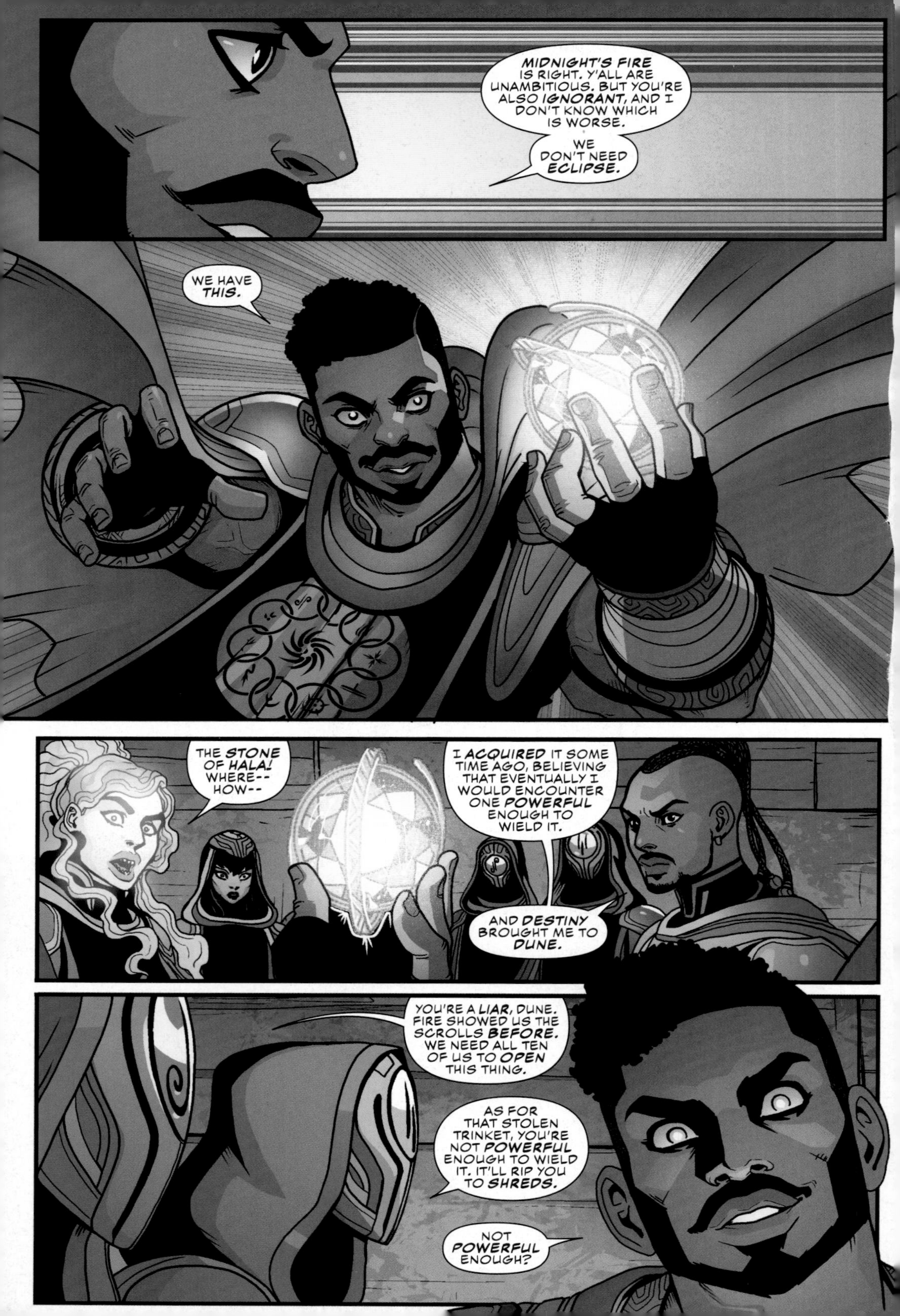

MIDNIGHT'S FIRE IS RIGHT. Y'ALL ARE UNAMBITIOUS. BUT YOU'RE ALSO IGNORANT, AND I DON'T KNOW WHICH IS WORSE.
WE DON'T NEED ECLIPSE.
WE HAVE THIS.
THE STONE OF HALA! WHERE-- HOW--
I ACQUIRED IT SOME TIME AGO, BELIEVING THAT EVENTUALLY I WOULD ENCOUNTER ONE POWERFUL ENOUGH TO WIELD IT.
AND DESTINY BROUGHT ME TO DUNE.
YOU'RE A LIAR, DUNE. FIRE SHOWED US THE SCROLLS BEFORE. WE NEED ALL TEN OF US TO OPEN THIS THING.
AS FOR THAT STOLEN TRINKET, YOU'RE NOT POWERFUL ENOUGH TO WIELD IT. IT'LL RIP YOU TO SHREDS.
NOT POWERFUL ENOUGH?

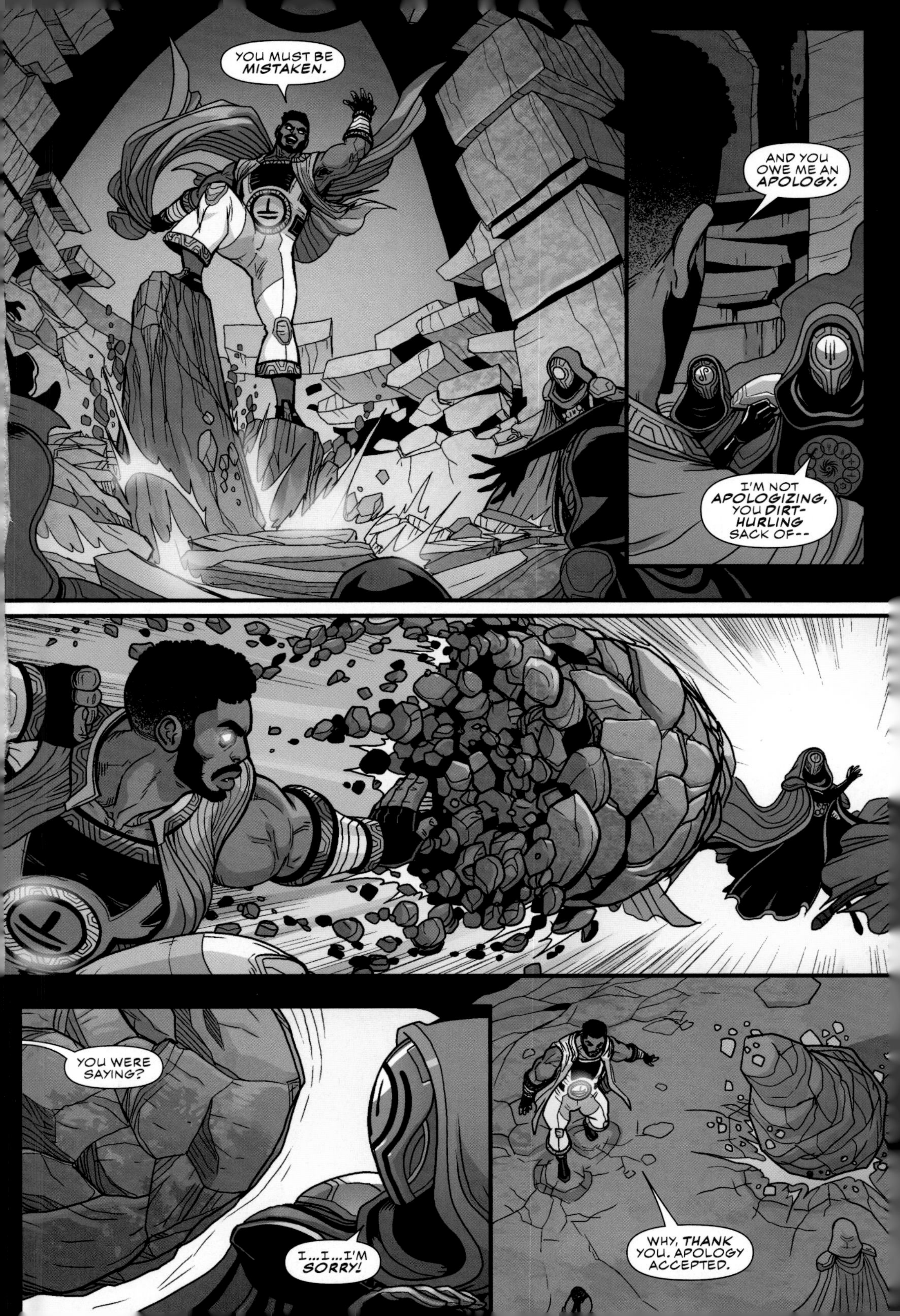
YOU MUST BE MISTAKEN.
AND YOU OWE ME AN APOLOGY.
I'M NOT APOLOGIZING, YOU DIRT-HURLING SACK OF--
YOU WERE SAYING?
I...I...I'M SORRY!
WHY, THANK YOU. APOLOGY ACCEPTED.

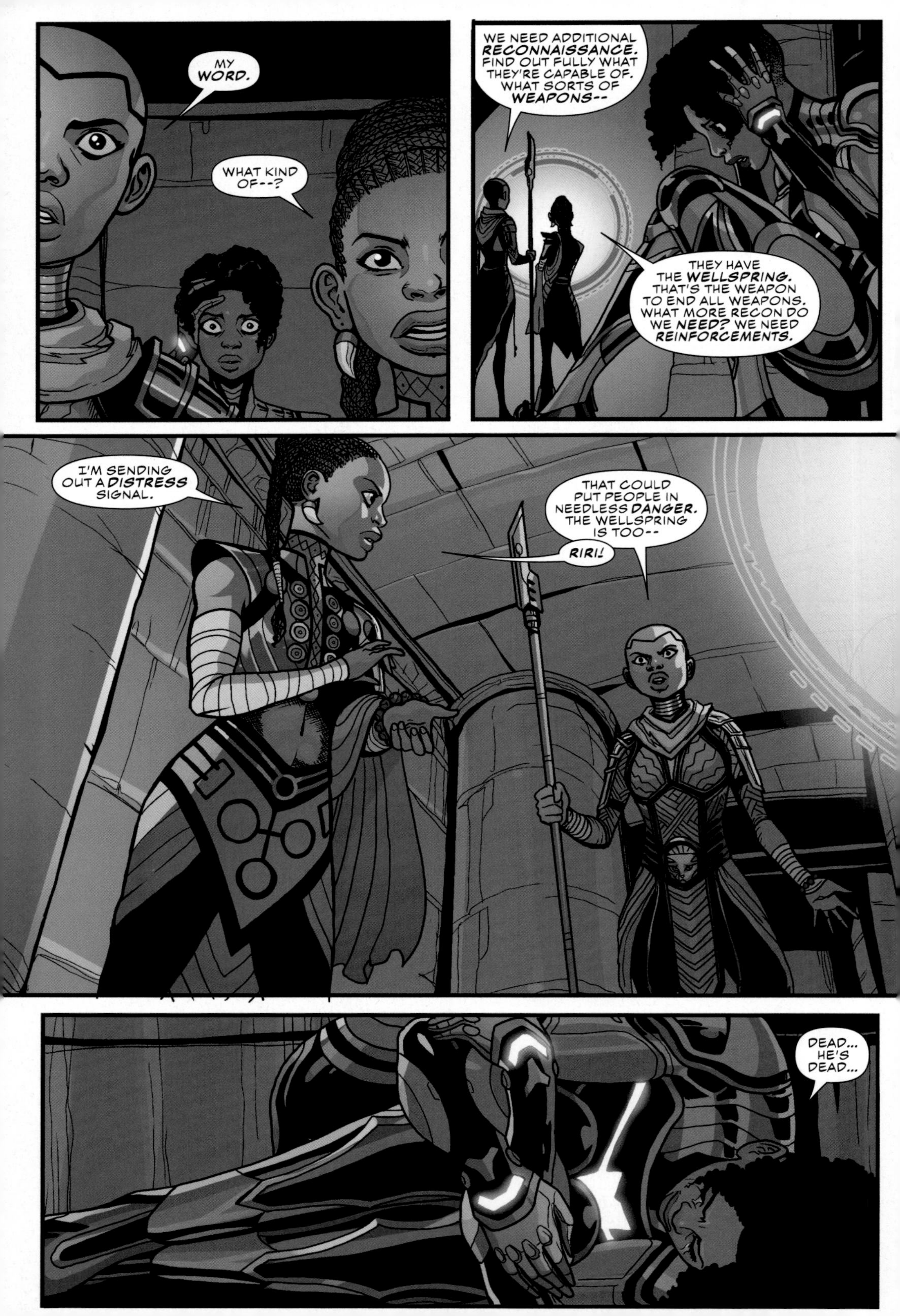
MY WORD.
WHAT KIND OF--?
WE NEED ADDITIONAL RECONNAISSANCE. FIND OUT FULLY WHAT THEY'RE CAPABLE OF. WHAT SORTS OF WEAPONS--
THEY HAVE THE WELLSPRING. THAT'S THE WEAPON TO END ALL WEAPONS. WHAT MORE RECON DO WE NEED? WE NEED REINFORCEMENTS.
I'M SENDING OUT A DISTRESS SIGNAL.
THAT COULD PUT PEOPLE IN NEEDLESS DANGER. THE WELLSPRING IS TOO--
RIRI!
DEAD... HE'S DEAD...

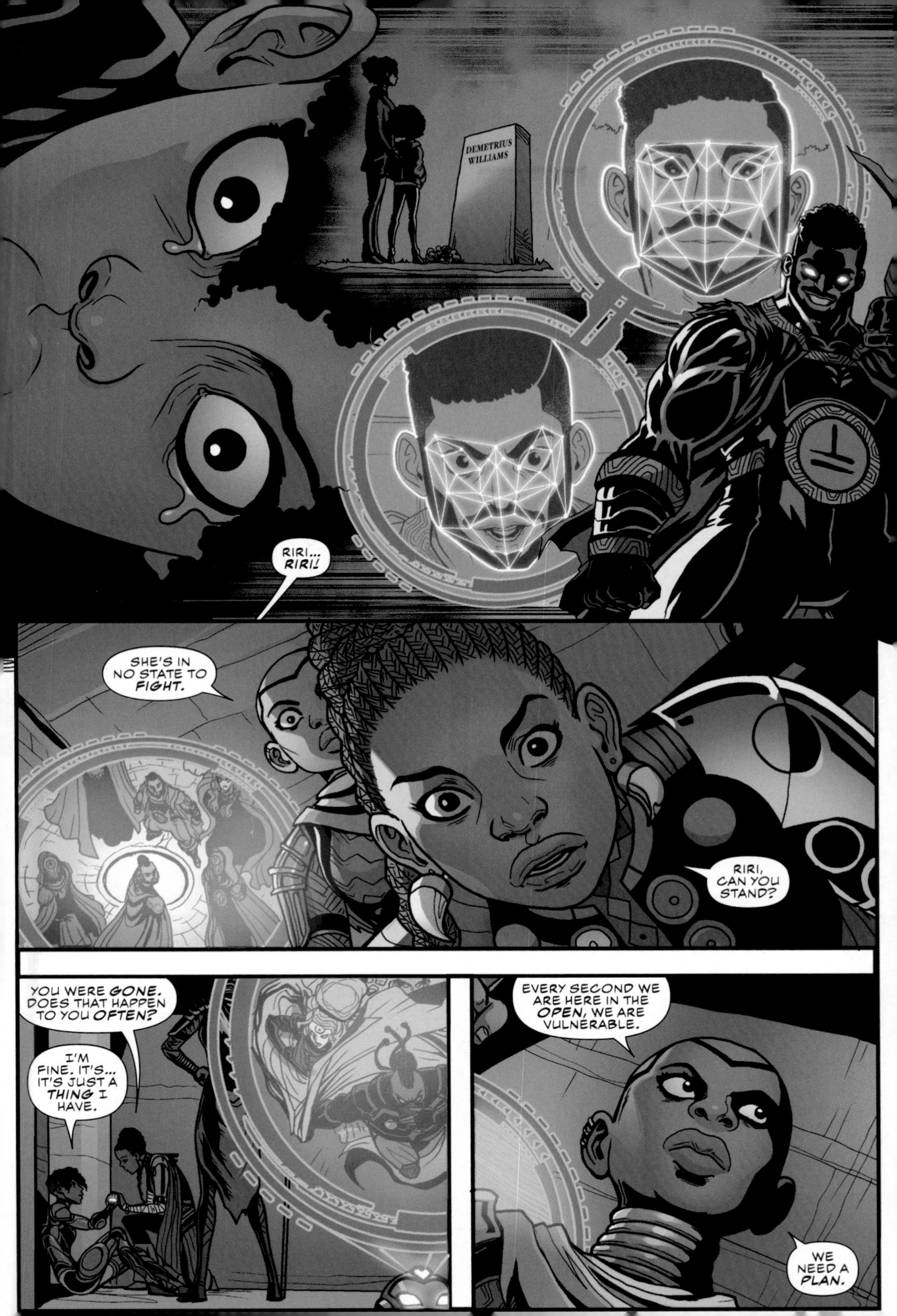
DEMETRIUS WILLIAMS
RIRI... RIRI!
SHE'S IN NO STATE TO FIGHT.
RIRI, CAN YOU STAND?
YOU WERE GONE. DOES THAT HAPPEN TO YOU OFTEN?
I'M FINE. IT'S... IT'S JUST A THING I HAVE.
EVERY SECOND WE ARE HERE IN THE OPEN, WE ARE VULNERABLE.
WE NEED A PLAN.

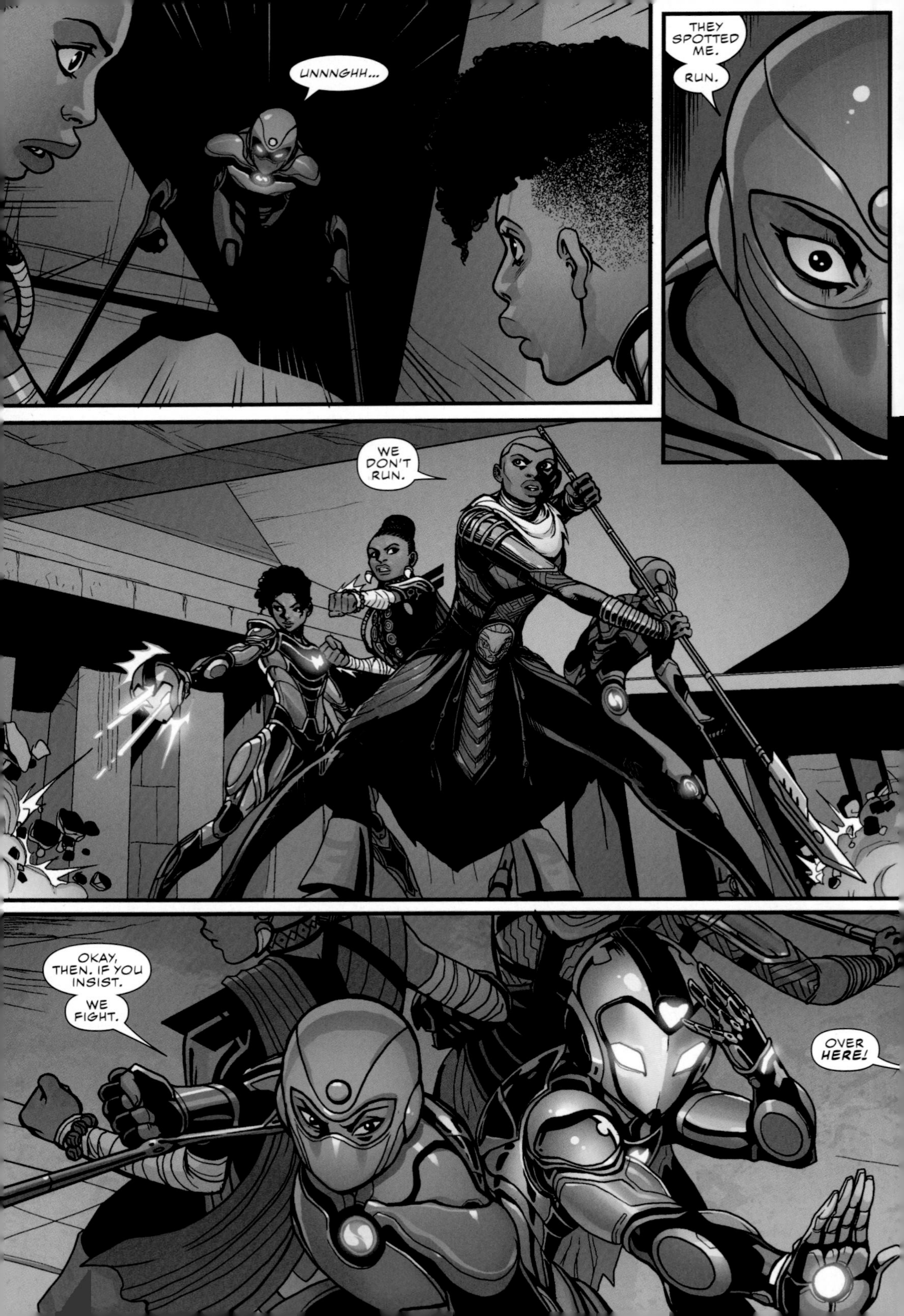
UNNNGHH...
THEY SPOTTED ME.
RUN.
WE DON'T RUN.
OKAY, THEN. IF YOU INSIST.
WE FIGHT.
OVER HERE!

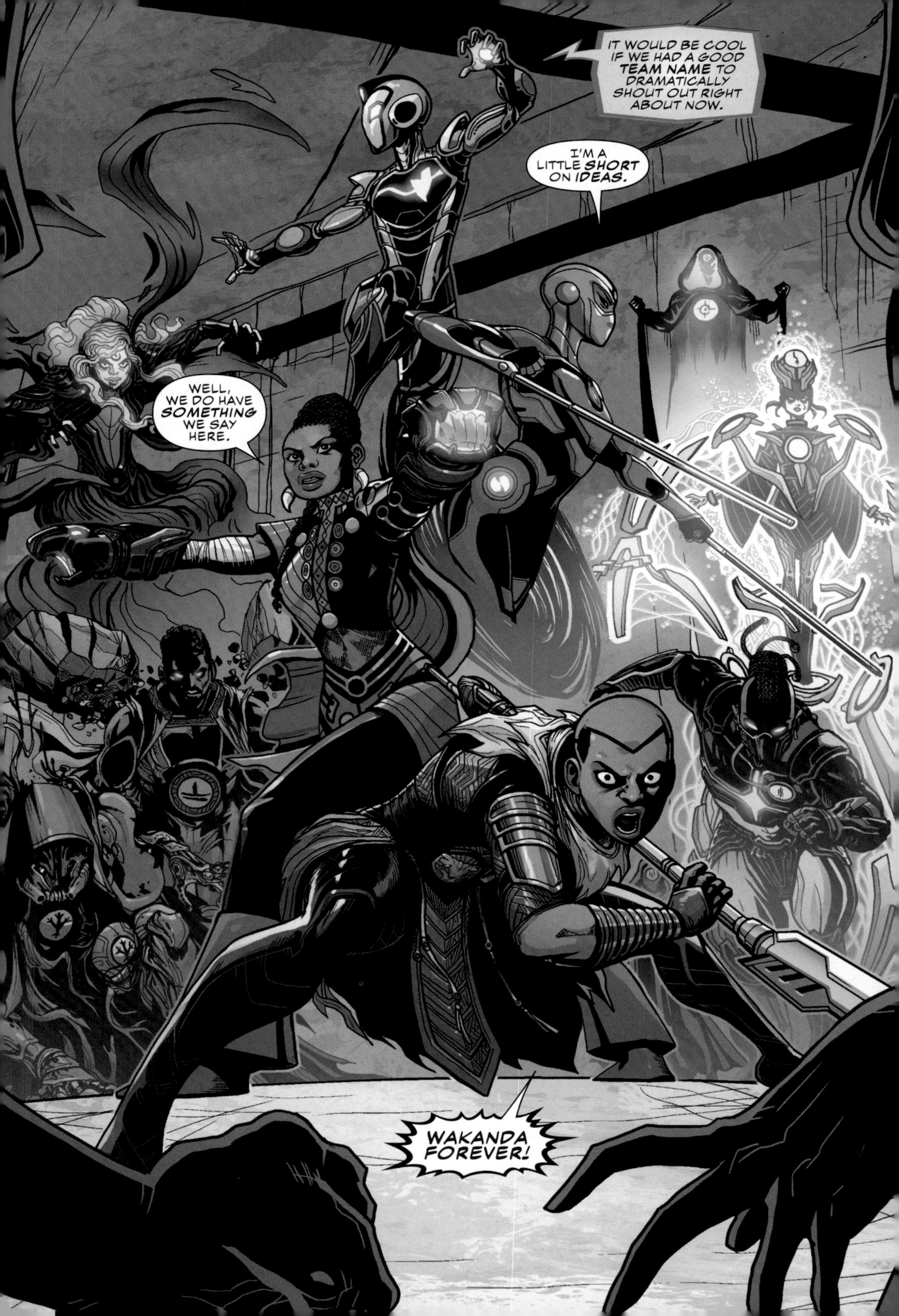
IT WOULD BE COOL IF WE HAD A GOOD TEAM NAME TO DRAMATICALLY SHOUT OUT RIGHT ABOUT NOW.
I'M A LITTLE SHORT ON IDEAS.
WELL, WE DO HAVE SOMETHING WE SAY HERE.
WAKANDA FOREVER!

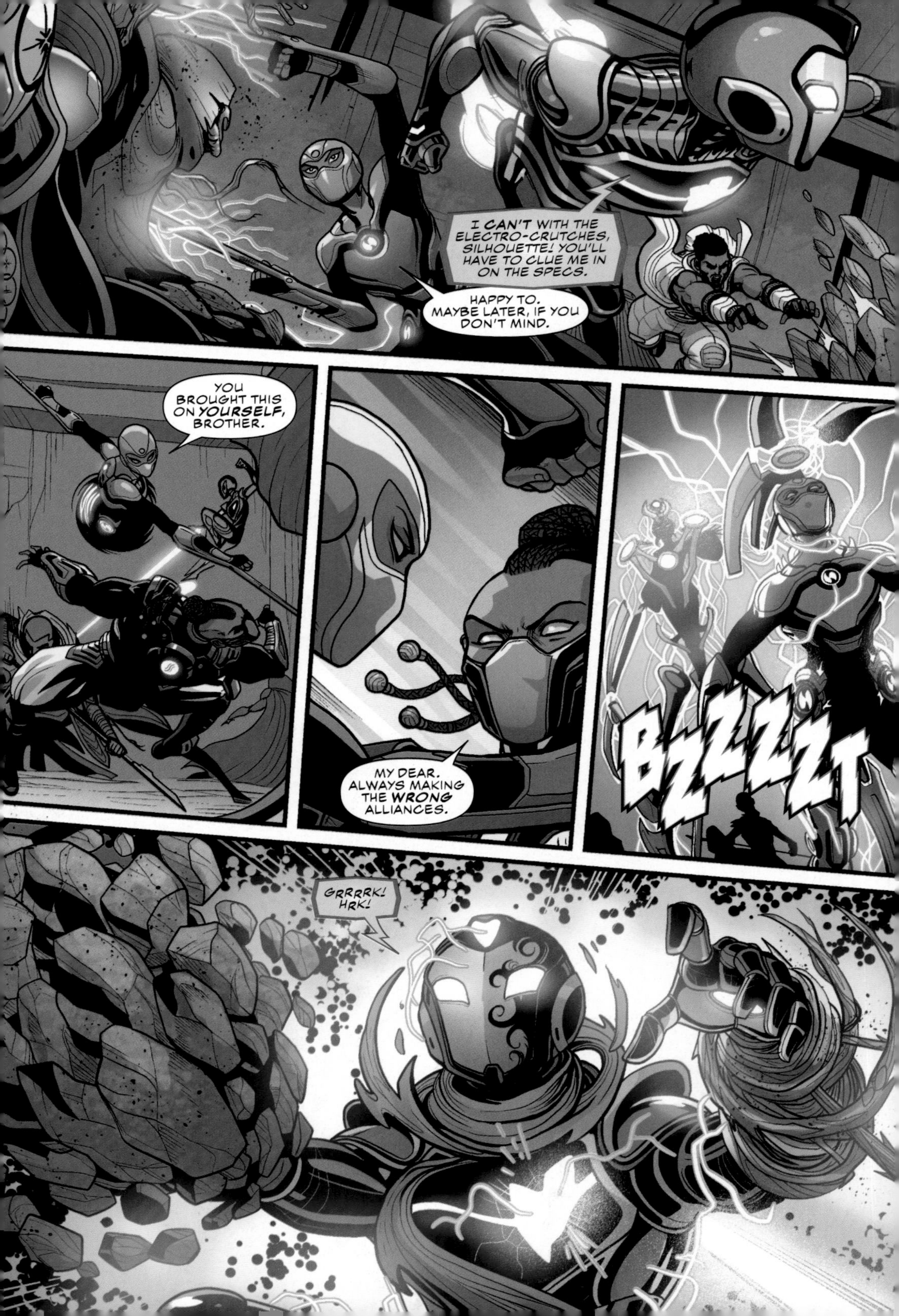
I CAN'T WITH THE ELECTRO-CRUTCHES, SILHOUETTE! YOU'LL HAVE TO CLUE ME IN ON THE SPECS.
HAPPY TO. MAYBE LATER, IF YOU DON'T MIND.
YOU BROUGHT THIS ON YOURSELF, BROTHER.
MY DEAR. ALWAYS MAKING THE WRONG ALLIANCES.
BZZZZZT
GRRRRK! HRK!

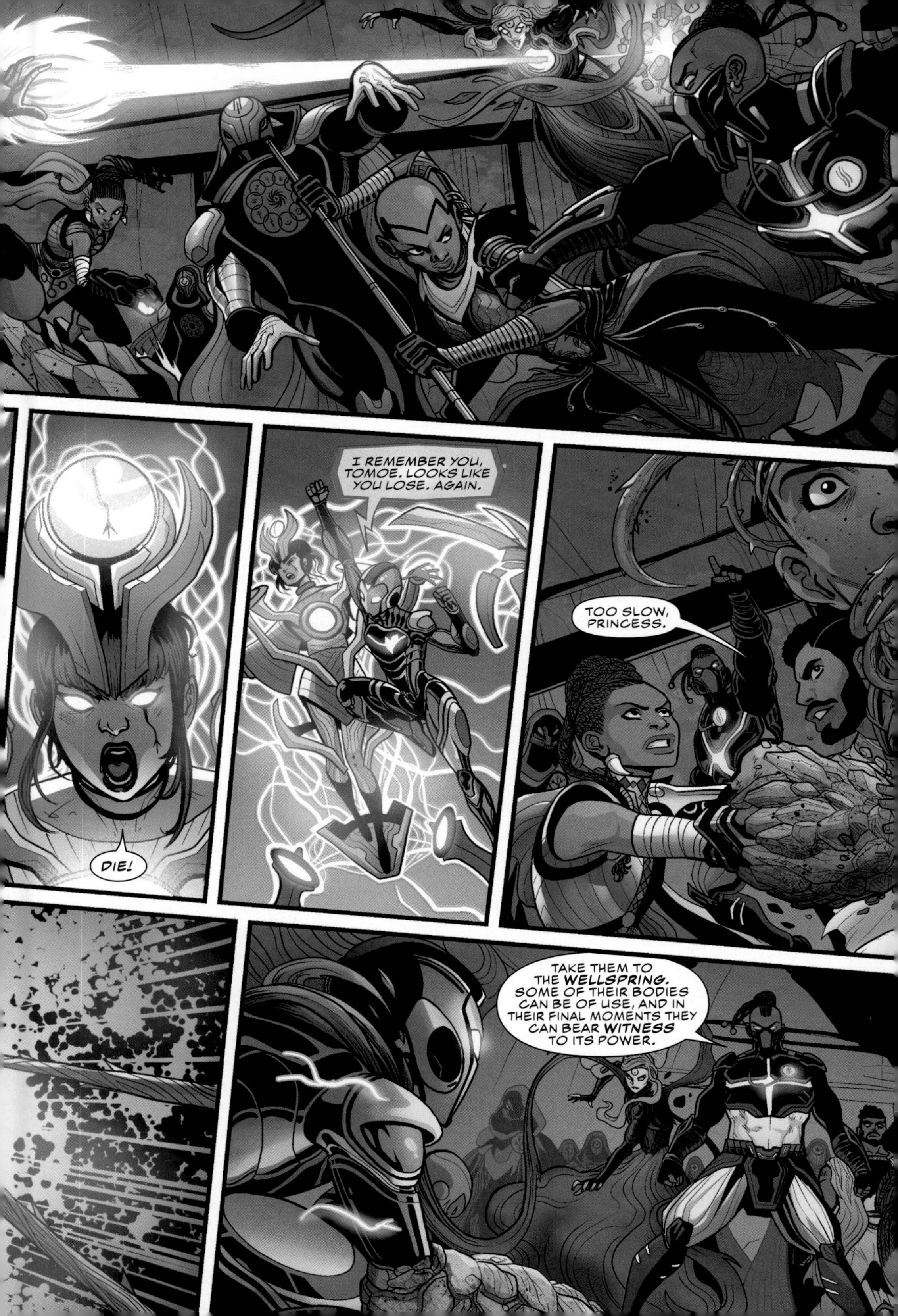
DIE!
I REMEMBER YOU, TOMOE. LOOKS LIKE YOU LOSE. AGAIN.
TOO SLOW, PRINCESS.
TAKE THEM TO THE WELLSPRING. SOME OF THEIR BODIES CAN BE OF USE, AND IN THEIR FINAL MOMENTS THEY CAN BEAR WITNESS TO ITS POWER.

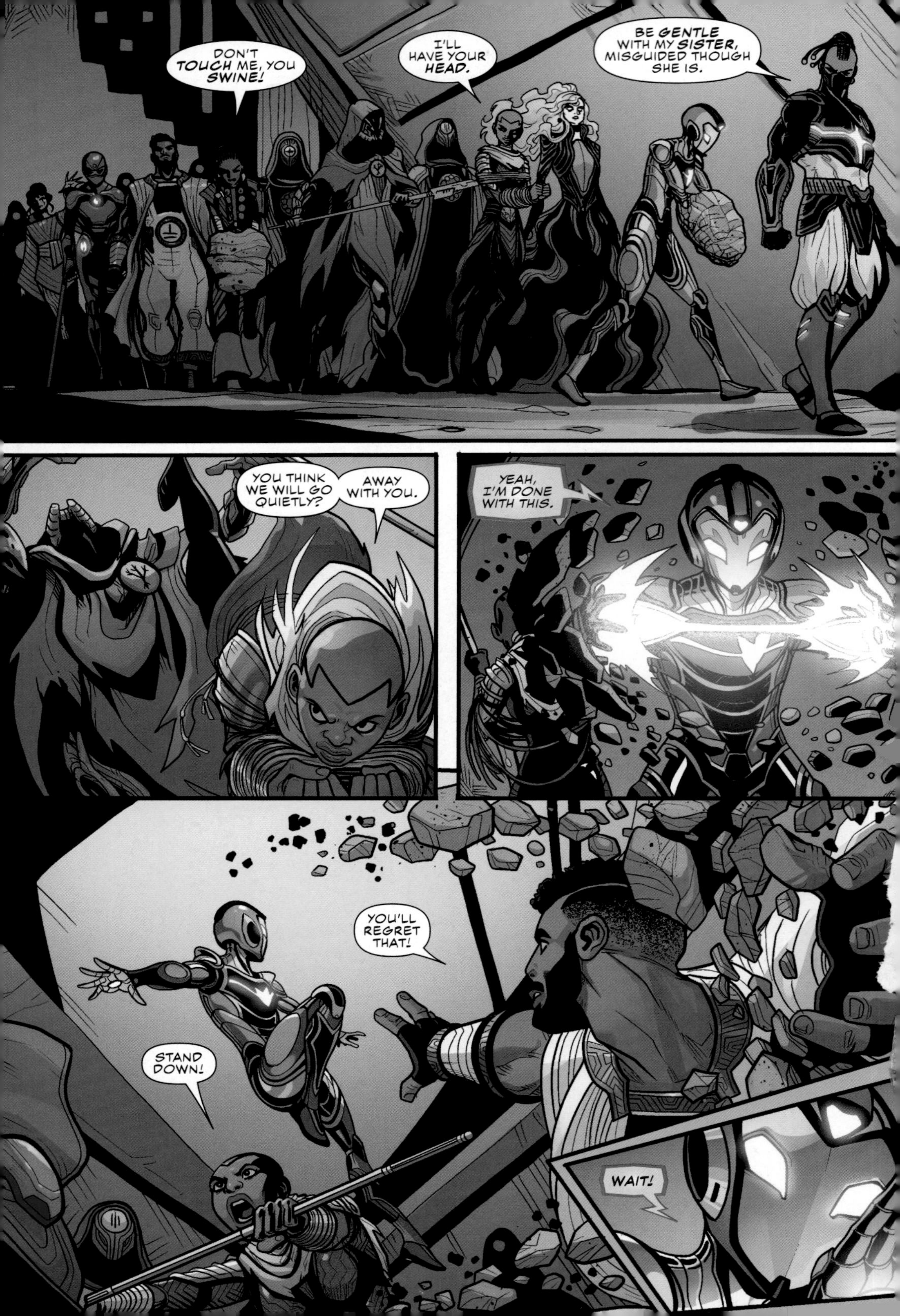
DON'T TOUCH ME, YOU SWINE!
I'LL HAVE YOUR HEAD.
BE GENTLE WITH MY SISTER, MISGUIDED THOUGH SHE IS.
YOU THINK WE WILL GO QUIETLY?
AWAY WITH YOU.
YEAH, I'M DONE WITH THIS.
YOU'LL REGRET THAT!
STAND DOWN!
WAIT!

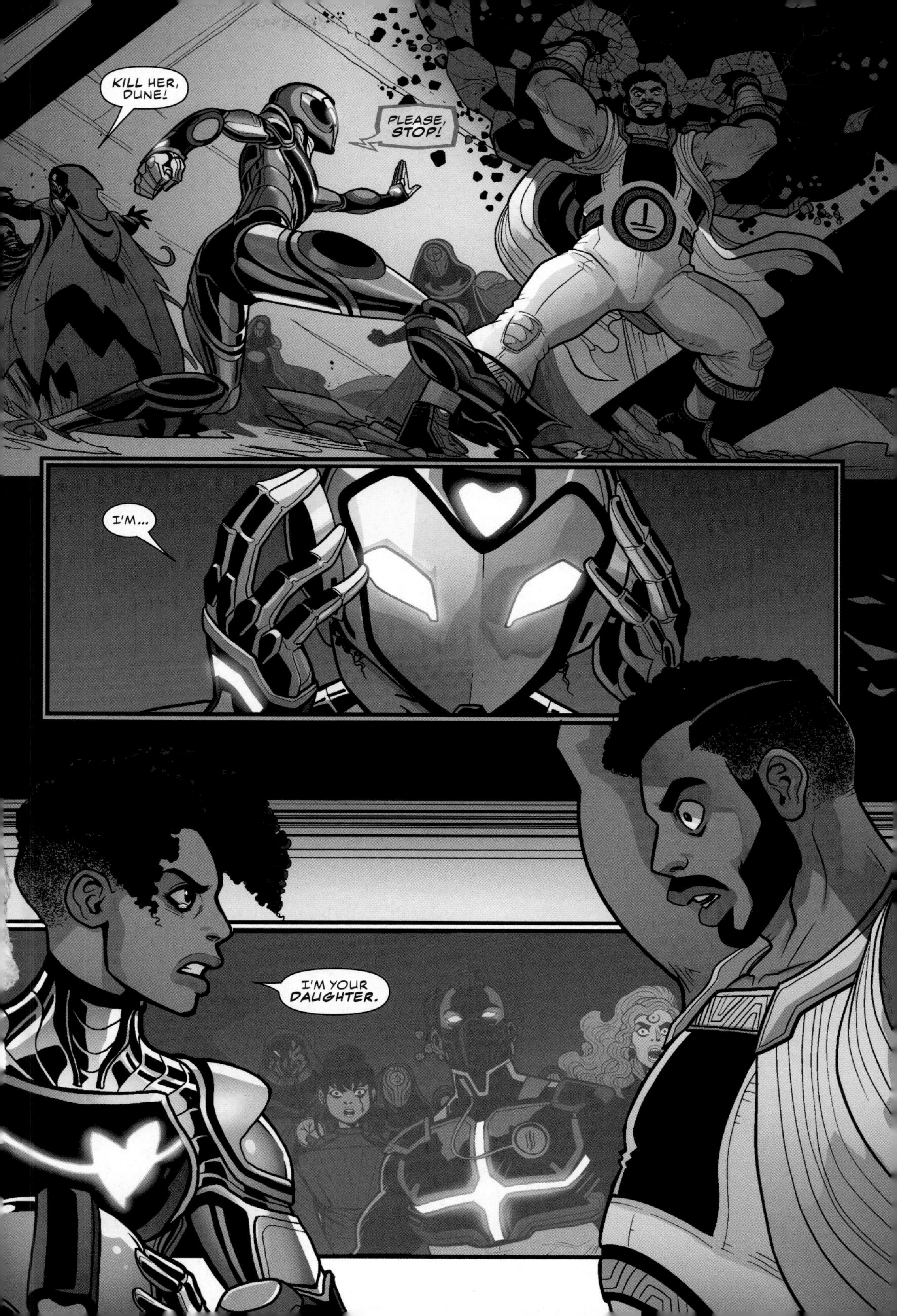
KILL HER, DUNE!
PLEASE, STOP!
I'M...
I'M YOUR DAUGHTER.

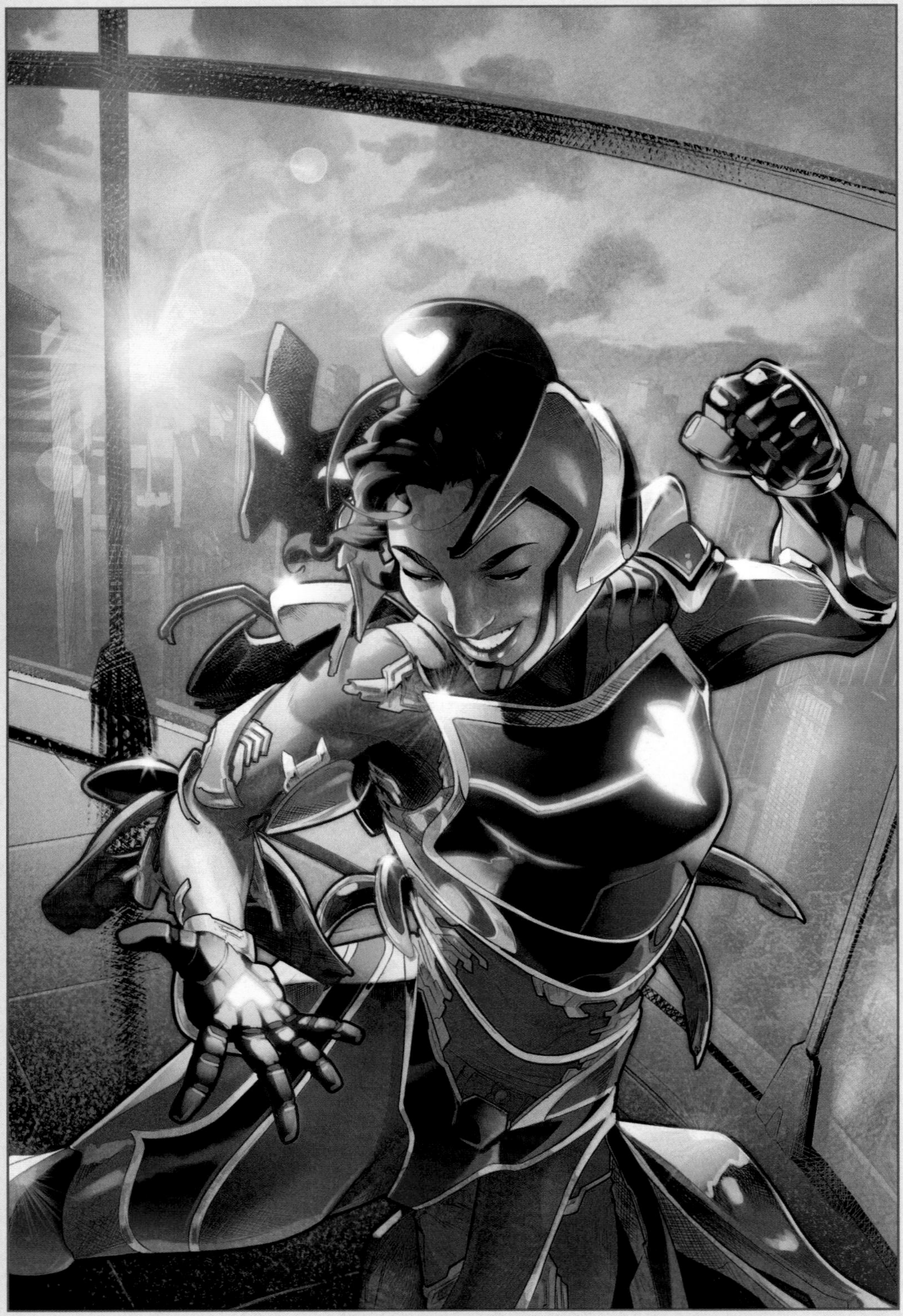

#1 VARIANT
BY JAMAL CAMPBELL

12

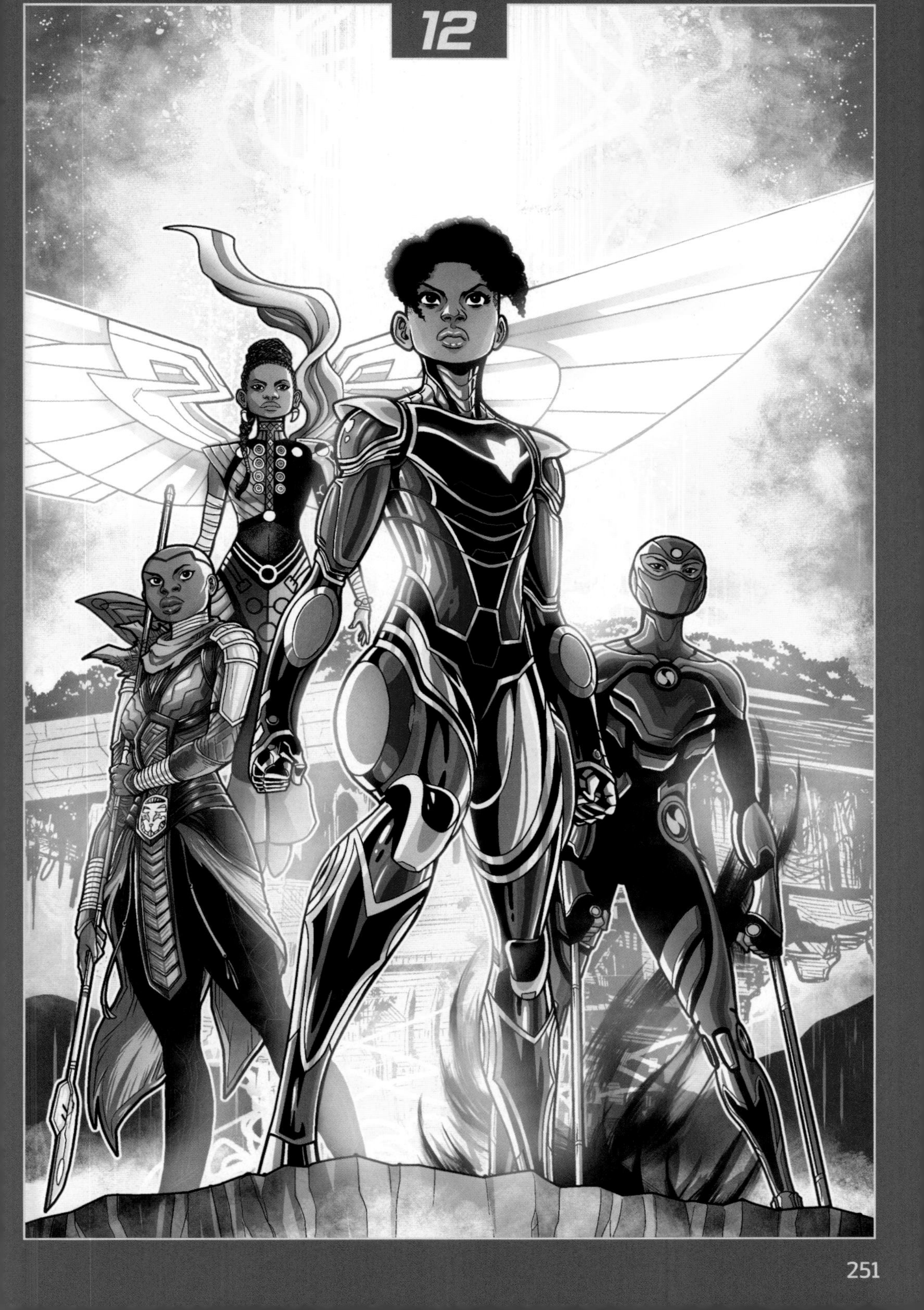

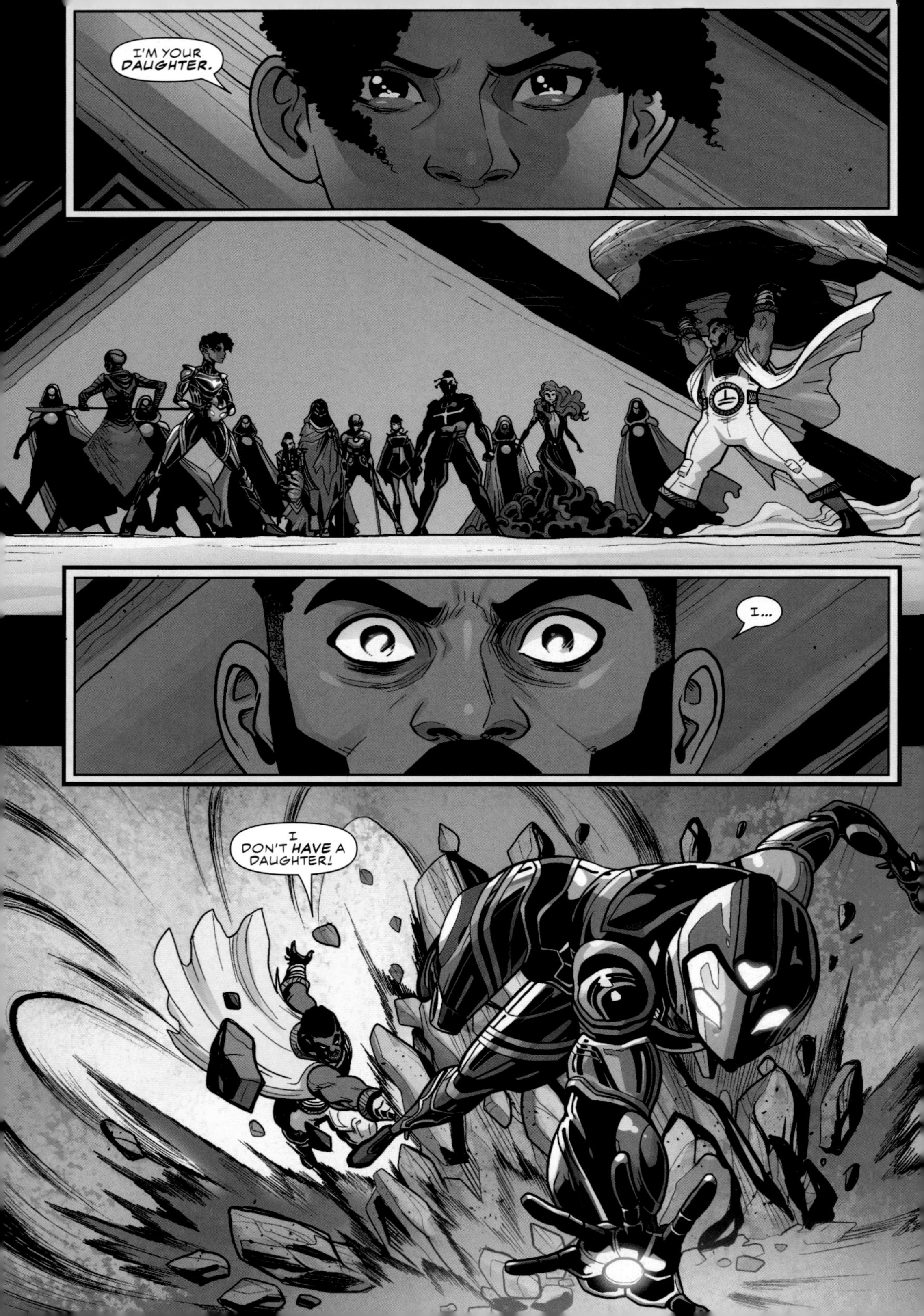
I'M YOUR DAUGHTER.
I...
I DON'T HAVE A DAUGHTER!

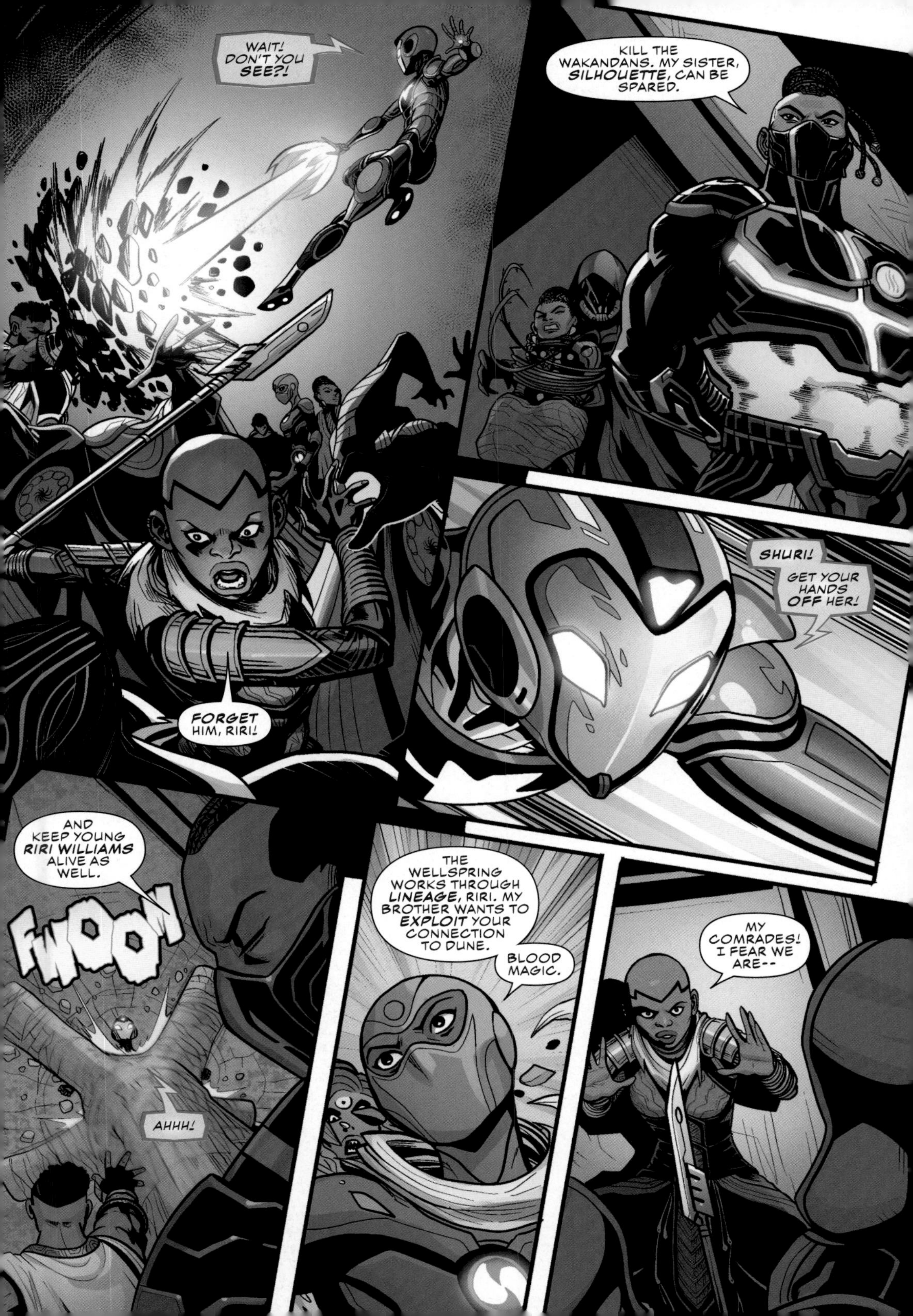
WAIT! DON'T YOU SEE?!
KILL THE WAKANDANS. MY SISTER, SILHOUETTE, CAN BE SPARED.
FORGET HIM, RIRI!
SHURI!
GET YOUR HANDS OFF HER!
AND KEEP YOUNG RIRI WILLIAMS ALIVE AS WELL.
FWOOM
AHHH!
THE WELLSPRING WORKS THROUGH LINEAGE, RIRI. MY BROTHER WANTS TO EXPLOIT YOUR CONNECTION TO DUNE.
BLOOD MAGIC.
MY COMRADES! I FEAR WE ARE--

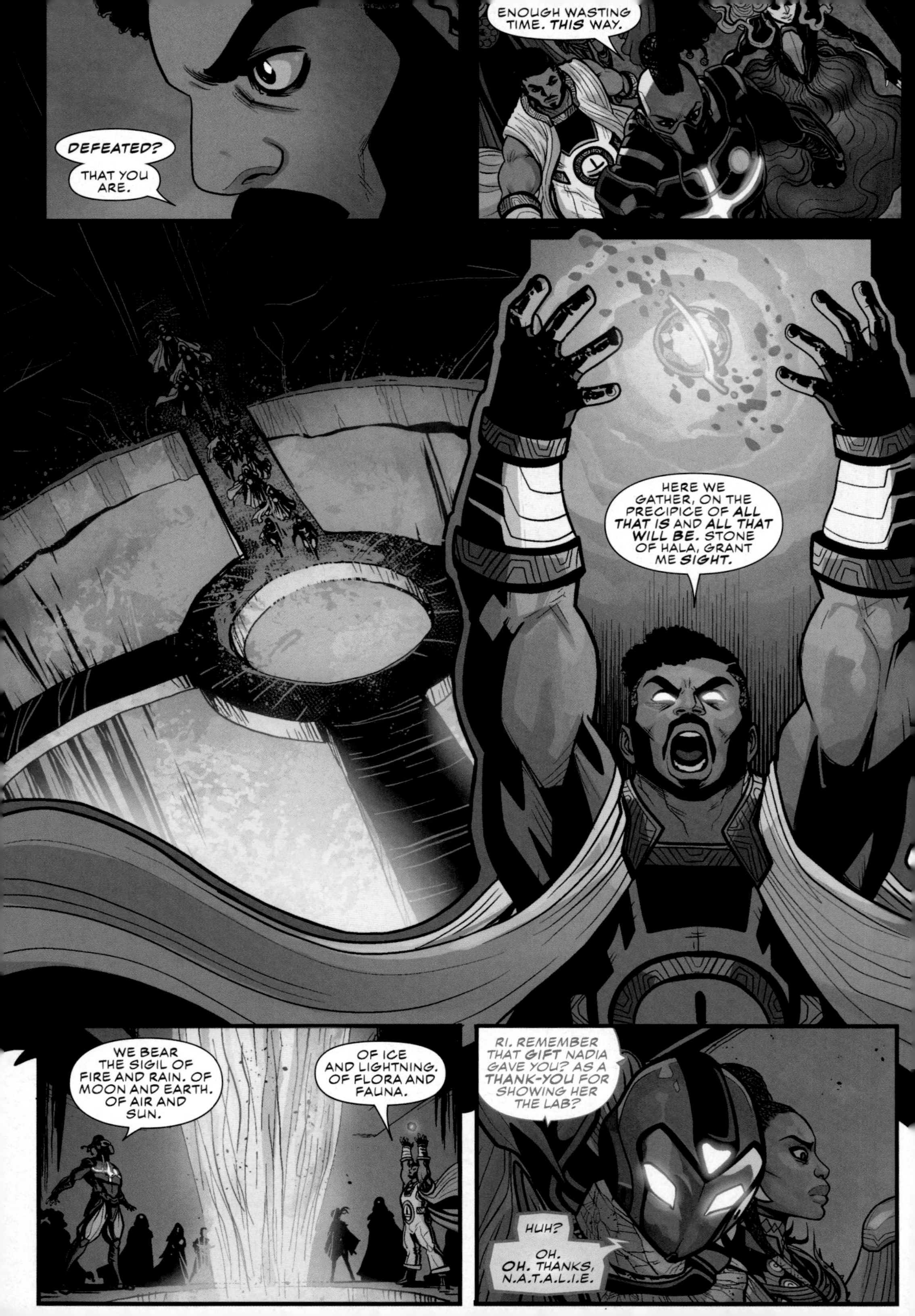
DEFEATED? THAT YOU ARE.
ENOUGH WASTING TIME. THIS WAY.
HERE WE GATHER, ON THE PRECIPICE OF ALL THAT IS AND ALL THAT WILL BE. STONE OF HALA, GRANT ME SIGHT.
WE BEAR THE SIGIL OF FIRE AND RAIN. OF MOON AND EARTH. OF AIR AND SUN.
OF ICE AND LIGHTNING. OF FLORA AND FAUNA.
RI. REMEMBER THAT GIFT NADIA GAVE YOU? AS A THANK-YOU FOR SHOWING HER THE LAB?
HUH?
OH. OH. THANKS, N.A.T.A.L.I.E.

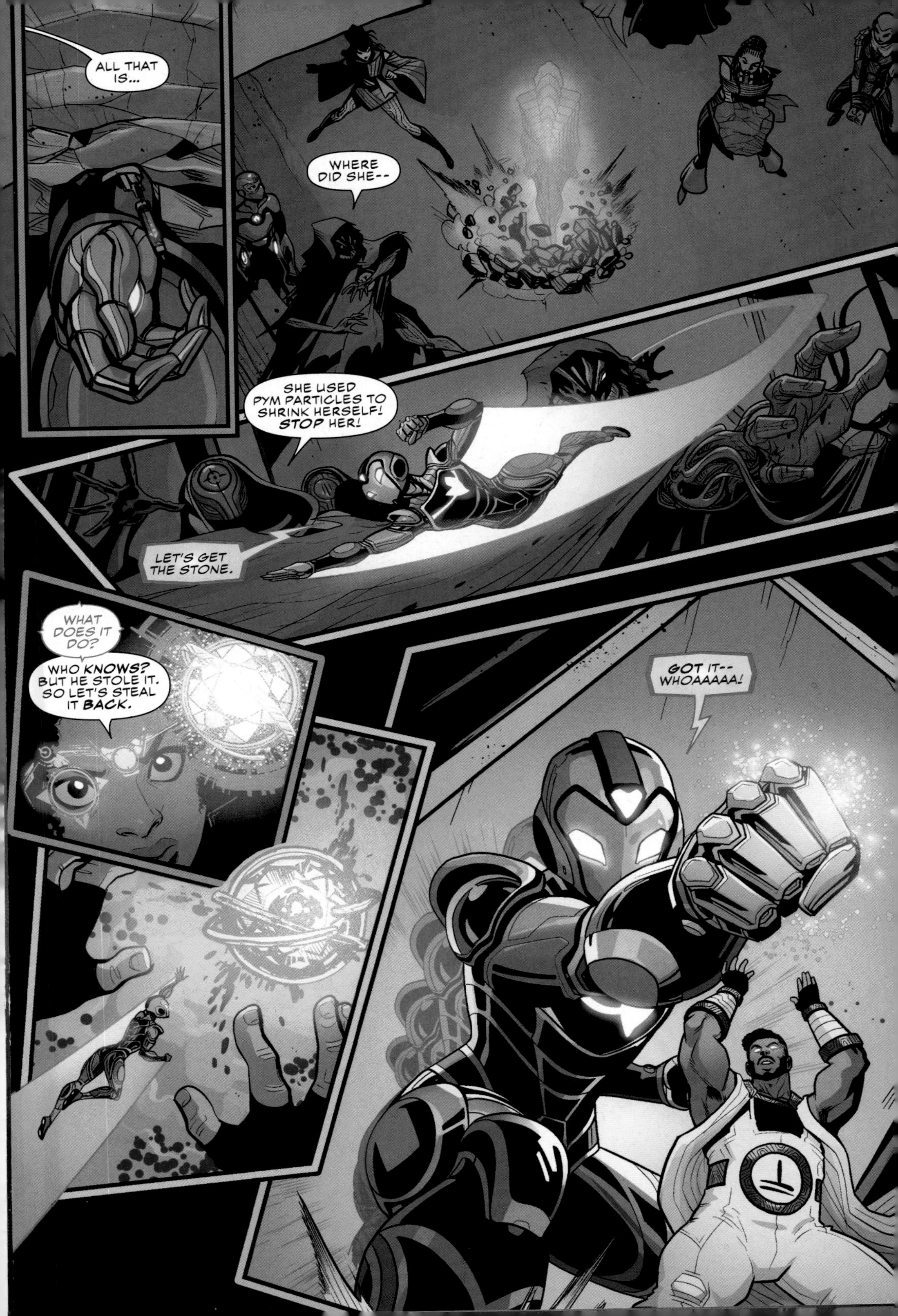
ALL THAT IS...
WHERE DID SHE--
SHE USED PYM PARTICLES TO SHRINK HERSELF! STOP HER!
LET'S GET THE STONE.
WHAT DOES IT DO?
WHO KNOWS? BUT HE STOLE IT. SO LET'S STEAL IT BACK.
GOT IT-- WHOAAAAA!

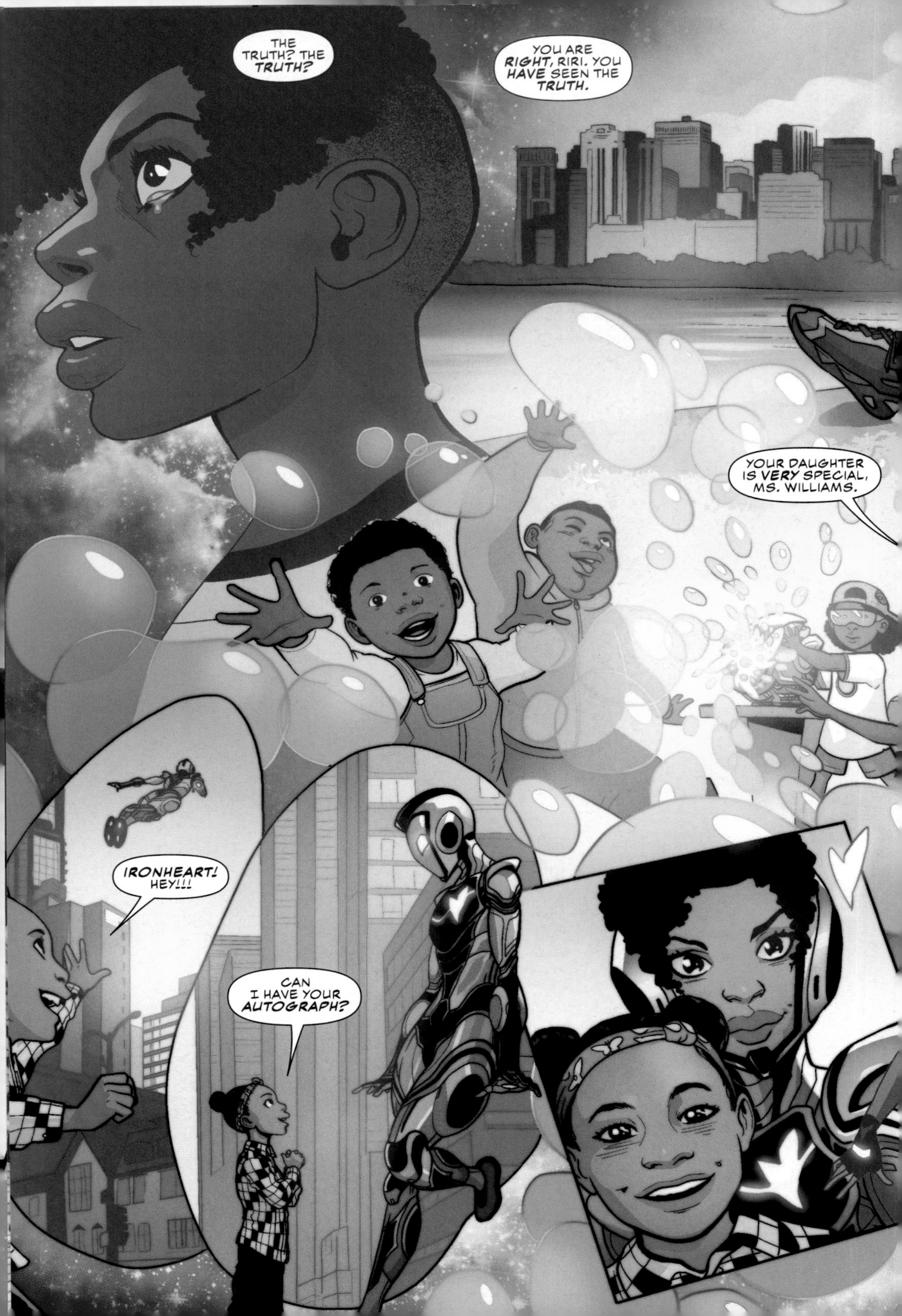
THE TRUTH? THE TRUTH?
YOU ARE RIGHT, RIRI. YOU HAVE SEEN THE TRUTH.
YOUR DAUGHTER IS VERY SPECIAL, MS. WILLIAMS.
IRONHEART! HEY!!!
CAN I HAVE YOUR AUTOGRAPH?

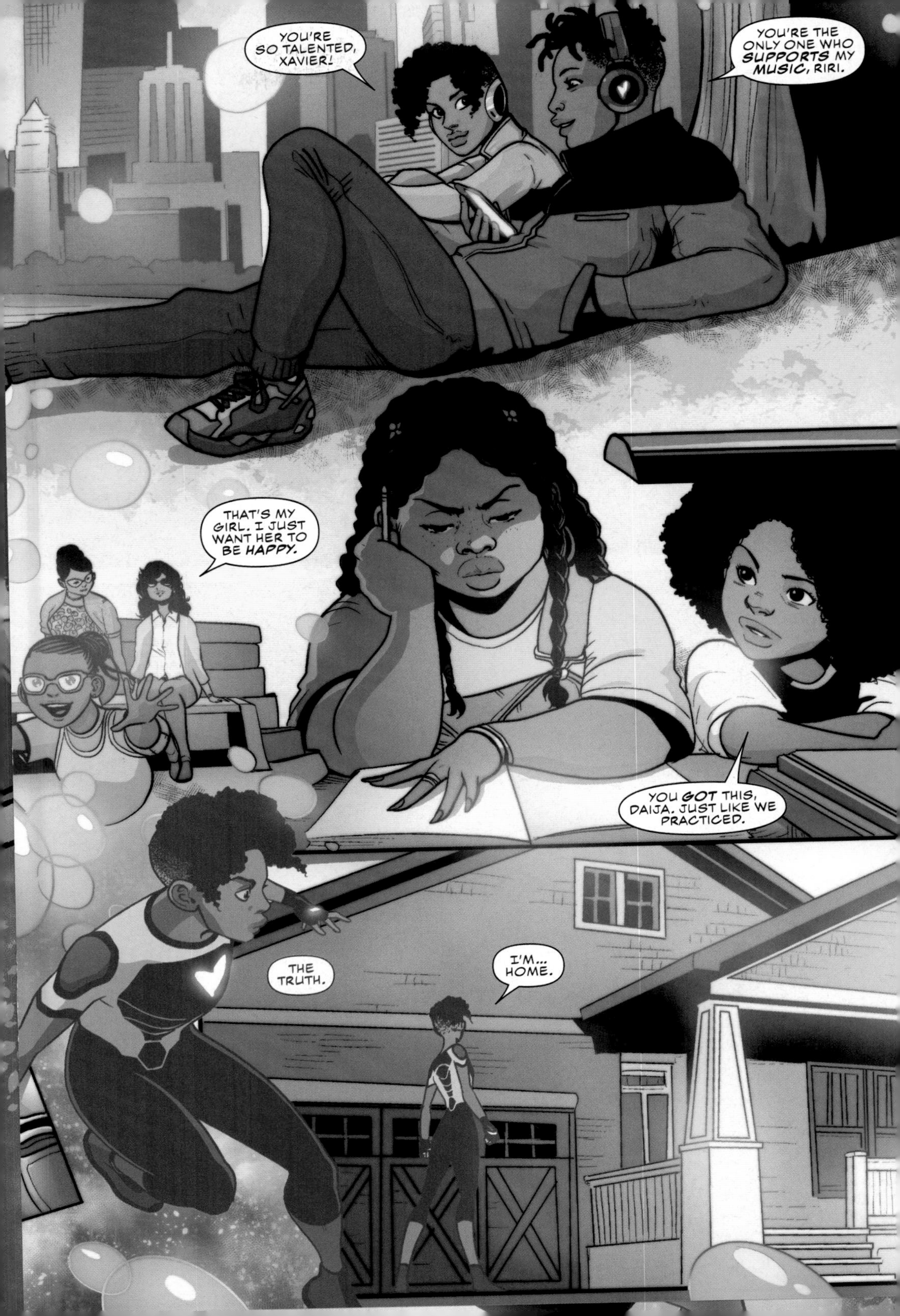
YOU'RE SO TALENTED, XAVIER!
YOU'RE THE ONLY ONE WHO SUPPORTS MY MUSIC, RIRI.
THAT'S MY GIRL. I JUST WANT HER TO BE HAPPY.
YOU GOT THIS, DAIJA. JUST LIKE WE PRACTICED.
THE TRUTH.
I'M... HOME.

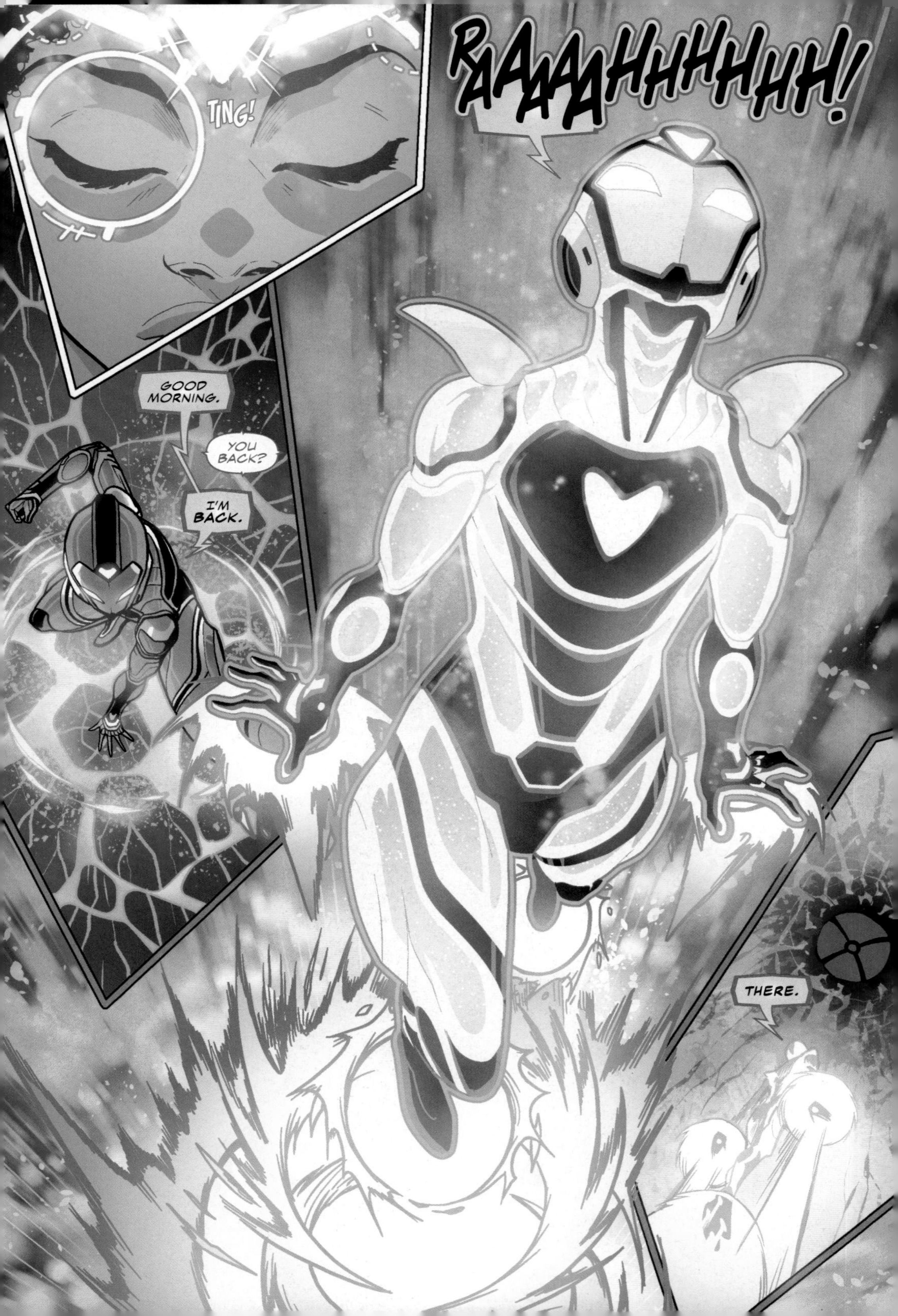
TING!
RAAAAAHHHHHHH!
GOOD MORNING.
YOU BACK?
I'M BACK.
THERE.

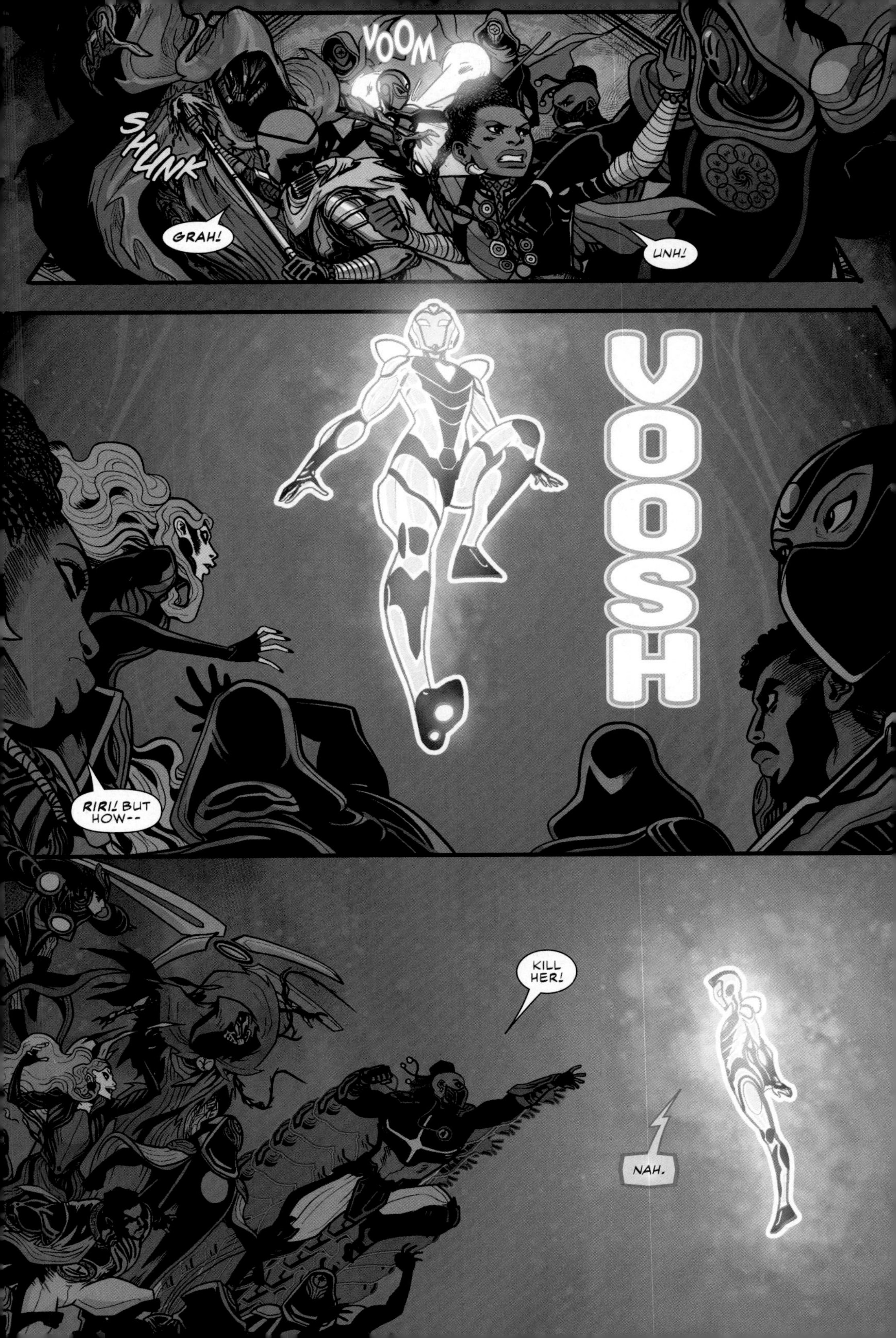
VOOM
SHUNK
GRAH!
UNH!
VOOSH
RIRI! BUT HOW--
KILL HER!
NAH.

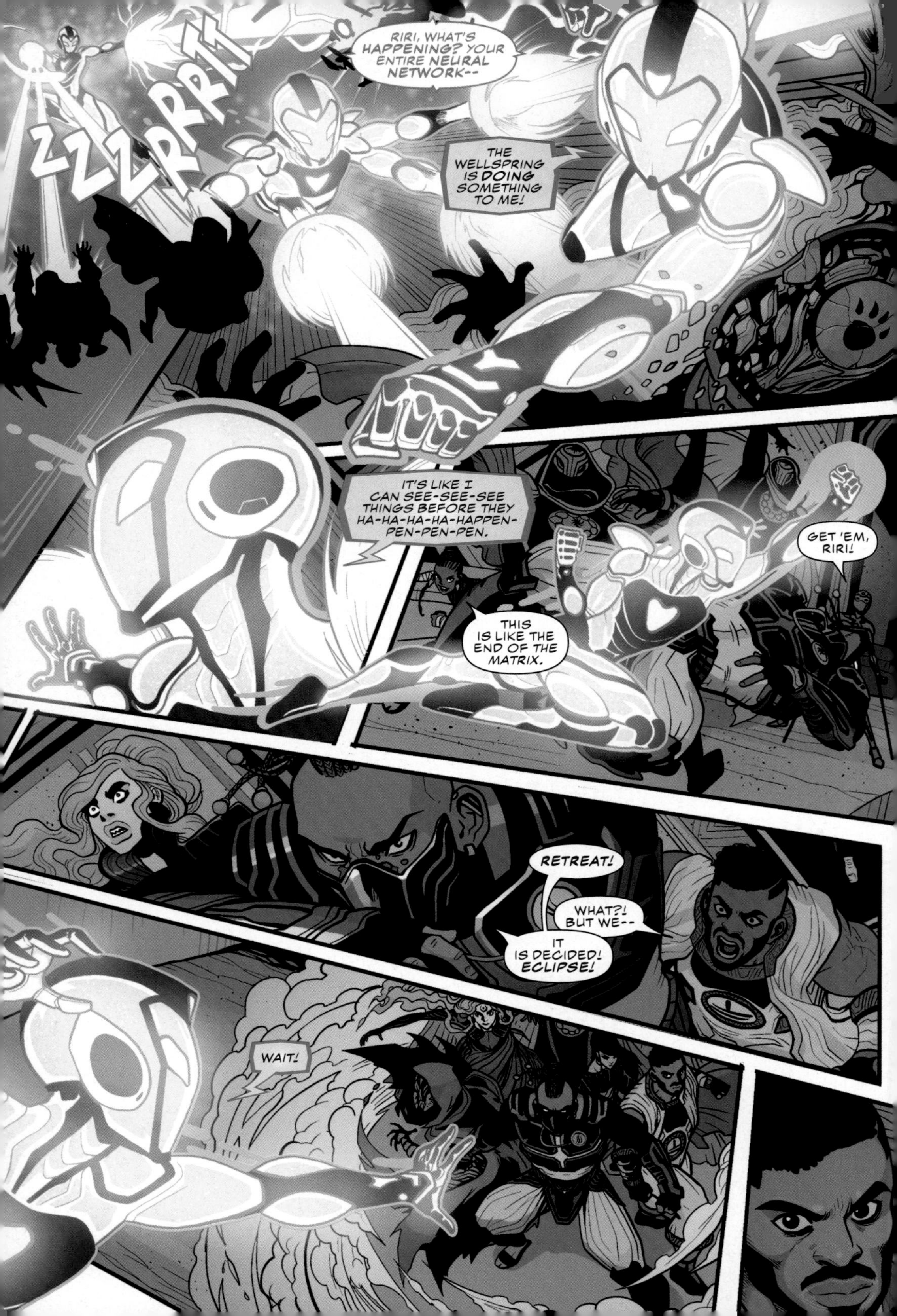
RIRI, WHAT'S HAPPENING? YOUR ENTIRE NEURAL NETWORK--
ZZZRRRT
THE WELLSPRING IS DOING SOMETHING TO ME!
IT'S LIKE I CAN SEE-SEE-SEE THINGS BEFORE THEY HA-HA-HA-HA-HAPPEN-PEN-PEN-PEN.
GET 'EM, RIRI!
THIS IS LIKE THE END OF THE MATRIX.
RETREAT!
WHAT?! BUT WE--
IT IS DECIDED! ECLIPSE!
WAIT!

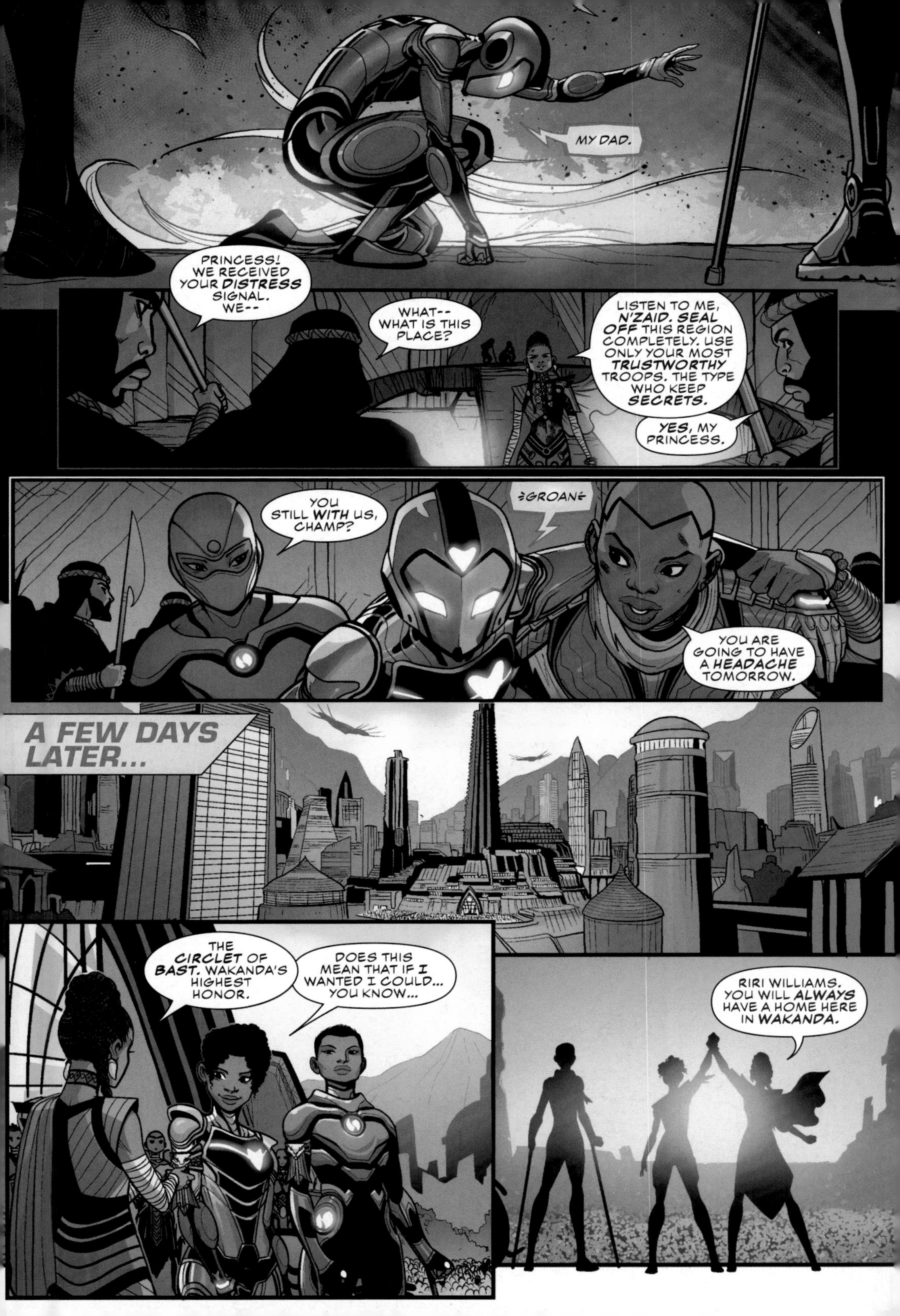
MY DAD.
PRINCESS! WE RECEIVED YOUR DISTRESS SIGNAL. WE--
WHAT-- WHAT IS THIS PLACE?
LISTEN TO ME, N'ZAID. SEAL OFF THIS REGION COMPLETELY. USE ONLY YOUR MOST TRUSTWORTHY TROOPS. THE TYPE WHO KEEP SECRETS.
YES, MY PRINCESS.
YOU STILL WITH US, CHAMP?
GROAN
YOU ARE GOING TO HAVE A HEADACHE TOMORROW.
A FEW DAYS LATER...
THE CIRCLET OF BAST. WAKANDA'S HIGHEST HONOR.
DOES THIS MEAN THAT IF I WANTED I COULD... YOU KNOW...
RIRI WILLIAMS. YOU WILL ALWAYS HAVE A HOME HERE IN WAKANDA.

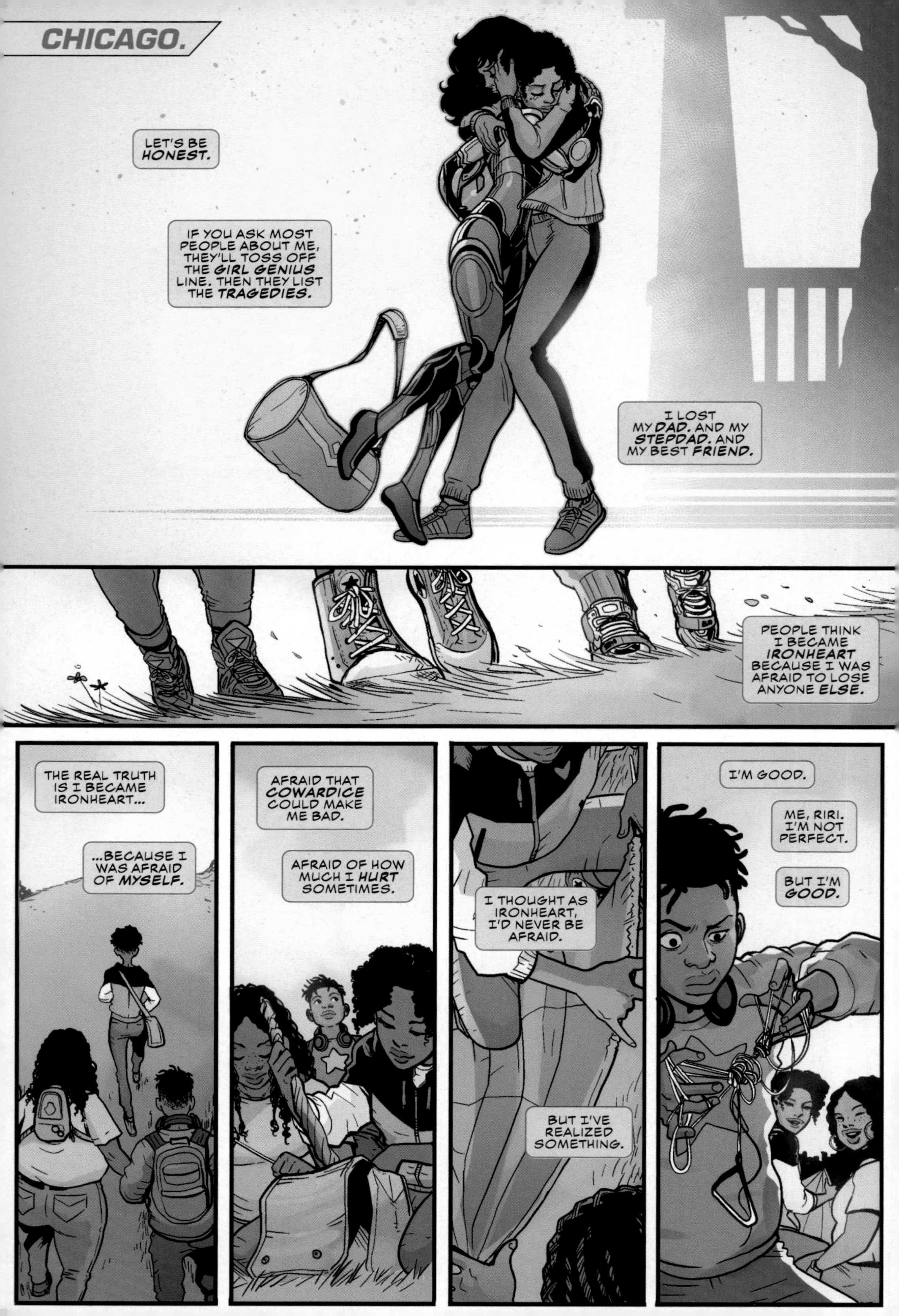
CHICAGO.
LET'S BE HONEST.
IF YOU ASK MOST PEOPLE ABOUT ME, THEY'LL TOSS OFF THE GIRL GENIUS LINE. THEN THEY LIST THE TRAGEDIES.
I LOST MY DAD. AND MY STEPDAD. AND MY BEST FRIEND.
PEOPLE THINK I BECAME IRONHEART BECAUSE I WAS AFRAID TO LOSE ANYONE ELSE.
THE REAL TRUTH IS I BECAME IRONHEART...
...BECAUSE I WAS AFRAID OF MYSELF.
AFRAID THAT COWARDICE COULD MAKE ME BAD.
AFRAID OF HOW MUCH I HURT SOMETIMES.
I THOUGHT AS IRONHEART, I'D NEVER BE AFRAID.
BUT I'VE REALIZED SOMETHING.
I'M GOOD.
ME, RIRI. I'M NOT PERFECT.
BUT I'M GOOD.

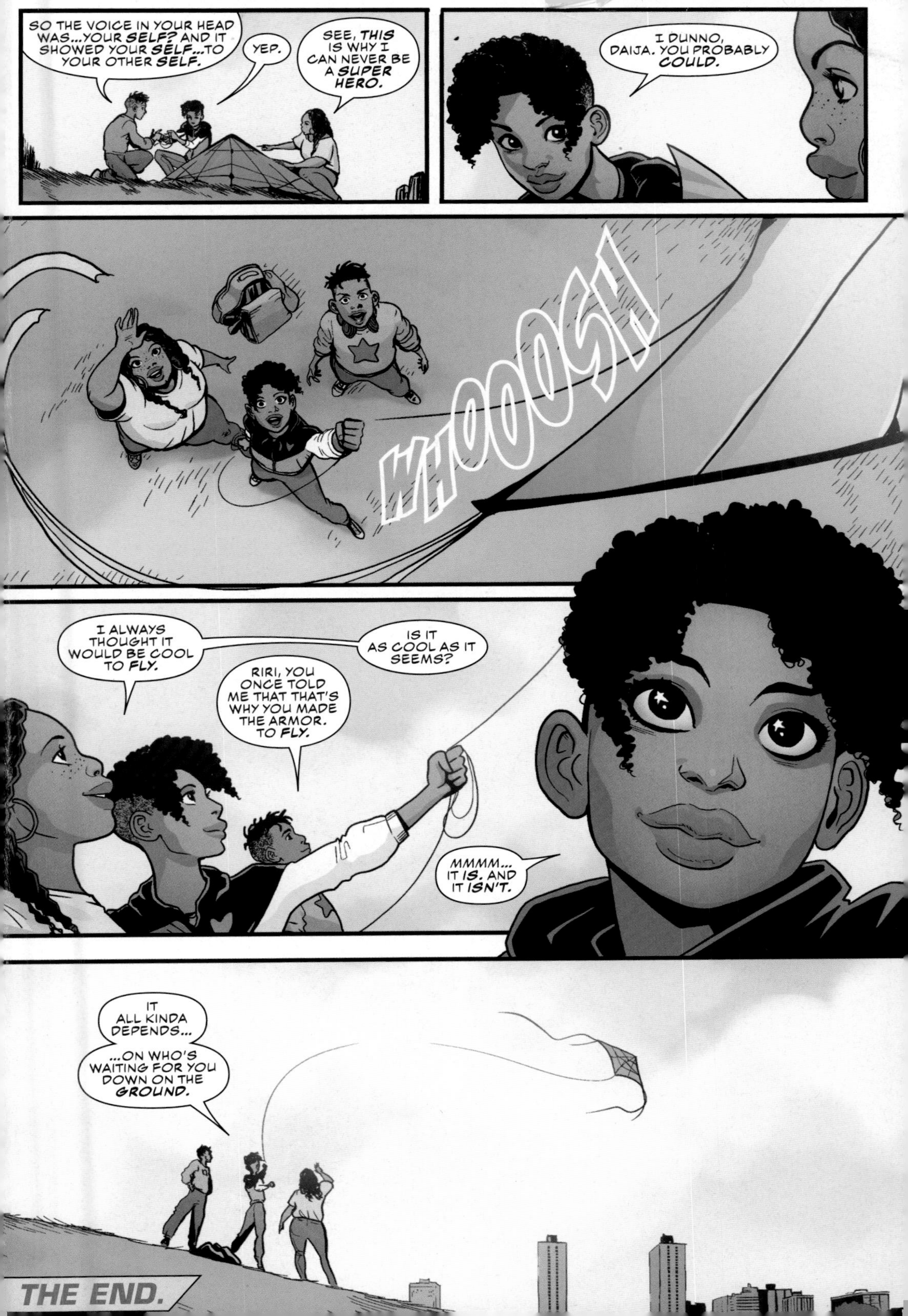
SO THE VOICE IN YOUR HEAD WAS...YOUR SELF? AND IT SHOWED YOUR SELF...TO YOUR OTHER SELF.
YEP.
SEE, THIS IS WHY I CAN NEVER BE A SUPER HERO.
I DUNNO, DAIJA. YOU PROBABLY COULD.
WHOOOSH!
I ALWAYS THOUGHT IT WOULD BE COOL TO FLY.
IS IT AS COOL AS IT SEEMS?
RIRI, YOU ONCE TOLD ME THAT THAT'S WHY YOU MADE THE ARMOR. TO FLY.
MMMM... IT IS. AND IT ISN'T.
IT ALL KINDA DEPENDS...
...ON WHO'S WAITING FOR YOU DOWN ON THE GROUND.
THE END.

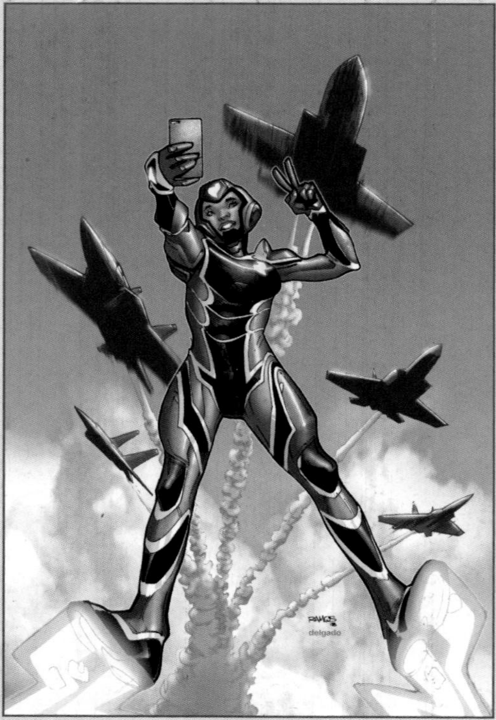
RAMOS
delgado

#1 VARIANT
BY HUMBERTO RAMOS & EDGAR DELGADO

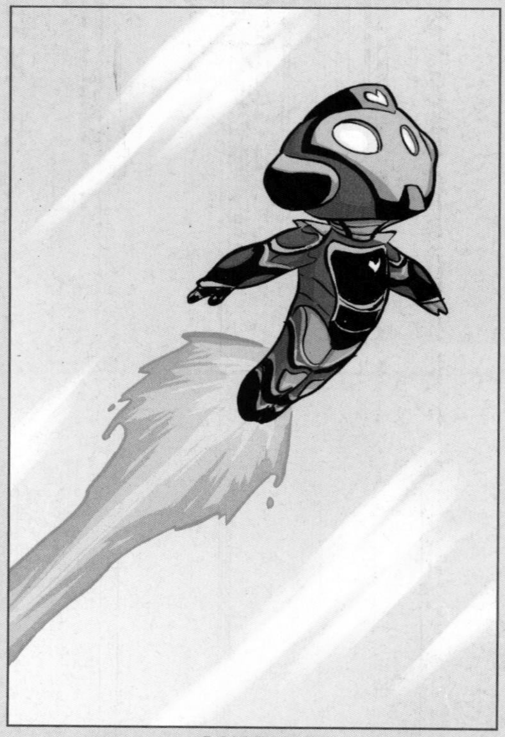

#1 VARIANT
BY SKOTTIE YOUNG